Tower of Gaij

UnderVerse Book 9

By
Jez Cajiao

Jez Cajiao

Published through MAH Publishings Ltd
Editing by Michelle Dunbar
Editing by Faith Williams
Cover by Marko Drazic
Typography by May Dawney Designs
Formatting and additional editing by Christine Cajiao

This is a work of fiction, all characters, places, spells, realities and secrets of the Upper and Lower Realms are entirely my own work, and if they offend you, it's not intentional. Probably.

CONTENTS

THANKS

Hi everyone, well, just as a point here, we're working on getting the audio and the eBook releases closer together, which means that I'm writing this further in the past—subjective to where you are now—than usual.

In fact for me, this is *July*. Yup, that's right, long, long ago, this book was finished, and as such this means that things like my usual heads-up on Patreon will be markedly out, most of my Patreons are currently reading this book now, though some on the highest tier have even finished the next book as well! (To be clear, I have anything and everything I've written available to the highest tier not as a 'you must join here to get everything, but instead because if someone chooses that tier of support, then I damn well feel like I should give them anything and everything I have. It's the same point, but viewed from a completely different reasoning and perspective.)

Now, we're currently getting ready to run our first Convention (LitRPG Con) in conjunction with our partners Soundbooth Theatre, and as such I want to draw attention to the huge amount of work that our partner in Legion; Geneva, has put into this.

She's taken the con from rough sketch and plan to literally two weeks away from launch, and She's done so with far too many sleepless nights, has made incredible efforts and has drank a truly horrific number of coffees. She and Emily Labes-Royce (Freshly back from her maternity leave, congrats Em!) are the powers behind the throne of the con, and when you read this, and you look back to the event, I hope you realize just how much effort was put in to make it as incredible as it was (will be)!

Oh bugger it you all know what I mean! I'm talking in the past dammit, I might as well be a ghost! Whoooo!

Heh, seriously though, Congratulations and thank you Geneva.

-Jez
03/07/25

UNDERVERSE BOOKS 1-8 SYNOPSIS

BOOK ONE:

Jax is working a dead end job, in a semi-stable relationship, and searching for his missing brother, while plagued by dreams of the UnderVerse. This terrible alternate reality is where he, and his brother Tommy, are pulled against their will on occasion. When in the dream they inhabit artificial bodies and fight to protect abandoned villages and more, standing between the inhabitants of the Old Empire and the creatures of the night.

They awaken back on earth once the threat has passed, or they've been killed, with their injuries following them. While they heal at a tremendously accelerated rate, it still requires days to recover, and in that time, they hide their injuries, lest they be locked away for self-mutilation.

After one such session, Jax decides to come clean to his GF and explain everything. Badly injured and bleeding heavily, he arrives at her home, only to find her in bed with another man. He loses control, half beating the man to death, and having his skull shattered in turn by her, using the baseball bat he'd bought her for self-defense.

Jax comes to in the hospital, chained to the bed, and is interviewed by the police and warned he faces a significant jail term. While alone and contemplating this, an unknown doctor slips in and assures him it has all been taken care of, before drugging him.

When Jax wakes up this time, it's to find himself restrained, again, but on an airplane heading to meet 'the Baron Sanguis'. A lawyer assures him that should he carry out the reasonable requests of his new employer, then not only will all legal concerns be a thing of the past, but he will find his brother as well. Jax accepts, warned that refusal means death, and meets the Baron, an inhuman monster who admits to being an interplanar traveler, and a member of the original nobility of the UnderVerse, the Realm that Jax and his brother dream of.

To be free and to find his brother Jax must travel to that shattered Realm, and open a stable portal back to this Realm, as the mana here is simply too low in concentration for the portal to be held open for more than bare seconds. Alternatively, a portal from that side, to here, would be secure and enable the nobility to return with servants and forces intact, ready to reconquer their home.

Over the next several months, as Jax is trained for the 'little task', he discovers more about the past of that Realm, including that the voice of madness that occasionally speaks to him, and that he'd written off as himself being mad to some degree, is actually the voice of the Eternal Emperor Amon, a fragment of His soul being all that's left, clinging to the genetic line.

Amon was murdered, by the Baron, His son, and others of the nobility, with the aid of the God of Death, Nimon. In the process, and as his price for this, the followers of the other nine greater gods were purged and their temples cast down. Leaving the God of Death, who dragged one of the moons down to impact the

Realm, with a powerful enough surge of His 'aspect' (death) that He managed to banish the other Greater Gods.

Jax grows to hate the Baron, but has nothing left in his life beyond his missing brother, and so takes the opportunity, training heavily, before facing eleven other nobles' choices in the arena to 'earn' the right to go to the UnderVerse. He wins, barely, and trades the remains of his opponents and their personal items to their sponsors, in exchange for several magical artifacts, before passing through the great portal.

Once on the other side, and having made a deal with an opposing noble 'house' for access, he finds himself in a ruined tower. The Great Towers were bastions of the old Empire, powerfully magical, self-sustaining and intended as entire self-contained cities. At half a mile wide at the base, two to three miles high, and sustained by their own mana collectors they acted as garrisons and secure imperial bastions in places of danger.

The Tower that Jax finds himself in, however, was never inhabited fully. It was finished, intended as a research and security station, but had only a skeleton crew when it was assaulted by a SporeMother. The SporeMother, a multi-limbed monstrosity of legend, flooded the defenders with undead and possessed creatures, birthing DarkSpore creatures, parasitical clouds that could puppet flesh, turning the unprepared defenders into attackers, claiming the Tower. The few remaining survivors, beleaguered on all sides, ordered the Tower's controller Wisps to shut the entire structure down, sealing the Wisps themselves away, and preventing the creature from being able to feed on the mana of the Tower to grow stronger, expecting that the Tower would be assaulted and retaken shortly by the Imperial Legion.

Then, before reinforcements could take the Tower back, the Cataclysm came. Seas and mountains rose, islands vanished and the creatures of the deep and of nightmare were set loose to roam. When Jax arrives at the Tower he finds it dark and silent, populated by the ancient dead, with only occasional more recently killed adventurers scattered here and there. He also encounters Sporelings, immature SporeMothers, hidden in the portal chamber, fighting them and locking himself away in a side room.

Jax uses one of the spells he gained, resurrecting one of the Sporelings he killed to form a companion to fight alongside him. Using his new companion, Bob, and his weapon of choice, a bastardized naginata, Jax proceeds to clear the Tower partially, discovering the 'Hall of Memories' and its sleeping Wisp, Oracle. He is gravely injured, and alone, Bob having perished in the fight to enter the room, and when he awakens the Wisp takes the chance it unthinkingly offers, to use some of the stored knowledge of the Hall of Memories, in the form of spellbooks, to enable him to defeat the undead outside the room.

Unfortunately, all magic he has accessed so far has been through books such as this, impressing outside knowledge across his brain and damaging it each time. This final spellbook is one too many, and results in scarring, internal bleeding and more. Jax is dying and Oracle, the newly awakened Wisp, bonds herself to him in an attempt to save him, gaining access to his manapool and enabling herself to cast the needed healing spells to save his life.

Over time Jax recovers, and with Oracle's guidance, reawakens and grants the name 'Seneschal' to the Wisp that controlled the tower. They reactivated the mana collectors and began the basic repairs the Tower required, as well as awakening the Goddess of Fire, Jenae.

This in turn awakens the SporeMother, now ancient and decrepit, but still powerful. In the fight that follows between Jax, Oracle, the newly reformed Bob and the SporeMother and her minions, the Eternal Emperor Amon makes contact with Jax, guiding him to use an artifact recovered in the Tower earlier. This Silverbright potion (Dragon's blood) transforms his weapon from a standard construction into a basic magical, but evolving, weapon. Jax kills the SporeMother, but is gravely wounded. Over the next day, as he is healed, the companions clear the remaining sections of the Tower, and find the creature's nest underground, along with the remains of the Golem Construction Cradles or Genesis Chambers.

They also find the Wisp responsible for the golems, name him Hephaestus, and take the time to reclaim the single working Genesis Chamber. This begins the construction of the most basic of stone golems to protect and rebuild the Tower. In the process, HeartStones are uncovered, a magical way to send a memory, as a method of communication. Most are long drained of mana, but the fragments that remain make it clear that Barabarattas, lord of one of the two nearby cities, has been trading slaves to the SporeMother in exchange for Sporelings, hoping to raise a captive army of SporeMothers.

The Wisps sense an intrusion higher in the tower and Jax explores, finding a group of slavers, heavily armed, using their slaves to loot an old armory. Jax attacks when seeing a child beaten, killing the slavers, with Oracle's help, and driving off the two airships that had been docked on the balcony. One is damaged and crashes in the courtyard below, while the other escapes to land at a nearby lake to effect repairs.

The freed slaves pledge allegiance to Jax, and while they rest, he takes one of their number, Oren, the captain of the crashed ship, down to the courtyard. He discovers that they were pressed into service, and had no desire to work with the slavers. The remaining surviving crew swear as well, and inform Jax that there is a third ship. This is the warship that was enforcing the City Lord's will, and it was still incoming, having stopped to raid a village along the way. Jax and the slaves use the weapons they have, the remains of the damaged ship and subterfuge to lure the warship in to land, while Oracle disables their engines.

Jax and Bob, aided by some of the former slaves, fight and kill the soldiers aboard the warship, capturing the crew, freeing a group of slaves taken from the villages and locking the crew in those same cages. Jax formally claims the Tower as his, and through the right of blood, having found that he is an illegitimate son of the Baron Sanguis, and therefore noble in his own right, he begins the right of Imperial Succession.

Barabarratas, like all nobles remaining in the Empire, with no Imperial House to swear to, had been unable to lay claim formally to the Imperial Throne, but once the succession has begun, sees a way to claim the throne. He threatens war against Jax, unless he surrenders. Jax, being short of patience and self-control, as well as occasionally being an asshole, in turn declares war on Barabarratas and his city of Himnel, taunting him before leading his people in a wake. The end of the book comes to Thomas, Jax's brother, languishing and injured in a jail, before being sold as fodder, the lowest caste of soldier, to the Dark Legion of Nimon.

BOOK TWO:

Thomas fights his abusive jailor and draws the eye of a Paladin of Nimon, who grants him a chance to prove himself. Thomas is happy to take that chance and prove his worth in battle to escape the rank of fodder.

Jax awakens with a hangover, the wake having gone well, and proceeds to set about trying to repair the Tower. Two of the new recruits, now citizens of the Great Tower, Oren the Dwarf airship captain, and Cai, a Panthera humanoid with a skill for organization, assist him. Teams are formed for hunting and defense, with a personal squad geared around Jax. This is formed from ex slaves who are determined to never be cowed again. Lydia leads them (mace and shield, heavy armor), with Jian (dual wielding swords), Arrin (mage), Cam (axeman), Miren (archer), Stephanos (archer) and Bob. Jax and his new team go to try and capture or recruit the escaped second airship, but upon arrival at the lake, find the ship deserted.

They are attacked as they search by small four-armed amphibious creatures known as the 'Mer'. In the course of the fight, Jax realizes they are young, ranging from a young adult, to a child, and they were attacked by goblins prior to Jax's arrival, attacking him in pre-emptive self-defense. The young ones are joined by older, more experienced warriors, who agree to a truce at first, and then request help to deal with the nearby goblin horde.

Jax agrees, and three of the Mer join them, assaulting the goblin camp. In the course of the fight, Jax saves the life of one of the Mer, the oldest of the younglings, and upon clearing the ruin, and rescuing the surviving crew of the airship from them, claims the land as part of the Empire. In the process, the goblin cave is revealed as a buried outpost, complete with basic golems, which are claimed and returned to the Tower.

The Mer village remains neutral, but several of their people join Jax, including the youngling, Bane. The leader of the Mer that join the Tower is Flux, an accomplished adventurer, and he supports Bane's desire to be Jax's bodyguard. Several of the older Mer decide to join the Tower, many of whom are skilled, but crippled. Jax heals them, magic being increasingly rare in the UnderVerse since the fall of the Empire, and his abilities and the knowledge stored at the Tower are revealed as being incredibly valuable. The rescued crew join Jax, bringing their ship and joining the resurgent Empire.

The older banished Gods are awakened, and Jax has a disagreement with one, Tamat, the Lady of Assassins. Using a draconic legacy from Amon, Jax manages to beat Her in Her weakened state, before being forced back by Jenac, who begins the process of spreading the worship of the original Gods again. The Gods are weak, but They have abilities They can grant, and information from the past that is relevant. Nimon is unaware They are back.

Jenae, after an earlier disagreement with Jax, helps him to find that his brother was recently in the city of Himnel. Oren and the others implore Jax to free their families, to bring them to the Tower from Himnel. He agrees, pausing only long enough to have his body inked with tattoos, guided by Jenae, Ame, a Mer runesmith, and a tattooist named Renna.

While attempting to find a hidden entrance to the city, used by smugglers, Oracle, who has fallen in love with Jax and he with her, is captured and taken deep underground by the drow, a race of Dark Elves that are scouting the city for an unknown reason. Jax catches some of them, and in a bout of frantic insanity, imbues his body with sufficient mana that he gains a new ability 'Mana-Overdrive' speeding his movements and strength up, but it is short lived, and results in a 'crash' afterward. Jax uses this ability to kill two of the drow, and then, driven mad by Oracle's capture, pain and fear allows his darker side to come out as he tortures the drow for information.

Bane calms him down, hides the body from the others, and guides Jax back to himself. Jax's group, now including Barret, a former soldier and a member of Oren's ship's crew, dives underground, hunting the drow. Over the underground trip, they meet Ashrag, an ancient Cave Spider, who remembers the Empire, and despite her monstrous appearance, was once an Imperial Citizen. Jax resurrects ancient Oaths, claiming them as his own at Amon's direction, and passes out from the mana drain. This convinces Ashrag and, after fighting a group of her brood, she swears allegiance. She agrees, on the condition that Jax free the tunnels of the drow who view her kind, and their bodies, as a great delicacy.

Jax eventually leads his team through the various dark places, and finds Oracle, captured by the drow leader, a Drider. The half woman-half spider, has several smugglers held captive and fights the group. Jax is triumphant, but Cam dies at the hands of the drow. Oracle is freed and the smugglers are mainly compliant, save their leader, who ends up making a comment that Jax disagrees with pointedly, and dies.

The last few drow fight a retreat, until they are killed by a new threat coming the other way along the tunnel. The three newcomers slaughter the drow, then, after a tense standoff, are revealed to be Imperial Legionnaires. The Imperial Legion has been dismissed and derided since the Cataclysm, slowly dwindling in numbers and through several bad apples in leadership, have become outsiders in their own homes. They are disliked and disrespected by the locals, even as they march out to fight the creatures that nobody else can.

The Legion is falling apart, its members lost and despairing, until Jax resurrects the Oaths, and finally a chance at a future is given back to them.

The three scouts, Yen, Tang and Amaat swear to Jax, and reveal that they are even now, below the City of Himnel.

BOOK THREE:

Jax leads the group to the surface, fighting off a group of local thugs who attempt to hunt the Legionnaires, and eventually reach the Arena and Arena Master Mal, one of the local leaders of the Smuggler's Guild. This is the man Oren had recommended as the best choice of an ally in the city. At the same time Jax is in the process of capturing a small group of Djinn, who offer allegiance in exchange for freeing their captured clan mother from the Skyking.

Mal agrees to help, for a fee, and introduces his team; Soween, his right hand, Jay his muscle and Josh his mage and Soween's husband. While Jax is resting, and about to finally get some 'private time' with Oracle, who can assume human form and size at will, Mal receives a message from the local crime lord, the Skyking. He demands Mal turn over the 'Legion' having discovered that it was Legionnaires that killed its people. Mal refuses, and instead, to gain the time they need, arranges a series of arena fights with the 'captured' Legionnaires, including Jax, and betting games.

While Mal makes these arrangements, Jax and his team visit a local healer, intending to get some of the deep seated injuries to his brain that are slowing his ability and level growth addressed. Along the way, Jax is surrounded by the enslaved, seeing the casual cruelty of the people, the way that nobles laugh and stroll, while slaves on the verge of starvation carry their bags. Amon sees this and their twinned rage escapes control, resulting in a temper-tantrum of epic proportions, leveling a section of the city and freeing the slaves, while also releasing Amon to face Jax inside his own mind.

Jax manages to defeat Amon, but in the process, discovers that he's had an unrecognized parasitic inhabitant all this time. He tears it free, gutting himself in the process, and only survives through the intervention of his team getting him to the healer, and the divine help of Jenae.

The Legion, having lost contact with their scouts, and seeing the devastation in the city, send a small, but elite team out to investigate, and with their help, Jax is returned to the Arena. The Legion settles in to protect him.

Jax is drained by the healing, and Centurion Primus Augustus, one of the four Primus of the Legion, fights in his place in the Arena that night, slaughtering all thrown against him.

Jax awakens and meets Mal and the others, works to integrate himself with the Legion and meets the non-human members of the shipyards who've been brushed aside by Barabarattas and his kind as 'sub-human'. They are recruited, and a plan formed. Rather than escaping with everyone through the hidden Smuggler's Path and robbing the city for the Tower's needs, a new more daring plan is concocted.

The airships are built in the shipyards, and Himnel's greatest weapon is under construction, the battleship. Currently it's a bare structure, open to the elements, but under the plan, additional volunteers are brought in, and the battleship is sealed up, and made, minimally, airworthy. The Legion are contacted and given orders, in three days they are to capture the shipyards.

Having little alternative, and no love for the city, as well as a legitimate authority encouraging it, the Legion agree.

Jax fights and recovers that night and trains, dragging Grizz, the Legionnaire into his group, as well as Yen and Tang. The next night, after the fight, he leads his team to raid and rob the Magical Emporium, a golem secured shop. The presence of the golem leads Jax and the others to discover a hidden section below the main shop, unknown by all. They realize that long ago it wasn't a shop, but a golem repair and construction facility. The golems are claimed, the construction facility below ground being ordered to begin repairs and construction, while golems there are used to repair ancient mining golems, which are sent to the Tower, burrowing underground. The rest of the golems are sent to wait in the river for the assault on the shipyards.

The following night the Arena fight is 'fixed', but Jax, with the help of his team, wins, and they launch the assault. Combining the assault on the Skyking with the one on the shipyards, Jax and the small Legion team, along with his own, take the Skyking's tower, killing them all. Halfway through the fight, when confronted with the rarely seen Anubai, a heavily magical species, Jax activates his trump card, his Tattoos. Rather than being decorative, they are in fact magical runes enabling him to channel mana through them, helping him to turn the tables on his foes.

In the fight, they capture the first of the airships circling on 'overwatch' over the city. To capture the others, Jian assumes control of one of the ships and accidentally, being unfamiliar with the controls, fires a giant fireball at the tent city of recruits around the Dark Citadel of Nimon. Jax, as the leader of the group, is blamed and declared Apostate, and a holy war begins.

The ships are brought under Jax's control, and return to the shipyards, to be crewed by his people. In the following confusion, Jax is hit in the head and injured. The ships flee Himnel, having stolen the vast majority of the city's manastone store, which are needed to power the engines of the ships.

Without stones, Barabarattas is unable to give chase, and the ships head out to sea, hoping to leave the impression that they're not from the Tower, and as Jax had ordered. Unfortunately, Nimon is aware of the truth.

The Dark Legion attacks the stragglers leaving the city, and their latest recruit, Thomas assists in killing some of Jax's Legionnaires. Jax awakens when they are far out to sea, close to the Sunken City, a flying city from the old Empire that crashed into a seamount. He confirms the orders to land there, to make the ships secure, and then to make for the Great Tower. He also finally gets some 'private time' with Oracle.

BOOK FOUR:

Jax meets the Legion leadership, Prefect Romanus, and Alistor, his right hand, as well as the crew of the battleship and many of the refugees. While in transit, Jenae informs Jax that knowledge he needs is lost in the Sunken City, and he vows to find it. Jax is still recovering, but by the time the ship lands, along with its much smaller escorts, at the Sunken City, he attempts to meet the two local parties from both Himnel, and its enemy city Narkolt.

Both are found to be led by 'nobles' but Himnel's is using slave labor, as well as being offensive, and suffers an 'accident' involving a sword. Narkolt's group are slightly more respectful and are given twenty-four hours to come back and discuss their intentions. The remaining guards from the Himnel group are given the same chance. As part of the discussion Jax uses an Imperial Ability, freeing the city of the souls of the unquiet dead that were condemned to roam it eternally, granting them their peace.

Once this is realized by the nobles, they ignore Jax's warning, and lead their people into the city's depths, searching for loot and artifacts. Jax orders the Legion into it as well, then leads his team in. In searching the depths, they are trapped by a landslide and explosions, set off by one of the nobles from Narkolt, and are forced into the depths.

Jian uses one of two books Jax gives him at this point and summons a demon to assist him, although it becomes clear the demon cares little for anything but gaining its own power. In the search, they are attacked by a group of feral Gnomes, explorers trapped long ago by the undead revenants and worse. These Gnomes were forced into a small pocket that, with typical gnomish ingenuity, they made into a livable space. They were then enslaved by a Skinwalker and its controlled Leviathans, forced to give their water and more to it, leaving them a water source heavily contaminated by metal, to drink and to raise crops from. The result is that the Gnomes essentially are driven feral, regressing and attacking each other. A small group is preserved as best as they can, while the greater population succumbs to madness.

These mad Gnomes attack Jax and, in the process, he and Oracle heal one of them, at least partially restoring his mind. Giint is broken by the things he's seen and done, and joins Jax, not knowing what else to do. The remaining feral Gnomes attack, and are driven back, as Jax and the team attack the Skinwalker and its pets. Jax wins the fight, but the Skinwalker, unbeknownst to them, is inside the creature they just killed, and escapes.

Back with the Dark Legion, Thomas, wounded from long ago injuries, is offered up to the Dark God, allowing His blood to mingle with Thomas' and regaining his magic, as well as sparking to life a dark seed, as he begins to fall in love with Belladonna, his squad leader.

Jax uses an Essence Core and gains the ability of flight and increased mana regeneration through meditation. Jenae reaches out, informing them that a hidden force is incoming, led by the drow, with captive SporeMothers. Jax orders Oracle to go to the fleet resting overhead. They are to leave immediately and fly at full speed to the Tower to defend it. Jenae makes it clear that the Gnome's original ship, while hidden, is still usable, but the DarkSpore the SporeMothers could release would result in massive casualties if the fleet doesn't leave.

A small number of the Gnomes have been swayed by Giint and wish to join Jax, agreeing to lead him to the hidden ship. He leaves them to prepare, attacking the nearby camp of the undead, led by a necromancer from Earth, a previously sent through 'volunteer'. Bartholomew the Lich, or 'Barry' as Jax refers to him, appears and traps the team, only to have Lydia, in a burst of desperation, seize the hidden power of the Valkyrie, turning the tide of the battle and beginning her own ascension. Barry is killed in the fight, and Jax, when he recovers the rest of the loot from the vault, also awakens a slumbering Wisp. Jax, his team, and the Gnomes race to reach the ship, receiving injuries along the way, but reach it just as the enemy arrives overhead.

The ship is powered up, and the Wisp is permitted to bind itself to the Gnome's ship, gaining control. They use explosives from the Gnomes to free the ship of its hidden location, and then fight their way out of the Sunken City.

One of the enemy ships crashes in the fight, releasing the SporeMother and leaving it behind, while the others follow. In the fights that come, Jax and his team are badly injured, and Stephanos dies, killed by a drow. Just as all seems lost, Mal appears, flying his own ship and driving the drow back, having left the fleet to come and help.

Jax and the others start to recover, only to have Jenae reach out, informing them that Nimon has dispatched His Dark Legion, an advanced force, to make a portal close to the Great Tower, and plans to assault it. With that, Jax orders Tenandra, the name the gnomish ship's Wisp has chosen for herself, to get them to the fleet with all haste.

BOOK FIVE:

Jax transfers ships. Along with his team, and he orders the fleet to land as soon as they are over land again, cross-loading the most skilled Legionnaires and his own team onto a small number of the fastest ships. He leaves the fleet under Romanus' control, and names Augustus as his heir, in case anything happens. Miren, Jian's lover and the surviving archer of the team, quits, unable to keep going.

The faster group flies ahead, securing the Tower and using the majority of the stolen manastones to repair the structure in a massive burst of magic. The next few days are filled with training and meetings as Jax tries to get the Tower's structure, both physical and command, established. Then quests are given by the awakened Gods, and as the Tower is secured. Jax raids the other locations in the path of the oncoming Dark Legion, determined to prevent them from uncovering the golems that could make a massive difference in the upcoming confrontation.

While these are being stripped, Denny, a Legion trap smith, takes an advance force and sets up an ambush for the approaching enemies. Jian's demon rebels and is banished, leaving Jian weaker and furious. He turns to the second book on demon summoning, and heartbroken at the news that Miren has run straight into the bed of a Legionnaire, binds a succubus, Sehran. When Jax finds out, he and Oracle question Sehran, but permit her to stay as a part of the team on a trial basis.

Thomas, unbeknown to Jax, is a member of the closing Dark Legion, and on a side mission, discovers he has a rare gift. As a Dark Berserker, his own nascent power as a berserker is corrupted by the dark gift.

Jax joins Denny and the others, and the trap is sprung, annihilating the majority of the Dark Legion, and Jax, after injuring Belladonna, is beaten back by Thomas. The pair fight each other, unknowing, and Jax escapes, setting off a magical attack that kills several of Thomas' friends in the process. Jax and the Legion take their airship and fall back, while the Dark Legion flee and Jax proceeds to clear local sites of interest.

A hidden interloper, Ronin the Bard, is discovered in the Tower, and joins Jax's team, bringing knowledge, music and a little magic to the team. The Arbuton, a sentient tree, is found living atop one of the old outposts, and deals are struck, with Jax sending a golem to aid the Arbuton, and the Arbuton sending Woodite, a Grove Tender, and its mate, Ha'zel, along with two guardians to assist the Tower.

In the exchange, Jax is separated from the team and dragged underground through a river, only to find a long-buried city filled with kobolds who summon their revenants and attack him. He uses his ability to free the souls of the enslaved within the kobolds' weapons, trapped and ensorcelled revenants, and strips the city of life.

When Jax awakes, having been overpowered by his ability, he finds one of the spirits waiting for him and it offers to guide him out. On the way however, Jax is contacted by Malthus, the 'Administrator of Pelath's View'. The being claims to be bonded to the city, much in the way that Seneschal is bonded to the Tower, and is alone, having been buried for long ages. He offers knowledge and artifacts, as well as a safe fallback position for the Empire should it need it, all in exchange for company. And a song.

Jax agrees, and several hours later, reaches the surface, meeting Oracle and the others, before returning to the Tower, finding that the rest of the fleet has arrived.

Thomas throws caution to the wind, determined to save Belladonna, and has her bound to his back, an IV drip botched together using a vampire's teeth and worse, to share his own blood, and hopefully the healing ability that he shares with Jax, with her. He sets off running to the Dark Citadel, as Jenae informs Jax that She found traces of Thomas… as a Dark Legionnaire.

Jax dispatches Mal and Augustus to Narkolt to try and recruit the Legion garrison there, then returns to clearing the surrounding areas. He and Amon face each other again, this time Amon comes out ascendant, and faces an ancient evil, devastating it, the village, and the land around for miles. Jax has his power torn out of his control, and has a split second to fight Amon, or save Oracle and Bob, who, as bonded companions, need his mana and health pool to live. Jax chooses them, and uses his rising understanding of magic to free them both, forcibly evolving Oracle into a new species.

Lydia faces her past, as well as her father and husband, who sold her into slavery. Jax and the rest of the team watch as she beats them half to death, then the team travels to the slave markets of the Habieen, following the path her mother was taken on to be sold. The resultant fight includes a mana-hurricane, and only the intervention of the Gods keeps Jax alive, but badly broken. Tenandra takes the ship and flies away, attempting to get reinforcements and to draw attention from Jax as he's carried by his people, surrounded by hundreds of freed slaves, into the forests.

The Dark Legion, guided by Nimon, chases Jax, who has recovered consciousness, and his people. Jax sends Lydia and Grizz to free the soul of the last Valkyrie, claiming her armor, rather than letting the following Dark Legion stumble over its resting place. With the rest of the team sent away, Jax is down to Bob, Ronin and Bane, and he sends Bob and Ronin to guide the freed slaves, sending Bane to hunt the Dark Legion's scouts.

The Dark Legion advance teams kill the slowest of the refugees, showing no mercy, and Jax makes a decision, asking for volunteers. They slowed the advance, killing several dozen, but seeing that there's no chance, with the numbers arrayed against them. Jax sends the volunteers on ahead, ordering them to protect the others, as he remains behind to buy them time.

He uses his flight ability, 'Soaring Majesty' to conduct a series of hit and run attacks, drawing the enemy to him, before folding together the most powerful spell he can, literally drawing a firestorm down upon himself, while screaming a challenge to Nimon, the Dark God himself. Then Jax attacks the Dark Legion, determined to sell his life as dearly as possible.

In the course of the fight, the brothers come face to face again, this time Thomas wins, pinning Jax to a tree with a spear, removing his helm to see the light in his enemy's eyes die… only to look into his brother's eyes.

Thomas rebels against Nimon and his weakened blood, drained heavily into Belladonna, allows him to swear to Lagoush, Goddess of Water, and he is accepted as Her champion. The brothers fight the Dark Legion together, but no matter how valiant, skilled, and dangerous, two men cannot defeat hundreds.

At the end, as they both believe it's all over, Augustus steps forward, Mal having gathered all those that he could, and brought them when he realized what was happening at the slave camp. The Imperial Legion faces its antithesis, and wins, driving the Dark Legion back. Jax is collected, and the forces fall back to the Great Tower, the refugees being shepherded by Legionnaires and airships.

Bane, however, is missing…

BOOK SIX:

Jax and Thomas have been reunited, and although the return to the Great Tower was painful, both of them being badly wounded, they have made it back to a secure location and start to rebuild their relationship.

Sint, God of Light and Order, had tasked Jax with recovering His Chosen Champion, and the airship bearing Lucian, Restun's Great-Great uncle arrives. A confrontation between uncle and nephew ensues, as Restun has spent his entire life, battling against the stigma of an uncle that was not only infected with vampiric essence, but that was banished from the Legion.

In the ensuing argument, and with the confirmation of Lord Sint, it is made clear that Lucian was made a scapegoat centuries ago to cover for the then Legion-General's excesses.

The result was an innocent man sent wandering the continent in the aftermath of the Cataclysm, battling evil wherever he found it. Lucian is elevated to Chief Justicar, and set to establish an order of Justicars to enforce the laws.

Jax and Tommy, now going by Thomas, set off and took the fragment of Lagoush, Lady of Water, to the Mer nearby. They continue on to reclaim the tools of Svetu, the God of Gnomes, long lost to the world in an ancient ruin.

The ruin, now populated by insane Goblins and Orcs, is hidden high in the mountains, taking up the front and publicly accessible section of an ancient Imperial production facility.

Jax and his team, assisted by Thomas, loot and recover the site, eliminating most of the inhabitants, and ending up with several Orcs that had been captured and enslaved, as new citizens. The production facility requires several tons of rare ores however, to regain functionality.

These ores were long ago mined by a lost mining golem, and Jax and his team set off to recover the golem, finding, in the process, a clan of Amilith. The mining golem (and the accumulated ore) is recovered, and the Amilith are left in their valley, all save two who are determined to reclaim a member of their tribe back at the Tower.

On the way back to the Great Tower, several fleeing airships are seen, also heading for the Tower, and under attack by demons. Tenandra, in her ship-body, is able to get Jax and his companions close enough to fight the demons and save one of the ships, though the others are lost.

Rewn, City Lord of Narkolt is aboard the lead vessel, having been chased from Narkolt by an assassination attempt by the drow. Rewn swears to Jax, and agrees to relinquish the city to his control, but in the process of the discussion, is revealed as being a puppet.

Rewn has been 'guided' by his advisors for his entire life, provided a wiling harem, drink and drugs, and told what to say in public. He is utterly unprepared for the realities of life, and breaks down on learning he will actually have to work if he expects to rule in truth in Narkolt.

Bane, missing from Jax and the others since the battle in the forest against the Dark Legion, is found to have been diverted by Tamat, Goddess of Assassins and Dark Deeds, and is currently slaughtering her hated brother Nimon's priests. He rescues a trio of Dwarven women, and they assist him in his slaughtering of the priesthood, as well as their escape, as Bane attempts to return to Jax and his friends.

Rewn attempts to involve himself in the plans for retaking Narkolt, and is handled by one of his concubines, Carmen. He is removed from any kind of leadership position in the short term, while Jax and the Legion assault Narkolt.

Mal is sent ahead, along with a small team of spies, all of whom are captured on arrival, after Mal's lover Alyssa, the owner of the 'Kneeling Lady' whorehouse, mistakenly arranges monitoring of him.

The assault on the city is hard fought, but ultimately successful, and a drow Drider, a massive half Dark Elf, half spider tears free of the City Keep, revealing the drow presence for all to see.

In the ensuing fight, a great many good people are lost, but eventually, the city is taken, and Jax turns to mopping up. The drow, attempting to flee from the city, use a heavily modified transport to try and collect their remaining forces from the 'Kneeling Lady'. They release an immature SporeMother into the city, and Oracle is injured. Jax loses his shit and beats the SporeMother almost to death with his gauntleted fists.

Oracle is exposed as having been changed by the spells and bonding that Jax was forced to bind her with when Amon had torn his connection apart in their last altercation.

Days pass as Jax consolidates his control over the city of Narkolt, and Rewn finally arrives, attempting to declare his ownership, and refusing to learn his place. This results in him being stripped of all rights to the city, and his former lover Carmen, now imprisoned by his hand, being raised up instead to rule the city in Jax's name.

The City interface grants a true Imperial Noble with access rights, a way of monitoring all illegal actions in the city. Jax and his people make use of this to gut the Smuggler's Guild, wiping out the majority of the corruption that has festered in the nobility since time immemorial as well.

Many of the nobles refuse to swear fealty to Jax, and are banished, fleeing with their forces into the surrounding forest. Mal is named a noble, and proceeds to name Alyssa his lady, then brings his father, Hannibal, in to finish gutting the Smuggler's Guild, using the pretense that he was banned from all the 'good bars' by them when he was declared a traitor for helping Jax.

The ancient Imperial Armory under Narkolt is uncovered, and a sleeping Elder God, the original Valspar, is accidentally set free, before being summarily killed in the ensuing chaos when the Gods lend a hand, fearing the result should such a creature regain its strength of old. The Armory contains some working facilities, and they are turned to producing golems and weaponry.

Bane arrives during the fight against the Valspar, and helps to turn the tide, before retaking his position as leader of Jax's personal bodyguard.

The city manastone mine is also recovered, an ancient deposit of stones that had been continually converting the city's sewage to manastones since the Cataclysm. This fact had been long lost, and the sewage had been allowed to continue building up, until Jax and his team, literally swimming through the sewage at times, cleared it out and reclaimed it and started repairs.

Barabarratas is inducted into the order of Vampyrs by his assistant Cletus, who in turn is a supporter of Akanji, Lucian's brother. Barabarratas, seeing that his enemy Jax has claimed and secured both the Great Tower, and the city of Narkolt, changing the balance of power on the continent, makes a deal with the Dark Legion and Nimon's priesthood. In exchange for them protecting the city, he cedes some control over it to them.

As Jax and his forces prepare to assault Himnel, a Wisp colony is discovered far to the north, with several of the Wisps being captured by Himnel's forces. One is forcibly bonded to a young girl that is found to have enough of the noble Imperial bloodline. Through Nimon's blessing, she is able to assume control of Himnel, in name only. She is, however, able to command the golems in the city to fight Jax and his forces when the assault begins.

Thomas is sent with Tenandra and a small team to rescue the Wisps, while Jax, with Romanus advising, leads the assault on Himnel. The airship battle is short, the new weapons and methods of manufacturing that Jax has brought to the UnderVerse result in the annihilation of Himnel's forces.

Once the Legion is flown into Himnel's territory, they are deposited and create a beachhead, protecting the area as the Himnel army and elite forces are flown in as well.

Barabarratas orders an assault on their position, one that takes the lives of many Legionnaires, but is ultimately unsuccessful. Romanus is badly injured and Jon takes over as leader of the assault above ground, while Jax and Augustus, along with the remaining Legionnaires and his team, use a mining golem to assault Himnel from below, thinking to avoid the walls, and the deaths of innocents that would come if they were to assault the city directly.

Under Himnel, Jax and his team meet Barabarratas's secret weapon, a captive SporeMother breeding ground, along with hundreds of possessed undead.

Jax fights the SporeMothers, and eventually kills Cletus Thane, Barabarratas's assistant and handler. Several of Thomas's old Dark Legionnaire team are exposed as having been transformed into monsters to track and kill him for abandoning Nimon, and one of them is found and eliminated.

Jax takes control of the SporeMothers, and the hunt for the Vampyrs begins, resulting in several of the coven being killed off, and Alistor, the former Tribune of the Legion of Himnel, being exposed as a traitor and a secret adherent of Nimon.

In the following assault on Himnel's keep, Jax forcibly converts the golems to his side, but only after the deaths of many of the Legion. Jax and the remaining forces assault the remaining enemy forces in Barabarratas's throne room, and in the fight, Jax and Amon bond.

The Eternal Emperor augments Jax's abilities and knowledge, enabling him to easily exert his will over many of those there, and in a pitched battle, Lucian defeats Akanji.

The City of Himnel is taken by Jax and the Dark Legion, along with their surviving priesthood, flee to their citadel.

With the twin cities of Himnel and Narkolt held by Jax, and the airships as well, the Dark Citadel is gradually reduced in power, starving their forces, until after a few days of constant attrition, Nimon takes a direct hand on events.

The Arch Lich Ghastool, empowered by Nimon, leads his forces out of the depths of the ocean and assaults Himnel, Jax and his forces having deployed already before the city in the defensive emplacements they'd been preparing to fight the Dark Legion from.

Grizz is killed in the fighting, and the horror of his failure, the realization that many of his mistakes and the deaths caused by them are down to his own refusal to admit his differences from the others, drives Jax to take a final step, and to accept his power. He bonds himself to Amon.

Jax saves Grizz, returning him to life, and as a newly born Master of Mana. He then lifts into the air, slaughtering the Lich's army and the Arch Lich himself, tearing the mana that was sustaining the ancient undead free in a single act, using that mana to raise his 'Genetic Viability' overall by more than twenty percent though a single spell.

The Heliogifts, magical claymore mines, that had been hidden in the field ahead waiting for the Dark Legion's advance, are set off as the Dark Legion, well, advances…

Many of the Dark Legion elites are slaughtered in the ensuing explosion, and more are killed as Jax unleashes his own war golems, before finally unleashing a spell crafted by one of Amon's highest mages.

The Dark Citadel is destroyed, and Nimon, in a fit of rage, challenges Jax to a battle for his soul. Jax agrees, and the Gods gather round, ensuring a fair fight, reforming his armor and healing him, preparing him for the battle ahead.

Nimon and Jax have equal points agreed, all of Jax's stats are totaled, and Nimon creates a physical avatar with the same points. Unfortunately for Jax, the physical avatar has no need of such things as Intelligence, Charisma or Wisdom, being controlled by Nimon himself.

As such the avatar is physically far superior to Jax, and Jax wins only through a combination of blind luck, and trickery, thanks to his razorwire belt. Jax kills Nimon, cutting His head free, and orders that it be made into a goblet, just because he can.

That night, in the celebrations and festivities, Oracle drops the bombshell to Jax that, regardless of all the perfectly good reasons why it shouldn't have happened, including their being different species, and her having never previously had a body capable of it, she was indeed, pregnant. His life, never simple, got far more complicated.

BOOK SEVEN:

Jax, having survived to claim the continent of Dravith, was now officially heir primus to the throne of the empire, and had one year in which to hold to his title, before he may climb the crystal steps to the throne of the empire.

Provided, of course, he survived long enough, and could travel to the heart of the empire to do so.

That wasn't the most terrifying change in his life, though. The Prince of the Empire, Imperial Scion and Master of all Dravith, had been struck with an entirely unexpected—albeit not unwelcome—new title as well: father-to-be.

Oracle, his love, his wisp and soul mate, was pregnant, and after sobering up and realizing the implications of this, he turned to the only being he felt he could speak to frankly, and that wouldn't be over-awed by him, or forced to sugarcoat an answer.

The God of Light and Order, Sint.

Unfortunately, due to his divine nature, Sint had never had to deal with such matters, and so gave little advice beyond the immediate to secure the throne and the continent, and to deal with any and all threats as quickly as possible.

He did, however, also give Jax a quest, and a great deal of information, as well as advice, on the next step, regarding the fragment of divinity that Jax recovered from Nimon.

Jax had two choices before him. The first was that he absorb the fragment, and gain a significant boost in power. Although Jax was instantly tempted by that, he was warned that this was, in fact, the lesser of the two paths open to him.

The second was to bind the fragment to his soul, and begin his ascension to godhood.

Ten fragments were required to lift him into the ranks of the lesser gods, on par with Darakin and Issa, Illoth and Asmodeus, among others.

When Jax decided to bind the fragment, and attempted ascension instead of absorbing it, Sint offered him a quest to do so, and then left him to find his path.

Over the ensuing days, Jax battled to bring stability to his fledgling and resurgent empire. He named Thomas as Leader of the Imperial Senate, and others to high offices, before turning control of Himnel over to Duke Augustus and Clan Mother Hellenica.

While trying to bring order to the city, and hand over responsibility for it, an attempted assassination brought to his attention that not all in the city were either devoted, or at least apathetic to his rule.

Instead, in the ancient and forgotten "wizards tower" in the center of the city, a new force had taken up residence…one that had successfully hidden from his forces and his abilities.

In the ensuing fight, he discovered that the notification advising all that he had formally claimed his place in the succession of the empire wasn't limited to only the UnderVerse.

The banished and escaped nobles of his own realm, Earth, had also received such information, and, in a fit of rage, had begun to return, en masse, through forbidden blood magic rituals.

The destructive nature of blood magic meant that the portals used to return them were rendered to scrap afterward, and no control over the location of the far portal was possible.

As such, many of the nobles emerged into long forgotten or ruined locations. There was no way to control or maintain the connection, and many died in transit, but some—including his father—made it through.

Their locations were hidden, but as Jax explored and then destroyed the Himnel tower, he found that it was not the only local emergence point.

Travelling to Narkolt, he led a stealthy search of the area around that city's tower, finding that it, too, had fallen to the enemy.

Although the majority of the legion were training at the Great Tower, and Thomas and his team had been dispatched to secure the imperial production facility—whose portal was also active and under enemy control—Jax was counterattacked by forces of the old nobility.

In the fight that followed, Jax learned more of the secrets behind the fall, and that although Narkolt appeared strong from the outside, even with the infiltrators purged, it stood at the brink of collapse.

Raiders, escaped smugglers, Dark legionnaires, and the local and now displaced nobility who refused to serve the empire had fled into the nearby forests.

There, they raided the villages and caravans that made up the lifeblood of Narkolt, and after the war with Himnel, its own forces were severely depleted.

Jax worried about the team that had been sent to the prax Glorious Retribution—now known as the sunken city—far off the coast, but agreed to hold off on travelling to secure it. Instead, he led his forces to secure the forest, as Restun and Romanus, of the legion, brought in reinforcements to assist.

In the ensuing battle, an ancient harp, the Cursed Harp of Athelas, was discovered. The party nearly succumbed to its lure, abandoning all control, before Ronin, the bard, saved them.

Other camps hidden in the forest were drawn to the sounds of battle. Jax and his party led the rescued and sworn guards saved from the harp's influence to defend the camp, until Tenandra arrived, her ripple fire cannons clearing the field.

Over the next several days, the party recovered, and although emotionally damaged through the influence of the harp's evil magic, they grew closer, as they travelled to the sunken city.

Once there, they found that it, too, had been invaded by the nobles. The party that held the control center had access to a portal, and had captured the group Jax had sent ahead.

In the fight to save them, and to take control of the site, a panicking son of the noble who had laid claim to the structure triggered an artifact, suppressing all use of mana in the area, and trapped Jax in a collapsed section, after they used explosive weaponry from Earth.

Jax, cut off from magic, with his abilities suppressed, spells not available, and significant injuries, was forced to battle his way down to the lowest levels of the prax, to then return upward through a different, and less damaged section.

During the trek, he recovered several large and powerful manastones, giving him limited access to mana but at a horrifically inflated cost, faced foes who had taken over the lower reaches of the city and who had been mutated by the constant exposure to mana, and finally, discovered and rescued a group of semi-feral gnomes.

Using the gnomes, and their knowledge of the prax, Jax recovered some ancient Praetorian armor, and, wearing it, fought his way through the remaining guards of the invaders and to the control room.

Blinded, he attacked, desperate to reach Oracle and his friends, feeling that she and Sehran had somehow been sent far from him. Unable to see, he was forced through a portal to a hidden location, before the portal was again shut.

Trapped on the far side, he discovered Sehran, starving and cut off from her lover, Jian. He bound her to himself, giving her access to his mana and saving her life.

He was, however, surrounded.

Hundreds of both the long dead and the more recently captured attacked him, and he discovered the terrifying reality of the buried city he had been cast into.

It was a long forgotten, and hated, outpost of a creature that was old when the gods first walked the land. For it, mana was inimical to its form: a sentient, distributed liquid intelligence. In forcing its form into these bodies, and the bodies of the soldiers and the other nobility who had been caught exploring its depths, it had learned much about the realm, and now was ready to attempt to lay claim to it once again.

In the deep past, far greater gods than those who currently walked the UnderVerse died in their attempt to cleanse reality of its infection.

Now, with them long gone, the Dark Tide, Xenefier, was returning. In discovering Oracle, a creature both of magic and of flesh in a way it had never encountered, was pregnant, it realized it had found a way to both survive the hated touch of mana and evolve to its highest possible state.

All it had to do was take Jax and Oracle's unborn child and contaminate it with its own form. As that child grew, with its inherited mastery of mana at an instinctual level and access to the imperial throne and all of the abilities that inferred, it could finally claim the realm and rule over all.

Jax, Oracle, and Sehran managed to escape, and in doing so destroyed much of the city, fleeing into underground caverns and along long-buried and forgotten passages. But Xenefier survived, wounded, driven back…but not destroyed.

In their escape, Jax and his now much smaller party encountered a second city, though this one was far more recent in creation—a living city, one that was in a constant state of war with Xenefier and its creations, and also with the creatures known as S'barrr, huge reptilian things that hunted the city's inhabitants, the Xon'dike.

The Xon'dike—survivors of a second, much more heavily damaged, crashed prax—had devolved, losing much of their technology and knowledge, reverting into a superstitious and fanatical group, one built around the worship of…the empire.

When Sehran fed on an injured S'barrr and discovered—too late—that its blood was in effect a highly concentrated alcohol, she let slip Jax's identity, and far from falling to their knees and worshipping him, they declared him a blasphemer and heretic.

Jax, Oracle, and a cleansed Sehran were forced to flee, not wanting to kill a bunch of misguided fools who might be recoverable, and after many hours, finally found their way to the surface. Unfortunately, what they found, as Oracle recognized a distant landmark, was that they were even farther from home than they feared.

They were not even on the same continent.

Instead, as they stared out across miles of rolling sand dunes, the heat of the barren desert shimmering, and making the remains of the ancient buried city in the distance seem to hover, they realized that they were alone, far from home.

BOOK EIGHT

Following the events at Narkolt and the defeat of Nimon, Jax, Oracle, and Sehran found themselves unexpectedly transported thousands of miles away to the continent of Carrmor. Separated from their companions and the Imperial Legion, they quickly realized they had a decision to make.

They could hide and hope for rescue, or take action.

First and foremost, they knew that they had to learn about this continent, navigate this new hostile territory while protecting Oracle and her unborn child, and only then could they make a decision about the next step.

Their arrival dropped them in the middle of a vast desert after their first encounter with living Xon'dike. Unfortunately for Jax and the others, the Xon'dike were also religious zealots.

After the party escaped through a tunnel collapse into the desert above, Oracle realized that a distant city and its distinctive buildings were once in the midst of fertile lands before the cataclysm.

Making their way to the ruined Dome of Truth, they battled desert creatures, including massive sand wurms and wyverns, before finding the strange "Changed Ones."

These humans had been experimented on and were magically modified with insect-like mutations through an attempt to alter them to better live in the spreading desert, as well as to give them a chance to survive and counter "what walks between."

Whatever that was though, records have long forgotten, and after destroying the binding machine and freeing a few surviving Changed Ones from their mental slavery, they encountered an angry horde of giant scorpions. Fleeing the city, they teamed up with a small group of survivors led by Finna and Toren, who guided them to the rest of their party, a band of refugees from a caravan that was attacked by slavers working with the Caravaneer's Guild, which maintained a ruthless monopoly on trade routes.

Jax convinced the survivors to swear allegiance to the empire in exchange for protection, revealing himself as the imperial prince. In exchange, he agreed to lead them to retrieve the rest of their group, now held by the same slavers, and they crossed the desert to rescue them, battling massive desert predators along the way.

At the slaver camp, they discovered the "Sons of the Deep," a particularly vile organization that used necromancy to turn their dead slaves into soldiers. Jax used his imperial ability to free all the slaves by shattering their control collars, and in the process discovered a few imperial legionnaires who had been surviving in Carrmor for centuries.

The legion, however, retained little of their vaunted former glories. Instead, forced by unwise additional oaths inflicted by a well-meaning—but foolish—noble in the past, the legions of Carrmor had been compelled through their oaths to throw themselves into battle against unwinnable odds for centuries.

Due to their extreme experiences and as it was their only chance at survival, for long years the legion grew stronger, simply given no alternative beyond success or death.

But as all things must, the centuries of poor support, increasing threats, and the decimation of their ranks reduced the legions to a fraction of a fraction of their once vaunted strength.

No longer feared by the slavers, they had become the ultimate prize instead, for a legionnaire captured, forced to obey and carefully permitted only to see certain things, made a perfect guard for those who could afford them—or better yet, fodder for the arenas.

As such, few legionnaires now survived outside of captivity, and if Jax wanted to save them, he had to hunt the slavers even more desperately than before.

Worse still, the slaver camp victory came at a cost, as Jax's use of his imperial power drew Nimon's attention. Though the Dark God attempted to confront Jax directly, the protection of Jenae and other gods of the pantheon shielded him, and Nimon declared Jax a blood enemy to all his followers—again—though this time it was obvious it was simply to make it clear to all that Jax was no longer on a distant continent, but here, far from support, and within His reach.

The goddess Lagoush revealed that the Cradle of Feshcan'un, an ancient place of power, would be the safest location for Oracle to give birth. Unfortunately, that journey would be long and arduous, as well as taking them through dangerous territory, including the slaver-controlled town of Marrow and the nomadic tent city of Sonra, where a massive annual slave market was rapidly approaching.

Leading a growing army of freed slaves and exultant legionnaires, Jax battled against the Sons of the Deep.

After liberating the town of Marrow, he discovered that Earth nobles had also found their way to Carrmor and were competing to establish power bases.

When the group set up an ambush to free the last of the caravan's missing members, Jax faced off against a necromancer claiming to be thousands of years old. The ancient elf's contempt for the empire and his twisted view of necromancy as a misunderstood art were revealed and his teeth were kicked in, along with the rest of him. After a desperate fight that cost almost as many legionnaires their lives as they rescued, Jax prevailed, but time was fast running out.

In a moment of rash stupidity, Jax had publicly challenged the goddess Illoth to single combat at Sonra, with control of territories on Carrmor as the stake.

Thanks to Sint, if Jax was victorious, any city declaring for him would be instantly cleansed of drow influence, potentially allowing him to claim vast swaths of the continent without setting foot in them.

The caravan continued its journey across treacherous plains toward Sonra, battling the elements and slogging through dangerous bog lands. Along the way, Jax received training from Darakin, the God of Battle Himself, who materialized each night to spar with him in preparation for the coming confrontation with Illoth. These brutal training sessions left Jax battered but increasingly skilled.

Upon reaching Sonra, a vast tent city centered on nomadic herds, Jax's caravan was placed under observation by the city's leadership. As political maneuvering began, Illoth struck first, surrounding Sonra with an army of drow, driders, and spiders while sending assassins to eliminate Jax before their formal combat.

The assassination attempt failed when Darakin, Sint, and Tamat intervened, their divine presence forcing Illoth to honor the terms of the challenge. Escorted to the sacred inner ring of Sonra—a hidden sanctuary for endangered species shunned by the outer world—Jax entered the mystical Elsecaller, a pocket dimension between life and death where Illoth awaited in her terrifying drider form.

Despite Illoth's overwhelming size and strength, Jax used his alchemical poisons, tactical training, and growing connection to the divine fragment he took from Nimon to gradually turn the tide. In a brutal fight that tested every skill he'd learned, Jax ultimately won, claiming a second fragment of divinity and earning the loyalty of Sonra's people.

Best of all, the damage done to Illoth both in losing ten percent of her strength to Jax, and in the damage done to the perception of her in the minds of the realm, was immense.

With Illoth's defeat, Jax had secured his claim over any territory that swore allegiance to him, banishing all drow influence from those lands. The continent of Carrmor now lay open before him; he'd gained allies, grown stronger, and was poised to expand into this new land…

But in his rash challenge, others were made aware of his location, and given time to prepare…

PROLOGUE

"Hell would I know?" Mal snapped, sitting up, and accidentally knocking a pile of clothes from one of the chairs in his captain's cabin with a misplaced boot. "Dammit, what's a man got to do to get a damn cleaner in here! The rest of the ship's spotless—how come my cabin's always the last to be cleaned!" he roared, throwing his hands up in frustration.

"Sorry about that, Mal," Soween replied blandly, not looking up from the upgraded map on the captain's table. "I'm sure we can get the cabin boy in to clean your quarters for you."

"Damn right," Mal grumped, somewhat mollified and nodding to himself, even as he picked up the pile of clothes and looked around the room for somewhere to dump them that wasn't already covered in detritus.

The captain's cabin aboard his airship was a wonder: light, airy, and wide enough to fit his table, three chairs, and a built-in drinks cabinet, a bed large enough—in his professional opinion—for at least three, and two wardrobes.

Best of all was that the rear wall was made up almost entirely of windows, enabling him to open them mid-flight and get a truly breathtaking view for his morning coffee.

No matter what he did, though, the damn place was *always* a mess! Every day, he had to chase bloody cabin boys out at stupid times, the idle little sods complainin' that they'd been told to clean all things, yet tryin' to do it—of all times—when he was relaxing!

It was ridiculous!

Now, when he needed the place spotless so that he could think, there wasn't so much as a clear spot on a single surface to put down his clothes. And as to the wardrobes?

He grabbed a handle and yanked it open, staring in dismay at the complete lack of any fresh and clean clothes hanging ready for him.

"What the hell am I paying these people for?" He groaned, before tossing his armload of dirty washing in and slamming the door again before more than a handful of things could tumble free. Turning his back on the fresh trap, he washed his hands of any responsibility for it. "Right, dammit, I need this place cleaned, my clothes sorted, and right goddamn now!" he snarled.

"Sure, Mal," Soween replied absently. "So shall we go somewhere else to talk and plan?"

"What?" He frowned. "Why the hell would we do that? This is the captain's cabin!"

"The cabin boys need to get in here to clean it," she pointed out in that reasonable and calm tone that she damn well knew he hated. "So, if we're here planning, and they're trying to mop the floors, clean the windows, and straighten the place out, we're going to have to work around them, or—"

"Fine!" he snapped. "As soon as this meetin' is done, though! No more excuses, ya hear me?"

"I hear you fine, Mal." She nodded. "As soon as this meeting is done, the cabin boys can get in to clean, and you can have your midday meal in the galley."

"What?" He grunted in shock. "But—"

"So, do you think this is accurate?" She pointed at the small atoll on the map that she'd found.

"How in the hells would I know?" He sighed, moving over and peering down at the map. "I mean, the map was made by Himnel, and it's marked up as a random island, so, could be, I guess."

"We'll find out in a few days," she said. "Comparing the location to the original islands, and after what your father said about, what was it…?" She paused, trying to remember the strange name that he'd used.

"Catastrophic subsidence," Mal muttered. "He said that the cataclysm must have caused catastrophic subsidence, and that the original island would still be in roughly the same area, but that it'd be anywhere from a few meters to a mile deeper now. No way of telling."

"Well, if there's an atoll here…" She tapped the map, then pulled out the old map that she'd managed to bargain for not an hour ago, and jabbed her finger onto a badly drawn landmass on that one for emphasis as well. "And this map is right, then that's what's left of the island of Imshi."

"Still don't see why the hell that was important," Mal admitted, peering down at the two points. "I mean, sure, old maps can be useful, like treasure maps, and like this one for findin' our damn way around and back, but why do we care if that's the top of some old island? It's not like we can drag it back up into the sun, can we?"

"No sir, we can't, but if that's the top of the island, then it means that the whole place wasn't buried as deep as it could have been. Most likely, and more importantly for us, it means that should we find some who are comfortable in shallow water exploration, then we could still search the place."

"I mean, sure, if it's an old island that sank, people won't have managed to get much off it, but the chances that there's anything that can just be found by divin' in and having a little swim? If there was anythin' there, it'll be long gone by now. You can't tell me that people back then will have just shrugged and gone 'Oh well, that's Mickail's home gone; no need to send a boat and see if there be anything to salvage,' right?"

"That's just it, sir. What did the bard tell you about the fight between Jax and the lich? The one right before he fought Nimon?"

"Bad luck mentionin' *His* name," Mal muttered out of habit, squinting at the map and trying to remember. "He said somethin' about the lich sayin' he'd a massive stash, didn't he? I stopped listenin' when he said it was out of reach under the sea."

Mal shrugged, then scratched the back of his neck as he went on. "I mean, sure, yeah, a massive treasure that a lich that was plunderin' the corpse of the empire in the early days managed to get together would have been great, but there's a lot of ocean out there, and anythin' beyond a heated bathtub is too damn deep. You seen the shit out there? I have. One voyage as a boy, never again."

"I have," she agreed, smiling to herself as she stared at the little nub of an island. "And let's use a little common sense, shall we? If you were a lich—so you didn't have to breathe or have any worries about things like food and so on—would you want to live on the ocean floor?"

"Well…"

"Not where the sun gives you some light, not where there's a nice palace or anything…no, I mean literally at the bottom of the ocean?"

"What, where it's gonna be all muddy an' stuff?"

"Silt, I'd imagine, sir, but yes." She nodded encouragingly.

"Hell no. I'd be settin' up in a palace on the land. Get a load of walkin' corpses together, an' make them check the place out, give it a lick of paint, some nice views, that kinda thing. Bottom of the ocean's got to be shit for views."

"Exactly. So let's take it a step further. It's after the cataclysm, and you've got necromantic magic, but all the old laws and the whole world seems to be falling apart. You don't know if the nobility, the legion, or anyone else is going to leave you alone, decide to kill you and burn all your corpses, or keep coming to you with their problems.

"Remember that the legion enforced all the laws with a harsh boot. So if he's a lich, or even just a necromancer before this, he's going to have known that if the empire hears he's been breaking the laws, then they'll come for him…imperial mages, entire legions, the works."

"Right?" Mal nodded. "They didn't fuck about in those days."

"So, either you're a scumbag and you're used to hiding from the legion, or you're possibly an ex-imperial servant who knows that if you're setting up for yourself, you need to do it as far away from everyone as you can. Right?"

"Makes sense."

"So, you don't have concerns about the living—not about your body needing the same things they do, anyway—but you do know that you need bodies. A lot of bodies, and there's this whole island that's just sunk off the coast. Sure, getting to it might be a problem, but if he manages that, once he's there, he doesn't need to breathe or anything, so what's the issue? He can probably see in the dark, or make light or whatever, but is he going to want to live at the bottom of the ocean in all the silt and dead things that float down?"

"Maybe it'd be good for his magic?" Mal mused.

"It'd be rotting," she pointed out. "You remember that leviathan corpse we saw washed up along the coast last week?"

"Gods, yeah, that stank." Mal grunted. "Even the reagents we recovered had to be burned in the end…too big to go in bags, and too rotten to carry."

"Exactly. Plus, as we said, sir, why set up at the bottom of the ocean, when there's an entire island's worth of buildings that were sunk along with it? Why set up a new palace or something, when instead he could literally take one of them over and do what he wants? It's not like anyone else is going to come looking. And if they do? Free fresh bodies."

"And best of all, he gets to loot the entire island," Mal breathed. "Makes sense."

"That's what Jax thought."

"The boy knows about this?" Mal glared at her. "Dammit, you got my hopes up already. I was going to go looking!"

"Would you, sir?" she asked, carefully concealing her smile. "If, for example, we could get there ahead of any recovery party that was being sent, I'm sure that Cai and your father, in their official roles, could turn a blind eye to a recovery fee…"

"Ah, it'd not be worth it," he groused. "What'd we get? As a fee, I mean?" he added, looking away, then glancing back at her.

"Ten percent," she said firmly. "They were talking about giving a captain who could make the run five, of course, but if we were to do it, and being the first to see the connection between the atoll and the original islands, we could get there ahead of anyone else. I think that'd warrant double what they were offering."

"Bah. Barely worth the cost of the mana crystals to get there," he grumbled.

"Of course, sir," she agreed, folding the old map up and shaking her head, as she stared down at the captain's table projected map with a regretful air. "It's a shame. After all, an entire island chain's loot, plus all the ships that could have been looted over the centuries. Then there'd be the lich's own artifacts and treasures. Ten percent could have been enough, oh, to entirely fill our holds alone, I'd think."

Mal froze, staring at her.

"And, of course, imagine the look on Jax's face when he found out that someone had managed to recover double the platinum and precious metals that were needed to make those legendary buildings he had the entire continent stripped to make?

"When he finds out that a captain of a ship who loots all of that has only gotten five percent of it as a finder's fee, he's going to love it, I imagine."

"Five percent is a damn insult!" Mal growled.

"It would be, sir," she agreed blandly.

"Ten percent, well…" he grumbled.

"I'd imagine that ten percent would be the official fee, only as well, sir." She went on smoothly. "There'd be other things on top of that. Spellbooks, first access to the increased training facilities of the Imperial Academy, possibly even an upgrade to the ship."

"That thing that he did to his ship? Where it can recharge its mana from storms an' shit. I want that," he added, nodding to himself.

"I think that'd be something he'd *have* to agree to." She nodded. "After all, you'd have just doubled the treasury overnight, recovered the armor that he needs for the Valkyrie corps, and brought back more magical artifacts than he's ever seen.

"And you'd have it done before he gets back, so that he doesn't even see how easy it'd be. Instead, he'd just have to listen as you tell him how you've fixed all his problems in one fell swoop," she prompted, fighting to keep her face straight.

"Yeah, he'd have to be all respectful at that, and thank us, and every time he sees it all, it'll eat him up inside that it was me who brought it all back." Mal stared into the distance, grinning to himself.

"Exactly, sir." Soween sighed regretfully, straightening and tucking the map away. "And we could have made his people do all the work as well, considering that there are a bunch of mer who have joined the empire now. We could have asked them what they wanted to get more of their villages to go out there to do the actual work of recovery. Then had *Cai* pay them, so it cost us nothing, and we could have simply parked up on that little atoll, relaxing in the sun, while they searched the sea for us."

"Yeah…" he agreed, nodding again, his grin at risk of splitting his face.

"Oh well, I'll explain what I found and pass it to your father and Cai instead." She turned and headed for the door. "Don't mind me, sir. I'll get the cabin boys moving now."

"Whoa, whoa!" Mal cried out, frantically surging to his feet and shaking his head. "Why the hell would we do that?"

"I thought you said it wasn't worth our time?"

"For five percent?" he snapped. "Hell no. But for all that we're going to get? I'll damn well get us ten percent and bonuses!"

"Very well, sir." She stifled a smile again. "I'll get the ball rolling with the crew, make sure we're outfitted for a long journey, as we'll need to have supplies for at least a month at sea."

"A month…" He paused, looking conflicted.

"Perhaps Alyssa and her daughter would care to come with us?" Soween suggested. "I know that she's commented before about how hard ship life must be?"

"Yeah…no! Dammit, no, not if we're gonna be relaxin' aboard ship while everyone else is doin' all the work. I don't want her seeing that…"

"Perhaps we could talk a few of the gnomes into accompanying us, and take the time to expand the vessel as we discussed instead?" she suggested smoothly. "That way, you'd have ample time to relax, and yet it'd be obvious that this was only because of the ship being worked on. And on both the flight there and back, she'd be able to see you in your element, commandin' the crew and rescuing the empire."

"Yeah…" He nodded.

"Very good, sir. I'll make it happen." She stifled another smile, finally heading out onto the deck of the ship and marching along. She let loose a sharp whistle.

"Yes, ma'am?" one of the cabin boys sprinted up to her side.

"Arrange a meal for the captain in his cabin, then he'll be off to a meeting. Get his cabin cleaned as soon as he's out of it and fast. We're about to have guests. And find me Jay. It's time to round the crew up. We'll need a carpenter, and some tanks of freshwater installed for the mer, and…"

She hurried along, issuing orders, sending the crew running this way and that, making sure that the ship was ready, before passing word to Cai and Hannibal that Mal was on board with their plan.

They knew better than to act surprised when he came to them and "demanded" the perfectly reasonable price they'd already offered as their fee.

Her life was very different from what it had been when she and Mal first started smuggling together. But no matter what, she'd make damn sure that their little family stayed together, as safe as she could make them, and always growing.

CHAPTER ONE

"Booyah!" I roared, holding the head of Illoth's avatar aloft in my right hand. The cheers that rose on all sides surged at the sight, as well as the sudden ripple that flowed out from me, even as I pulled off my helm and dumped it in my bag.

It passed through the air and the ground, a warping of space that left almost everything just as it had been.

The only difference was made clear as I pulled up my notifications, grinning to myself as I saw what I'd hoped to see.

Let all be aware!

Jax Amon, former son of the disgraced House of Sanguis, and Godslayer, has defeated Illoth, Goddess of the drow, now officially known by the Empire as "Lolly the Turd Spider" in formal combat.

As Prince Jax Amon of Dravith has won, he lays claim to one-tenth of her power, condensed into a fragment of Her divinity, and, as per the previous challenge, claims the Continent and strips his opponent of any access, but not others of the Pantheon of the Dark.

HOWEVER, the continent of Carrmor is classed as contested, and not currently under his direct control. As such, each territory that is claimed by the Imperial Throne and Prince Jax shall be cleansed of Illoth's hand, only once it declares for him. Should Prince Jax succeed in claiming all the continent, then she—and by right of connection, any others who bear her mark—shall also be removed.

Prince Jax has been awarded dominion over the local area—100 square miles—and all who dwell within those bounds.

The Imperial Succession continues!

All those who wish to contest the rise of Jax now have less than one year to state their grievance and face him.

If, at the end of this time, he still stands in control of a Greater Territory and as a Prince of the Empire, then and only then may he ascend the Crystal Steps and be proclaimed Emperor!

All Hail Jax Amon! All Hail the Prince of the Empire!

Others popped up, and I quickly skimmed them, needing them out of the way, considering that I was currently surrounded by people.

Most of the notifications were unimportant unimportant in detail, anyway. This skill had increased, as had that, and again, most were swiped aside.

I'd pulled them up and dismissed them right before the fight with Illoth, not needing any distractions before I went into it. But now? I saw one that I'd need to deal with, and soon, which was the kill notifications, but *damn.*

As the circular border that was usually around the inner ring of Sonra shimmered and started to reform, I was reminded of the secret these people had been hiding for forever.

Or at the very least for hundreds of bloody years.

The great tent city of Sonra—the massive, constantly moving herd, and basically a walking, manure-generating, massive *fair*—was actually a goddamn *ark*.

I banished the last of the notifications, feeling it as a few more tried to surge up. I forced them down, just as my Goddess Jenae spoke. The sound of her voice was both pitched for mortal ears, and yet rumbling and charged with divine power that couldn't be ignored.

"Jax, prince of the empire and my champion, again, you rise triumphant in our battles against Nimon and his allies. We, the gods of your ancestors, thank you, and reach out our hands in benediction.

"All of those you guide to our worship shall receive our bounty and our attention. As proof of this, we remind all those who hear our voice that by the efforts of the imperial prince and ourselves, the drow, their servants, and all those who bear Illoth's foul grace have been banished from this territory.

"For one hundred square miles from this spot, not a single creature of Illoth now draws breath. And for those who already mourn loved ones, lost to the foul drow and their mistress's machinations, know that we mourn with you.

"Rise, Jax…rise and advance. Claim this continent, free it of our enemy's disgusting touch, and when it is done, ascend the steps as Emperor.

"As Amon did of old, so shall you revel in our blessings, as the Eternal Emperor. The empire shall once again be granted our divine favor, guiding and protecting. Congratulations, Prince, and know that we are proud of you."

The benediction hung in the air for a few seconds, and I carefully kept my face smooth, and as much amusement from my voice as possible.

"Thank you, my lady Jenae, Goddess of Fire and Hidden Knowledge. I'll guide those who revere the empire, and swear as citizens, in praying to yourself and your divine brethren later tonight," I called.

"We shall look forward to it. And, again, Jax, most favored of our disciples, know that we are proud."

There was a brief silence as the crowd stared in awestruck wonder while Jenae spoke to me alone.

"Was that too much?" she wondered.

"Nah, you did great," I assured her.

"Thank you. Jax, you should be proud, incredibly so. As a Godslayer, you are one of only a tiny fraction of a tiny fraction of all the beings who have ever lived, who have earned that title. That you did it to defend others, and to free the children of the empire, is a feat that is worthy of true benediction and respect."

"Thank you," I said, not knowing what else to say.

"You're welcome. Now, before you go and enjoy the spoils of your battle, my sister wishes a moment of your time. Be well, Jax, and know that we are truly thankful for all that you have achieved."

As the words of Jenae faded, a new voice spoke; again, I sensed it was for me alone.

"Jax, as Jenae said, you did well. But, to bind a fragment of divinity requires access to a place of power of comparable focus. Illoth styled herself the spider queen, but she reveled in stealing from me. Both she and Nimon took aspects of my focus, claiming them for themselves. The fragment you have, I believe is like this, and must be attuned to you in a place of true darkness, and the darkest of deeds, lest its power be wasted..."

"Thank you for the warning, Tamat," I sent to her. *"Do you have any suggestions? And when do you want the head?"*

"I'll take the head soon, but not yet. Show it off...let the others laugh and spit on her supposed power a little first. And I've already made provision for the rest of her corpse to be collected from the Elsecaller, and to be disposed of."

I didn't say it, knowing that I couldn't afford to piss her off right now, though that corpse could have been damn valuable…

"The corpse is not usable in terms of alchemical components or anything similar," she said, still apparently sensing my thoughts. *"It was created for this battle and this alone, making it useless in any other way. But as a tool of propaganda? I shall have her corpse delivered in recognizable chunks to every latrine across this camp and others as you establish them."*

"I knew I liked you for a reason," I breathed, a wide smile coming to my lips.

"Thanks in part to my leather pants, I believe." She laughed in the silence of my mind as that traitorous image rose in my head. *"Regardless, I would make you an offer now, one that I suggest you spend a few days considering. Don't bind that fragment. Instead, trade it to me for one of my own. I'll make it a fragment you can use, meaning you'll still gain, but so will I. Ask the others for advice, and know that I offer this in the hope of both growing closer to the empire, and gaining power that can be used to defend us both."*

"I'll...think on it, Goddess," I offered, and felt the sense of her retreating from me.

With that, the overwhelming sense of presence that the gods brought with them dissipated. I took a deep breath, then blew it out in a laugh as Oracle hit me from the side, wrapping her arms around me, barely suppressing her tears as she clung on.

I dumped Illoth's head on the ground, wrapping both arms around my future empress, and kissed her soundly, grinning as the others crowded around me.

"You did it," Oracle whispered, beaming up at me. The pride in "her man" and the love that shone forth was enough to keep me warm in the depths of Siberian winter, never mind here, on the great plains. "You beat her."

"Like her ass was a drum!" Sehran crowed, jumping in for a cuddle as Oracle shifted around. Being Sehran, the comment was slightly wrong, as I'd certainly not beaten Illoth's ass like a drum—it made 'em think that come hell or high water, I would be doing that and more to Oracle's at some point tonight.

The second thing that was slightly wrong—and yet oh so goddamn right at the same time—was that it being Sehran who was giving me a cuddle, she'd half climbed me like a spider monkey, and was attempting to smother me with her highly impressive chest.

I wasn't sure whether I should be fighting to come up for air, or burrowing deeper. But considering that I damn well knew she was doing this to get a rise out of me, and there was nothing more than that involved, I finally got free.

Then I laughed at the ridiculously joyful look on her face. As a succubus, burying my head in her cleavage literally was her "normal" way of giving me a cuddle; although those around me might have been a little uncomfortable had she done this on Earth, this was the UnderVerse.

My staid and more uptight upbringing—in comparison to hers, anyway—was the one that was out of place here. I shook my head and dragged her into a one-armed hug as well, making sure that she was now lower on my body so that I could actually see and still breathe.

That meant that Oracle was suddenly subsumed by the same pillows, and I sighed happily at the view.

"Ah, my prince?"

I looked over, seeing Daralen trying to hide a smile. As soon as she had my attention, she—and the other handful of legionnaires behind her—dropped to one knee, clapping a fist to their chest in salute.

"Congratulations on your mighty victory, Prince Jax," she repeated in a louder voice.

"Thank you, Primus Daralen," I said formally, knowing that here too, just like in that ridiculously phrased bloody speech by Jenae, she wasn't really speaking to me at all.

She—and Jenae—had been speaking to those around us, and as I gestured for the legionnaires to stand, I shifted my attention to them.

The Elsecaller was at my back still, and a good four or five hundred meters ahead of me, I could see the rising wall of wind that worked to obscure the inner ring from the outer world.

Filling that space were hundreds of beings, of which humans were by far in the minority.

Elves, dwarves, and gnomes were there, of course, though the percentage of gnomes was higher than anywhere I'd seen before. There were also other races, dozens of them, from an apparently ancient, blue-skinned pair that looked to be male and female, and barely able to stand under their own strength—a pair hovered at their sides, ready to support them—to massive orcs.

There were tiny elfin characters that made me think of the elves of British folklore, the kind that were supposed to make bloody shoes and so on, all the way up to mighty centaurs.

Minotaurs stood next to goblins, and a single red-skinned creature with three eyes and a beak, but entirely humanoid beyond that, stared at me with its head cocked to one side.

All these races and more were on display, and I was struck by the bloody incredible planning that must have gone into this.

This was literally an ark. All the species that, as far as I knew, were typically hunted and treated as targets or enemies by "normal folk" were here. Hidden in the center of a constantly moving herd.

Better yet, their "sort of" acceptance of the slave trade on their doorstep?

It meant that slavers came to them to sell their wares.

Where any of them would have had to search high and low normally to find and recover these races to protect them, now instead they'd managed to set it up so that the bloody slavers came to them!

Even better, they made it so that the slavers knew not to fuck with them, so they'd even be offering them better rates! No wonder none of the freed slaves left.

Those who were trusted enough to be brought into the inner rings—or that were of a race deemed necessary—would find a literal safe paradise.

I saw it all in an instant, and as I looked around at these people, I saw both the pride, the concern, and the outright fear on their faces.

Was I going to be like the others? A noble in name but someone who would turn my face from the "lesser races," as I'd heard them called? Or would I punish them?

They'd killed legionnaires, after all. Probably thousands over the centuries. The only way that they could keep this secret safe was to make sure that the legion didn't know it, considering that the legion were constrained by those bloody stupid oaths to "protect the innocent at all costs."

That had sounded reasonable, and when it was given, and added to the legion oaths, it was probably intended so as well.

In practice, it'd meant that a single legionnaire, badly injured, even completely unarmed, would be forced by their oaths, to attack an army if they harmed an innocent in sight of the legionnaire.

It'd probably done more in a single goddamn phrase to drive this entire continent into the toilet than anything else.

As the legionnaires were forced to attack slavers on sight, no matter the odds, of course Sonra had to keep them out, and even execute those who broke their laws. Not for the first time, I wished I could reach out and drag that stupid, sanctimonious asshole of a noble who had inflicted those rules on them out of the grave, just to put him back in again.

"I am Jax Amon," I said loudly. "I take it you are the Council of Sonra, and the reason that the inner ring is kept hidden?"

I looked around; those I was guessing were the council were at the front.

The first four I could pick out were, as before, the elderly woman—grey-haired and grim-faced—I knew to be Ilena Vhyrakai, matriarch of the Vhyrakai clan.

Then came the brothers—thank fuck for Othair's careful descriptions—Daven and Malik Kreonar, the heads of their clan, both lean, and their cheeks bearing the signs of ritual scarring and an absolute fuckload of rings in their ears.

Then came the leader of Sonra's guard force, the outriders. Reth Suntari was a lean man as well, but for him, it looked like rather than just being healthy and fit, it was because he pared away every single excess bloody calorie in the search to make his mount a hair faster.

He wore a blackened and studded leather chest piece, his eyes and hair were black as pitch, and he had a hell of a tan that spoke of a life in the saddle.

Besides them, though, were four others: two goblins, an orc, and a centaur that towered over them all.

"I am Cleq." The first of the goblins stepped forward and bowed quickly, before straightening up again, standing slightly taller, despite barely coming to my waist, and obviously both uncomfortable and yet too proud to allow another to speak for her.

"I lead the Council of Sonra," she went on. "And yes, the races in the inner ring are the reason we hold to our privacy."

"I don't blame you," I agreed, nodding as Oracle and Sehran moved to stand on either side of me; Daralen moved up to stand by Oracle's side. "Having seen how some races treat each other, I bet you've had damn good reason to shelter inside."

"You have no idea," the centaur said grimly, before lowering her head. "I am Sharn, and we greet you, Prince Jax, and ask your intentions."

"I'm intending on a beer, a goddamn sit-down and a bath," I said. "After that, a good meal. And yeah, there's going to be a lot to talk about, including that the local area is now cleaned of the drow and all her"—I kicked the side of Illoth's head on the ground—"kind. Beyond that, I think we've got a lot to talk about, don't you?"

"There is much to discuss," Cleq agreed, nodding. "But first, before anything else, we must understand your intentions toward Sonra."

"Answer carefully, human," Sharn said calmly. "We have ways of proving your words, and understand that although we mean no insult to you or your empire, we will judge you on this." She folded her arms and stared down at me.

I nodded, liking the no-bullshit approach.

"Sounds good to me," I said with a slight smile. "Well, first of all, yeah, all I said before, but regarding Sonra? I want allies. I don't like having to conquer places as I go…" I saw the frown on a few faces at that and saw the way they had all moved to hold something in their hands. Guessing it was some kind of truth stone like the outriders had carried, I snorted and rephrased that.

"Okay, when people are arseholes, sometimes yeah, I enjoy conquering them. A nice little fight and some arrogant fuckstick brought down to ground level—yeah, all right, I do enjoy that on occasion. What I'm here looking for, though, isn't a fight with Sonra. I came looking to free my legionnaires and any slaves.

"I have access to imperial abilities, and one of those is that, as I told your assistant Ren…" I looked at Ilena, and she nodded. "One of those abilities is to free slaves. When I do so, any who hold a control collar's leash or artifact will receive the backlash. A lot of those people die instantly, and frankly, as fucking slavers, they deserve it."

"And those around them when it happens?" the second goblin asked. "And I am Greg."

"Nice to meet you, Greg." I nodded to him. "Well, I won't lie…if an innocent is holding the collar, they suffer that backlash." I looked around the group. "I don't like that, and if I could make the magic more specific, I would, but I can't. At the end of the day, although I know that some will inevitably be injured who shouldn't be, if they're holding a slave collar, I don't really think 'innocent' is the best description for them.

"My intention in coming here was literally to free the slaves, recover my legionnaires, and then, after the challenge with Illoth was issued"—I carefully didn't say that it was issued by me—"then I decided I'd quite like to kill her as well. Plus, I'll be having her head made into a goblet for the Goddess Tamat, who I'm intending on getting drunk as a skunk with at some point soon."

The looks on their faces at that were comical, and I pressed on.

"After that, well, as I say, I'd like to have the people of Sonra as my allies. No, I won't spread the word of what you are, and who, but I also won't help you if you choose to stay neutral. I know the legion has had some…issues here over the last seven hundred years. Are you aware of why?"

"The oath." Cleq spat on the floor.

"Give that woman a fruit basket." I nodded, pointing at her, then waved the confused looks aside. "Sorry, goblin. Fuck it. Regardless, though, yes, that bloody stupid addition to the oaths. That has been removed from all the legionnaires I've had swear to me. And as soon as I can gain access to another source of mana that's strong enough, I'll remove it from *all* legionnaires on this continent.

"As such, the whole 'running into battle against insane odds' thing is over. As is the way that they've been shit on by many people. My intention is that we'll be raising the imperial standard again, and basically conquering, recovering, and damn well claiming anywhere I can on this continent. Why? Because that way, I can kick Illoth off it, I can keep my people safe, free the slaves, and last and most personally important, I can keep Oracle, my love, and my future empress, as well as the mother of my unborn child, safe as well."

There was a long silence as the council apparently digested that and decided whether they were happy with it, before Cleq spoke again.

"You appear human, and yet aren't. May we ask as to your species?" She directed it at Oracle.

"I was a wisp." She smiled sunnily. "When Jax found me, I was bound to the Great Tower of Dravith, a tower that had been captured by a SporeMother, and I was bound in slumber. He woke me, badly injured, and after I had accepted that he had the requisite authority to claim the tower, and seeing his injuries, I bound myself to him."

"You mean he enslaved you," Sharn growled.

"No, I don't," she snapped back, going from happy and beaming to glaring in an instant. "He freed me, as best he could, and offered each of us, the four other wisps who are currently sworn to the empire, our freedom. He healed me, and I him. Then he shared and bound his soul to me. He gave me both physical form and authority over the empire. And before you ask, no, me becoming pregnant wasn't planned, and no, we have no clue how it's possible. But even the gods acknowledge that it's true, and that I'm to be the mother of a new race.

"So, as I know that this is going to be high in your concerns, no, he's not a 'humans first' type. Daralen here is the primus of the local legion, and she is obviously not entirely human. Sehran is both a friend of ours and a member of Jax's personal squad." Oracle paused, then shook her head.

"And I'm just going to say it, because I know it'll come out and be wondered over by you all. Yes, she's a succubus. No, she's not sharing our bed—"

"A lie." Cleq interrupted Oracle.

"She's— Wait, what?"

"You lied," she said. "Forgive me, but we can sense that."

I burst out laughing, and they all looked to me. "Sorry, yes, she shares our bed on occasion, but we haven't had sex, nor do we intend to," I clarified. "She's one of our closest friends, and is in a relationship with another of my squad and another wisp. When there's not enough beds to go around, she's cuddled up to us, so I suppose in that sense, it could be a lie."

"Truth." Cleq nodded. "Forgive me. A lie was obvious, but not what it concealed."

"I think that makes things clear then," I smiled around, "and I hope it addresses at least some of your concerns. But seeing as you've been so blatant about it, allow me to reply in kind. First of all, how do you know when a lie is spoken?"

"An old device, copied by our artificers." She held a stone up. It was a grey-blue color, and smooth like a pebble that had spent long years in a river. But as she held it and spoke, it flared red and gave off a slight shiver. "I am a giant," she lied.

She tossed it underarm to me, and I caught it. "My name is Thomas," I tried, the first obvious lie that came to mind, and nothing happened. I looked to him in question.

"You must channel mana into it, to activate it," she said, a slight smile on her lips.

"Of course I do, dammit." I sighed, focusing and feeding my mana out through my hand like I did with my naginata. The stone grew instantly cool to the touch. I repeated my lie, smiling as it gave off a pulse of heat and shuddered in my hand. "May I?" I asked, and she nodded, twisting and accepting a spare from another.

"Very well. So now that you know my position, what is your intention toward me and my empire?" I asked bluntly.

"We are unsure," she replied smoothly, before smiling toothily. "We are certainly not hostile to you, and yet we are aware that the position agreed to today with your empire may not be the position that exists tomorrow, and that your heir, should you be blessed with one, may choose to dissolve any alliance we make. As such, considering our position, and secrets, we are cautious."

"Jax is the heir to the Eternal Emperor Amon, acknowledged by both Amon and the gods, and he possesses fragments of divinity that are helping him ascend to godhood," Oracle pointed out, smiling. "Any concerns that he might pass the empire along to a son or daughter who could break its laws are…unlikely to come about." She phrased it carefully, but it was clear to everyone.

"Jax, with the blessing of the greater gods and their alliance to him personally, is likely to still be ruling the empire in a thousand generations' time. So, although we understand your position, I think if anyone should be concerned about the future likelihood of the other changing their mind and being unreliable, it's not going to be from this side."

"Ah…" Cleq appeared stunned. "My apologies. We were unaware of the situation."

"So it's true then?" the older woman, Ilena, barked suddenly. "You have claimed fragments of divinity from both the God of Death and the spider goddess?"

"I have." I nodded. "And I've been given a quest by the gods to collect more, to fuel my ascension."

"A living god who will sit atop the throne of the empire." Sehran spoke up, her voice clear. "Can you imagine a better ally, or one you'd rather have by your side?"

"We can see the advantages," another of the group said.

I nodded to one of the brothers, noting that the fucker didn't identify himself. But considering they were twins and dressed identically, I just knew they were going to confuse me regardless.

"We see the disadvantages though as well." His brother spoke up. "You have started a war with the gods, and you want us to pick a side. We prefer neutrality."

"Enjoy your neutrality then." I smiled, and he blinked.

"We weren't…" he started, and I snorted.

"I know. You haven't *committed* to neutrality," I said. "But you'd like to not be involved. I don't blame you. Personally speaking, I'd quite like to be back on Dravith with the people who asked for my help and who I'm responsible for, rather than tens of thousands of miles away, but fuck it, that's life.

"If the dark dickhead hadn't betrayed everyone and pulled down a fucking moon, that'd be nice as well. But regardless, I'm here, you're here, and we have to make the best we can of a shitty situation. If you want neutrality, that's fine. You can move on. And although I'm sure you'll be safe from Illoth for a while, good luck when you try to move outside of my territory."

"We could always remain inside the bounds…" one of the brothers started, then fell silent.

"Except that you can't." I nodded. "Once your herds have eaten everything, it's going to take a while to regrow, the crap will take time to be absorbed, and your entire business model of being paid to move to a new location will be fucked.

"Alternatively, you might choose to just tour here. After all, a hundred miles of territory sounds like a lot, except that it's focused on me. Right now. As far as I know, it's not going to move, but it means that fifty miles in any direction, the territory ends, and that's a lot more limiting. Add in then that I'm moving on to Gaij next…and well."

I left unsaid that yeah, this territory would probably stay here; it wasn't going to continually move with me, and I damn well hoped at this point that Illoth hadn't figured out that she could set up at the fifty-mile point between me and Gaij, and start preparing her forces for round two.

They obviously missed that little detail, though, and I saw it on their faces.

"So, personally, I'd like us to be allies and friends. After all, in my lands, which I'm constantly expanding and that will be patrolled by the legions…"

"And protected by the Godslayer," Oracle added archly.

"Slavery and so on is illegal. In fact, as an imperial citizen—which you could be if we form an alliance—there's a specific law which I think you'll appreciate."

"Oh?" Cleq asked.

"*Don't be a dick*," I replied. "I know, I know, it's a pretty open-ended law. But it's enforced by an oath, and damn, it's effective. See, things like discriminating against you because you're a goblin…well, that'd be firmly in the 'dickish behavior' category. It's not something that's going to kill anyone, thanks to the way the oaths work, but it's something that's going to force people to not be such, well, dicks."

"A refreshing, if vague, law." She nodded.

“I know, right?” I beamed. “It’s such a simple concept, and so fucking easy to understand. If I argue with someone, am I a dick? Depends on the point of view. If I believe I’m not, then I’m fine. If instead, though, I do something that I know to be dickish, like I deliberately spread slander about goblins, when I’ve met a sentient and upright citizen who’s a goblin? Well, I’m going to regret that.

“The same works for theft, for assault, and for all our laws. The worse the transgression, the worse the response. You try to stab another citizen? Well, that’s going to end very badly for you. You do it by accident—you turn around and they step in close when you had no clue they were there? Accidents happen. It’s a very open-ended law, but fuck me, it works. Now, before we get into the nitty-gritty, because we clearly are, how about this? My people are in the second ring, can’t remember the area, but fuck it. I need to return to them. We lost damn good people to Illoth’s ambush, and I need to be with them.

“As such, how about we get together for a meal later this afternoon or better yet, later on? Something informal, where we can actually talk to each other openly, and none of the shit that comes when people try to speak in riddles?”

“An excellent suggestion.” The orc inclined his head. “I am Bravimoth, and Sonra accepts. Perhaps you could return here at sunset?”

“I’d be happy to.” I forced a smile, thinking internally that considering the sun had barely risen that it was going to be a long-ass day. Then I remembered my plans for a damn bath, and to pound Oracle’s arse, and I cheered right up.

Who knew, maybe I’d even have time for a little food?

CHAPTER TWO

Exiting Sonra's inner circle was an experience. Stepping up to the wall of rushing wind that looked like it was a literal hurricane a few inches from my face gave me the willies, but as Ilena explained, it was a shield and illusion both. In this case, all I needed to pass through was to be welcomed formally by a member of the council.

She did that for every member of my much-reduced party, and then I reached out, touching the spinning vortex of winds, only to feel…a cool breeze.

Sure, it was fast-moving air, but as I stepped into it, it was more like a headwind, or when you stuck your arm out of the car while driving and the passage of the air forced it up or down.

Considering the transfer point was only maybe six inches deep, if that, once I stepped forward properly, I was already out the far side, staggering slightly, but none the worse for wear.

Oracle and Sehran followed. And Daralen, of course, had stepped through ahead of me, determined to secure the far side.

I joined her and the four legionnaires who had come with us; Othair and Marteen formed up close around Oracle, Sehran, and me, and we started forward through the camp.

The area we'd stepped through to enter the inner ring, passing through the shield that protected it, was clearly a specific access point, as we'd been led out near the same area that we'd entered. I'd noted the great wagons that surrounded the camp, drawn up tight against the shield as well.

On the inside of the ring, the wagons were monstrous things, easily as large as a four-bedroomed house back home, and yet incredibly well made.

The hundreds of meters that formed the inner ring were tightly encircled by these enormous wagons, both—as I'd imagine—not only a convenient parking place and to form a line of demarcation, but also as a literal physical wall to prevent anyone who accidentally somehow made it into that area from seeing anything they shouldn't.

Once you were past those massive wagons, there were a lot of differences between the inner and outer rings, including that there were so many different beings and styles of dwelling.

The freakiest bit, though, was undoubtably the ten pillars, and the Elsecaller.

That the inside was as magically active as it was, and that it somehow managed to create a safe space where the bloody pillars could stand in apparent serenity, firmly planted into the ground, was only part of it.

Clearly, the interior moved magically each time the camp travelled; that was just obvious. They couldn't be taking the bloody pillars down and then replanting them, as well as regrowing the grass every two days when they moved, after all.

Or hell, maybe they could—buggered if I knew. All I did know was that, earlier on, when I'd looked at the pillars on my way past, heading both inside and then again when I was heading back out, they looked like they'd easily been there for a thousand years.

They were also at least three meters across, perhaps twenty high, and looked to have been painstakingly carved over the passage of those centuries with hundreds of thousands of symbols.

I recognized them, or what they were supposed to be, anyway.

Things like the Flame of Jenae. It wasn't anything particularly special—I'd seen it a thousand times: on her altar, on things in the Constellation of Secrets, popping up here and there in the tower, now that it was consecrated to her worship…all sorts of places.

I'd barely noticed it, if I was being honest, and for a "divine symbol," it was a bit shit. A simple line to represent the ground, then a slightly wavy teardrop shape atop it with a smaller one in the center.

That was it. Bare-bones and basic as shit. But it was clearly also *Her*. It was a symbol that stood for Her, and that was simple enough that even a child could draw it.

Well, tens of thousands had, it seemed, all over her pillar, and those drawings spiraled round and round. They overlapped and they formed a confusing mélange of images, all over a single pillar that was obviously supporting tens of thousands of individual prayers.

These were visible signs of these people, desperately begging for help, for hundreds of years, casting their prayers out into the silence. And the tenth pillar? It was blank.

All the others had desperately scrawled, carved, inked, and painted symbols.

The tenth, that was presumably there available for oh, say, *a death god*, was conspicuously fuckin' empty, and I had to stifle a grin as I made that connection.

Sonra was a city that moved forever, never stopping in one place for long. It was a home to herders and merchants, refugees and hopes. Most of all? It was home to a persecuted population who were desperate.

I'd get them. I damn well knew it. If they really wanted to stay neutral, they'd not be urgently pleading to just nine of the gods. They'd have reached out to Nimon as well, and they'd deliberately left that fucker out of it, that was clear.

No, they were looking for reassurance, for deals and for a promise, that was obvious. They'd not expected what had happened overnight. Now that it had?

They were as good as mine.

Oracle and I walked side by side, our fingers interlaced, as Sehran took off, flying overwatch, and the legion pushed out to force people back and to provide a little privacy.

Daralen, Marteen, and Othair walked slightly behind us, and we walked in the center of a small, but very determined ring of steel.

The four legionnaires and Daralen were on high alert after what had happened on the way in. And after the gods had vanished, for a little while, as we headed for the exit from the inner ring, it'd felt a hell of a lot safer than it had earlier.

That was when Marteen, of all people, dropped the bombshell.

"So…when it forced Illoth and the drow out, did it force out anyone else?" he asked. His voice was raw—and so were his eyes—clearly trying to make conversation and to not think about the fact that when we reached our section of the camp, it'd be to face the body of his mother.

"Like whom?" Othair asked curiously, glancing over at his younger companion, and unconsciously smoothing one hand down the front of his slightly battered-looking suit.

"The other gods." Marteen shrugged, still staring ahead, his eyes hollow and empty, distracted.

And just like that, my butthole puckered.

"No," I admitted flatly. "The dark dick can still send people after us. And the exclusion isn't foolproof, either. When we gained a similar one on Dravith, it was phrased slightly different and forced only the gods out. Their servants were left inside, easily able to range wherever they needed to.

"In this situation, I'd bet that the trade-off for not pushing the others out when I won was that the power needed to push just one of them and all their followers instead was so much higher. Remember, that's every spider that follows Illoth, every drow, everyone who's sworn to or is following her…all of them shoved out in a heartbeat." I scratched at my chin in thought, then nodded as I put two and two together.

"It's a good point, though. I bet if I was to fight one of the other dickheads and defeat them, I could get them added to the exclusion as well. Wonder who Baphomet or Asmodeus counts as followers?" I mused.

"Baphomet is a full-on nature deity, and not one that many civilized people admit to following. He's primarily represented by Minotaurs, satyrs, and fauns, but with the emphasis on nature *against* civilization," Othair replied calmly, before going on.

"Where the goddess Lagoush is the closest in the spectrum to his sphere of influence, dealing as she does with healing, water, and change, he is focused solely on nature and specifically, he revels in the more violent aspects of it.

"Where a storm may be needed and perfectly natural, for example, if Baphomet is involved, it will be far more violent than expected. His followers are not all the Minotaurs and other beastkin, of course, but he is the traditional god they deal with and dedicate their worship to."

"Joy, and we just met a fuckload of the more…" I paused as I glanced around at the people staring and listening in. "Interesting people," I finished lamely.

"Quite."

"Wait, if that's the case, why the hell didn't he have a pillar in there? I mean, sure, okay, if you don't want him getting a big pillar like the greater gods, you'd still have a lesser one, right?" I asked.

"It's probably because of personal mentality," Oracle suggested, sounding unsure. "Those we met were more…advanced? More civilized?"

"And you think that they're further from their roots, and less inclined to worship him?" I guessed, then nodded again.

"Actually, that'd make sense. You remember the mosaic in Production Facility One?" I glanced at Oracle, getting a firm nod of the head, before I spoke slightly louder to the others so that they could hear clearly. "We discovered a hidden, pre-cataclysm site that was sacred to the god Svetu," I explained.

"Inside, there were huge mosaics that showed members of all races working together, and a lot of those we met were there as well, despite the more commonly known of those races not really…" I fumbled with my words, having to be careful about what could be heard by others, before sighing.

"Let's just say that those who were on the wall were as civilized and good at engineering and creation as any other. And looking at those we've met, we probably have a situation where they were judged as their less civilized cousins act. That'd be a good reason to hide. And if you were forced into that, worshipping a god you know has gotten rid of the god you were worshipping and who's revered by your less civilized cousins...yeah, that's probably not in the cards."

"It's a roundabout way to say it, but it makes sense," Oracle agreed.

"Okay, and what about Asmodeus?" I asked, hoping to jog things along, now that I'd realized that things weren't necessarily going to be all sunshine and light in the negotiations after all.

"Infernal," Othair said. "I suspect that your companion Sehran may be able to provide more information on him, but he is a primarily infernal and control-oriented god. Things like contracts were traditionally viewed as his purview, and of course the cambions."

"The what?"

"Cambions," he repeated, blinking when he realized that I didn't get the reference, not that I'd misheard him in the sound of the crowds. "Ah, half-breeds of an infernal and another race."

I glanced back at him, seeing that he was obviously uncomfortable saying it, as the phrase might offend Daralen, but it was the most accurate one.

"Okay, anything you can tell me about them?" I pressed.

"They're rare, but not hugely so. Most cities will have a handful of them. Due to their natural gifts, they tend to seek work in the legal and accountancy professions."

"Natural gifts?" I asked.

"He means they're sneaky, underhanded, and love to use the powers that they inherit," Daralen said for him. "It's rare that a succubus becomes pregnant, though I'd heard of it, and they tend to show up thirteen months later and drop the child off on the father's doorstep, then vanish again. Their contracts forbid them keeping anything they gain from here beyond power, I've been told."

"Is that true?" I sent to Sehran, relaying the conversation to her, and she sent back a quick, but curt response.

"It's not accurate, as we can retain gifts we take from here, but we're forced to do that because a half-breed child of this world would never survive there."

I took the hint and pushed a sense of love and reassurance toward her, then continued with the conversation with the others.

"Okay, so then what?" I asked.

"They tend to grow up as relatively normal inhabitants of the realm, save that they have a little more aptitude for magic, right up until puberty hits." Daralen snorted. "I'm not saying they're all sex-crazed, underhanded scumbags, but that's because I've not met them all. All the ones I have met? Well, they'd sell their father for a button to be made into glue, and not understand the issue. They're the most unfeeling, uncaring creatures you'll ever meet, and it's only blind luck that they're almost always mules."

"What?" I frowned, confused why a fuckin' ugly horse had anything to do with it.

"Mules...ah, sorry, I wasn't sure if you understood the term. Like when a horse and a donkey breed, the result is alive and grows up just fine. It can fuck all it wants as well, but they don't produce offspring," she clarified, and I snorted.

"Ah, I get it." I nodded. "We call them a jaffa."

"Jaffa?"

"It's a type of orange where I come from, but it's seedless." I grinned, then sighed, seeing it'd gone right over her head. "Dammit, Tommy would have got that," I muttered, shaking my head disgustedly, thinking of John, a chef we'd worked with whose wife had him "fixed" and we'd called him Jaffa from that day on.

"Regardless, due to their long lives—usually three to five hundred years—and that incubuses who are summoned have no need to take the resulting child back with them, it means that they are, as I said, rare, but not overly so."

"And they do what?" I asked.

"As followers traditionally of Asmodeus, they tend to focus on contracts, legalese, and accountancy. Wherever there's someone breaking the absolute spirit of the law, and yet doing it legally, or the spirit of the contract, and yet you can't punish them? That's generally a follower of Asmodeus."

"Fucking lawyers." I groaned. "We've got a goddamn God of Lawyers!"

"Exactly. And I'd recommend not challenging him, if possible, my prince," Othair said.

"Why?" I asked, fully intending to kick that god's fucking arse.

"Because the contract that he would insist upon would inevitably favor him. No matter what the outcome, he would win, as he'd have planned it that way from the start. Personally, I'd suggest an alliance, or an attempt to draw him into neutrality instead."

"But I can fight Baphomet?"

"Of a certainty." He nodded. "Though, if I am honest, Baphomet is a god who is more likely to challenge you first, and is likely to be on par with Lord Darakin in that he would fight for the love of the contest. Where Illoth and...others," he obviously didn't want to slag Nimon off, "they may choose, or be able to be manipulated into unfamiliar bodies to face you, Baphomet would glory in it. He was once readily seen across the empire's outermost boundaries, according to myth and legend."

"Coolio, I'll need to sort that out then." I sighed. "There was another god Jenae mentioned, I'm sure..." I racked my brain, trying to remember.

Oracle spoke up. "There are a dozen more, my love, but the one Jenae mentioned was Ardat. The others have either remained neutral or have chosen exile, I expect. We should ask her when we get the chance."

"Okay, Ardat?" I prompted.

"A shapeshifter and changeling goddess. Ardat, although never particularly popular in the way the others were, is known as a seeker of secrets," Othair mused. "Where the Lady Jenae is a seeker for hidden knowledge, seeking to share it with the world and learn, building upon it, Ardat is more..." He hesitated, and Oracle went on for him.

"She's the goddess of Peeping Toms and stalkers. All the weird stuff that you told me about the internet from your home? She'd love it. She'd be the goddess of that in a heartbeat, and love spreading disinformation as much as anything else."

"Great set of gods you picked, Nimon." I snorted. "Fuck me, the goddess of degenerates, stalkers, and secret conversations, and the gods of lunacy and lawyers. You must have some truly awful parties."

There was actually an answering rumble of thunder, but for the first time I could remember, it didn't sound angry and threatening…more resigned and grumbling agreement. I snorted a laugh, getting the second, much angrier roll of thunder I was used to. He presumably realized what he'd done.

The next half hour was more or less of the same: small talk while we passed through the second ring, and then stepped carefully across the fields of the great herds.

Oracle lifted from the ground and flew, only a few inches off it, but it was enough. The rest of us?

Meadow muffin central, unfortunately, especially as the depth of the literal crap we were striding over was now several inches, and there was almost no chance of avoiding them.

I'd noted the knee-high boots that a lot of the outriders wore. Now, looking at the sheer depth of the literal shit they had to wade through every day? I was either getting some boots, or I was activating my new spell and churning the goddamn earth as I walked.

Well, that or I was flying and to hell with it all. The reason I wasn't right now was that it'd be a kick in the teeth to the others who had come with us here. It would also give away the fact that I could fly, which I didn't want all my enemies knowing—I'd done it a little in the Elsecaller but that could be chalked up to magic in there, after all. And lastly?

It made me a bigger target for more people.

If I was marching along, it limited the people who could actually see me thanks to the size of the tents, wagons, and so on, not to mention the crowds that were even now marching back and forth.

Sure, the whole 'godslaying' thing had been news last night and this morning as well, but most didn't know who I was or which way I'd be marching, it seemed, so it wasn't until I reached the third ring and headed along inside it toward our section that word started to spread again.

Until then, the normal business of the camp had resumed and as it was apparently the buildup to a massive seasonal fair, or sales time, it was…well, it was manic.

Tommy and I'd once spent a season in the North Yorkshire Dales, earning extra money—cash in hand—working at the massive sheep sales.

We'd basically been muscle, doing nothing but keeping an eye on the crowds and making sure things were all right, because the amount of money that changed hands in those places was frankly insane.

The kind of farmers who bought and sold sheep that were valued in the hundreds to thousands of pounds sterling, and sometimes, by the literal hundreds, were also often the kind of farmers who didn't want to disturb the hardworking tax man.

Instead, there'd be a lot of ready cash changing hands at these places, often in the tune of hundreds of thousands an hour. The kind of money that would normally only literally be moved by specialist bank transports with armed guards was instead stuffed in the pockets of ratty old jackets. And when it piled up in the auction houses?

Well, when there was that kind of money changing hands, there were also pickpockets, thieves, and muggers, not to mention less kindly types.

We weren't important enough at that point to be worth paying for protection, not for the real money, but a friend had gotten us in for a few days to act as muscle where we were needed.

As such, the sight of thousands of people in a space that looked like it should hold a hundred, if that, was familiar. And as more and more turned, recognizing that we were the ones who had caused all the uproar and interest overnight?

The effect spread quickly.

People shouted things; other surged forward, wanting to speak, to meet me, to threaten me, to make deals…all of them.

This was a massive merchant hub, one that was still building to the "main event" of the market that was only a few days away. That was why the slavers had been heading here.

The market—Othair had explained as we marched here—was held annually, and although it wasn't intended as a slavers' market, it'd ended up having that tagged on. And then, as time passed, and the slavers found just how convenient an annual market could be, it'd massively grown.

Now, the main annual market for the herds, as it was planned to be, was probably smaller than the one for the less savory livestock.

There were also a hell of a lot of other merchants here, though, as the slave trade wasn't the only one to see the possibilities. Everywhere I looked, I saw merchants, guards, porters, and customers travelling.

Surrounding them were the tents, wagons, and who knew what else of Sonra. And on top of, underneath, and in every gap in between were the flies, maggots, and shit of the millions of animals.

There was a lot I loved about the UnderVerse—genuinely, there was—but the one thing that they'd not managed to do was figure out sanitation.

In every camp, ours included, there were latrines—basically a quickly made hole to shit into that was covered over when you moved on.

In the cities? There were sewers, which was a bloody relief, and in the places like the Great Tower, there were even toilets, which was wonderful. But here?

The best that the vast majority of the inhabitants here had were the occasional latrines that were set up around the outside.

That meant, that as a lot of the stalls we passed were also selling wine, ales, and more, that the reek that surrounded us wasn't just limited to animal…waste.

The entire experience made me want to activate Flames of Wrath and walk through the screaming filthy lot of them. I did my damn best to keep my mouth shut now and limit my breathing to my mouth.

That meant I could taste it, which was nasty, but it was ever-so-slightly better than the goddamn smell.

People pressed in against us on all sides, and as word spread more and more, so did the crowds. The shouting wasn't that bad at first. Questions could be ignored, after all. Every so often, someone decided to make a show of how tough they were, and that the legion "wasn't really that tough."

The results were certainly memorable, as trying to push forward, spit, throw filth, or scream abuse at members of the imperial family *really* triggered the legionnaires.

Most survived with only a dozen or so broken bones and missing teeth, though the one drunk who literally stood directly in our way, shoved his hand down the back of his pants and shit in his own hand, and then acted as if he were about to throw it?

Daralen didn't get to kill him, but that was because the outriders of Sonra, who had seen the way things were going, stepped in before she could.

He screamed, once, and his remains were dragged aside.

That wasn't to say that it was all doom and gloom, though, because as we passed another group—now much larger and clearly set up ready to move—they started to recite the imperial oath.

This time, I did stop, accepting their oath as Oracle pushed the full one out to them, and then gave my own.

Fifty-odd people swore the oath then and there, and that was on top of the twenty-odd who had done it originally as I passed on my way into the fight with Illoth.

They gathered their gear once we started off again, and they travelled to our camp with us, cheering Daralen up no end, as they were apparently a group known to be friendly to the legion, and as they'd sworn the oath, they were trustworthy as well.

She kept the ring around us with just the legion, but quickly co-opted the new citizens to form up and clear a path.

By the time we reached our camp again, with the outriders of Sonra now in the lead and behind us as well, seventy-odd heavily armed merchants and travelers, and then my small party, it was a massive relief.

"What are your orders, my prince?" Daralen asked formally as we stepped into the camp, and the outriders turned away.

"Secure the camp, make sure everyone's okay, and then get some rest." I turned to Othair and Marteen. "You two as well. We'll have a ceremony for our dead tonight, at two hours to sunset, but for now, please, help the new people get settled in the camp and then get some rest yourself."

I could already see people outside the camp who were trying to get my attention, and I grimaced. "Get our forces ready, and make sure the camp is as well protected as we can make it for now," I said. "I'll speak to the council about it in our meeting, but there's no way this can continue, now that people know who we are."

It was already starting to look more like a mosh pit out there than the border of an encampment. And the only reason people weren't already dying was because the legion had set to, and had already created earthworks.

The standard legion camp in enemy territory—provided they had enough people who could do it—was a design that harked back to ancient times, much like the Roman legions had done it.

A deep trench was dug around the camp, and the displaced earth was used to raise an earthen berm around the camp; where there were trees, they'd be felled. Depending on how long the legion expected to be there for, they'd range from creating an overlapping wall of branches, vines and more, to a full-on wooden wall with a parapet to walk.

The trench would get sharpened stakes driven into the ground to dissuade people without an invitation from attempting entry. There was even a collapsable bridge that could be constructed and set out to allow us to cross over the trench on entering and leaving the camp.

How the Roman legions had done it was with packtrains and massive quantities of supplies; the Imperial Legion did it with special backpacks, bags of holding, and a ridiculously gung-ho attitude.

Either way, though, crossing that line made me feel a hell of a lot better, even if one of the legionnaires had to literally stomp back across the little bridge and start shoving people off the far side, in order to retract the bridge.

I followed Oracle into our massive wagon, hearing it as she reached out to Sehran and asked her to join us. A handful of minutes later, we were all stripping off.

It wasn't for "fun time," either. We were all filthy, stinking, and there was no way we were going to be relaxing and resting like this.

That meant the bath that we had in the main wagon was getting filled, and we were damn well making the most of it.

Yes, all right, the water was magically summoned; it was a fountain of healing waters. I waded in manfully and held a fire spell in my hand and literally passed the water through it.

It caused some of the water to erupt into steam. The spell needed so much more mana to do it this way that it was unreal, but it was fast, and it really heated the water well.

It also had the slight advantage of literally creating water that was bubbling with healing energy, and damn.

It was a massive relief to damaged and battered muscles, and was the magical equivalent of a fucking spa.

Why did we summon Sehran to join us in the bath? Well, as much as there was always that bit of "gnawing on my knuckle and trying not to look," it was because there was limited water that we could summon and heat because of the mana costs. Besides, we'd all seen each other naked more times than we could count.

That meant when it came down to it, either we shared a bath and all got a lot cleaner, or we had a bath after her, and getting into a bath with the scum of the last person floating on the top was not a great experience.

Or, she got in after us, and considering I was most definitely the dirtiest, that wouldn't be very nice for anyone.

Finally, the bath was in the bedroom, and I fully intended to have some fun with Oracle afterward to get over the stress and pain of the last few hours, and that meant if we had Sehran go after us, then she'd be trying to find excuses to hang around and watch for as long as possible.

Being a succubus, she had no such hang-ups about sex that we did—or, more accurately, that *I* did—and I was having all off at the minute keeping her from watching Oracle and I as it was.

As such, we shared the bath, and then I kicked her out to go relax in the main part of the wagon, while I bounced Oracle—carefully—off all the walls and broke a fold-down table.

Several hours later, when we'd both had the chance to work out a little frustration, had a few hours of sleep, and had dressed again, we ate some food. Then Oracle went to deal with the business of the camp and Sehran flew back up and resumed her place on overwatch. As for me?

I rested and meditated for a while, then worked my way through the notifications that I'd choked off earlier.

The first that popped back up was annoyingly that I'd not yet managed to complete the last quest from Jenae. I read over it quickly, frowning, while lying back in a deep and actually surprisingly comfy chair. Then I grinned as I looked at the next one.

Congratulations!

You completed your quest: What Secrets does Sonra Hold?

There were many possible reasons that the tent city of Sonra and its council had granted special dispensation and have offered faith to the Imperial Legion, and now, upon seeing the true inhabitants of the inner circle, you know them.

Reward: 257/257 followers, 50,000xp

"Not bad," I muttered. "I was hoping for more, but still…" I moved on, pulling up a notification that I wanted to see a hell of a lot more.

Congratulations!

You have killed the following:

- ***1x Greater Divine Avatar, level 48 for a total of 3,500,000xp***
- ***141x Slavers/guards of various levels for a total of 204,112xp***
- ***503x Drow of various levels for a total of 9,781,375xp***
- ***1,357,096x Spiders of various levels for a total of 2,111,771xp***
- ***3x Drow Spiderkin of various levels for a total of 88,629xp***
- ***43x Drow priests of various levels for a total of 1,122,301xp***
- *27x…*

I didn't bother reading all of it, unable to keep the spreading grin from my face. I realized that not only had the gods decided that "remove from this territory" had also meant "remove from this plane of existence," but they'd apparently somehow wrangled it to mean that as it was my action that led to it, I should receive the goddamn experience as well.

Fuck to the yes.

I started to laugh; then, unable to hold it in, I threw back my head and yelled at the ceiling of the wagon, "Thank you, everyone!" Knowing, and I mean *knowing*, that Jenae and the others would understand exactly what I meant.

The total, as I pulled up the next notification, had been enough to net me several levels, and damn that was a relief! Fighting gods was goddamn profitable when it came to levels. If anything, I was only sorry I'd not discovered this secret when I was lower leveled!

Congratulations!

You have reached level 49-51.

You have 64 unspent Attribute points and 1 Meridian point available.

Progress to level 52 stands at 2,114,423/12,000,000

"Hell to the fucking yes. That's gonna sting, but hey, I'll be a big boy and take it," I muttered, looking at the points that I had to invest. Fifty of them came from hitting level fifty, the multiple kicking in and then my seven points per level for the others, which I was going to have to think long and hard about using, considering the massive slowing of my growth of late.

That being said, though, was I really slowing that much in my growth? It felt like it'd been ages since I gained a level. But when I thought about the effect of kicking a god's teeth in had?

My real level growths from now on were likely to be coming from either making major discoveries in my professions, from quests, or from large-scale battles, I guessed.

At least I had that option, though, because most in my place weren't going to be picking fights with the gods.

Moving on, though, the next one? Well, that was damn nice to see as well, as was the one after it.

You have been offered a Divine repeatable Quest: My God is Better than your God (5)

Jenae and the Pantheon of the Flame have offered you a Quest: Travel to the City of Gaij and conquer it, throw down Nimon's altar, as well as those of the Pantheon of the Dark, and dedicate the Tower of Gaij to the Pantheon of the Flame.

Bonus: Recover the Legion Encampment of old and return its foundries and constructors to operational status: 0/1

Kill the Leader of the Dark Legion in Gaij: 0/1

Kill enemy Priests, Clerics, and Paladins: 0/20

Capture the City of Gaij: 0/1

Capture the Tower of Gaij: 0/1

Bonuses will be given for exceeding these numbers.

Reward: Territorial Claim increased, 30,000+ Citizens, Access to City treasuries and capabilities, 3,000,000xp

*

Congratulations, Eternal!

You have reached level fifty, and have a Class Choice waiting.

Class Evolution Recommendations

Common:

Exploratory Alchemist: You've found that the secrets of life may very well lie at the bottom of a bottle, after all! Choosing this as your latest evolution will grant you a one-off bonus of ten points to Perception, a randomly chosen recipe, and a chance to automatically discover a recipe by drinking a sample of it in potion form.

Brawler: Where many in your position would have grown, they would have changed their mindset and who knows, perhaps even have learned that their strongest weapon isn't their forehead, you remain woefully ignorant of these details. What you have found, however, is that deep down, regardless of the reasoning behind it…You. Just. Like. To. Fight. Choose this, and your latest evolution will grant you a one-off bonus of ten points to Constitution and five points to Strength, along with the ability, once per day, to absorb up to 1000 points of damage, then redirect it into a single blow. (Must be unleashed through your forehead.)

Paladin: You're on first-name terms with a variety of gods, as well as being a Champion for one. Perhaps it's time to take the plunge? Choosing this as your latest evolution will grant you a one-off bonus of ten points to Endurance and five points to Strength, along with a boon from your chosen god.

Rare:

Fleshweaver: The Fleshweaver has been injured and healed themselves, or been healed by others so frequently, that they've learned to get by with horrific injuries, simply by pulling together the most pressing wounds and

keeping on going. Choosing this as your latest evolution will grant you a one-off bonus of fifteen points to Dexterity, along with the Ability; 'Pain? What Pain?'

When all seems lost, your pain will suddenly vanish, and through the hidden art of Blood Magic, your injuries will reverse, condensing into a single cast spell that will transfer all your injuries to your target, stealing their health in turn. This Ability may be used once per 144 hours.

Arcane Knight: The Arcane Knight class is based around heavily armed, heavily armored warriors with a high understanding of magic. Choosing this as your latest evolution will grant you a one-off bonus of five points to Endurance, five points to Strength, and five points to Wisdom, as well as the Ability Stand Fast. Once per 24 hours, the Ability Stand Fast can be used, granting all allies within hearing range a boost to their Endurance of 10 points for one hour.

Sorcerer III: Magic is no longer within your blood; instead, it is diffused throughout your essence, through your very soul. You stand upon the cusp of the greatest discoveries of the age, and you inch your way closer with every breath. No longer do you struggle to cast; no longer must you battle every spell to ensure it does as you wish. Instead, you guide the threads with an innate mastery that's born of thousands of hours of careful study…even if they were done by someone else, and with another's memories!

Choosing this as your latest evolution will grant you a one-off bonus of fifteen points to Intelligence, boosting your second manapool in your companion's body to a grand total of twelve hundred mana in addition to your own.

Unique:

Soul Sovereign: You have developed an unprecedented mastery over the boundary between life and death, allowing you to command not just bodies through your necromantic endeavors, but the very essence of those who have passed. Choosing this as your latest evolution will grant you a one-off bonus of fifteen points to Charisma and five points to Intelligence, along with the Ability Soul Claim, which allows you to bind the soul of a willing wraith to serve you in spectral form with all their skills intact but at 50% effectiveness, for 24 hours, once per week.

Mage Imperator: You have a long way to go, but you have demonstrated your ability to become an unholy terror upon the battlefield. Trained and experienced as both a legionnaire and a mage, the time has come for you to set aside the games of youth, and instead become the living embodiment of the Emperor's will upon the battlefield. Choosing this as your latest evolution will grant you a one-off bonus of five points to Intelligence and five points to Constitution, along with access to five imperial war spells. Note: This class begins the quest chain: "Rise of the Imperial War Mage." This class quest cannot be refused.

<u>Imperial Overlord II</u>: You have claimed dominance of the continent, but as yet, your claim is still contested. Perhaps a boost is just what you need? Choosing this as your latest evolution will grant you three additional Titles of your choice to award to your followers.

<u>Please see the Examples below:</u>

<u>Arch-Priest</u>: You are currently the highest-ranking member of the Pantheon of Flame. Laying claim to the position of Arch-Priest formally will create the ability to induct others into the upper Priesthood, granting them bonuses, depending on their deity of choice.

<u>High Inquisitor</u>: People lie, even the best of them. Perhaps it's time to bring the burning light of truth into the darkest places of the soul? Using heat, pain, and sheer brutality, you shall scour the land of their filth! Granting this Title will give access to the repeatable quest: Renounce thy Sins.

By the time I finished reading it, I knew what I wanted to take, but I also knew that I'd be limiting Oracle if I did it. I opened my mouth, thinking to call to her, before she beat me to it.

"Do it!"

"What?" I asked.

"Do it, Jax!" I got the mental image of her shaking her head, a fond smile, and then a kiss on my cheek. *"Jax, I know you, and when you get notifications, we're soul bonded so I get them too. You need to decide on your class evolution, and that you'd even considered another class choice is sweet and all.*

"But we both know which one you want, and which one is both the best for us, and the most likely to keep our baby alive. Yes, selfishly, I went straight to the sorcerer three option first, wanting to improve my manapool.

"Then I looked at the others, frankly, hoping they'd be poor choices. They're not. There's some incredible ones here, and that includes the Imperial Overlord class, as it'd give our people a solid boost as well.

"As for the Soul Sovereign, it sounds a bit strange, I know, but considering you've got access to the Elsecaller, you could literally step in and speak to the spirits of the unquiet dead. You could summon them through the veil for a day of life again. That doesn't sound like much, sure, but you could summon one of the long-dead legion armorers; you could search for the souls of mages from the height of the empire, and even alchemists who bottled the secrets of life itself.

"Any and all of them who you find, you could bind to you on your terms, enabling them to live for a day, and they could spend it teaching our people! Imagine the benefits, when Restun could meet the greatest Primus Praetoria of the past?

"The very best, though, and I mean for all of us, is the Mage Imperator. I know you! You're considering everything else first, because you don't want to just jump in. So come on then, explain your reasoning."

"Dammit," I growled. Then I snorted and turned, smiling as Oracle opened the door and stepped inside, moving across and sitting opposite me, waiting, having presumably set off as soon as she felt me going through the notifications.

"Fine." I sighed. "Yeah, I'm tempted by the others. A lot of them look cool, but it comes down to the Exploratory Alchemist, Sorcerer Three, the Soul Sovereign, and the Imperator."

"Why?" She smiled, damn well knowing she was being my damn duck in this as I needed to work through my choice before I made it.

"Okay." I glared at her, struggling with my irritation…and trying not to laugh. "So, Alchemist first. We're on a new continent and we're going to find more new potions. That could massively speed up our increases in skill, which in turn will keep our people safer and alive longer."

"Boring, though, and you've already learned to see and sense the pattern behind things, so the alchemy is nothing that you can't figure out yourself, and probably better," she pointed out, and I snorted.

"Which is why it's a no," I agreed. "Okay, then, well, Sorcerer Three—"

"Isn't really an option here." She cut me off. "We both know it'd increase my manapool by a lot, but it's not enough to make it really worth it, so let's move on."

Her waving aside that choice so determinedly made me smile. "Yeah, all right. So Soul Sovereign is basically a lich class, and yeah, I *could* call the greatest warriors of the past through, it both ties us to the Elsecaller to use the skill properly, and it relies on us being able to actually find those souls. Sure, in time, I bet I can learn to do it, but when I first stepped in? I saw our friends. I saw those who had died for me, and I heard them calling out. I looked, and suddenly I couldn't see which they were, or who. There were dozens of the dead all wearing the same faces and sounding like Stephanos and the others.

"That's what I'd be up against—the dead who are desperate for any experience, any hint of life again—and who would literally say and do anything to get it. Then add in that I'm pretty sure that any soul who's left wandering the other side of the veil and who would be drawn to places like that, is doing so because they can't settle?"

I shook my head, struggling to put what I felt into words and explain it.

"When you pass through the veil, you either move on and you rest, you sleep away the ages, before whatever happens, happens. Perhaps you're reborn…maybe you just drift away and dissipate. I don't know. But what I do know is that that option is always left for you.

"If you can't rest, it's because you left something undone in this life that's so incredibly imperative it's preventing you from resting in the afterlife, and that's either insanely important, like it was for the wraiths and spirits aboard the prax, or it's because you can't rest from fucking fear and anger.

"Those who walk the halls of the dead aren't looking for *rest*—they're looking for absolution, for payback, or they're terrified of the next step. They can't let go and move on, because so many of them are terrified of facing judgment!

"Those who can? They're likely to be the ones we desperately need. Do you see Restun dying and then saying 'Oh well, I don't fancy resting in peace; instead, I'll spend the next few millennia fighting to torture other souls and feed off them.'?"

"It is Restun…" She pointed out quite reasonably.

I hesitated, and then changed what I was going to say, choking off a snort of disbelieving laughter. "Okay, yeah, bad example," I admitted, remembering his face when he discovered burpees. "So yeah, he would torture the living, but it'd be to make them into immortal fighting machines, not to feed off their suffering…" I broke off again, unsure for a second, then plowed on.

"Anyway, you know what I mean. I can use the ability once a week, and as soon as they realized what I was looking for, every soul who couldn't rest in the afterlife would be battering down the gates, trying to lie to me to get a second chance.

"Then once they'd had a second chance for twenty-four hours, they'd be desperate to get another, and another. It has the potential to be incredible, but the time lost to it?" I shook my head. "I don't think it's worth it, not without some way to either verify that the soul we get is the soul we want, and certainly not without access to the Elsecaller no matter where we go."

"So that leaves us with Imperator, and gets us five points in Intelligence and five points in Constitution. But what we really want? Five new spells. Spells that are specifically aimed at a class that sounds like the coolest possible of all classes, a Mage Imperator," Oracle finished for me.

"We get more mana regardless from our Intelligence, and even if we didn't, that wouldn't *matter* because you got so many points from that insanely overpowered kill notification. No, this gets us five spells, and they're awarded from the imperial throne and the system, so they shouldn't damage your brain. They're rewards, after all."

That last bit was said with a little uncertainty, but fuck it.

I grinned at her, then nodded. "Okay, let's see what we get. And uh, Oracle?"

"Yes, Jax?"

"Be careful, but…" I wasn't sure how to say it, worrying that it might put her at risk.

"I'll stay in your mind and connected both through the bond and by your side, my love. Don't worry, we're safe. And even if it wasn't, there'd be no way I'd leave you."

"Thank you," I whispered. "Okay, fuck it, here goes…"

CHAPTER THREE

I selected the Mage Imperator class—I mean, come on, who was I kidding—and yeah, the result was…impressive. Where the other classes had been minor changes—I mean, hell, my original choice of Spellsword was mainly just the difference in Intelligence and so on—the stats were most of the award, and that was it.

When Oracle suddenly got access to her own dedicated manapool with Sorcerer One, that was a hell of a difference, but beyond that? Not a huge one.

The knowledge that came with the class choice, though?

That was fucking insane.

As soon as it started, I saw the reason behind it, and why the hell it was marked as unique as well.

That had caught my eye before, but I'd figured that wasn't that big a part of it. Now, though? Now, I damn well understood that the reason it was unique was exactly the same as it'd been for Lydia.

There were no imperators left to give me the training required for the class, which was why the quest came along with it. As the information, the memories, and the knowledge began to download into my brain, I hissed in pain.

I saw the colleges, the academies, and more, places of learning from a thousand years ago, when the empire was at its height, filled to overflowing.

I saw them all, and I saw the absolute contempt that the imperial imperators held them in.

I felt the memories, I felt the sneers from some and the amusement from others, as they watched the little magelings, apprentices and masters and students, gifted amateurs or not, as they struggled to understand the "deeper secrets of the cosmos."

They were taught so little, and told they'd learned so much.

The imperators were to normal mages, what the Praetorian Guard were to city guards and basic soldiers.

Yeah, they were sort of the same, but the gulf of experience and knowledge was horrifically vast.

For me, as I sat there, seeing the past through the eyes of ancient masters, I saw it all and was absolutely horrified. At the same time? I damn well *wanted* that knowledge.

These were the mages who would be sent out by Amon to deal with "minor" things, such as revolutions, armies from kingdoms that were attempting to throw off the yoke of imperial subjugation, and of course, rampaging dragons.

Not greater dragons—of course not…that was crazy. For a rampaging greater dragon, Amon himself would take care of it. But for a minor one? A lesser dragon, as opposed to a wyrm, would be something that the legions and their personal mages and battlemages just couldn't deal with. Occasionally a battlemage would get lucky—they'd make a breakthrough or they'd just be that fucking good that they'd survive such an event, and the reward for such a monumental fuckup?

They were sent to train as an imperator.

The standard classes for an imperator started where the average mage had reached their absolute limit. They would be weighed, measured, and their focus assessed. If they survived the first term of acclimatization, then they'd be given a personalized path aimed to bring about their ultimate ascension.

If they were ice-focused? They'd end up training in places that made the Antarctic seem like a fucking tropical holiday destination. Fire? Welp, get ready, there's an exchange program going on in hell just for you, my son. And when I say hell? I mean they were studying literally in hell, surrounded by demons that viewed them as a nice snack.

That was the level of dedication and insanity involved. One in ten thousand battlemages would be selected for imperator training, and one in fifty might make it. One in half a million battlemages.

Considering the average mage would spend their whole life working toward being acknowledged as good enough to be classed as a battlemage?

I suddenly realized exactly why the warning about the quest being non-refusable was there.

The level I needed to get to, just to *start* my training? Fuck me!

On the upside, though, I had access to the starter spells that the imperators were offered. Although I needed to do a hell of a lot more to reach the heights I thought I was getting close to, I now had a path and a series of targets to hit, thanks to the quest.

Also, if I was honest, I couldn't wait to fucking see Restun's face. Because along with the knowledge that I'd gained on who and what the imperators were, I'd also gained a lot more information on the realities of the Praetorian Guard, and their armor.

I paused, refusing to look at the spell list and at the quest yet. Instead, I climbed to my feet and stepped over to my armor standing on the crude armor stand that Aellin had cobbled together for it, and took a deep breath, before pushing my mana out of my palms and into my armor itself.

Part of the information that had come to me had been a hint of the different paths available: Glacial Imperator was the ultimate evolution of the ice mage, Infernal Imperator for the warlocks, Solar was the light path, Phoenix was that of the fire mages. And when it came to the armor?

The Artifice Imperator was a legion armorer who had gone so far down the path of enchantments that they'd been picked free of being a 'mere' armorer and instead was directly responsible for the creations that were worn by…

The Praetorian Guard.

Grenelda was one such, and suddenly it all came home to me that the reason that bloody necromancer was so pissed off seeing me wearing armor that had apparently shown signs of her work? It wasn't that I'd scratched and dented the shit out of it—it was that I was wearing a set of it without a goddamn clue what I was doing!

Our armorers had tried working on it. They'd improved on some dents and they'd managed to buff out a few of the scratches and so on, but that was it.

Now, as I wrapped my hands around the left vambrace and focused on it, I felt it.

How the hell I'd not felt it before, I couldn't imagine, but now that I was looking for it, I poured mana out of my palms and into the metal, seeing an almost instantaneous reaction.

The deep blood-red plates of the armor had been scratched, scraped, and basically battered to hell over the last few weeks, the dust of the desert was ingrained in places, and here and there, the enameled plates looked like they'd been hit with a sandblaster as the movement of just my arm against my leg when walking had ground away at it.

Now, as I fed a hundred and then another thousand mana into it, I saw the reason he'd been so pissed.

The deep blood-red reappeared, surfacing like it was rising through the depths of a muddy puddle, and god*damn.*

I knew the armor was gorgeous; I knew it. But seeing it now, after weeks of getting used to it, after seeing it first in the depths of the prax and now? I cut off the feed of the mana, not because it was fixed and polished up—because it wasn't. No, I stopped because I'd damn well drain myself a dozen times over to fix it up.

Best of all? I felt the armor attuning itself to me, adjusting ever so fractionally.

I realized that if someone was far enough along in their skill set that as a warlock they could summon the dukes of hell itself, then the equivalent armorer wasn't going to just be creating self-polishing damn armor.

There was going to be a *lot* more to the armor that I'd not even scratched the surface of yet, and fuck me sideways I was going to find out *exactly* what that was.

I left the gleaming red spot on the vambrace. Eleven hundred mana invested, and it looked like I'd fixed and polished perhaps ten percent of the left vambrace and that was it. Still, I couldn't help but grin as I sank back into the seat, sensing Oracle's unspoken prodding to get on with the "good stuff."

I couldn't help myself.

Pulling up the spell list, I nearly shit myself, though. A good fifty spells appeared, along with a handful of evolutions for each, and I just wanted them all.

The issue?

The lower-end spells were a thousand mana…*each.*

They cost nearly half my damn manapool, per casting, for the cheapest of the spells! Firebolt, for example, which when I'd started out, I was so proud of? Ten mana to cast.

Oracle sensed my disbelief and my horror and quickly adjusted the screen for me, separating them out into spells I could actually afford. I cursed as they were cut down to ten, and yet I was damn thankful as well.

The first spell was sort of boring, even if it was a massive upgrade to my arsenal if I chose to take it, and yet…well, frankly, it *was* boring.

1) Mana Lance: The standard offensive spell taught to all Mage Imperators upon initiation, Mana Lance has remained virtually unchanged since the height of the Empire due to its perfect balance of efficiency and versatility. The caster channels concentrated mana into a brilliant spear of energy that can be held to be used from a

mounted role, hurled, or even fought with in close combat to produce strikes with devastating precision.

Unlike more elemental attack spells, Mana Lance delivers pure arcane force, bypassing most common magical resistances. The spell can be charged by holding the casting position longer, increasing both range and penetration power proportionally to the time/mana invested.

Elite Mage Imperators can manifest multiple lances simultaneously, allowing them to engage several targets or concentrate overwhelming force on a single threat. The spell's signature crimson hue serves as a psychological weapon in itself, as its appearance on the battlefield has historically signaled the arrival of imperial elite forces.

Note: Both the size and devastation of the Mana Lance is variable. Minimum casting cost is 1000 mana due to the containment structure and the cost of solidifying mana into a viable weapon. However, once formed, the physical creation is malleable until it is released from the caster's control.

I wasn't that impressed. I mean, seriously? A thousand mana for a fucking lance? That was when I saw Oracle's grin, and I forced myself to reread the details.

Variable. That was the important word here, I decided. If I could summon the lance, and then shift its design? The massive burst of information that I'd received on accepting the class surged in my mind, linking up with the incredible amount of magical information that Amon had shared as well. Slowly, oh so slowly, it started to dawn on me.

If I took away the word "lance" and instead substituted the word "naginata"?

That made a lot more sense.

Or sword. Or fucking banana, dammit! It was literally a case of whatever weapon I chose to form with the spell, I could! I could adjust it on the fly as well.

A sword that was a longsword until someone went to parry it, then a short sword to pass their guard, before lengthening again, this time into a greatsword? Now that would be lethal!

Sure, it'd be an absolute nightmare to learn to fight literally again from scratch, but once I was used to it? Damn. Moving on, I couldn't wait to see what was next!

2) **<u>Tactical Displacement:</u> This versatile battlefield manipulation spell allows the Mage Imperator to instantly reposition themselves or their target across the battlefield. Unlike crude teleportation magic, Tactical Displacement involves a precise calculation of battlefield dynamics, allowing for strategic placement rather than mere escape.**

   When cast, the target is enveloped in a swirl of crimson energy before instantaneously appearing at the designated location. The spell can

be used defensively to extract wounded allies, offensively to position strike teams behind enemy lines, or tactically to rapidly redeploy forces in response to changing battlefield conditions.

Masters of this spell can perform multiple displacements in rapid succession, orchestrating complex maneuvers that leave enemies disoriented and vulnerable.
Note: The unique magical signature of this spell can be countered if the opposing force is aware ahead of time and recruits a suitable temporal or void magus.

That was…okay, that was fucking insane is what it was. It was literally a short-range teleport, one that was incredibly expensive, considering the thousand mana cost, but as it could be scaled up or down? I could step into the shadows here and step back out behind the enemy commander's back, behead him, and then back, all in less than a second.

Better yet? I could do that with my damn squad with a few mana potions to hand. Literally jump our entire squad across a short distance and fuck shit up, then booyah, back out of sight again.

I had no clue how insane it'd be to be fighting on a battlefield and have someone with a massive manapool literally create a portal like this in front of a charging line of cavalry, and then have them appear behind their own lines…

That made me grin even more. Why the hell put our own cavalry at risk, after all? Why not let the enemy charge, and then cast it against them? Have their own cavalry suddenly vanish from the battlefield, only to reappear behind their command tent and run their own leadership through or ride over them?

Fuck me, no wonder these imperators were considered the swinging dick of the battlefield! They wouldn't even need a fucking army. Just rock up, and boom!

You could create a portal in front of the enemy elites, and then reopen it a hundred meters above the rest of their army and just drop them all through! The force that the enemy were relying on to counter the best of the best are suddenly screaming and falling on their friends, crushing half of them to death and breaking bones everywhere.

Then you just pop a potion and do it again!

With enough mana, you could beat an army to death with itself while drinking rum on a fold-out lawn chair you brought along for the show!

I couldn't help it. I wanted it desperately, and yet…I knew, just *knew*, both from the manapool I had and the shared information that I already had, that there was no way I'd be doing that for a while.

No, these were the *entry-level spells.* I sensed the possibilities of these, but there was no way I could pull off that kind of an effect yet. Thinking about it… I nodded slowly. I could do this; I could create the displacement field or portal, but the size I'd be limited to? I'd have to get good with it, and I'd have to damn well practice and level it like nobody's business.

Moving on, I pulled up the third spell in line.

3) **Imperial Command: The most distinctive spell in the Mage Imperator arsenal, Imperial Command channels the ancient**

authority of the Empire into a powerful compulsion effect. The caster speaks a single, clear command infused with Imperial mana, their voice resonating with supernatural authority.

Targets within range feel an overwhelming urge to comply with the command, fighting against their own oaths if necessary. The effectiveness varies based on both the target's willpower and the caster's innate strength, with true masters of Charisma and Wisdom capable of commanding even powerful beings.

Unlike crude mind control, Imperial Command works through the innate recognition of authority embedded in the metaphysical structure of the realm itself—the same principle that powers Imperial oaths and bindings. This makes it particularly effective against constructs, summoned entities, and any beings with historical connections to the Empire.

That one…well, that was a little harder to get, but it was basically using the imperial oaths to force compliance, without the target having agreed to the oaths? It was compulsion, a single insanely powerful order that I could give to someone. I felt dirty even thinking about it, and not in a good way.

Though, I could see the advantages. Using it, for example, I could order a noble who had no allegiance to me to confess their sins and unless they had a higher investment in Charisma and Wisdom than I did? They'd have to do it.

I saw the advantages, but also, not for me. Just…no. I had enough issues with the oaths as it was, and this was just a step too far. Despite knowing the potential uses I could put it to, I also didn't want to go further down that line. Hard pass.

4) **Mana Cascade: This tactical area-denial spell transforms the battlefield by destabilizing ambient magical energies. The Mage Imperator puts out a wave of crimson energy that creates a zone of fluctuating magical distortion.**

   Within this field, enemy spellcasting becomes unpredictable and hazardous—minor spells may fail entirely, while more powerful incantations risk backlash against their casters. Imperial mages, linked to the caster and therefore to the specific resonance pattern of the Cascade, remain unaffected, giving Imperial forces a decisive advantage in magical combat.

   Advanced practitioners can "tune" their Cascade to specific magical forms—e.g., fire—creating targeted disruption against known enemy specializations while leaving even the magic of those not yet allied untouched. The visual effect of the failing spellforms across the battlefield serves as both tactical indicator and psychological warfare.

Now that? That sounded damn good. To literally deny my enemies access to their spells, and yet to still cast for my team? Hell to the yes, I could see the advantages of that!

5) **<u>Legion Enhancement:</u> A potent battlefield support spell that temporarily infuses allied forces with enhanced capabilities. The Mage Imperator raises their staff or weapon, releasing waves of crimson energy that wash over nearby targeted Imperial forces, granting them supernatural Strength, Endurance, or Agility according to tactical needs.**

   Unlike crude berserker enchantments, Legion Enhancement maintains and has even been known to sharpen the affected soldiers' discipline and coordination. Enhanced troops move with uncanny precision, their attacks striking with perfect timing and their formations adapting with heightened tactical awareness.
   The spell's effectiveness scales with the targets' existing training, making it particularly devastating when cast upon elite imperial legionnaires already operating at peak human capability. The enhanced troops emit a subtle crimson aura, striking fear into enemies familiar with its significance.

That was impressive. I mean, battlefield support wasn't really my role, I had to admit, and through the filtering knowledge and the background I had, I damn well knew that the thousand mana cost was only going to scratch the surface of its effects; and for a small team at that, never mind entire legions. But *damn.*

To buff a thousand plus people to a level that was classed even here as supernatural? What was that going to be? Not a measly five or six additional Strength. I mean, fuck me, a bard could do that.

No, this was going to be the kind of spell that boosted the receivers' Strength by fifty or more points, I was betting.

It literally called out the berserkers as "crude," for fuck's sake, and I'd seen the difference that the buggers could make when they activated that ability! They gained half again their Strength for a short period, and if I could do that for an entire squad?

Even better because they'd not be bulking out of their armor thanks to it being a magical force multiplier?

"Fuuuuuck," I whispered. "That could be…"

"You could literally power through entire armies," Oracle agreed in a hushed voice. "You could activate that—if you could have used it in the fight with Illoth, you could have ripped her leg off and beat her with it. You would have boosted yourself to the same stage as Nimon had been…"

"There's no way I could have used this in that fight, could I?" I was grinning already, before a second point leaked through and I groaned. "Dammit, no, I couldn't." I realized that I'd need to continually guide the spell, and for as long as it was active, I wasn't going to be fighting.

It was a buff spell, one that required constant adjustment, and while Oracle could do that in the field, she wasn't able to take part in the divine fights.

Plus, if I did it, what was to stop the other side doing the same? I had to imagine that bloody Nimon would know at least a fraction more magic than I did, after all!

No, I liked it, but it wouldn't be the trump card I'd been hoping there.

Moving quickly on, I pulled up the next and squinted at it curiously.

6) **Arcane Diagnostics: This sophisticated analytical spell allows the Mage Imperator to assess battlefield conditions with supernatural precision. When cast, the mage's vision is overlaid with a complex array of magical indicators, revealing hidden information crucial for tactical decision-making.**

   Though this spell requires a focus with each casting, some examples of the uses it can be put to are:

- **Active magical effects and their approximate power levels**
- **Hidden enemies and invisibility effects**
- **Structural weaknesses in fortifications**
- **Lingering magical residue that might indicate traps or ambushes**
- **The general condition and capabilities of visible forces**

  This information appears as intuitive visual indicators rather than raw data, allowing for instant tactical assessment without overwhelming the caster. Elite Mage Imperators can share these insights with commanding officers through linked focusing crystals, enabling real-time strategic adjustments.

Now that was cool, and yeah, that kinda hinted at the other roles of the imperators…not just walking nukes, but support staff and even artificers. Nice, but not for me. I moved on.

7) **Pact Bond Manifestation: This signature warlock-adapted spell allows the Mage Imperator to physically manifest aspects of their patron entity directly into battle. Creating a rift of variable size, through which emerges a manifestation of the pact—tentacles of void energy, wings of infernal flame, or whatever form best represents the patron's nature—that obeys the caster's commands with perfect precision.**

   Unlike traditional mass warlock summonings that risk the summoner's autonomy, these manifestations are bound by Imperial contract with the relevant ducal signatory of the hell planes, ensuring absolute control.

These manifestations can attack enemies, defend positions, or create zones of their patron's influence on the battlefield. Each manifestation carries the distinctive magical signature of both the patron and the Empire, creating a unique hybrid energy that most conventional counter-magics cannot properly identify, nor dispel.

That was a nasty one, basically a trap situation where you could make specific areas of the battlefield totally unusable to your enemies because they'd be full of flame or writhing tentacles, or fuck knew what really.

I had a momentary thought about the kind of shit that would come about if this was cast by Jian, with his bond being to a succubus, and the area of effect potential…then I shook my head and moved on. I had no words for the mental image, and damn.

There'd be nobody interested in a fight, that was for sure. Waiter? Check please.

8) <u>Essence Bargain:</u> **This tactical exchange spell channels the warlock tradition of reciprocal sacrifice through the Imperial Right protocols. The Mage Imperator activates a whole-essence bargain, in which the entirety of the essence in a given location is transferred to their bonded partner.**

What distinguishes this from crude warlock bargains is the precision of the exchange. The Mage Imperator specifies exactly what power they require—healing, destructive energy, specific knowledge—and receives exactly that, with no hidden costs or interpretative loopholes…PROVIDED that a reciprocal amount of essence is channeled in return.

Should the spell fail, the enemy escape, or the targets survive, then the essence is drawn through the imperator and returned to the hellscape.

Note: This requires a secondary contract with a willing participant of the hells, along with a significant infusion of mana. Consider carefully the costs of this spell. You have been warned.

This one was an interesting one. Expensive, sure, and dangerous? Fuck to the yes. The potential gains, though? If we could find a partner in the hellscapes who was up for it, we could essentially say we wanted a fuckton of orichalcum and in exchange? We're giving up the essence, what I knew as the souls, of our enemies.

We could offer up the literal contents of the battlefield, slaughter them all, and then booyah, get paid in the converted amount of precious metals.

That sounded fantastic, sure, but the risk?

What if I misplaced a decimal point? I was shit at math, always had been. If I put down a kilo extra of material, how did that equate? Was I going to lose my leg? Was it going to be utterly unknowable? Shit, would it mean that if I was an eyelash out of specification then I'd just drop dead? Fuck to the no. I know that

Sehran was good people, but the dukes of hell? I had to think that if I fucked up, they'd kinda say no, and take the exact measure deliberately.

Like when internet deliveries first started to gain popularity and people received half a sachet of ketchup by weight for their order and a ton and a half of grapes thanks to hitting the wrong keys.

I was labelling that one as a hard pass.

9) **<u>Five-Element Convergence:</u> This devastating offensive spell channels all four primary elements—Fire, Water, Earth, and Air—into a single, concentrated attack.**
   As each of the relevant elements are both in spectacular opposition and at once capable of conversion with one another, they can create a significant detonation.

   Like other similar spells, the four primary elements are compressed into a small-scale reaction, held in place until they reach critical levels and forced to coexist through the interaction of a fifth force: gravity.

   As the spell reaches completion, the caster hurls this unstable convergence at their target. Upon impact, it detonates in a spectacular cascade of sequential elemental effects—targets are simultaneously burned, frozen, crushed, and drowned as each element expresses its destructive nature in turn.

   The resulting attack carries aspects of all four destructive natures, and although many targets have developed an immunity or resistance to at least one of the elements, it is highly unlikely they will have developed such to all four primary elements.

This one in comparison, well, it was a bit shit. Not "shit," all right—it was probably the local equivalent of a nuke—but we already had a variant of this, and it was incredible, not to mention homemade.

That was a point, I realized. These were the basic spells of the imperators, and they were designed as almost training wheels spells, something to start them off and help them to serve the empire.

That was great and all, but I was from a world with science, which meant I knew damn well what could happen if we split the damn atom somehow and fucked shit up.

That, in turn, made me wonder about just how much magic told science to go suck a barrel of dicks, and I started to get a headache.

Moving on.

10) **Winter's Judgment: This devastating offensive ice spell channels the implacable nature of winter itself through Imperial authority. The Mage Imperator draws down a concentrated beam of biting cold that then disperses into seeking tendrils of azure-tinged frost.**

These tendrils unerringly track designated targets, wrapping around them in constricting bands of supernatural cold. Victims find their very life essence freezing: blood slows in veins, thoughts crystallize in minds, and movement becomes increasingly difficult as joints stiffen and muscles seize.

What makes this spell particularly feared is its inevitable nature. Once the tendrils have locked onto their targets, the cost to continue the attack is no longer taken from the original investment. Instead, it continues through the use of a sigil burned into the target at the point of contact.

Only the destruction of the sigil can stop the target's mana being converted to fuel the attack. No amount of heat or conventional magic can fully counteract their effects. Only specific mana conversion, temporal countermeasures, or the death of the caster can halt the progressive freezing before it runs its course.

Now that one? It wasn't really my style, but that you could inflict a sigil on a target and then make that target fuel its own destruction with its own mana? That I liked. Yeah, that could be useful.

"Well, any thoughts?" I asked Oracle, staring over the list, then looking at her when she remained silent. "What?"

"Jax, I'm bonded to you, yes, but these are your spells, and—"

"Don't give me that shit," I growled. "Fuck's sake, Oracle, you know better."

"I do." She smiled impishly. "I just wanted to distract you, and we've not got the time for a better way of doing that."

"You evil…" I groaned as she went on.

"Okay, so option one, for me, would *have* to be Tactical Displacement. No matter the situation, being able to zip across the battlefield in the blink of an eye? Or to literally open a rift in space in front of an enemy mage as they unleash their most potent spell, then have it impact their commanders? That's a yes."

"Damn right it is," I agreed with a grin. "Next?"

"Well, we're not warlocks, so that's those two out, unless you want to bring in a third wheel?" She glanced at me curiously, and I shook my head.

"No, I mean, I care about Sehran, and to keep her here and with us? Sure. Long term? Not something I'm interested in."

"Same," she said. "Though she is a tease far too often, but moving on! Winter's Judgment I'd say, more so for the sigil and the knowledge that comes with that, I think…"

"Okay," I agreed. "I suppose it'd be awesome for crowd control."

"Yeah, and that I like," she said. "What about Arcane Diagnostics?"

"Not one I was really considering," I admitted. "Why?"

"I was thinking it would augment your pattern ability and the background information might help evolve our identification and examination abilities, especially for some of the relics that we're looking for."

"The quests?" I remembered Lagoush had given us one and that we'd been recommended to head to the Cradle of Feshcan'un, whatever the hell that was, to help Oracle safely give birth. "Yeah, actually that makes sense." I nodded. "Most of the stuff we're gaining here isn't going to be hugely helpful, but that's because we can literally cast them twice in a fight and that's it."

"True, but we can take the information we learn, and use it to improve our other spells," she countered.

"Yeah, fair point." I sighed. "Just feels like a waste, not taking the spells that we could, even when we can't afford to use them."

"The other forty spells?" she asked. "I can—"

"No." I stopped her with an outstretched hand. "Please don't unlock them. You know me."

"I do." She smiled brilliantly. "You'd pick something far too powerful and use it in every battle, despite the cost in health, just because you want to use a nuke to deal with everything."

"And that's why you hid them." I nodded. "You know me, and I know you. All right, so that's three. What are the last two?"

"What do you want?"

"Honestly, as boring and shit as they are, Legion Enhancement and Mana Cascade."

"Why?" She cocked her head to one side curiously, resting her chin on her knuckles and drawing her legs up under herself as I spoke.

"Legion Enhancement because it'll make a hell of a difference to our people, and Mana Cascade, because when we eventually come across mages who know what they're doing, and people who know how powerful they can be, I want a counter that leaves them fucking useless so that we can curb stomp them into the ground."

"That is incredibly evil and I'm there for it." Oracle sighed. "Okay, that's the more fun things out of the way, I'm sorry to say. Is there anything else you need to do?"

"This afternoon?"

"Yeah."

"Not that I know of. I mean, I need to face our people when we talk about our losses, but…" I frowned, wondering where she was going with it all.

"Okay then, when you select the spells, they're going to fill your mind, Jax, and then the final prompt—don't look at it yet!"

I jerked to a stop and looked at her in concern.

"It's the beginning of the imperator questline, but when you start it, it's going to fully dump all that information into your brain, so get ready, okay?" she finished.

"I am." I sighed. "How bad is it going to be?"

"Pretty bad," she admitted. "You remember how Lydia, when she first accessed her ability and her new class, went nuclear and then crashed out for a day?"

"Yeah?"

"That was because there was nobody to teach her, so she got the basic class information from the realm. That's what you're going to get, except instead of learning how to summon a pair of wings and to call upon her most basic abilities, you're going to be accessing a master's degree in magic."

"Fuck." I grunted. "I never even managed a fucking diploma."

"Well, look on the bright side." She sighed, settling back in the cushions.

"What's that?"

"At least I have a meat-based form now to help cushion some of the knock-on effect."

I couldn't help but wince at that. Then I took her hand in mine and took a deep breath, and knowing through the bond that we were both as ready as we could be, I accepted the spells, and moved to the final notification.

Congratulations, Mage Imperator!

You have resurrected one of the greatest weapons in the imperial arsenal, a specific class choice that were famed, far and wide, as completely insane magical lunatics with almost zero morals.

When you absolutely, positively have to sink an island to the bottom of the sea, and yet still burn everyone atop it to death as punishment for non-payment of their taxes? This is the class you go for!

Once the Mage Imperator class has been unlocked, there are no further options beyond succeed in your class, or die! All Mage Imperators may select a single form of mana to use as their primary focus; please select this now:

Fire

Earth

Water

…

You have selected *Fire*!

You have gained an innate resistance to fire and all fire-based attacks. Spells of this school will now do 10% less damage to you, and inflict 10% additional damage to your target!

Due to your position as Chosen of Jenae and her realm-bound champion, this has been upgraded to 20%!

Beware, the pretty coals and flames may appear to do less damage to you now, but only a fool tries to swim in the lava!

As an ascendant fire-focused Mage Imperator, you receive the quest specialization most appropriate to your class; *fire!*

Grow, learn, and excel…for the only way to live through this quest is to earn it!

- ***14/30 - Reach minimum level 30 in Fire Mastery***
- ***0/5 - Select and evolve 5 spells of Mage Imperator level or below***
- ***0/1 - Provide/create a site for the training of the next generation of imperators.***

Reward: 1x Greater Boon, 1,000,000xp, Survival.

You cannot refuse this quest.

I read it all, the last sections through blurring vision. I hissed, the precursor pain I'd received earlier being as a summer breeze to a fucking tornado in comparison to what came next.

As the seconds passed, and the pain only built, I heard Oracle whimpering. I swallowed hard, hating this side of it, and that she was now forced to go through the pain with me.

"Worth…it…!" she gasped.

I blinked, forcing one eye to focus on her, as Sehran crashed through the door, having felt part of what we were going through and thinking there was an assassin here. That was the last I remembered for several hours, though, as the demon, one of our gentlest friends, dropped to her knees, taking Oracle in her arms and holding her as she began to weep.

CHARACTER SHEET

Name: Jax Amon				
Title: Godslayer				
Class: Mage Imperator (Fire Focus)			**Renown**: Imperial Scion, Prince of Dravith, Master of Himnel and Narkolt, Godslayer, Mage Imperator	
Level: 51			**Progress**: 2,114,423/12,000,000	
Patron: Jenae, Goddess of Fire and Exploration			**Points to Distribute**: 64 **Meridian Points to Invest**: 1	
Stat	**Current points**	**Description**	**Effect**	**Progress to next level**
Agility	83	Governs dodge and movement	+730% maximum movement speed and reflexes	4/100
Charisma	61 (56)	Governs likely success to charm, seduce, or threaten	+51% success chance in interactions with other beings	29/100
Constitution	125 (123)	Governs health and health regeneration	2460 health, regen 160 points per 600 seconds (each point invested now worth 20 health) Gained: Genetic Storage	N/A
Dexterity	93	Governs ability with weapons and crafting success	+83% to weapon proficiency, +93% to the chances of crafting success	21/100
Endurance	73 (67)	Governs stamina and stamina regeneration	2190 stamina, regen 53 points per 30 seconds (each point invested now worth 30 stamina)	4/100
Intelligence	206	Governs base mana and number of spells able to be learned	2260 mana, spell capacity: 102 (100 + 2, +200 mana from items)	N/A

			Gained: Hyper Cognition & Mana Manipulation	
Luck	72	Governs overall chance of bonuses	+62% chance of a favorable outcome	41/100
Perception	71 (61)	Governs ranged damage and chance to spot traps or hidden items	+61% ranged damage, +61% chance to spot traps or hidden items	11/100
Strength	77 (74)	Governs damage with melee weapons and carrying capacity	+77 damage with melee weapons, +77% maximum carrying capacity	3/100
Wisdom	100 (90)	Governs mana regeneration and memory	+1350% mana recovery, 15 points per minute. Gained: Mana Manipulation	N/A

CHAPTER FOUR

It took a while to recover. I'm not gonna lie…by the time I could actually see again, and focus both eyes at the same time, not just one and then have to close it to focus the second? That was awhile longer.

On the upside, though, the panicked sprinting by Sehran, and then the explanations given when she realized what was going on, meant that when I did manage to get back into the land of the living, the others had all gotten their heads around me probably not being much use for the rest of the day, and had moved ahead with what needed to be done.

I was fairly sure that Othair and Cai were either going to hate each other on sight, or become the very best of friends. They were both such efficient bastards that they were either going to rule my goddamn empire, or be the death of me.

Othair had—with the help of Marteen, who'd apparently been desperate for something to focus on—organized everything to within an inch of its life.

There was food, there were lights, and apparently the traditions here on this continent now included paper lanterns with a simple candle lit inside to carry your words to the departed as a final goodbye.

There were lanterns prepared for each and every one of the lost, and though it shamed me, I couldn't even remember the names of half of them.

When I left the wagon, dressed again in my armor and ready to speak, the camp was eerily silent, with even the hush of the surrounding camps slightly lessened out of respect.

Hundreds of lanterns were in the air already, as many chose to celebrate the loss of those they loved at different times.

That meant that given the many hundreds who had been lost in the tent city to the saboteurs and the drow scumbags, there were no shortage of people mourning.

For me, it seemed a bit weird. I'd picked two hours before sunset, not in a "fuck you, my schedule is more important" but because I didn't want to make everyone from the camp wait until then. There were children in the party, after all, and despite it being nearly midwinter back on Dravith, it was high summer here.

That meant it was around eleven at night here when the sun set, and fuck me, by that point, everyone was going to be unconscious who could be.

Even I was finding it difficult keeping going by the end of the day. And as for holding off until then to eat in a "more informal manner" with the bloody council?

I wasn't looking forward to it.

Thankfully, beyond saying a few words as the candles were lit, I didn't have much to do here tonight, as it was custom for the closest to the lost ones to do the speaking on their behalf. Marteen spoke about his mother, telling a short tale of how she'd come to be a merchant, and how successful she'd been, before ending on how much she'd loved that I'd conned them into swearing an oath to "the prince" who she and the others had believed to be on another continent at that point.

Another of the armorers—a tall elf by the name of Vasimarn—gave a speech about Aellin, and it was filled with love for her lost friend and regret that their ongoing competition to see who could level their skills using only a single hammer would cease.

The details of the competition were lost on most of us, but the other armorers laughed, and then finally, just before the pyre was lit to burn the bodies, Vasimarn produced the hammer in question, laying it atop her friend's hands.

It was tiny, looking more like a household thing that'd be used to hang a damn picture on the wall, but, as she stepped back, tears streaming down her cheeks and she clapped her fist to her chest, I couldn't help but feel for her.

On all sides, the action was being repeated. Dozens spoke of their loved ones, and they had been doing so for an hour when the pyre finally burst into energetic life. Those who had been burned or buried along the route—as per their choices—were remembered tonight as well, and by the time everyone started to drift away, I was already late for my little dinner.

I wasn't concerned, though. Considering these people had lost their lives to protect and see me through, the very least I could do was stand here and think of them, sending my respects after their souls into the afterlife.

Lanterns rose around us, vanishing into the wine-dark sky, ashes and cinders floating upward in a soaring dance.

Half an hour later, as I entered the inner ring—again, with glares from those who believed not only was it disrespectful for me to be allowed in, but even more so Oracle, Sehran, Daralen, and the twenty legionnaires she'd brought—I was hungry enough to eat the hind leg of a scabrous horse, and entirely out of patience.

Perfect time for me to do complex negotiations then really.

"Prince Jax." Cleq the goblin greeted me, bowing from the waist and straightening as I inclined my head in response. "We were concerned when the appointed hour came and went…"

I bit down on my irritation. "I'm sorry," I said. "We lost a great many on our way here, and tonight was a ceremony for them. As such, it overran."

"Think nothing of it," he said quickly. "We should have considered the losses, and made adjustments. Do you wish to rearrange this meeting?"

"No," I replied, then sighed. "I'm sorry, Cleq. I'm trying to be reasonable and respectful, but the truth is I'm exhausted, and I have very limited patience. I've suffered many losses, and every minute that I lose here in meaningless arguments and debate costs the lives of more of my people.

"Out there, right now, I have no doubt within a few miles of where we stand, there are imperial legionnaires being held enslaved. I told you last night where I stand on slavery, and I think you feel the same, so you'll understand how little I value the niceties of polite society, when those people are, frankly, fucking dying."

"We understand," Cleq said slowly. "Perhaps tonight will address those concerns, but regardless, please join us. Food has been prepared." She gestured toward a surprisingly large pavilion nestled between two of the gigantic wagons.

Unlike the gaudy decorations I'd seen outside in the merchant sections, this was elegant in its simplicity—dyed canvas with embroidered symbols I recognized from the pillars.

Inside, a low table stretched the length of the space, surrounded by cushions and what looked like adapted seating for the different species represented on the council. Sharn, the centaur, had a wider area where she could comfortably rest her body while still reaching the table. And despite everything, I still forced myself not to ask her how she'd wear trousers if she had to.

Fucking stupid thoughts that spring to mind when you're tired, I mused.

"You honor us by attending." Matriarch Ilena rose as we entered, her silver-streaked hair gleaming in the lantern light. "Even in your grief."

I glanced at her sharply, then nodded, forcing a smile as I reevaluated the situation. Either they knew what we'd been doing and that comment from Cleq was a hidden barb, or…

No. It was bloody stupid to think they'd not have had watchers on our camp, and regardless of Cleq and her comments, better to just move forward, and try to remember that I was tired, and needed these people on our side.

The entire council was present. Besides Cleq, Ilena, and Sharn, I spotted Greg, the second goblin, sitting next to Bravimoth the orc. The Kreonar twins, Daven and Malik, were still totally unknown as to which was bloody which as they were identical down to their facial scarring. Reth Suntari stood apart from the others, looking uncomfortable as I noticed that his right hand was resting where a sword belt should have been.

Looking around, I realized that they were all unarmed. I mentally cursed, guessing that in showing up with everyone in full armor and armed, I'd probably set this off to a bad start.

"I apologize for my lateness," I said formally. "Tonight was an opportunity to say goodbye to those we lost. Also, I apologize for coming armed. As my life has been of late, I simply didn't consider not."

"We understand," Cleq said quickly. "We suspected as much."

"Could have sent bloody word, though," one twin grunted.

"And you could have come and fucking asked, but hey, here we are." I smiled toothily at him, daring him to make a comment, and he paused, then snorted. To my surprise, he inclined his head.

"You're right. I'm sorry, my prince," he admitted, looking like the apology had to be dragged out of him. Even so, it was more than I'd expected to get.

"Ah, it's all good," I said. "I think we've all had a bit of a stressful week."

"Decade, more like." He smiled wryly. "Thank you, though."

I waved it aside, then Oracle slipped her hand into mine, giving it a reassuring squeeze as Daralen positioned her legionnaires strategically around the perimeter of the tent. Sehran stepped in close, smiling around at the others, before speaking into the bond.

"I'll take off and circle the camp, make sure we're not about to be attacked again," she offered, and I nodded, smiling my thanks as she made a point of pressing her fist to her chest, then leaving.

"Will your companion not be joining us?" Greg asked pointedly, and I shook my head.

"No, she's going to keep an eye on the camp," I said, making no bones about it.

"Very well. Please, be seated," Bravimoth replied after a few seconds where they all looked at one another in concern, then gestured to the cushions obviously set aside for us. "Eat first. Then we will talk."

I settled down awkwardly. My armor that I'd redressed in was incredible, sure, but damn, it was a pain to get into certain positions in it. Crossing your legs to sit on a damn cushion on the floor? Difficult.

Oracle sat beside me gracefully, while Daralen stationed herself directly to my right, acting every inch the protective bodyguard.

The food arrived almost as soon as we sat: platters of roasted meats, exotic fruits, and bread that looked nothing like what I'd seen in Dravith. My first instinct was to dive in, and the smells that rose were enough that I really wanted to literally faceplant a damn serving dish of what looked like chicken and noodles. But I hesitated, waiting for our hosts to begin.

"The food is safe," Sharn snorted, obviously reading my suspicion. "We don't poison guests."

"Glad to hear it." I grinned. "Sorry. Where I come from, it's considered rude to eat before everyone is ready, and I just realized I have no way of knowing what rules you followed."

"The highest ranking in the room starts the meal." Cleq smiled, and then went on. "But considering the obvious and understandable concerns over poison, forgive me, but I shall start."

Cleq reached for a platter first, serving herself a small portion and biting down on it, before passing the platter along to me as a clear demonstration that the food was indeed safe. I nodded my thanks and dug in, my stomach practically howling with gratitude.

For several minutes, we ate in relative silence. The food was exceptional—spiced differently than I was used to, but delicious still, making me think more of Cantonese than anything I'd had recently, and damn I loved it. I noticed the twins watching me with barely concealed interest, while Matriarch Ilena seemed more focused on Oracle.

"My congratulations to your chef." I smiled as I wiped my mouth after another tiny baked bun. "Damn, I love these little ones. We have a high-level baker at home, and I missed his creations. Tell me, have you ever heard of doughnuts?"

"I don't think so," Greg admitted, looking unsure. "Most of the other races are less enthusiastic over the…" He gestured to the buns, and I held up a hand quickly to stop him saying anything else.

"I don't want to know what's in it," I said, having noticed after the first one that none of the other humans were willing to eat them, while the two goblins and the orc wolfed them down. "I just like them, and I'll worry about the ingredients later."

I had a momentary concern that it was something like monkey bollocks or whatever, and then shook it off. Best just not to know.

"Your victory over Illoth was…impressive," Reth Suntari finally said, breaking the amused silence. "Though it's left us in an unusual position."

"Unusual how?" I asked between bites.

"The spiders are gone," Malik Kreonar—or maybe it was Daven—replied. "Gone from a hundred-mile radius of Sonra, apparently. That creates both opportunity and concern."

"Opportunity because the drow were always a threat," his twin continued, "but concern because the power vacuum they leave might be filled by something worse."

"Like me, you mean?" I shot back, taking a swig from my cup.

Cleq laughed, a surprisingly deep sound from such a small frame. "You are direct, Prince Jax. Yes, like you—but not just you. The Dark Legion, other gods' followers…many will see this territory as available now."

"It's not available," I corrected her. "It belongs to the empire."

"An empire that hasn't existed for seven hundred years," Ilena pointed out gently.

"An empire that's rising again," Oracle countered. "With Jax as its prince."

"Yes, but—"

"Tell you what…anyone who disagrees with my empire, I'll fight," I suggested amiably. "How's that?"

There was a brief pause as the whole "fuck me, he kills gods" thought revolved around more than one mind, I was sure, and then I moved on.

I set down my cup, leaning forward. "Gods, that was good. Thank you all. Okay, let's cut to it. You've hidden here for generations, protecting refugees that the rest of this continent would hunt down or enslave. You've preserved species that might otherwise have been wiped out. I respect that, honestly, more than you know. But you're living on borrowed time."

Sharn's tail swished irritably. "We've survived centuries. What makes you think our time is running out?"

"Because I found you," I replied. "And if I can, others will too. Not to mention, you're running out of space. The inner circle can only hold so many, and you can only migrate so far with the herds before someone starts asking questions."

A heavy silence fell over the table. The council members exchanged glances, and I could see I'd hit a nerve.

"We have…concerns about capacity," Greg admitted reluctantly. "There are always more that we wish to save but the risk to us all should we overreach is far higher."

"Not to mention the increasing aggression of the slaver guilds," Bravimoth added with a growl. "They grow bold, believing themselves untouchable."

"They're not," I said. "Not anymore."

"You are a man who appreciates directness, that much is clear, so, I ask you this." Cleq studied me, head tilted slightly. "What exactly are you proposing, Prince Jax?"

I took another bite, chewing slowly as I considered my next words. "An alliance. Sonra becomes an official ally of the empire, and you swear fealty. Yes, I know, allies and swearing fealty are usually two different things." I held a hand up to stop the complaints and growls that had already started at that suggestion.

"The reason is simple. As I said before, all the empire is united under the oaths. When you've sworn, you literally can't stab one another in the fucking back. The first group of caravaneers I rescued from the desert had been hit by slavers, and until they swore, they had no clue that they had a few spies in their damn midst.

You'll gain a way to prevent *anyone* from the outside, anyone at all who's part of the empire, from spreading your secrets. Add to that, you get both our protection and you get to come out of hiding. You maintain your autonomy, but under my protection. No more hiding, at least not from me and mine."

"And what do we gain from this arrangement?" Reth drummed his fingers on the table.

"Beyond that? My oath that no imperial citizen will harm your people. Access to imperial magic and training. And most importantly"—I leaned forward again—"my guarantee that any territory that swears allegiance to me will be cleansed of Illoth's influence. Permanently. And you get access to those lands."

"We've just seen the proof of that," Sharn acknowledged grudgingly. "But the lands..."

She hesitated; clearly there was something there, and I could see it. I'd added that at the last second, having thought about the limiting factors of such herds. After all, they travelled the plains here in a constant, if slow, rotation. That was all well and good, but what if the reason they stayed on the plains wasn't just that it was best for them—what if it was that they couldn't travel elsewhere?

After all, the nobles who currently paid them to come to their lands and spread the fertility and walking manure factories were vying for their attention up here, but down in the lands that we'd passed through?

Fuck me, the thought of the changes in the lands bordered by the desert these could bring about?

I'd learned in my history classes that the Sahara had originally spread due to the entire area being massively overgrazed in the deep past.

That sort of made sense. But what if, instead of that happening, we reversed it?

If the herds were fed on hay or whatever and grass seeds were spread behind the migration? A single year of their travels could roll back centuries of neglect and damage.

The terrible heat there was in part because of the reflection of the sand, and the rivers that were nearby were long dried up, I knew, but there were solutions to all of that.

We could create fountains with the aim of healing our people and to provide water. Frankly, it was cheap enough I'd stopped noticing the cost long ago.

A few high-level mages could summon entire damn rivers, I had no doubt. And as to people like Ame? With access to runes and a single mana collector, there was no reason we shouldn't be able to start rivers flowing again long term, using the ambient mana of the realm.

That the areas had failed in the first place, I believed, was because of a lack of focus and will to do anything about it, until it was too late. Then, with thousands of people to support in the area, the little work done to reverse it had failed.

Add on that there was a form of magic in the area fucking the place up? Yeah, not good. I had plans for that though, and there was a good chance that the effects had only been strengthened by that, not that it'd been enough to do it on its own.

I'd not be looking at starting in the heart of the desert, though. I'd start on the borders, working to roll it back year by year. This could be the first step to that, and in the meantime, they'd get access to entirely new markets as they travelled.

I blinked as the others argued on, oblivious of the sudden tangent my mind had gone off on.

"But the slavers," Ilena was saying. "*They* are the immediate problem. Many of our…less visible citizens were once slaves themselves. As Sonra approaches its annual market, the number of slavers and their captives increases dramatically."

"As I said before, I can free them," I said. "All of them."

The twins glanced at each other. "How does this work?" one asked. "You mentioned it, but…"

"It's an imperial ability," I explained. "I can shatter all slave collars within my reach, healing the enslaved and freeing them, while those holding the leashes suffer…consequences."

"Your reach being how far exactly?" Cleq pressed.

"Depends on the mana I have available," I admitted with a shrug. "With enough mana potions and stones, I could cover the entire continent in one go. Provide me a hell of a lot of mana? Some powerful stones or potions? I can reach hundreds of miles."

Another silence fell, this one more contemplative.

Bravimoth cleared his throat. "Such an action would bring chaos. The slavers would retaliate."

"Against who and with what?" I replied with a grin. "Their forces would be decimated by the backlash. And they'd be facing not just my legionnaires but thousands of newly freed slaves with very fresh grudges, plus your outriders."

"And the Dark Legion?" Reth asked. "Nimon won't take kindly to your continued interference. They claim that their way of dealing with the slavers is better; they purchase all that they can, and then force them to serve."

"Nimon can go fuck himself," I said bluntly. "I've beaten him once. I'll do it again if necessary."

Oracle laid a hand on my arm. "We've fought the Dark Legion before, and yes, we accept that they are both a significant threat and they are well equipped, while our forces here are…less than we'd like. But if not now, then when?" She glanced from one council member to the next.

"When would you decide that the time has come to try to live free? To rescue those who suffer already under the pain of slavery? The literal prince of the empire is here, offering his protection, immediately after fighting Illoth herself to the death…"

There was a pause as the others glanced at me. I took the opportunity to drag the head out of my bag of holding and set it on the table with a clang and crash of cutlery and glassware.

Her head, like the rest of her had been, was three or four times the size of a regular human's, with a dozen eyes set across her face like those of a spider. Her hair was matted and bloody; her mouth sagged open and blood dripped from her severed neck.

I looked around curiously. "I know none of you really got a good look last night, so feel free to stare now." I gave a wide smile. "This will be the last chance to see it, though, since as I mentioned last night, it's going to Tamat to be made into a fucking goblet. *That's* where I stand on the gods, to be clear. Some are my valued and honored allies, and the others? If they're not with me, then they're against me. There is no neutral in that war."

"And that brings another interesting point to bear," Oracle added with a smile. "The gods have returned, and we count several of their champions as part of our forces. Jax is the Champion of Jenae, and her Chosen as well. Through joining us, you gain access to the gods, and with their help? Additional quests and more.

"As an example, on the march here, Lord Svetu gave quests to the refugees to make little things like shoes to help them. The Lords Sint and Darakin as well as Lady Tamat intervened personally when we were attacked to stand by Jax's side. He's literally fought hundreds of the Dark Legion, alone, and routed them. So, the question may be better looked at as this: can you afford *not* to join us?"

Cleq nodded slowly, then reached into a small pouch at her belt. She withdrew the truth-detecting stone I'd seen earlier, activating it with a pulse of mana, and obviously not willing to take any more on face value.

"Prince Jax," she said formally. "If we were to ally with your empire, would you guarantee the safety and continued existence of all races currently under our protection?"

"As far as I can, yes," I replied without hesitation, watching as the stone remained dormant. "I can't swear that you'll all be safe, because only a fool swears a promise they can't keep. But those who can't be protected will be avenged, and I'll do the very best I can. All beings capable of reason receive the same rights under imperial law, and receive the same punishments if they break it."

"Would you demand we relinquish our independence entirely, becoming subjects rather than allies, upon our swearing?"

"No," I said. "Though I'd hope in time you'd choose to fully join of your own accord, and I'd happily include a clause that if I tried to pull some kind of a trick like that, then it breaks your oath to me. I've included that before for others." I stifled a smile when I remembered that mad bastard Nigret and the effect on him when we'd had to explore the sewers.

Still no reaction from the stone, as it continued to glow a solid blue.

"And if we refuse your offer?" Sharn took over the questioning. "What then?"

I met her gaze steadily. "Then we part ways peacefully. I'll still cleanse the area of slavers because that's what I do, and you continue as you have been. But you lose the protections I'm offering, and I lose valuable allies. Add to that, I won't come to protect you when you leave the limits of my protection and the drow come for you, or the Dark Legion and others.

"Remember that you hid until recently, sure, but when Illoth chose the Elsecaller as the place for the fight, the gods all saw you and this location. Think about how many of them will just shrug this off and won't decide to make an example of you, or send their people here to recover, oh, say the artifacts, the wealth you possess, or you as prizes."

The stone remained glowing steadily.

Cleq exchanged glances with the other council members, a silent communication passing between them. Finally, Matriarch Ilena spoke.

"We have survived by remaining neutral, Prince Jax. By staying *hidden*. What you propose would fundamentally change our way of life."

"Your way of life is already over," I countered. "The old gods are returning. The balance of power is shifting. You can either be part of shaping what comes next or be swept aside by it."

Oracle nodded. "The gods have chosen to support Jax's claim. Even Sint, Tamat, and Darakin themselves walked among you yesterday."

"And through our alliance," I continued, "your people would gain legal protection under imperial law, not just behind a veil of secrecy that could fail at any moment. Remember that as I conquer territory here, anyone who wants to stay within it will be swearing the same oaths. That means that should you choose to travel with us, to tour those territories moving forward, you won't need to hide at all. Your people would be free to walk outside, to visit the scummiest areas of the shittiest cities, all in perfect safety."

"From citizens," Oracle added quickly. "If an outsider was to enter—a trader, for example, with some guards who attacked—there is no way to prevent that, but they'd be held to account and punished for attacking a citizen of the empire, regardless of who they were or what race."

Another silence fell, this one longer than before. Finally, Cleq spoke again.

"We would need to consult with our people. Such a decision cannot be made lightly or quickly."

My patience frayed. "How long?"

"Until morning," Reth surprised me by saying. "The council can call an emergency gathering of its representatives tonight."

I nodded. "Fair enough. But there's one thing I won't wait on. Like I said before, those slaves in the market camps? They need freedom now, not after deliberations."

"You would do this regardless of our alliance?" Bravimoth asked. "To be clear."

"Yes."

Cleq tapped her fingers on the table, then looked at Ilena. The matriarch nodded almost imperceptibly.

"Then perhaps, as a gesture of good faith, we could agree to assist you in this endeavor, regardless of the decision made to ally with you," Cleq said carefully. "Sonra has…resources. Manastones and potions among them."

My eyebrows shot up. That was unexpected.

"You're sitting on a stockpile?" I asked.

"We trade," Malik—or Daven—explained. "We have done for centuries. Much of what passes through Sonra is moved on, but some items we keep. Strategic reserves, yes, but we could look to provide a portion of them to you, to use in this."

"And you're willing to part with some of them?" Oracle asked, clearly as surprised as I was.

"Consider it an investment," Ilena said with a thin smile. "In a potential ally."

"This is dangerous," Bravimoth rumbled. The big orc towered over most of the figures at the table, including the diminutive Cleq seated next to him, and he held up one hand, gesturing to everyone to let him speak. "Please understand, Prince Jax, I do not speak to refuse this alliance. I support much of it, though I have concerns with the oath of fealty as a citizen of the empire, and our situation as allies, rather than subjects. I believe that to be unworkable, but that is a separate issue.

"No, my concern is that if we help you to do this, and then we choose not to join you, we have removed a system we spent long centuries building, as those slavers will no longer travel to Sonra for the annual fairs. We lose access to those slaves we could rescue, and it is that which concerns me. I was bought from such a caravan, and although I am not one of those born into Sonra, due to my race and the need to keep my identity and existence secret, I was permitted into the inner ring.

"Where others view Sonra as their home, and love it for this, I view it as the only hope for many races to be maintained. This is a perfect system, one that was damaged by your fight with Illoth, and through it, we have already lost much that we spent so long working to maintain.

"I do not speak to dissuade you from freeing the other slaves. Indeed, I wish to help with it, and would accept my exile from Sonra as a cost to do so, if need be. Instead, I argue for a plan to deal with the fallout, should you fail in your quests, and should all return to what it was, save our identity be exposed."

As he rumbled to a stop, I couldn't help but nod. They were fair points, and despite his brutish appearance, he'd managed to put it across damn well. Probably better than I'd made my argument, to be fair.

"Simplicity in itself." Ilena smiled. "What we do, should we decide not to assist Prince Jax moving forward, is blame the events on him. We explain that after killing a goddess before our eyes and with a significant legion presence in the heart of our city, we were forced to assist him, then we put out a call and instead of, as we have done until now, keeping the slavers at arm's length, we give them a dedicated section of the outer ring to call their own."

The look of horror on a few faces made her smile even more as she went on.

"Don't judge me on that. In doing so, we would then counter the influence of any survivors who see our involvement in the slave raid. It brings us back to a position where we can gain access to the slaves, and then we also work to increase the outriders," she finished.

"You have opposed the increase in outriders that I requested at the last four meetings of the council. Why change now?" Reth asked, surprised.

"Because until now I saw no need to further increase the number of those who could learn our secrets. The prince is right. The God of Death at least must now know of our position, even if the others don't, and his Dark Legion alone presents a bigger threat to us all than any other. Regardless of where we choose to go from here, in joining the empire or refusing it, we will become a target.

"The location of the Hall of the Nether, if nothing else, will be a target for the Dark Legion. And should He have examined our camp at all? He would have seen the artifacts we possess. There is much that could be used to advance His legion, and that discounts the wealth. No, I don't see Him leaving us be. Regardless of the outcome, we need a larger fighting force, and of those, I think we must increase the inner guard first."

"Very well, with that understood, then I don't oppose the use of the outriders in freeing the slaves as well." Reth nodded decisively.

I leaned back, considering their offer. It made sense from their perspective—helping me free the slaves would demonstrate both goodwill and power, attesting to the benefits of our alliance without fully committing them yet, and it shows them just how the power works…from the outside, at least. If I could prove that it was as successful as possible, it should shut down any concerns as well.

"How many fighters, mana potions, and stones are we talking about?" I asked.

"We could provide six hundred outriders, to augment the legion," Reth said after the others looked to him in question. "More than that and we risk removing them from locations that must be protected, as well as causing significant harm to Sonra."

"And we will need to maintain a reserve, as we agreed," Greg said. "Four hundred mana potions of varying strength, and twenty-seven high-grade manastones."

I nearly choked on my drink. That was a fortune by any standard.

"That's…generous," I managed.

"It's practical," Sharn corrected. "We have as much interest in ending the slave trade as you do. More, perhaps."

"When would you want to do this?" Cleq asked.

I exchanged glances with Oracle and Daralen. "Dawn," I decided. "Most of the slavers will still be sleeping off their night's revels. The slaves will be awake, preparing for the day."

Reth nodded approvingly. "Tactically sound. We can position our outriders to contain any who try to flee."

"My legionnaires can do a lot despite their small numbers," Daralen added. "But we are already a target to many, and in removing them from protecting the camp, I'm concerned about the safety of our charges."

"Perhaps your camp could be relocated at dawn to the outer edge of the second ring?" Sharn suggested. "We cannot admit you to the second ring, not yet, not without a formal alliance and possibly not even then. But we could move you to the edge of the ring, on this side of the herds, and then from there, should you need aid, our forces would be faster to assist?"

"That works," I agreed.

"How many slaver camps are there?" I asked.

"Eleven, of true size," Reth admitted. "With around four to five hundred guards on the largest, and anywhere down to six or seven on the smallest. Plus there are the fighting pits, and…" He looked around at the ladies, before going on in a slightly uncomfortable tone. "And there are the brothels and slaughterhouses."

"So several thousand to fight, and less than a thousand on our side." I nodded. "That's fine."

"Fine?" Reth repeated. "How is this 'fine'?"

"I'll take, say, fifty of the legion to the largest camp?" I asked Daralen, looking over at her.

She smiled wolfishly. "Fifty of my best against six hundred slavers?" she asked, and I nodded. "It'll be a slaughter, my prince."

"Exactly..." Reth started, and I snorted.

"A slaughter of the slavers," I clarified. "Look, I'm sorry, but you're all used to seeing a single or a handful of legionnaires charge a fucking camp and get slaughtered, right?"

"Exactly..." Greg sighed. "Please understand we mean no offense, but—"

"But you've never seen a coordinated and well-provisioned, equipped, or incentivized group of legionnaires, when they've not been forced by a fucking stupid oath to march to their deaths," I finished for him. "Believe me, with only six hundred of the enemy against fifty of the legion, that's not a fight. Add in, how many of the enemy are going to be slave fighters who are forced to fight through the use of the control collars?"

"There are many," he admitted, suddenly seeing the point.

"And they'll all be freed. They'll all be armed, ready, and healed, right in the middle of their hated enemies, with a chance for revenge. Even without that, the legion could do this, and definitely with me and mine backing them. But truthfully? I don't see this the way you do. I'm concerned that too many innocents will be injured. But even there, the risk is low enough that I think we have to take it."

"And we've been training the legion as we go, so many of the legionnaires have access to magic now—healing spells, Magic Missile and more. They can both heal and eliminate the enemy with ease," Oracle pointed out with a predatory smile. "How many slavers' guards are elite? Ready to lay down their lives to protect their masters and have access to spells?"

"Almost none, in fact." Greg smiled.

The planning continued as we finished our meal. The initial tension gradually gave way to a sense of cautious cooperation. Maps were brought out, positions discussed, contingencies planned for. Despite my exhaustion, I felt a surge of energy. This was something concrete, something immediate that would make a real difference, and that would prove that we could do this.

That the empire could really make a difference in these people's lives.

As the planning session concluded, Cleq approached me directly while the others were examining maps with Daralen.

"There is one more thing, Prince Jax," she said quietly. "Something we would ask in return for our assistance tomorrow, and that will increase the likelihood of the council voting to support you."

I tensed slightly, waiting for it to be something fucking ridiculous. "What's that?"

"There is a tower," she said, "three days' journey from here. The Tower of Gaij. It was once an imperial outpost, but has long since fallen into...other hands."

"The succubai." I nodded. "Yeah, I know."

"Well, those who hold the tower are not as many believe. They are..." She struggled for the words, and I held up a hand to stop her.

"My companion Sehran who took off to keep an eye on the camp is obviously a succubus, so just say it."

"We want you to claim it." She sighed. "As prince of the empire, it is rightfully yours anyway. But its strategic position would secure this entire region—if it were held by a friendly power—and it is the seat of local control. If you claim it and take control of the area, you should be able to increase your territorial control as well, and that in turn…"

I nodded slowly, understanding dawning. "It means that the drow and Illoth, as well as any she commands, will be pushed out of that territory as well. And if I held the tower, your alliance with me would mean protection for your people across a much wider area."

"Just so," she agreed. "The council's likely decision will hinge greatly on whether you commit to this task, but the condition is, and we feel a lot more confident in it given your companion, that you do not harm the succubai. They, like us, have been forced into a symbiotic relationship with the slavers and gangs, as well as the nobility. Unlike us, they could not hide who and what they are, so instead they have been forced to perform and to—" She looked concerned as she again struggled for words.

"They have been forced to turn the legion aside, and to deny them protection in a site that would have meant that many more survived to date. The succubai are not inherently evil, no more than we are, and yet they have been forced to acts that may not meet with your approval. I ask that you show them mercy, and listen, before you judge."

I considered it briefly. Another great tower meant more resources, more security, and a stronger foothold on this continent. It was a win-win. I'd been totally planning to claim the damn place anyway, though he didn't need to know that, and I already had a quest as well. Might as well get paid twice…

"We can agree to this, I think," I said slowly. "After we free the slaves, we'll make preparations to head to the tower."

Cleq's face broke into a wide, sharp-toothed smile. "Excellent. Now, I believe we've kept you from your rest long enough, Prince Jax. Dawn comes early, and we all have preparations to make."

As we prepared to leave, Matriarch Ilena approached Oracle, speaking too quietly for me to hear. Whatever she said made Oracle's eyes widen briefly before she nodded in understanding.

Outside the pavilion, the night air was cooler and the stars blazed overhead with remarkable clarity. The inner ring was quiet, most of its inhabitants having retired for the night, though there was a solid guard presence still positioned all around the ring.

"Do you think that went well?" I asked Oracle as we walked back toward the barrier, directing it to Sehran, who swooped in low and landed nearby. *"What did the matriarch say to you?"*

Oracle smiled at Sehran in greeting, as the legionnaires stepped aside, letting her move in to walk alongside us. *"She said that the tower is badly damaged, and she wanted us to not have too high hopes for it, as she's heard from others that it's on its last legs."*

"Well, between Sehran and our authority, I think we should be able to get inside, if nothing else, and then from there we can figure it out," I guessed. *"It'll all come down to the succubai and their take on it, but however they're keeping the nobles from claiming it is concerning."*

Sehran leaned in closer, smiling as she spoke through the bond. *"I'm sure my sisters will want to speak to me at least, though whether they'll let you in without a fight, it's a bridge we'll have to cross when we get there."* Then she spoke aloud, noting Daralen marching alongside but clearly missing everything we were saying. "So, we're really doing this? Taking on every slaver in Sonra at dawn?"

I nodded. "With the potions and stones from the council as well as their fighters, we can free them all at once. No more piecemeal rescues."

"And afterward, on to the Tower of Gaij," Daralen added. "I like it. Decisive action, clear objectives."

"And potential allies who can make the trip a lot easier," Oracle pointed out. "Though that's a point—if they decide to travel with us, they won't be able to travel very fast. How long would it take us to reach Gaij with the entirety of Sonra with us?"

"Weeks," Daralen replied. "From here to Gaij for us is around three days at a hard push. For all Sonra? They can barely travel three miles a day, and although they'd be able to push that a bit more once they were up to speed, I'd be surprised if they could do more than five."

"Damn." I sighed. "There's always fuckin' something, isn't there?"

Stepping across the barrier out of the inner ring and into the second was a bit weird again, the buffeting of the wind, everything, but I was starting to get my head around it being just one more bit of magical bullshit. Some guards on the far side—Sonra's outriders—formed up to guide us back to our camp. Word had apparently already been spread. As we moved through the second ring, a section of the herds was being moved back from the edge, and a space was being made for a large party to move in.

"Damn." I sighed. "We'll need to clear the land."

"Otherwise, most of our people are sleeping on shit," Oracle agreed.

In seconds, a new plan was made. Instead of heading back to the camp and getting a few hours of shut-eye—there'd have been little beyond that, considering the attack was in six goddamn hours—now Sehran was dispatched to the camp with orders for Othair, Toren, and Marteen.

They were to get the entire camp ready and get moving. A contingent of Sonra's outriders were already on their way to provide assistance as well. Although the camps on either side would no doubt be rubbing their hands at the sight of us "being moved on" by the outriders, they'd soon change their tune when they realized that we were moving to the other side of the herds instead.

Daralen and the four legionnaires with us rested a little, as those closest to our new location made some room and offered drinks and somewhere to rest that wasn't covered in shit, while I, well…

I, frankly, terrified the animals…although not in the way the sheep were used to in Wales.

Instead, I surrounded myself in flames, and Oracle guided me, as I used the new spell we'd learned recently—Environmental Cleanse—to sort the ground that was being cleared for us.

The spell flowed out, covering me in a swirling flame forced into the rough shape of a dome. The sight was one that set the nearby animals freaking out, but the herdsmen were ready and they managed to calm them, while I started to walk along.

As the leading edge seared and burned the shit, it also broke it down; then a second layer rolled the earth, a third compacted it, and a fourth smoothed, so by the time my feet crossed it, there was a clear, clean stretch of dry, slightly steaming ground. It wasn't a cheap spell, but damn, it was worth it.

By the time the first of the wagons turned up an hour later, our new camp was ready for them, and I was damn well ready for a very, very brief nap.

"Get some rest," I told my companions. "Tomorrow, we bring the empire back to Carrmor, and remind the slavers the risks they run."

"With our boots and blades." Daralen grinned, and I winked at her.

Morning arrived with urgent knocking at our wagon door. I sat up, instantly alert despite the early hour. Oracle was already moving, summoning clothes as Sehran's voice called from outside, as she'd apparently not felt a need for sleep.

"Jax, Oracle—they're here! The council's representatives with the mana potions."

"I'll be out in five," I grumbled, though in truth I was excited as well. I hated the slavers with a passion, and getting to do this? It came with a side order of nerves, mainly because I was always a little nervous that the power wouldn't work. But I forced that thought away and dressed quickly.

My mind still felt raw from yesterday's pummeling by new knowledge and the aftermath of accepting the Mage Imperator class, but the promise of action pushed the discomfort aside.

Outside, the pre-dawn air was crisp and alive with purpose. A small delegation from the council waited—Reth Suntari himself with four of his outriders. He held a pair of pouches, magical in nature, that I just knew were filled with potions and stones.

"Prince Jax," Reth greeted me with a curt nod. "The council spent the night in deliberation. We've reached a preliminary decision, contingent on today's outcome."

"Which is?" I asked.

"Sonra will ally with your empire," he announced formally. "Provided you successfully claim the Tower of Gaij within the month. The freeing of the slaves today will be considered the first act of our alliance. And as a token of our esteem, should you succeed today, then you will be formally admitted to the second ring, as will all those sworn to you."

A slow smile spread across my face. "Consider it done."

Daralen stepped up from where she'd been waiting nearby, her legionnaires formed up behind her in perfect ranks despite the early hour. "My prince, our forces are ready to move into position around the slave markets as discussed. We await your command."

I nodded, turning to Oracle and Sehran. "Ready?"

They both nodded, determination evident in their stances. I glanced over at Reth as well, who, for the first time, smiled widely before nodding.

"Then let's do it. Let's end slavery around Sonra." I turned to Daralen. "Legion Primus, there appears to be a lot of slavers in the area. Start moving your legion, and at dawn, and my signal, do your duty."

"Yes, my prince!" She crashed her fist to her chest and inclined her head, before turning to her forces. "LEGION!" she roared.

For the first time, I noticed people at the edge of the camp, the inner edge, and clearly of Sonra, watching in hushed silence.

"Today marks the next step in reclaiming the empire! As of right now, no slaver is safe! By the grace of our prince, those who are enslaved shall be freed. And as for us? Well, we get to be the instrument that teaches the unworthy! You know and I know that there will be brothers and sisters of ours out there right now, held captive by the slavers.

"Well, we get to be the ones who march into those camps, put a sword in their hands, and point them at the enemy! There can be no greater day for a legionnaire than today, freeing our brothers and sisters, stomping on the slaver scum that defile these lands, and raising the standard of the empire! ARE YOU WITH ME?"

The answering roar was something I felt more than heard, it was that powerful.

"Optios, you have your targets. Centurions, do your duty! *Quiiiiick*, march!" she bellowed, and the legion dissolved in an ordered mass of glorious purpose.

CHAPTER FIVE

"Okay, looks like it's time." I sighed to myself, an hour and a half later, as the sky truly began to lighten. The table before me held a dozen of the most powerful mana potions, and the five largest manastones, as well as half a dozen of the weakest and smallest.

It was going to be Sehran's job to literally force-feed me potions and hand more stones to me as I needed them. When I was deep in the zone of manipulating the mana needed for this, there was no way that I was going to see anything else.

Oracle, who'd usually have been the one to handle things like this, was instead going to be working with me, helping to guide the power as I fed it out, as after a lot of discussion, we'd both concluded that there just had to be a better way of doing this.

In the past, I'd literally drained the local area of all mana to do it. Other times, I'd been fine with a few potions or just doing it with a manapool that shouldn't have been enough to do anything like what was needed, but I'd knocked myself out with the backlash.

A backlash that we knew was only because I didn't understand the power I was wielding at the time.

As such, she was going to help me do this. As I stepped up, tugging the cork free of the first potion and hefting it with my other hand, her hand intertwined with mine.

"Remember," Oracle whispered, "don't try to force it all at once. Just relax. Let me guide the flow."

"It's time," I said. My voice sounded weird, even to my own ears. "Get the signal flags ready."

Reth Suntari nodded from where he stood with his lieutenants, and one of the outriders raised a bright pennant. Across the camp, I could see the same ones being hefted again and again, spreading the word. Both the outriders and the legion would be watching for it, knowing that it was the sign to start moving.

I stepped to the edge of the platform, aware that hundreds of eyes were now on me. The sun was just breaking the horizon, its first rays catching on my armor, which I knew everyone around me could see.

Time for the speech.

"Seven hundred years ago," I called out, my voice carrying farther than it should have been able to, "the empire fell. The Eternal Emperor, Amon, was murdered, and its towers crumbled. Its legions were scattered, and its people were left to fend for themselves against the darkness."

I paused, letting my gaze sweep over the watching crowd: a mix of my own people—who, though they'd not been told what was happening, obviously knew me by now and could probably guess—Sonra's citizens, and representatives from the council.

"In that darkness, the worst of the survivors flourished. Slavers. Warlords. Those who would build their fortunes on the broken backs of others.

"They took my citizens, your brothers and sisters, and instead of helping them, instead of building something better, they squatted in the corpse of the empire and they fed on it. They raped, they tortured, and they pillaged.

"The innocent were taken prisoner and were forced to serve their new masters' twisted desires, be that as slaves who were worked until they died, or in other, some would say far worse, ways.

"Men, women, and children—forced to do the unspeakable, starved, beaten, and murdered, by those who had no compassion. Where only greed flourished. They fed on that corpse; they lied and cheated and they claimed what they could steal as their right.

"Noble houses that were established by the emperor himself, descendants of our own families, not only abandoned their sworn duty in permitting this, but many reveled in it. They led the worst of these in excesses that would become the stuff of nightmares for their victims, and they fucking *liked* it."

My rage began to build—not the hot, uncontrolled fury that had once governed me, but something deeper, more focused. A righteous anger that Oracle helped me channel into the mana surging beneath my skin as I chugged the first potion, knowing that the initial rush of mana would be lost, but that the regeneration rate would help.

"Seven hundred years of suffering. Seven hundred years of chains."

I lifted my free hand, letting the first wisps of power leak from my fingertips, a white light that curled and twisted in the morning air.

"That ends *today*. Not just for a handful, not just for a lucky few. For all those I can reach! And tomorrow? MORE! We draw a line here, now in the fucking sand, and we shout 'NO MORE.' This far and no more! Now, we march into the future with our heads held high. No more will we hide who we are!"

I reached into my core, into that place where the imperial bloodline's power resided, drawing it forth as Oracle steadied the flow.

"The empire falls no more. From this day forward, it RISES!" I roared, even as I slammed my boot down on the platform. The mana erupted from me in a visible shock wave, rippling outward across the ground. The earth buckled and trembled, not in destruction, but as if the land itself was shaking off centuries of accumulated pain.

"By the authority I hold as Prince of the Empire, by the blood of Amon that flows in my veins, by the power of the oath that binds us all—I declare this age is OVER. Those who are enslaved, those who have been forced to kneel to unjust masters, those who are even now bound by chains on both souls and their bodies…I declare you to be FREE!"

The wave of power expanded faster now, racing toward the slave camps. As it passed, the air warped. People screamed as it passed through, around, above, and below them; here and there, hidden in the third ring, explosions started already.

Screams rose, not just in surprise, but in shock, in pain and horror, and lastly, in joy.

I could feel every collar, every manacle, every tool of bondage within my range like points of wrongness in the world that needed to be corrected.

The power flowed onward, hitting the outside, as Sonra termed it, the land beyond the third ring, where their supposed control ended, and it hit the first camp. I saw through my connection as the slaves there were surrounded by a bright, white light, lifting from the ground as though gravity itself had surrendered its hold on them. Their collars began to glow, first red, then white-hot, before crumbling into ash that spiraled away, even as that same light flowed outward. For the first time, as it ran down their bodies, healing their injuries, I felt it, and felt Oracle's understanding of it as well.

It wasn't just pulling magic out of my arse to heal them—oh, no. What it was doing in the destruction of the collars wasn't just destroying them…it was *converting* them. The reason they tended to collapse, becoming as fragile as poorly fired clay, wasn't because they'd been magically turned off or whatever.

The collars were incredibly magical artifacts, and they were using that mana, the power contained within them, to flow across those bodies and to heal them in turn.

For those who were constrained by mere iron and so on? That was where most of the cost of freeing them came from. For those held with control collars? Unless they were actively badly injured as well, then as they were released, there was more power flowing out and into the ring to continue!

That was one of the reasons for the variable bloody costs!

At the same time, I felt the backlash—the owners of those collars, the controllers of those leashes—screaming as the magical feedback tore through them. Some dropped instantly, their hearts stopped mid-beat. Others clawed at their own control devices as they melted into their flesh. But most?

For most, the control device simply exploded, detonating into shards that were flung free with abandon, even as the flesh nearby was pulverized.

I didn't flinch. This was justice, long delayed.

"Pour your rage into it," Oracle whispered, her voice cutting through my focus. "But keep control."

I nodded, accepting another manastone from Sehran, who watched me with a huge grin on her face.

The wave continued to expand, reaching the second camp, then the third. More slaves suspended in golden light, more collars turned to ash, more slavers falling.

The stone crumbled as I sucked the mana from it, ten thousand mana gone into me in a second. A second, then a third was pressed into my hand; each fractured and collapsed to dust as my mana bounced like a hooker's arse. My health surged and dipped, as my very life force was taken in the seconds between the mana's replacement.

The glass of a potion vial was forced to my lips, and I took it, even as another stone was pressed into my hand. Instead of seeing them, though, I saw the camps. I saw the power that was rolling out.

I could feel wounds healing as the power passed through the freed slaves—broken bones knitting, infections clearing, even the deeper wounds of spirit beginning to mend. They would remember the pain, but their bodies, at least, were made whole.

"LEGION, ADVANCE!" I sensed Daralen's voice booming across the fields. The legionnaires surged forward, no longer held back now that my power had swept through the camps.

The outriders moved with them, hundreds of riders, many on what looked like strange, lean horses but were actually something else entirely—beasts that I couldn't even remember the names of. But I did remember they were basically predatory horses, gifted with fangs and claws, instead of teeth and hooves.

I was dimly aware of Sehran forcing another potion between my lips. The liquid spilled down my chin as I struggled to swallow while maintaining concentration. The power reached farther now—touching the outer slave camps, the fighting pits, and both in the third ring and far outside in the camps, I felt the effect on the brothels.

"More," I growled, feeling the strain as the distance increased.

Oracle's grip tightened, and she pushed more of her own mana into the connection. "Draw from me," she urged, reaching out and apparently doing something—touching a manastone, I guessed—as her mana surged again as well. "Use what I have."

I did, opening myself to her completely. Our manapools merged until I couldn't tell where mine ended and hers began. The glow around us intensified, bathing the command area in ferocious light.

In the distance, I could see the freed slaves beginning to move; confusion gave way to realization, then to a wild, desperate joy. Some fell to their knees, weeping. Others immediately turned on their former captors. Many were unarmed, seizing discarded weapons. For hundreds, though, they'd been kept as both slaves and guards, forced to obey by the collars; now, as they turned on their weeping, injured, and confused masters, they let loose with all their righteous hatred and rage.

Worst of all were those who had been forced into the brothels. There and then, although many of those who were visiting weren't the actual slavers, those who were freed by my power put their rage, their pain, and in many cases, their teeth, to good use.

The legionnaires were there to provide guidance to the slaves, to prevent chaos from turning into slaughter—though I noticed many were doing exactly what I'd have done, grabbing the surviving slavers or their guards and holding them while the slaves screamed and attacked.

Good. Let them have their vengeance.

I reached for another stone, but Sehran shook her head. "That's the last one, boss," she said. Her voice seemed to come from very far away.

I nodded, feeling the power beginning to ebb. The wave had reached its farthest extent, touching every slave camp, every pen, every hidden chamber where human beings were kept as property. I could sense their freedom blooming like thousands of tiny flames in the darkness.

Beyond them, the wave front of the power hurtled on, growing fainter and fainter with each passing mile. But here and there, despite the distance, despite everything, I grinned as it washed over caravans of slaves who had been bound for Sonra.

I felt the wave as it slammed into them, and I felt it as Oracle did…something.

"Speak quickly!" she sent to me, and I did.

"Come to Sonra, come to the empire, and be free." I felt the air reverberate over the freed slaves, those marching alongside wagons tens of miles away, forced by their masters to toil as they marched to their own sale, and now, suddenly freed.

Then it was over. I blinked, feeling light-headed, weak, and fuck me, as a fresh potion was pressed to my lips and I chugged it, I was suddenly and heartily sick of the minty fresh taste of a bloody mana potion.

"It's done," Oracle whispered, her face streaked with tears I hadn't noticed her shedding as I turned to her, unable to keep the smile from my lips. "We did it."

I swayed on my feet, suddenly aware of how drained I was. Sehran caught me before I could fall, her strength easily supporting my weight.

"Not done," I muttered. "Need to…explain to them."

Distantly, I knew the first groups of freed slaves would already be guided toward our location by legionnaires and outriders. Thousands of them, moving in ragged lines, still dazed by their sudden freedom. Some would be lost, uncertain what to do with themselves now that the collars were gone.

"At least sit down," Sehran suggested softly, but I shook my head.

"No. They need to see me standing." I straightened, drawing on reserves I didn't know I had. A wash of strength and a burst of stamina suddenly surged in me, making me draw a deep breath and stand taller.

I glanced at Sehran, who winked, removing her hand from where she'd pressed her fingertips to the skin of my neck, and I smiled.

"Thank you," I said.

"Anytime," she whispered. "But remember, the crash when that wears off in half an hour…"

"Then we have until then." I sighed, forcing myself to remain standing, as already, in the distance, I could see people pushing their way free of the third ring and stepping out amongst the herds, staring at our camp in open wonder and hope.

The first to make it across, with the herdsmen already moving and chivvying their animals out of the way, was a young woman, a blanket wrapped around her shoulders, blood drying on it and her obviously naked flesh beneath, as she staggered uncertainly forward.

"I'm…free?" I heard her ask one of our people—Marteen, I saw, when he turned, nodding and gesturing to the center of our camp.

The passage had been deliberately left free from me to the edge, and she saw me standing there, the small guard of legionnaires Daralen had insisted on keeping around me, and the others who stood ready.

"Come," Sehran called, her voice reverberating with promise and hope, her magic bleeding into it. "Come, join us, and be free."

I held on for the half an hour I'd been warned about, using a stamina potion and even chugging a potion of Legionnaire's Might that I'd remembered I had in my bag. But when I couldn't take any more, I spoke.

My voice was raw, but I pushed power into it anyway, making sure it would carry.

"People of Carrmor! You are SLAVES NO MORE!"

A ragged cheer went up from those close enough to hear.

"The empire has returned, and with it comes this promise: No citizen of the empire shall again be enslaved without imperial reprisal. Those who swear the oath today join a brotherhood that stretches back millennia, a legacy of protection and justice. And for those we cannot protect? We will avenge! This I swear!"

I gestured to where Daralen watched proudly over her legionnaires, many of them now escorting former slaves.

"The Imperial Legion stands ready to protect you. To teach you. To welcome you as brothers and sisters under the imperial standard, and to guide you so that, should you wish it, you won't need another to protect you ever again. We can teach you to face the slavers, and fucking gut them!"

I paused, seeing the mix of hope and fear on so many faces.

"I know many of you have nowhere to go. No homes to return to. The empire offers you a place. Those who wish to swear the oath, to become citizens with all the rights and responsibilities that entails, will be welcomed. Those who wish to travel elsewhere will be given supplies, and wished good luck. None will be forced to join us against their will, even now, when we have freed you!"

I took a deep breath, my strength beginning to give out.

"The choice is yours. Freedom means nothing without choice. But know this—from this day forward, every slaver, no matter how powerful, no matter how wealthy, lives on borrowed time. This I swear, as Jax Amon, Prince of the Empire and heir to the Eternal Throne."

As the last words left my lips, my legs finally gave way. Sehran caught me again, and this time I didn't protest as she and Daralen guided me down to sit, before I could smash the chair. Oracle, not being as bloody stupid, was already sitting by my side.

"Nice speech," Sehran murmured. "Very princely."

"Fuck off," I managed with a weak smile.

From our position, we watched as the legion and outriders continued their work. Some of the slave camps had seen horrific fighting break out—former slaves turning on guards who hadn't been killed by the backlash, or slavers who had survived trying to flee with whatever wealth they could carry.

Lastly, unsurprisingly, there were plenty who moved in and tried to loot the camps as soon as the legion or the outriders moved on with the survivors.

But the operation was going mostly as planned. The outriders had formed a tight perimeter, cutting off escape routes, while the legionnaires moved methodically through each camp, securing weapons, gathering the newly freed, and executing summary justice on slavers caught in the act of resistance.

"How many did we free?" I asked Oracle, my voice barely audible.

She closed her eyes briefly, sensing through our connection. "Thousands. Perhaps ten thousand or more. The final count will take time."

"And the cost?"

"We'll know soon," she whispered. "But Jax—this was worth it. Look at them."

I followed her gaze to where a group of children, their collars gone but the marks still visible on their necks in rings of dirt if nothing else, were being gently guided by legionnaires toward food and water stations that had been hastily set up. Their faces were still drawn, their eyes haunted, but there was something else there too. Something I was willing to bet hadn't been there for a very long time.

Hope.

"Yeah," I whispered in agreement. "Definitely worth it."

Daralen approached, her armor spattered with blood but her posture straight and proud. "My prince." She saluted with fist to chest. "The main camps are secured. We've encountered significant resistance at only three locations, but it's being dealt with. Casualty reports are still coming in."

"Our side?"

"Minimal. The backlash took most of the slaver leadership. The rest are disorganized, fleeing where they can. Those who've taken wounds are even more thankful than before for the gift of spells that Lady Oracle has provided."

I nodded, too exhausted to say more.

"Rest," she said, her voice softening slightly. "We have this under control. When you've recovered, there will be many who wish to speak with you, both to thank you and to swear the oath."

"Give them food and shelter first," I rasped. "Oaths can wait until tomorrow, and I think they need a little care."

She smiled. "Already being done, my prince."

As Daralen left to continue coordinating, I leaned back against Oracle, feeling the warm sun on my face. Around us, the camp was transforming into a vast processing center, with legionnaires setting up stations for food, medical care, and registration of the newly freed, even as it was being filled with volunteers from the second and first rings of Sonra.

"I need to get up," I said after a few minutes, trying to push myself to my feet. "There's not enough room. We need to cleanse the field…"

"You need to rest," Sehran countered. "You just channeled more mana than most mages see in a lifetime."

"Just help me stand for a minute," I insisted. "They need to see that we're okay."

Sehran and Othair exchanged a look, then reluctantly helped me to my feet. The world swam alarmingly for a moment, then steadied, while Oracle… She shook her head, and I saw just how much the magic had taken out of her.

Standing, I could see more clearly what was happening. The legion had established a perimeter, with the freed slaves being guided into organized groups. The wounded were being treated, many with obvious fresh wounds from fighting, which I assumed had come from the battles to take down the slavers.

Though it was rare, the shouts that lifted to the air from where children were being reunited with parents made everything, absolutely *everything*, worth it.

I smiled, seeing that even those who had nobody else were cheered by the sight of food being handed out.

In the distance, smoke rose from several of the slaver camps—whether from fighting or deliberate destruction, I couldn't tell.

As I watched, in the distance, Reth Suntari directed his outriders to escort another large group of freed slaves toward our position. Among them were a sight that made my heart leap—the look of legionnaires, their bearing unmistakable even in slave rags.

"Daralen!" I called, my voice cracking. "Look!"

She turned, following my gesture, and her posture instantly changed. "Legion!" she barked at her nearby people. "Form honor guard! We have brothers and sisters returning!"

As the legionnaires hastily assembled, the group drew closer. There were perhaps twenty of them, men and women with the unmistakable bearing of the legion despite their ragged appearance. Some were injured, leaning on their fellows; some had lost limbs—and in the case of one who bore the marks of a hastily healed wound and still wet blood covering her side, it was recent—but all walked with heads high.

When they reached our perimeter, they stopped as one, their eyes finding me. For a moment, nobody moved. Then, as if by unspoken command, every one of them brought a fist to their chest in salute and knelt.

"Prince Jax," the apparent leader called out, a tall woman with a scarred face and eyes that had seen too much. "The Thirteenth Legion, formerly of Romesh, Fifth Cohort requests permission to return to duty."

My throat tightened. "Permission granted, Legionnaire. Welcome home."

CHAPTER SIX

I woke to the sound of muffled conversation and the earthy smell of brewing tea. My head felt like it had been stuffed with cotton, and my mouth tasted like I'd been licking the bottom of a mana potion barrel, which, considering yesterday's events, wasn't far from the truth.

"He's awake," Oracle's voice came from nearby, and I felt her cool hand on my forehead. "How do you feel?"

"Like shit," I croaked, struggling to sit up. "But alive. How long was I out?"

"About eight hours," Sehran's voice answered from across the wagon. "Which is pretty impressive considering you channeled enough mana to level a small city. Most mages would be in a coma for a week."

My eyes finally focused. I was back in our wagon, lying on the bed. Oracle sat beside me, while Sehran lounged against the wall, idly coiling what looked like a brand-new whip with a lot of obvious pleasure. Primus Daralen stood near the door, her posture stiff but her expression relieved.

"Morning, Daralen…anything to report?" I asked, my voice still rough and my head fuzzy. I checked quickly and let out a sigh as she started to speak. I had a blanket covering me, so at least the prince of the empire wasn't flashing his cock around.

Daralen stepped forward. "The operation was a complete success, my prince. Final count shows we freed twelve thousand, four hundred and thirty-seven slaves from the markets and camps around Sonra. Slaver casualties number approximately two thousand two hundred, with another four hundred or so captured."

"And our side?"

"Seventeen legionnaires wounded, three critically but stable. Nine outriders killed, twenty-two wounded. No civilian casualties among the freed slaves, though many required medical attention due to the fight."

I nodded, absorbing the numbers. Not zero losses, but far better than I'd feared. "And the freed legionnaires?"

At this, Daralen's expression brightened noticeably. "Thirty-four in total, from three different cohorts. Most have been enslaved for less than a decade, though a few for longer. All have reaffirmed their oaths to me, and have asked to make a formal swearing to you when possible, and are already assisting with organizing the others."

"Good." I accepted a cup of water from Oracle and drank deeply, listening because yeah, it was incredibly important, but when I looked into Oracle's eyes, I could see just how tired she was still. "What about the council? Any word on their final decision?"

"They've formally voted to ally with the empire," Oracle answered. "Cleq came personally to deliver the news while you were unconscious. They were apparently impressed by what they witnessed."

"I fucking hope so," I muttered. The display of power had been incredible, and it damn well cost me in terms of the way I felt right now, not to mention possible backlashes. It was worth it, though—not just to free the slaves efficiently, but to demonstrate exactly what the empire could bring to the table.

"There's more," Sehran added. "The freed slaves have been talking. Word is spreading about the 'prince who breaks chains' and the 'return of the empire.' People are excited, Jax. They're shit scared, confused, but excited."

"How many want to swear the oath?"

"Most of them," Daralen replied. "We've been organizing them into groups, explaining what the oath means, making sure they understand it's a choice. The first ceremony is scheduled for sunset, if you're well enough to do it."

I pushed myself further upright, wincing at the dull ache that seemed to permeate every muscle. "I'll be there. What about preparations for the journey to Gaij?"

"Already underway," Oracle said. "Othair and Marteen have been working with the council representatives to secure supplies and map the route. The key question is timing."

"What do you mean?"

"Sonra's leadership wants to move with us," she explained. "At least as far as they can. They're conscious that the edge of your protection zone ends about forty miles from the borders of Sonra. As such, they're arguing over whether they should stay with us all the way, or move slower and then hopefully remain inside the border of cleared territory when you claim Gaij. But as we discussed last night, their pace would slow us considerably."

I frowned, considering the options. Speed was important—both for establishing our position at the Tower of Gaij and for Oracle's safety as her pregnancy progressed. After all, as the first of her kind, we didn't know whether she was going to go nine months, three, or five hundred.

But, leaving Sonra behind meant potentially abandoning them to whatever threats might move in once we'd gone.

"We need to split our forces," I decided. "The main group travels with Sonra at their pace. A smaller, faster group—us, our core team, and most of the legion escort—presses ahead to secure the tower."

Daralen nodded approvingly. "A sound strategy. I've already checked the legionnaires, and I'm pleased to report that between the recovered armor from the slave camps and the armor retained from those we lost, we have enough to outfit one hundred and fifty-four of the legion in full field gear."

"Good. And we'll need to—" A wave of dizziness washed over me.

Oracle immediately pressed a hand to my chest, urging me back down. "You need more rest," she said. "Your mana levels are full, but that level of drain isn't meant for a mortal body—" She glared at me as I opened my mouth to protest and went on. "And even a demi-god like you needs to rest now and then."

I wanted to argue, but the room was starting to spin. "Fine. You're right. Daralen? We take a hundred and fifty of the legion. Between our refugees in training, and the fighters we've gained from the slavers, and the outriders, that should be more than enough to protect Sonra, right?"

"Easily, unless they face a literal army." She smiled. "There are over two thousand now freed slaves who list their occupations as 'warrior,' 'adventurer,' or some variant on 'gladiator.' That's how many have expressed a desire to sign on and swear the oaths, anyway. Another five hundred have asked to return to join us once they've located their families.

"Having two thousand hard-taught and experienced warriors added to Sonra's forces means that it'll take a hell of a force to take them out now. Frankly, I'd like to take a small party of the freed slaves with us as well. Not many, a hundred or so. That number won't make much of a difference to those we leave behind, and it'll significantly improve our chances should we encounter any kind of larger force."

"Fine." I sighed. "Daralen, you're in charge of the fighters. I trust you—make the call you think best, but make sure these people are safe. Then, wake me in two hours. Oh, and ask Cleq and Reth to meet us here—we need to finalize arrangements before the oath ceremony."

As I settled back, Oracle's cool hand returned to my forehead, and a gentle pulse of healing magic flowed through me.

"Oh, what a brave prince," she murmured. "Even half-dead, still finds the strength to be issuing orders."

"Oh, fuck off." I snorted. "I know you love me for my charming personality, really," I mumbled as sleep began to reclaim me.

"That's one of the many reasons I love you," she whispered.

That was the last thing I heard before darkness took me again.

The next time I woke, the wagon was filled with the golden light of late afternoon. I felt marginally better—my head clearer, the muscle aches reduced to a tolerable throb. Oracle sat on the side of the bed, looking down at me, and having recently shaken me awake, while Sehran was nowhere to be seen.

"Better?" Oracle stroked my hair back from my eyes.

"Getting there," I groaned, carefully sitting up. This time, the room stayed mostly stable. "Damn, I feel like I've been hit by a damn truck. Are you okay?"

"I'm okay. Tired, don't get me wrong, but I was only guiding the mana a little, tweaking the spell. You were doing the heavy lifting."

"Meh," I muttered, then grinned and pulled her to me, kissing her.

"Hey!" she yelped, before bursting out laughing. "Now I know you're feeling better! Sehran suggested we have a bath together and massage each other to see if that got a rise out of you later, or if you were too exhausted."

"I'm not too exhausted," I blurted, before cursing. "I mean…"

"I know what you meant, and it's fine." She kissed me again.

"You're a cruel tease." I sighed. "Okay, did you bring Cleq and Reth?"

"They just arrived and they're waiting outside. I wanted to make sure you were actually coherent before letting them in."

"I'm lucky to have you," I whispered with a small smile and stole another kiss. "Yeah, I'm coherent enough. Let's not keep them waiting."

"Pants first or not?"

I snorted. "Okay, maybe one more minute…" I sighed, before sighing again, as Oracle pointed a finger at a simple top and trousers combination that rested on a nearby table.

I dressed quickly, nearly falling over only once, before rubbing at my face. "Gods, what does it say about my damn life that I still can't get underwear that doesn't make my balls feel like they're being rubbed by sandpaper? Seriously, of all the goddamn races out there that had to have the best tailors, why the hell was it the whisky-dicked drow?"

Oracle laughed. Then, when she was sure my rant was over and I wasn't about to start "adjusting myself" again, nodded and moved to the door.

A moment later, Cleq entered, followed by Reth Suntari and, to my surprise, Matriarch Ilena as well.

"Prince Jax." Cleq greeted me with a formal bow. "It is good to see you awake. Your display of power yesterday was…most impressive."

"Indeed." Ilena smiled slightly. "In seven hundred years, no one has dealt such an unexpected blow to the slavers. They will not be happy, and that alone brings me more pleasure than you know, my prince."

I nodded an acknowledgment, gesturing for them to take seats. "I'm glad to hear it," I said. "Making slavers regret their life choices is one of my favorite things, I admit. So, I understand the council has voted to formalize our alliance?"

"Unanimously," Cleq confirmed. "With the condition we discussed regarding the Tower of Gaij, of course."

"Of course," I echoed. "Speaking of which, I've been considering our approach. My team and I need to move quickly to secure the tower, but I recognize Sonra can't match our pace."

Reth leaned forward. "We've been discussing this as well. The council proposes that Sonra begin moving toward the Verdant Valleys, which lie roughly in the direction of Gaij. The journey will take us several weeks, but the valleys offer good grazing and natural protection."

"Meanwhile," Ilena continued, "you and your elite forces can move ahead to secure the tower. Once established, you can expand your zone of protection to encompass our route."

It was essentially what I'd been thinking, though I wasn't sure about the timing. "How far are these valleys from Gaij?"

"Approximately a hundred miles," Reth answered. "Close by the border of your current protection radius, but within reach if you can claim the tower."

I nodded slowly. When I claimed the territory, that should more than cover that stretch of land, but I needed to make the details they seemed to be ignoring clear as well.

"That works out, but don't forget it's only Illoth who's forced out, and her supporters. Not Nimon or any of his dark dicks."

"Correct, but in these lands, the lady of spiders is by far the greater threat. When you head south, into the central and lower plains, there are many bastions of the Dark Legion, and ten miles from Gaij—fortunately, on the far side—there is a Dark Legion encampment, one of the permanent ones."

"The old legion base," I growled.

"Correct. However, traditionally, only a small force holds it. It relies more on the sure knowledge that anyone who should choose to attack the Dark Legion would be hunted down by its reinforcements and made an example of, for its protection, instead of the actual forces stationed there. Should they be sent out to attack us, there should be sufficient outriders to defeat them here, and in doing so, they would have to leave that base defenseless. We judge it unlikely."

"And you're happy to help the freed slaves?" I asked. "I'm willing to leave the majority here to assist you—the fighters, I mean—as well as those who aren't capable or interested in defending themselves, but I'll need you to help them."

Cleq exchanged glances with her companions before answering. "Many wish to follow you personally, Prince Jax. However, we've been explaining the realities of a fast-moving military expedition versus the more gradual pace of Sonra. Most understand they would be better served staying with us initially, especially those with children or medical needs, and of course, we expect to assist them."

"Thank you," I said. "I've asked Daralen to take a hundred and fifty of the legion and a few fighters as well, though the rest are to remain here with you."

"A wise compromise, and we thank you." Ilena gave an approving nod, relief clear on her face. "We will ensure they are well cared for."

"What about the captured slavers?" Oracle spoke up for the first time. "I assume you don't plan to bring them along."

Reth's expression hardened. "We've been…dealing with them according to our traditions. The worst offenders have already been executed. The rest are being processed."

I raised an eyebrow. "Processed?"

"Those who committed lesser crimes are being offered a choice," Cleq explained. "Death, or service in restitution. Those who choose the latter will be assigned to labor for the benefit of those they once enslaved, under strict supervision."

"No," I said. "Guards and their assistants, camp followers and so on, yeah, they can be processed as you say. But slavers? The penalty for slavery in the empire is death."

There was a long silence as they processed this. Reth and Cleq looked mightily pleased by my proclamation, while Ilena hesitated.

"Ah, they are wealthy individuals, members of the noble houses," she pointed out. "Traditionally, they would be punished in a few ways, but ultimately they'd be ransomed back to their houses and—"

"Get their names, any identifying marks or explanations as to their behavior, and then hang them," I said. "If anything, they should know better. And fuck letting them off when they've been slaving. No, if their daddies have an issue with it, I'll string them up by the balls in the same tree."

"The mental image is incredible." Reth sighed, smiling wistfully. "I can only hope to be there when you meet the nobility of this realm, as clearly those you're used to dealing with are more honorable."

"You'd be surprised." I snorted. "The last city I captured—no, wait, the one before actually…Narkolt? They'd been pretty much running the city and manipulating the city lord for years. They thought they'd get away with it, and I had to hang half of them before the survivors got the message."

"I so wish to see you take Gaij," Reth whispered, his eyes bright.

"Oh, and in Himnel, I named a primus of the legion to the position of duke, and told him to hang everyone who crossed him. They started behaving themselves pretty quickly, actually."

"I've died," Reth said softly, grinning widely. "I've died and this is an afterlife as a reward for good behavior."

"Stick with me, mate." I grinned back. "I'll pass you the rope…you can tie the knots."

He just grinned and rubbed his hands in apparent glee.

"Now, about tonight's oath ceremony—" I started.

A knock at the wagon door interrupted me; Sehran poked her head in, her expression serious.

"Sorry to interrupt, but we've got a situation. A large group is approaching from the east—looks like a caravan, but heavily armed. They're flying white banners, but the outriders are nervous. They've sent a party toward us, should arrive in ten minutes or so."

I exchanged glances with the council members. "Expecting anyone?"

"No." Reth was already rising to his feet. "But word of yesterday's events has spread quickly. It could be merchants seeking protection, or something else entirely…" Then he shook his head. "No, that's not right. Nobody who's within a ride of us since we started should be able to have dispatched a force, not yet."

I pushed myself up, ignoring the protest from my still-recovering body. "Well, let's find out. Oracle, help me with my armor. Cleq, would you like to join your companions to receive these visitors? I know you traditionally keep out of sight, but I'm guessing you being here is a point to show those days of hiding are done?"

"With pleasure." She nodded, smiling a little nervously. "Yes, though not all agree nor wish to reveal their presence yet."

"Sounds good." I sighed. "Fuck, okay, the manastones and potions sent to help me in freeing the slaves…do we have many left?" I asked the room generally, and Oracle spoke up.

"Plenty of potions left, but no manastones."

"Is this a problem?" Cleq looked over at the other two. "Do you believe we will need…"

"No," I assured her. "Our forces are sufficiently strong that I'm not worried about that, but my armor is battered to shit." I gestured to where it stood on its stand. "More mana would enable me to repair it fully to make a better first impression. As it is? It'll have to do."

"Jax, we have the resources of the slaver camps at hand now." Oracle smiled at me. "Sorry, I didn't realize what you were thinking there. I'll have Othair bring one of the bags over."

"One?" I asked.

"Everything that was of value and recoverable was taken from the slaver camps," she assured me. "Sonra has claimed that which was recovered by their forces, but the rest is ours."

I looked to Reth, the leader of Sonra's outriders, and he cleared his throat, looking a little embarrassed.

"Obviously some is due to you in tribute, but as your allies, not sworn vassals, I believe we are entitled to keep some?" he tried nervously, clearly hoping I'd not push for too much.

"I think that's fair," I agreed. "Considering the situation and how many people we need to outfit as well as the various costs, what do you think is fair?" I kept my gaze on him as he squirmed.

"Twenty percent?"

"That's a little low," I said.

"Forty?" he tried again.

"I think that's fair." I nodded, seeing the relief on his face, and how Ilena started to smile widely. "You can keep forty percent, and the rest goes to the imperial treasury."

I pretended not to notice the sudden horror and the way the others winced at that as I stood. "Okay, I need to dress, so unless you're sleeping with the imperial prince here, I'd appreciate some privacy."

"Of…course." Reth sighed, forcing a smile, before joining the others and leaving the wagon.

"Did they really just try to give us twenty percent of the loot after we did most of the work?" I asked Oracle.

"They're merchants and craftsmen." She nodded. "I think we're lucky that they started that high."

"Cheeky fuckers." I sighed. "Damn, I can't wait to get a portal opened and get Hannibal over here. That fucker will tear them a new arsehole if they're this stupid."

"What's wrong?" Oracle asked me. "I felt the way you reacted when Sehran said there was a white flag."

"What does a white flag mean here?" I asked, and she hesitated.

"Nothing as far as I know," she admitted.

"It's the national flag of France from back home," I said. "Well, it's not, but it's the favorite flag of the cheese-eating surrender monkeys, and that means that someone from Earth is coming."

"And in force." Oracle nodded. "Okay, I'll get you the stones and—" She broke off, obviously reaching the same conclusion I had.

"But we can't risk using them just to fix my armor up a bit, when we might need them for a fight with the nobles from back home," I finished for her. "If they're anything like the shitheads we've faced so far? They sacrificed people in their thousands to get here, and they'll have brought as many weapons as they could. That means this continent might be about to find out what a suitcase nuke can do."

CHAPTER SEVEN

"Are you ready?" I asked Daralen as the riders appeared in the distance.

"I am, my prince, but—"

"Trust me, it's needed," I said. "Keep them spread out, and their shields at the ready. I'd rather they defended themselves and survived long enough to counterattack, rather than got the first hit in."

"As you say." Obviously, my orders that the legion were to spread out, rather than form a wall to defend me, weren't going down well.

I wasn't letting them die in their dozens, though, if one of these fuckers had an RPG or something hidden in his bags. I squinted around, suddenly wondering about drones, an entirely new feeling of existential terror at the thought of that little bit of technology making the leap across the divide.

What the hell could an enemy do with a drone and a low-yield tactical weapon, after all? It'd be the end of the empire in short order.

After a few seconds as the riders drew in, I'd managed to remind myself that no, the higher the tech item, the higher the likelihood it'd explode in transit. And there was no way that the baron or any of his dickish friends would allow a nuke through the portal with them close enough to be caught in the ensuing explosion.

As to a drone? Sure, if there wasn't the cost limitation on any mass coming through, but with that, and then the higher likelihood of an explosion, rather than filling that space with say, a fuckload more of ammunition?

Then add on that once any battery was depleted, it couldn't be charged again here unless there was something I was missing or a fuckton of solar cells, and again, that brought the space and weight constraints back around, and yeah. That was the end of that.

Conventional weapons were likely to be the only kind I'd face, as even the most virulent bioweapons were unlikely to survive against even low-level spells, so fuck it.

As the riders climbed down and bowed jerkily to me, then began reporting to Reth, I listened in carefully.

"A hundred or so, sir. Most are guards, and the pair who lead them are in strange clothing. They all carry metal things, strapped across their bodies and they hold them as weapons, but…" She shook her head in bewilderment.

"Describe them," I ordered. "The metal—what color, what they look like."

"Uh…about so long…" She gestured to three-quarters of a meter long and maybe a quarter that high, then described what sounded a hell of a lot like an assault rifle.

"Do they have any other weapons?" I asked. "Like a short spear in a tube?"

"Some, though they hold them strapped to their horses' saddles," she admitted. "Their armor is black and tan, with many pockets and pouches, and strange metal strapped here and there. It looks hot, and they wear helmets that are…" She gestured around in a half circle, clearly flummoxed at the design.

"Okay, thank you." I sighed. "Reth, you and the rest of the council will need to be brought up to date on these people if they're who I think they are. But the quick version is that they're from another realm, and their weapons are far more deadly than you're used to. A single well-trained soldier with one of those metal weapons is more than capable of killing hundreds of your people.

"They fire pieces of metal around the size of your thumbnail very, very fast. If they're good at what they do, they can fire them from far enough away that it'd take you an hour or more to run to them, and they can kill you with a single hit." I paused at the look of shock on a lot of faces, and I went on.

"The upside of this is that your armor provides some protection against their weapons, and they have very limited ammunition for them. Think of them like crossbows, smaller ones that can hold hundreds of bolts, but once they have been used, that's it. They can't be reused or rebuilt, not unless they brought a hell of a lot more equipment than I'm willing to bet they managed.

"Instead, they'll use them in limited engagements, and mainly as a shock-and-awe tactic. Their leadership are likely to be the worst kind of nobility, and apart from a very small number, they see absolutely no value in your lives. They are the nobility who fled the realm when Amon died, his sons and daughters, and for the last seven hundred years since they murdered their father, they've been hiding."

"And now they return?" Cleq asked. "At the same time as you do?"

"Yeah, and no, it's not a coincidence. As I say, more to bring you up to date on when we get the chance—and when you're all sworn to me, not before—but they're here in direct retaliation to me claiming the throne. Expect them to hate me and attack as soon as they can."

"Then this alliance shall be tested before it has even begun." He sighed.

"Outrider!" Reth barked, making the leader of the small group jerk to attention.

I suddenly realized the way they'd all been staring at Cleq as details slid into place.

They all knew Reth, Ilena, and the twins of course—they were the public heads of the council and the ostensible rulers of Sonra. But unless they were born into Sonra, and then trusted above others as well, they still weren't permitted into the inner ring, to discover that those three families were only part of the council.

The non-humans in that council were going to come as a hell of a shock to most of Sonra, and I couldn't help but wince at that thought.

Regardless, though, the outrider was speaking again.

"Yes, Commander?" She tried not to look concerned or confused.

"What did they tell you?" he asked.

"They claim to be representatives of a great house—Granth, I think they said—and they ask leave to approach and meet with the prince. They claim guest right and swear that provided no hand is raised against them, then they shall raise no hand against us."

"Granth?" I squinted. "Fuck's sake, why's that name familiar?"

"William," Sehran whispered in my ear, and I laughed.

"Wil*helm*," I corrected as it clicked. "Damn, yes! Okay, Reth, this might not be a complete shit show then. There's one I've had a meeting with before, and he swore an oath to stand aside and not support any action against me. He's the scion of that house, so I hope that's him. Damn, we might have just gotten lucky."

"Do you wish them to be admitted to the outer ring?" he asked. "We cannot admit them to the second. Not even for you."

"You don't know them and you've had those rules for a long time." I nodded. "I understand that. We're on the edge of the second, though, so this camp is mine. I'll not try to bring them deeper, but I need to speak to them and quickly. Ask them to bring only ten of their guard, the rest can stay back, but promise guest rights and that they'll be allowed to leave without being hindered, provided they don't break the rules of the camp or act like dicks. If they agree to that, then bring them into the camp, but be ready. It's not like they couldn't lie about which house they're from, after all."

He nodded and passed the orders along, as well as giving additional orders for stealth and what were apparently a limited corps of assassins and spies to be made ready.

When I asked where they were and if he had many, he smiled and told me that until the oath was sworn, that was information that he couldn't share.

That was when I noticed that those who had been working with us since we moved here? The ones who had come to help us prepare the new camp and who were the most friendly?

Yeah, they were all in sight and clearly ready to charm the pants off the new arrivals.

"You sneaky bastard," I muttered. "They're *all* spies?"

"I cannot discuss this," he said.

But I saw the little quirk of the lips, as he was pleased I'd not guessed it before.

"Fucker, I'll get you for that." I sighed, moving on. "Okay, people, let's get ready for guests. I don't know how this usually works, but there's a not small chance this is going to be an assassination attempt, so be ready."

That was all that needed to be said for the legion to go on high alert, and a handful of the legionnaires without armor to volunteer to act as animal handlers and so on, with weapons secreted about their person.

In a matter of minutes, the camp atmosphere had changed to one that was about to be attacked, and frankly, I winced as I looked around.

We were doing everything short of marking up signs saying "we don't trust you, fuck off" and waving it at them, but I didn't know how to make it less obvious.

A few times, I considered just telling everyone to stand down, or me marching out to meet them. And then I was reminded forcibly that if I tried that, Oracle would come with me and that I'd be putting her and our unborn child in that danger without the backup we had here.

Then I nearly doubled the guard.

Half an hour later, when the feeling had honestly reached a level of paranoia that was borderline psychotic, the first of the horses rode into view.

There were three guards in the lead. One held an assault rifle across his chest, and the others held a spear aloft with a pennant attached that flapped and fluttered in the wind: one with the black cloth and golden design; the other was clearly a white flag. As to the riders, though?

They wore full battle rattle, what looked to be a careful mix of modern antiballistic and armor plating, something right out of the super-soldier stuff that used to get shared around on the military forums about the army's next-gen shit.

I'd never expected to see it for real, as no matter what the government claimed in press conferences, investing a few billion in brand-new, state-of-the-art gear was never going to happen.

Not when they could kick it down the road a little farther and the "only" cost would be a few hundred servicemen and women's lives.

That these people were wearing it made me nod in appreciation, even as my balls shriveled up. They'd be a nightmare to take down in that gear. And their weapons? As they rode into the camp, I noted that they all had an assault rifle across their chest, a handgun on their right hip, a dagger on the left, and a sword across their back.

Their horses were local, I'd guess, and obviously not very well trained…or, at least, not used to their riders yet, by the way they shied and tried to split off. But their saddles had multiple bags attached, as well as a bedroll, and each had a secondary weapon there too: a mace or an axe.

I noticed it all in an instant, my increased Perception allowing that, as I triggered my Hyper Cognition.

As time seemed to slow down, I watched them, examining what I could see of each rider, waiting for the inevitable betrayal, the attack, even as I readied to counterattack and…

The fourth rider in reached up suddenly, flicking a clasp under the helmet's chin and sliding it free.

I fought an immediate urge to fireball him in the face for the sudden movement, until a familiar face emerged.

"Ach, I never zhought I'd zee you again, Jack." Wilhelm smiled, before clearing his throat and trying again. "Prince Jax of Dravith, I am Wilhelm of House Granth, and I acknowledge both mine oath to stand aside in any dispute between your house and our own, zhat I shall never fight you again, and lastly, I add to mine oath freely, zhat none sworn to me shall attack you unwarranted, by mine order or lack of action."

The air rippled with the oath he swore, and I sighed, cancelling my Hyper Cognition and nodding to him. I stepped forward, pulling my helm off as well.

"Wilhelm," I greeted. "I didn't expect to see you either, mate. Welcome to the UnderVerse!"

He grinned, clambering down from his horse. Two others did the same while the rest of his guard stayed where they were on horseback, watching us with obvious suspicion.

Wilhelm was a big man, easily six two, and wearing the same armor as his guards. But where he'd seemed huge to me when we'd met last time, now he seemed…well, human.

I noticed the way he stared at our size difference, probably comparing me to when we'd met last and we'd been around the same height, but he'd been far heavier with muscle.

Now, he looked like the supporting character alongside the hero.

Heh.

I turned, reaching out and taking Oracle's hand, drawing her forward and speaking as I did so. "Wilhelm, this is Oracle, the love of my life. Oracle, this is Wilhelm. We fought in the arena, and he was both a gentleman afterward and honorable, which meant more to me than I can say, considering the utter cockwombles I mainly met there."

"Mine lady." Wilhelm bowed his head and took Oracle's hand, pressing his lips to her fingers in a display of old manners that just fit him to a T. "It is mine honor to meet one zo beautiful."

She smiled. "Wilhelm, son of House Granth, the honor is mine."

"Behave yourselves, you buggers." I snorted. "Wilhelm, you want to come inside? We can get a drink out of the sun and out of sight while we talk."

I gestured to my wagon a little farther back, and he smiled, the sweat on his face clear from both the heat, and presumably the insulation of the armor he wore.

"I vould appreciate zhat, ja," he admitted.

"Excellent. Before we go, this is Sehran, my good friend—we'll explain more about her nature a little later, perhaps—and Primus Daralen of the Imperial Legion. Then these are representatives of the ruling council of Sonra…Reth, Cleq, and Ilena." I named them in turn, and he inclined his head to each.

"Unlike what I said about the nobles before," I said to the others, "this is perhaps one of a very small number of their ranks who wasn't a complete waste of skin, so here's hoping he doesn't change my impression of him in the next hour." I grunted, drawing a laugh from him.

"I shall do mine best," he assured me, his Germanic accent clipped and precise as always.

"Perhaps one of us might accompany you, but the others are needed elsewhere," Reth suggested.

"Sure. Which of you wants to come?" I asked, and Cleq smiled, stepping forward. "Let's go then." I gestured to the wagon, before speaking to Daralen clearly. "Stand down our forces, and continue with whatever preparations you need for tomorrow. We can discuss it in more detail later, but you're in charge."

"I understand, my prince. Do you wish me to accompany you?"

"No, we'll be fine," I assured her, confident that should Wilhelm attack when it was just the few of us, that I could handle it.

She nodded, but then added, "I understand. I'll provide drinks for his guards, and the three who will be taking up station *outside* the wagon as well."

Subtle that, adding that his guards wouldn't be joining us inside, I realized. I nodded in respect to her, as Oracle led the way to the steps, opening the plain wooden door and disappearing inside.

I followed her, with Sehran on my heels, then Wilhelm and Cleq, before Daralen pointedly closed the door in the faces of the guards, remaining outside as well.

They'd obviously accepted that as a done deal, though, because as we moved inside, none tried to follow.

That could have been because Daralen glared at them, though. I genuinely believed that regardless of their fancy armor, if she decided to pick them up and break them over her knee, she could have.

She might not have had the suppressed "dynamo of terror" feeling that Restun gave off, or the effortless perfection of Augustus, but damn, she was a primus all right.

Inside the wagon, Wilhelm was clearly impressed, and I couldn't blame him.

There were three rooms, including the toilet—just that existing in a medieval magical fantasy realm was severely underrated.

The main suite was the size of a large family room, about three meters across and five long…not ridiculous, but also considering it held a handful of seats, a table that I used for my alchemy, and a long couch that Sehran usually slept on, it was a damn nice room.

The rear of the wagon was slightly larger, with a very nice double bed for Oracle and me, and a bathtub that somehow was recessed into the floor, yet didn't hit the ground underneath, even when I just bloody knew stepping down into it, I should have been literally embedded in the ground.

Then there was the armor stand, the sunken window with a ledge wide enough that Sehran often perched on it to enjoy the breeze, a wardrobe, and a pair of chairs in here as well.

That it was all so luxurious was incredible, and I saw the look that Wilhelm gave the place as he sat down.

"It's better than you were expecting?" I asked.

"Significantly," he said. "Our own wagons are much less impressive. Perhaps you could explain vhere we might purchase such? Or you might have some for sale?"

"I…don't know if we have any," I admitted, only just realizing that actually, we had five or six of these at least, and that was before we came to Sonra. "But we recently claimed some more wagons, so we might have some."

"I know not vhat price zhey vould fetch here, but depending on your needs, I know I vould appreciate one, and my mine father and mother as vell." He nodded.

"Well, that's the rub, so let's start there, mate." I shrugged. "You and your parents came to the UnderVerse, how?"

"Zhere vere…" He hesitated. "Methods used zhat we do not approve of," he finished. "Ve had long stockpiled manastones to prepare for a crossing, but zhe numbers we had, and zhe availability of mana in zhat realm, not to mention zhe draw needed, meant zhat it vas insufficient. I vas only informed of zhe additional methods after arrival."

"Yeah," I said. "There's a lot of that going around, I hear."

"Zhe transfer between zhe realms is something zhat I cannot say more about, but zhe decision vas made, and I came, as I vas left vith zhe choice of stay zhere and allow a single guard in addition to travel in my place and reduce zhe effect on others not at all, or to come, and…well."

He looked genuinely uncomfortable about it, and as much as I didn't like it, I decided to move on. After all, in his place, I totally got it. If I'd fought against going, my father, the bastard Baron Sanguis, would have forced me. And if he hadn't? He'd not have rethought his actions for even a second.

"So your parents were fine with it then?" I asked.

"Nein." He shook his head. "Ve are a minor branch of zhe House of Granth, accepted for our skills, and mine potential, and zhey, like me, vere informed only after zhe transit of zhe methods used. Zhey, like me, are unhappy, and yet ve have no choice."

"So what brings you here then?" I asked. "Besides shopping for a new wagon."

"Vhen you made contact vith Arlo, he explained vhat he'd seen in you and vhat you told him, upon his return to zhe family. Mine parents and I vere summoned before Gaspar, zhe patriarch." He paused, rubbing at his beard, before reaching into what was obviously a bag of holding on his hip and pulling free a bottle of wine. "Do you have glasses?"

"Dammit, I said we'd get the drinks," I muttered.

Sehran smiled, climbing to her feet. "We have mugs, and I'll get more drinks." She pulled out a collection of small mugs from a side compartment.

"I wish I had coffee left," I apologized as Wilhelm poured, and he nodded.

"Ja, I too find myself missing zhat, zhough I have been assured it is available here, but vhere, alas, ve do not know," he agreed.

"Oh, shit, no, sorry, man—I mean I've got some basic coffee…I meant the good shit." I grinned, dipping a hand into my bag and bringing out a small bag of "normal" coffee that I'd gotten as part of my general camp gear ages ago.

I underarm tossed it to him, and he snatched it out of the air, peering at the bag with a smile on his face as I went on.

"You know that coffee that's made somewhere in South America? Where it's made from cat shit?"

"Ja?"

"They have something similar here. Freaked me out the first time I tried it, but damn, regardless of the method of making it, it's incredible."

"You have zome?" he asked hopefully.

"We've finished it." I lied, having a single carafe left, and about six cups of it in total. That was enough for one for each of us here, but I was fucked if I was wasting that on someone I wasn't sure of yet.

I tasted the wine that he'd brought, and I winced.

I'd never been a wine drinker, not really, though I had it now and then; mainly I just had whatever was handed over. But this? I glanced at the bottle and then nodded in recognition.

It was an Earth vintage, something that looked old, and considering how limited that had to be? I appreciated the gesture, before taking another drink.

Sehran returned, a small keg under one arm and a few more mugs in her other hand. She poured out what was clearly ale instead, and I took that as well, setting it down next to the wine glass.

I figured I'd smile, play nice and down the wine in a minute—no need to be rude, after all—but Earth vintages compared to UnderVerse just weren't in the same league.

Wilhelm accepted the mug Sehran offered with a nod of thanks, then tasted it, and sighed. "Zhis is more zhan generous, Jax. Ah…"

He hesitated, and I shook my head before he could be more formal.

"Just Jax is fine, Wilhelm."

"Zhank you. As for zhe better coffee you mention…" He took a sip of the ale, savored it briefly, then continued. "Perhaps ve might trade for zome in zhe future? I find myself missing many comforts of Earth, zhough none so much as decent coffee."

"Once things are more sorted here, we can probably help with that," Oracle chimed in. "Though the quality varies. I've not tried many, and the normal compared to the special stuff is…well, it's a big difference."

"Any vould be velcome, my lady." Wilhelm's smile was genuine. "Our supplies from home are strictly rationed, and myself and mine immediate family are not highly zhought of enough to receive such luxuries yet."

I leaned back in my seat, studying him. "So, Wilhelm, tell me about your family's situation. You said a minor branch of House Granth?"

His expression shifted, becoming more guarded. "Ja, zhat is correct. Mine parents and I are…how vould you say it? Zhird cousins to zhe main line. Mine father vas uninterested in a martial pursuit, and instead served zhe family as upper management for one of zhe family investments, and my mother managed zhe breeding program for our horses. Ve have some standing, but little real authority vithin zhe house structure."

"And yet here you are, apparently speaking for them?" I prodded.

Wilhelm shifted uncomfortably. "I am here because Gaspar Granth, our patriarch, believes I might receive a…varmer velcome zhan others. Given our previous encounter."

"He's not wrong," I admitted. "Though that doesn't explain why House Granth is reaching out at all. Last I checked, most of the noble houses that fled would happily see my head on a pike."

"Many vould, yes, but Gaspar is pragmatic," Wilhelm acknowledged with surprising frankness. "Also, zhe situation has changed from vhat zhey expected, zhough not greatly. Zhe great houses vere always prepared to accept serving one of zhe others in zheir climb to zhe throne, in exchange for access to zhe realm again. Your claim to zhe throne has created…complications, being as you are not serving your house's interests, but instead your own, zhough little beyond zhat has changed."

Cleq, who had been sitting silently and observing our exchange, leaned forward. "What sort of complications would drive nobles from another realm to cross into ours in such numbers? And with such weaponry?"

Wilhelm sighed, setting down his mug. "When vord reached us of Prince Jax's claim to zhe succession, it triggered vhat you might call a panic among zhe houses, as you clearly had no intention of opening zhe portal to us to return. For seven hundred years, ve have maintained zhe fiction zhat zhe empire could be restored under proper noble guidance vhen zhe time was right. In truth, zhough zhe leaders vere not, zhe lesser branches of zhe families vere mostly content to remain vhere zhey vere, building vealth and power in zhat realm."

"Until I fucked up their plans," I said with no small amount of satisfaction.

"Indeed." Wilhelm nodded. "Your claim—a legitimate one, by blood—meant zhat any noble house vishing to contest zhe succession had to do so vithin zhe allotted time frame. According to imperial law—"

"One year," Oracle finished for him. "From the moment of claiming a greater territory."

"Just so." Wilhelm spread his hands. "Zhe houses vere not prepared. Zome, like mine, had dedicated entire generations to preparing a minor stockpile of manastones, planning for an eventual return. Others had nothing. All vere desperate."

"Which explains the blood rituals." Oracle's tone made it clear what she thought of such methods.

Wilhelm's gaze dropped briefly to the floor. "Yes. I do not defend zhese actions. But I must explain zhem if you are to understand our position. Again, ve vere ordered to move, and zhough ve suspected zhat zhe methods of opening zhe portal vould be terrible, ve also knew zhat should we refuse and flee, zhen all zhat vould happen vas zhat ve vould never have a second chance to come here. Zhe families vould lose zhe more moderate voices zhat may yet dissuade zheir less controlled members from zheir actions, and nothing beyond zhat vould be achieved."

I drained my mug and set it down harder than necessary. "So what does Gaspar want from me? I'm guessing he didn't send you just to catch up on old times."

The corners of Wilhelm's mouth twitched slightly. "Zhe patriarch of mine house, Baron Gaspar Granth, vishes to…discuss zhe succession. He believes zhat a bloodline zhat has maintained itself in purity for seven centuries has a stronger claim zhan—" He paused, obviously reconsidering his words.

"Than a bastard son of the disgraced House of Sanguis?" I finished for him, my tone dangerously light. "Is that what you were going to say?"

"Zhose vould be his vords, not mine," Wilhelm replied carefully, clearly not happy with the words. "But ja, zhis is his intent, and I must convey his position."

Oracle's hand found mine, squeezing gently. A warning to keep my temper. I took a deep breath, though in all honesty, I wasn't surprised in the slightest.

"And what exactly does Gaspar propose? That I just step aside? Surrender my claim after everything I've done to restore the empire?"

"In essence, ja." Wilhelm's frank admission surprised me. "He offers you recognition as a duke in your own right, vith dominion over zhe territories you've claimed on Dravith, and a seat on his council. In return, you vould acknowledge him as zhe rightful heir to zhe Eternal Throne."

The room fell silent for a moment. Then I laughed. Not a chuckle, but a full-throated laugh that had me doubling over. Oracle's lips twitched in amusement, while Sehran didn't bother hiding her grin. Only Cleq maintained a neutral expression, though her eyes were watchful.

"I'm sorry," I managed when I could finally speak again. "But that's just fucking ridiculous."

Wilhelm didn't seem surprised by my reaction. "Ja. I told Gaspar you vould most likely refuse."

"And yet he sent you anyway?" I wiped tears from my eyes.

"Ja, I vas under orders to make zhe attempt, and to phrase it as best I could." Wilhelm gave a slight shrug. "And now I have done so." He reached for the wine bottle, refilling his mug. "Let us consider zhat particular discussion concluded."

I raised an eyebrow. "That's it? No threats? No ultimatums?"

"Nien. Vould zhey serve any purpose?" Wilhelm countered. "You have zhe legion at your back, zhe blessings of zhe gods, and if rumors are true, fragments of divinity. Gaspar may be proud, but he is not a simpleton."

"And yet he thought I'd give up my claim for a dukedom," I pointed out.

Wilhelm smiled thinly. "In truth, I doubt he expected you to agree, but could not keep himself from attempting it. He also asked me to make clear zhat should it help his cause in persuading you, zhat he hates Sanguis vith every fiber of his being, and zhat he would happily assist in his capture, as vell as hand him over to you, bound and gagged, fingers and tongue removed, to do vith as you vish."

That drew a surprised snort from me.

"In any case, I am authorized to discuss other matters, should zhe primary proposal prove…unpalatable."

Cleq stirred. "What other matters might interest the prince, when your master has already insulted him so thoroughly?"

Wilhelm turned to the goblin and frowned, clearly unsure as to her position with being a council member, and yet a goblin. "An alliance, uh…Cleq, vas it? House Granth has resources zhat could benefit Jax's claim for zhe empire—veapons, knowledge, trained fighters. And ve have a common enemy in many of zhe other houses."

"Other houses that are already here, and that you know about?" I asked, suddenly more interested.

"Four major houses have successfully transported zignificant forces and are in zhe area to mine knowledge," Wilhelm confirmed, nodding. "House Granth, as I represent. House Korvanis, led by Duchess Eleanor. House Vexen, under Lord Bartholomew. And House Malakai, commanded by Count Lucius."

Oracle's expression tightened. "Malakai. I recognize that name. They were enemies of House Falco, who were responsible for the Great Tower of Dravith."

"That's a point." I nodded. "Where does Granth stand on Falco?"

"Zhey vere our allies in zhe great game, though ve have lost contact since coming here." He frowned. "Are you allied or against?"

"Neither. But they gave me good advice, and they gave me a way to make sure of my arrival at the Great Tower. So, considering they could do that, I doubt that they just ended up anywhere at random."

"Zhey vere known to have greater control over zhe portals zhan others," he agreed. "Zhey offered a key to Granth, but…"

"But you didn't know if it'd be a quick way to eliminate you or a genuine key and you passed on it?" Oracle suggested.

"I believe so, ja." He sighed. "In truth, zhe last few months have strained many of zhe alliances of old, and have encouraged outright var between many of zhe weaker or less prepared houses. Sanguis vas known to have resorted to raiding zhe veakest for zheir resources before zhey came through."

"Of course that cockwomble would," I muttered.

"Regardless, both Sanguis and Malakai are both against Falco." Wilhelm nodded. "And zhey also remain bitter enemies of House Granth. Zhere is no love lost between any of zhe houses, in truth. Each sees itself as zhe rightful heir to zhe empire."

"And where are they now?" I demanded. "These other houses?"

"Scattered," Wilhelm said. "Zhe transfer process was…imprecise. According to zhe limited information ve have, House Korvanis emerged somewhere in zhe eastern mountains. Only one member of zheir house made it free of zhe site, and zhey vere delirious vhen found. Ve believe zhat line to be extinct now. House Vexen reportedly arrived in a region now called zhe 'Blighted Marsh,' zhough on our maps, it vas once a veritable paradise. As for House Malakai…" He hesitated. "Our intelligence suggests zhey arrived near Gaij, and zhey along with two other houses have been attempting to claim it, zhough who zhe others are, I know not."

That got my attention immediately. "The Tower of Gaij? You're certain?"

Wilhelm nodded. "As certain as our limited intelligence allows. Count Lucius vas reportedly moving to secure it as his base of operations, zhough again, not an ally. And even if zhey vere, ve vould be unsure if zhey vere being truthful."

I exchanged a meaningful look with Oracle and Cleq. We'd already agreed we needed to get there quickly, but fuck's sake, nothing was ever easy.

"This is…concerning," Cleq said slowly. "The tower is important to our own plans."

"And it's where we're headed next." I watched Wilhelm's reaction carefully. "I told Arlo to let you know where we'd be, both because it was pretty fucking easy to figure out, and because I'd hoped to see you again, I'll admit. Though I wasn't fucking happy to have an RPG fired at me by a slaver dickhead."

"I imagine not. Nor vere ve to find zhey had killed and looted our men," he agreed. "But you intend to continue to Gaij?"

"We do." I saw no reason to hide it, considering as soon as we set off, it was going to be obvious.

His expression remained neutral, but I detected a flicker of interest in his eyes. "In zhat case, perhaps our interests align more zhan it may seem."

"How so?" I asked, suspicious but willing to listen. I tossed back the wine, then winced and replaced it with the ale. *Gods, what I'd do for a decent energy drink instead of this crap.*

"House Malakai's forces are formidable, but not in huge numbers," Wilhelm explained. "Should you choose to confront zhem, House Granth could provide…assistance."

"In exchange for what?" Oracle asked with a smile.

Wilhelm spread his hands. "Recognition of our imperial rights. Not zhe throne—ve accept zhat negotiation has failed—but acknowledgment zhat House Granth maintains its noble status and traditional holdings under imperial law."

I considered this carefully. "These 'traditional holdings' being what, exactly?"

"Zhe northern provinces of Trent, specifically zhe regions surrounding vhat vas once called zhe Granite Spires," Wilhelm replied. "Territories zhat are, I believe, far from being currently claimed by your forces."

Sehran leaned forward. "Convenient that you're asking for lands you know Jax hasn't reached yet."

"It is practical," Wilhelm countered. "Ve seek no conflict vith Prince Jax or his forces. Ve merely vish to reestablish ourselves vithout unnecessary bloodshed, and zhen begin to actually *live* here, instead of just survive."

I drummed my fingers on the table, thinking it through. "And what would this 'assistance' against House Malakai look like?"

"Perhaps twenty of our fighters, armed vith limited veapons from Earth," Wilhelm said promptly. "Plus intelligence on Malakai's forces and tactics. And my personal service, if you vould accept it."

That last part surprised me. "Your personal service? As what?"

"As advisor, fighter, vhatever role you deem appropriate," Wilhelm said. "I have sworn not to raise arms against you. I vould extend zhat oath to serve you directly in zhis campaign."

Cleq cleared her throat. "A generous offer, but one that requires careful consideration. The prince cannot make such decisions hastily," she interjected.

I looked at her sharply, then concealed a smile at the clear panic in her eyes. Of course, she and her people hadn't yet sworn to me, and they were planning to claim a position as allies, not members of the empire directly. They wanted me to try to take Gaij, but if it came with me taking other lands in short order through this alliance…

"Maybe we should push them to join as vassals instead?" Oracle suggested through the bond. *"As allies, they don't have any land, and they have to keep moving, unless they want to do a deal for some land. But as vassals…"*

Wilhelm nodded. "Of course, I do not expect an immediate answer. But time is not our ally, ja? Count Lucius vill be preparing to attack as we speak."

"Fuckers," I muttered. "He's there already?"

"He is and ve suspect still at least von other house. Zhere vere three zhat attempted to claim Gaij, vith one of zhem simply marching in and demanding zhat zhe succubus serve zhem from now on and hand over all control.

"Zhey tried to claim zheir imperial right of access, and somehow it failed; zhen zhe demons butchered them. We know not more or vhom zhey were, only zhat zhey vere from Earth and as such, zhere vas limited equipment recoverable. House Malakai bought it all, and zhey've made zheir intentions clear, zhough for vhatever reason, zhey've not yet attacked, or hadn't vhen ve last heard from our spies."

"And what about the other houses?" I asked. "Where do they stand in all this?"

"House Korvanis is traditionally insular und defensive, and as far as ve know, zhey have all been viped out. Zhough that may yet be a ploy. If she survives, zhe duchess vill likely focus on establishing her territory before making any moves against others," Wilhelm explained.

"House Vexen is more ambitious, but hampered by zheir unfortunate arrival location. Both, however, vould oppose House Malakai gaining a significant foothold—and by extension, vould not object to your efforts to keep zhem from zhe tower."

I leaned back, considering everything Wilhelm had said. The offer was tempting. Twenty armed fighters with Earth weapons would be a nasty surprise for anyone who fucked with us, and Wilhelm's personal service could prove valuable. But I didn't trust any noble house farther than I could throw them—especially not one led by someone who thought I'd give up my claim to the throne for a dukedom.

"Here's what I'm offering," I said finally. "I'll consider recognizing House Granth's claim to the northern territories of Trent—*after* we've dealt with House Malakai and secured the Tower of Gaij. In return, you provide the assistance you've offered, including your personal service, and you get me a fucking map that explains where the hell bloody Trent is, and why you want it."

"And we would want Gaspar's oath that he will support Jax's claim to the throne, and serve the empire," Oracle added. "Binding for the entire house."

Wilhelm looked thoughtful. "I cannot commit to such terms vithout consulting mine Lord Gaspar. But I believe he vould consider zhem, at least, given zhe alternatives."

"Which are?" Sehran asked.

"Var vith zhe other houses, vith no allies, in a realm vhere ve have little in zhe vay of reserves of ammunition," Wilhelm said bluntly. "And eventual confrontation vith Prince Jax after he has further consolidated his power."

"Sounds like a shit deal for House Granth," I observed.

Wilhelm smiled thinly. "Ja, indeed. Vhich is vhy I believe Gaspar vill see zhe visdom in an alliance. However, I cannot promise."

"How quickly can you speak with him and return with an answer?" I asked.

"Perhaps, three days, if I leave immediately?" Wilhelm replied. "We have established a base camp approximately forty miles northeast of here, and zhat vould permit me time to travel zhere, for consideration, and to travel back."

I nodded. "Then that's what we'll do. You return to your camp, speak with Gaspar, and bring back his answer. Meanwhile, we'll continue our preparations to march on the Tower of Gaij."

"Ah, perhaps four, possibly even five days if you are to head directly zhere zhen…I meant if you vere to remain here." Wilhelm apologized. "And I have to ask, if he refuses, and ve meet along zhe way?"

"Then we'll reassess," I said. "But I won't delay our plans for Gaspar's convenience."

"It might be more prudent to vait. After all, ve have both zhe information you vill need and zhe troops…" he suggested.

"And if it was more likely that Gaspar would agree? I'd do that," I admitted. "As it is, though, and let's be clear about this, he and your house will be swearing to the empire and me personally as vassals. He's gonna choke on that for a bit before he decides. And considering it's a fifty-fifty if he'll agree or tell me to go fuck myself, I'm not leaving an enemy to get ahead of me without good reason."

Wilhelm nodded, seemingly satisfied with this arrangement. "Zhen I shall leave immediately. Ah…" He paused, then sighed. "Jax, I believe you to be an honorable man, and I cannot, nor vould I vish to stand against you. *I* see zhe advantages of this offer, as vell as zhe potential, but Gaspar may not. Please know, I cannot force him to accept."

"I know," I said. "Wilhelm, if he decides not to, and comes after me? I've killed other nobles, and their entire guards. I wasn't aware of the larger families. Those I've dealt with so far have been smaller groups, but I will tear him a new arsehole if I have to. Tell your parents that if this comes to a fight, they need to step back, because if they take part, I'll kill any who stand in my way."

"I vill, and I zhank you again for zhe understanding. Lastly, from myself only, and not on behalf of zhe house?"

"Yeah?"

"Congratulations." He shrugged. "For vhat it's vorth, I believe you to have zhe potential to forge an empire from zhe ashes, and I hope to live to see it."

"I hope so too, mate." I shook his hand, before bidding him goodbye.

As he stood, Cleq did as well, smiling and saying that she needed to return to her responsibilities and would come back later.

As they left the wagon, Oracle leaned closer to me. "Do you trust him?" she asked quietly.

"Wilhelm personally? Somewhat," I admitted. "Gaspar and House Granth? Not a fucking chance."

Sehran stretched, her wings flexing slightly. "At least we know what we're heading into now. With House Malakai already at the Tower of Gaij."

"And with Earth weapons," I added grimly. "This just got a lot more complicated."

Oracle's hand found mine again, squeezing gently. "When isn't it complicated with you?"

I couldn't help but laugh at that. "Fair point. But even by my standards, fighting a noble house armed with assault rifles while trying to claim a tower full of succubai is a bit much."

"If you think I'm bad, just wait till you've got an entire tower of my sisters sworn to you." Sehran laughed huskily. "We both know that's why you're doing this, really."

"Oh no, whatever will I do…" I pretended to be horrified. "How big is that bath again?" I made a point of peering over my shoulder toward the sunken bath, and she laughed.

"You say that now, but remember I'm happy with Jian, and I know my place isn't contingent on you being happy with me. A tower full of succubai who think it is?" She shook her head.

I paused, the jokey side falling away as I realized just how bad that was going to be.

"Oh fuck," I groaned.

"Exactly," Sehran purred as she and Oracle laughed.

CHAPTER EIGHT

The rest of the afternoon was spent working hard, and not in the way I'd have preferred to, with Oracle bent over the bench before me.

Instead, I spent a grand total of five hours working on my alchemy skill. And when I finished, I was seriously pissed at not having gained any new skills—I was only one away from my next evolution—through sheer bloody-minded grinding.

Two hundred and fifteen mana potions sat gleaming on the table before me, and that represented not only the entire stock of mana ingredients that I'd been able to lay my hands on, but it was also the entire stock of damn containers I could get.

I'd hoped to make a load of health, stamina, and possibly even poisons as well, but Oracle, when I'd told her my plan, had recommended these.

She was spending her afternoon teaching more legionnaires Magic Missile, Complex Healing, and Explosive Compression, but she was right.

For healing potions, thanks to the capture of the slavers' wagons and basically everything they'd had, we currently had enough for three healing potions per legionnaire, and one per volunteer.

That sounded unfair, I knew, but the legion would be fighting again—and soon—and the others would basically be on guard duty, without the expectation of a fight in the near future.

That we'd given them potions at all was a hell of an expense, and one that I'd not have risked had we had less available. But, fortunately, the sheer number of potions recovered was a relief.

Then came the mana potions. Fifty-seven of them, and all either very low strength, or very high.

That sort of made sense, as either the slavers had no use for magic, it being a very expensive skill set to obtain without a resident wisp to share the knowledge, or they were desperately focused on it, in the case of one small caravan.

Magic was, after all, a force multiplier.

It was a hell of a relief, therefore, that the ones who had access to that magic were also the ones who had the control devices, and had died in spectacular fashion.

So, we were back to the mana potions, and that giving them to the limited number of legionnaires who could either cast all three spells, or at least healing, just made sense. That way, they could heal their brothers and sisters, and we could save lives.

It did mean, though, that I was stuck spending hour after hour peeling the fucking furry underside from leaves and chopping roots up.

By the time I'd finally finished, repeatedly casting Heal and Scour to get rid of the sticky goop that covered my fingers, I still had the ghost of a stiff neck and back, and I was mentally exhausted.

That was when Sehran sent word through the bond that Reth was approaching, from where she stood atop the wagon, watching over both me inside and the next wagon along, where Oracle was teaching.

I sighed, forced myself out of the wagon, and blinked in the late afternoon brilliant sunshine.

"Fuck's sake, if I lived here, I'd be barbecuing all damn year," I muttered, imagining Tommy here with me, the long days and equally long evenings, the balmy air, and the masses of meat on the hoof on all sides.

We'd need a brewery, obviously, and it'd have to run full bore every day to keep up, but…

That was when a fresh wave of the surrounding scent, best described by the moniker of simply "brown," was carried to me atop the wings of a hundred flies.

They swarmed incessantly, and I waved them away, blinking and cursing, before finally spotting Reth as he hurried over.

To my surprise, he wasn't headed for me at all. Instead, he made a beeline for Othair, who was seated at a small table beneath a hastily erected canvas awning, a ledger set out before him as he apparently meticulously cataloged our supplies.

"Commander Reth," Othair greeted, smiling and looking up from his paperwork. "I presume this is the inventory?"

"It is," Reth confirmed, pulling a rolled parchment from his belt. "Though it's larger than I was worried it'd have been earlier. If I'd known we could get this from the slavers before now, I'd have led the attack years ago."

Curious, I wandered over, nodding to them both. "Inventory of what?"

Othair looked up; surprise flickered across his face as he quickly struggled to his feet. "Ah, my prince, my apologies! I thought you were still working on your alchemy. Commander Reth has brought the complete accounting of seized goods from the attack on the slavers and the goods that were recovered."

"All of it?" I raised an eyebrow. "I thought we'd just grabbed what was immediately useful."

Reth smiled thinly. "What was immediately useful was indeed taken first, but the outriders have been hard at work since then conducting a thorough sweep of all slaver encampments. The total haul is…substantial. Though, if I'm honest, it was more a case of needing to do it now, before anything else could vanish."

"The camps were raided as soon as you left?" I guessed.

"They were raided while we were there," he growled. "We had to keep moving, but despite orders to stay clear, and the setting up of boundaries, merchants on virtually all sides of the camps attacked as soon as the riders moved an inch!"

"And how are you dealing with that?" I asked.

"Sanctions, warnings, and beyond that? There's little we can do," he grumbled, before shaking his head. "Forgive me. It's frustrating that there's just no way to prevent this. It's only because of sheer luck and bloodstains that we were able to recover the damn *wagons*, never mind anything else. Thankfully, the outriders and legionnaires grabbed bags of holding where possible so we recovered a lot of the highest value items there."

"Well, there's options there, but we can go over that in a minute. For now, don't keep me in suspense." I grinned, pulling up a camp stool and sitting down. My back thanked me immediately. "What'd we get?"

Othair cleared his throat. "Perhaps it would be best if Commander Reth simply reads through the major categories, as it is, in the main, his men who led the recovery efforts?"

Reth glared at him, before nodding, and unrolled the parchment, which extended far longer than I'd expected, nearly reaching the ground. "First, there are the wagons," he began. "Ten luxury transports, formerly belonging to the highest ranking or the richest of the slavers. Three retain significant bloodstaining that will need to be addressed, but all are structurally sound and are, well, they should fetch a high price, should you have no need for them."

"That's our portion?" I asked.

"Yes," Reth confirmed. "After we've taken our forty percent, these are your share. Many of these were either moved as soon as we left the camps, or had been parked away from the general slave markets. The smell apparently was an issue for them." He sneered at that, and I snorted, thinking that the poor fuckers who lived here permanently had to have lost their sense of smell years ago. "We've also recovered well over four hundred ordinary wagons in varying states of repair. Of those, your share is just shy of three hundred."

I whistled. "Three hundred? What the hell are we supposed to do with three hundred wagons?"

"Many of the freed slaves will need transport," Othair pointed out. "And with the plan to travel to Gaij, any supplies we need will need to be carried. Add in as well, that although the legionnaires and our original group were trained to run alongside the wagons, for this many people…" He shook his head. "Many are simply too old or too young to do that for more than an hour a day."

"Fair enough," I conceded. "What else?"

Reth consulted his list. "Mounts. Approximately four thousand horses, most in good condition, though all are in desperate need of grooming. Two hundred and seventy-three mixed exotics, including razor-tusked boars, scaled ridge-runners, and three pregnant dire wolves."

"Pregnant dire wolves?" I repeated incredulously.

"They're often prized as guard animals," Reth explained with a shrug. "Far more valuable with offspring on the way, but they're also banned from Sonra, given that most of our herds are prey animals and both sides tend to react as soon as one scents the other. Had we known they were here, we'd have banned the fool who brought them on the spot. Instead, as it is, we have given them to you, and ask that you take them to Gaij with your advance party."

"What the hell am I going to do with them?" My voice rose. "Just have them waddling alongside the horses? Fuck no, we're going to be riding hard, man."

"Failing that, and should you refuse them, we'll cull them tonight."

I winced, not liking the thought of killing anything that was pregnant, until Reth went on.

"They'll attack as soon as they see prey," he repeated. "Look at our herds, Prince Jax, and tell me what you think will happen when they scent them."

"Stampede." I sighed.

"Exactly."

"Can they be tamed?"

"Not to the best of my knowledge. The only known method so far is to imprint on the newborn at birth, and force another, similarly strong hound type to accept it as their own. The drawback of this method is that it requires the mother of the dire wolf and the original offspring of the hound be killed and their blood smeared on the other in the two-way bond.

"By which I mean that the hound mother is to be smeared in the dire wolf blood, and the dire wolf pup is to be smeared with the hound's blood. This is the only known success, and it was recorded at a one in ten success rate."

"I thought you said they were used as guard dogs?"

"They are, mainly in places that you don't ever intend to return to yourself."

"Fuck," I muttered. "At least tell me they're tasty?"

"Perhaps, though most describe dire wolves as tasting, and I quote, 'like ass.'"

"Dammit." I sighed, rubbing my face as I thought. I didn't like it, but if they couldn't be tamed and they were essentially unusable in any way, as well as likely to drive the herds and horses mad, then there was no choice. "Fine, cull them."

"There's more," Reth continued. "Two Fenris-class mechanical warhorses, gnomish manufacture, with intact manastone cores. We have claimed one; two are yours."

That got my attention, and I looked up disbelievingly. "Fenris models? Are you serious?"

The mechanical warhorse I'd stolen from the drow back on Dravith was a hell of a thing—an armored, tireless mount that could charge through battle without fear or fatigue. I'd reached out to the gnomes to try to get them to make me a fucking cavalry corps of them. They were apparently a labor of love, though, with each taking literal years to build. As such, we'd moved onto claiming all that we could and now we had two more. Thorn was gonna shit a brick.

"Quite serious," Reth confirmed, almost smiling at my obvious enthusiasm. "Both appear to be the Mark III variant, slightly older than current models but reportedly more reliable."

"That's…that's actually incredible," I admitted. "Are they functional?"

"According to the gnomes we had look at them, yes, though they appear to need minor repairs and their manuals are locked out. The activation key for one is missing as well, so we have claimed that one, as our…more unusual members are gifted in these areas." He smiled, and I did as well.

"Thank you." I knew he could have just as easily left me the locked one and said it was my problem.

I immediately wondered whether I could claim one for myself, then felt slightly guilty for the thought. There were probably better uses for such valuable assets than giving me a second mechanical mount when I already had one back home.

"They are a wonder indeed." Othair smiled. "I have only seen one in the past, and that was both a terror on the battlefield, I'm told, and a wonder for transport."

Reth nodded. "Next, currency and valuables. Approximately four thousand, two hundred and three platinum, twelve thousand gold, forty-three thousand silver marks, and various lesser coinage, mostly copper, though some knuts and zari as well…approximately another ten thousand in those. Trade goods valued at roughly twenty thousand platinum equivalents, primarily consisting of spices, preserved substances, and enchanted textiles."

"Enchanted textiles?" I asked.

"Primarily self-cleaning and temperature-regulating fabrics," Othair clarified. "Highly sought after by merchants who spend extensive time traveling."

"Huh." Self-cleaning fabric sounded pretty damn appealing after spending days in armor, all right. "Go on."

"Manastones," Reth continued. "One hundred and thirty-seven in total, ranging from tiny to significant in size. Roughly worth about another ten thousand gold, should you wish to sell them."

"Fuck no." I snorted. "The value of them is in the mana, not the coins."

"After seeing what you managed earlier, I'd agree," Reth said dryly. "Weapons and armor," he continued, moving further down his list.

"Ah, instead of listing all the individual weapons, perhaps it would be easier this way," Othair interjected. "We have three thousand volunteers who require weapons and armor. How many of them can we outfit?"

"Three thousand…?" Reth mused, reading over the lists quickly. "Perhaps half that fully, all of it with a weapon, such as daggers and spears, but only half with armor or a weapon of choice. Then there are several enchanted weapons or armor that you'll probably want to give away as rewards?"

"Not me." I shook my head. "I barely know a fraction of the people, and although I'll meet more of them as time goes on, better not to waste them. As they'll need to be sorted, I'd say let Daralen take care of it, and she can pass them down the chain from there."

"Are you sure?" he asked. "Some of these will be quite valuable."

"Yeah, give them to her. If she wants me to look at something, I will. But the weapons we've already had have been mainly handed out, though that reminds me…" I pulled out Soulrend from my bag of holding and looked it over.

"That is…an impressive weapon," Reth whispered, his eyes wide.

"Yeah…" I muttered, using my identify spell and then reading the details out to the others.

Soulrend	**Further Description** ***Yes***/*No*
Details:	This greatsword has changed the fate of kingdoms on three separate occasions. Its blade is forged from enchanted ice that never melts, bound to a hilt of ancient ironwood wrapped in the preserved skin of a frost wyrm. The guard is crafted from platinum inlaid with sapphires, and the pommel holds an orb of condensed ice mana. The sword emits a constant chill that forms frost on nearby surfaces and can unleash waves of freezing energy that slow and gradually petrify enemies. Those slain by the blade rise temporarily as frost wraiths that serve

		the wielder for a short time before dissipating. The sword's most terrifying ability is to trap the souls of particularly powerful enemies within the sapphires, allowing the wielder to consult them for knowledge or torment them for eternity.	
Rarity:	**Magical:**	**Durability:**	**Charge:**
Legendary	Yes	47/100	3/5

"We'll need to try to figure out who is trapped in the sapphires at some point, but, honestly? I think we're going to need someone who knows about this kind of shit," I admitted. "If I try to question them, I'm more likely to hurt them than not. Have you got anyone?" I asked Reth, who was still staring, wide-eyed.

"Ah, I believe so?" he whispered. "Ilena has people who have such specializations, and Greg has a cousin who is gifted with magical crafting."

"Fair enough." I slid the weapon back into the bag. "When you've sworn to me, I'll pass it over then and they can try to figure this shit out. Oh, I should probably say, I got the weapon from a dick who was one of the founders of the Sons of the Deep, a necromancer."

I saw the look on Reth's face and grinned as I went on. "Don't worry—he's very dead now. But he made some comments about claiming the souls of skilled people, or those with extensive knowledge and secrets. As such, we need to be careful when investigating this."

"I will…we will be very careful," he whispered. "You would truly hand over such a weapon?"

"Fuck yes." I snorted. "I use a naginata, mate…a bloody murderstick and a *proper* weapon. That thing? It's a glorified butterknife in comparison. I don't need it, and I don't want it. Once we know the souls are either helping us or released? I'll probably just give it to Daralen or someone. I think she used a sword?"

"You could ask for any price for a weapon like this," he pointed out.

"You think as the prince of the empire I give two shits about coin?" I asked. "Back home, the only use I have for platinum, for example, is melting it down. I spend ingots like water to make things like the Imperial Academy. As for coin? As long as the economy is rolling, it's all good."

I noted the disbelieving look on his face, and I went on.

"Besides." I shrugged. "For me, there's an entire continent to reconquer, and you better believe there's a lot of loot out there."

"Well, yes, but most is in the hands of the nobility," he said.

"Glad to hear it." I smiled. "Makes it a lot more convenient when I only need to kill a few nobles to get it all rather than chasing everyone else down."

There was a long pause, as Reth looked from me to Othair, who smiled smugly at him.

"Do you recall the town of Marrow, perhaps, Commander?" he asked.

"Yeah." Reth nodded, his brows knitting and a twist to his mouth as he apparently remembered something unpleasant.

"Excellent. We passed through there on the way here. Prince Jax freed me, hanged the former lord, then burned the town to the ground."

"That was a fun one." I sighed. "Daralen and a lot of the legion were being held there, so I kinda let them work out a little stress on the former lord as well."

Reth stared at me for a long few seconds, then started to smile.

I shrugged. "Anyway, moving on…any Earth weapons, like the kind of things that Wilhelm's party had earlier?"

Reth shook his head as if in a daze, smiling slightly. "None. It seems the slavers hadn't yet acquired any such weaponry, or had hidden their stockpiles elsewhere."

That was both disappointing and relieving. The last thing we needed was for random locals to start running around with assault rifles.

Reth continued through several more categories of recovered items: medical supplies, preserved foods, luxury goods, and various contraband. By the time he finished, the sun had noticeably shifted in the sky.

"That's…a hell of a haul," I admitted, somewhat stunned by the sheer volume. "How many people are working on processing all this?"

"Nearly two hundred," Reth replied. "Both outriders and your legionnaires, along with volunteers from among the freed slaves. It's being cataloged, repaired where necessary, and stored according to priority."

I nodded slowly, digesting this information. The damn visit to Sonra had been even more successful than I'd realized. We'd not only freed over twelve thousand slaves but also acquired a small fortune in resources, and hopefully more.

"Well done, both of you," I said, genuinely. "Make sure everyone involved gets proper rest, though, and then, I guess, we need to start with the oaths."

"Of course, my prince," Othair replied with a slight bow.

Reth cleared his throat. "If I might have a moment of your time privately, Prince Jax? Regarding those oaths?"

I glanced at Othair, who tactfully gathered his papers. "I should check on the potion distribution, my prince, and Lady Oracle expressed a desire to discuss the methods of gathering people for the oath with me as well." He rose to his feet. "By your leave, my prince."

Once Othair was out of earshot, Reth relaxed slightly, although he also started to chew on a lip, apparently unsure where to begin.

"Perhaps, I should say that instead of speaking as commander of Sonra's outriders," he said quietly, "I speak, instead, as simply a man concerned for the future of my people."

"All right, go on." I frowned.

"The council is divided on certain matters," Reth admitted. "While we have agreed that officially allying with the empire is needed, there are…differing opinions on how close that alliance should become."

"Understandable," I agreed, waiting and hoping.

Reth nodded. "Some think that we should go no further than was agreed—becoming allies rather than subjects—and that this gives Sonra its best hope."

"But you don't."

He hesitated, then nodded, dropping the act and just coming out with it. "I believe it is short-sighted," Reth said bluntly. "You offer aid provided we serve; we accept this, but most of what we gain is limited. If we are allies, you come to our aid, and we come to yours, but little else. After all, what do we get? We have agreed to split the loot, and you give us leave to travel in your lands, but beyond that?

"We still travel over great distances, thousands of miles, if we continue as we have been, and while we can stay inside your territory, we are protected from the drow. That's it, though. If the Dark Legion comes? What then?"

"Then you run, or you fight," I said.

"And as allies, you would come to our aid?"

"I would, but as and when I can."

"But the meeting earlier suggested that there was a higher value in being fully part of the empire," he pointed out. "Better weapons, lands of our own, magic, power, training and more."

I leaned back, studying him carefully. "So you're suggesting Sonra could consider becoming imperial subjects rather than allies?"

"Others have suggested that the benefits could be substantial," Reth clarified. "But I need to understand what those benefits—and obligations—are."

Smart man. He wasn't committing to anything, but I was willing to bet that this wasn't just him. For a military man, I could definitely see the attraction. He'd have access to the legion, to magic being taught by Oracle and others, and he had to be shitting himself knowing that he now needed to protect Sonra with a hell of a big target drawn on its back.

As allies, we'd come to help, but he was responsible for protecting them. As subjects? I'd be responsible for making sure they had enough of a force to do it.

"Fair enough," I said. "As allies, Sonra gains our protection when our forces are nearby, trade agreements, and mutual defense in times of crisis. But there are limitations. Imperial resources are directed first at imperial citizens and territories. Allies receive what's left, when available."

Reth nodded, clearly following my meaning. "But we still have to swear the imperial oath? That seems…well, it's making us obey you, but we're getting little in return."

"You get to stay in my lands, and have my support as allies," I corrected. "You get to know that any other citizens you encounter will help you, and literally can't fuck you over. As I claim more territory, you get to stay inside it, kept safe from Illoth's reach, and as I kick the ever-living fuck out of the Dark Legion? You'll be free of their boot on your neck as well. Most of all? You get our help."

"But not as much as we would as imperial subjects?"

"As imperial subjects, rather than allies, Sonra's people are my people, with all the rights and protections that entails," I explained. "Training programs for your fighters. Legion support. Magical education for those with aptitude. Land for settlement. Access to imperial artifacts and manufacturing techniques."

I paused, making sure to be absolutely clear. "You're aware of the imperial facilities like the towers, and you've seen the golems, right?"

He nodded.

"Imperial citizens are identified as 'friendly' to the golems, regardless of the situation. Imperial citizens can't—thanks to the oaths—attack each other. That means that if you stray into an area protected by an imperial golem? It'll help you. If you're being hunted by someone? It'll take your side.

"Hell, if there's a genuine need and we have enough, we'll even assign some to Sonra, perhaps a dozen war golems. That'd be enough to take on, oh, several hundred Dark legionnaire elites if they were used well. You wouldn't need as many guards, and when the shit hits the fan…well, I once told one to tear the arms off a cave troll and beat it to death with them. It did it. Literally.

"Then you'd also have access to imperial facilities—within reason—and protection, as well as access to the artifacts that the old empire once controlled and that have been laid moldering ever since.

"But, on the other side, it also means accepting imperial law and governance—not just you follow these laws and that's it…you do you, boo.

"Instead, if something happens and I need you to take Sonra to the desert and start touring there, or into the mountains, you'd do it. I'd not issue orders like that on a whim, and you'd have the chance to explain to me why it'd be a mistake. But if I decide you still go, then you go.

"You'd retain local autonomy in most matters, just as you do as allies, but major decisions would require imperial approval. You'd pay imperial taxes, though considerably lower than what most realms extract. Lastly, those dealings with nobles and so on you mentioned?

"No longer your problem—now they're mine. And as to your council, I'd be willing to accept a member from it on *my* council as a representative. That comes with imperial titles, and instant higher authority over the local nobility."

Reth considered this carefully. "And our…unique situation? The inner ring and its inhabitants?"

"Would remain under your control," I assured him. "Look, as I've said before, all beings capable of reason receive the same protections under imperial law. And frankly? I don't have the time to be involved in any of your shit unless I have to be.

"For me, the ideal solution is that you all swear to me, we move on, and you appoint one person who I deal with, mainly because I won't have the time to deal with councils and I'll be moving on fairly soon. As it is, your council deals with all your stuff internally and I will occasionally issue orders and request if I have to. That's it.

"Ninety percent of the situation remains the same when it comes to your own people. But if you swear to follow me, you get my people backing you as one of our own. I have a responsibility to make sure that you're safe, and that if things are happening, like a drought, I need to make sure you all get enough food.

"As allies, you stand on your own two feet, and we'll help you as and when we can. Either way, though, your people would gain legitimacy and protection, not lose their identity."

"And the oath?" Reth asked. "It is…concerning."

"The oath prevents citizens from harming one another." I sighed. "It doesn't control your thoughts or force obedience in all things. You'd be protected from betrayal by your fellow citizens and they'd be protected from you. What's it worth to know that if some of your more unusual members decide to go for a walk, through the streets of Gaij, once we take it, that they'll be safe?"

"Will they?" he asked bluntly.

"From any imperial citizen, yeah." I nodded. "And tonight, we start with that oath here. The people out in the camps get the choice of agreeing, or fucking off. If they want to stay, then, as you agreed, they swear that oath; they become imperial citizens. After that, when we know that those with you are safe, the next step is healing. We'll teach a small handful of your people a healing spell, and they can literally start healing any citizen, on request, for free.

"I mean that bit as well—*for free*. Healing is free in the empire, and the healers are compensated by the empire directly. So remember that when people ask, please."

Reth fell silent for a moment, weighing my words. Finally, he nodded. "I…you have given us much to think on."

"I assume you'll be reporting this conversation back to the council?"

"Of course," Reth admitted without shame. "Though, as I said, it's a personal question, not an official one."

"Your secret's safe with me." I snorted, both of us fucking knowing that it was as official as it could be. "But be clear on this: I'm not pushing Sonra to change the nature of our relationship. The choice is entirely yours, and I'll honor whatever decision your council makes. Lastly, if you wanted to swear to be allies tonight, and that you would become full citizens on my taking control of Gaij, but that if I fail you remain as allies? I'd accept that."

Reth blinked in surprise. "That attitude alone may sway more votes than you realize. Most expected demands, not an offer."

"I'm not in the business of forcing people to join me, just that if they want to live under my banner and gain from the blood and sweat of the empire, then they contribute to it." I shrugged.

"Personally, I don't damn well like the way the oath is, and the way it forces people to play nice, but I like the alternatives a lot less. Back where I came from, there's a vote-based system of ruling, or there was. It failed a lot because of the manipulation of the system, but the saying was that 'democracy was the worst governing system ever invented…except…for all the others.'"

"I…see?"

"No, you don't but that's fine. What I mean is that it's a shitty system, but it gives you and me the best balance of protection and freedom we can get. And besides, as a bonus, join me, and you'll get to watch me kick the living fuck out of the noble houses that won't live by the same rules as everyone else. That has to be worth the risk, right?"

That drew a genuine laugh from Reth, brief but sincere. "Knowing that we will all be equal under one ruler is itself a relief." He rose to his feet, offering a formal bow. "Thank you for your time, Prince Jax. I shall return to the others."

"Good talking to you." I smiled. Then, once he was gone, I let out a sigh and retreated back into the wagon.

"Reth's just been by, sounding me out about what the difference between being allies and citizens is," I sent to Oracle and Sehran.

"And?" Oracle sounded distracted.

"And I think he'll go for it," I admitted. *"I offered a condition where they get to swear as allies, and the full citizenship only becomes active once we take Gaij."*

"That's generous," Sehran pointed out uncertainly.

"Not really," I replied. *"If we can't take Gaij, we're fucked. We're already behind enemy lines, and with Sonra and our newly freed people, we've got what? Fifty thousand people here? At least twenty, and that's if only a small number of Sonra actually swear.*

"That's too many to move fast in any direction, and we need to get to the Cradle. We've got to get there soon, and the sooner the better, considering we genuinely don't know if the baby is going to make an appearance this weekend or in a year from now. If we can't set these people up somewhere safe, then they're fucked. We can't take them with us either. And, lastly, even if Sonra didn't swear, there's over twelve thousand people we rescued this morning.

"I have to think there's a lot of them who are going to want to swear, and that is going to clean us out of fucking every manastone we can get our hands on, and a hell of a lot of the potions as well. If only half of them join us, that's still an insane number of people, and we can't protect them all the way to the Cradle, not and expect the majority to survive anyway, even besides the months it'd take," I finished, my mood darkening.

"So we take Gaij, set it up as a bastion of the empire and just hope that nobody comes knocking while we're away?" Sehran asked, apparently a little uncertain it'd work.

"We take the city, and the tower," I confirmed. *"The base of the tower is intact, but it's lost most of the upper levels, and especially the control facilities. What I think that means is that the lower floors, and specifically the golem creation systems, will be there still. If we can take them, that opens the door to us creating higher-leveled war golems. Those can hold the city, even against Earth-based weapons."*

"They can, but my sisters would have tried it," Sehran pointed out.

"Sure," I agreed, grinning in the quiet of the room. *"But they won't have the authority to use them. And if the wisp who controlled the systems is sleeping or doesn't have the authority to help them? That leaves them locked out. But any controller, be it a wisp or a golem or whatever, should accept me."*

"But only if there's someone there who can listen," Oracle pointed out. *"This is a lot of 'if' and 'maybe,' Jax."*

"I know." I stared at the ceiling. *"But the alternative is that we just bypass the city and head straight for the Cradle. Better to try to claim it and see what we can recover, rather than assume there's fuck all worth the effort."*

"We're with you," Sehran said reassuringly. *"Always."*

I sent them a feeling of thanks and love, and then cut the connection, settling back, only to have Oracle reestablish it less than a minute later.

"My love, I think we need to start with the oaths," she said. *"I know the legionnaires need this, but the effect of so many oaths tonight on your mind...well, it's going to be exhausting, more than we've ever done in one go. If it leaves you unconscious, then we need to be ready to deal with it. Better we start in smaller*

batches this afternoon instead of taking the oaths from both the new people and Sonra, as we don't know how many of Sonra will be willing."

"Point." I sighed. *"Well, we might as well get this over with."*

CHAPTER NINE

The crowds stretched as far as I could see. A literal ocean of faces: some hopeful, others nervous or uncertain. They were being broken down into clusters of five hundred at a time—thank fuck—and Othair and Daralen were working well together, while Marteen was apparently still busy working on the merchants out in the third ring.

The process had begun about four million years ago, or so it felt, and now as the sun dipped toward the distant horizon, my head pounded and my mana channels felt like someone had opened them up and rammed a scouring wire brush along them. My throat was raw from speaking, and my mind hummed with the thousands of new connections already formed.

Oracle sat by my side, her hand latched on to my own in a death grip as she saw, well, who knew what. She was so deep in the zone of mana manipulation that it was insane.

Sehran circled overhead, keeping watch. Daralen stood nearby, with fifty of the legion on guard and ready, just in case, as hundreds of people streamed in and out in what felt like an ongoing wave.

Oracle and I were reduced to sitting on a dais, hastily erected, and peering out across those faces. It was exactly how I *didn't* want to look: a prick sitting on a throne and looking out over everyone's heads, like I was too good to stand and greet them properly.

After five thousand people and—only—ten oath bindings so far, with who bloody knew how many thousand more to come, though?

The choice was I could stand for a short while, and then collapse from the strain and be unable to move, or I could sit for most of the time, stand and give out the oath and my response, and then sit again.

Or, you know, considering the work I had to do beyond being a focal point and a mana battery, I could lie in a bed and let Oracle do all the work…but we weren't married yet and that seemed unfair.

The eleventh group stood before me now, a mix of former slaves, refugees, and those who'd traveled to Sonra with various caravans and had moved off, streaming through the camp to join the massive gathering that still surrounded our camp like a tumor.

Sonra's outriders and herdsmen were getting pissed off as well, as no sooner did they move their animals along, then more people arrived and they had to do it again. For the vast majority, they had nowhere else to be, beyond here, with us.

Considering the loop of animals were in between the second and third rings, that limited the space that they had to expand into around our camp, and so the movement of Sonra—a gradual march that took place every few days, and that had been put off for longer than normal already—had begun out of necessity as well.

I stared out, noting that the expressions on the faces of these people ranged from reverent to skeptical, but they all shared that same hungry look. They were a people desperate for protection, for belonging, and for something to believe in.

"You know why you're here," I called out, my voice croaky but still carrying across the hush that fell. "You've seen what happened with the slavers. You've seen the legionnaires. You've heard what the empire offers."

I paused, looking at the faces before me, searching for doubt, for fear. There was some, of course. Who wouldn't be afraid after what they'd endured? But there was something else too—hope. And that was what kept me going.

Hope that'd long been missing from the faces of too many out there.

"I won't lie to you," I continued. "The oath you're about to take isn't just words. It's *binding*. It will change you. You'll gain protection, both from the outside world and from each other, as no citizen can harm another without consequence. You'll gain rights, from me personally and my empire, to justice, to aid, to vengeance if you fall. But you'll also gain responsibilities."

A murmur rippled through the crowd. This was the part where some usually drifted away. I gestured to the perimeter, where Othair and several legionnaires stood ready to escort any who chose to leave.

"This isn't for everyone. If you'd rather make your own way, go now, please. Go with my blessing, with my wish of good luck and supplies for your journey." That'd been Othair's doing, and damn it'd been good. It was a basic pack—some food and little else beyond the bare necessities—but it was both an offering to those people who couldn't swear now—they needed to find families or more—and a way to differentiate them. Nobody who had fuck all was going to put a bag of free food down and just wander off, leaving it alone, as it'd be stolen in seconds.

That meant we could pick those who refused out of the crowd even easier.

A handful who had clearly come along more out of curiosity than anything else moved toward the edges, but fewer than I'd expected, and it was getting less with each speech. If I was honest, though, the whole warping of the air and the slavers exploding earlier probably helped too.

"For those who stay, know this: the empire isn't just about power. It's about standing together. It's about looking at the person next to you and knowing they've got your back. It's about building something that will last long after we're gone."

I scanned the crowd again, feeling the weight of their expectation.

"So, make your choice. Stay or go. But know this: if you join us, whatever comes next, whatever armies march against us, whatever gods think they can break us, we face it together. As citizens of the empire. As free people. And for those ready and want to learn to fight? As legion aspirants."

I turned to Oracle, nodding slightly. "Ready?"

"Better to sit down," she replied softly, and I complied, settling back into the seat, embarrassed but damn well knowing that it was needed.

Four greater mana potions sat ready on a small side table for me, each capable of restoring four thousand mana at once. Based on the last few hours, that should be enough, but the strain of binding so many at once was growing, even with all the experience we were getting.

"My partner Oracle will share the oath with you now," I called. "Those who don't wish to take it, that's your choice, and again, I wish you good luck. But please, leave now. Those who do wish to become citizens of the empire, who want to gain more than they lose, speak the oath, and be welcome!"

As Oracle projected the words into their minds, my mana plummeted immediately. The first voices rose, hesitant at first, then stronger, until damn near five hundred voices spoke as one:

"I swear upon pain of death, to faithfully execute all that the Emperor decrees. I swear upon my soul that I shall stand for the Empire when it calls. I shall be strong when the weak need me, generous when the poor are at hand, and merciless when my fellow citizens are threatened. I shall worship the gods of my fathers, respect my elders, and raise up my children to stand tall.

"I am an Imperial Citizen. I claim the right to call upon the Legion in my hour of need, to hold those who wrong me to justice, and to be avenged if I cannot be saved.

"I swear to obey Prince Jax and those he places over me; I will serve to the best of my ability, speak no lie to him when commanded otherwise, and treat all other citizens as family.

"I will work for the greater good, being a shield to those who need it, a sword to those who deserve it, and a warden to the night.

"I will stand with my family, helping one another to reach the light, until the hour of my death or my lord releases me from my Oath.

"Lastly, I will not be a dick!"

As their voices faded, I downed the third mana potion, gulping it to replenish what had been drained, having barely even noticed as I chugged the first and second. The minty flavor I used to enjoy tasted like ashes now as I responded:

"I, Lord Jax, do swear to protect and lead you, to be the shield that protects you and yours from the darkness, and the sword that avenges that which cannot be saved. As the Empire grows in strength, so shall you."

Almost five hundred new threads formed in my mind, connecting me to each new citizen. I could feel their dedication, their hope, their relief—iron and silver threads shading toward gold, a tapestry of loyalty and devotion, love and awe. To be on the receiving end of it was humbling and terrifying all at once.

"You'll note that important last line there in the oath," I added, forcing a smile despite my fatigue, as I lowered the fourth bottle. "That you won't be a dick. For those who aren't sure what that means, it's simple. Look at the things you do and the way you live your life. If you flip it around, and you were on the receiving end of that, how would you feel? If you ask yourself 'am I a dick' and you don't understand the question, chances are then yeah, you're a dick."

That earned a ripple of laughter, easing the solemnity of the moment.

"The simplest way to think of it is that you need to think of everyone around you as family. You might not like your brother very much, and hell, the gods know there's plenty of days I don't like mine. That's fine.

"Anyone who wants to hurt him, though? They come through me first! That's *family*. That's us and the rest of the world defined right there. We look after our own, always.

"So, I ask that you remember that, moving forward, but most of all, welcome!" I called out, my voice echoing as Oracle did something to it. "Welcome, citizens, to the empire!"

I'd gotten the speech down by bloody rote now, and I settled back, smiling as people started to move, some cheering. I waved to them, but most were just curious and if anything, a little confused and looking for something else. Some kind of difference beyond the oath.

They'd learn, I knew, as the reason this took so bloody long wasn't just the time for me to recover between each swearing. No, it was because Othair and the others were sorting people into groups as they left and arrived.

Dozens were working the crowd now, and the line of legion aspirants grew by the hour. They were being led off to one side of the expanding camp, where legionnaires experienced in training were waiting, ready to take command of the group.

Back home, I'd been reduced to barely double digits of "real" legionnaires by the end, or so it felt. They'd moved from the principal fighting force to a training and leadership cadre, bringing the next generation of the legion along as quickly as possible. Here, although we hadn't yet lost so many, we were following the same pattern.

The aspirants would be taught legion discipline, trained to fight, and they'd move from freed slaves and basic guards or fighters, to lethal warriors in short order.

They'd be rebuilt from the ground up, with good food, good equipment, and a damn reason to fight—beyond coin—and they'd excel. Within a year, I was hoping that they'd be a literal army the likes of which hadn't been seen in centuries.

Not just legionnaires—no, they'd *all* be mages as well. They'd be living legends, each capable of taking down entire caravans of slavers and worse, and they'd bring order and safety to the empire again.

Most of all, they'd be an army of the maddest, baddest, hardest, and most dedicated babysitters the realm has ever known for my future child.

My plan was that these people, once they were trained, would be augmented by the best equipment we could produce. They'd be trained as mages and legionnaires, and people like Restun would spend their lives making damn sure that when a legionnaire got jumped, alone, miles from help, it'd be the legionnaire who walked away after the fight. The attackers would pull back a bloody stump with no body attached.

As the newest citizens dispersed, guided by the legionnaires to receive their supplies and assignments, I saw Daralen waving the next group to begin assembling. Five hundred more faces, five hundred more souls to bind to the empire, and five hundred more nails scraped through my damn channels.

"How are you holding up?" Oracle asked softly, her hand taking my own again.

"Been better," I admitted, pulling out another set of mana potions. "Been a lot worse too. How about you? You're the one guiding this shit show."

"We've done more than five thousand already," she said. "That's incredible compared to how long it took us even a few months ago."

I nodded, squinting at the sun. "I know. Still doesn't feel any better, though. Let's keep going and see if we can speed it up at all. We need to finish the freed slaves today, if we're to set off in the morning."

"To the right," Sehran whispered through the bond.

I glanced over in response. Daralen had broken off from arranging the incoming groups, instead leaving that to an optio, and was headed over.

Cleq walked beside her. The diminutive goblin looked unusually formal in what appeared to be ceremonial robes, and with Ilena and the twins, as well as Reth behind him, and most interestingly, Sharn.

People were moving aside, but where they looked at the short-arse goblin in confusion and even a few with disgust, most stared in open surprise at the centaur.

"My prince." Daralen bowed slightly, after I'd gestured her up to stand with us on the dais. "The council requests a moment before we proceed with the next group."

I raised an eyebrow, glancing from Cleq to the massing numbers below. "I'm not gonna complain at a delay," I admitted.

Cleq stepped forward, hands folded before her. "Forgive the interruption, Prince Jax, but the council has reached a decision that we believe you would wish to hear without delay."

That got my attention, and I nodded, hoping this wasn't going to be a "thanks, but no thanks" chat. "Go on."

"After extensive deliberation," Cleq announced, standing straighter and speaking loudly, her voice carrying surprising authority for her size, "the Council of Sonra has voted to accept full imperial citizenship, with the condition that our status as subjects rather than allies will activate only upon the claiming of Gaij and its surrounding territories, and we request a seat on the Imperial Council!"

I blinked, surprised despite myself. I'd expected them to take days more to decide.

"That's…excellent news," I managed. "I didn't expect it, though, or at least not so quickly. Can I ask why?"

"Your actions yesterday spoke louder than any words could," Cleq replied loudly, taking the chance to spread that she was a member of the Council of Sonra, and not just a random goblin who had wandered in, while wearing stolen curtains.

"The council has agreed—the freeing of the slaves, the manner in which you dealt with the slavers, and your treatment of those under your protection…these things were carefully observed. But so was the humility that you showed, and the respect that you have shown to the mixed races of Sonra."

Oracle smiled widely, and spoke up. "How many from Sonra will be taking the oath?"

"All eight hundred and eleven from the inner ring," Cleq said. "Fifteen thousand and more from the second ring, we believe, and beyond that, all citizens and visitors of Sonra who wish to remain so. With your permission, we will begin informing those in the third ring and beyond that they must either swear to the empire or make ready to depart."

I couldn't hide my surprise. "That's…fuck me, Cleq, that's a surprise, and it's a shitload more than I expected."

Cleq's mouth quirked in what might have been a smile. "We've lived for centuries in the shadows, Prince Jax. The chance to step into the light, protected by imperial law and might, is not one we take lightly. We're well aware of the risk it poses, but it is one we embrace."

I exchanged glances with Oracle, who gave a slight nod. *"The math works,"* she sent through our bond. *"We have the mana potions, barely, but we need to ask them to provide some of the cost, or we'll have nothing left."*

"This, ah, shit, this changes our plans," I winced, thinking aloud. "We can't do this in a day and still leave tomorrow."

"No," Daralen agreed. "But if we stay a day, or even two more, it gives us the chance to better organize our forces and supplies as well as—"

I nodded, knowing what she wasn't saying: that it meant that those who might change their mind if we left it until later wouldn't have that chance to back out.

"We could also use it to send a party of advance scouts," she suggested as well. "Good horses, and an escort of skilled riders would make a hell of a difference…"

The hint was obvious: let's make use of the outriders and begin folding them into the chain of command.

I nodded slowly, then turned back to Cleq. "When would you like to begin?"

"The representatives of the inner ring are prepared now." She smiled. "The others will follow as you direct."

I looked over his shoulder. Sure enough, a group of perhaps fifty beings stood waiting—a mix of races I'd rarely seen in one place, from towering centaurs to short-arse goblins, from proud orcs to beings I couldn't even identify. The hidden heart of Sonra had decided to step into the light, and the looks they were getting, not just from my people, but from the masses on either side of them?

Fuck, there was a reason they were nervous, I knew.

"Well then," I straightened and forced myself to my feet despite my fatigue, "let's welcome them home."

The next two damn days blurred together in a haze of oaths, potions, and endless faces. The eight hundred from the inner ring had been the easiest. We'd had the five hundred who were moving in next step aside and wait, and we'd done the first fifty, and then the remaining seven hundred plus as they could be gathered. They'd been quick to gather, and the collection of weird and wonderful beings had sworn with solemn dignity. Then afterward, they seemed split almost equally between those who immediately scampered back into the protection of the inner ring, and those who moved through the crowds, clearly delighted to be seen and to see the outside world.

The remaining twelve thousand volunteers and freed slaves and the fifteen thousand from the second ring had taken *much* fucking longer, proceeding in batches through what was left of the day and deep into the night, their oaths illuminated by torchlight and magic.

We had to stop them coming when I couldn't see any more from the pain. And then, as soon as I'd woken the next morning, it'd been to thousands waiting, most of whom had bloody camped out in place, not even bothering to move back to the spaces set aside for them. We got working as soon as I was dressed and had a bite.

I'd felt each new connection forming, hour after hour, the weight of responsibility and of those thousands of souls, but as I thought I was nearing the end?

It was the merchants and traders from the third ring who truly surprised me. When word spread that those who didn't swear would lose access to Sonra and its markets, there had been a moment of shock, followed by something approaching panic.

"Did you do this?" I asked Marteen as we watched yet another group of merchants being organized for the oath. "Damn, man, your mother would be proud."

He shrugged, a sad smile playing at his lips. "Sonra has been the trading hub of the great plains for centuries. I just dropped a few hints, after Reth passed the word that they were going to lose access, that you protected your merchants, but that any others? Well, if they got in the way, and maybe looked like they worked with the slavers, then there was nothing to stop you raiding them if they weren't sworn. Then I pointed out that you were from another continent, one that I'd heard was incredibly rich, and that your merchants were naive and had survived the cataclysm intact. Few were going to risk losing access to that.

"Lastly, well, I made out that once you were out of sight, who was to know if they'd sworn the oaths, and as they were common sense ones, what was the harm? You'd be leaving soon, and then everything could go back to normal. The only real difference would be that Sonra would be closed to those who'd not sworn the oaths…meaning those who did would get the very best of everything."

"They're swearing loyalty to an empire they barely understand, just to keep their trading rights," I marveled. "And you lied through your damn teeth to make it happen. No offense, but when Hannibal and Mal, not to mention Hanau and the others, get their hands on these merchants, they're going to pluck them like chickens."

"They're swearing loyalty to something powerful enough to break the slavers overnight," Reth corrected, having moved up to stand nearby. "Never underestimate self-interest when aligned with self-preservation."

"And ignorance," Marteen added, smiling evilly. "These are the kind of merchants who deliberately fucked me and my family over. They're the kind who helped to build the guilds into the monolithic things they are today."

"And you want to burn them all down and piss on the ashes?" I asked him, getting a curt nod. "That I can work with." I smiled. "By the way, any representatives of the guilds here?"

"There were four," he said grimly. "Three were killed by their control devices exploding. The fourth claimed guild privileges and the outriders allowed him to leave with what was left of his caravan."

"They did fucking what?" I hissed, my irritation rising fast into anger.

"There were no slaves, and although he was in the same party as confirmed slavers, he was also a guildmaster."

"So he got off because he's powerful?" I asked. "That right?"

"Essentially."

"Sounds like I'm gonna have to deal with that."

"He was heading to Gaij."

"Really?" I perked up. "Daralen, what's the chances of catching him?"

"If he was travelling by caravan?" she mused. "If I was to dispatch a fast-riding scout team, it's possible. It'd depend on the wagons he has and the route taken, though."

"Do it," I ordered. "They need to explain their presence with the slavers, and frankly, I need to understand the guild structure and their place in it. If they're slavers, then I want one to question so we know where we need to focus. If he's innocent—I don't believe he is, but let's be clear, there's always a chance—then we can scare the shit out of him and use him to open doors for us. Either way, though, I don't want him getting to Gaij first and turning the city against us."

"Consider it done." Daralen clapped a fist to her chest and then turned, calling out to one of the nearby legionnaires, barking orders.

By midday on the second day, we'd processed nearly nine thousand more merchants, traders, and their entourages than we'd expected. Our camp had expanded from a clearly delineated group, into just part of the overall sprawling city of tents and wagons, with the legion and the outriders working tirelessly to maintain order.

I slumped in my chair, halfway through the latest batch, when Sehran's voice cut through my fatigue and the cracking mana migraine I had. *"Something's happening at the perimeter."*

I followed the sense of her attention to where a commotion had broken out at the edge of our improvised oath-taking grounds. Sehran dropped from the sky beside us, her wings folding as she landed.

"A large party approaching from the north," she reported. "Maybe a hundred and fifty, heavily armed. They're flying the banner of House Granth and a second banner I'm not familiar with."

I frowned. "Wilhelm again? What's he playing at? Wait, this is fucking fast, isn't it?"

"He's in the lead, and he's carrying that French flag again."

"The white one?"

"Yeah."

"Heh." I grinned despite everything, knowing that when Tommy found out I'd identified the international flag of surrender as the French national one, he was going to laugh his arse off, and simultaneously, any nobility from home who were from France would be furious on general principles.

CHAPTER TEN

"Perfect timing," I muttered. "Just what I need when I'm practically running on fumes."

Oracle laid a hand on my arm. "We could postpone the next batch. You need rest, Jax."

I shook my head. "No. If they're coming in force, I want as many people bound to us as possible before they arrive." I turned to Daralen, who stood nearby. "Get ready, just in case. And tell Wilhelm himself and any representative he's brought, ten guards, no more."

"At once, my prince." She saluted before moving to relay the orders.

I drained another mana potion—my counting had gotten fuzzy, but it must have been at least my hundredth since we'd started and fuck, by now, I had to be at serious risk of poisoning from them—and gestured for the next group to approach.

"Let's get this done," I told Oracle. "Then we'll see what the noble houses want."

Wilhelm and his party arrived as the sun was kissing the horizon again, just as we finished binding the last of the day's oath-takers. I remained seated on my makeshift throne, deliberately not rising to greet them. For some, it'd be seen as a power play, I knew, but the truth was simpler.

I wasn't sure I could actually stand without falling over.

Oracle stood at my right, Sehran just behind, while Daralen positioned her legionnaires in a protective formation.

Wilhelm led the delegation, still in his combat gear but with his helmet removed. Behind him walked a handful of others I didn't recognize, their clothing a blend of Earth military styling and local fashions—practical, expensive, and designed to intimidate.

"Prince Jax," Wilhelm greeted me with a formal bow. "I bring vord from my grandfather to discuss in private, as vell as from mine own section of zhe house, und I have been asked to introduce zhe countess of House Kazimir, who vishes to discuss certain...arrangements vith you."

I raised an eyebrow. "Arrangements? That's an interesting choice of words."

A woman stepped forward, tall and severe, with steel-grey hair pulled back in a tight bun. "I am Countess Yelena Kazimir. I represent a coalition of the true nobility, who have recently arrived on this continent."

"I'm aware of how you arrived," I said coldly. "And the fucking blood price paid for your passage."

Her expression tightened minutely. "Necessity sometimes demands harsh measures, 'Prince' Jax. But that is not why we are here."

The sneer as she named my title and the obvious contempt she held for me was grating, and I forced myself to remain civil.

"Then get to the point," I said. "I've spent the last few days slaughtering slavers and binding nearly fifty thousand people to the empire. I'm not in the mood for diplomatic shite."

She stared at me, nostrils flaring, before clearing her throat and going on. "Put simply, we are here to propose a division of territory. This continent is vast, with resources enough for all. We suggest establishing clear boundaries to avoid…unnecessary conflict."

I stared at her for long seconds, then laughed. It wasn't entirely genuine—I was too tired for that—but their confused expressions made it worth the effort.

"Let me make sure I understand," I said when I'd composed myself. "You arrive on this continent through blood rituals that cost who knows how many lives, and now you want me to agree to just carve it up between us? Like gentleman thieves dividing the spoils? Just ignore the people who are here already, and the reality that you've got what, at most, a few hundred on your side?"

"This is a serious proposal," Countess Kazimir insisted. "Our houses have considerable resources, both from Earth and acquired here. We control significant territory to the east and south. A formal agreement would benefit all parties."

I leaned forward. "Let me be perfectly clear. I don't recognize your right to *any* territory on this continent or any other. You're thieving shitehawks who murdered Amon and then ran away when there were consequences for your actions. The empire is reclaiming what was always ours. Those who stand with us will prosper. Those who stand against us…"

I let the threat hang in the air.

Wilhelm shifted uncomfortably. "Mine prince, vhile I am bound by mine oath not to oppose you, I must advise zhat zhe strength of zhis house is substantial. Perhaps some accommodation—"

"No." I cut him off. "Here's what I'll offer instead. Any noble house that wishes to swear the imperial oath and join us as citizens will be welcomed. Depending on your ranks, you can keep your titles, even some autonomy in how you govern your people. But you will answer to the empire. You uphold its laws, and you'll be bound by them as any other is, and you accept that your people will have the same rights as any other citizen, sworn to the empire, and directly, ultimately, to me."

Kazimir and I exchanged glances, before she responded.

"That is…not acceptable," she said stiffly.

"Tell me, 'Countess'…" I made it clear I didn't care about her self-bestowed title. "Do you know where Sanguis is?"

"No," she spat. "We have no contact with the likes of him."

"Then we have nothing to discuss," I replied, settling back in my chair. "Be thankful, though. Had you said that you were one of his, I'd have sent you back in a fucking matchbox.

"Now, you're welcome to try your luck elsewhere on the continent. But be warned—as I claim more territory, any who have refused this offer will find no welcome within imperial lands. And when I'm done with my present target, I'll be moving to deal with you."

"You're making a mistake," Countess Kazimir said, her voice like ice. "We could be valuable allies."

"I already have allies." I gestured around to the sprawling camp. "Fifty thousand of them, bound by oath and choice, not by accident of birth or wealth stolen across worlds. And, let's face it—you're not one of the originals, are you?"

I could see the calculation in her eyes, the reassessment. She'd expected to negotiate from a position of strength, not to be dismissed outright.

"I am of the primary bloodline, and—"

"And you're fucking expendable," I snapped, sitting forward. "That's why they sent *you*—not to negotiate…don't flatter yourself. You were sent to see if I would accept and move on for a simple life, or if I'd squash you like a bug."

"This isn't finished." Her voice was thick with anger. "You've made powerful enemies today."

"Bitch, I've been making powerful enemies since I got here," I replied with a tired smile. "It's becoming something of a fucking hobby. Let me make my position clear, though, all right? Just so you know what you're reporting when you get back.

"I fucked up Nimon in one-to-one combat. I just beheaded Illoth, and I already conquered Dravith. I am the recognized heir to Amon, while you, your family, and all their titles, at fucking best, are secondary nobles. Most of your old ranks have already either been stripped entirely, or you've 'just' lost your places in the imperial succession. I, on the other hand, have the personal blessings of eleven gods on my ascension."

I let that linger in the air for a few seconds before going on. "I have well over a hundred thousand people behind me, I have the support of the legion, and the right to claim and exert my authority over any and all imperial citizens, sites, and fucking resources, including golems and more.

"If you claim them and I turn up on your door? I have the greater authority, and they will literally change sides at my order. This isn't a theory—it's a practiced fact.

"So. Go back to your family, and tell them this from me. Bend. The. Fucking. Knee. Accept imperial rule, and rise as members of the empire, perhaps even with your authority returned to you and your place in the succession reconfirmed once you've earned it. Failing that, at least have the balls to face me openly. And then, when I've wiped you off my goddamn boot, I'll conquer what's left.

"Oh, and remember for next time—if you want to negotiate, bring something to the table. If you want to try to threaten me? Don't do it with fuck all in your hand."

As they turned to leave, Wilhelm lingered, waiting until the others were out of earshot.

"I…zhat vas…unexpectedly brutal. You have to know zhat zhey vill move against you," he said quietly. "Perhaps not immediately, but soon. Zhey've discussed falling back to get room und establishing a base at vhat vas once Eastreach, about two hundred miles from here."

I eyed him tiredly. "Then I'll conquer them next." I sighed, rubbing at my face. "Seriously, mate, why bring them here, and tell me this?"

"Mine oath," he said. "I cannot fight you, nor can I stand by and allow zhose sworn to me to do so. Varning you of danger, however, does not violate mine own obligations to my house."

"Thank you." I sighed, meaning it. "Your honor continues to impress me, Wilhelm. So, why are you here, and again, why bring the idiot brigade?"

"I…" He paused, then managed a half smile. "Might we speak in private?"

"Yeah," I agreed. "Two minutes, mate. Daralen?" I turned to the legion primus and saw the concern in her eyes.

"Yes, my prince?"

"How many do we have left to go, any idea?"

"About four thousand." She winced. "Though that's a rough estimate, as more keep arriving. Best to work on a plan of five."

"Okay, fuck it. I'm having a break. I'm sorry but I damn well need one, and I'm fucked. I'll be back in an hour. And don't worry, he's sworn an oath." I nodded to Wilhelm, who straightened, and spoke up quickly.

"Nein, Jax, you are not safe, even vith one vho has sworn. Mine oath vould ensure retribution vould be swift, but I could still power through und injure you, should I desire, zhough it would likely cost me mine own life in retaliation. Zhe oath I gave you vas not a full oath of citizenship, after all…it vas a personal oath only."

"And that you felt the need to warn me of that is why I'm willing to extend a little trust." I forced a smile, before clambering down from the podium to head toward the wagon. Oracle stumbled down along beside me, at least as exhausted as I was.

I was about to reach out to her, but before I could, Daralen was there, offering Oracle a hand, and then blinking in surprise when Oracle not only accepted it, but shifted herself into a princess carry using both her ability to fly and the massive half-orc's strength.

"We trust you," I said to Daralen with a smile, noticing the shock on her face. "What, you think we'd trust you to watch over us and to run the legion, but not to carry the woman I love and our child?" I asked, and the hard-bitten primus smiled uncertainly, but she cradled the exhausted Oracle gently, carrying her.

"A shoulder?" Wilhelm suggested, stepping in close, and I took the offer, putting one hand on his shoulder and relaxing slightly. "Mein Gott, you look terrible," he breathed. "Ve can talk in zhe morning, but…"

"But you've got shit we need to hear and now's the best time." I nodded. "Don't worry. I've had meetings while I've been flayed alive before. A little exhaustion is manageable."

I said it with a smile and he frowned at me, obviously not getting it, until Oracle spoke up.

"He'd had his armor seared into his flesh by a bolt of lightning from Nimon—directly, I mean—and then he'd fought several hundred Dark legionnaires in that condition," she explained. "The mess was horrific, and so was the cleanup. We had to cut him free of the armor and peel him like a grape before we could heal him."

"Zhat is…zhat's horrific." He winced, and I nodded.

"Fucking well hurt, that did," I admitted. "Though the look on Hannimish's face was hilarious."

"Ah…?" He raised an eyebrow in question, and Oracle answered tiredly.

"A local noble who was trying to make a deal. He got in the room, expecting to see Jax just doing what most nobles do, drinking wine and complaining over a splinter in a finger. Instead, Jax had his organs on display while Primus Augustus was cutting the melted clothes and armor free, and was still giving orders."

"Hannimish threw up." I grinned. "Ran away and threw up. Though, after that, he was a lot more respectful."

"That was even after you'd cut off your arm, but he saw you do that, too, so it left an impression, I think," Sehran pointed out. "Jian told me about that. You know, before you gutted his nephew as well."

"It seems you have endured much," Wilhelm murmured, looking downcast. "Since ve have come here, I have been mainly consumed vith minor tasks of administration, gathering reports, und only occasionally trusted to run errands or ride vith zhe guard."

"Really?" I blinked.

"I am of zhe great House of Granth, but I am also a minor scion. Far removed," he admitted as we entered the wagon.

Daralen laid Oracle in a chair then stood at parade rest as I sank into another.

"Fuck's sake, you two, sit," I growled. "You're making me feel worse watching you."

"Zhank you." Wilhelm smiled. "Very vell. You are exhausted und I have little time before I am missed. I took zhe opportunity to escort zhe countess because it both got me out to meet you, und it got me out of zhe camp und away from prying eyes. I am sworn to mine family line, und cannot leave zhem, not under almost any circumstances. However, I got Gaspar to agree to a slight compromise.

"He is unwilling to accept imperial servitude, unless he is convinced of your eventual success. He is also, unsurprisingly, unvilling to relinquish his guard. I got an agreement zhat should you succeed in claiming a greater territory, und in eliminating House Malakai, zhen he vill meet vith you und negotiate personally. I…I tried for more, but he vould not grant it."

"It's pretty fucking little," I said softly. "And it shows what he thinks of me as well, in that he's willing to meet me to *discuss* it, despite me gutting two gods and having to conquer a city and kill one of his rivals to earn that?"

Instead of the anger he'd obviously expected, I was…empty. Almost disappointed. I knew that in itself was a bad sign, even more so that I couldn't be bothered to even care about it.

I'd had zero patience for the posturing bullshit that whatsherface had tried only ten minutes ago, and yet now? I couldn't be bothered to even be angry.

"Zhere is one more zhing."

"Oh?" I forced myself to put a faint smile on my face, knowing I had to look a mess.

"He agreed zhat I, und my parents, vould be permitted zhe status of emissaries to your court, should you ask it."

I blinked, seeing both the badly concealed hope on his face, and wondering where the hell that had come from.

"Why?" I asked bluntly.

"He zhinks so zhat we might report back to him and bring him advantage over you in zhe negotiations, as well as using zhe situation to compel you to accept his imperial rank." He looked ashamed.

"And yet you want this?"

"Vith all mine heart, ja." He snorted. "In our own camp, ve are second-rate citizens, too highly born to be permitted close relationships vith zhe guards or locals, und yet too lowly born, as an outer branch family, to be permitted near zhe 'true nobility' beyond to be used as servants. I spent mine life training, and yet I barely get to fight. Zhat is not to say zhat I revel in death, but…"

"But you want to test yourself," Daralen said softly. "You spent your life preparing to fight and now that you have the chance to do so, instead you are useless."

"Ja," he admitted, bowing his head. "It is a shameful thing."

"Daralen?" I looked at her. "Could you make use of him?"

"I could, my prince, provided he was willing to join the legion, and swear the oaths."

Wilhelm's head snapped up. "You vould permit me to join you?" he asked incredulously.

"Can you swear the oaths?" I asked brusquely. "Because I'm willing to give you a little trust here, mate, but if you can't, you could murder my people with impunity, not to mention the risk to my friends, as you've sworn no oath not to."

"I could swear zhe oath of imperial citizenship, and I could tell you of zhe oath zhat I have vith my family, including zhe loopholes, but I could not swear to serve you directly as a vassal. Once you ascend zhe throne, zhen zhe family oath vould automatically include you as emperor over mine familial loyalty to Gaspar, zhough, und I and mine parents vould be free."

"What do you think?" I asked Oracle.

"He seems genuine," she admitted. *"And if he swears the imperial oath, then although I can see the conflicts he's talking about with a family oath and you being the prince, there should still be enough residual cover from the oath itself that we'd be safe. We'd need to be careful about what we say around him, though."*

"Is it worth the risk?" Sehran asked. *"Knowing that he's going to report things back to his family?"*

"Maybe," Oracle mused. *"If we let him see what we want, it means that we at least have the opportunity to guide the narrative. After all, you know that there are spies here—there have to be. And if there aren't, then there will be soon when we reach Gaij."*

"So we take him on, learn what we can of the houses from him, and accept that he's going to be reporting on us back to Gaspar?" I asked.

"Well, considering you're going to be conquering the city either way, at least this way you know who's watching you, and what they are reporting. And if things are the way he says, then we have the chance to develop his loyalty. He seems…"

"He seems like he's not an absolute cockwomble." I sighed.

"Exactly."

"Fuck it," I said aloud. "What do you bring to the table, Wilhelm?"

"I…can provide advice on zhe various families, a breakdown on zhe general feeling und zhe alliances zhat vere in place before zhe transfer. Und, of course, I offer mine martial skills."

"You'd fight alongside my people?" I asked.

"Happily."

“Fine. Just you or did you say that your parents wanted to come as well? And what did you say they did before?”

“Mine father is an investment manager, typically put in place in medium to large companies to make sure zhat zhe investments are made and spent wisely, while mine mother vas a breeder, horses primarily.” He smiled.

“Well, no clue what they’ll be able to do here, but we’ll take them,” I agreed. “Do you need to ride back to get them?”

“Ja.” He straightened and spoke formally. “Prince Jax of zhe Empire, mine house patriarch has agreed zhat I, und mine parents, may serve at your pleasure, as both ambassadors und an example of zhe faith of House Granth. Vhile neither I nor mine parents can swear an oath to you, ve are all imperial citizens, and may swear zhe imperial oath, provided you acknowledge zhe patriarch Gaspar as head of House Granth und his place in zhe succession.”

I paused at that, realizing what I’d missed before, although Wilhelm *had* said it, and it’d been on me missing it.

To accept Wilhelm, and his parents, I needed to accept—as the imperial prince—that Gaspar was an imperial noble. Doing so would transfer the formal control of his house back to him, if any nobles currently claimed that title here, and it’d give him the right to command imperial citizens and equipment. The fucker. He *knew* that and had almost got me.

That was why Wilhelm had been so surprised when I agreed.

“All right, let’s see how this goes.” I smiled despite myself. “Wilhelm, please return to Gaspar and pass my response to him. And then, if you’re permitted to come to me still, get your parents and bring them and anything you need back. You’ll need to catch us, as we’ll be setting off tomorrow morning, on the road to Gaij, and we’ll be pushing hard. Please pass word to Gaspar, that as the prince and heir to the empire, I’d be happy to confirm his place in the succession, formally.” I smiled wider.

“If he wants me to do it now, however, before we’ve even opened negotiations, I’ll make it clear that his position will be at the very end of the line, right after the last remaining other imperial citizen dies, and that his formal title will be of a level to make that clear. Possibly as Imperial Squireboy or something similar. If he expects anything else, then he is to present himself to me, *formally*, in Gaij at noon in four days. Failure to attend will be considered as him forfeiting all imperial rights and obligations, and instead of me being willing to speak to him about a joint future with the empire, at one minute past noon, I will formally strip House Granth of any place in the ranks of imperial nobility, and order it disbanded.”

“Oh, mein Gott.” Wilhelm closed his eyes and looked to be praying, considering the way his lips moved.

CHAPTER ELEVEN

"Gods, I needed this," I called to Daralen, as I bent low, grinning as the wind streamed past, the feeling of the horse below me intoxicating.

I'd wanted to bring the Fenris pair, but then I'd had an attack of conscience when I remembered that the damn things could pull several wagons at a time, with ease, as opposed to normal horses.

Also, we'd be able to outride everyone, which was great, right up until you remembered that we were riding as part of a group and that wasn't a good thing.

Instead, I'd left the pair with Sonra with the understanding that they were a loan, not a gift. When I had enough to make a full unit of the fuckers, though, I was going to.

"It's been too long!" she called back, a bright smile on her face as she, too, bent low over her own horse's neck.

The grassland was thundering past now, with five hundred of us on horse, varm, or mammoth.

That was in itself a fucking glorious sight, and one that I'd never have expected to be very fast. But whoo-boy had I been wrong.

The varm were the light scout mounts, carnivorous deerlike creatures, or maybe antelope would be more accurate. They were a little smaller than the horses most of us rode.

Those were special warhorses that had been bred for the legion, and Sonra had kept most of them as their personal stock instead of selling them.

They were both larger than the average horse and fucking aggressive, as well as smarter. They could carry a fully armored legionnaire all day every day, and provided you looked after them, groomed them and fed them well, as well as weren't stupid enough to antagonize them, they'd be excellent mounts that were lethal to everyone else, not you.

The varm were a good hand or two smaller, much more nimble, and had the outriders scout corps on them. Fifty of them that could outdistance us like we were standing still, instead of at a full gallop.

They had fanged teeth, claws instead of hooves, and they tended to look at everything, and I mean everything—including their riders and the other members of the herd—as food.

They were also tamed, or at least as far as they could be, which was a bit of a relief.

That meant they only tried to take a bite out of their riders occasionally, and the riders spent as much time watching their mounts as they did anything else.

They were, though—I'd been assured—an absolute terror in battle as they liked to maim their enemies and move on, rather than kill them outright to ensure there was plenty of food.

So fuck with the varm, and expect them to sever hamstrings and so on, then go onto the next target, while their riders simply worked to keep their battle frenzy as much under control as was possible.

That meant that I was really looking forward to seeing what they were like in battle, which was cool. But behind us? There came the *real* cavalry.

Mammoths. Massive ones with long tusks, shorter hair than I expected from mammoths in our world, but beyond that, they looked like highly aggressive, short-haired elephants with serious goth tendencies.

Heh.

That was what I decided they were, from now on, as their hair was predominantly dark, and they were invariably grumpy and hostile to anything and everyone, barely deigning to acknowledge their riders, never mind anyone else.

Goth elephants.

They had a shitload of metal on their tusks and legs as well, thick bands that encircled their ankles with sharp spikes on the outside. And best of all?

Thanks to the trail song—something that I'd been informed by Daralen that was copied imperfectly by the Dark legionnaires—they weren't lumbering along slowly.

Oh no, they were keeping up with us at a full gallop!

Marn, the leader of the goth elephants, said that they could, with a little notice, rig them with even heavier armor, mainly leather, treated with special compounds to make them harder to burn.

The only thing they feared was fire apparently, but it took a seriously brave fucker to hold position with something that was flammable when a fucking goth elephant was running at them.

Even if a mage got one or two with fireballs, the result wasn't likely to be what they wanted, because for these creatures, "fear" translated into "stomp it into paste."

Anyone who hit them with fire was likely to be pounded into a pancake by the next one in line in outrage.

All in all, I was really enjoying my ride, especially when we crested the next hill, and I got to stare out across the plains.

The rolling sea of golden-green grass stretched out before us, broken only by the occasional stand of trees that dotted the landscape like islands. In the far distance, hazy blue mountains marked the horizon, their peaks lost in clouds.

"Goddamn, I love this," I muttered, before turning and looking over my shoulder. Oracle urged her own horse forward to join me at the crest, then plunged down the far side.

Her horse was skittish around mine, probably sensing the predatory nature of the massive legion war-bred mounts. Ilena had suggested that instead, as Oracle wasn't wearing heavy armor, she'd be better off with one of their more prized personal mounts.

She'd taken one look at the snow-white beautiful horse and had refused to ride one of the aggressive beasts, claiming—rightly, I had to admit—that her focus needed to be on protecting our child, not fighting her damn transportation.

It was nothing to do with the fact that she apparently fell in love with the damn thing, and was already doing damage to our supplies by constantly feeding it bloody apples.

"It's beautiful," she called, her eyes scanning the vast expanse. "How much farther to Gaij?"

"Two days at this pace," Saracen, the leader of the outriders called over, pulling alongside us. "We'll reach the foothills by nightfall, then follow the old imperial highway through the pass tomorrow."

I nodded, taking a long drink from my waterskin. The day was hot, but the breeze created by our movement kept it bearable. We'd left Sonra only a few hours ago. The larger contingent of refugees, freed slaves, and the remainder of our forces followed behind at their slower pace, slowed even further by the plodding speed of the bloody tent city.

"Any sign of trouble from the scouts?" I asked.

Saracen shook his head. "Nothing yet. The varm riders report the plains are clear all the way to the foothills. Though they did spot some smoke signals about ten miles east—probably nomad clans tracking our movement."

"Friendly?"

"Unknown. The nomads here shift allegiances quickly. They might be waiting to see if we're worth trading with or raiding. Generally, they want to keep on the right side of Sonra, though, so when they see us, they're more likely to talk than just attack."

"Let them come." Sehran swooped down to hover beside us, her wings beating steadily against the air. She'd been flying ahead, acting as our aerial scout. "A few desert raiders would make this journey less tedious."

I grinned up at her. "Getting bored already?"

"I've been promised succubai sisters and a tower full of mysteries," she replied with a theatrical pout. "Instead, I've spent the last few hours watching you bounce around on a horse."

"We'll be there soon enough," Oracle assured her. "And you'll have all the succubai company you could want."

"Speaking of which," I said. "What should we expect when we get there, Daralen, Saracen? You've both been to Gaij before, right?"

Daralen's expression darkened slightly. "I was stationed in Gaij for a year, dispatched from the legion I first trained in, to take up a position as their primus. I lasted four months before my party was ambushed and I was taken, much to my shame. My experience with it was limited, as the legion was forced from the surrounding area almost before I arrived, and it has been long since then. The tower is…not what it once was."

"I gathered that much from what Cleq said."

"It's more than just the damage," she explained as we began moving again, our mounts picking their way down the hillside. "The tower was never fully functional again after the cataclysm. The portions that survived are a city unto themselves—a vertical warren of chambers, workshops, and dwellings—but they're also empty. The succubai permit only limited access, and for a set period of time. Outstay your welcome and the golems remove you."

"But the succubai rule it?" Oracle asked.

"They do, but only for the tower," Daralen corrected carefully. "The nobles of the surrounding lands have been trying to force the succubai into what they see as their 'correct' positions as entertainers, courtesans, and worse for centuries.

"The tower remains technically independent, and yet a part of the city. Basically, they keep control of the tower but nothing else. To keep that, they must constantly maintain a watch to fight off anyone who tries to access its grounds by force."

Sehran's expression hardened. "So they're prisoners in all but name."

"More or less," Saracen agreed. "Though they've found ways to turn their position to advantage where possible. They're survivors. They also have a finger on the pulse of the city and a claw on the throat of every criminal. They've survived by making sure that all the criminals and nobility alike know that they're too weak to fight them off directly, but that they'd injure any attacker severely enough that the others would immediately stab them in the back.

"Then there's the imperial golems. There's few of them, and they're not seen very often, but when they're seen, people run," Saracen finished, gesturing widely. "The golems don't care who you are. If you're on tower grounds and there's an attack, the golems clear you out, be that by ordering you to leave, or stomping you flat and throwing what's left over the walls."

"Tell me about the walls," I called.

"Tall, and magical, they run in a circle around the tower, and look to be the original walls, with the section where the tower fell outward rebuilt. I've been told it looks different, like the main walls and the tower itself is made of marble and quartz, all gleaming, but worn away. The repaired areas have more like granite in them, but they're carefully maintained. Or so I've heard! They don't like anyone getting too close!"

I nodded my thanks, then pondered this as we rejoined the main column. Our force was spread out across the plains. The legion horse and aspirant corps that we'd brought were at the front, followed by the wagon train carrying our supplies, and the mammoth cavalry bringing up the rear. Overhead, Sehran returned to her scouting pattern, occasionally dropping low to speak with the varm riders ranging ahead of us.

"What about the laws?" I asked Daralen after a while, as we dropped to a walk to rest the mounts and we could finally carry on a normal conversation. "If they're independent but under pressure, how do they govern themselves?"

"The Mistress of Gaij is the official ruler," she replied. "Or she was, last I heard. She sits atop the succubai, and they run the tower. But as I said, they have very little say in the running of the city. In theory, they control everything within the tower and a small radius around it, as they set up most of the city and they provided shelter on a lot of occasions in the past. But the various factions moved the council out of the tower and into a building in the city to force the succubai to either accept that they had no control, or that they'd have to leave the tower to attend."

"And they can't do that, can they," Oracle growled. Clearly her protective instincts over Sehran came to the fore with the thought of her sisters being taken advantage of.

"No, the golems protect them as guests inside the tower's limits, and they'd travel a little—like, they'd probably run out to help one if they were attacked in their sight. But the succubai can't fully command them; they only have guest rights. That means that if the succubai leave the tower, they're never seen again, and the rest of the city knows that."

“So in theory they all work together, but in practice…” I shook my head.

“In practice, as we discussed before, the nobles have taken over the city that the succubai built. They claim to be working with them, but they spend most of their time scheming and fighting to gain more control. Mainly in the hope that they can support larger forces than their enemies, so that one day they can take the tower and the rest of the city.”

I snorted. “Fucking nobles. Same shit, different realm.”

“The succubai aren’t going to give up control willingly,” Oracle said. “Currently they might be trapped in the heart of the tower, but over the time they’ve spent there, they have amassed tremendous wealth, and they’re the mistresses of their own destiny. They were never imperial citizens, so they’re not going to just celebrate when we walk up to the front door, Jax. They’re going to fight us tooth and claw.”

“That’s why Sehran is going to be a trump card.” I shrugged. “Seeing her, they’re going to at least want to hear what she has to say, even if nothing else. As much as I’d rather do it with their approval, we’re taking that tower one way or the other. The golems will have to accept my bloodstone, won’t they?”

“In theory, yes,” Oracle said slowly. “But, Jax, if they have orders to fire on anyone who crosses a line we don’t know about, you could be dead before you get the chance to even start.”

“And that’s why we try to do a deal. But one way or another, the Tower of Gaij, and the city, are the center of this territory, and we need it.”

The next day and a half passed without incident. We made camp in the foothills that night, the massive bulk of the mammoths forming a natural barrier on the windward side of our position. The legion established a perimeter with practiced efficiency. By the time the sun had set, the camp was secured and meals were being prepared.

I sat with Oracle, Sehran, Saracen, and Daralen around one of the campfires, a map spread out between us that I compared to my internal, magical map.

“The highway passes through here.” Daralen traced a route through the hills with her finger. “It’s an old imperial road, so the stones, although buried, are still more or less intact. It’ll take us down into the valley where Gaij is located.”

“Any natural choke points we should worry about?” I asked, thinking of potential ambush sites.

“Just one—the Bridge of Sorrows.” She pointed to a narrow pass still high in the hills. “It spans a deep ravine about midway through the journey tomorrow. The bridge itself is sound, but it would be an ideal place for an ambush.”

“We’ll send the varm riders ahead to secure it,” I decided. “And keep the mammoths as a rear guard until we’re clear.”

Oracle leaned forward, studying the map. “What about the city itself? What’s the layout?”

Daralen sketched a rough circle on the map. “The tower stands at the center, and the city has grown out from it like ripples in a pond. The outermost ring is mostly markets and warehouses, then comes housing for the common folk, then the noble district closest to the tower itself.”

“Seems backward,” I commented. “Usually the rich want to be farthest from the rabble.”

"The tower provides protection," Daralen explained. "And access to the succubai. The closer you are, the more status you have."

"So everyone's competing to be near our objective," I mused. "That's going to complicate things."

"Not necessarily," Sehran countered. "If the nobles are already there, it just means we know where to find them."

I grinned. "Good point."

As the fire died down, I found myself staring up at the stars, Oracle nestled against me. The constellations here were different from those on Earth, or even those visible from Dravith. Everything felt slightly off, like a familiar song that I loved when someone sang a cover version.

"You're thinking too loudly," Oracle murmured against my chest.

"Sorry," I replied, kissing the top of her head. "Just wondering what we'll find tomorrow."

"Whatever it is, we'll handle it together."

I smiled into the darkness. "Always," I whispered, before closing my eyes and falling asleep.

The Bridge of Sorrows lived up to its name—a narrow stone span arching over a ravine so deep that its bottom was lost in shadow. The ancient imperial engineering remained intact somehow, the massive blocks fitted so perfectly that not even a knife blade could be inserted between them.

The ravine it crossed was an ancient fault line, a sharp, jagged crack that ran for miles in every direction, at the foot of a valley we were descending. Our path wound down the hillside in long switchbacks, giving us plenty of time to observe the bridge as we approached.

And what we saw confirmed the bridge's ominous name. It stood wreathed in flames and smoke.

We made it more than halfway down before the wind twisted to carry the smoke away from us, and we could finally clearly see the length of the bridge. We paused by the side of the road, me squinting to make out the details even with my incredible Perception, as Daralen checked through her eyeglass.

"Those are legion bodies—ours," Daralen growled, lowering it and urging her mount forward to meet our returning scouts.

I cursed, pushing up to ride alongside her as we picked up the pace.

It took another ten minutes, the horses kicking up great streams of pebbles and clouds of dust as we turned back upon ourselves time and time again, before we reached a point where one of the scouts joined us with a report.

The rider galloped up, then reined in sharply. His varm snapped irritably at his leg as he reported, but he barely seemed to notice as he casually freed a foot from his stirrups and kicked it in the side of the head.

"The caravan, my prince," he called, shaking his head. "According to the survivors, it was them."

"This was a caravan?" I exchanged glances with Oracle.

"Guildmaster Tevin," Daralen spat. "The only guildmaster who survived the freeing of the slaves. The outriders let him pass because…"

"He was a guildmaster and exempt or some such bullshit," I finished for her, annoyed. "I remember, but a fucking caravan did this? I was starting to think he must have changed direction. How did he get here so fast?"

"Who knows. He must have pushed hard, though. I was starting to think we were chasing a ghost." Daralen continued before pausing and glancing at the rider who took over.

"There were six outriders and two legionnaires. Only the legionnaires survived, thanks to what looks like their heavier armor and healing potions. As it is, they're unconscious, and the others were giving them more potions when I left to report to you."

"What could you tell?" Oracle asked the rider.

"Well, the bridge is ablaze. We'll need to give it a few hours to die down," the rider replied grimly. "From what we could see—because we can't get too close to the blaze—the advance riders tried to stop them for questioning as you ordered, my prince, but I'm guessing the guildmaster didn't feel like talking."

"Casualties?" Daralen's voice was clipped.

"As I said, all the horses and six outriders dead. Both legionnaires were alive when I set off, but it was a close thing. They were riddled with crossbow bolts. If I had to guess, a spell or a scroll trapped them in place while the guards fired. That anyone survived is a miracle. Four of the enemy dead that we can see. The rest scattered into the hills on horseback. They blocked the bridge with the wagons and set fire to them. They've been burning for a while now. I'm guessing Alkai's Flame for them to be still going and as hot as they are."

"What's—" I started to ask.

"A very hot burning concoction," Daralen replied grimly to me. "Lasts about twelve hours and costs around twenty gold per bag. You need to mix the contents, throw it, and run—and you run very, very fast." She studied the flames. "Judging from the condition of the wagons and the intensity, this happened at least eight hours ago."

"Motherfucker," I spat. "Daralen, I want that dickbag's head."

"Prince, do you want us to try to circle around?" the rider asked.

I considered it briefly, then shook my head. "No. We need to secure the bridge first. Form a perimeter just in case this is some sort of a trap, and let's get our people across. Oracle and I can cast spells to dispel the flames. Once we're over and know there's nothing else to this, we send enough men to get the job done."

"Kill or capture?" Daralen asked as calmly as she could, though fury at our murdered people simmered beneath her words.

"Both," I growled. "Catch him if you can. We need to know what he knows and why he's so desperate to reach Gaij. Then nail his balls to his forehead and kick him over the edge to the ravine."

"I'd rather be a little more personal," Daralen muttered, and I shrugged.

"Question them however you want. To be clear, I don't give two shits how you do it or how they die. If they're our enemies, then they'd do it and worse to us if they could. Just don't waste time and do anything that you might regret later."

As we approached the bridge, evidence of the fight became clear. Dark bloodstains marred the pale stone in dozens of places. Though hours had passed, the blood was still sticky enough to attract insects that rose in panicked clouds as we drew near. The bodies lay where they had fallen—all six of our dead too close to the flames to recover safely. The two survivors had dragged themselves off the end of the bridge before collapsing out of sight of the far side. The scattered bolts that lay around them made it clear they were under fire when they'd done so.

They lay motionless as Daralen crouched beside them, speaking in a voice too low to hear from where I stood. Despite the potions and spells used by the advance team, their blood loss and general condition meant they'd need more time to recover. Oracle swung down to help as well, while I stared at the far side, knowing that my insane Perception could be all the warning we'd get.

The enemies—caravan guards by their clothing—lay scattered about. The legionnaires and two outriders had all fallen within a small area, evidence of how suddenly they'd been ambushed.

The varm scout riders who had found them had established a defensive position at the bridge's foot. Their mounts prowled restlessly, nostrils flaring at the scent of blood.

"Spread out," Daralen ordered as the rest of our forces reached the bridge. "Scout the area and make sure there are no surprises!"

"Saracen?" I addressed the bearded man, who stared at the distant bodies on the bridge, tears streaking his cheeks.

"My prince," he acknowledged hoarsely, wiping his face with the back of his hand.

"I'm sorry for your loss," I said automatically. "You knew them?"

"There." He pointed to a figure sprawled in death, a crossbow bolt protruding vertically from its forehead. "That's my eldest son, Ethan."

"Oh fuck." I sighed. "I… I'm sorry." The words felt wholly inadequate, but they were all I had to offer.

I glanced Saracen over quickly. Soot and dried blood stained his clothing and hands. I'd mistaken his reluctance to approach the bodies as shock, but now I realized he'd already been there and had likely been driven back by the intense flames.

"We'll get him," I promised, gripping his shoulder once in support before nudging my horse forward.

"Sehran, can you see anything?" I asked through the bond.

"There are a dozen different tracks. It looks like bandits live somewhere close by or at least people who spend most of their time in the woods. I sense five life-forms large enough to be people watching us. Considering how spread out they are, I think we're best sending in the legion."

"Don't risk yourself," I agreed. *"If you approach any of them, you don't know if they still have poisoned crossbows or spells. Fall back and keep watch."*

"Will do," she whispered, clearly angry at losing more people in this senseless violence.

"They'll live, but they're going to take a few hours to recover enough to do more than cling to their saddles." Oracle climbed back up into her horse's saddle. "Jax, if this is like that Greek fire you showed me, water will only make it worse. I'll need a few minutes…"

"Okay, people," I announced. "Oracle and I are working on a spell to handle the fire. Once we cross to the far side and secure the area, I want a report on the tracks. Are they still reachable, or will they be at Gaij by now?"

After receiving affirmative responses, I dismounted, sat cross-legged on the ground, and closed my eyes.

"I'm thinking we use the base that turns the earth from the Environmental Cleanse spell, and we—" Oracle spoke through our bond, sharing mental images and half-formed theories.

I glimpsed weaves of air meant to smother and lift earth, while transport sections of the spell would move the earth from here across and—

"You know what?" I blinked, then rolled my shoulders. "Fuck this shit," I said definitively. "EVERYONE BACK!"

One look at my grim face sent people running.

"Oracle, can you…?" I sent her a mental image. My spell was refreshingly simple compared to her complex plan of transporting earth from this side of the bridge to smother the flames while drawing out the heat.

She understood immediately and snorted, shaking her head. "Now why the hell didn't I think of that?" She sighed, before using simple weaves of air to grab our people's bodies and drag them clear of the target area.

Once they were safe, I cracked my knuckles and began to cast.

The first spell was something I'd had in mind for a while but hadn't found a use for—not when compared to spells like Pyroclastic Blast. And although I liked the idea of Battlefield Displacement, one of my new spells, I knew from experience it would cost me dearly to cast and the more space I needed to transport, the more mana it'd cost.

The cheapest version cost a thousand mana to open the portal, and the cost climbed depending on how many people were moved, how far, and how fast. With a much larger manapool, it might be worth it—and I cursed as I realized I still hadn't used those damn points. I resolved to do so soon.

For now, though, there was no way to quickly transport everyone and their horses across the bridge.

So, being the highly intelligent, sensible, and careful man I am, I opted for a nice, simple "blast" spell.

It used the firebolt base, but with air as the main component. I added a pop of gravitational magic at the end to create outward force, then fired it off, all wrapped in a barely cohesive shell.

I felt Oracle making changes even as I unleashed the first version, tweaking it and adding layers of complexity. She suppressed certain elements, enhanced others, and rewrote the spell into a more polished version than my "spit and sawdust" original.

That's why the first version, which hit the rearmost caravan's axle, merely shattered it and nudged it a few inches sideways. The second impact, however…

My version cost thirty-five mana per casting; Oracle's improved version cost fifty. Not an enormous difference, and with our mana potions and pool of over two thousand, we could fire continuously.

Once Oracle and I hit our stride, it was like operating a grenade launcher. Each improved spell streaked through the air for about a second before impact, then exploded, hurling the target away from the point of contact.

We coordinated to push sideways rather than straight ahead. Within ten seconds, we'd shoved the now-shattered, frequently detonating, and still merrily burning mass to the left of the bridge.

Oracle created a funnel of air that pulled up and over the side, aiming toward the gorge and the river far below, while I fired dozens of shots at the mass.

A minute later, both the bridge and the river below were ablaze, with fragments of burning wreckage shooting in all directions. I was starting to grin like a fool, thoroughly enjoying myself, when Sehran added an Explosive Compression spell.

That final push shoved the last remaining "intact" caravan aside, leaving it tilted ominously over the edge of the bridge's crenellations.

Oracle unleashed the last spell—a supercharged air blast that tipped it out and over. We watched as it fell, crashing into a rocky outcropping and bursting into fragments that cartwheeled free, still flaming, until they hit the rocks and river far below.

Within seconds, parts bobbed to the surface, almost too distant to see clearly already in that frantic frothy river, yet still burning. I couldn't help but sigh, feeling a slight drop in my stress levels as the wreckage floated merrily away—right until Daralen spoke.

"You're aware, my prince, that the gorge leads somewhere? And that the flaming wreckage is being spread along that path, still burning?"

"Crap," I muttered, suddenly seeing things from a different perspective as I wondered what lay downriver.

"The river travels below the earth soon," Saracen said softly, stepping up to my shoulder. "There is a community of dark kobolds that make their home in the depths there, known for assaulting travelers…"

"Oh, well, that's okay then!" I cheered right up.

"So this will likely drive them out to raid the area, should their home burn. And they will view this as an attack, that they will go looking for revenge," he finished.

"And we're back to crap," I muttered, looking at the now well-spread but barely diminished material still burning as it bobbed and spun along.

Oracle was already using threads of air to pluck more flames free and pile them against the side of the bridge as I sighed and sank back down to begin meditation.

Half an hour later, the bridge was cleared, and judged both sturdy enough and clear on the far side, that we could cross.

When we finally made it, it was to find that yes, it was a spot beloved of the local banditry, and there were literally hundreds of tracks on the far side; no, it appeared that the merchant guildmaster wasn't one of their friends, and again yes, he'd managed to piss them off, as he apparently used more of his limited supply of poisoned arrows and crossbow bolts to take at least half the gang down.

Then what was left of the gang had closed on him, and he'd used what was hopefully his last spell.

The Vinefield was an AOE spell that created grasping vines in a set location. They then crushed the bones of anyone caught in its range, which had further endeared him to the bandits.

When Saracen rode back with Daralen by his side, there was a battered, badly injured bandit who was sweating profusely atop a mount between them.

He looked like shit, was literally bleeding to death, and by the smell had recently shit himself and was incapable of cleaning himself at this point.

I hit him with a Scour on general principles, and he sighed as Oracle did the same with a Heal.

"Oh, thankee, lord!" He smiled wanly. "Ah do be just tellin' yer men 'ere ah wus just rydin' past, on me way home, iffin' yer get me?"

"He claims not to be a bandit, and he was merely lost, trapped between the flames and the bandits, and is a simple farmer," Daralen informed me, offering me what appeared to be his sword.

I took it and looked it over. It was well maintained, and obviously was an expensive one, judging from the damascene patterning of the blade.

"A fam'ly ere'loom!" he said quickly. "Passed from ma gran'daddy te ma daddy, an' then te me, gods rest 'is soul!"

"Whose?" I asked conversationally.

"Eh?"

"You said 'gods rest *his* soul,'" I pointed out.

"Aye?"

"Not 'their.' 'His.'" I smiled again. "Listen, friend, we're passing through. We need to get to the city of Gaij, and frankly, I don't have the time to fuck about, so a quick few questions and we'll be on our way."

"M'kay?" He nodded, trying to hide his smile, thinking he was getting away with it.

"First of all, the merchant who passed through here, is he alive?"

"Fer now." His face darkened in anger before he could stop it. "Ah mean—"

"That's fine. Is he heading to Gaij still?"

"Aye, 'e were."

"Are you a good imperial citizen?" I asked.

"Oh, aye." He nodded, clearly having utterly no concern who I was beyond that there was a legionnaire on one side of him, and outrider on the other, and a nutter in blood-red armor watching him.

"Glad to hear it. Only a few last things and then we can get on. So, the Prince of the Empire is coming, and we need to make sure the path is clear. As such, you'll need to swear the imperial oath…you know, the one that you already *must* have sworn as a good imperial citizen. To make things a little easier, and because there's not much time, I'll accept that you can just swear to obey Prince Jax of the empire and those he places above you, etc., etc., if he comes before you and declares himself as the prince. Good enough?"

"Uh…" He started, until Oracle spoke up.

"But the prince said that anyone who wasn't an imperial citizen was to be killed." She lied. "How do we know he is?"

"Oh, I think I can tell the difference between an honest man who's fallen on hard times and a bandit," I said with a fake and very wide smile. "So what do you say, friend? Are you happy to swear the oath, or do we chop your head off here and now as the enemy?"

"Ah'll swear!" he promised frantically.

"Excellent. The first oath please, Oracle, the one that we offered to Marteen and Zyenna and their friends in the cave."

Oracle sighed, shaking her head while pretending not to agree, and secretly sending me amusement through the bond.

Ten seconds later, as he shuddered over the oath settling into him, I spoke up again.

"Excellent. Well, we're nearly done here now, so, just to make things clear. *I* am Prince Jax of the Empire, and I command you to speak the truth to me and those present here now. You are to obey their orders as if they came from me, do you understand?"

"Yes!" he cried out, eyes bulging.

"Great. Are you a bandit?"

"Yes!" he blurted, terror on his face as I nodded.

"Now we're getting somewhere. So, Daralen, question him please. Then execute him as a self-professed bandit. Everyone else, let's move on!"

And that was that. Half an hour later, Daralen caught up to me and drew in close, passing word that yes, the bandit and his friends had been heading after the last two survivors of the caravan, and that one of them was Tevin, the guildmaster, the other apparently being his chief bodyguard.

They'd escaped, but only just, and were last seen riding hard for Gaij aboard two more Fenris models, which was apparently at least half of how they'd managed to keep ahead of the others this long, though whether they'd make it was uncertain.

Especially considering there were still at least one more group of bandits between here and there, and they were down to two men on horseback without equipment.

We picked up the pace, knowing that the bandit couldn't have lied to Daralen. I deliberately didn't ask what had happened to him, because frankly I didn't care.

The only reason they'd not attacked me and my party was because they'd already been busy and they'd have to have been suicidal to do it.

As such, I viewed it as a favor to society.

We continued to ride hard, settling into a cold camp only after it became too dangerous to the mounts to keep riding in the dark. We were off again at first light.

Again, there were the occasional signs of banditry—tracks, Sehran passing word that life signs were strong in the bushes to either side of the trail…that kind of thing—but considering we were five hundred plus professional killers in full armor, it was unsurprisingly decided by the watchers to fuck right off and live another day instead of attacking.

I contemplated attacking them instead, sending the legion out to sweep through the forest, but Sehran and Daralen convinced me against it. First, Daralen pointed out that we'd invariably lose legionnaires, because if they had crossbows, at close range they'd punch through armor, and we didn't know for sure these were bandits, though it was likely.

Then Sehran pointed out that her sisters, after so long in the tower, might be thankful for a brief trip out, and that she already knew of several legionnaires who had approached her with serious questions about the bonds involved with succubai.

Yes, some of them had been unable to keep their eyeballs from tumbling down her cleavage, but most had been more interested in the tactical advantage it gave, rather than just company in their bedrolls.

As such, better to leave them for now, and then, if there was a deal to be made with the succubai, maybe a "hunting trip" would be an option.

By midday, we were out of the hills entirely and descending into a long, broad valley. And there, rising from the plains in the distance, was our first clear glimpse of Gaij; the hills, valleys, and occasional mist or heavy rainclouds had conspired to shield the reality from me until now.

Even with all of that, it was clear that the way that my own tower had a spell woven into the very stone of the tower to hide its view from more than about ten miles out, this had something similar, but less effective.

I was guessing it was because of the damage the tower had sustained. But either way, now that I was a lot closer, I could finally see it in all its "glory."

"Holy shit," I breathed, pulling my mount to a halt.

The Tower of Gaij was both magnificent and terrible—a vast stump of what had once been an impossibly tall structure. Even with two-thirds of its height gone, it still dominated the landscape, rising at least half a mile into the sky.

Like our own tower, its base was easily half a mile across, a massive circular foundation that seemed to grow directly from the bedrock, that conspired to make it less a tower, and more a cube, when seen from this distance.

The surface was a patchwork of original imperial architecture, grown in place, and makeshift repairs, giving it the appearance of a colossal, wounded creature that had been badly stitched back together. Scaffolding clung to its sides in places, and massive buttresses had been constructed to support sections that might otherwise have collapsed.

Around the tower, the city of Gaij spread outward in concentric rings, just as Daralen had described. The buildings nearest the tower were grand, with tiled roofs and stone walls. As distance from the tower increased, the structures became progressively more modest, until the outermost ring was little more than a sprawling market of tents, temporary stalls, and warehouses, and most of them were on the outside of a second, apparently the "main" wall.

"It's…not what I expected," Oracle admitted.

"It's better than I feared," Sehran countered, having landed recently. The joy of so much flight had worn off after such hard days, and she was riding one of the spare horses beside us. Her eyes were fixed on the tower with an expression I couldn't quite read. "At least it's still standing."

"Home again." Daralen sighed. "When last I was here seems forever ago, and even then, the succubai were barely willing to speak to us."

As we drew closer, more details became visible. The tower's surface was dotted with windows, balconies, and even the occasional external staircases—some original, others clearly added later. Massive openings punctuated its sides at irregular intervals, likely where entire sections had collapsed and been converted into open-air areas; one looked like a market, another a massive restaurant area.

The most striking feature was the massive rent that ran almost the entire height of the structure on its eastern face—a jagged wound that had been partially filled in with newer construction, creating a bizarre scar.

"What happened there?" I pointed to the rent.

"That's where it broke," Daralen replied grimly. "When the cataclysm hit, the upper portions sheared away along that line and fell eastward. What you're seeing is the internal structure exposed, then built back into over the centuries."

The weirdest part? The "original" sections of the tower were gleaming and apparently pretty much pristine, or so they looked at this distance. The sections where it had been apparently fixed by hand were clearly not covered by the tower's self-maintenance capabilities.

As we approached the city outskirts, I could see activity at the gates. Word of our approach had preceded us. Mainly, if I had to guess, because despite pushing damn hard, we'd not caught that fleeing bastard. He'd been visible in the distance, riding into the gate, less than an hour ahead of us.

"They're mobilizing the city guard," Daralen observed, squinting at the walls. "Not a full alert, but definitely a show of force."

"Good." I straightened in my saddle. "I'd hate for them to underestimate us."

Oracle gave me a sidelong glance. "Are we going with diplomacy first or intimidation?"

"Why choose?" I growled. "We'll be exceedingly polite while looking absolutely capable of tearing down their walls."

"The more traditional imperial approach, then." Daralen sounded pleased. "If that's how this visit goes, then I'll not complain. The nobles here were responsible for bringing the Dark Legion in and our defeat."

"Yeah, I think there's going to be a lot of debts paid by our visit here." I shrugged.

Daralen signaled, and our formation tightened. The legion horses formed up around and behind us, the legion aspirants behind them with the varm riders flanking and the mammoth cavalry bringing up the rear in a display that even I had to admit was impressive as hell.

"Forward," I commanded, and our massed ranks of madness resumed its advance toward Gaij.

"My prince, if you need to make an impression?" Saracen said in a low voice, still clearly depressed over the loss of his son, but determined to do his duty, despite the body that we carried strapped to its horse at the rear of the party. "Raise your right hand, fist clenched, and then drop it, moving it to the right, like this." He showed me, though holding it close to his chest where the goth elephants and their riders couldn't see it.

"It's trained into the mammoths, and they'll stand on their back legs, trumpet, and then come down as one."

"I like it." I grinned at him. "Thank you."

As soon as I'd said that, he passed orders, having the mammoths spread out to either side as if in a battle line. Regardless of anything else, it was fucking impressive.

As we drew closer, I could make out more details of the city's defenses. The walls were a hodgepodge of imperial remnants that were clear back around the tower's base and high over most of the nearby buildings, and newer construction, suggesting multiple expansions and repairs over the centuries. Guards lined the battlements, their armor catching the afternoon sun, as they stood, looking ready to attack.

But as much as I knew I should be watching the fuckers, I kept finding my eyes drawn back to the tower itself, looming over everything like a wounded giant. Even damaged as it was, it radiated power.

"Look," Oracle said softly, pointing upward.

Near the top of the tower, something was moving. At first, I thought it might be birds, but as I watched, I realized they were too large and moving too purposefully. Flying humanoids—at least a dozen of them—were circling the upper reaches of the structure.

"Succubai," Sehran confirmed, her eyes gleaming. "They're watching us."

"Good," I replied. "Let them see exactly who's come calling."

The city gates loomed ahead, massive wooden things reinforced with iron. They remained open, but a line of guards stood across the entrance, pikes at the ready.

I urged my mount forward. Oracle and Daralen flanked me; Sehran stayed just behind me, her magic suppressing her more demonic traits and a cloak serving to hide her face. Behind us, two hundred of the Imperial Legion, two hundred and fifty aspirants, and fifty of Sonra's finest followed, a force that could quite possibly take the damn city if it had to.

But that wasn't my goal. Honest.

"Move aside, guardsman," Daralen barked.

"What's your purpose for visiting the city?" a tall, well-muscled, and obviously senior guardsman asked loudly. His companions formed up, ready to try to repel us, even though that was clearly not their intention. After all, if they'd not wanted us to come in, the first step would have been to close the fucking gates.

No, this was theatre, pure and simple, and it was designed to get something from us. The problem was, we didn't know what.

Was it a bribe? Was it to try to demean us, to force a confrontation? To just delay us while the guildmaster vanished into the city?

I didn't know, and it fucking grated.

"I warn you," Daralen ground out. "You won't like how this ends. You know us. You can see the armor—we're the Imperial Legion. This is imperial territory and the city council will hear of this, unless you get your pretty little guards out of the way by the time I count to three."

"I'm sorry," he replied. "You *look* like imperial legionnaires. But I don't know you, and another traveler reported bandits dressed as legionnaires were chasing him. So, I'll ask again, who are you, and what's your business here?"

"I am Prince Jax Amon." We halted before the guards, my voice carrying across the suddenly silent gateway. "Heir to the Eternal Throne, Champion of

Jenae, and Godslayer, twice over," I announced, kneeing my mount forward. As I started to move, so did the others.

"I'm entering a city that's in the middle of imperial territory, built around an imperial artifact, and chasing a suspected slaver. I have the right, the authority, and the strength to pull this pathetic wall down atop you all, and then march into the city regardless. So I'll ask you this, guardsman—who?"

"Who?" he repeated, blinking and confused, suddenly looking a lot less sanguine as the guards on either side of him shifted uncomfortably.

"Who told you we were coming? Who claimed we were bandits after a bridge was deliberately set aflame and left to spread burning wreckage to the river, just to stop our passage? *Who* told you this, *where* are they, and who the *fuck* are *you* to fucking bar *my* path, guardsman?"

I growled, feeling it as Oracle did something and our mana bar dropped slightly. Sehran, behind me, started to sing…a low, threatening sound that made the guard back up in response.

"My prince, perhaps our heavies might open the gate for you?" Saracen asked from behind me, and I smiled and nodded, raising my hand as he'd suggested.

I held my fist clenched in the air as the guard stammered out a reply that was wordy as all hell and answered precisely dick of my questions. Then I lowered my hand, sweeping it to the side, as I'd been told, and was almost blasted from my feet as the mammoths in sight reared up on their hind legs, pawed at the air, and let loose a trumpet blast fit to demolish the bloody wall. Or so it felt.

"Heavies!" he barked. "Clear our prince's path!"

"Ah, I'm sorry." The guard tried again. "But you can't…"

He was brave, I had to give him that, and even standing at the front, directly before us, he stood his ground, despite the sudden shudder that could be felt through the earth as the goth elephants started forward.

They marched on either side of me. The gate was wide enough to permit multiple wagons to pass at a time, and fucking stupidly, as they narrowed into a line two abreast, nobody rushed to bar it shut.

Unfortunately for him, directly behind him, his men had decided that discretion was the better part of valor, and had started quietly melting away as the behemoths stomped closer.

When one member of the second row of guards saw that his companions were hurrying back, he panicked and tried to follow, dashing after them, and catching the unreasonably long, twelve-foot pike as he tried to maneuver it.

He tripped and it fell from his hands, crashing into one of the few remaining guards who had stood still in the front row and nearly knocked him out, as unexpected as it was. Suddenly, they, and the guard captain, realized that the rest of their colleagues had remembered urgent appointments elsewhere.

"Stop!" the guard barked desperately. Then, as he spun back, he saw the mammoth that was only feet away, and he yelled in panic, turning and starting to run.

The first of the great beasts to reach the gate didn't bother to slow, despite the five or so guards who had finally come to their senses and were trying to push the gate closed. Instead, it ducked its head, drove its tusks into the gate, and smashed it backward, half ripping the gate from the mounting, before storming through.

The trunk that caught the guard captain in passing was gentle—more or less—but it was also inexorable, and *far* stronger than he was.

He was picked up, carried through the gate at the urging of the mounted rider who barely managed to duck his head to clear the top, and then the captain was tossed aside.

As with all cities where a lot of animals were the main mode of transport, there were significant piles of…evidence…left of their passing. To prevent the roads becoming impassable through it, most cities employed people whose job it was to clear and pile this evidence to one side, before carting it out early in the morning or late at night, to the fields.

Gaij was no exception, and the pile of stinking horse, oxen, and fuck-knows-what shit that steamed silently to one side of the gate, was, at least, a nice soft place for the captain to be thrown.

"I told you you'd regret it," Daralen called down, as we rode past the flailing and cursing guard captain, before continuing into the city.

CHARACTER SHEET

<table>
<tr><td colspan="5">Name: Jax Amon</td></tr>
<tr><td colspan="5">Title: Godslayer</td></tr>
<tr><td colspan="3">Class: Mage Imperator (Fire Focus)</td><td colspan="2">Renown: Imperial Scion, Prince of Dravith, Master of Himnel and Narkolt, Godslayer, Mage Imperator</td></tr>
<tr><td colspan="3">Level: 52</td><td colspan="2">Progress: 417,882/13,000,000</td></tr>
<tr><td colspan="3">Patron: Jenae, Goddess of Fire and Exploration</td><td colspan="2">Points to Distribute: 64
Meridian Points to Invest: 1</td></tr>
<tr><th>Stat</th><th>Current points</th><th>Description</th><th>Effect</th><th>Progress to next level</th></tr>
<tr><td>Agility</td><td>100</td><td>Governs dodge and movement</td><td>+1000% maximum movement speed and reflexes. Gained Temporal Fluidity</td><td>N/A</td></tr>
<tr><td>Charisma</td><td>61 (56)</td><td>Governs likely success to charm, seduce, or threaten</td><td>+51% success chance in interactions with other beings</td><td>51/100</td></tr>
<tr><td>Constitution</td><td>125 (123)</td><td>Governs health and health regeneration</td><td>2460 health, regen 160 points per 600 seconds (each point invested now worth 20 health) Gained: Genetic Storage</td><td>N/A</td></tr>
<tr><td>Dexterity</td><td>100</td><td>Governs ability with weapons and crafting success</td><td>+100% to weapon proficiency, +100% to the chances of crafting success Gained: Master Craftsman's Touch</td><td>N/A</td></tr>
<tr><td>Endurance</td><td>73 (670)</td><td>Governs stamina and stamina regeneration</td><td>2190 stamina, regen 53 points per 30 seconds (each point invested now worth 30 stamina)</td><td>89/100</td></tr>
<tr><td>Intelligence</td><td>206</td><td>Governs base mana and number of</td><td>2260 mana, spell capacity: 102 (100 + 2,</td><td>N/A
.</td></tr>
</table>

		spells able to be learned	+200 mana from items) Gained: Hyper Cognition & Mana Manipulation	
Luck	79	Governs overall chance of bonuses	+69% chance of a favorable outcome	92/100
Perception	110 (100)	Governs ranged damage and chance to spot traps or hidden items	+100% ranged damage, +100% chance to spot traps or hidden items.	N/A
Strength	90 (87)	Governs damage with melee weapons and carrying capacity	+90 damage with melee weapons, +90% maximum carrying capacity	88/100
Wisdom	105 (95)	Governs mana regeneration and memory	+1400% mana recovery, 16 points per minute. Gained: Mana Manipulation	N/A

CHAPTER TWELVE

We rode into Gaij like we owned the place…which, after all, if I had any say in the matter, we soon fucking would.

The stunned faces of the citizens as half of the mammoth cavalry pushed through first, clearing a path wide enough for the rest of us, were almost comical. A mix of terror and awe played across their expressions.

Add to that, most people had only ever seen a handful of imperial legionnaires in their lives, and I was willing to bet that many of them would have been in, well, less than great condition when they saw them.

Here we were, all fully armed and armored, locked, loaded, and ready to fuck shit up.

The streets nearest the gate were packed, a churning mass of humanity and other races that parted in front of us like water before the prow of a ship. Market stalls lined both sides, their colorful awnings flapping in the breeze; the scent of spices, roasting meat, and the ever-present stink of too many bodies in too small a space filled the air.

More than anything else, though, the hairs on the back of my neck stood on end at both the thought of how many people surrounded us on all sides, kids running underfoot and hoof, and just how easy it'd be to sit in one of the nearby windows with a drawn bow.

This place was an assassin's wet dream, and riding as we were? We'd set ourselves up as even easier targets. I was probably fine in my heavy armor, as were the legionnaires, but Oracle and Sehran? I felt her agreement as the thought occurred to me, and the shield she cast over the pair of them was powerful enough to slightly warp the air, if you knew what you were looking for.

I let loose a slight sigh of relief and checked my potions. We still had plenty, but when I hit halfway down my capacity, I was popping one, just in case.

"Eyes up," Daralen murmured as we passed deeper into the first ring. "Notice the buildings?"

I followed her gaze and spotted what she meant. Although most of the structures were typical fare—timber frames with plaster walls, thatched or tiled roofs—every twenty paces or so stood something distinctly imperial. Old mana lamps, their crystals long since burned out or stolen, adorned some corners. Doorways carved with the imperial crest decorated taverns and shops, as they'd clearly stripped the fallen and shattered sections of the tower to build the city.

"They built on the bones of the past," Oracle observed.

"They always do." I kept my voice low. "Fuck knows back home that what's left of Hadrian's Wall is almost entirely in farmers' villages now."

The streets grew slightly less crowded as we moved inward, the homes of the poor and the market district giving way to more permanent buildings.

Here, the city's wealth began to show itself. Shops displayed enchanted equipment behind glass windows, and guards stood by them, glaring at anyone who came close.

Hell, the glass was a rarity in itself. Most places I'd been on Dravith had wooden shutters, rather than actual glass.

We passed a jeweler's window that featured a necklace shimmering with an inner light that couldn't possibly be natural. I snorted at the instinctual thought I should get it for Oracle, considering I knew that unless it came with an actual bonus to something that mattered, like a stat or her spellcasting, she'd not be interested in the same way that my exes would have been with "oooh, sparkly."

A weaponsmith displayed a sword that hung suspended in midair, slowly rotating to catch the light through some magic.

"Magic is rare, but not as rare as some places," Sehran noted from beneath her hood. She'd pulled her cloak tight around herself, hiding her wings and more demonic features. "I can feel it much more here."

"The tower," Oracle said simply. "Unlike ours, even before the fall, it was old, and would have been filled with artifacts. I bet there was a long time when all people did was dig and raid the ruins."

I nodded, keeping my eyes moving, watching everything and everyone. The crowd observed us warily, some ducking into doorways as we passed, others boldly staring. A few children ran alongside us until their parents snatched them back.

"You think they've figured out who we are yet?" I asked Daralen as she moved in close, her shield held ready and her head constantly on a swivel.

"They know what we are," she replied distractedly, not looking over. "The legion armor is unmistakable. As for who you are specifically? Hard to say. Depends if word has travelled this far yet. The notifications will have made it clear you're on the continent, so…"

We reached a broad thoroughfare that carved straight through the city, leading directly toward the inner wall and the tower beyond it. Unlike the meandering, organic growth of the outer districts, this was clearly planned—a road that had survived the centuries.

"The primary thoroughfare," Daralen supplied. "The main approach to the tower, mostly reserved for the nobility and the rich."

"Well, isn't that convenient?" I grinned. "Since I'm the heir to the imperial throne and all."

As we continued down the road, the buildings grew more impressive—three and four stories tall, many with stone facades and proper tile roofs.

Some showed signs of having once been grand structures that had slowly decayed over centuries, with newer, cheaper additions grafted onto ancient imperial stonework.

The people here were becoming notably better dressed, their clothes finer, their bearing more confident and with jewelry on display that would have been snatched in the outer city in a heartbeat.

There was wariness in their eyes as they watched our procession, and I noted more than a few guards standing at attention outside what appeared to be noble homes.

"Local aristocracy," Daralen said, following my gaze. "Minor nobles mostly, working for the handful of families who control the city."

"How many major players?" I asked.

"Four, maybe five houses of any significance," she replied. "Though I couldn't tell you who. While my legion was the Legion of the Tower of Gaij, we were—" She shook her head and changed what she was about to say. "The legion was banned from the city years ago, and even then, we were constantly on the move, trying to hold the area. When we lost our encampment to the Dark Legion of Nimon and the nobility's scheming, that marked the end of our knowledge of the city. Now, with the old nobility returning from Earth, I have no clue who'd be rising and falling, as houses."

"Well, we'll address that as well." I growled, making a mental note to fuck some of the nobility up as an example.

We were now close enough to the inner wall to get a proper look at it. Unlike the outer city wall, which was a patchwork of original imperial construction and centuries of repairs, the inner wall was pure imperial architecture—gleaming white stone that seemed to shimmer slightly in the afternoon sun.

It stood at least sixty feet high, a smooth, unbroken circle from what we'd seen so far, surrounding the tower. No visible mortar lines, no obvious joints—a continuous band of stone that had been grown rather than built, just like the tower had been originally.

I switched my gaze from the silent and apparently unmanned wall to the massive edifice beyond it. The tower loomed, impossibly tall, even in its truncated state.

"The wall is active," Oracle said suddenly, her voice tight with concentration. "I can feel some kind of defensive enchantments, not just the usual maintenance ones that we had back home. They're active and waiting."

"Waiting for what?" I asked.

"Probably for someone to try something stupid, I'd imagine," Sehran whispered. "You know you want to."

I shot her a grin, and she winked at me from inside her hood. She rode half hunched over, a great big cloak over her that made her look like she was deformed; her magic reducing instead of removing her wings meant that she hunched forward, and she was apparently leaning into that.

As we approached the gate in the inner wall, I could see that we weren't the only ones with an interest in the tower today. Three distinct groups had formed a tense standoff before the massive gate.

To the left, perhaps two hundred soldiers in black armor stood in rigid formation—the Dark Legion. Their armor was a twisted mockery of imperial designs, with spikes and dozens of them having added grotesque faces worked into the metal. Each bore the symbol of Nimon on their breastplates, and had highlights that ranged from bronze to gold, depending on their rank.

On the far side, a larger force of city guards and what appeared to be noble household troops formed a ragged line between the gates themselves and the other two parties. Their armor was a mismatched collection of styles and qualities, but they had numbers on their side, if fuck all else…three or four hundred, at least.

And directly opposite the Dark Legion and before the guards, was a smaller group that made the hairs on the back of my neck stand up. About a hundred men in modern tactical gear, the sunlight glinting off their assault rifles.

They'd arranged themselves in a defensive perimeter, their weapons pointed outward. I recognized their insignia immediately from the arena when I'd been thrown through to this realm, and I guessed at the name—House Malakai.

All three groups turned to watch as we approached, the tension in the air thick enough to cut with a knife.

"Well, shit." I sighed. "Looks like we're late to the party."

"What's the play, my prince?" Daralen's hand rested casually on her sword hilt.

"We make our presence known," I replied, urging my mount forward. "Keep it loose, but be ready. I want to talk before we fight."

Our force reorganized smoothly, the legion horses forming a half circle behind us, the varm riders ranging to the sides, and the mammoth cavalry creating an imposing wall at our back. I rode forward with Saracen and Daralen flanking me, Oracle and Sehran staying carefully positioned within the protective bubble of the legion.

As we came to a halt, a brief silence fell over the gathered forces. Then, predictably, everyone started to shout at once.

A Dark Legion commander stepped forward, his face concealed behind an ornate helm shaped like a snarling beast. "The tower is claimed by Lord Nimon! All who approach do so under pain of death!"

From the city forces, a fat man in expensive but ill-fitting armor pushed to the front. "Nonsense! The tower and all within the city limits belong to the Council of Gaij by right of seven centuries of stewardship! You are all intruders, and have no standing!"

And from the Earth contingent, a cold voice: "The tower belongs to the empire, and we are the nobility of the empire, the only *true* nobility present. Stand aside, pretenders."

I recognized Malakai immediately, remembering him standing with my asshat of a father in a booth and sneering as they gambled, placing bets on me and the others, wagering fucking vineyards and more over life-and-death struggles that went on below them.

He looked tired and furious, instead of languid and sneering, uncaring and unbothered as the sons and daughters of the "great houses" bled and died for their amusement below.

But his eyes—his eyes were the same. Cold, calculating, and utterly pitiless.

I let them bicker for a moment, then raised my hand, clenched my fist, where I hoped the mammoths and their riders could see, then dropped it, dragging it to the right in a smoothing gesture again.

The sound that erupted from the mammoths as they reared up was like thunder, drawing all eyes to me, before they came crashing down almost as one.

"I am Prince Jax Amon," I announced, my voice carrying across the suddenly silent gathering. "Confirmed Heir to the Imperial Throne, Champion of the Goddess Jenae, and Godslayer twice over. By right of imperial blood and the mandate of the original pantheon, I claim the Tower of Gaij and all imperial territories surrounding it."

I knew the realm wouldn't respond to me—I wasn't in the control center or anything like it, after all—but the point was made.

Malakai's face contorted with rage. "You! Sanguis's bastard upstart! You have no right—"

"I have every right." I cut him off. "My claim has been recognized by the gods themselves, and my authority confirmed by conquering the continent of Dravith. The succession is underway, and the empire rises again."

The Dark Legion commander laughed, a hollow sound from within his helm. "The gods? You mean the weak pretenders who Nimon cast down? Their blessing means nothing! Only the Dark One's will matters here, and he declared you apostate!"

"How did that work out for him when I killed him?" I asked conversationally. "I mean, shit, I use his avatar's head as a fucking goblet. Want to see it? I had it specially made."

That shut him up, though I could feel the ripple of outrage and shock that went through his troops. Most of them probably didn't believe I'd defeated Nimon in personal combat—not that death of their avatars was particularly permanent for gods around here.

The loss of a fragment of their divinity had to be fucking painful, though, and I still needed to trade the fragment I'd recovered from Illoth to Tamat yet.

Dammit. I made a mental note to speak to Jenae and possibly Sint about it first though, because let's face it, the Goddess of Assassins and Dark Deeds was named that for a fucking reason. Those two I trusted. Her? Not so much

The chubby—and apparently local—noble cleared his throat. "Regardless of these…religious disputes…the fact remains that the city of Gaij has been administered by the council for generations. Any claims must be adjudicated through proper channels."

"And those would be?" Oracle asked coolly.

"The council itself, of course," the man replied, as if speaking to a child.

Daralen snorted. "Convenient."

I studied the gate behind them. It remained firmly sealed, with no sign of the succubai we'd seen circling the tower earlier. They were watching, certainly, but clearly had no intention of involving themselves in this mess.

Smart.

If they weren't here and neither were the golems, then I couldn't present my bloodstone and command them, and neither could the others.

"I declare you apostate and formally chal—" the Dark legionnaire commander started to say, and I cut him off, speaking quickly.

"Consider your words carefully, asshole," I called. "I gutted Nimon's avatar, a creation of your supposedly all-powerful god, in single fucking combat. Three days ago, I gutted Illoth and banished her from all territories claimed by me. Now think about that, and just how likely I am to break a fucking sweat in carving my way through you all.

"I know what your elites, and your fodder, are truly like to fight. I've faced them. In their fucking *hundreds*. By my oath, I have slaughtered hundreds of Dark legionnaires, and it took the personal intervention of Nimon Himself to stop me carving my way through an entire legion of yours…*alone.*"

The touch of mana that I felt Oracle infuse my words with made them ring out. The fact that I was still standing, that no ill effect came about and that Nimon, dark dick that he was, remained silent, despite the feeling of a sudden oppressive presence, made it clear I was telling the truth.

"Think about your words, and then ask yourself…are you feeling lucky?" I smiled inside my helm, not stupid enough to not wear it here, where at least several hundred people were willing to try to kill me if they thought they stood a real chance of success. "Because you better be fucking lucky, or a better, more dangerous fighter than the god you serve if you want to finish that fucking sentence." My words hung in the air.

"This is getting us nowhere," another of the nobles cried out finally, even as more troops jingled into sight. "We all have claims, and none of us is willing simply walk away. I propose a parley—neutral ground, representatives from each faction, tonight."

To my mild surprise, a murmur of tentative agreement went through the gathered forces. Even Malakai seemed to consider it, though his expression suggested he was calculating the odds of simply shooting me where I stood.

The chubby noble stepped forward again. "As a member of the council, I can offer a neutral location for such discussions. The Grand Hall in the noble district would be suitable, and I can ensure fair treatment for all parties."

"And you are?" I asked.

He drew himself up importantly. "Lord Havelton, Third Seat of the Council of Gaij, Master of Commerce and Taxation."

Of *course* he was. Always follow the money.

"Very well, Lord Havelton," I said. "We accept your offer of a neutral location, provided everyone moves back from the entrances here while we talk. *But…*we'll need accommodations for my forces in the meantime. Or, of course, you can just save us all some time and get the hell out of my way."

Havelton looked as if he'd swallowed something sour, clearly doing mental calculations of how many troops we had and where to put them. "There is…the old Varnen estate. It has fallen into some disrepair since the family's fortunes declined, but the grounds are extensive enough to accommodate your people."

"And where is it?" Daralen asked.

"Three streets back, still in the inner ring," he responded.

"That will do," I agreed, having absolutely no idea whether it would. We needed somewhere to regroup, given that the only other choice was a massive fight right here, and knowing that if it came down to it, I needed Oracle at the very least well back from the opening salvos.

Fuck's sake, some of the assholes with Malakai had shoulder-mounted RPGs.

If they fired those into our ranks, at least half of the legion and probably Oracle and Sehran would be dead before anyone could do anything.

No. The more I considered this, the more I accepted that I needed to retreat from here, in a way that kept our fucking heads held high, maintained our dignity, and left us able to stab every bastard one of them in the back and stomp on their throats when they weren't pointing those at people I loved.

After a bit more posturing and the setting of a time for the evening's parley, the standoff began to disperse. The Dark Legion withdrew first, marching in perfect lockstep back toward the far end of the street and what appeared to be a makeshift fortress they'd established in the noble district.

It was obvious watching them that every single one of them was feeling both that they needed to be doing anything else, considering their own god had demanded they attack and kill me, and yet knowing that if they tried it, they were all dead men.

The city forces made it clear they were going nowhere, setting up camp directly before the gates as other forces rushed up and took up position with them. But that was fine; they'd been here for seven hundred fucking years and had made zero progress in capturing the tower, so realistically none of us were worried about *them*.

House Malakai's troops were the next to move, with the dickhead himself giving me one final venomous glare before ordering his men to fall back to whatever hole they'd crawled out of.

"Well, that went better than expected," Oracle commented as Lord Havelton sent a messenger to lead us to our accommodations.

"Nobody died." I sighed, relief filling me. "But hey, the night's still young."

There were a few moments of existential dread as we started moving. The horses, mammoths, and varm needed a lot more space to turn around than the average idiot in crappy armor. It was when we were right in the middle of the clusterfuck of turning that I felt the prickle on the back of my neck that suggested a crosshairs being drawn on me…

But it turned out to just be paranoia, and a few minutes later, we were off again, travelling a few streets over and then along to our destination.

The Varnen estate was, as Havelton had said, a place that had seen better days. The once-grand mansion's stonework was crumbling in places, with missing roof tiles and windows that had been poorly repaired. The grounds, however, were extensive—easily large enough for our forces to set up camp.

As we rode through the rusted iron gates, a nervous-looking man hurried down the cracked marble steps to greet us. He was tall and thin, with the bearing of nobility but clothes that had been patched one too many times to maintain the illusion of prosperity.

"My lord prince," he said with a deep and clearly fucking nervous bow. "Erasmus Varnen, at your service. My humble home is yours for as long as you require it, of…of course."

I dismounted, studying him carefully, waiting to see whether he was about to pull a fucking knife or a gun or…then I shook myself clear of it, and spoke. "Lord Varnen, I appreciate your hospitality, especially on such short notice."

He gave a strained smile. "When Lord Havelton explained the situation, I was only too happy to offer what little I have to such an honored guest!"

"I'm sure you were," Daralen muttered under her breath. The outriders moved up, taking charge of the horses, as twenty legionnaires formed up into a guard for us. The rest started moving horses, mammoths, varm, and the various packs, pack beasts and general crap, out to the grounds to set up camp.

Varnen led us inside, apologizing profusely for the state of the mansion as we walked through halls that might once have been grand but now showed signs of decades of neglect.

Faded tapestries hung on the walls, their colors dimmed by time and dust. The marble floors were cracked in places, and many of the rooms we passed were empty of furniture.

"My family once held considerable influence in Gaij," Varnen explained as he showed us to what appeared to be a study that had retained most of its furnishings. "But fortunes change, as they say. The Varnens were the stewards of the imperial gardens and surrounding areas of Gaij in the time of Emperor Amon himself. Our lineage is unbroken, even if our wealth is…somewhat diminished."

"And your allegiance?" Oracle asked pointedly.

Varnen hesitated, his eyes darting between us. "My lady, in times like these, a wise man keeps his options open. But I have always been a supporter of…stability. The return of imperial authority could bring that back, provided it's exercised with wisdom."

In other words, he was hedging his bets, seeing which way the wind would blow. I couldn't exactly blame him—his family was clearly hanging on by a thread, and backing the wrong horse now could finish them off completely.

"We'll need to discuss the situation in the city," I said. "I assume you have intelligence that might be useful?"

Varnen brightened at this. "Indeed, my prince. While my family's fortunes have declined, our information network remains quite…functional. I would be happy to share what I know."

"Let me be blunt, Varnen." I turned to him. "Do you own slaves?"

"Ah, no…" He shook his head, though he looked nervous.

"Probably not because he doesn't agree with it, and more that he can't afford them," Oracle sent.

"I'm glad to hear that." I nodded. "Varnen, I'm sorry but I'm not a courtier, so let's make our positions clear. I'm here to assume control of the city, that much is obvious. My people and I will only be staying here as long as it takes to sort that out, but you have the opportunity to gain by it, or not. We will not share any information with you regarding who we are or what we can do, unless you are an imperial citizen.

"Swear the oaths and serve the empire again, and provided you haven't broken any imperial laws, then you'll do well out of this. For a start, we'll pay you for our time here, for food and lodgings…"

"Oh, that's not necessary," he protested weakly. "You are imperial guests and—"

"And we'll pay you in platinum," I finished, stifling a smile as he broke off sharply. Yup, looks like I'd found a lever for this one straightaway. Either the dickhead who sent me here was a fool, or he didn't care about anything I might gain in the short term.

"Platinum…?" Varnen asked slowly. "My prince, the costs of simple lodging on my family grounds would be…"

"I'm paying not just for the lodging, but for you," I said. "I need allies here who know what's going on and the lay of the city, Varnen. I'm willing to pay for it in platinum, and believe me, my pockets are deep. I have no need for most of the wealth I gather through conquering cities and continents.

"What I need are *allies*, and people I can trust, so I'll ask you just once, Lord Varnen of Gaij—are you an imperial citizen? Can I trust you to help me here, both to navigate the area, and to help me rule this land?"

There were a few seconds where you could feel the silence as his mind raced.

On one hand, he was poor as shit…that was obvious; on the other, I had zero fucking doubt that he had skeletons in his closet. He was a noble, even if he was poor as fuck and didn't look to have so much as a handful of servants to maintain the manor house. If he supported me, and I failed?

He'd lose everything.

If I won, though…

I could almost see the cogs turning behind his eyes, and thankfully, he decided to reach out with both hands and grasp the lifeline that was being offered.

"I am an imperial citizen," he said softly, before kneeling creakily. "Though I am old and poor."

"Good man." I smiled. "You'll swear the oath, and then, when we know we can trust you, it'll be time to fix at least one of those situations."

I smiled at him, as Oracle pushed out the oath, and he started to speak in a voice that grew firmer as he did so.

The first step was confirming that he had no nefarious plans to fuck us over, and that he was indeed, the noble of the house, just in case—as we were in the city of Gaij and no longer in our territory—that shitehawk Illoth had replaced him with a drow.

That done, Oracle hit him with a heal, and then another when she found deep-rooted cancers, and Daralen carried him to a nearby seat as he lay there, stunned.

"Welcome to the empire." I smiled at him.

"What…?" he managed, taking probably deeper breaths than he'd been able to in years.

"A wasting disease," Oracle offered, not really feeling the need to go into the whole cancerous genetics conversation. "A little bonus of imperial service is healing."

"I suspected," he admitted, one hand pressed to his chest, rubbing unconsciously as he spoke. "The cost of healing, though…" He shook his head.

"How bad is it?" I asked. "Your house's finances, I mean."

"I am the head of a house that only includes two others," he said. "And while my wife and son are out at our country house, preparing to sell it, I was forced to remain here, lest squatters attempt to claim it."

"How many do you have employed?" Daralen asked, and he shook his head. "Nobody?" she asked incredulously.

"The last of them left two months ago, when I could no longer pay her."

"Was she trustworthy?" I asked, and he nodded firmly. "Okay, how many do we need to run the house here?"

"As it should be run?" He cocked his head to the side, and I nodded. "Half a dozen at least. A butler, cook, and groundskeeper, two maids, and at least one guard."

"We don't need the guards." Daralen snorted. "As an imperial citizen and a sworn supporter of the prince of the empire, I think I can pry a pair of legionnaires loose when needed," she assured him dryly.

"If you know people you can trust, and who are willing to swear the oath, hire them," I said to him. "How much do you need?"

"For what?" he asked, the changes coming too thick and fast for him.

"To get the food you need in, hire the staff, and anything else." I smiled. "Just tell me a number."

"I…" He hung his head in shame. "My wife and son are working to make our country estate as pristine as can be in the hopes of attracting a buyer, as I owe debts on this house. Given the choice, we would rather live there, but the value of this property is higher, and the protection the city walls offer mean we must be here."

"How much do you owe?" Oracle asked him gently. "Don't be ashamed, just tell us."

"A hundred and forty gold marks," he whispered.

"Daralen, can you send a small team with him? You'll need to pay off the debts entirely, and hire whoever is needed. Here." I gave him two hundred gold, looking at him in question. "Is that enough?

"More than enough." He nodded his thanks, his cheeks flushed with embarrassment.

"Take another fifty," I decided, before giving him that and then giving the same to Daralen. "Tell whoever you send that they're to get a list of equipment that's needed by our people. Spend it all, and if you need more, just let me know."

"How much do you want us to dig in?" Daralen asked me, and I smiled.

"Make this the legion camp for now. When we take the tower, we'll move there, but this is now an imperial holding, of House Varnen, of course," I assured him. "As such, make it clear that anyone who enters uninvited leaves in bits."

"With pleasure." She smiled.

"Is there anyone else in the house?" Oracle asked Varnen, and he shook his head. "Are you sure?" she pressed. "I'm going to use magic to scour the building clear of any uninvited pests. If there's anyone else here who hasn't sworn the oath, they'll die."

"There's nobody here," he assured her. "Or, if there is, they're not here with my blessing, anyway."

"Do it, my love." I nodded.

Oracle started to cast the spell that we'd used before, a variant on the Frostfire Circle of Cleansing but larger and geared simply to clear away any intruders, like Illoth's spiders. It took only a few seconds to cast, but she had to refresh it twice before she moved to cast it across the grounds, due to how many spiders, rats, and various pests were eliminated.

Given the realities of life, they probably weren't actually supporters of Illoth, just regular spiders, but they were creepy fuckers anyway, so I viewed it as a good thing they were dead.

"Okay, go get what you need," I ordered Varnen. "And send word to your family. They might become a target if they're out of reach, so better they're here where they're safe—if you're willing—and there's no need to sell off the country house." I handed over a further five platinum coins. "Consider this our rent for the next few days."

"Thank you." He stood slowly, clearly having lost the stress and fear that had been part of him for a long time. "You won't regret this, my prince," he assured me, and I smiled.

Over the next few hours, as our forces established a perimeter around the estate and set up camp on the grounds, Varnen returned quickly with the staff he'd wanted to rehire—apparently they'd all been with him for years and he'd had to let them go only recently—and the legionnaires who had accompanied him returned with two dozen former slaves as well as all the food and gear they believed we needed.

When I asked, the legionnaire simply said that he believed there could be no better way to gain help we could trust in the city than by freeing the slaves.

That'd been my intention all along, but I was going to hold off on doing it until I was in control, so I didn't complain. Instead, Oracle healed them, took their oaths, and they started work.

Varnen proved surprisingly knowledgeable about the current state of play in Gaij, and I was quickly damn relieved that dickhead Havelton had thought to try to piss me off by putting us up in clearly the poorest of the nobles' houses.

The city was officially ruled by a council of twelve noble houses, with the most powerful being House Durnell, House Havelton, and House Tessian. However, real power was increasingly in the hands of the guilds—particularly the Merchant's Guild and the Caravaneer's Guild, which controlled trade in and out of the city.

The Dark Legion had established a presence years ago, but they'd been gradually decreasing their numbers until they represented a fraction of the force that had taken the legion encampment about ten years back. They had a small force that held and operated that outside the city, and the rest were on patrol or doing whatever the dark dick wanted, the rest of the time.

They'd been summoned back to Gaij, though, and three guesses who'd done that and why. Rumor also had it that these were only the first to arrive, with much larger forces on their way.

They technically operated under the council's authority, but everyone knew they answered only to their commanders and, ultimately, to Nimon Himself.

And then, just weeks ago, the first of the Earth nobles had arrived, another house initially, who'd tried to claim the tower; then two more, of which only House Malakai had survived to date.

"And the succubai?" Sehran asked, speaking for the first time since we'd entered the mansion. She'd kept her hood up, even indoors, and positioned herself in the shadowy corner of the room.

Varnen's expression grew guarded. "They remain…isolated. The tower is their domain, and they permit no one to enter without invitation. Even the council must currently communicate with them through intermediaries, though they cannot keep that up for long."

"When was the last time anyone from the city entered the tower?" I asked.

"Officially? Weeks ago," Varnen replied. "Though rumors suggest that certain…clients…are still occasionally admitted. The succubai have always provided certain services to those with sufficient wealth or influence."

"And unofficially?" Oracle prompted.

Varnen hesitated. "There have been attempts to force entry. None have succeeded. The tower's defenses remain formidable, even after all these centuries."

"What do you mean, 'formidable'?" I asked. "Be specific."

He swallowed, clearly uncomfortable. "The golems, my prince. The original imperial sentinels. There aren't many left—perhaps a dozen that anyone has seen—but they're…devastating. During the last attempt, by House Tessian about twenty years ago, a single golem killed thirty armed men before they retreated."

I exchanged glances with Oracle. The plan—although, yeah, all right, "plan" might be generous—was still the same. We needed to make contact with the succubai directly, which meant getting Sehran to them without anyone else catching on.

"Lord Varnen," I said, "thank you, both for your honesty and your support. I hope we can continue to have more conversations during our stay, but if you don't mind, I need some time with my advisors now."

He bowed quickly and nodded, climbing to his feet. "Of course, my prince. And if there's anything else you require, please don't hesitate to ask."

He left at the obvious hint, presumably to supervise the arrangements for our troops or to…fuck knows, actually. I'd never had to run a noble house like this, so for all I knew, he was off to polish the candlesticks. I turned to my inner circle: Oracle, Sehran, Daralen, and Saracen.

"Thoughts?"

"He's terrified," Oracle said immediately. "And he was desperate, but now? It's all he can do to keep the smile off his face."

"I feel bad, considering we literally rocked up and claimed everything, but well, he's certainly gaining out of it," I admitted. "I just hope he doesn't turn out to be a dick when we find out more."

"He knows this city," Daralen added. "And his information seems solid."

"We can use him," I agreed. "But it's only because of the oath that we can trust him."

Sehran moved from her corner, lowering her hood now that we were alone. "The parley tonight is probably going to be a waste of time. None of the factions are going to back down, and unless we've missed something, none has enough strength to force the others out without weakening themselves too much."

"It's a fucking Mexican standoff." I sighed, then realized nobody would understand the reference. "It's a stalemate," I clarified. "And the succubai are content to let it remain that way."

"Then we change the game," Oracle said. "Tonight, while you're keeping the other factions occupied at the parley, Sehran makes contact with her sisters, and you…" She smiled. "Don't push them into outright attacking you, but act a little…mad. Just enough that they're not certain what you'll do next. Throw them off a little, and they'll be too busy watching you to pay attention to anything else. Daralen can act as your handler as well, make everyone think you're some kind of mad dog."

"It's risky." Daralen frowned. "If we go too far, or if any of the factions spot her and tie her to us, they'll act, even without knowing what we're planning. They'll assume that we're in contact even if the succubai refuse to deal with us."

"Which is why we need a distraction," I replied. "Something big enough to keep all eyes on the parley instead of the skies, so that I can add to it."

A slow smile spread across Oracle's face. "I think I might have just the thing."

CHAPTER THIRTEEN

The Grand Hall lived up to its name, although the sheer amount of wasted wealth was almost enough to make the ceiling collapse under its own weight.

It was a massive stone structure near the center of the noble district, with soaring ceilings supported by intricately carved columns.

Ornate tapestries and banners ranging from the city's history to celebrating this noble or that prick in tinfoil hung from the walls, and enchanted chandeliers provided warm, golden light.

Despite its grandeur, I couldn't help but notice the subtle signs of decay that stood out here and there: cracks in the marble floor, washed-out colors in the tapestries, a general sense of faded glory desperately clinging to respectability.

Each faction had been directed to its own entrance and seating area, with a central round table for the primary representatives. The symbolism wasn't subtle, but it was effective, and it helped that there was no sodding way I'd have come here without the legion backing me up. Fifty of them, with all of them now having access to at least one spell, and many the standard three.

I'd brought a small delegation—Oracle, Daralen, Saracen, my legionnaires as guards. Sehran had remained behind at the estate, supposedly feeling unwell after the journey, but in reality preparing for her covert mission to the tower.

The Dark Legion had sent their commander, now revealed as a gaunt man named Vectus, accompanied by what appeared to be some kind of high priest of Nimon and a hundred elite guards. The city was represented by Lords Havelton, Durnell, and Tessian, along with a woman introduced as Magistrate Kora, apparently the head of the city's justice system.

House Malakai had sent their leader, who turned out to be called Darius, along with what I assumed was a younger relative and thirty armed guards carrying modern weapons, which, in all honesty, anywhere else would have been overkill.

Fortunately, though, when it came to heavy armor and magic, they weren't punching as hard as they apparently thought they would be.

The atmosphere was tense from the moment we all entered, with none of the factions willing to be the first to take seats at the central table. After a brief, awkward standoff, Lord Havelton took the initiative, gesturing graciously toward the table.

"Perhaps we might begin these discussions in a civilized manner?" he suggested, his forced smile not reaching his eyes.

Reluctantly, we all moved to take our places—myself opposite Darius Malakai, with the Dark Legion commander and Lord Havelton to my left and right. The others arranged themselves behind their respective leaders.

"The purpose of this parley," Lord Havelton began, "is to address the competing claims to the Tower of Gaij and to establish a framework for—"

"Let's not waste time with pointless pleasantries," Darius Malakai interrupted. "We all know why we're here. The tower is imperial property, and House Malakai represents the true imperial nobility. Our claim is self-evident."

Commander Vectus laughed, a dry, rasping sound. "Your claim is meaningless. The old imperial nobility fled when the true power of Nimon was revealed. You abandoned your duties and your people. You have no right to return now and claim what you discarded."

"Rich words from a worshiper of the god who caused the cataclysm in the first place," I remarked. "How's Nimon doing these days, by the way? Still sucking his thumb and whining from our last meeting?"

Vectus's face contorted with rage. "Blasphemer! Lord Nimon cannot be truly harmed by a mortal, no matter what tricks you employ to fool the non-believer!!"

"Didn't look that way when I was holding his severed head," I replied with a shrug. "In fact, I have a lovely goblet made from his skull. I'd have brought it to drink from tonight, but I didn't want to be rude."

Lord Durnell, a heavyset man with an impressive beard, sitting next to Havelton, cleared his throat. "Perhaps we could focus on the matter at hand? The Council of Gaij has administered this city for centuries. We have maintained peace, prosperity, and order. Any change to the status quo must be carefully considered and implemented gradually, and, frankly, you'll have to explain why we should permit it, and what's in it for us."

"You've maintained your own power and wealth," Daralen countered. "While allowing slavery to flourish and the surrounding territories to fall into chaos."

"Harsh accusations from those who have only just arrived," Magistrate Kora said coolly. She was a striking woman, tall and lean, with silver streaking her dark hair. "The council has done what was necessary to ensure the city's survival in a hostile world."

"And as for slavery," Lord Tessian added, "that institution exists throughout the continent. Gaij is hardly unique in that regard."

"It exists because the empire fell," I said. "And it will end now that the empire is rising again."

Darius Malakai snorted. "The empire? You mean your pathetic collection of refugees and mercenaries? You're no more the empire than these provincial nobles."

I turned to face him fully. "Want to challenge me on the grounds of imperial rank, Darius? Come on, tell me where you once claimed…let's see if my rank is high enough to strip you of it."

His face flushed with anger. "You dare!"

"I dare a fucking lot." I cut him off. "You ran from Nimon—I came here and bitch-slapped him off my continent. Remind me, what's Malakai famous for? Oh wait, that's right, fuck all of note. You might have noticed that I've brought the legion with me. The *real* one, not whatever mercenaries you've managed to outfit with Earth weapons."

Darius's hand twitched toward the sidearm at his hip, and the tension in the room spiked dangerously.

"Go for it." I smiled, leaning forward and nodding. "Try shooting me with that peashooter, and I'll ram it so far up your arse, you'll be tasting what I had for breakfast."

"Gentlemen, please," Lord Havelton snapped. "Violence will solve nothing. The tower remains sealed, and none of our forces have been able to breach its defenses. Perhaps we should discuss practical matters—how to approach the succubai and negotiate access?"

This, at least, was a topic that all parties seemed willing to engage with, if only because they all had the same problem.

"The succubai have refused all communication since the arrival of the new claimants of nobility," Lord Tessian explained. "Previously, they would at least accept messages and occasionally respond to the council, as well as being open for business. Since your arrival—and I make no accusations, Lord Malakai; I state facts—but since your arrival, they have sealed the tower. Now, they simply…watch."

"They're waiting," Daralen observed.

"For what?" Commander Vectus demanded.

"For us to destroy each other," I said simply. "So they can deal with whoever's left standing."

A contemplative silence fell over the table as everyone considered this.

"It would be consistent with their historical behavior," Magistrate Kora admitted. "The succubai have always preferred to let others fight while they remain secure in their tower."

Daralen and I barely bothered to argue with the others, waiting for the opportunity and mainly focusing on keeping the arguments going whenever it looked like they might settle on something. But despite the lack of a damn watch, I kept track of the time. Oracle had planned for her "distraction" to begin approximately two hours after nightfall, which should be right about…now.

A massive boom shook the building, rattling the chandeliers and sending dust drifting down from the ceiling.

"What in the hells was that?" Lord Durnell exclaimed, half-rising from his seat.

A guard burst into the hall. "My lords! There's some kind of magical battle disturbance to the west!"

Perfect timing.

Everyone rushed to the windows and balconies to see what was happening,

It was also *exactly* the kind of distraction we needed.

"Who, or what is it?" Lord Havelton murmured, his eyes fixed on the display. "The scale of the power…"

"An attack," I growled. "A distraction by one of you!"

That got everyone back to the game at hand, and they immediately had hands on weapons.

"Please, my prince!" Havelton snapped. "At least try to engage in civilized discourse! Who would be attacking? And even if so, that is miles beyond the city!"

"I don't trust you." I glared at the Dark Legion representatives, as Vectus suddenly cursed.

"You did this!" he spat. "A distraction so that you could attack our encampment!"

That was more or less right, mainly because their encampment—which they'd stolen from the real legion—was indeed in that direction.

He was also dead wrong, though, because what it was, was a single, very simple spell that Oracle had cobbled together after a conversation with Jenae about it.

The Goddess of Hidden Knowledge couldn't really teach us spells without taking more of a hand in things than she was allowed to, but…she'd enjoyed a friendly discussion with Oracle over the various effects of air and fire magics, when placed just so.

The spells that even now were rattling the windows weren't actually doing anything.

They were just very loud, and very bright, and they were being cast by a trio of legionnaires who had impressively large manapools, and who Oracle had spent an hour painstakingly teaching this spell.

Best of all? The message I received as I stared at the distant flashes.

Sehran was on the move.

SEHRAN

While the nobles, Dark Legion, and Earth forces stared out at the magical light show, Sehran crouched in the shadows of the Varnen estate's roof. Her wings were unfurled but still, her muscles tensed for flight. She'd shed her concealing cloak, revealing her true form—the violet skin, curved horns, and bat-like wings that marked her as a succubus, though now without any effort at hiding her demonic nature and the more…expected features.

Her skin was grey in some places, mottled green in others, and the violet?

What had once been her "natural" skin tone was now a striping that was both a clear warning and perplexing, even to her. It'd come about after she evolved—after feeding on the SporeMothers—and she both felt it disgusting, as it made her look almost diseased, and incredible.

There was something about it, like a tiger's stripes, that just said "danger" and that was intoxicating, as was the desire to show it off for the first time to those who might understand.

From her vantage point, she could see the Tower of Gaij looming in the distance, its upper reaches lost in darkness. Occasional flickers of movement suggested her sisters were still circling, watching the city below.

She watched the magical lights and flashes in the distance. Grinning as she saw that Oracle's distraction was in place, she then crouched, spreading her wings. It was time to move.

With a powerful beat of her wings, she launched herself into the night, staying low at first, using the buildings for cover; her natural magic helped to obscure her from casual observation. The few citizens still on the streets were too busy gawking at the light show to notice a shadow passing overhead.

She waited until she was closer to the outermost ring of the city, far from where she should be heading—just to be sure—and then banked, suddenly climbing, *hard.*

Now, in theory, if anyone saw her, they'd think it was a succubus who had been out having some very risky fun, rather than paying a visit to Jax at least.

She looped back and beat her wings harder, climbing quickly as she approached the inner wall surrounding the tower. The wall's enchantments might detect her, but they wouldn't target her—not with her heritage. At least, that was the theory.

She passed over the wall without incident, feeling the magic wash over her like a warm breeze. Recognition. Acceptance. Caution, but the tower knew what she was.

Now in the open space between the wall and the tower itself, Sehran beat her wings harder, climbing rapidly. The tower was vast, its surface a patchwork of original imperial work and newer additions. Occasional windows and balconies dotted its face, some lit from within, but the vast, *vast* majority dark and seemingly abandoned.

She aimed for the upper reaches, where she'd seen her sisters flying earlier. As she ascended, the magical display behind her continued to paint the sky with color, reflecting off the tower's polished surfaces.

Movement caught her eye—shapes detaching from the tower's heights, flying toward her. Her sisters, coming to investigate.

Sehran slowed, then hovered in place, making no threatening moves as three succubai approached. They were beautiful and terrible in equal measure—their bodies perfect, their wings powerful, their eyes glowing with inner fire, but…they also looked tired. Curious, cautious, but dog-tired.

"Greetings, sisters," Sehran called out as they circled her. "I come seeking audience with your mistress."

The lead succubus, her hair a flowing river that was as dark as a raven's wing, narrowed her eyes as she called out above the wind. "You are not one of ours. Where do you come from?"

"I was summoned here months ago," Sehran called back. "I've come with one of my masters, Prince Jax Amon, heir to the imperial throne."

The three exchanged glances. "Another thief coming in the night," one said dismissively.

"This one brings a succubus," the fiery-haired second succubus noted. "That's…different, and wiser."

"I'm neither his prisoner nor his slave," Sehran said. "I'm his ally. Though he holds my bond, it is another who I call mine, and he's permitted me to serve and love, living here, openly. I bring a message directly for the Mistress of Gaij, one that may save both your home and his birthright."

After a moment's consideration, the leader nodded. "Follow us. But know that at the first sign of betrayal, you'll find yourself back in the hells."

Sehran inclined her head in acknowledgment. "I understand. But sisters?"

"Yes?"

"If you try to send me back, I'll gut you all before I go." Sehran smiled, her teeth glinting in the moonlight. "If I go back, they'll never let me return—I've grown too much. So try it, and I'll make you regret it."

There was a long silence, as the other three watched her. Then the leader inclined her head, both in acceptance and, from the angle of her horns, in respect. Sehran couldn't help but smile as she joined them.

The four succubai flew toward the tower, not to its peak as she'd had expected, but to a large balcony about two-thirds of the way up. The balcony led to an ornate doorway, fashioned in the imperial style but clearly modified over the centuries.

As they landed, the door opened, revealing a succubus older than the others. Her wings showed signs of battle damage; her face bore scars that even their kind's natural healing couldn't fully erase. She wore a simple black dress that contrasted sharply with her crimson skin.

"Lilandra," the flame-haired succubus addressed her. "This one claims to come from the claimant prince. She requests audience with the mistress."

Lilandra studied Sehran with ancient eyes. "You smell of this plane," she said finally. "But also of something else. Something older."

"I've been bound to Prince Jax for some time," Sehran explained with a wide smile. "He recently took Illoth's head. That leaves a mark."

Lilandra's eyebrows rose slightly. "Indeed it does, young one. Come. The mistress will want to hear what you have to say, and certainly any news you have."

She led Sehran through a series of corridors and chambers, each more opulent than the last. Despite the tower's external appearance of decay, its interior—at least in these upper sections—was immaculately maintained. Ancient relics blended seamlessly with later additions, creating a space that felt both wondrous and alive.

The handful of other succubai they passed regarded Sehran with curiosity, some with suspicion. None interfered as Lilandra guided her deeper into the tower.

Finally, they reached a set of double doors made of some iridescent material that seemed to shift colors as they approached. Lilandra paused.

"The mistress sees all that happens in Gaij," she said quietly. "She knows of your prince's arrival, of his forces, and of the standoff at our gates. What she doesn't know is why she should care when so many others have come with similar claims."

"My prince doesn't just claim the tower," Sehran replied. "He offers you all freedom and respect, not to mention a place in the reborn empire."

Lilandra's expression remained neutral. "Bold words. We shall see if the mistress finds them persuasive. But be warned, little one: annoy her, and she'll be picking bits of you out of her teeth…"

She pushed open the doors, then stood back, smiling darkly as Sehran tried to keep the smile on her face, despite the sudden knotting in her stomach.

CHAPTER FOURTEEN

A foolish trick," the priest of Nimon suddenly snapped, drawing all our eyes. "Our encampment remains safe. Should any of your weaklings attempt to attack it, they'll be taken as slaves, gelded and sold!"

"I'm sorry, are you talking to me?" I asked after a few seconds, cocking my head to the side as if just realizing, and he sneered. "Okay, just to be very sure about this, let's be clear on our positions, shall we? Are. You. Talking. To. Me?" I smiled widely.

"I am, fool! The pretender prince, coward, and...*erk*!" He broke off as I triggered Mana Overdrive and burst forward, grabbing him by the throat and squeezing.

"Unhand him!" the local magistrate barked.

"Fuck off," I replied conversationally as the Dark Legion commander drew his blade and glowered at me.

"Release him now, or..."

"Or what?" I asked him, squeezing harder, before catching the priest's flailing right hand and snapping his fingers back, preventing him from finishing the spell he was trying to cast.

He choked, eyes rolling back in his head as the backlash from the failed casting tore at him, and I smiled to Vectus. "Come on, I asked 'Or what?' By which I mean, you're *already* standing before the apostate. The one man above all others that your god has ordered you to kill under any circumstances, so what more do I have to do? Obviously, you're a fucking coward."

"I am no coward!" he hissed.

"Bullshit. Has Nimon revoked my status?" I angled my head back and shouted at the balcony and up toward the sky. "Oi! Fuckface!"

Thunder rolled instantly.

"Yeah, you! You decided that you're sick of getting your arse handed to you and you want to make friends?" I yelled, and the thunder suddenly cut off. "That's right!" I barked. "You want to sit down and negotiate with me and the gods? See if we can move forward? I mean, that must be the case, right? Otherwise, you'd never have revoked my status as top of the target list. I mean, the *real* Dark Legion back on Dravith attacked me on sight.

"Surely you're not so lacking in actual warriors that this is the best you've got, is it?" I called, grinning widely. I turned back to Vectus, and then dropped my voice. "Tell me, how often do you speak to your god, really? I mean, is he really as disappointed in you as it looks right now?"

The sudden feeling of Nimon's attention vanished, drawn aside by who knew what. In that brief split second, I snapped the priest's neck, then dropped him on the floor between us.

"Try it any time," I whispered to Vectus, seeing the way his face was mottling through the slit in his visor. "If you think you're hard enough, anyway."

There was a brief silence, before it was broken by another.

"Parlor tricks," Darius Malakai sneered, dismissing the now dead priest on the floor with a glance. "Designed to distract us from the matter at hand."

"My lords…there was a guarantee of safety here!" Havelton burst out. "A neutral ground, with no fighting allowed!"

"Was there?" I asked, acting surprised. "You said neutral ground. You never said anything about us not attacking each other."

"It was implied!" he snapped.

"Oh, I thought we were just playing nice." I shook my head and let out a little laugh. "Forgive me, everyone. I misunderstood."

"My man is dead," Vectus snarled.

"Very," I agreed cheerfully. "And yet you're not, and neither's anyone else, yet. If you want to keep it that way, maybe don't try to fucking goad me, eh?"

"My lords, we are here for a much more important matter!" Havelton cried, trying to get the conversation back on track.

"And what matter is that, exactly?" I took advantage of the break to move away, back around the table and to my own chair, sitting down comfortably. Then I leaned back as if none of them in the room were worthy of my attention, and again, switched up my mannerisms and speech. "We've established that we all have competing claims, and none of us can access the tower without the succubai's cooperation. Unless someone has a magic key they've been keeping secret?"

The Dark Legion commander, Vectus, hissed, clearly forcing himself to let go of his rage and need to attack me, before kicking the now dead priest in the side of the head, as he gestured for one of his men to take the body away. "There are ways to breach the tower's defenses. Lord Nimon's power—"

"Couldn't stop me from cutting his avatar's head off," I interrupted, shaking my head as if regretting I needed to remind him. "So forgive me if I'm skeptical about its effectiveness against imperial defenses that have held for seven hundred years."

Vectus's face darkened with rage. But before he could respond, Magistrate Kora cleared her throat.

"Perhaps we're approaching this from the wrong angle," she suggested. "Instead of arguing over whose claim is strongest, we might consider what each party brings to the table. An alliance, perhaps?"

"With heretics and usurpers?" Vectus scoffed, as a second priest moved up and sat in the other priest's space, clearly watching me as if I were a hungry lion.

I smiled at him and gave him an unsubtle and cheery wave, before speaking in a stage whisper and deliberately acting unhinged. "Might be best not to mention the atrocities you committed against my people, eh? I might get angry next time!" Then I winked and slouched back in the chair.

Silence fell again, and this time I deliberately let out a little giggle.

Fucking hell, I was *really* enjoying this. Oracle had suggested I act a little mad, and I do it to throw them off, but if I'd realized it'd work this well, I'd have done it ages ago in meetings with the nobles. At least I'd not have been as bloody bored in them, if nothing else!

"We each have complementary strengths," Kora started again, clearly watching me and attempting to redirect the conversation. "The local nobility knows the city and its people. The Dark Legion has numbers and divine backing.

House Malakai brings technology from the other realm, and Prince Jax…brings the imperial bloodline and legitimacy."

I had to admit, it wasn't the worst idea I'd heard. It also wasn't going to happen, but it kept the conversation going, which was all I needed right now.

"An interesting proposal," I said, careful to switch suddenly, sitting up as if I'd never been slouching, and trying to project an air of split personality, as I changed my tone to formal and neutral. "Though I imagine the implementation would be…challenging."

"More like fucking impossible," Darius snarled, for once finding something we could both acknowledge. "The fundamental interests of our factions are incompatible."

"Are they?" Lord Havelton wondered. "Perhaps our goals are more aligned than we realize. We all want stability, prosperity, and power. The details may differ, but the broad strokes are similar."

This launched a fresh round of debate, with each faction laying out what they considered their nonnegotiable requirements. The Dark Legion wanted recognition of Nimon's supremacy and the right to ban the imperial legionnaires from the territory. I'd guess they'd have also asked for my head, but they were wary that saying it might cause me to attack again—a feeling that was made even worse when I kept giving more little waves to the priest and winking at him when I caught him looking.

The local nobility wanted to maintain their privileges and authority over day-to-day governance. House Malakai wanted acknowledgment of their status as the "true" nobility and ultimate control over the tower.

And what did I want? The tower, of course, and the elimination of slavery. Then preferably all their heads on pikes. But more immediately, I wanted to keep this charade going until Sehran completed her mission.

So I engaged, countered, proposed, and opposed as needed to keep the conversation alive without actually conceding anything meaningful. I even occasionally argued against myself, pretending that the other side had asked for what I'd just been demanding, and telling them that it was unreasonable.

Oracle occasionally added her own thoughts, her diplomatic skills proving invaluable in smoothing ruffled feathers when tempers flared, and adding to the overall confusion.

Two hours into the discussion, with the others at the table now fully convinced I was an unstable lunatic who was being handled by Oracle, the real power behind the throne, a messenger slipped into the hall and whispered something to Lord Tessian. His face paled slightly.

"My lords, ladies," he rose from his seat, "I'm afraid I must temporarily withdraw. An urgent matter requires my attention."

As he hurried from the hall, I caught Oracle's eye. Something had changed, and I damn well hoped it was a good thing for our side.

"Perhaps this would be a good time for a brief recess," Lord Havelton suggested. "We've been in discussion for some time, and refreshments have been prepared in the adjacent hall."

I nodded my agreement, and the parley broke up into smaller groups as servants opened doors and the smell of food and drinks wafted invitingly through.

I spoke to Oracle through the bond, feeling it as Sehran sent a "not yet, busy" sensation through the bond to us. *"What do you think happened?"*

"Not sure," she replied quietly. *"But something's shifted. I was hoping it was Sehran, but..."*

Daralen joined us, her expression neutral but her posture tense. "My prince, we may have a problem. My people report unusual movement near the tower. The Dark Legion appears to be repositioning some of their forces."

"They know something we don't," I murmured. "Or think they do."

"Sir," one of our legionnaire guards approached, saluting sharply. "A message from Lord Varnen. He reports that his family have arrived safely, but that they were mere minutes ahead of a drow raiding party."

"Fuck," I hissed. "Just what we need. Illoth's little spiders coming to join the party."

"The territorial claim from defeating her doesn't extend this far," Oracle reminded me. "We're well outside the hundred-mile radius."

"I'm aware," I replied grimly. "Which means this just got a lot more complicated."

I glanced across the hall, where Darius Malakai was in deep conversation with someone I guessed was a younger relative, their expressions suggesting they were discussing something of utmost importance. The Dark Legion contingent had clustered near one of the windows, Commander Vectus periodically looking outside as if expecting something.

"They all know," I said. "Something's happening, and they've all got pieces of the puzzle we don't."

Oracle placed a hand on my arm. "Jax, we need to get back to the Varnen estate. If there's going to be trouble, I'd rather have our full force at our backs."

I nodded, decision made. "Daralen, make our excuses. Say I'm bored and need to go gut something. We're leaving."

"My prince," she acknowledged, moving to speak with Lord Havelton, who nodded quickly, shooting uncertain looks my way.

The situation with them might not have been productive, but considering I knew they'd never support us without our boot on their throat anyway, I really didn't give two shits what they thought.

As we prepared to depart, Darius Malakai caught my eye from across the room. The smirk on his face made my blood run cold. He raised his glass in a mock toast, his eyes never leaving mine.

The bastard definitely knew something.

SEHRAN

Sehran stepped into a chamber unlike anything she'd seen before. The circular room occupied what must have been a full quarter of the tower's circumference at this level, its ceiling soaring upward in a perfect dome. The walls were lined with bookshelves, interrupted occasionally by tall windows that offered panoramic views of the city below.

At the center of the room stood a raised dais, upon which rested a throne-like chair fashioned from what appeared to be a single piece of crystal. And in that chair sat the Mistress of Gaij.

She was, without question, the most beautiful succubus Sehran had ever seen—and that was saying something. Her skin was a deep, midnight blue, nearly black, with gold patterns that seemed to shift and shimmer, like they were floating across the surface of a pool. Her wings were enormous, easily twice the size of Sehran's own, and instead of the bat-like membrane that most succubai possessed, hers appeared to be made of living shadow, stars occasionally twinkling within their depths.

Her face was ageless, her eyes pure gold without pupil or sclera. When she spoke, her voice was like honey poured over gravel: sweet, but with an underlying roughness that sent shivers across the skin of all that heard her speak.

All those marked as prey or lesser guests, anyway.

"So," she said, studying Sehran with those unsettling golden eyes. "You come to us from this realm, bearing the banner of yet another claimant to our tower."

Sehran bowed deeply. "Mistress, I come on behalf of Prince Jax Amon, true heir to the imperial throne and—"

The mistress waved a dismissive hand. "Yes, yes. Heir to the throne, champion of the gods, slayer of Nimon. I've heard it all already." Her eyes narrowed. "What makes your prince different from the dozens who have come before him? Frankly, why should we care?"

"He's actually succeeded," Sehran replied, dropping the formal act. "Where others have claimed, then failed, he's conquered. Dravith, another of the continents of this realm, already belongs to him. The Great Tower there recognizes him as its rightful master, and it's recovering. Where it was on the verge of collapse, now it's thriving. Lastly, he defeated Nimon and Illoth both in single combat, claiming a fragment from each god's divinity for himself."

This, at least, seemed to give the mistress pause. "A fragment of divinity? That is...unusual, though hardly a surprise, and not something unique."

"He holds two," Sehran continued. "Nimon's and Illoth's. He defeated the goddess of spiders just days ago, and claimed Sonra, with the citizens there all swearing to follow him."

A murmur went through the room—there were other succubai present, Sehran realized, hidden in the shadows at the edges of the chamber, over a dozen, many laid on lounge chairs or reclining in deep piles of cushions.

"Bold claims," the mistress said, though her tone had shifted slightly. "Even if true, what does that matter, and why should we care? We have maintained our independence for seven centuries. Why should we surrender it now?" She shook her head.

"Make no mistake, child, you are young, and although impressively strong for your age, you haven't walked our path. We know what these mortals are like. You ask us to permit him entry, yes, but we all know what will happen then. He, as the prince of the empire, will try to throw us out. Thinking the tower will bind to him and accept him in a heartbeat. And then what of us? If he believes this, and when it fails, what will he do? Attack us? Break his oaths and attempt to banish us?

"We'll fight, and if we win, we're back where we were yesterday. If we lose, we lose our home, our independence, and for what? Where would we go? It's not like we can just return to the hells. Once there, even the weakest of us would be bound to never return. Stuck serving this prince or that duke for eternity! You think we remain here because we can't return? We *want* to be here, so why would we give any of that up?"

"Independence?" Sehran countered. "Or isolation? You're trapped here, Mistress. Unable to leave the tower without risk of capture or worse. Your sisters can't travel beyond the gate without fear of being hunted. Is that independence?"

She shook her head. "We both know it's not. You're prisoners here. It's a gilded cage, but it's still a cage."

The mistress's eyes flashed dangerously. "We have survived."

"Survival isn't *living*," Sehran pressed. "Jax offers more than just claims of ownership. He offers partnership. Protection under imperial law. Freedom to move throughout the empire without fear of persecution. And as to the tower?

"What, you think he wants to live here? He doesn't! He's moving on—we all will be—but what he'll leave here is a tower that could accept your *imperial* authority!"

"I have no imperial authority." She scowled. "We cannot—"

"We can!" Sehran cut her off. "Look at me! Look at what I have become!" She released the blocks on her power, and allowed the transformation to take hold fully, making the others stare in wonder.

Her skin darkened and her claws elongated; her hair shifted and fangs lengthened, even as her wings shivered and stretched. The restrictions she normally forced on them were cast aside as her legs, her arms…all of her grew.

"I was summoned by Jian, a warrior who serves Jax," she rumbled out, as the others stared at her. "For weeks, I served him as we all do, enjoying my visit and thinking little more of it. Over time? We spoke of synergy. Of how we could grow. We spoke of power and how he was bound to the prince, a man who spent every drop of blood and mana he could raise to free those who were enslaved…"

"Pretty words," the mistress said. "But words are wind."

"You want to know why you should trust him? Then shut your mouth and listen!" Sehran hissed. "I served Jian, seeing little beyond his bedroom ceiling and being banished back when he was busy, right up until Jax and Oracle found out about me! Instead of insisting I be dismissed, instead of fearing me, he set me to a test! Prove myself to him, and to Jian, and I'd be permitted to stay with Jian as long as we both wished. I didn't have to hide in a room as if a shameful toy!

"Jian is one of Jax's personal squad, so I literally ended up in the field, travelling with Jax and his team as he conquered cities. He beat a SporeMother to the brink of death, and because I'd proved myself to him, he left the experience he could have gained and gave it to me instead!

"I have my place in his team on my own merit, and, despite everything, when he knew that his guard and friend loved me, instead of banishing me and refusing to allow it? He celebrated!

"When we were forced through a portal, far from my Jian, and I was starving, he fed me on his blood and bound me to him. He and his love, the one who will be the next empress when he ascends, the woman who bears his unborn child—I am bonded to! And fed me without reservation!

"Who else in this realm would ever permit such as us to roam free, never mind access to such a bloodline! You know what he ordered me to tell you?"

"What?" The mistress watched Sehran carefully.

"Nothing."

"What?"

"He didn't tell me to tell you anything, or that anything was off the table. He told me to talk to you and to try to convince you to join him, and serve the empire. That's it. No *how* to do it, or the costs, not what I can tell you or promise. He trusts me, actually trusts me, to negotiate for the empire, and to speak the truth.

"Now, when my prince is surrounded by enemies, I'm here, telling you what you need to hear, instead of being there to protect him, and I RAGE!" she howled.

"You want to know why you should give it all up? Why you should meet him, and serve? Because he will give you freedom and he will raise you up! You say you have no authority to rule here? Then ask for it! Make it a demand that in exchange for handing him control of the tower, you get to be its steward, that you need a seat on the council of the city, and that he needs to make the city welcome you, rather than trapping you!"

"He is but a mortal…" one of the succubai scoffed.

Sehran rounded on her, hissing in rage. "Mortal?" she spat. "What mortal fights the gods and has them ally with him? Not the empire—*him* directly. He is no more a mortal than his ancestor Amon was. And if anything, Jax will rule longer! He has two fragments of divinity already, and the gods themselves want him to claim more! The greater gods want the empire ruled by a literal god. And if that comes about, what do you think will stop him from smashing everything in his path?

"You say that you'd be forced to remain in hell if you were to return there somehow? So would I!" she snarled. "Except that he refuses to accept this! I explained it, and why. You know what he did with Nimon's head? He made it into a goblet! That one detail, that one artifact, could grow in power to rival anything that has ever been made by the empire, and do you know what he promised me?"

She turned slowly, making eye contact with the succubai as they sat or stood, staring back at her hungrily. "He swore that if I was somehow banished, I was to wait, because he'd find a way for me to return. Because he would offer that artifact, the skull of a divine avatar, in exchange to whatever prince of hell I was bound to, so that I could return!" She sagged suddenly, and went on in a much quieter voice.

"I am allowed to love, to live, and he has given me hope, my sisters. I am bound to him, yet free. I serve him by choice, not compulsion. He knows our nature, understands our needs, and respects me, as more than my body or my willingness to obey. He refuses me, no matter the offers I made at first, nor those I make now in jest. All that I am valued for…is me. Tell me, my sisters, what more can I ask?"

"And what would he say, if he were to find that we cannot give him the tower?" a voice asked from the shadows. An older succubus stepped forward, her face lined with age in a way few of their kind ever showed. "That, for all we might wish it, we cannot gift him it?"

Sehran hesitated, confused and thrown. "You can't?"

"When we came here, it was as guests. We were permitted to visit the tower, and we were given its protection, though at the time it was superstitious peasants who we were expected to be protected against.

"When the cataclysm came, most of us were here, enjoying our brief interlude on this side, permitted to step across the realms and to stay, just as you were summoned. When the cataclysm struck and the tower shattered, the majority crashed across the land, bringing horrific damage to the surrounding area, including the local nobility and their guests.

"The mistress of those days was at the party, as were most of our kind. Our masters and companions were there; our guards and those we cared about, all fell.

"And as for us? We were the most recently arrived, or worse, those who had transgressed and were being punished, not permitted to attend the ball, though that saved our lives."

"So?" Sehran asked.

"So we cannot leave the tower," the mistress growled, drawing Sehran's attention back to her. "How do you think it still stands? It stands because we feed it!"

"What?"

"The mana it requires? It has to be given! We cannot leave, just like we cannot give it over! You think we don't know of the potential of a structure like this? The mana it produced back when it was active was incredible, and would be more than enough to change the tide in a war. You think we are unaware of the situation out there? We see it all!

"To survive, we built networks of assassins, spies, and thieves, and we know all! There are armies massing, ready to march in and slaughter your prince. All he needs is the mana to claim the territory and he will remove at least one of those, banishing the spider goddess from the battlefield. With her gone, her allies can be defeated, but to do that?"

"He needs the mana…" Sehran whispered. "What armies?"

"He needs the mana!" the mistress echoed. "Yes, he does! Mana that comes from us and feeds us! We draw out the mana we need to survive, and we channel every drop we can back into the tower! We feed it and keep it together—not the wisps! They fell with the tower!"

"Oh no…" Sehran's eyes widened as she understood.

"We can't leave the tower, because it'd collapse as soon as we did! If we're not here to feed it, it'll collapse. There's no great riches of mana to use to claim the area, because all the tower gets is split between feeding us and being fed back into itself to keep its walls intact. You wonder why we're here? Instead of ruling this land?

"We're trapped! We couldn't maintain the tower, and the more those outside came, the more they wanted! Every single one of them, from the water they drank to the tread of their feet in its halls…they were like parasites, draining the tower, inch by inch and day by day. And so we banished them! We've got a single golem left, active, because it's all we can afford to maintain.

"Even now, you look around and you see wealth, but it's all fake! They're the trappings of wealth. Every single coin we gain is spent on buying manastones to feed the tower, so that we can rest, to take our turns, and take a single night off, to relax, to not be pestered and pawed at by drooling, jumped-up, anxiety-ridden monkeys!

"To not be forced to channel and meditate endlessly, moving constantly, feeding a drop here and a drop there back into the structure. Have you never wondered why a magical building that grew itself is still a ruin? Because instead of repairing itself, every drop of mana it gains goes back into regrowing! If we stopped siphoning off the mana, stopped guiding it to the areas that were most damaged, we'd starve and the tower would instead collapse in days!"

Sehran stared at the mistress, her mouth open in shock as it all clicked into place.

"Sometimes, we wish for that," the old one whispered. "That the tower be permitted to fall, and then that we could just *sleep*."

Sehran hesitated, looking around, then sighed as she realized that it was a combination of the worst-case ideas that the little group had bandied around, while travelling, but it wasn't necessarily terminal, not unless…

"Wait, you said *armies*. What armies!" She spun back to the mistress, as that little detail clicked into place.

CHAPTER FIFTEEN

The journey back to the Varnen estate was tense. Our group moved swiftly through the darkened streets of Gaij, the legionnaires drawn up in formation. As we jogged, the feeling of impending doom grew stronger with every meter we passed. The legionnaires on all sides stared out, weapons drawn and ready, their shields bouncing with each step.

The city felt suddenly unnerving: the shadows deeper, the air heavier with the threat.

"Something's wrong," Oracle murmured as we turned down a narrow side street, one of the legionnaires having spotted an incoming Dark Legion patrol.

I could feel it, too. The months of constant fighting made it second nature to know when someone nearby had unfriendly aims on you…a subtle wrongness, like the pressure drop before a storm. "How far to the estate?"

"Another ten minutes, five if we really push." Daralen's hand rested on her sword hilt.

We continued in silence, each of us alert for any sign of danger. The streets were eerily empty, the usual nighttime revelry subdued. Even the taverns we passed seemed unnaturally quiet.

"Everyone knows something's about to happen," Saracen observed quietly. "They're staying indoors."

We were passing through a small square when Oracle suddenly froze, her head snapping up. "Jax!"

I followed her gaze upward just in time to see a dark shape hurtling down from a rooftop. I threw myself sideways, dragging Oracle with me as the figure crashed into the spot where we'd been standing and rolled, popping back to its feet as others burst out of the shadows on all sides.

The legion fell in around me. For a few seconds, it was all swinging blades and screams, the crash of weapons and the cries of pain as people fell; arrows streaked in, punching into weak spots in armor, even as our people fought back.

I was in the middle, surrounded by legionnaires who desperately fought to keep us safe, despite the fact that I was at least as dangerous as any of them by now. Instead, as I felt Oracle doing, I cast, as quickly as I could. Three Frostfire Circles of Cleansing raced out, driving what were quickly revealed as drow back, burning those that were caught inside their range, and beginning to heal the legionnaires and the small contingent of riders with us.

Eventually, as both sides separated, their apparent leader stepped forward, staring at me malevolently.

It was a drow—tall, lithe, with skin black as night and hair white as bone. She wielded twin curved daggers that gleamed with a viscous purple liquid that could only be poison.

"The Godslayer," she hissed, her red eyes fixing on me. "The Spider Queen's *murderer*."

"That's me," I confirmed, tightening my grip on my naginata, lifting it and banging the metal-clad base down hard on the cobblestones. "Though I think 'murderer' is a bit unfair, considering it was a duel, and she was ordered into it by Nimon. Fuck it, though. So, you're a long way from home, spiderfucker."

She bared her teeth in what might have been a smile. "Home is wherever Her will takes us, and Her will demands your death."

More shapes appeared on the surrounding rooftops—at least a dozen more drow assassins, all armed and ready, bows already drawn back. And scuttling out into the moonlight beyond them?

Spiders.

Hundreds of spiders, from things the size of Great Danes all the way down to barely larger than a regular one They burst free of the shadows on all sides, racing for us. I was just damn glad there weren't any that were the size of Ashrag.

"Fuck," I muttered. "Daralen, defensive formation! Oracle, behind me!"

The legionnaires moved quickly, forming a protective circle around Oracle as Daralen stepped to my side, her sword drawn.

"The fragment," the lead drow called down. "Surrender it, and your death will be quick."

"Counteroffer," I called back, knowing there was no chance of that happening. "Go fuck yourself, preferably with something spiky."

She laughed, a sound like breaking glass. "You're surrounded, outnumbered, and far from your army. What makes you think you have a chance?"

I smiled thinly as I realized the only reason we were talking. If I died, and the fragment was unbound, it'd collapse, as Sint had once told me. The power would be returned to the realm all around me, and it'd be wasted. No, she needed to capture me, to hold me ready for her mistress to harvest, and that wasn't going to end well for them. "Bitch, I've killed your *goddess* already. Her lackeys don't scare me."

Her face contorted with rage, and she hissed something, as on all sides the drow unleashed their arrows.

Oracle hadn't wasted any time, though, and while the legionnaires had braced shields to take the impacts, she'd been casting and holding two more circles, as well as, wonder of wonders, a shield.

That she was a creature of magic was clear in the multicasting. I could just about manage two spells; that she did three like this was incredible. But there was no time for awe.

Both slammed out, and spiders in their hundreds died in flames as the spells were drained in seconds.

More replaced the first, but again, the spiders came, tromping across the border of the spell and bursting into brief flashes of flame and soot. The next and the next did the same, the spells failing under the onslaught.

"Jax, I need to power them!" Oracle sent me, and I grunted, sending her back a fast *"Go for it."*

She switched from passively powering and letting them go, to powering the circles constantly, flash burning the spiders in their thousands. But as she did that, my mana dropped like a rock.

The legionnaires all had magic now, but unlike my own legionnaires back in Dravith, they had it—they knew that intellectually—but they'd spent years learning to use their weapons in a fight. And until they were ordered to, and reminded to, they fell back on cold, hard steel.

That was their biggest mistake, as the first wave of spells landed, not cast by one of us, but by drow mages—and they were *vicious*.

Three spells impacted in short order, each exploding and sending legionnaires hurtling from their feet. Black flames crackled across their bodies as dirt and debris flew in all directions.

The houses hemmed us in; the drow had the high ground, and the bastards made the most of it.

Oracle cut from powering the circles—they'd served their purpose already, most of the spiders having died now—and instead she started dual casting, healing and shields, even as I reached out and triggered my tattoos, dragging the mana out of the spells that were burning my legionnaires—the drow ones, anyway.

Black flames gutted and died, and I grinned, unseen behind my helm. "My turn."

As Oracle focused on healing, I leapt forward. The legionnaires behind me closed ranks around the injured and kept her safe.

"Come to me!" the drow shrieked. "Meet your death!"

I snarled and bounded over a shocked and groaning legionnaire, triggering Hyper Cognition and Mana Overdrive at the same time. The world slowed for me, and I used it to pick out my targets.

The drow—besides being a race of whisky-dicked assholes—were preternaturally graceful, and stronger than normal elves and men. They moved like greased fucking lightning, and when they fell, they twisted in the air like cats. They were beautiful, tall, lithe, and yeah, if the drow men couldn't get it up for their women? It was clear that there was just no fucking chance of it functioning at all.

The non-spidery women, anyway.

All of this meant that the drow had a single, massive weakness, though. *Arrogance*.

They believed that they were the premier race in all of existence, and they fucking showed it. So, when the stupid bitch lunged forward, her blades extended, I moved slowly.

Literally, I had to move like I was pretending to pass through treacle. Then, when I extended my naginata and she shifted a tiny fraction aside to avoid it and drove her daggers for me, she was totally fuckin' unprepared for me to suddenly speed up, roll my wrists, and rotate my naginata in a fast spin.

The metal-clad base came up; it caught her extended forearms halfway to the elbows, smashing them aside, and sent her daggers with them, flipping past my face and into the alley nearby.

Then I nutted her.

Well, it wasn't just a headbutt. She'd leapt forward, and so had I. Her daggers should have taken me in the throat, and she'd been expecting to land her feet on my outstretched leg, then probably flip over me and look really cool.

She'd probably been planning to land in that three-point stance that Black Widow did and having everyone admire her ass in the leather.

Instead, her arms were suddenly going to her left—my right—and she was unarmed. And, because she was an arrogant fuckstick, instead of a helmet, she had a single tiara-looking thing that held her hair back out of her eyes.

My shoulder probably hit her chest at the same time as my armored forehead hit her nose. And, really, that was all she wrote at that point.

The feeling of breaking cartilage and deforming face was a familiar one to me by now. And as I then threw my arm upward and hurled her back, it was into the nearest wall.

The sound she made as the back of her head impacted the stonework suggested that her intellectual prowess was unlikely to ever attract Mensa's attention...if it ever could have before.

The way she then crumpled to the floor made it clear that she'd not be getting back up either. But, unfortunately, that was when I found that I, too, had a minor issue with arrogance, because it'd all been a fucking trap.

I was out ahead of the legionnaires and exposed, as I spun my naginata and sliced through drow like butter. A touch of fire mana fed into the weapons, causing it to barely snag as it severed limbs and took heads.

I actually had a split second where I thought about trying to kill them all as cleanly as possible, in the hope that we could loot some really nice goddamn spider silk pants again, and maybe some material to make Oracle something nice for the bedroom, when the first round hit me.

It was a high-powered sniper round, and I was damn lucky that it was a glancing blow that hit the crest of my helmet and snapped my head sideways.

I staggered, hit the wall and shook myself, turning, just as the gunshot registered. Then, still having both abilities active, though the cost was significant, I twisted. The second shot hit the wall next to me and sent stone fragments exploding out as I searched.

There!

As soon as I saw it, I stepped to the right. A third shot barely missed, and I snarled. But the flash of the barrel for the fourth came too fast, and the impact staggered me again.

This one had hit my right pauldron. I hissed, before shouting out a warning, trying to give directions and an explanation, when a drow hit me from the side and stabbed down at my throat.

I spun, ducking my chin and barely covering the gap between the bottom of my helm and the chest piece, before the next round slammed home and the drow's innermost thoughts and feelings redecorated the wall.

That was when the sound reached me. I spun, staring in horror at the trio of RPGs streaking toward us.

I reacted on instinct, not even having time to form a spell. Instead, I threw up a shield, powered partly by the knowledge I had of mana, and partly by the rock-solid demand that it be formed *right-fuckin'-now*. But it wasn't enough.

Unlike when I had Amon in my mind, I wasn't yet a master of mana in my own right. The half-formed shield took the first blow, but failed.

The second hit the failing shield and detonated. The force was directed almost all outward at the street below and the mouth of the alley—an area filled with my people, all still fighting for their lives.

The third explosion tore through our ranks, sending legionnaires flying like rag dolls. Blood and fragments of armor rained down as the shock wave hit me, driving me back despite my enhanced strength. My ears rang, vision blurred, and for a moment, the world seemed to move in slow motion.

Through the smoke, I could see Oracle—thank the gods she was still standing, her own shields having protected her and the legionnaires closest to her. But others weren't so lucky. Bodies lay strewn across the square…many moving, some not.

"Oracle!" I shouted. My voice sounded distant and muffled in my own ears. "Get out of sight! Earth weapons!"

I scanned the rooftops again, searching for the source of the RPGs.

There—a flash of movement on a balcony three buildings down. A figure in tactical gear was setting up another RPG launcher, and I snarled as I hurled a spell back at him, even as more fire came pounding in.

Malakai's men. It fucking *had* to be. Either he knew about the drow incoming and made use of the situation, or worse, he was coordinating their attack.

"Daralen!" I bellowed. "Rooftop, to your right! You've got magic—USE IT!"

She followed my gaze, then barked orders to the legionnaires. Spells appeared in seconds as she roared out commands, bringing order to the chaos, even as Oracle frantically formed another shield.

Ten seconds later—an eternity in combat, but one bought for them by Oracle's shields and me jinking left and right to draw the sniper's fire—and the legionnaires fired in unison. A great wave as damn near a hundred gleaming magic missiles soared upward and lit the sky, streaking back along to punch into the figures lining up return fire.

They fell, but there were the sounds of more fighting close by. I knew that if fucking Malakai was making the most of the drow incursion, so would the Dark Legion.

I needed to end this. Fast.

I chugged first one, then a second mana potion. The appearing mana almost vanished as soon as I got it, as Oracle made the best use of it she could.

"Move!" I shouted to my people, gesturing toward a narrow side street that would take us back toward the Varnen estate. "Oracle, shields! Daralen, rear guard!"

We began a fighting retreat. Oracle maintained a protective bubble around us as legionnaires supported wounded comrades, or cast and healed each other.

I slammed out two more circles, one ahead that we could march over and one behind, providing healing to us and burning the shit out of our enemies. But the confusion wouldn't last forever.

Dozens of drow had been reduced to kibble in the attack, and houses on either side of the street were collapsing.

I heard cries, shouts for help, and pleas, screams from those unconnected to us and who simply had the bad luck to have been living nearby.

I heard it all and, hardening my heart, I turned away from them.

It was horrible, I knew it was, but right now we were the target. If we stayed here, trying to help them? We'd bring more fire in and more losses to the innocent. And as for the drow?

More forms flitted across the roof of a nearby building and I realized that the small group we'd fought so far were nothing more than the advance party.

Sure, we'd probably taken out most of the spiders, but the drow were scattered all across the city. An RPG streaked from a distant building, exploding in the streets far from us.

Tonight had turned into a bloodbath.

As we reached the mouth of the side street, another explosion rocked the square behind us. More goddamn RPGs. I didn't know how many the fuckers had, but damn, they were clearly determined to make the most of them.

"Jax..." Oracle sent to me, and I paused, falling back as I realized I'd done my usual, and I'd taken point. *"We can't win this defensively, and as much as I don't like it, I think it's time we changed."*

"What do you mean?" I sent to her, frowning.

"I think it's time the new imperator came out to play."

I froze, then started to grin, evilly.

"Daralen, I want you to protect Oracle with your life," I ordered. "I hold you personally fucking responsible for my love and our child, you get that?"

"I do, my prince!" she shouted from behind her shield and straightened. "Might I ask where you'll be?"

The legionnaires were clustered in around us—already a fucking terrible mistake if another RPG launcher found us—but I grinned nonetheless and rolled my shoulders ostentatiously.

"I'm gonna pick the city up and give it a little shake," I said, plans already forming. "Let's see what falls out."

"Very good, sir." She nodded, apparently of the opinion that was all that needed to be said. "Please try to leave the Varnen estate intact, if possible, then. We'll need somewhere to hold the victory celebration."

I looked at her, seeing that gleam in her eyes through the little slit in her helmet, and that she was playing this up for the legionnaires and the survivors of the outriders clustered around us.

Realizing suddenly that they'd just seen horrific weapons they could have never imagined unleashed on us, their friends being literally blown apart, and that they were about to have to run out across open ground again, I nodded.

They needed a little "pick-me-up," that was true.

Fuck it.

I checked my bag and then smiled. I was feeling fed up to the back teeth of the damn things, but I did have eleven mana potions left. Nine of them were greater ones, replacing up to four thousand mana at a time.

I hesitated, then shook my head. I couldn't risk it.

I *wanted* to just slam all the points I had available into my Intelligence. I had more than bloody sixty, after all. Although that sounded like an incredible number, it was also a case of even though it was high, it would realistically only give me six-hundred-odd points more than I currently had. And if I used them more wisely? I should be able to get at least two more centuries under my belt.

That would hurt, and I certainly couldn't do it right now—especially after the last time I'd done that, I'd basically been off my face in pain for about seven hours.

That was why I kept putting it off, because I couldn't guarantee that it'd "only" be that, and not ten or twenty hours next time.

But as soon as we had some security? Damn right I was going for it.

Regardless, as much as I wanted to do that, I couldn't. I pulled out the first potion, a common one, that replaced seven hundred.

After my little potion-popping situation a few minutes ago, I was eleven hundred at the minute; that'd get me eighteen. That gave me at least one use, with a second to be provided with another potion, so to hell with it.

I chugged the potion like it was tequila at the start of the night, lifted my helmet, and gave Oracle a fast, hard kiss. I stepped back, crouched, and launched myself into the air, using my Soaring Majesty.

CHAPTER SIXTEEN

The feeling of flight just never got old. Even now, with blood spattered across my armor and the sounds of battle on all sides, there was something exhilarating about leaving the ground behind.

I rocketed upward, a small drain on my mana and health, but it was negligible compared to what I was going to unleash.

The city spread out below me like a macabre diorama. Fires had broken out in several districts; their orange glow cast dancing shadows across the cobblestone streets as the heavens above opened, the first splatters of rain falling.

I could see figures moving through the shadows—drow assassins, Dark Legion patrols, and what had to be Malakai's men in their tactical gear.

My gaze locked onto a particular rooftop about seven hundred meters from where I hung suspended. That shitebag sniper who'd taken shots at me was still there, in a little cupola atop the building. A massive bell left him barely enough room to move around it, and left him exposed as he leaned out. His rifle glinted in the moonlight as he scanned the streets below, probably looking for me.

He'd missed me darting up and out of the alley, and even now, he hadn't spotted me hovering above—why would he look up, after all? He was already on the highest of the local "normal" buildings.

Perfect.

I focused, channeling a massive surge of mana into one of the new spells I'd gained with my Mage Imperator class. A thousand points of mana—nearly half my entire normal pool—condensed into a crackling vortex of energy around me as I let the arcane phrases and finger twisting gestures flow.

The more I grew used to the spell, the less I'd need the crutch, but for now? Best to do it the way the spell had been gifted to me.

Battlefield Displacement wasn't something I should risk fucking up, after all.

The world blurred, stretched, then snapped back into focus as I materialized directly beside the sniper. The rush of displaced air wasn't subtle; it'd announced my arrival with a loud *crack*, causing him to start turning. But it was too little, too late.

I didn't even bother with my naginata—not this close, this personal, and not with a stone wall behind him.

I punched, and damn hard. My fist slammed into the front of his helmet, and then pile-drove through the ceramic layers, the high-tech sections, and then through the meat behind it.

I'd heard once that we were electrical signals piloting a meat-based mecha, and if that was true? Fuck, he was gonna need to take his for a replacement control center, because I had to brace my left hand—still grasping my naginata—against his shoulder to hold the body still enough to rip my fist free.

I shook the blood and unidentifiable last thoughts and feelings of my victim from my gauntlet and immediately dropped to a crouch, scanning the nearby rooftops for any sign that I'd been spotted. Nothing yet.

With quick, practiced movements, I rifled through the dead man's gear, finding another small mana potion—a pleasant surprise—and then helped myself to his rifle.

It was a sleek, modern sniper rifle with a high-powered scope. I checked the magazine—seven rounds left, and no replacement mags, unfortunately, but it'd have to be enough.

Downing the dead man's mana potion first—it was common, but lower grade than mine, replacing five hundred only—I then slid my naginata into my bag of holding and took up the rifle.

Through the scope, I quickly located one of the RPG teams setting up on a balcony about three blocks away. They were focused on the street where I'd left Oracle and the others.

Not today, fuckers. I grinned.

I steadied my breath, lined up the shot, and squeezed the trigger. The rifle kicked against my shoulder as the round tore through the air, finding its mark in the bearer's skull. Before his companion could react, I'd cycled the bolt and put another round through his chest.

Two down.

This was a hell of a nice rifle, considering I'd been, at best, average with the things when I'd been in the army. Oh, for the difference enhanced Perception and Dexterity made! Mind you, the Strength that enabled me to hold the rifle like it weighed nothing at all helped too.

I swung the rifle to the left, where another team was visible on a rooftop garden. They were more alert, already scanning the area after hearing the shots. No matter—they weren't looking at me yet.

Instead, they were looking to see who I'd been shooting at, and I grinned to myself as I lined up on the first.

Two more shots, two more bodies.

The rifle was a good stopgap, but I knew it wouldn't be enough. I needed to keep moving, to keep the enemy off-balance. I scanned around, deciding that it was better not to waste the opportunity after all; I located a party of Dark legionnaires and shot the obvious leader in the crotch.

Dishonorable? Yeah. But was it hilarious? Definitely.

I waited until he managed to get the healing potion almost to his lips, then shot him in the head, and his friend as well for good measure. Then I dumped the rifle and pulled my naginata back out, after pocketing one more thing from the corpse at my feet.

A grenade.

I smiled. I much preferred being the hunter to the hunted, I decided. Time for round two.

I spotted a cluster of drow moving across a rooftop about a hundred meters away, or two streets over. They were too spread out for a single attack to get them all. But I had a better idea.

Channeling another thousand mana, I cast Battlefield Displacement again, appearing twenty feet above their position. They looked up in shock at the sudden crack of displaced air, then yelled in surprise as I descended, my naginata already spinning in a deadly arc.

The first three died before they could even raise their weapons. The fourth managed to loose an arrow that scraped across my pauldron before I separated his head from his shoulders. The fifth attempted to flee, but a quick sweep of my blade through his hamstrings dropped him to the rooftop, where a final thrust ended his struggles.

Nearby, I spotted movement—more drow, these ones down in the street and accompanied by Dark Legion troops in their distinctive black armor. They'd spotted me and were pointing, shouting orders. I pulled the pin on the grenade, then threw it at them, loving that they just ignored the small cylinder when it bounced into their midst and did nothing at first.

Another mana potion down my throat and I was back to full, another thousand mana channeled. I was suddenly behind their formation, my naginata already in motion. Three went down in my initial assault, blood painting the rooftop in wide arcs. The others turned, drawing weapons, but as they did, Mr. Grenade explained that he was no longer their friend, and the resulting explosion on the far side of their party…*well.*

That threw them off their stroke, that was for sure. More than half spun, looking for the attack; a third more were dead or dying. And the ones that faced me?

They were too slow, too confused.

I switched tactics, triggering Hyper Cognition and Mana Overdrive. I rammed my blade into the gut of one of the drow and pinned him to the figure behind him; then I abandoned the naginata momentarily in favor of raw brutality.

I grabbed the next nearest—a Dark legionnaire—by his helm, yanking him toward me as I drove my armored knee up into his groin. As he doubled over, I wrenched his head around with enough force to snap his neck, then used his body as a shield against the crossbow bolt that flew at me from one of his companions.

Dropping the corpse, I lunged forward, catching the crossbowman by the throat with my gauntleted hand, lifting him bodily and slamming him down onto the cobbles hard enough to crack them. His chest caved in from the impact, and blood bubbled from his lips.

A drow came at me from the side, twin daggers flashing. I caught her right wrist mid-thrust, batted aside the left, and twisted until the bones shattered. Then I drove my forehead into her face, her nose collapsing under the impact.

She staggered back, but I didn't let go. Instead, I grabbed her head, pulled her toward me and drove my knee into her sternum with enough force to crush her heart. That'd teach the fuckers to not wear proper armor.

The last two drow tried to push back into their companions and flee. But instead of allowing that, I reclaimed my naginata and cast a Pyroclastic Blast into the literal middle of the still reeling group.

Arrows streaked down toward me as the small band of Dark legionnaires basically became "No. 27 without rice, extra crispy." And I chugged another potion, then triggered the spell again, this time appearing in the air a hundred meters up; then I triggered Soaring Majesty, flashing down into the midst of the four drow archers. I killed the first before he'd even seen where I was; the second grabbed his companion and shoved him into my way, gaining himself a few precious seconds as I threw the betrayed drow off the side of the building headfirst. I gave chase, covering the distance in a few bounds.

The backstabbing bastard fell as I severed his spine with a horizontal slash. The other reached the edge of the roof, preparing to leap to the next building—

But I wasn't done with him yet. One more mana potion later, I had eleven hundred mana and climbing, thanks to the sheer amount of regeneration I was receiving from so many potions.

"Battlefield Displacement," I growled, vanishing and reappearing directly in his path as he jumped. The look of terror on his face as he realized what had happened was priceless. I caught him midair, my hand closing around his throat.

"Tell your friends," I snarled, "the Prince of the Empire is coming for them all."

Then I hurled him from the rooftop, his screams trailing off as he plummeted to the street below.

I paused, taking stock. My mana was running low again, but I still had several potions left. More importantly, I'd created chaos among the enemy forces. They no longer knew where I would strike next, and that uncertainty was working well. I could hear sporadic gunfire, spells and shouts from the distance that I damn well knew was away from anyone who had sworn to me, thanks to the threads that bound the sworn and me together.

Through my bond with Oracle, I could sense that she and the legionnaires were making progress toward the house. Good. I needed them out of harm's way for what came next.

I drained another potion and took to the air again, scanning the city below. There—a larger contingent of Dark Legion troops was setting up some kind of perimeter around what looked like a command tent in a small plaza. Perfect.

This time, I didn't bother with stealth. I soared directly overhead, drawing their attention deliberately. Crossbow bolts and arrows flew toward me, but I moved too fast, too erratically for them to effectively track.

I cast Battlefield Displacement once more, this time appearing directly in the center of their formation. The moment I materialized, I unleashed a spinning attack with my naginata. The blade trailed fire as I channeled mana through it. Blood and severed limbs flew in every direction as I carved through their ranks like a thresher through wheat.

A Dark Legion commander charged me, his sword raised high. I parried his strike with the blade of my naginata, then drove the butt end into his crotch hard enough to lift him from his feet, doubling him over. As he gasped for breath, I drove my knee into his face, sending him reeling backward to crash to the ground. Before he could recover, I stepped in close and drove the blade of my weapon through his chest, lifting him bodily into the air. He thrashed, then I shucked him off the blade, back down onto the cobblestones.

More came at me from all sides, their black armor gleaming dully in the firelight. I switched to a more defensive stance, letting them circle me, waiting for their attack. When it came, I was ready.

The first two attacked in tandem: one high, one low. I leapt over the low attack, twisted in midair to avoid the high one, and then landed behind them. Before they could turn, my naginata had claimed both their lives with a single sweeping cut, and I grinned.

I fucking loved magic. They wore heavy plate armor, and my blade—yeah, sure, I was channeling into it, and it was fire, which I had affinities and gifts with, but for it to treat their armor like gossamer threads?

It was wonderful, and as much because of my insane strength as it was the blade.

Three more rushed me from different directions. I channeled even more mana into my weapon, causing the blade to glow white-hot. As they came within range, I spun in place, creating a whirlwind of flaming death that caught all three. Their armor melted into their flesh as they fell, screaming.

I laughed, feeling unstoppable, a god of war made flesh. Each enemy that fell only further fueled my rage, driving me to greater feats of violence. Blood soaked the cobblestones, turning the plaza into a scarlet reflection of my wrath.

And then I saw him, the commander of this particular Dark Legion contingent, I guessed, standing at the entrance to what must have been their command tent. Unlike his troops, he wore no helmet. His scarred face twisted in a mixture of rage and fear.

"Face me, apostate!" he bellowed, drawing a wicked-looking blade that pulsed with dark energy. Those on either side fell back, clearing the way.

I grinned, lifting the bottom of my helmet and drinking another mana potion as I strode toward him, then tossing it over my shoulder and resettling my helmet. "With fucking pleasure!"

Our blades met with a crash that sent sparks flying. He was good—better than his underlings by far. And, more importantly, the blade wasn't just steel or iron.

Whatever it was, it was reinforced enough that it took my strikes and deflected them in a shower of glowing sparks that lit the night. Each strike was calculated, each parry executed with precision, rigorous training obvious with every stance he shifted from or to.

He was good, I had to admit.

I feinted left, then struck from the right; my naginata slipped past his guard to score a shallow cut across his ribs. He hissed in pain but didn't falter, countering with a low sweep that I barely managed to jump over.

We traded blows for what felt like minutes but was probably only seconds. The world around us faded away as we focused solely on the dance of death. He managed to land a blow on my left arm; his enchanted blade gouged into my armor deep enough to sear the flesh beneath. I retaliated by driving my knee into his gut, forcing him back.

"You fight well," I acknowledged, circling him warily.

"I was trained by Lord Bartholomew himself," he spat, blood flecking his lips.

"Seriously? Lord fucking Bart?" I snorted, then cast Complex Healing. I spun my naginata, twisting it from an overhead flick into "beating the grass," where you slipped from left hand dominant to right, over and over, driving him back as I grinned ferally. Then I lunged forward in a burst of speed enhanced by the now available again Mana Overdrive.

My naginata drove through his defense, piercing his shoulder and pinning him to the tent pole behind him. He screamed, dropping his sword as he clutched at the shaft impaling him.

"Your god is weak," I whispered, leaning in close. "And so are you."

I twisted the blade, widening the wound, then pulled it free, allowing him to slump to the ground. As he gasped and clutched at his ruined shoulder, I snatched up his sword and slid it into my bag of holding, then grinned at him, though he couldn't see it with my helmet on.

"Good fight," I congratulated him, before raising my voice and speaking to those on all sides. "Now, I've already had a bunch of you dark dicks swap sides when I proved I could beat you like a redheaded stepchild, so, before I slaughter you all, any takers?" I turned slowly, looking at the silent group.

Dozens of legionnaires stared at me, literally, and I couldn't help but grin.

I knew I shouldn't be feeling this way—I shouldn't. I wasn't supposed to revel in the slaughter like this; these were real people, real lives that were ending, all because I decided that they should. But honestly?

It was both an intoxicating mix of danger and skill, adrenaline and…and I didn't know what. I just knew it felt incredible, and the more I did it, the more I wanted to do it.

I was becoming a god amongst lesser men, and fuck me, I deserved this! I was doing incredible and I was…

…

……

……….

I was a fucking idiot.

That was the first thought that came to me, long seconds later as the world fuzzed back into focus. I stared muzzily up at the dim shapes that strode closer, out of the darkness.

I blinked, or tried to, finding that I could taste copper pennies, that the air smelled of ozone, and yeah, my muscles were still unlocking.

Symbols flashed in my vision, symbols I barely managed to make sense of, before thankfully, they faded.

They were clear in one way, though: between "concussed," "stunned," and "burning," I was both incredibly lucky that the pain was somehow choosing to remain distant, and damn close to the edge, considering that my health bar flared and flashed an angry, almost empty, red.

As the last of the debuffs faded, I managed to focus my right eye. I realized that the reason my left was feeling weird was that there was no input coming from that side at all.

Blinking? Yeah, a little fucking hard when you've only got one eye.

I felt the presence of the gods and how the thunder rolled. The pressure of divine presences as the nine "greater," but oh so much lessened, gods and their two lesser, and weirdly currently stronger companions, all roared and fought with Nimon and his pantheon of dickheads.

"Yu fuckin' di' it ag'in…" I mumbled, realizing as I pushed myself out of the crater that, first, yeah, I was in a fucking *crater*.

One that had been hammered into the ground by some incredibly powerful impact from above.

Secondly? On all sides, I saw burned, charred, smoldering, and obviously dead or dying Dark legionnaires.

That dark dickhead had hit me with something—probably that fucking black lightning again—and in a high enough power level that it'd killed everything around me…probably because he'd been worried I was about to make some more of his soldiers change sides.

I mean, I'd been sort of joking about it, but I didn't believe any of them would have done it. Not again.

The only reason they had last time was that Thomas was my brother, and those who had switched over had all been loyal to him, more or less.

They'd certainly been shit on from a great height by the Church of the Dark, put it that way.

Now, though? As I realized that the dick genuinely didn't understand people at all, and he'd apparently thought that they were going to do it? I started to laugh.

It was more wheeze than a laugh, admittedly, and yeah, there was still smoke rising from me and the area around me.

Sure, I couldn't fully focus my eyes—my eye, I mean—and everything was a bit dim and hard to make out. But I could deal with that, I decided. I saw movement, and this time I managed to kickstart my brain into more or less a semblance of activity. I hit myself with a Frostfire Circle of Cleansing first; then, as the shadowy figures cried out and backed up, and shouts rose again, I managed a Complex Healing, and then a second one.

As the last one kicked in fully, a pain ran through my head, like a pressure building higher and higher. Then, with a pop, the pressure suddenly vanished. I blinked, then shook my head in shock. A final debuff—fractured skull—that I'd been unable to make sense of before faded away.

Now, with that done, I could tell three things.

First, I was surrounded by a mixture of Dark legionnaires, Malakai's people, and the fucking drow. But that was okay, because they were apparently arguing over who got to do the honors, having thought I was brain-dead or some such. Staggered throughout the crowd were a bunch of lunatic priests chanting some stupid atonal bullshit.

Secondly, the gods were *really* pissed, and that was also adding to the whole "what the hell do we do now" situation, as the rolling thunder alone was enough to make the air feel like a drum.

A final roll almost shattered my eardrums again, and did manage to shatter a nearby window with the pressure. I wondered whether that was a one or a twenty…that the thunder had rolled.

Then I shook that stupid thought off, because the third thing presented itself front and center in my brain again.

"JAX!" Oracle yelled into my brain.

I flinched, sending a wave of shock, concern, nervous guilt, and confusion out to both her and Sehran.

"What?" I asked.

"I am going to KILL you!" she seethed. *"Stop picking fights with Nimon!"*

"But—"

"You might have started a true war of the gods, Jax!" Oracle snapped. *"We won't win that, but Jenae and the others can't let this slide! They've appealed for intervention!"*

"What?" I asked, even more confused. *"From who?!"*

"They won't say, but they're insanely pissed at him, at you, and at this world, so, Jax, just get out of there and let whatever happens, happen!"

That, of course, was when the last RPG hit.

I was picked up and hurled through the air and into a wall. When I crashed to the ground, it was with the wall joining me, ramming down atop me, in a wave that only the armor saved me from being crushed by.

As it was, though, I was left battered, bruised, and pinned. My health wasn't bad, but it was far from full. And at some point, I'd already lost both Hyper Cognition and Mana Overdrive.

I struggled, my brain feeling like it was more mush than meat, as I forced myself, step by painful step, through the healing, until it was nearly done. I paused, trying to get a mana potion free of my bag.

I was trapped under a section of rubble that was vaguely triangular—a corner of the wall, I was willing to bet. But whatever was happening out there—I could still hear goddamn chanting—I was definitely going to need just one more potion, and then I'd kick their arses.

My mana was redlining. I snarled. If Oracle had needed to use it so much and so suddenly—I'd had almost a third of it left when I cast the healing and should still have plenty, surely—then I had to get the potion in me fast and my mana back up to…

My hand stopped dead, as my fingers reached the bottom of the bag, shoving frantically, and I froze.

Carefully, I checked the pouch, and then the location on my hip. Fear rose in me as I confirmed that yes, that was where my bag of holding should be, and that it was both the right size and shape.

What it wasn't, though, was noticeably fuckin' magical, considering that I could feel cloth and sod all else!

Absolute terror overtook me for a handful of seconds, as I remembered being back in the prax. The feeling of no magic, of being trapped in the dark and in the deep, the fear of knowing that no matter what I did, my magic wasn't there.

I'd learned from that. I'd survived it; I'd found ways of doing things. But the one thing that I hadn't managed to do, not yet, was get over that sudden fear of losing my magic.

And worst of all, right now, as Oracle's distant voice faded like radio static, as the last of my mana bottomed out, was the feeling of weakness that flowed through me.

I was trapped, under stone and brick, metal and rubble, and as the chanting went on and on, I felt myself growing…weaker.

Shit.

The reality of all of this suddenly crashed in on me.

I spent so much of my time running, racing from one place to the next, adjusting my plans on the fly, and then changing them again, that I just…I got used to always being in motion, and the feeling that because I never knew what was going to happen next, there was no way anyone else could either.

Now, I realized, hearing that chanting again, that it just wasn't true.

They'd prepared for me. They were casting some kind of area effect spell designed to interfere with mana manipulation, or perhaps even to stop my mana specifically. Though how that was possible, I just didn't know.

I swallowed hard. If I didn't get the hell out of here, out from under all the rubble and soon, then this was going to end badly for me. I started to push the rocks and rubble aside.

I should have been able to shoulder my way through this with ease. Hell, I'd thrown rocks like this aside on many an occasion. The first time I'd fought a drider, I'd used a rock that had to weigh more than all this crap, to squash her like the bug she was.

Now, though, as I strained and heaved, moving first the smaller rocks, and then the larger, second by second, minute by painful minute, I heard it: a slow, mocking applause from somewhere beyond the rubble pile.

A hulking figure was suddenly revealed, dragging the largest rock aside, then dropping it to the side, staggering and moving back to expose…a shape that stepped out from the shadows of a nearby building.

He wore the ornate armor of a Dark Legion high commander, his face hidden behind a helm shaped like a snarling demon. On all sides, across the courtyard that I found myself in, dozens of figures stared at me with derision and contempt clear on their faces.

"Impressive." His voice echoed oddly through his helm. "Most impressive. You've slaughtered what, thirty? Forty? Fifty even, of my soldiers? A pity we brought hundreds, with thousands more on the way."

I tried to respond, but found my voice weakened by the field. The chanting grew louder, and a fresh wave of exhaustion washed through me. All I could manage was a hoarse whisper: "Who…are…you?"

He reached up, removing his helmet to reveal a face I recognized—it was Vectus, the Dark Legion commander from the parley. His lips curled into a smile that never reached his cold eyes.

"I am the Voice of Nimon, here and now, and I bring His words," he said. "I am the chosen instrument of His will. And you, apostate, are His enemy."

I tried to lunge at him, but my limbs felt like they were moving through molasses. I barely managed to get to my knees, before I fell forward and crashed to the ground, trapped there by the incredible weight of my armor.

The anti-mana field was reaching its peak strength now, rendering me weaker than I'd ever felt in my life. And as I was? My incredible armor—armor I loved and that had seen me across the damn continent and through I didn't know how many fights—was pinning me to the ground.

Vectus laughed at my struggles, circling me with predatory grace. "You truly thought you could challenge a god and walk away? Nimon is eternal. Nimon is patient. He knew you would come here, to this city, to this very courtyard."

"Bullshit," I managed to force out.

"Is it?" he countered. "Consider this—why did the drow attack tonight, of all nights? They knew you were coming, so why not ambush you on the bridge? Why did a spider not creep into your bedroll and simply bite you as you slept, paralyzing you? Why did they not do this in their tens of thousands, night after night, preventing you from ever sleeping, from recovering your mana? Why were Malakai's forces so perfectly positioned? Why did my legion have an anti-mana ritual prepared and attuned specifically for you?"

I didn't answer, conserving what little strength I had left.

"We did it, because Nimon showed us," Vectus continued, his voice taking on a fervent, almost ecstatic quality. "In visions, in dreams, He revealed your coming. He commanded the drow, through their mistress, to obey. He made deals with the nobility to delay you, with House Malakai to goad you. Every step you've taken since facing Lady Illoth has been according to His design."

He gestured, and more Dark Legion troops emerged from the surrounding buildings, forming a perimeter around the courtyard. There had to be at least fifty of them, all armed, all watching me with expressions ranging from fear to hatred.

"Great Lord Nimon wanted you to feel powerful," Vectus explained, drawing a wickedly curved dagger from his belt. "Wanted you to believe you were unstoppable. So that when the moment of your fall came, it would be all the more crushing."

He approached me slowly, the dagger gleaming in the firelight. "You will release your fragments of divinity to me, and they shall be returned to the Great God Nimon, their ultimate rightful owner. Your head will adorn the gates of the Dark citadel as a warning to all who would oppose the true god of this realm."

I managed to lift my head, staring directly into his eyes. "If…Nimon's so…powerful," I gasped, "why…doesn't He…come Himself?"

Vectus's expression darkened. "Blasphemy to the end. It will make your suffering all the—"

He never finished the sentence. A dark shape plummeted from the sky, crashing into him with enough force to drive him to the stone with a crunch of breaking bone.

There was a flash of violet skin and the gleam of curved claws. Suddenly, Vectus was missing his head.

Sehran stood over his body, her wings spread wide. Her form radiated power and fury I'd never seen from her before. And she wasn't alone.

Half a dozen other succubai descended from the night sky. Their forms blurred as they moved with inhuman speed among the Dark mages and troops. Screams erupted as claws tore through throats and flesh with equal ease; blood sprayed in wide arcs as the demons unleashed their full fury.

The mages maintaining the anti-mana ritual were the first to die, their throats torn out before they could react, but they were far from the last. As they fell, the oppressive field began to weaken; my strength returned in a surge that left me gasping.

Sehran was at my side in an instant, her clawed hand extended to help me up. "Sorry I'm late." She grinned, her fangs gleaming. "Had to convince some new friends to join the party."

"You know, I think I love you," I croaked up at her.

Her grin widened. "Now that's familiar—a man on his back, looking up at me and telling me he loves me…" She shrugged. "I mean…I *am* just that good…"

"Plus, that skirt is short enough I can just about see your breakfast." I snorted. "Fuck's sake, Sehran, thank you."

I took her hand and struggled to my feet as the last of the anti-mana field failed, my mana no longer blinking like I was at an all-night rave on acid. Around us, the surviving Dark Legion troops were trying to fight. But as the succubai beheaded their victims, they screamed, wave after wave of sonic screams that made the very air shiver as the succubai continued their slaughter.

A bowel-loosening terror rose in me, and then, suddenly, as Sehran reached out to me, laying one hand on my shoulder and crooning something without words, the fear faded, a new strength growing.

"Perfect timing," I managed, retrieving my naginata from the corpse currently holding it for me. "How did you find me?"

"You weren't exactly subtle," she replied after a few seconds, as the succubai stopped singing and she could drop her own song. She gestured to the fires and destruction I'd left in my wake across the city, and smiled. "Plus, the mistress has been watching everything from the tower. She sent us to fetch you."

"The mistress?" I asked, confusion momentarily replacing exhaustion.

"Seraphina," Sehran explained. "Mistress of the succubai of Gaij. She wants to meet you. And after what I told her about you, she's willing to offer an alliance, subject to some conditions and a conversation. But first…are you okay?"

"I…will be." I forced a smile, knowing that she could feel it through my bond, much as Oracle did as I opened myself to her as well. There was so much to say, to explain, but for now it was better to just share myself and feel her reaching to me, sensing everything that was going on.

I glanced around at the carnage in the courtyard, then at the succubai who were now regrouping, their forms silhouetted against the night sky. They were magnificent and terrifying in equal measure, their bodies perfect engines of destruction.

"An alliance sounds good right about now," I admitted. "But what about Oracle and the others?"

"Already taken care of," Sehran assured me. "The mistress sent another team to guide them to safety. They'll meet us at the tower."

I nodded, relief washing over me. Then I paused, looking at the succubai more closely. There was something different about them—an aura of power that seemed almost…desperate, and oh so very hungry.

They grabbed onto figures left and right, biting down forcefully and draining them, literally ripping their life free, and I swallowed hard.

"What aren't you telling me?" I asked Sehran.

She hesitated, then sighed. "The tower…it's not what we thought. The succubai aren't its masters—they're its prisoners. They've been sustaining it with their own essence for centuries, trapped inside because if they leave, it'll collapse."

"So no great source of mana to claim the territory," I realized aloud.

"No," she confirmed. "But Seraphina thinks you might be able to help them. And in return, they'll help you claim the city."

I considered this, looking out over the burning cityscape toward the Tower of Gaij, its massive bulk silhouetted against the night sky. The situation had just become vastly more complicated, but also potentially more interesting.

"Well then." I slid my naginata into my bag of holding, feeling incredible relief as it worked. I tugged a potion free, popping it and chugging it. "Let's not keep the mistress waiting."

One of the succubai approached—a striking creature with hair like living flame and skin the color of polished obsidian. "We must move quickly," she said, her voice musical yet edged with steel. "The Dark Legion will regroup soon, and Malakai's forces are already throwing off the compulsion."

I looked to Sehran, who nodded in confirmation. "Lead the way," I told the flame-haired succubus.

She and her sisters took to the air, their wings beating powerfully against the night. Sehran offered me her hand.

"I can fly on my own," I pointed out.

"Can you?" she asked. "You look like shit."

She was right. My mana reserves had been dangerously low, and my physical body had taken more punishment than I cared to admit. It was surging up faster and faster—the potion had been enough to fill me—but even as I received the mana, it was siphoned off by Oracle…healing others, I sensed.

There was no danger, not right away, or at least not to her, but I felt her desperate need to be back with me, and her wish that whatever I do, I not fucking waste mana needlessly, not now.

I nodded and accepted her hand, powering my flight with Soaring Majesty, but letting Sehran help as well, half dragging me into the air. We rose after her sisters, and left the carnage behind.

CHAPTER SEVENTEEN

Flying through the night air, even with Sehran half-carrying me, reminded me again of how damn much I loved having access to magic. My mana reserves were recovering, but they also felt like someone had rammed a wire brush through them, *again.*

And the anti-mana field had left me feeling like I'd been hit by a truck, then backed over, and then the driver had gotten out to take a piss on me. But still, I was flying!

"We're almost there," Sehran called, her voice carrying easily over the rush of wind. "Do you see the tower?"

I looked ahead and snorted softly. The Tower of Gaij was a monster, so of goddamn course I could see it. It wasn't as impressive as the Great Tower back on Dravith, though here, set in the middle of a city and half a mile high, it certainly stood out, that was for sure.

Where the Great Tower in Dravith had been a solid pillar of imperial might, this one was battered, truncated, and the top floor of it had been finished off with a crenellation that made it look like a squat, round medieval castle.

Even as damaged as it was—obviously fixed and botched together, with entire sections missing or crumbled away—it was fucking magnificent.

"Impressive," I admitted. "Though it's seen better days."

"Seven hundred years of neglect after a collapse will do that," Sehran agreed. "But just wait until you see the inside."

We flew over the outer wall. A tingle of magic washed over us as we passed through whatever wards were in place.

The succubai seemed unbothered, and by extension, the wards ignored me as well, making me wonder—again—what the hell they were, and why we didn't have them back home.

We landed on a large balcony about two-thirds of the way up the structure. The flame-haired succubus who'd led our flight—I still didn't know her name—gestured toward a set of ornate doors.

"The mistress awaits within," she said. "She's…eager to meet you."

Something about the way she hesitated on the word "eager" made me instantly wary. I exchanged a quick glance with Sehran, who gave me the smallest of shrugs, and I returned it.

"Give me a minute." I blew out a long breath and then sunk to one knee, reaching out to Jenae.

"The mistress…" The succubai had barely started before she choked off her response, the feeling of a divine presence filling the air.

"Jax," Jenae said shortly. ***"I cannot explain the situation, nor our response, but understand that Nimon crossed a line that cannot be crossed without consequences and it has already cost him greatly. When I can explain, and if, I will. Until then, please, do not push this."***

"I…all right." I heard the warning and the stress in her voice, and decided that as much as I wanted to have this out—that dickhead had hit me with a lightning

bolt *again*, after all—I was better off trusting her with this one. *"Just let me know what you can."*

"I will, and thank you."

A sudden warmth spread through me, and I noted that my Constitution, Perception, and Charisma had been bumped by five points each for the next hour, due to a blessing of my goddess, and I smiled despite myself.

Alrighty then, time to meet the boss, I decided, waving for the slightly dazed succubus to lead the way.

The doors opened onto a corridor lined with imperial-style tapestries, though these depicted events I didn't recognize—as well as giving more prominence to the non-human races that had served the empire. Interesting change compared to the ones in the chambers at Dravith, where the leaders were clearly human and were surrounded by those other races.

They were also armored to fuck, and seemed to be making the point: let's be friends…*or else*.

We stepped in through the balcony doors and then through a second set of closed doors, making me snort as I got the layout. Just like back home on Earth, we might have a porch to stop the weather outside getting in, they'd done that here with the little entrance.

A stupid thing, sure, but it made me laugh.

Next, we entered a vast circular chamber that had to occupy a quarter of the entire floor. Bookshelves lined the walls, interrupted by tall windows offering panoramic views of the still burning city below. A domed ceiling soared overhead, and a raised dais in the center had a reclined chaise lounge, one of those weird half-couch, half-bed things.

The being seated upon it was, without question, the most striking succubus I'd ever seen. Her skin was midnight blue, nearly black, with shifting gold patterns that reminded me of the aurora borealis. Her wings were enormous—at least twice Sehran's size—and seemed to be made of, well, the thing that sprung to mind, considering she was barely decent and a succubus, were the old black silk sheets I'd once spent a damn fortune on.

They'd been comfy as hell, nice and cool…and impossible to get goddamn stains out of. A terrible waste of damn money.

Still, her wings were like that: silk with actual fucking stars twinkling within them. Her eyes were solid gold, no pupil or white…just pure molten gold that fixed on me with unnerving intensity.

"Be welcome, Jax, Prince of the Empire." Her voice was a throaty purr that ran up and down my back. "I am Seraphina, Mistress of Gaij. Your companion has told me much about you."

I gave a slight bow—this was her home, after all. "The pleasure's mine, Lady Seraphina. I understand we've got a lot to talk about."

"Indeed we do." She rose from her throne with fluid grace. "Starting with why you believe you should control this tower, and why we should aid you rather than the dozens of other claimants who have made similar boasts."

"Because unlike the others," I replied bluntly, "I don't want to use you. I want to free you."

Her golden eyes narrowed slightly. "Bold words. Sehran has spoken of you, and your position, and warned that subtlety was not your way."

"It saves time," I agreed. "But before we continue, my companions? Oracle and the others?"

"They are being guided through the city by my agents," Seraphina said. "They'll arrive at the tower's old entrance within the hour. Your Oracle is…most remarkable. A wisp in physical form, carrying your child, no less."

"She is," I confirmed, unsurprised that Sehran had shared that. "And yes, she's pregnant."

Seraphina circled me slowly, studying me like I was a particularly interesting specimen. "Remarkable indeed. The children of succubai and mortals rarely survive to term, and we are forced to abandon them when they do. Yet despite the obvious issues, you've somehow created life with a being that should have no reproductive system at all."

"Well, if it's any consolation, it wasn't planned, but it's very much all natural," I said dryly.

She laughed, then shook her head and straightened. "Well, regardless, congratulations. Have we been formal and polite enough, or shall we continue to fence?"

"Definitely long enough." I snorted. "Sorry, Seraphina. Honestly, I'm just not very good at this side of things. I have people who help me with it, but…" I shrugged. "Being blunt saves a lot of time, and it worked for Amon."

"That it did, right up until the end. Might want to remember that." Her eyes twinkled. "Come, Jax. We have a lot to discuss, and little time before your enemies regroup."

She led us to a side chamber where a table had been set with food and drink. Other succubai were already present, including a scarred elder who smiled toothily, and stared at me like I was a burger and fries and she was starving. They watched me with expressions ranging from curiosity to outright suspicion.

I accepted a goblet of wine but shook my head at the offered food. "Honestly, we can eat later. I had some shitty food at the meeting I had earlier and it's still not sitting right. So, Sehran mentioned something about prisoners?"

Seraphina's expression darkened. "Yes. Not prisoners of others, but prisoners of the tower itself." She took a sip from her own goblet before continuing. "When the cataclysm struck, the wisps who maintained this tower were destroyed—the first two from the physical collapse of sections where their anchor points were, the third from feedback shock as it tried to hold it all together, and well…we don't know more. It's not exactly our area of expertise."

She gestured around us. "We were here on an exchange program. Several of your warlocks were visiting our home, and we were here, though in admittedly larger numbers, as your realm, well, it's a bit nicer to visit for outsiders." She smiled ferally. "The empire had just begun allowing limited planar travel for those willing to abide by its laws. We had been granted temporary residency in exchange for certain…services, and to assist the researchers."

"And that's how you became guests of the tower," I guessed.

"Among other things," she agreed with a slight smile. "When the tower began to collapse, those of us who survived faced a choice—flee and watch it crumble completely, or stay and try to preserve it. We chose to stay. The contract that we'd sworn was nebulous enough on certain points that we didn't foresee damage to the tower in its possibilities. We had sworn to assist in protecting the tower should there be a need. Between a full legion and it being the central location for training of warlocks? We considered it about as safe as it was possible to be."

"Why not just return to the hells?" I asked.

"Because we could not." The older, scarred succubus—Lilandra, I'd learned her name was—spoke up. "Both because our oath bound us to assist the tower and leaving it to collapse would count as breaking that, and because despite the limited gains we've made—considering how long we've been here—once we return, we would never be permitted to leave again. The dukes and princes of hell guard their power jealously. Any succubus who has grown to our level would be considered…dangerous."

"And you'd grown to like it here," I suggested.

"We had grown to *love* it," Seraphina corrected. "For the first time, we were not merely servants or tools, but respected members of society—at least within these walls. The wider world might have viewed us as exotic curiosities or worse, but here, we were citizens of the realm, and our lot was more pleasant than many of us had known for most of our time."

She gestured to the chamber around us. "So we made our choice. We would preserve the tower, using our own essence to replace what the wisps had provided, and channeling the mana of the realm into and through ourselves, forming conduits that fed the tower, and slowly staved off its inevitable entropy.

"When you consider the size of the original tower, and the significant weight that was pressing down, it would have failed. The pressure alone, without the mana to repair and augment the stone below? Impossible. But with us feeding the little we could, and with the greater structure gone, it was enough. We became the pillars holding up this remnant of the empire."

"And that's why you can't leave," I realized. "You're literally part of the tower's foundation."

"Precisely," she confirmed. "Every succubus you see here channels the majority of her mana into the tower each day. It has stunted our growth, prevented us from reaching anything like our full potential. Where we should have grown in power over these centuries, instead we have merely…existed. But we live for the time we have here to relax, to feed, and more."

I frowned, thinking through the implications. "So there's no massive reservoir of mana here that I could tap to claim the territory, that I get, but to see that the reason it all still stands is you? Damn."

"Exactly." Seraphina sighed. "Just us, feeding on the tower and then slowly draining ourselves to keep these walls from crumbling completely."

"Fuck," I muttered. "I know exactly what you're saying as well, to be clear," I admitted, scratching my chin. "The Great Tower in Dravith? It was intact, the wisps having channeled everything they had into the shields just before the cataclysm. But it wasn't out of blind luck. Or at least not quite.

"The tower was under attack and falling to a SporeMother. The legion hadn't yet taken control and the limited defenders were being slaughtered. The mage in charge ordered the wisps to drain the mana banks into the tower's structure and shields to stop the SporeMother gaining access to it and feeding, and then they were to sleep.

"That's how I met Oracle, as one of the tower's original wisps. The tower itself survived the cataclysm, but mainly because Dravith wasn't as developed as this continent. So, the tower was lost, forgotten about...as was the SporeMother, who'd lost most of her forces and stayed, squatting in it.

"Then I came along, finding an utterly ruined and collapsing tower. I killed the SporeMother, then claimed the structure, starting the repairs," I finished.

"You repaired it?" The mistress sat forward and fixed me with those peculiar eyes.

"I did, but don't get your hopes up." I sighed. "First of all, the tower was degraded, but more or less intact. Sure, a bad storm could have finished it off, but the majority of it was solid, more or less. Most importantly, the mana collectors were there. They were just shut down...hmmm..."

"What?" she prodded.

"I'm wondering if I could jump start the tower," I admitted. "Funnel enough mana into the structure that it kicks in the self-repair functions, and that stabilizes the structure, then have Oracle adjust the seed or whatever it has.

"I mean, she'd told me ages ago that the towers were built from special seeds. In theory, all we need to do is make a change to that seed and tell it that the roof, with all the mana collectors, is actually the roof you currently have, right? Give it the raw materials and enough mana and it'll grow a replacement. Right?"

"You could do this?" she asked. "Repair the tower?"

"Honestly, I don't know," I admitted. "When I did it last time, I had a team of wisps who knew what they were doing, and they worked on it, consuming an absolute fuckton of manastones as well. Without those two points, I'd be slamming a shitload of mana into the tower and just hoping that it can make it work."

"We can do this." She sighed. "Forcing mana into the structure of the tower is not something we have an issue with. The sheer quantity of mana needed, though? That is the issue. It would take hundreds, if not tens of thousands, of willing people to drain their mana into the tower to make an appreciable difference."

"Or—and this is because of my abilities, mind you—maybe just me," I muttered, before smiling at her. "Tell me more about us working together."

"We would be willing to accept you as master of the tower and assist you in taking the territory, through claiming the city, provided you in turn accept that I rule the tower as your second, and day-to-day ruler. I receive an imperial title, and a position on whatever council you put in place here, as well as my people and myself being accepted as imperial citizens, not playthings.

"Lastly, your wisp...she was joined to that tower? Then she joins to this one, and she will see what is required. If all else fails, and we cannot repair the tower, then you release us from the oath here and we go our separate ways."

"That last one is a hard pass." I shook my head. "I love Oracle, and even if I didn't, there's no goddamn way I'd force her to bond to the tower and stay here, not even considering that she's the love of my life, a free person in her own right and pregnant with my child. I'll do you one better, though."

"Go on."

"You accept me as master of the tower; you help me take the city and the territory. Once those are done, if you want to stay here, I'll do what I can to make the city cover the costs of maintaining the tower. And, if for whatever reason, we can't repair the tower and we have to accept its collapse, I have legionnaires who have expressed interest in bonding succubai. I'll introduce you to them, and depending on how many of you and them there are, either I'll detach them to help here, or you can come with us, and I'll free you from the bond to the tower, once you swear to me."

"An…acceptable counter." She nodded. "But I require an imperial…"

"A title, and your people and you to be imperial citizens…yeah, sorry. I accept that."

"Very well, there will be details to work out, such as the title and our position in the city, but your broad offer is acceptable. What is the first step?"

I smiled. "The first step is that you help me get my people inside these walls, safely and quietly," I said. "Until Oracle is safe…"

"We have already made plans," she assured me. "The outside world suspects there are at most a dozen of us here. In reality, there are nearly fifty, with thirty working on channeling into the tower at any one time.

"We have dispatched twenty of them to shield your party, using our gifts to hide their passage from all eyes. And should they be discovered? We will fight for them."

"That…works?" I mused.

"Jax?" Sehran interjected. "Believe me, although I'm not that skilled at it, my sisters have spent centuries practicing…it's how they've been able to visit the city outside at all, through using our inherent magic to conceal themselves. In this case, they can make the legion look like something else…Dark legionnaires, for example, or guardsmen, and they can simply march through the streets as if they were on patrol. Trust me, and know that Oracle will be as safe as we can make her."

"I trust you." I smiled at her, my fear falling away. "In that case, we need to make a change. Oracle and her party were going to come here and that was it, but now we might as well get everyone moving then. No sense in waiting for a second chance. Could you…?"

"I'll go with them, and I'll stay with Oracle," she promised, standing and looking to the mistress quizzically. "May I…?" she asked, clearly wanting us both to sign off on her joining their party.

"Of course, child." Seraphina smiled languidly. "Go and serve your prince."

We both watched Sehran leave. Three other succubai stood and left with her at the mistress's gesture, before I turned back and nodded my thanks.

"All right, I might have some ideas, but first, tell me about the city. Who controls what? Who are the major players besides the Dark Legion and House Malakai?"

Seraphina nodded to one of her sisters, who produced a detailed map of Gaij and spread it across the table. "The city is divided primarily between the local noble houses—Varnen you know, though they are amongst the smallest, and are currently suffering as part of a plot by Havelton, to claim their manor. The major players, however, are Tessian and Havelton. Beyond them are Durnell, Coombs, Renalth, and Xenin, with Basheir as a distant runner-up. There are a half dozen minor families sworn to one or the other, and two dozen unaligned but considerably weaker houses beyond that, who are basically merchants and skilled artisans." She looked to me to see whether I was following, and I nodded.

"Middle class, we'd call them." I grunted. "Basically, they get a seat at the table because they're rich enough or have worked hard and been damn lucky, that's it."

"Exactly. Then House Malakai has established a foothold in the eastern district, using their strange weapons to intimidate the locals and claim the city is theirs, while doing things that are unclear. The Dark Legion controls the southern quarter, and they have also begun claiming religious laws have been broken, and are punishing those they deem a threat."

"Are they a threat?" I asked.

"No." She shook her head. "With our situation, we spent centuries building a network of eyes and ears in the city, and now our little birds tell us everything. These people were merely in possession of items or luxuries that the Dark Legion desired, so they took them. They have also claimed a shipment of manastones that was bought and paid for, in transit to us. We believe they suspect how badly we need the stones, as they've been attempting to negotiate with us by offering bribes of stones to open lines of communication."

"Typical dickbags. And the common people?" I asked.

"Caught in between, as always," Lilandra, the older succubus said with a sigh. "Many wish for the restoration of imperial authority, at least in theory. In practice, they support whoever keeps them fed and relatively safe. As your actions have generated notifications, the people speak of them in taverns and in hushed whispers, but they also see the risks. Slavery is common here, and should the slaves be freed, many would have reason to fear for their lives."

"How bad is it?" I asked.

"Bad," she admitted. "The city is a cesspit, and the only ones who rise to the top are always the ones who are the least deserving or compassionate. If you chose to behead every third person in every building of the city, you'd still barely register on the scale of atrocities."

"Joy, another shithole city. Why the hell can't we meet nice people, just once?" I muttered.

"The city requires jobs be done." She shrugged. "If they cannot be done by willing workers, then they'll be done by slaves. It has ever been this way."

"No," I growled. "It hasn't, and it won't continue. If I have to break the city, I damn well will."

"The city is more fragile than you know," the mistress pointed out, and I snorted.

"It is," I agreed. "But so were the others. Just taking the slaves out of the equation won't end things here, but what will is paying the workers, putting the coin back to work in supporting them."

"You would need tens of thousands of gold for that." She snorted. "Should you simply free every slave and they continued to serve in their roles? The sheer cost would bankrupt half the nobility."

"It would, wouldn't it." I smiled. "Okay, let's leave that for now, though, beyond one last question: are the local nobles claiming their authority as supposed imperial nobility? Swearing the oaths publicly and then rocking on with their lives, or not?"

"Not," she said. "This land has been claimed as part of three separate short-lived kingdoms since the fall. Two of which are still in evidence in the other territories, though this city broke free of the last three decades ago."

"Damn. Shame that," I muttered. "Ah well, when I take the city, that'll change."

"And what of the other claimants?" Lilandra asked. "You say 'when,' but they will not simply surrender their ambitions. And when you are seen to rule here, and the territory remains unclaimed, will that not show them that it is the city that is needed, not the tower?"

I smiled grimly. "No, they won't. Which is why we're going to trick them into thinking they've already won, and then pull the rug out from under them. They fooled me, after all, and turnabout is fair fucking play."

For the next hour, as we waited for Oracle and the legionnaires to arrive, I outlined my plan. It was dangerous, perhaps even fucking reckless, but it just might work. The succubai listened intently, occasionally offering refinements or pointing out potential pitfalls, especially when it came to manipulating people, or getting access to them.

My original idea had involved smash and grabs, then threats and police-state terror tactics, while their suggestions were a little more…elegant.

By the time a messenger arrived to inform us that Oracle and the others had reached the hidden entrance, the plan had taken solid shape.

Seraphina stood, her decision clearly made. "Prince Jax," she said formally, "I believe we have an agreement. The succubai of Gaij will pledge our allegiance to you and the reborn empire, conditional upon your support and our place as rulers of the city, in your absence."

I nodded solemnly. "And I pledge, as Prince of the Empire and heir to the Eternal Throne, to free you from your burden and to grant you your rightful place as citizens and members of the new nobility."

The mana we injected into the agreement was enough that I felt the bonds forming, but it was far from the oaths required. This was just something to get the ball rolling, and I couldn't help but grin, as she and the others did as well.

"Now," she said, "let us welcome your Oracle and prepare for tomorrow's feast," she finished, and fuck me, she looked downright predatory, as she led the way back out into the night.

The "hidden entrance" to the Tower of Gaij wasn't exactly hidden.

I mean, it wasn't seen as an entrance, not anymore, but hidden?

It was the mirror to the main gate in the wall that surrounded the tower, just like we had back home. There were two gates in the wall that looped around inside the city, massive and clearly, well, a fucking gate.

The difference was that it'd been sealed for centuries, the gates overgrown with stone somehow and then covered with centuries of vague neglect until it was practically part of the landscape.

It took ten minutes and fifteen thousand mana from us all poured into the gates to make them revert to their original form. And when they did, and they were opened? The dust and debris that fell free was incredible.

We opened it enough for Oracle and the group with her to pass through. As soon as they were inside, we simply sealed it again—with a single golem on our side to pile a shitload of rock against the inside of the gate, to make it very, very hard for the gate to be opened without us being aware.

It was a bit of a shame that we needed to do that, I'll admit, because the stone we used was part of the inner decorative area.

The succubai had been here for seven centuries, operating basically a giant brothel, bar, and restaurant combined for a very rich city. As such, the structures that were dotted around? Incredible.

And they all had such convenient little nooks and seats, too, for "entertaining" and I *liked* it.

More importantly, though, when the massive stone door had finally swung open, revealing Oracle in the middle of our battered but determined force, a wave of relief washed over me. She looked exhausted but unharmed. The moment our eyes met, her love flowed into me, warm and reassuring.

The legion quickly rode forward, streaming into the gardens and forming a protective bubble around us as the golem waited, then shoved the gate shut again. The silence outside was only broken by the sounds of confusion at the loud noise as the gate crashed closed.

The succubai who had shielded them all the way were mingling with the legionnaires, but I only had eyes for Oracle.

"You're alive." She stepped forward to embrace me. "I felt the magic being pulled from you, and I was terrified."

"It'll take more than an ambush and some sneaky magic to keep me down," I lied, holding her tight. "Though, maybe not a hell of a lot more. If Sehran and her sisters hadn't arrived when they did…"

"I know," she murmured. "I felt it through the bond. You need to be more careful, Jax. I know it was the right call at the time, but… I was terrified I was going to have to raise this baby on my own!"

I nodded, releasing her but keeping her hand in mine and being careful not to point out that she'd feckin' encouraged me to go have fun before this. "How are our people?"

"Seven dead," she reported grimly. "Eighteen wounded. But all major wounds are healed, and the legionnaires are healing minor ones themselves. It's experience for them, after all. Daralen has them organized and ready for whatever comes next."

"Good," I said. "Because we have a plan, but it's going to take all of us working together to pull it off, and well, you're probably going to need to polish it a bit."

"It's your plan—of *course* I'm going to need to polish it." She smiled at me, and then hugged me again. "We need to stop doing this," she whispered. "Just stop…everything."

"I know," I agreed. Yeah, we did need to because one of these days, I'd not get rescued by a friend, and instead I'd be dead. But until then? We couldn't stop.

As the legionnaires filed into the tower itself, the succubai guided them to quarters that had been hastily prepared. The tower was vast, with enough space to comfortably house our entire force—hell, half the city, never mind our piddly little group—but much of it was in varying states of disrepair. The succubai had maintained only the sections they actively used, and that was mainly with bought items, the mana reserved for the areas that needed it structurally, letting others fall into ruin to conserve their energy.

Once our forces were settled, I called a council of war. Oracle, Daralen, and Saracen joined me and the succubai leadership in the central chamber where I'd met Seraphina earlier.

"Before we begin," I said, "you all need to understand the tower's situation."

Seraphina nodded and explained again about the wisps' deaths and how the succubai had been sustaining the tower with their own essence for centuries. My people listened intently, their expressions growing more concerned with each revelation.

"This changes everything." Oracle sighed when Seraphina had finished. "Without functional mana collectors, the tower can't generate its own mana in anything like a real quantity. And without wisps to direct that mana properly…"

"That's where you come in," I told her. "You're the only wisp we have, but I'm not expecting you to do too much, I think."

"Go on." She sighed. "I just know this is going to be bad…"

"The tower already directs mana fed into it to maintain itself, and the succubai basically just keep directing the mana by feeding it directly into the worst-affected areas. That way, it doesn't spread to, say, trying to regrow the upper floors."

"Got that." She nodded.

"Well, what if…" I explained our little plan, and by the end? Oracle was laughing.

"Jax!" she managed to get out, through semi-hysterical giggling. "Not asking that much? You're expecting me to 'just' tweak a design that was created by mages who were masters of their craft! I can't just lop off sixty floors from the original design and call it even! I wouldn't know where to begin, never mind selectively modifying 'just' the collectors. Even if I chopped the rest of the tower off and just slapped that top on top of the current sections, the connections wouldn't fit. And the first thing that the tower would try to do is build the Hall of the Eternal!

"The portal would have to be built, and that requires tuning, something that I have no clue how to do. I don't think *Seneschal* could do it, and he has a working section to compare against. No. I'm sorry, Jax, but this…this is madness."

"This is Sparta," I replied unthinkingly.

"What?"

"Dammit, nothing." I groaned. "Fuck's sake, we're back to square one."

"No." Daralen was the one who spoke up, surprising everyone. "Forgive me, my prince, but I don't think we are. If you were to attach mana collectors to the roof, would they work?"

"They'd have to be tied into the tower," Oracle said slowly. "And they'd start the whole growth cycle of the tower over again, but yes, the first stage would be repairing the existing sections and fully integrating them. The tower seed has everything it needs, if it can get enough mana."

"Everything?" I asked.

"The seed can construct the original blueprint of the tower," Oracle confirmed. "The issue is that without the materials, it will take far longer, as each material would have to be grown from scratch. And changing from one kind of material to another takes forever, or so I remember Seneschal whining about. That's why we needed the ingots to make the academy. Although the Great Tower could in theory create it all, it'd take decades, and the first step would be the integration of those plans into the seed.

"Instead, Seneschal essentially used a built-in system to carve out changes in the seed's layout that were then tied…" She saw the glazed eyes on everyone and shook her head. "You know what? It doesn't matter. All you need to know is that yes, if we could get the mana collectors back and attach them to the roof, it'd be enough, provided we were happy with the tower taking thirty to forty years to regrow.

"The first issue is that with the tower drawing in even the highly limited amount that the tower does from the collectors that are sunken into the ground, its first priority is to begin what it sees as the most pressing repairs. It doesn't think in the way that you do. It doesn't really 'think' at all. Instead, the missing two-thirds of the tower are marked as the primary priority, and all mana is channeled toward repairing that, as the limited awareness can identify that the lower levels are there. As such, if they're complete, its priority is the upper floors, just as it was when it was grown.

"That means that it will automatically continue to try to regrow the tower. And without active mana collectors that can draw down, that's all it'll do. After all, the seed was created to do just this. With more mana in the mix, it'll shift to secondary priorities and that'll include strengthening the remaining section of the tower while the regrowth goes on."

"I'm fine with that," Seraphina said quickly.

"Me too." I nodded. "We can find a solution to the wisp situation later, but fuck it, at this point? Just 'not falling down' would be a bonus."

"Then all we need to do is recapture the legion encampment, and bring the collectors here then." Daralen sounded like it was simple.

"Oh is that all?" Seraphina asked, then she shook her head. "I understand the wish to retake it, Daralen, I do. It was the legion's home, but…"

"But we take it and destroy it." Daralen spoke over her. "This isn't me attempting to retake all the legion has lost. This is me offering a solution. Sonra is coming, though not until this area is part of your territory. When it is? The goblins and gnomes of Sonra, not to mention the handful of slaves we have already rescued from those races, will be overjoyed to assist. And with your imperial authority, my prince, you can shut down the collectors, enabling them to be moved intact and safely.

"The gnomes can study the ancient artifacts and you can attempt to remake them here, inside the tower, ensuring that the tower will never again be without a dedicated fighting force to defend it. Legionnaires who are too old to campaign can instead be stationed here, training the next generation, and the city of Gaij and the city of Sonra can be merged."

She went on, looking embarrassed as everyone stared at her.

"That spell that you used to turn the earth over? The one that got rid of the shit and smell?"

"Yeah?" I asked.

"Could you teach it to others?"

"Easily," Oracle agreed.

"Then you do that. The herds could settle here and migrate around the city. They always have to shelter for the winter. Regardless, they only move because they need to; they need fresh fodder and to clear the ground to let the shit be absorbed. If instead you had a team who rotated the fields around Sonra, then turned the earth behind them, the fields would be much more productive, and Gaij would grow in wealth as well."

"And with more money, Gaij can pay for the food and armies it needs," I finished for her. "Damn, Daralen, it's a simple solution, but a damn good one. It'll need some work, but it'd also mean we could stabilize the economy, because all those jobs that the slaves are freed from, those who settle here will be happy to do because it's not a 'slave's job' anymore, it's just a 'job.'"

"They won't have the memories of it as a slave's role," Oracle agreed.

"Well, we're going to need to do something, because that's the second 'minor' detail that Seraphina shared with me," I said grimly. "Not only are there a lot of others here in the city making themselves unwelcome, but there's a full legion of the dark dicks on its way." I turned to Seraphina. "Do you want to explain it?"

"We are aware of three forces that may choose to march upon the city," Seraphina said. "The raider city of Kronk to the east has gathered its forces and appears to be massing for an attack, though there are more likely targets than us.

"The city of Lembiq to the southeast has a significant force, though primarily of archers, and its one that has been called up in preparation as well, though that is more likely in response to the third and final force.

"The Dark Legion, a full legion of five thousand, was seen marching approximately fourteen days' march from here to the southwest. Any of these forces may have different aims. In fact, I'm sure that Lembiq has called in their levies to defend themselves against one or the other of these forces, given that it is still in a state of war with Kronk, and they are no friends of the Dark Legion. But we need to be ready in case one of them turns toward us."

"Great." Oracle groaned. "Please, Jax, don't try any diplomacy on them. We can't afford to fight all three…"

"I resent that." I snorted, then waved it off. "Seriously, though, we might end up with one of them coming after us, but probably not. As Seraphina explained it, Kronk and the Dark Legion hate each other, so more likely they'll fight each other and Lembiq will stand their army down, or go after the mauled survivors of that fight. Regardless, though, we need to be ready."

"I agree." Daralen nodded firmly.

"If they do come after us, though, don't forget we have our own army, or we will have soon. We have more than ten thousand who want to train as an army, after all. Daralen has begun training them as legionnaires, but if we make Gaij their home, a permanent one, then we don't have to worry about anyone else trying to take it." I added.

"No?" Seraphina asked. "It's concerning me, as you're essentially drawing a great big target on my city."

"We are," I agreed. "But it's a target that will take a full army to take advantage of. The Dark Legion would need at least twenty or thirty thousand to take a city that's protected by ten thousand regular troops. Is that the math, Daralen?" I asked her, and she nodded.

"On average, a fortified position adds four to five times the defenders' strength. Here, it would be against seasoned and highly trained troops, so that would be reduced though. The longer we have to prepare, the better the odds."

"And how much would those odds be improved if we managed to teach, oh, say five thousand of those troops basic spells, like Magic Missile?" I purred. "Five thousand times five missiles, twenty-five thousand missiles that streaked across the skies, and hammered the Dark Legion into ash."

"That…would make a significant difference." Daralen cleared her throat.

"Jax, it takes an hour for me to teach three!" Oracle wailed. "This would be months of work, months that we need to be travelling to the Cradle!"

"It would," I agreed. "But that's only if you had to do it yourself."

"What?" She blinked.

"How are spells usually taught?" I asked.

"Well, by mages to other mages, or by spellbooks," she said, suddenly getting it. "Could we do that?"

"Do what?" Seraphina asked, not following.

"Make the city's mages teach the army." I grinned evilly. "And yeah, I'm betting I can, once they've sworn to the empire."

"But they'd refuse, surely?" Seraphina shook her head.

"They can't," I said. "Not if they want to remain in the city and take advantage of all the good shit we're going to be bringing in. All the advantages the city is going to get are for *citizens* only. Those who won't swear? The gate is that way." I pointed vaguely at the outer walls.

"We make them swear, and we give them access to new spells and so on. We make sure it's worth their while, but we also make them teach as we need, in great big fucking classes. We have the troops undergoing legion basic training in groups of a hundred, and then they split off for one-hour classes with the mages. The mages won't be able to teach them all…not realistically. Some will fail, others won't have any aptitude, but I bet you I know one group that will manage it."

"How can you be so sure?" one of the succubai asked me, and I grinned at her.

"You've seen nobody so dedicated to improving themselves, as a newly freed slave. They'll work to the point of collapse to protect their freedom," Daralen said. "Those who joined us already have proved some of the most dedicated aspirants I have ever seen."

"Exactly. Now give them a chance to learn magic, to get proper equipment, and to earn a place in the teams we send out to hunt down slavers? Freeing their brothers and sisters?" I grinned evilly. "You better believe they'll throw their heart and soul into it."

"And you have five thousand like this?" Seraphina asked.

"Oh no." Oracle shook her head, grinning. "Better."

"More like *twenty* thousand." Daralen smiled. "And if we're offering magic as well? I imagine the average citizen would happily learn given the chance, on the understanding that they serve as a militia when needed."

"So, let's say a hundred thousand missiles in a volley. Even if the average person only managed five volleys, that's five hundred thousand magic missiles slamming into the attacking enemy." I smirked. "Just how long do you expect even a fully equipped Dark Legion to last? One minute? Two?" I shook my head. "Shields would pop instantly. Armor would crumple with the first wave, baking the wearer alive."

"And that doesn't count those who actually have an aptitude or more powerful spells," Sehran added. "The Explosive Compression you taught me? A thousand of those would eliminate any army as a threat in a single volley."

"You permitted her to learn magic?" Seraphina stared at me hungrily.

"Of course." I smiled. "Magic is open to *all* imperial citizens."

"I look forward to swearing the oath then," Seraphina said, taking the bloody obvious hint.

CHAPTER EIGHTEEN

I outlined the plan for everyone present. The succubai would publicly announce that the tower would hear all claims to its ownership the following day, with each faction given the opportunity to make their case. This would lure all our enemies into one place.

"Meanwhile," I continued, "the succubai will use their network of spies and assassins to clear a path and then they'll visit the leaders of the local noble houses here, one by one, tonight. Each will be told the same thing—that they and only one other are being offered a special deal: swear allegiance to me, and they'll retain their rank and possessions. Refuse, and they'll lose everything."

"They'll think they're the only ones being offered this deal?" Daralen asked.

"Exactly," I confirmed. "Well, they and one other. We get Varnen to publicly swear first…that should get the ball rolling. When they see their peers doing the same thing tomorrow, they'll assume they've each made the same private arrangement with us, and with a little luck, it'll trigger a panic…"

"And House Malakai? The Dark Legion?" Lilandra inquired.

"We don't bother trying to turn them," I said. "They're too committed to their own causes. When the local houses declare for us, we'll be in a position of strength. The Dark Legion will likely attack—and that's when we spring the trap.

"They'll come here, all of them will, but Malakai especially, because he'll believe that as soon as he's inside the walls, he'll be able to claim the tower. Just like we did. The only difference is, we know that without the control centers or the wisps, it's impossible. There's nothing to claim."

The most ambitious part of the plan involved using my imperial abilities, enhanced by the Mage Imperator spells I'd recently acquired. Using the spells, I'd disrupt the mana. And then Oracle, linked to me, would help me to link my imperial ability that we used to free the slaves outside of Himnel. The combination of that and our joined abilities would pull the mana in from all around us.

As nobody else could draw on the mana, I didn't have to worry about being interrupted, and I would create a massive funnel, absorbing the ambient magic from the surrounding area and channeling it into Oracle, who would in turn be in place above an uncovered mana conduit that fed directly into the tower.

"This will serve three purposes," I explained. "First, it will provide the power surge we need to temporarily rejuvenate the tower, allowing us to activate its remaining golems and defenses. Secondly, it will demonstrate our power in the most dramatic way possible, and with the golems active, the locals will realize that they don't dare fuck with us. And third? When the Dark Legion and Malakai see us channeling this much mana, they'll assume an attack."

"It's risky," Oracle warned. "Channeling that much mana could be dangerous for both of us, especially in my condition."

"That's why we're not doing it alone," I replied. "You, with the help of the succubai, will work to distribute the load, and we'll use the tower's inherent structure to guide the flow. It won't be perfect, but it should work long enough for our purposes.

"And when they attack us, we stomp them into jam, or the golems do, and we claim the city, as either the locals will have declared for us, or they can join the jam brigade," I finished.

"It's brutal, underhanded, and I'm impressed." Sehran smiled. "I can't wait to see what happens."

Seraphina nodded in agreement. "We've sustained this tower for centuries. We can certainly help direct a surge of external power through it."

"And afterward?" Daralen asked. "What's our long-term strategy?"

"We take control of the city. With the power that we'll be pulling in, and how visible this will be, Oracle will siphon off a small section of it and push that out, offering it to the people. Not all will swear, not the first time, I understand that, but enough will," I said.

"With the local nobility behind us or dead and the tower's resources at our disposal, we'll only need a small number of the surviving nobles and the people to support us, as we already have all of those who swore for us from Sonra in the area.

"Sure, they're farther out than I'd like, but they're also inside the territory. The relevant issue is that more than ten percent have to be actively hostile to us, not how many are supporting. So we'll be in a strong position. The succubai will serve as the tower's stewards, no longer its prisoners. And once we've claimed the territory? Fuck it, we can send the golems to stomp the Dark legionnaires at the encampment into paste as well. Then we strip it and we'll begin recovering the mana collection system from the encampment to bring here to replace the one destroyed in the cataclysm."

I looked from one to another as I went on. "We need this foothold on Carrmor, and the succubai need their freedom. This accomplishes both."

After finalizing the details, we went to our various tasks. The succubai set out to bring in the noble leaders, while Oracle and I descended into the tower's depths to examine what was left of the wisp manawell.

Unlike our tower, the lower floors here were intact, so it was kinda weird to take the original stairs, not the ones that we'd made to cover over holes and so on, and then pass down into the depths of the third sublevel of the tower, before finding the manawell.

It was also seriously weird to be there, seeing the equipment, the old genesis chambers, and most of all?

The manawell, that was clearly not Heph's, and yet, should have been.

Approaching it was like walking up to a grave, made even worse by the utter identicality between it, and the one that a wisp I considered a friend inhabited.

"Is it dead?" I asked in a hushed whisper.

"It is," Oracle replied softly, and I reached out, taking her hand in mine and squeezing gently.

"Did it…did they have a name, or a gender?" I asked. "I mean, can you tell if…" I was unsure how to ask whether it had been an identity-less slave like they had been when I first met them.

"I don't know," Oracle said sadly. "There's nothing here. Even the wisp well back in the desert had a fragment left behind. Here? It's just…empty."

"What do we do?" I looked up at the strange structure. It was clearly the same as Heph's, and…different.

All manawells were the same in that they had a small suspended well that would fill with solidified mana when the well was active. It looked a little like sentient quicksilver, and the inside of the well was slightly tiered, apparently made of grey and black striated rock, and had a wide lip that ringed it.

Also, like Heph's, this one was about a meter high, and stood atop a small, fluted pillar. Unlike Heph's, though, this one had flat panels alongside it, angled in toward an ornate chair.

If I was reading it right, these were something like the magical version of monitors, and the wisp would be in the well, controlling the system, while its masters got to sit and give direction.

Back home, the SporeMother had smashed all that she could. And then, when she couldn't move or break the well, she'd instead used it as literally a toilet for seven hundred years.

Heph had not been amused when I woke him, but as the guy who had nostrils? I was even less so.

"*We* don't do anything, Jax." Oracle sighed. "*I* do, though this is going to be very strange. Jax, can you…I don't know, can you not watch?"

I blinked, surprised. "Okay?" I agreed, turning my back as she moved closer, then cursed. "What's wrong?"

"We need to activate the well. It's not as much as it needs to wake a wisp, only five hundred instead of a thousand, but still."

"Here." I reached out blindly, and then felt Oracle guiding my hand to the well.

I didn't really get why she didn't want me watching, considering everything and that she was at least as human as I was now, probably more, considering how much my DNA was messed up with other creatures being added into it. But I respected it, and when I felt her guiding my hand back away from the well, I kept my back turned, instead looking out over the cavern.

Like back home, the genesis chamber—I didn't know their name for it, but Heph had liked that name for it when I suggested it, and it'd stuck—but regardless, the chamber was big.

Like, *really* big.

Easily two hundred meters across and roughly squared off. There were storerooms on the far side, their great doors apparently locked up tight. Beyond that?

The room was filled with row upon row of the imperial version of manufactories.

They were specialized, like the five in the heart of the chamber that were positioned in a rough circle around the manawell. Those were designed to build golems, specifically war, construction, servitor, or crafting class ones.

I could see at the back, positioned closer to the storerooms, were tunnels that presumably led out from the tower and deeper into the earth.

Two dust-covered mining golems sat silent and long dead, and I couldn't help but smile as I slowly peered around. Dozens of other systems were set up, many which had hoppers or containers to hold materials, until they were needed.

I'd seen similar equipment before, though it'd been horrifically damaged after ages housing a Valspar.

Here? They looked like they'd probably long since seized up. The dust was deep enough that kids could probably build dens in it. But beyond that?

They looked to be intact.

A grin stretched my cheeks as I remembered what I'd found in that long-forgotten armory as well.

Slayer arrows.

There was a manufactory that was set to make a load of different arrows, including ones designed to kill fucking ghosts, though how that worked I had no idea.

The slayers, though?

They were horrifically violent things. They split into six different arrows mid-flight and were enchanted to where they'd spread out and not just hunt the target, making minor adjustments in flight, but shock, stun, and silence them as well.

It had a banshee wail attack, a shield killer…fuck, I couldn't even remember it all. But I remembered Tang, and the way he'd practically begged to bear my children in return for those arrows.

Now, looking around? I realized that provided I could get the systems working again and also some materials?

When they arrived here, I could have gear ready to kit my team out to hunt the gods.

I could give Bane equipment that he could use to go hunting Illoth and expect to kill the bitch. I could… I could…

The empire had all of this back then, I remembered. They had *all* of this, and they still died. They fell, when the world ended, and we were left wondering over the fucking remains, thanks to those dickbag nobles.

I drew in a deep breath, the happy feeling crushed as I glared around, silently vowing that I'd make this right. I'd use what they had here to save my people, and then we'd conquer these assholes and sort this shit out.

"Jax?" It was Oracle, and I spun to face her, knowing that it was okay now.

Whatever she'd done, she now stood by the edge of the well. The "water" that filled it was again liquid quicksilver, and her fingers were dipped into it.

Tendrils of the silvery mass crawled up her arm, and pulsed under her veins. But as soon as she saw the worry on my face, she shook her head.

"It's not active, and it's not poisonous," she assured me. "If anything, I think this would be good for the baby. It's literally the magical side of my heritage, just without any form of awareness."

"Really?" I blinked.

"Oh yes, just well…not until they're finished growing?"

"Like twenty-one?" I frowned, and she snorted.

"No, more like, 'solid and human shaped.'" She smiled at me, then took a deep breath. "Okay, so onto the more important details. Yes, I can direct the flow of mana from here, and I think I can even add in some safeguards, as well as specifics. But no, it's not a full system access at all.

"I think the best way to work here would be to guide the mana through the channels, and then have succubai on each level who then draw it from these channels and into specific areas. Think of the channels sort of like pipes: the mana flows through them, and then the succubai pull it out.

"Then they direct it back into the tower in specific areas, and use it to repair as much as we can." She turned slowly, then pointed to a larger genesis chamber off to one side. "And then, we reactivate that one," she said.

"It's the least damaged higher system, and can create up to a class four, advanced golem. There are systems here that could create class five, greater golems, but the materials and costs involved in terms of time and mana?" She shook her head.

"No, if you're okay with it, I'd say we make a single class four, and then have that begin making a creation table. Once that's ready, we can bind it to the tower, and that'll allow more granular access, and specific changes to be made."

"Sounds like a plan." I nodded. "What was all that about, with not wanting me to watch?"

"I didn't know if I'd change." She looked embarrassed. "It's been a long time since I was anything other than my humanoid form with you, and I didn't want you to look at me, and well, be reminded that I wasn't real."

"You daft bugger." I moved in close and wrapped my arms around her, kissing her and holding her tight. "You were always real. You weren't always human, that's all."

"I was a creature of magic, that's all, and when you don't have a form, existentialism questions become really important," she said quietly.

"Oracle, I barely understand what you just said, and even I know that's bullshit," I disagreed. "You could be anything. That makes you more than regular meat sacks in my book, not less, so don't be so bloody stupid."

She snorted a laugh against my armored chest, then sighed and looked up at me. "You know, you're really not very good at this," she said, despite the smile putting the lie to her words.

"What?" I asked, bewildered.

"Being just another meat sack." She shook her head. "You always saw me with your heart, never your head, didn't you?"

"Well, I wouldn't say it was always my heart that was pointing me at you…" I waggled my eyebrows suggestively and made her snort in laughter.

I leaned down and kissed her, holding her in my arms for a long minute, before we eventually broke off.

"Okay, so from here, I think we can do this." She nodded determinedly. "Once we have the mana coming in, anyway. The first phase will be the disruption, and you're going to need a lot of mana for that. I'd suggest you get any manastones you can, and have them ready. Then, from there, once you're pulling the mana in, you feed it to me, like how I used to be the link between you and the tower to feed mana into you at home to manage things like this. Except here, it'll be reversed."

"Okay, then what?"

"Well, normally I'd handle it all. I'd form the link between you and the tower—it needs to come through the bond, after all—but if I was down here instead…yeah, actually, I'm going to have to disengage somehow and then get down here, and…" There was a long few seconds before I could see her brilliant white teeth gleaming in the dim light as she smiled at me.

"Or…" she whispered. "I teach Sehran."

"Can she do it?" I asked. "She's not a creature of magic—is it dangerous?"

"It is, but her sisters are going to be doing it anyway, and they had to learn somehow. And she's linked to us both. But it's…well, it's going to mean she'll be even deeper in us."

"Usually it's the other way around," Sehran's throaty chuckle rang out from behind us, "and my master is deeper in me!"

"You daft bugger." I snorted, having sensed she was nearby and not really thought about it before now, so used to her presence as I was.

"Sehran…" Oracle started, and the succubus strode out of the shadows, holding up one hand.

"Yes, I know what you need. Yes, I'll do it. And yes, I am incredible, thanks for noticing." She smiled.

"There's a risk—" I started to say, and she cut me off.

"There's a risk every day." She shrugged. "This way, I can help, so teach me."

And that was that.

We spent the next several hours working together, channeling mana into the dormant systems, following faint patterns Oracle could sense. Gradually, sections of the machinery began to illuminate, dim at first, then with increasing brightness, as once again I grew to hate the taste of bloody mana potions.

"We're making progress," Oracle said, her voice exhausted. "But we're just jump-starting the most basic functions and warming it up. Without a proper mana collection system, this is all temporary."

"Temporary is all we need right now," I reminded her. "Just enough to put on a good show tomorrow and power the remaining golems as well."

By midnight, we'd managed to awaken three war golems and a pair of servitors as well. It was a fraction of what the tower must have once contained. But for facing regular troops, and with the one war golem that was currently active still as well?

It'd be enough.

It had to be.

The succubai had returned with reports that most of the local noble houses had accepted our private offers, believing themselves to be the sole beneficiaries of our generosity.

Admittedly, with it being succubai spreading the word, and how it was done? I imagined they'd have agreed to anything at the time.

The ladies of the night had hidden themselves well, slipping out and into the bedchambers of the various noble houses. For some, it'd been easy, because the lords and ladies basically lived separate lives. For others? Their partners were drugged, enthralled, or in two cases, invited into the bed and had joined in very willingly.

Then after, when those who had been regular visitors to the tower and guests of the succubai, were recovering, they were distracted. The succubai crooned to them, dropping them into a very suggestive state.

Then, they'd blink and suddenly a legionnaire, handpicked for this, would be standing before them.

The offer was made, as was the unsubtle hint: the tower wasn't up for claiming; it already had been. Now all that was left was the inevitable fallout of who would rise and who would fall.

But wait, a little lifeline was offered just as the sudden fear of losing everything started to bite.

"Tomorrow," they were told, "you and the others will be summoned to the tower to make your claims on it, but you know, now, that it's already been claimed. What do you think is going to happen to those who fight against the Godslayer? There's room for one or two of you to survive, and to help rule here, though. The prince will be moving on, after all, and who will be left here to watch over you?"

Then, when the sudden surge of greed got higher than the fear, the fear was brought back.

"Of course, for those who wait too long to proclaim themselves? Well, an example is going to have to be made…and the succubai are always hungry…"

Then the legionnaire would leave, and the succubus would drop the now terrified victim into a deep sleep.

The whole thing reeked of cheap theatre, but when they woke up in the morning? The first thing they'd find would be the invitation from the succubai to attend the tower at noon, and to make a formal claim, or support another to do so.

The plan was simple, because I was both shit at planning, and the less complicated a plan was, the less likely it was to fail. That being said, though, I had high hopes.

"Everything is in place," Seraphina reported as we gathered for a final review of the plan at dawn. "The nobles have been visited at their estates, and the invites to attend the ceremony were left. Our spies report that House Malakai and the Dark Legion are also preparing to attend, each confident in their own claim, after we had their invites delivered as well."

"And the city?" I asked.

"Tense," Lilandra replied. "Word of last night's violence has spread. Many of the regular beings are staying indoors, fearing what the day might bring."

"They're right to be concerned," I said grimly. "But if this works, by tonight, Gaij will have a new order, and a better one."

We retired to quarters that had been prepared for us, though sleep was elusive. Too much depended on the coming day's events, and my mind refused to quiet. Oracle curled against me, drawing comfort from our physical closeness as much as our mental bond.

"I can feel your anxiety," she murmured in the dim light of the early morning sun.

"Just thinking through all the ways this could go wrong," I admitted.

"And all the ways it could go right?" she prompted.

I smiled despite myself. "Those too."

We dozed fitfully until ten, when a gentle knock at the door announced that it was time. Finally, the day of reckoning for Gaij had arrived.

CHAPTER NINETEEN

The weather had decided to play ball, which was a hell of a relief, as only an hour ago, Oracle had realized that for us to do what we needed to do, I needed access to the open air, and that was going to totally ruin the moment, if I had to suddenly jump out of a window at the end of my speech.

Instead, the rooftop of the Tower of Gaij had been prepared with meticulous care. Four sections of seating had been arranged for the claimants: one for representatives from the local nobility, House Malakai's contingent, the Dark Legion, and my own people.

At the front of the gathering, with their backs to the panorama of the city, Seraphina and five of her sisters had established a tribunal-like setting, all cushions and silk hangings, from which they would ostensibly judge the claims.

I took my place in the section assigned to me, with Oracle at my side and Daralen and a small honor guard of legionnaires behind us. The war golems were strategically positioned throughout the hall, currently appearing dormant but ready to activate at a moment's notice. More legionnaires waited in adjacent chambers, prepared to move at my signal.

"Nervous?" Oracle's hand found mine beneath the cover of my cloak.

"Who, me? Nah," I lied, giving her hand a squeeze. *"Just another day of conquering cities and facing down potential armies. All in a day's work for a prince."*

She raised an eyebrow but said nothing. Both of us knew full well that my heart was pounding hard enough to power a small town.

The local nobility arrived first, filling in with expressions ranging from nervous anticipation to barely concealed smugness. Each house leader who had received our "exclusive" offer glanced surreptitiously at me, clearly expecting some sign of our secret arrangement. I nodded slightly to each, maintaining the illusion and getting more than a few watery smiles in return.

I also had to stifle a grin when Varnen took his place at the back of the group of nobles, with many of them glancing from him to me, and back again.

House Malakai's contingent entered next, Darius at their head. They were dressed in a bizarre mixture of Earth tactical gear and more traditional armor, which meant that they had to be sweating like crazy. And when you included the additional silken sashes and crap that Darius had added to his, he'd managed to create a bloody stupid look.

Darius himself carried what appeared to be his own bloodstone clutched in his right hand, and I had to fight not to take mine out and compare it. His eyes met mine briefly, and the corner of his mouth turned up in a smirk I desperately wanted to punch off his face.

The Dark Legion arrived last, their new commander at the front. I didn't recognize him—evidently, Vectus had been replaced. I mean, he'd *have* to have been, after all. And as to the leader I'd faced whose sword I had in my bag now? I had to wonder how many leadership types they had left.

After all, they had to be running low by now.

The hatred in his eyes when he spotted me was unmistakable, as was the nervousness on the face of his priest.

It was the same one from the dinner last night, so just to throw him off, I acted incredibly pleased to see him and threw him a really unsubtle wave. That got a load of glares from those around him, and after clearly derailing his entire career, I promptly ignored him. The rest of their contingent took their places with military precision, hands never straying far from their weapons, though they had no idea how pointless that would soon be.

Once all were seated, Seraphina rose from her central position. "Representatives of Gaij," she began, her voice carrying effortlessly through the hall, "you have come to present your claims to the tower. For seven centuries, we have maintained this remnant of imperial glory, waiting for the day when worthy leadership would emerge. We believe that, finally, that day has come."

She gestured to the assembled claimants. "Each faction will present its case. We will hear from the local nobility first, then House Malakai, followed by the servants of Nimon. Prince Jax, as the most recent arrival, will speak last."

This announcement caused some muttering among the assembled representatives, but no open objections. While they spoke, Oracle and I would be working—preparing the mana disruption and funnel spell beneath their notice.

Through our bond, I felt Oracle already beginning the subtle manipulations that would enable the tower's systems to accept the coming surge. Sehran had moved closer to us, taking up a position where she could view the entire chamber while still remaining close enough to help, and coincidentally standing right atop a hidden section of the roof that led straight into the mana channels, ready to serve as the conduit once things kicked off.

The spokesperson for the local nobility, Lord Havelton, rose first. His argument centered on their centuries of stewardship over the city, their deep understanding of local needs, and their ties to the original imperial families through distant ancestry.

"For seven hundred years," he declared pompously, "the houses of Gaij have maintained order and prosperity in this city. We have defended its walls, fed its people, and preserved its traditions through the darkest times."

As he spoke, I began quietly channeling mana, feeling it build in my core as I prepared the disruption spell. Unlike normally, I wore the cloak that had come with my armor, something that I didn't bother with generally, mainly because it was ceremonial and would only ever end up covered in blood and guts. But it did, admittedly, look awesome. I'd have loved to show off more—if my armor didn't keep getting as battered as it did—but more importantly? One of the succubai had a very useful little hobby, it turned out.

She'd been moonlighting as a *seamstress*.

It wasn't a seamstress in the style of the veritable city of Ankh-Morpork. She actually knew how to sew.

As such, she'd sewn a collection of pockets into the inside of my cloak, and we'd filled them with the few manastones we could get our hands on.

I just had to hope it was going to be enough.

Through our bond, Oracle guided the spell, getting it as set up as it could be, without it actually kicking off, ensuring it remained undetectable until we were ready to unleash it.

Havelton droned on and on, his speech increasingly convoluted as he tried to establish why his house, specifically, should be given primacy. I could see several of the other nobles shifting uncomfortably, especially as, apart from him, we'd literally approached almost all of them last night. He clearly had no clue as well, which was fun.

House Malakai's presentation was next, with Darius himself making their case.

"The Tower of Gaij," he began, his accent clearly marking him as a posh wanker despite his attempts to sound local, "is merely one of many imperial assets that rightfully belong to House Malakai. I once ruled here, literally, seven hundred years ago. Through the perfidy of that man's father, the Eternal Emperor Amon himself was murdered, and we were forced from our homes." He pointed at me, sneering. "I knew this tower when it was new. I strode these halls, and I learned from its masters, as the head of the House Malakai. My own grandfather, Amon, sat atop the throne of the empire, and he gifted me with missions to expand the borders of the empire!"

He went on to speak of superior technology, of resources beyond anything the other claimants could match, and of restoring the tower to its "true purpose" as a bastion of dominance. Throughout his speech, he repeatedly fondled the bloodstone, clearly expecting it to give him some advantage when the time came.

The Dark Legion's new commander made the shortest presentation, essentially declaring that Nimon's will superseded all other claims and promising death to those who opposed it, so fuck right off, or else. It wasn't particularly diplomatic, but I had to admire the straightforwardness.

"The apostate," he spat, pointing directly at me, "has already been condemned by the Great Lord Nimon. This tower, this city, and all who dwell within it are hereby claimed in His name. Resistance will be met with destruction."

By the time it was eventually my turn to speak, the magical preparations were complete. The disruption field was primed and ready, the funnel was about as ready as we thought we could make it, and Oracle gave me a subtle nod, confirming everything was in place.

I rose and approached the center of the open-air gathering, taking a moment to lock eyes with each faction leader before speaking.

"Unlike these glorious windbags here, I won't waste your time with lengthy speeches about worthiness or destiny," I began. "My claim is simple: I am Jax Amon, Prince of the Empire and heir to the Eternal Throne. This tower, like all imperial holdings, rightfully belongs to me."

I paused, letting that sink in. "But ownership is not the same as stewardship. The succubai of Gaij have maintained this tower at great personal cost for seven centuries. They deserve better than to be eternal prisoners, bound to these walls by obligation and necessity."

Murmurs rippled through the audience as I continued. "Therefore, I declare that the succubai will be among the *stewards* of this city, no longer its prisoners. They will serve the empire as citizens, not as living pillars."

"Bold words," Darius Malakai called out, rising from his seat. "But words alone do not make a claim, and neither do attempting to bribe the succubai!"

"Well, shit, you know what? I think you're right," I agreed, pretending to be surprised. "Mind you, that's not all I came to say, so how about you sit down and shut the fuck up, you prick. *Now*, some of you might remember that we had a meeting last night." I glanced around at the various faces there. "Some of you might even have been promoted, after your predecessors met with untimely ends.

"You all know what I'm talking about, so let's drop the fancy talk, shall we?" I asked. "There was an attempt to take me and my people out last night. The drow were let into the city, the Dark Legion helped them, and so did both the guard and that useless cockwomble's men." I nodded my head to Darius. "All three of you, the other claimants for the tower, united and tried to take me and mine out, and you *failed*.

"That's fine that you tried, though…I was expecting it. Admittedly, the mana field? That was a nice touch. But let's be clear about what worked and what didn't, shall we? We killed over three hundred of the dark dicks. Two hundred drow, and ten thousand plus spiderkin. A hundred and seventy-seven guards of the city, and two hundred random people died, that I know of last night," I finished the numbers, having checked my notifications, and I plowed on.

"You know how many of my people died?" I asked, rhetorically, before going on. "Seven."

I let that hang there in the air for a few long seconds. "Seven of my people died, and you have no idea how fucking angry I am about that. These are people who marched and ran alongside me, who gave up their lives in the service of the empire, and who died because you shitehawks didn't know you were already *beaten*.

"You." I sneered at the leader of the Dark legionnaires. "I don't even know your name, and I couldn't care less. I killed your leader, your upper priests, and I gutted your god and I'm sure you've been made aware that I use his fucking skull as a goblet. When it comes to the decision whether *I* should permit you to rule a city in *my* empire? Fuck no. Denied!" I turned from him to Darius, who glared hatefully at me.

"You, fucknut." I snorted. "You claim kinship with Amon? I have his *memories*!" I shook my head, making a little of it up, admittedly, as I played to the crowd. "He regarded you with utter contempt, just like everyone here does. Hell, just like most of your own generation did back then. He thought you were a waste of skin, and that the best bit of you was thrown away when you were born.

"You say you left when my father killed the emperor and you think to tar me with that brush? You show your fucking ignorance! You *fled*, when Nimon empowered *Sanguis* to do the deed, and I've already promised to gut that useless fuck and mount his head over my fireplace.

"Is he my father? Aye." I looked around at the others who stared at me in shock. "Aye, as much as I hate the scum-sucking dog, he is. You know what that means, though? I am the son of Amon's firstborn. If we're ignoring that you and he were stripped of your place in the succession for fucking rebellion—which your entire claim lies under—then I have not only the greater right of blood, as just like you, I'm the direct grandson of Amon himself, but I'm also the son of his firstborn, so fuck you very much. I'd invite you to suck my balls, but we both know you'd like that.

"Now, though, let's take it a step further, because unlike the rest of you useless stains on the curtains of life, *I* am the *named heir*. Named BY AMON and therefore at the fucking top of the list of succession, a list THAT YOU'RE NOT EVEN ON.

"You?" I sneered at Darius, who had the grace to look slightly uncomfortable now. "You were *disowned.* Your entire generation who supported Sanguis were. You sit there, clutching a bloodstone, and hoping that it'll work for you, but it *won't*. You've even been trying to use it, since you walked in, haven't you?"

That got a blink from him.

I smiled. "You've not got so much as a twitch from the golems, never mind the tower! You want to know why?" I folded my arms and stared down at him as he scowled at me.

"I'll let you in on a little secret." I leaned forward slightly. "It might have been the succubai who invited you all, but they did so at my request. You can't claim the tower for two reasons. First? You have *no* imperial authority."

I'd wanted to strip him of his remaining formal rank here, but after a conversation with Jenae a few hours ago, I'd found that although she couldn't tell me where his lands were, they currently were outside of my control, which meant that I could bluster and lie, but I couldn't *actually* strip him of his nobility.

Not yet, anyway.

"As to the second reason, and it's a much more fun one, and yet oh so much simpler, can you guess?" I looked around, seeing the light dawning on a bunch of faces. "Yup, that's right—it's because *I've already claimed it.*"

I paused for effect, as the succubai stood as one, and the mistress spoke clearly and loudly for all to hear.

"We deny the claims of the false lords, and declare Prince Jax Amon, Lord of Dravith, to be master of the Tower of Gaij!"

I grinned, seeing the horror on the faces of more than half of the people in the gathering now. I couldn't help but say it, as I lifted my arms out to the sides, and then gave a bow to the crowd, before straightening up.

"It's *showtime*, motherfuckers!"

People surged to their feet. The hubbub of rising voices, confusion, questions, and denials were building, but they were all stopped dead as five golems pulled the ornamental draperies from their forms and stepped forward, making it clear just why the succubai had chosen to create a garden of silks and boudoirs on all sides.

I took a deep breath, reached out and in at the same time, and first of all? Triggered the Mana Cascade spell.

It was what Oracle had spent most of the last hour building and getting ready. Because no matter what its description looked like, it wasn't a simple thing.

Fuck, no. For a spell to literally cause disruption to all magic across a specified area, it needed to literally cover that area. In my case, instead of say, feeding out a disruption field across a room, or even a building, I needed to cover at least a few *miles*.

That meant Oracle had spent time creating specific weaves that spread out through the air, each and every one of them simply hanging there, floating along like a little puff of methane in an elevator.

Nobody knew it was there until it was too late, or until some evil bastard asked everyone whether they could smell popcorn and made them draw a deep lungful.

The weaves were everywhere, and that alone, before the spell had even started to take effect, had cost us almost ninety thousand mana.

Ninety-fucking-*thousand.*

Then, as I smiled at the stunned crowds, I activated the final stage of the spell. The manastones that I had sewn into the lining of my cloak crumbled to dust, and the two hundred thousand in solidified and purified mana they had held was absorbed into me as well.

Oracle was already moving. Her immediate part was done, and she needed to get the hell down to the ground floor and then below, to the manawell as quickly as possible. But before she did, she triggered the second spell, a shield of air—just in case—and held it, as she jumped off the side of the roof.

A handful of people saw her go, or saw the succubai who were streaming out. But the vast majority had eyes only for Seraphina and Sehran, who now stood behind me—Sehran still on the carefully positioned access point for the mana channels—and they missed most of those moving.

That was mainly because of the fact I was glowing--quite literally--and I'd taken off, buoyed aloft by the waves of power that I was feeding out into the weaves, as they went from neutral and inactive, all the way up to horrifically active.

To explain how the spell worked was akin to explaining why water was wet. "It just is" was the best description for that. But as the various magically inclined around the room tried to take action, what they found were weaves that floated everywhere and that formed weak patterns already in the air, the stone, and even passing through bodies all around them.

The effect when they were inactive was almost impossible to notice, and certainly it had been for the people summoned here today, because they were distracted by the pomp and ceremony, and, if I was being honest, by the fact that there were a lot of succubai who weren't wearing a great many clothes.

Now, as they tried to form spells, they found weaves that were sliding through and into their own, breaking them, tearing apart sections of their spells, and destroying the careful balance of mana needed to cast even the simplest of spells.

For most, they collapsed instantly—writhing, weeping, and generally suffering the backlash from failed spells. That was nice, because those who were trying to cast, by and large, were my fucking enemies, and that amused me greatly.

What they didn't realize was, though, this was only the *first phase.*

As I was lifted higher into the air on wings of light and glowing brilliantly, the weaves became brighter as they shifted, and the second phase began.

This was the dangerous one. This was the stage when it could all go wrong, and that was mainly because when we'd done this before?

We'd done it entirely on instinct.

Still, I did it then, and now, with the mana across the entire city permeated by ours, for a few handfuls of seconds, nobody else could cast a spell.

So, while we were still connected, I started to speak again.

"HEAR ME, PEOPLE OF GAIJ!" I roared, a subtle tweak of the spells magically carrying my voice across the city. "I AM JAX AMON, PRINCE OF THE EMPIRE, OVERLORD OF DRAVITH, AND THE GODSLAYER!"

I felt the shock that was carried at those titles, and I continued, no longer shouting. After all, I think that my start had gotten everyone's attention.

"I am here, atop the Tower of Gaij, called here to take my place, through the cries of imperial citizens long forgotten! For centuries, since the cataclysm, since the fall of the empire, your supposed 'betters' have ruled over you, claiming divine right.

"They have claimed they had the right to command you, at first, because they had imperial mandate, and then, in later years, through might alone.

"They beat and enslaved you! They stole from the people, they taxed you unjustly, and they forced many a better man and woman to kneel, simply because they could!"

I figured they were all pretty safe bets. There was never a man in history who didn't have a day when they were pissed at their bosses, after all. And as for the noble houses and taxes? Yeah, I figured I was on pretty safe ground with that.

"For decades, the succubai, guests of the empire, attempted to live side by side with those who sought refuge. In the end, they were forced to drive them out, as the demands upon the tower grew too great, and the support too little.

"Still, they showed leniency. Instead of ordering the golems to simply clear out the camps, and then the rising houses that surrounded them, they assisted the people of first the village, then the town, and finally the city of Gaij. They protected you. They opened their gates in times of trouble. And then, when they had to, they forced the people back from the tower and its grounds.

"For centuries, you have seen this tower, and you wondered why—why were *they* permitted to live here, granted guest right and protection, while outside, you labored and toiled. You were told that they were greedy, that they sucked the city dry, as well as those who could afford to visit them!" I paused, knowing a few would be snorting over the "sucked them dry" line.

"They did this not because they were greedy—they did it because they were forced! Forced time and again by the tower itself, a magical artifact that they were bound to. Every day, they have fed their mana, their essence, and all they could earn, into the tower.

"They did this not because the tower itself was greedy. No. They did it not because they desired wealth, or a life of plenty! No! They did it because as guests of the tower, they were the only ones who could! To allow another to claim guest right was to allow another to be bound!

"Those who called themselves your masters, those who have cursed the succubai, who have maligned them, claiming that the taxes they forced you to pay were onerous but that they would make things easier for you, that they would force the gates wide and let you live inside, plundering the tower and making your lives easier…

"They almost killed you all!" I let that hang in the air for long seconds.

"The tower is ancient, and powerful. It is a seat of rulership in these dark times, and a bastion against evil, as only the empire can be. But it needs mana. It must take mana, or the tower will collapse. And should that happen?

"How many of you would be killed? Crushed beneath these very rocks as they fall from the skies! Billions of tons of rock, falling this way and that, would destroy the city. Without the bastion of the tower to retreat to, as the succubai permitted you to in the past, the city would have been plundered long ago!"

"Now, imagine life here, if the tower fell? With the walls destroyed, with half the city killed by the falling rubble, and then with the roving gangs and bands of slavers you all know wait out there!"

I paused for dramatic effect, though mainly? I was shit scared of starting the next phase while Oracle was still rushing to the manawell and fucking this up. Time was running out, but I needed her there, and I needed these idiots paying attention to me for this to work.

"The succubai have protected you. Hundreds, possibly thousands a day would be required to feed the tower. Instead, they, with their greater mana capability, instead of feeding on a bonded partner, as the succubai would normally do, were tied to the tower directly!

"They managed to draw in mana, enough to feed them and keep them alive. But to do this? They had to then feed almost everything they could get back into the tower! They bought manastones, potions, and artifacts at horrific cost to feed the tower and protect you all. And the nobility?

"The so-called 'masters of the city'?" I saw the looks of concern on their faces as I singled them out. "They taxed you, and they taxed the things that the succubai needed to buy to protect you! They grew fat and rich on taxing everyone. And when it came to spending it on what mattered?

"Where were they, when the drow marched through your streets last night? Where were the guards who could have protected you? Did I say *guards*? As in the city guard? A tiny force that struggles to protect you, while being underfunded? I should say ARMIES! Where is the *army* your taxes paid for! Where was the army you needed to protect you, when the Dark Legion roamed through the streets last night with their allies, the drow!

"Where were your armies when false and cowardly nobles used weapons of light and fire to destroy sections of the city and left the innocent dead, all because they were trying to kill *me*?

"That's right! They turned your city into a war zone, they blew up streets, they killed hundreds, all to try to kill me and the Imperial Legion, when we returned to set this right!

"WELL, NO MORE!" I roared, as Oracle sent to me that she was nearly there. "No more, I say! I have taken control of the tower. The succubai have bent the knee to me. The Imperial Legion have bent the knee. And I will bring a new day to Gaij! My army marches even now to take up the defense of Gaij! Sonra, ancient city of the herds and innovation, has bent the knee to me, and more than thirty thousand approach the city to take up her protection, and to swell her coffers!

"You ask why does this matter to you? To all who hear my voice, as for most of you, it doesn't matter who rules the city! Taxes? There'll always be some, and the excuse for them will change. Laws? They change daily, and the rich don't care—they don't have to obey them, do they? Not like *you*!

"For one more group, the last and least, supposedly, of you all, I speak now, directly. For those who have been enslaved. Those who are trapped at the bottom, used, abused, and shit upon from a great height! You ask why should you care?

"You should care because this city is imperial! This is an imperial territory, and as such is under IMPERIAL LAW! In the EMPIRE, THERE ARE NO SLAVES!" The power had been building as I spoke, as my righteous anger ramped up and reverberated, seeking an outlet, a way to reach them all, to free them. Now I felt the first crackles as it started to burst free.

The imperial abilities, tied to the throne, and that only those who were in the direct line of succession, or Amon himself—as linked to him as I'd been originally—could access.

Now, power surged through me, and for the first time, because I was feeling for it, I found something that filled me with fear.

An emptiness.

A vast void—where once there had been what felt like unlimited power, now there was a void, as more and more of that reserve was drained.

It'd be enough, I knew, for this—there was more than enough—and it didn't even touch upon the mana that was being connected to me now by the funnel and the Mana Cascade as well. But in the future?

I shook that thought off and continued.

"I speak to you now, because as the prince of the empire, as the rightful ruler of these lands, I have come to restore ORDER. I have come to bring FREEDOM. And I have come to raise up the imperial standard!

"To those who have enslaved their fellow citizens, I say this: you are a criminal! You deserve no mercy from the empire, and you shall receive none! To those who have been broken, I say this: you will be healed. To the weak: you will be made strong. To the lowest: I will give you the chance to rise up!

"AND TO THE SLAVES? I SAY YOU ARE FREE!" I roared the last bit, even as I released the barriers that I'd been holding on my power.

It slammed out. The displaced air rolled like thunder, and this time? It'd definitely rolled a natural twenty.

CHAPTER TWENTY

The magic screamed out of me. The air warped all around as the force passed over and around, through and beneath all those surrounding me.

For the succubai, they gasped, the feeling of such power passing so close, and yet they were left alone, and safe.

For the legionnaires and the outriders, they felt the validation of their choices; they felt their future emperor's will manifest in the world, and the Eternal Emperor's gift.

For House Malakai? He got a nasty shock as he felt and saw power that he couldn't hope to beat. It screamed past him, though, and into the two last groups.

First, the Dark Legion: they saw the power; they felt the pressure. But they saw it as more of a light show—one by the apostate, no less—but that was all. Right until three of their number screamed out in pain, as their control devices detonated.

Their new leader was hurled from his feet as a priest standing by his side literally exploded. Two more, both priests again, though this time in the center of their group, died—one as a dozen devices exploded simultaneously, and the last one?

He survived, a few more seconds at least, as a bracer on his left forearm exploded, removing his hand and most of his arm, sending him to the floor with horrific burns and broken bones.

The last group, though, were the worst affected.

Varnen was at the back, and a small contingent of nobles he'd felt he could trust had been drawn up around him. Each and every one of them had made damn sure that if they had any slaves before now, by the time of this meeting, they no longer did.

The rest of the nobles? For them, it was a sign of visible wealth, of power, so they had the literal control devices bejeweled and sewn into their clothing.

They wore them as bracelets, as rings, and they traded them as thin rods. They had them in abundance, and each and every one of them detonated.

Of the forty-odd nobles who had climbed onto the roof, expecting to either switch sides to me or not, seven survived. And two of them, surprisingly, were high enough that they'd actually be useful.

The rest were rendered down to pate, or spread across the rooftop in various interesting ways.

While this was going on, the city beyond the tower was being hit with the same shock wave. And as it passed, with each and every meter it covered, those who had been enslaved were picked up, they were healed, and they were protected, while all around them, walls shook.

Cobbles rolled, buildings that were poorly built or damaged collapsed, and as thousands of slaves were freed, hundreds of slavers or slave owners died in terrible ways.

I felt the notifications and I shook them off. The hundreds of deaths—thousands, considering those who were invariably nearby when it happened—were what they were.

I hated that many innocents would be maimed and killed here; I did. But my heart hardened and my soul grew calluses, as I learned to live with it.

Moreso, as the power rolled out farther, the next stage was coming online.

Oracle reached out through me, through the masses of mana that were connected to me for these few seconds, and she then pushed the oath out from me. For miles on all sides, the oath was offered, appearing before the eyes of the stunned and terrified, the joyful and jubilant alike.

This was the time of the greatest risk. I'd have rolled the dice and come up snake eyes, if this didn't work. But I believed it would—I had to believe!

As the first voices rose, distantly, as the succubai here and the imperial subjects who had already sworn started the oaths rolling, the final stage began.

The mana that was roiling on all sides, that had been yanked in, that, even with all of this, had been spent in only small numbers compared to the ambient mass, was suddenly dragged inward toward me.

I drew in a deep breath, threw my head back, and stared at the clouds above. As the funnel went active, with my enhanced and now mana-tuned sight, I saw the mana of the world as it was connected to me.

A mist seemed to roll across the land, ephemeral and opaque at once. It existed in so much abundance that the simple truth of its presence had been missed by almost all forever.

Mana was a force, one that was everywhere and nowhere, like air or gravity. It existed, made solid and given form only when it was touched. But beyond that, it simply…*was*. Its presence was noted by most only when it was missing.

It filled and permeated the world, and I knew it now. The opposite of soul, the energy that was unique to each of us, and existed mainly through the veil or within us, that connected us with that distant and yet so near realm. No, mana was of *this* side.

Mana was life, though that was inaccurate as well.

What it was, though, at its very heart, was half of the energy that drove reality, and as I touched it, as I touched upon the simple fact of its existence, I felt it.

I drew it in, and I breathed it through me.

It entered, pouring into me, into my body, swirling past my soul and I felt the reaction I'd been looking for.

It wasn't that the knowledge of mana and soul was so secret that nobody could find it. It was that the knowledge of the two sides, the push and pull, the yin and yang, was so simple that most people overlooked it.

The soul was incredibly concentrated power…power that built throughout life. And then, when we passed through the veil, it existed on the other side, spreading out to fill the void. It dissipated slowly, breaking down to feed mana, on *this* side.

And mana? It was the same! It fed life; life begat souls; souls gathered energy and then, upon death, fed that energy into mana, creating the great wheel of never-ending energy that kept reality going.

The difference? The reason so few had ever guessed it?

Mana was *weak*.

Incredibly so. It could effect change in the realm; it could create fire, and then that fire could turn a living person into a dead person, or cook meat, or smelt iron, or a billion other things.

What it couldn't do was remove that person from creation.

It changed it instead. It changed a living man into a dead one, but he still existed. I felt it, and I knew that again, I was inching my way toward something, toward a secret that lay ahead of me in the darkness.

But not today.

Today it was enough, as I realized that the energy of all reality could be broken down into the simplest of terms.

Mana was a plus, and soul, a negative, on this side. On the other side of the veil? It was the opposite.

It was yin and yang.

Life and death, and always, balance.

Life mana and death mana were aspects of mana, and souls were possessed by the living and the dead alike. There was no place where the two sides didn't touch, and I knew it at an instinctual level.

Just like I knew that I was connected to so much mana right now, that the only limit I had with it?

Was how far I could reach.

With Oracle's help, we'd spread out the funnel—*the net* might be more accurate—across miles to ensure we could affect the entire city.

That was great and all, but had I realized this before? I might have spread hundreds of miles instead.

I reached out, and I *pulled.*

The sudden pressure as mana roared through me, into Sehran, through our bond, and then from her into the tower, was horrific.

On all sides, people were forced to their knees, and not least because the tower?

It shook.

Shook with *terrible* force, as the seed buried so far beneath, silent for long eons, awoke and did what it was supposed to do.

Its tower was found wanting, truncated, broken, and misshapen. That wasn't right.

That wasn't *acceptable*.

The tower was supposed to look like *this.*

All around me, people screamed. The stones of the tower slammed into my feet from below. I stood, tears streaming down my cheeks, held in perfect balance by the embrace of a power that could grind mountains to dust.

Up and up we roared. The land on all sides rumbled; more buildings shook and failed. But for this, the empire had laid contingency plans, though we discovered that at the same time as everyone else.

The same kind of bubble that was used to protect the slaves as the world around them heaved and flailed, as buildings collapsed and the city died, was suddenly active again, as those people were buffered from the falling stone and rubble.

They were dragged free, pushed out into the bubble of calm that surrounded the city beyond the falling walls, and they stood or sat, lay and screamed in wonder as the Tower of Gaij soared higher.

The lower floors were solidified first, sealed over, and the ruined and repaired sections smoothed into gold-flecked marble and obsidian instead as the minor repairs we'd planned for went well and truly beyond.

The great crack that covered one side, like a scar of the cataclysm, a mark that said forever, "we remember," was sealed over, transmuted back to perfection. As the tower continued to rise, the floor we stood upon, once not even a third of the way up the tower, was enveloped.

Stone rose from the land around—and, crucially, from the city that had until minutes ago surrounded the tower—and was ripped free to soar through the air.

That stone melted into the tower's walls and fed its exponential growth.

The world around me grew dark, as I was enveloped in the tower again. Walls rose past me; a ceiling formed overhead that glowed with strength and vitality, and then continued to grow.

The succubai, expecting to be used as conduits, were left stunned as the power that they'd expected to channel and work to feed through, suddenly passed them in great waves.

They backed away from the formerly ruined sections in shock, staring at pristine stone, before slowly, the great work decelerated.

The shaking of the earth was the first sign; it diminished, then grew quiet.

The mana that had poured from the world into me, and then from me into Sehran, and then finally into the tower faded and slowed, as billions of points of mana were absorbed.

The tower shuddered and gave a final lurch before settling. Stone ground against stone as long-dormant systems surged back to life. Lights flickered on in the hall we now found ourselves in; throughout the tower, long-dormant golems suddenly straightened, their eyes glowing with renewed power.

"What is this?" the Dark Legion commander demanded, his hand going to his sword.

"This," I said, my voice amplified by the last vestiges of power surging through me, "is what imperial authority truly looks like."

The entire structure hummed with energy; ancient runes and sigils flared to life along the walls as the tower drank in the power.

Then, as the world gradually grew silent, it began.

"I swear upon pain of death, to faithfully execute all that the Emperor decrees. I swear upon my soul that I shall stand for the Empire when it calls. I shall be strong when the weak need me, generous when the poor are at hand, and merciless when my fellow citizens are threatened. I shall worship the Gods of my fathers, respect my elders, and raise up my children to stand tall.

"I am an Imperial Citizen. I claim the right to call upon the Legion in my hour of need, to hold those who wrong me to justice, and to be avenged if I cannot be saved."

"I swear to obey Prince Jax and those he places over me; I will serve to the best of my ability, speak no lie to him when commanded otherwise, and treat all other citizens as family.

"I will work for the greater good, being a shield to those who need it, a sword to those who deserve it, and a warden to the night."

"I will stand with my family, helping one another to reach the light, until the hour of my death or my lord releases me from my Oath.

"Lastly, I will not be a dick!"

I could hear it: thin, distant voices called out the words; some mumbled in shock, and others yelled joyously. Still more were frantic, believing that they needed to swear and right now before I got more angry, pulled the heavens down and crushed the world.

As the power built, I sensed the moment when my will coalesced—a tangible shift in the magical landscape as my authority took root. It wasn't the same as defeating Nimon back home, but I could still feel it.

Lord Varnen was the first to rise from what was left of the local nobility, just as we'd planned. "House Varnen recognizes Prince Jax as the rightful ruler of Gaij," he declared loudly. "We pledge to the empire our support and fealty!"

This was the catalyst we needed. Another noble rose almost immediately: "House Tessian also pledges support to Prince Jax!"

The cascade we'd planned for began, as any surviving members of a noble house were desperate not to be singled out as the last to swear. Within minutes, every local house had declared for me, leaving only House Malakai and the Dark Legion opposed.

The Dark Legion commander realized what was happening and barked an order to his troops. They formed up in a defensive formation, weapons drawn, though each and every one of them looked fucking terrified. "We recognize no authority but Lord Nimon's," he blustered. "The apostate will never rule here!"

I smiled thinly. "Damn, that's a relief! I'd have hated to have to waste time on negotiating with you." I turned to the now-activated war golems that stood ready. "Eliminate the Dark Legion. No survivors."

The golems moved with surprising grace for such massive constructs. One minute, they were still as statues; the next, they were blurring forward to smash into hastily raised swords and shields.

A handful of the Dark legionnaires were elites, shifting as they took advantage of Nimon's Dark gifts. They screamed, muscles bulging as Dark berserkers grew inside specially designed plate armor.

Some of their number blurred, fading into invisibility; they bent light. They dove and rolled, ran and hid. And where a lucky few escaped the golems' first strikes, they didn't escape the succubai.

The Dark Legion fought, but they were outmatched in sheer size, ferocity, and power. Enchanted weapons, designed at the height of the empire, met iron and steel forged by the lowest bidder. Stone fists slammed down into panicking men and women with predictable results—blood, broken bones, and screaming that was cut short abruptly.

Darius Malakai, seeing the way the wind was blowing, decided to go for broke. He raised the bloodstone high, its surface glowing with an inner light. "Tower of Gaij! Golems!" he shouted. "I command you by right of my bloodstone! Obey your true master!"

For a moment, the entire hall seemed to hold its breath as the last Dark legionnaire died.

Then…absolutely nothing happened. I started to laugh.

The confusion on Darius's face was almost comical. "NO!" he screamed in disbelief, before rage contorted his features. "Kill them all!" he shouted to his followers. They drew their Earth weapons—pistols, rifles, and what looked suspiciously like grenades.

Oracle had guessed this would be the result, though, and the spell she'd cast before leaping over the side of the wall had been in preparation for this.

The shield spell she'd cast and fed with a fraction of the incoming mana bloomed into visibility with the first hits from Malakai's contingent as soon as they opened fire. The bullets struck the barrier and ricocheted wildly within the confined space, turning their attack into a horrific act of self-destruction, even as the grenadiers hurled their little presents.

As it tinted—and that was it…it fucking *tinted*—and only slightly, as opposed to the way a shield normally darkened as it approached failure…no, this *tinted* and then it became obvious to everyone that it wasn't a wall. No, it was a fucking inverted *dome*.

A dome that encircled the Malakai contingent, and that held and trapped the grenades inside. It redirected the bullets that ripped out in ricochets, and when the grenades bounced off the wall of the dome and rolled back to a halt before those men and women, who stared horrified and about to die, it held easily, as everything inside was killed.

The sounds of screaming and gunfire were mercifully brief. When the shield dropped, there was nothing left of House Malakai but bloody smears and shattered fragments.

The local nobility stared in horror at the carnage, then looked at me with newfound respect—not to mention outright fucking terror.

Good, I decided. That would keep them in line until that respect had time to grow.

Still, in the distance, the sounds of chanting, as thousands more took the oath, echoed up to the open windows.

"Gaij is now under imperial authority," I declared, letting the full power of the funnel flow through me. "Those who have sworn allegiance will be protected and raised up. Those who resist will be dealt with."

The last of the power surging through the tower reached its peak, briefly illuminating the entire structure with brilliant light before stabilizing at a more sustainable level. Through our bond, I could feel Oracle struggling as she desperately worked, guiding the flow.

Finally, I took a deep breath and popped the top off three mana potions, one at a time. I looked around at those who stared at me in various stages of horror, excitement, and hope.

"Here we go…" I breathed, as Oracle linked the tower to me and the hoped-for notification appeared.

Congratulations!

You have taken command of the Tower of Gaij and have the prerequisite authority and abilities to claim this city and the surrounding land (1,292 square miles), adding it to your territory as a claimed location.

Warning: Repairs must be conducted to bring the tower to full functionality.

Do you wish to annex this territory now?

Yes/No

Unsurprisingly, I went with Yes. The notification flared, then changed.

BEWARE!

Until the city and surrounding territory has been purged of dissidents and enemies, and the general morale has been raised from -7 (Distrustful) to a minimum of 0 (Neutral), this territory will suffer a penalty of 35% to all production, including life-forms.

(Time since morale was at 0 (Neutral): 22,992 days, 11 hours, 1 minute, 17 seconds.)

Do you wish to annex this territory now?

Yes/No

"Oh yeah, I think I fucking do, thank you very much." The second shock wave raced outward from the center of the territory, and I smiled evilly as I imagined just how many fucking drow, spiderkin, and beasty buggering shitehawks had been killed.

Attention, Citizens of the Territory of Carrmor!

The Tower of Gaij has been claimed by a worthy aspirant of ancient bloodlines!

All Titles, Deeds, and Laws in the claimed territories of Carrmor are held for review, and can be revoked, altered, annulled, or approved.

All Hail Prince Jax of Dravith and Carrmor! Scion of the Empire and Master of Gaij!

*

Congratulations!

You have claimed the Tower of Gaij.

Due to the lack of a creation table, and attendant wisps, this facility is unable to receive commands at this time.

*

Congratulations!

You have led your forces to formal war again, though this time you have used guile and cunning, diplomacy and magic to claim the territory. As such, you have earned a Title!

Diplomatic Developer: Level 1: Diplomats who reside within or are based from your territory gain +7 to Persuasion and Negotiation skills when dealing with outsiders. Trade agreements formed within your territory provide 12% increased value.

Arcane Administrator: Level 1: Your governmental structures operate with supernatural efficiency. Tax collection increases by 8%, while reducing citizen discontent by 5%. Reconstruction projects complete 15% faster.

That wasn't a hard choice at all. Considering the reconstruction tasks were going to be fucking huge, and that the morale issues were almost being sorted in one fell swoop there?

Plus, I got eight percent more taxes.

Admittedly, I had zero fucking clue where we were with taxes and more currently, and I had to guess that the real-world effect of that wasn't that everyone just spontaneously decided to pay me eight percent more.

More likely, with everyone being a little less pissed at me and my new government, they'd simply not be skimming as much off the top.

That was cool, though, and it was definitely better in my pocket than in the pockets of my enemies.

The stone of the tower beneath my feet gave one last shiver, and then it fell still. I blinked, letting out a breath as the mana that had sustained me until now drained away like milk from the bottom of a cracked jug.

The world around me tilted slightly, then righted, then tilted again. Before I knew it, I had a pair of succubai on either side, helping to hold me upright as a wave of incredible exhaustion tore through me.

I sucked down a shuddering breath and forced it out again, trying to stand straight. But my legs felt like jelly, my muscles were virtually water, and as for my brain?

I knew I had to do something, I was supposed to do something, but what the hell? I could barely operate my damn eyes to blink!

"Jax?"

It was Sehran, I knew that much, but beyond that? I just shook my head and forced the words out, my voice weak.

"Sehran speaks for me," I managed, barely.

In seconds, she was speaking for me, getting over the shock and doing what needed to be done. "Authority goes from me, to Oracle, Daralen and Sehran, Seraphina and down."

Seraphina took one look at the broken condition of me and Sehran and then gestured to Daralen, who stepped up beside her as she started to speak.

"You've sworn to Prince Jax, and this is now imperial territory!" Seraphina said, looking about as the two succubai—one on either side of me—helped me to a seat, while she said the things I'd spoken about me needing to tell the people.

"As such, you'll be receiving a list of imperial laws by the end of the day. If you've broken those laws, best that you speak to a legionnaire about it. Primus Daralen will designate someone for that."

"Optio Gilpin," Daralen declared. "He served as a speculatores for many years. He's aware of the laws and the punishments for transgression."

"So if you think you might have broken a law that's serious, I suggest you see Optio Gilpin, and he'll look to deal with it!" Seraphina went on. "If it was a minor law? It's in the past and we'll sort it out. If it's a major law, then I'd suggest you want to prove you're honorable by coming to the legion and having them discuss it with you, rather the prince sending the legion—or a golem—to get you."

There was a moment's silence while everyone looked from the hard-bitten and grim-faced legionnaires, and then to the golems, many of whom still wore the smears that was all that was left of their last opponents.

"Beyond that, I'm sure you all have other places to be. Spread the word about what happened here and get started on fixing the city up," Seraphina finished. "Prince Jax has just channeled more mana than any hundred other mages could try to do, and he did it to cast *all* the drow and their kind out of the entire territory, killing them in the process. So thank you for supporting him and the empire. Now get the hell out."

That was enough. Seraphina stood graceful and tall, but clearly accepting zero shit from anyone.

Sehran moved from my side, straightening and staring at her hands, then shaking her head in disbelief at the power she'd just fed through them. She staggered slightly, then sank gratefully into another seat.

The mistress of the tower placed a hand on her shoulder and smiled proudly at her, before turning and glaring at the assembled people. "Well?" she snapped. "MOVE!"

They did. Not a single one paused to ogle her as they usually would, making it clear that the old system of the nobles believing they ruled and that the succubai should dance and obey was long gone.

CHAPTER TWENTY-ONE

The dawn broke slowly, and I stared at the gently brightening light with a hint of confusion as I tried to replay the events of the day before.

The claiming of the tower and the surrounding territory had—unusually for me—actually gone according to plan. We'd even had a sort of plan for when it was all done as well, which I vaguely remembered as Seraphina taking over and getting started, along with Daralen.

Mainly because, although I'd known that I'd end up a bit fucked, I'd not really thought about the sheer amount of mana that I was passing through my body and through Sehran and Oracle's.

After Seraphina had kicked everyone out—literally, if they weren't part of our original party, then they were out, even including Varnen—then she and Daralen had seen to getting Sehran, Oracle, and me to a bedroom and to some rest.

There'd been talk about the succubai using their gifts to basically turbocharge my stamina and get me back on my feet to make decisions and get the ball rolling, but she'd discussed it with Daralen, and they'd decided against it.

Instead, we'd all been put to bed—Oracle and me in one room, and Sehran next door—and then we'd been allowed to sleep it off.

Now, as I lay there, my head feeling two sizes too big and stuffed full of cotton wool, I stared at the shutters and the light that streamed through them.

I could feel the tower around me, the strength and solidity of it, as well as see it in the vibrant walls and the gentle sparkles of quartz and gold in the marble.

The tower wasn't whole, not by a long shot, but it was intact enough that it wasn't going to collapse tomorrow, that much I knew.

As Oracle shifted against my side, I gently reached down and teased a hair free of where it'd lain across her cheek; she mumbled something, then apparently went back to sleep.

The tower was solid and intact enough that, provided we could get some mana collectors made or recovered and attached in the next year or so, there'd be no way to tell it wasn't fully up to strength.

That was a bit of a relief, mainly because the people who lived out in the city, I realized with sudden alarm, were going to be seriously scared shitless.

I blinked as the reality of that crashed down on me. Because yesterday? As part of repairing the tower, the magic had dragged in a fuckload of stone and more that had been part of the tower originally, and it'd used that to rebuild itself, which I'd not expected.

That was fine, great even, as it'd allowed the tower to do far more with the rebuild than it would have managed if the entire thing had been done just with mana.

The issue, though? Those rocks and blocks, the stones that were brought back to the tower? They'd been repurposed into building material for the city some seven hundred fucking years ago.

That meant we'd just ripped a fuckload of people's houses apart and left them homeless on the street without any warning.

Even with that, the reality that the people of the city were so happy to be part of the empire and the nobles being put in their place that the morale was "only" at minus two percent was *insane*.

I stared at the shutters, the golden light filtering through the light-brown grained wood, and I forced myself to think this through.

We had thousands, tens of thousands, now heading to the tower from Sonra. They'd need to be housed. This was a friggin' city already, one that hadn't had exactly an overabundance of spare houses that weren't being used before I'd ripped half of it apart.

A conservative estimate was going to be at least thirty thousand people living in the city, maybe fifty to sixty. And then, beyond that, there were the incoming people from Sonra, and that was…

Shit, I didn't even know. I knew we had twenty thousand plus of them between ex-slaves who had signed up as legion aspirants, the full legionnaires, and the outriders. In total, though? I thought there were about another twenty thousand, maybe?

I stared into space as I tried to imagine it. That many people who were suddenly homeless, not to mention Sonra coming and joining up with the city, and then…

"Though…" I murmured unthinkingly, "there's always the tower itself…"

"Hmmmm?" Oracle mumbled, still mostly asleep.

"Nothing, my love," I assured her, leaning down and kissing her, before sliding out of the bed and attending to the needs of nature in the attached bathroom.

Thank the gods for that being a standard thing in the great towers!

Returning to the room a few minutes later, I sorted clothing out, hit myself with a quick Scour—as I didn't have a shower designed by Seneschal in here and couldn't be bothered with a bath yet—and then tucked Oracle in, gave her a last kiss, and slipped from the room, dressed and ready to fuck someone else's day up.

I felt a little relief when I stepped out of the room to find four legionnaires on watch, fully armed and armored and clearly ready to slaughter anyone who tried to get past them. They stiffened on seeing me, and I shook my head, miming that Oracle was asleep and to stay quiet. I passed them, thanking them for watching over us, and asking that they keep her safe.

I could feel through the bond that Sehran was up and moving around in her room, as I passed it. I knocked lightly on the door, before closing my eyes and sighing when she opened it to see who it was…utterly naked and flashing the entire corridor.

"Fuck's sake," I groaned. "Seriously? It could have been anyone!"

"First, I could feel it was you through the bond." She ticked it off on her fingers as she grinned at me and bounced unrepentantly. "Second, I know how much this frustrates you and you still like to look regardless of what you say. And lastly, your societal hang-ups aren't mine." She shrugged.

"Seriously, Jax, you think we wear clothing like we do here in the hells? Believe me, we don't! It's either armor, deliberately teasing and provocative stuff that goes waaaaay beyond what I try to tease you with, or we're naked. This is my default, even when spending time around others, so don't blame *me* when you knock on *my* door and I'm naked."

"I…" I shook my head. "Yeah, you know what, you're right. Sorry."

"Besides, I love the look on your face when I do this…" She grinned evilly and bounced again.

"I hate you," I growled.

"No you don't." She laughed, before striding back into the room and plucking out some clothing, pulling it on as we talked. "So, are you okay? How's Oracle? What's the plan?"

"Oracle's asleep still, and I'm okay. Are you?"

"I feel like I've had my skin ripped off then a new set attached, and it doesn't fit right." She shrugged. "Like everything is a little 'off,' you know? Beyond that? I'm fine."

"Same," I agreed. "But as long as you're okay, we need to talk to the succubai, and we need to get the ball rolling with the city."

"I'm good. Do you want me with you now, or watching over Oracle?" she asked.

I hesitated, then shook my head. "With me. We have the legion again…Oracle's safe with them."

I had a moment of doubt as I said it. I barely knew half the legionnaires by sight, and that wasn't right, but…I also felt the bond.

I could feel these legionnaires and hundreds more in the tower, the city, and traveling toward me. I damn well knew that either I trusted them, or I had no business expecting them to trust and defend me.

Weirdly, I could also feel a single person out there "somewhere" headed toward me. I focused on that feeling, remembering them being in the desert when I resurrected the oaths when I first took the caravan, and they'd been sort of nearby. Now, weeks later, they were still around, still headed toward me, but slow as shit.

I shrugged and dismissed it. They'd catch up at some point, no doubt.

It didn't take long for the pair of us to reach the same formal area that I'd first met the mistress, only to find that unlike before, it was totally fucking empty.

Another hour was spent searching, and asking various succubai, until I found out that when we'd been basically put to bed like tired children, the succubai, released for the first time in centuries from having to feed the tower, had gone on an absolute rampage.

Daralen had been left as the token adult, and the sex demons had basically done what they did best, and were now spread far and wide.

I was a bit annoyed, but half an hour later, Daralen, Sehran, and I sat in a very nice pagoda-like structure in the gardens, with a hell of a spread of good food, tea, and fruit juices while we started to plan the next step, thanks to the employed staff of the tower.

And let's face it—after seven hundred years, I could hardly begrudge the succubai letting off a little steam. Amusingly, there'd actually been a pair asleep in the bush nearby when we'd taken up residence, and I mean "in" the bush. A pair of hairy legs had been sticking up and out of an ornamental hedge, and a much more attractive pair of legs had been on display, hanging out lower down.

It'd turned out to be the resident tower baker who owned the hairy legs, and one of his most ardent enjoyers of pastries who was slumbering a few inches below him.

It took the staff—most of whom were also hungover to buggery—only a few seconds of frozen, horrified recognition before they dragged him out of the bush and frantically covered him up.

The succubus, as one of the "little mistresses" of the tower, was left to sleep on, oblivious.

Daralen brought me up to date with the details, confirming that yes, there was significant widespread destruction of the city in the process of rebuilding the tower, and no, it wasn't as bad as I'd feared.

First of all, about a thousand people homes had received enough damage that they were considered demolished, dangerous, or otherwise unlivable.

Of them, the majority were people who made up solidly the "middle classes" of the city, and mainly the artisans, crafters, and the people who made the city "work."

Nearly a hundred had been the nobles, of which thirty were now dead, and their relatives were of the opinion that they'd really like me not to look too closely at them, and they would also quite like to move out to live in their country estates for a while, thank you very much.

Lastly, there were a few sections of the city that had been very poor and a single street of that had been demolished as well.

By the time Seraphina arrived, sliding into a seat with a tired but much happier expression on her face, we'd come up with a plan that I thought dealt with everything nicely.

We agreed to extend an offer to the people who had been disenfranchised that they could either have their homes or workshops rebuilt by us as and when we could—it wasn't going to be quick, but it'd be by golems and would be at a rate of about a house a day—or they could move into the tower.

Considering that these were the descendants of, or were themselves, people who had spent the last several centuries desperately trying to get into the tower to live in what they considered safety, it wasn't really a surprise when they all jumped at the chance.

Seraphina was a little concerned at it, but she had to admit, that as she'd be the mistress of the tower still, and the majority who were moving in were the better craftsmen and so on, it really wasn't an issue.

Also, the tower—we guessed, based roughly on the same dimensions of the Tower of Dravith and then sized down with the missing floors—could comfortably hold around a hundred thousand, and that wasn't even using the space that was set aside for things like the barracks, the cathedral, the large parade grounds, the training halls, etc.

That was only using the unused rooms in the newly extended area.

Considering that of that hundred thousand, there were roughly one thousand needing to find rooms and crafting spaces? Yeah, no stress at all.

Invitations were made and the people started gathering their things.

Next up were the incoming groups. Although Illoth and her kind had been banished, nobody else had been.

That was brought sharply to the front of our minds as Seraphina explained the real reason we needed to get moving, and fast, with the next stage: Those damn armies massing.

The nearest—according to her information—was almost directly to the east, some hundred miles out. For an army, that was about fifteen to twenty days' march.

This was a massive problem for two reasons. First and foremost, we needed to be setting off in less than a week, to get to the Cradle of Feshcan'un.

The issue? They were massing pretty much directly in the direction we needed to head, and that area was known for two things.

First? Mana was wildly unpredictable and spellcasting was both much harder and more costly, the closer you got to the Plain of Bones.

Secondly, according to Seraphina, the Cradle had been in that direction, once, long ago, and hadn't been seen in hundreds of years, because it was destroyed.

Asking how it was destroyed just got a shrug and an explanation that it had been, everyone knew that; nobody knew how, just that it was long gone.

Now, in what had been a lush and overripe valley filled with rolling hills and one of the greatest temples to life on the continent, there was only the desert of life, one that was so full of the bodies of those who had tried to cross it, that they now referred to it as the Plain of Bones.

There was a single city in the area, and that was Kronk. A stupid name for a shitty place, I'd been told, and one that I'd either need to deal with, or circle wide around.

Kronk was an old dwarvish town, one that had grown much as Gaij had. The only difference was that instead of being dedicated to trying to secure themselves through building high walls and trade, they'd done it through raiding the shit out of everyone.

It wasn't exactly on a line: Kronk was around thirty miles out of the way to the south. When it'd been discussed, it'd been planned that the group could simply travel fast and hard, and swing north a bit, before striking out across what was apparently now another desert.

That should have been enough to get us clear of Kronk, except that they'd already begun gathering their raiding forces into an army—again, something that happened now and then—but the timing…that was an issue.

According to Seraphina, they'd been making noises about marching on Lembiq—an elven city to the south and west of them—and as such, it would have probably actually worked out quite nicely for us, as they'd have been well out of our way. And without the raiding parties, we could have possibly even stopped off in the city to do a raid of our own.

Now, though, with us coming out of the blue and claiming a large part of the continent, there was a good chance that the army would be redirected to us. If that happened, first off, we needed the city here secure. And secondly, the whole point of going to Feshcan'un was to make the entire process of giving birth for Oracle safer and easier.

Traveling through a war zone into an area known for killing anything that walked through it, while dodging an entire army? That didn't sound so smart to me anymore.

As such, I decided that later today, I was going to have to have a conversation with the gods. If they could shed some light on why it was the right place to go, maybe we still would, and if not? Fuck it, the tower here with all the support we could manage would have to be enough.

We talked of practical changes, of food we'd need bringing in. Varnen was summoned and his wife and son along with him, and by the time they arrived, Oracle had joined us as well.

The next hour was spent first meeting them in a less hurried and manic manner, and then asking them questions around who, what, where, and how.

Who ran the various sections of the city and what they actually did: as in, were they the titular head of the district or were they the actual people who got shit done, and then where things were and how the city actually functioned.

There were a million details, though one fun little nugget that came out of the whole thing was that there had been a significant guildhall in the city for both the Caravaneer's Guild and the Merchant's Guild.

First of all, the Caravaneer's Guild had been basically gutted as half of it had packed up and ran when I'd arrived in the city—clearly that little shit who ran from Sonra had passed the word here as well—and then what was left had been raided by the Dark Legion in passing.

The Merchant's Guild, on the other hand, were sitting outside, or their representatives were, and they were pissed.

They'd not been invited to the little event yesterday to sort the city out, but they were very used to getting their own way in the city, so being told by a legionnaire to sit down and shut up or fuck off had left them furious.

I had no interest in talking to them yet, so I left them to cool their heels, and got on with important things instead.

Daralen showed me the dimensions of the original legion encampment, and Seraphina, despite suffering with a hangover, managed to review reports from her spies and get the current details together.

I hit her with a heal in gratitude, and she practically wept in relief.

After that, we moved onto the city, though now that we had a rough idea of the actual reality of the city and who and what made it run, there was a whole new plan to be made.

First of all, although people had been incredibly patient in a lot of ways, I'd freed the entirety of the enslaved population of the city earlier, and when I'd done it, I'd not only healed them all, I'd also slaughtered most of their worst oppressors in one fell swoop.

That was a great thing, truly it was, but it left a shitload of healed people who suddenly had no home, no way of feeding themselves, and absolutely nothing to their name, except that they'd been horrifically oppressed by "X," who was now dead.

They were leaderless and set adrift. While my people and I tried to get a handle on the actual reality of things, they…well, a lot of them went on a rampage.

They looted the shops they'd spent years being forced to guard. They burned down the houses of their former masters or people who'd oppressed them. They stole food, because they had nothing to pay for it with and no way to earn it. And lastly, a good number of them decided that if I'd freed them, it must be for a reason, and they came to the tower and camped outside the walls.

In response, I put Varnen in charge of one of the largest clothing empires—it'd been owned previously in conjunction between the Merchant's Guild and Havelton—and I told him to get started on clothing for the slaves, as well as the little things we needed, like bedding, beds, and everything fucking else.

The only "major" noble house to have survived more or less intact—Tessian—was surprising, considering they'd argued for the slave trade when I'd arrived here but didn't actually own slaves.

According to Seraphina, it wasn't a case of them having scruples; it was just that they dealt in money and banking instead, and the kind of slaves they could have made use of, besides those who cooked and cleaned, were instead owned by their subsidiaries.

Much as bankers did these days, they kept their hands clean by owning the companies that did the sneaky and underhanded shit, instead of doing it themselves.

That meant that when the time came to speak to the Merchant's Guild, I needed to deal with these scumbags as well.

Seraphina was fitting in well as my local factor, doing all the bits and pieces that I needed to make sure things actually worked. When I summoned the nobles, the Merchant's Guild, and the heads of both the city guard force and the Mercenary's Guild, she sent a dozen messages and more to get the ball rolling to get the freed slaves gathered for me to speak to after that.

They'd almost all sworn to me already—and another two hundred legionnaires had been freed, ranging from the vast majority being actual real legion aspirants when they were captured, all the way up to speculatores. The general from the freed "normal" slaves was among those who hadn't sworn; in exchange for their freedom, they owed me a chance to explain what I wanted.

She also arranged to have the heads of the various criminal families attend. Considering they were mainly also her spies, it amused the shit out of me.

The sun was still up, though the gardens were getting packed as the slaves and a great many citizens besides wandered in for the meeting, and we moved indoors to speak to the surviving nobles and various scumbags.

CHAPTER TWENTY-TWO

The council room in the Tower of Gaij gleamed with newly restored marble. I sat at the head of the massive table, tired but a lot better than I'd felt yesterday, admittedly. Oracle sat to my right, Sehran to my left, with Daralen and Seraphina flanking them.

The hall was long. People stood or sat in rows, and along either wall were legionnaires, fully armored and ready. At the far end, where they had to pass them to enter, were a pair of hulking war golems, advanced models.

Across from us, at the front, were the surviving original nobles of Gaij. A pitiful seven—out of what had been forty—squirmed in their seats, their faces a mixture of terror and naked ambition. Now, scattered through their seats were entirely new nobles, the survivors of the houses—if they had any—that I'd already eliminated.

Behind them stood representatives of the Merchant's Guild, with House Tessian's bankers at the forefront, all trying their hardest to look simultaneously important and absolutely unthreatening.

"Let me make this perfectly clear," I began, my voice still raspy from the strain of channeling that much mana and then spending the entire damn day speaking to people. "The only reason any of you are still breathing is because you had the good sense to support me when I took the tower.

"House Varnen threw in with me straightaway, which I appreciate, and that means that he's got a slightly larger amount of leeway than the rest of you, and a slightly better chance of climbing higher in the new imperial structure we set in place here. However, that also means that he needs to prove he deserves that spot."

I paused, letting the silence stretch uncomfortably. One of the younger nobles—a lanky bastard with a nervous tic—started to speak, but I cut him off with a raised hand.

"Your support so far has earned you exactly one chance. *One*. That's it." I leaned forward, resting my forearms on the table. "Fuck it up, and you'll wish you'd died with the rest of them."

Lord Varnen, sitting slightly apart from the other nobles, cleared his throat. "Prince Jax, what exactly do you require of us during this…probationary period?"

Smart man. He'd figured out the dynamic quickly enough, and was leading the others.

"Simple. This city is now the seat of imperial authority on Carrmor. It needs to be functional, and quickly. The people who lost their homes when the tower reclaimed its materials need shelter. The former slaves need food, clothing, and purpose. And we need to prepare for war."

That got their attention. Whispers and concerned looks flashed around the room.

"War?" one merchant asked, a stocky woman with shrewd eyes. "Against whom?"

"Anyone who opposes the empire," I replied bluntly. "To start with, there's an army gathering to the east at Kronk. Then there's the Dark Legion, who've retreated but are far from defeated. We're aware of their troops in motion somewhere to the south. Then let's not forget the drow—they've been banished from our territory, but they'll be looking for revenge, so I have no doubt that they'll be working to pull some kind of sneaky shit as well."

Seraphina gestured and a servant to one side stepped forward and began to distribute a set of parchments to each noble and guild representative.

"These are your assignments," she explained. "Each of you will be responsible for a specific aspect of the city's reconstruction and preparation. Lord Tessian, your banking expertise will be put into establishing a proper imperial treasury, one that will be receiving a significant seed of investment from Prince Jax, and that will be absorbing everything that certain former houses had owned. Lord Varnen, clothing and the textile industry. Lord Haseltine, your people will oversee food distribution and agricultural planning…"

She continued, assigning each noble and guild a task that matched their particular skills or resources. As she spoke, I watched their expressions, noting who seemed resistant and who appeared eager to prove themselves.

There was also a noticeable look of panic on Tessian's face. He cradled the parchment he'd received to his chest, clearly trying to stop anyone from looking at it, considering the crack about the property of "certain houses."

When she finished, I spoke again. "This is not a request. This is your duty to the empire, and the price of your continued existence. Perform well, and you'll find your position secure and even significantly improved. Fail…" I shook my head and let them fill in the blank.

"I'll make one thing clear here: I haven't always conquered and dealt with people as harshly as I do now," I said. "The reason I now do so is because every time I've attempted to rule with a lighter touch, people have pushed. They have lied, stolen, and backstabbed, and as such, now I rule with an iron fist.

"Prove yourselves to me, and to those I place over you, and I'll relax that significantly. But as the old saying goes, I'll give you plenty of rope." I looked from one to another. "What you do with that rope is up to you. You can relax and use it well, earn my trust and a place of potentially high office in the empire. Or you can fashion it into a noose and I'll damn well hang you with it. Like everything in life, this is your choice to make."

"You'll find we're devoted servants of the empire, my prince," Lord Tessian assured me, his voice rough as he tried to force out a smile.

I didn't trust the bastard as far as I could throw him, but fuck it, let him try to prove he could be useful.

"Good." I nodded. "You have until tomorrow morning to review these assignments and prepare your initial plans. Nobles, you are dismissed."

They looked shocked, and I quirked an eyebrow at them in question. Daralen stepped forward, one hand on her shortsword's hilt in obvious warning.

They took the hint and filed out.

I turned to the next in line, the guild representatives, who all hurried to move to the front of the room and take the freshly vacated seats.

"I've been informed that you try to ensure all business goes through you, and you penalize any who go their own way," I said without preamble, looking at the Merchant's Guild. "I don't personally mind unions, which is what your setups usually evolve into, because they often make sure the common worker isn't fucked over by their supposed 'betters,' like those overdressed idiots who just left…"

I got a few wide smiles from that and noted a lot of relaxing of shoulders and stances.

"However, every so often, these kinds of situations crop up where the guild—or the union, if you will—forgets that they exist to protect their members. Rather, they attempt to rule them, and like the fucking parasites you often are, you then end up stifling opportunity and instead of supporting the workers, you end up killing them.

"So, Zorbiah Zute'sh, are you here?" I tapped at a name on a piece of parchment before me. "Apologies if I've mangled your name."

"I am, and have no fear, great lord, I have—" a pale-skinned, beringed fat man started, smiling oily.

"I don't care. I was merely being polite." I cut him off. "You've sworn the oath, and so this makes things a lot easier. Have you ordered the beatings, murders, and destruction or suppression of your competitors?"

"Yes," he replied, before looking horrified as the word was torn from him.

"Was it for a valid reason, as in to defend others, or simply to ensure you gained more wealth?"

"It was to eliminate competition and to increase my wealth, or for me to gain in another way."

"Are you familiar with imperial law?" I asked cooly.

"I am. I studied it before arriving here today."

"Excellent. Are there any valid reasons for leniency under imperial law for what you've done?"

"No." He looked suddenly terrified.

"And there we have it, people—nice and straightforward. Thank you for your confession, Zorbiah." I nodded. "You'll all notice Optio Gilpin there off to the side—give a wave, Optio."

He did, then returned to parade rest.

"Excellent. To avoid any confusion, he is a member of the speculatores, an elite branch of the legion dedicated to rooting out corruption. You are all to respond with absolute truth when he asks you a question, and to volunteer anything you feel he is looking to find out, instead of hiding it, should he ask you as part of any formal questioning on his part." I smiled. "This is an imperial order from your prince."

The looks of horror spread across the room.

"As you can all see, the heads of the Merchant's Guild, the Mercenary's Guild and the city guard, as well as judiciary system are in this small group," I pointed out, raising my voice in the hushed and terrified silence of the rest of the room. "Optio Gilpin will be asking some questions, and then hopefully some of them will be returning to their homes and work after this meeting. If not, well, you'll all be able to guess why."

"You…you can't do this!" Zorbiah gasped. "You don't understand who I am!"

"I understand plenty." I snorted. "Any of you who are particularly eagle-eyed might have noticed two golems and a single legion rider atop one of my Fenris automatons leaving the city an hour ago. They're headed after the fleeing representatives of the Caravaneer's Guild, and they'll either return with them, or their heads. It being entirely up to that legionnaire and the guild representatives which."

There was a terrified silence.

I turned to the head of the Mercenary's Guild and nodded to him. "If you're still around after your meeting—and not incarcerated, obviously—I might have a great deal of work for you. But that will depend on your conversation, so good luck."

There was a brief pause and he nodded back, looking slightly worried, but interested, and I raised my voice again.

"You're dismissed!"

And as they filed out, the next group moved forward, the mages.

The mages of Gaij were a mixed lot—twenty-seven in total, ranging from ancient scholars with white beards down to apprentices barely into their teens. Unlike the nobles, few had sworn the oath during the initial wave. They'd been too cautious, waiting to see which way the wind would blow.

Now they stood before me, their expressions guarded as Daralen explained the situation with the armies.

"The empire requires your skills," she concluded. "You have two choices: swear the oath and serve, or leave Gaij with what you can carry on your backs. The prince offers safe passage out of the city to those who choose exile."

An older mage with a silver-streaked beard stepped forward. "And if we were to swear, what would our duties entail?"

"Some of you will assist with the city's reconstruction, depending on your skills and capabilities," I explained. "Others will train the Imperial Legion in basic combat magic and more. The most skilled among you will be gifted new magical knowledge and more, as well as being taught how to use ancient imperial technologies. The days of magic being an exclusive preserve of the rich and shameless are over. On Dravith, the entire legion has access to basic magic, which includes two offensive and one healing spell. Those who are gifted? They have a hell of a lot more.

"Some of you will no doubt be wondering at the magic you saw thrown around yesterday. The simple truth is that I am not only a prince, I am a legionnaire, and a mage imperator. Finally, I was gifted with a great deal of magical knowledge by my predecessor, Amon, the Eternal Emperor.

"As you'll imagine, that means that Oracle and I, my good lady here, have a great deal of knowledge of the most complicated and frankly horrific of the empire's war toys. That knowledge is available to those we choose to teach. And where we feel it is appropriate, there are also significant reserves of knowledge hidden, including the memories and spellbooks of some of the greatest mages of the past."

I paused, seeing the absolute naked greed on the faces of a great many of the mages. They exchanged glances, a silent conversation passing between them. Finally, the elder mage spoke up, apparently for them all.

"I am Magister Strasburg. I have served Gaij for sixty years, through three city lords and countless crises. If the empire has truly returned, then it has my allegiance." He stepped forward and knelt. "I will swear your oath, Prince Jax."

His decision broke the dam. Within minutes, twenty-five of the twenty-seven mages had agreed to swear. Only two—a pair of younger mages with identical stubborn expressions—chose exile.

After administering the oath, I instructed Daralen and Seraphina to begin integrating the mages into our operations immediately. Ten were assigned to help with the city, twelve to legion training, and the remaining three to work with Oracle on the tower's systems. The last two were to be taken to their homes, given the chance to pack up, and then would be kicked out of the city.

As they left, a wave of tiredness washed over me, a carryover from overdoing it yesterday, but I forced it back. There was still too much to do.

"Prince Jax, these are the last group." Seraphina smiled as the others were ushered from the room.

"Wait, you mean the spies and criminals?" I frowned dramatically, just for shits and giggles, and she nodded. "Oh, thank fuck…honest people," I finished, relaxing and getting a very confused series of looks from the people in the room now.

"Okay, look," I said. "Seraphina has vouched for you all. You'll notice that three of your usual number haven't attended?"

The group looked around, clearly trying to decide whether they should hide that they even knew one another, or whether they should be honest. Three hid it; two nodded.

"Great. That's because those other three were respectively murdering, raping bastards, and a slaver. As such, they're dead, and those under them who did such things are in cells, awaiting a hangman's time." I sighed. "See, the empire had a lot of laws, but at their heart, they came down to simple things, only growing more complicated when lawyers and other scumbags got involved and tried to manipulate the letter of the law to mean the opposite.

"Murder, rape, assault—be that physical or sexual—and blackmail are all illegal. The punishments fit the crime. A punch-up…well, maybe both sides get a clip across the back of the head and a day spent with the legion on punishment drill to teach a little self-control in future.

"You rape someone, you get hung. That's it. There's no need for a warning, because it's pretty fucking cut and dry that it's fucking wrong, and made more so by the involvements of the justicars, which I'll be bringing here soon thankfully.

"What I mean by that is that I'm well aware there are levels of sexual assault, but at the heart of it all is that really simple inclusion at the end of the oath of citizenship: '*don't be a dick.*'

"What I mean by that, is that rape? Solidly dickish move, and you fucking know it. Accusing someone of rape, when it's a lie and you fucking know it is? Also a dickish move. See how easy that is?

"Next, we have the various forms of assault, and the punishments match the crime; the more severe, the more straightforward the response. The laws are being nailed up all over the city and the criers are going to be walking around and making sure people who can't read understand those laws as well.

"There's one last thing to point out before we move on, and that's sexual assault of a minor. Fiddlin' with kids, in other words." I looked around grimly.

"That crime, there is no punishment severe enough for, so I'll make it fucking clear that it's not only a capital crime and results in death, but it's a case of a *very*, very painful death. I don't care about the ranks of severity and I'm not discussing them with you. See the previous comment about not being a dick."

I looked from one to another of the group, then nodded that I was satisfied they'd understood. "In this city, we have a very simple way of dealing with such, which is that the succubai have a very wide range of tastes, and some of them involve torture. Anyone who is found—like the head of the last gang—to be indulging in child abuse gets to spend their last days and fucking weeks as a guest of the succubai. And believe me, one of the first things they do is ensure that you have no hope or expectation of your death being brought about in a fun way."

"We understand," one of the heads of the crime families said, and I nodded to her. She was an older woman, well dressed, but in plain clothes, a single black onyx broach adorning her cloak and severely styled black hair that was greying.

"Glad to hear it, because this is where things get interesting for you. You, by and large, haven't been breaking imperial laws, beyond the obvious theft and murder level. You've also been spying for the succubai, and yes, I know, it's something that's usually hidden and not referred to." I waved my hands negligently. "So let's make our position clear. You're criminals, I'm the prince, I should be having you all hung on general principles, yadda, yadda, yadda."

"But you're not going to?" the second, a tall woman with long blonde hair and a look like a deer in the headlights asked, breathily, while adjusting her top.

"Please don't do that." I shook my head. "I'll be honest with you all in here and I'd ask that you are with me. Besides, I have a succubus in my personal entourage. Believe me, she's a lot better at pretending to be no threat than you are."

The woman paused and then inclined her head in respect, before straightening up and tucking herself back in.

"So, before I was interrupted, no, I'm not going to hang you. I'm going to recruit you." I smiled. "You all broke the laws here, but until I took over, it wasn't my problem, so I'm willing to consider this a situation of service to compensate and now, well, if you choose to stay, you'll swear the oath—if you haven't already—and then I'll ask you if you've crossed the line…and we all know where that line is now."

"And if we choose to leave?" a short, broad man with massive hands asked, cracking his knuckles.

"Same deal as the nobles and the others—a day's grace to fuck off with what you can carry on your back."

"And if we stay?" the first woman asked.

"You'll be made into literal spies. I'll have roles for you in my government—for one of you, anyway, as you'll be competing for the role of spymaster, and the others will be under them." I smiled around. "Don't get me wrong. I know you're criminals, and some of you are murderers as well. But the difference and the reason you're getting this chance is that you've also proved yourselves to have a code of honor, and as such, you're getting the chance to pay off your crimes.

"Again, just in case I wasn't clear, this isn't going to be an easy role. It's going to leave you against gods, never mind the lords and ladies who run the other cities. You've heard of the old nobility? The ones who were the original descendants of the Eternal Emperor? They're back. This role is going to pit you directly against them. You're going to be recruiting assassins, turning enemy agents and spies to our side, and you're going to be in incredible danger because of it."

I noted the looks on three of the six faces, as this little group was clearly split now between those who hungered for the chance to fight their way to the top, who could see a serious path to power, and those who were already at full capacity or near enough.

"You know how hard this will be," I said, speaking to the excited three directly and ignoring the others now. "You know it's going to be messy, bloody work, but that when it works, it'll save tens of thousands, possibly millions of lives. As Amon once told me, the things we sometimes have to do, so that others can look down on us and despise us, but from the safety of their ivory fucking towers, is terrible, but it's worth it."

I paused. "Prove that you deserve to play the great game, and I'll provide you with the tools you need to win."

I saw the hunger on the faces of those three, and I nodded; that seed was well planted at least. "Okay, that's it…oath time, then you get to see the optio, and any survivors who want to, get to move on with the plan."

Things moved fairly quickly from that point, and a few minutes later, they were out of the room and I sat back, sighing.

"Are you all right?" Oracle asked quietly, her hand finding mine beneath the table.

"Just tired, both from yesterday and a full day of this planning and people-ing bullshit," I assured her, smiling. "But we need to speak with Jenae before I rest."

"I'll help you prepare." She rose. "Daralen, can you make sure we're not disturbed while he does this?"

Daralen nodded. "Of course. I'll stand by the door myself."

"And that way we're close by in case he falls over again," Sehran added with a wide smile.

"Very funny," I muttered, though she wasn't entirely wrong. I seemed to do that a lot of late.

Mind you, I was also casting the kind of spells that people tended to think of as "once in a lifetime, mages of legend" castings, and I was doing it at least once a week on average, so fuck them all very much.

We set off walking, and I reflected on the tower and its current condition as we went, as well as the next steps.

When we'd discussed opening the tower to the people with Seraphina, I'd been clear on two things. First, that she'd unfortunately need to move her "throne room," which she'd been enjoying about a third of the way up the original height of the tower, because that was literally a perfect, if with a slightly small entrance, landing and maintenance area for the airships we were one day going to be docking.

Secondly, that the biggest room on the ground floor that she'd had tentatively pegged as a market, and that she'd been intending to use to make sure that the succubai—and the empire, of course—had access to anything and everything they wanted, was now going to be the cathedral.

It was the same layout for that section as back on Dravith, and it was both big enough and wide enough that it could fit a huge number of people, while still allowing the gods their space from one another.

Here, unfortunately, there was no Seneschal to make the place adjust itself to fit things properly, but there were plenty of other bonuses, such as it being blessedly quiet, now that the doors had been closed behind Oracle and me.

I moved into the center of the room, took a deep breath, and sank to one knee, setting out a small number of candles in the silence of the room, and Oracle lit them with a bare flicker of mana.

Then I teased free a single thread of fire mana and twisted it into the complicated weave to reach across the realm to the goddess I was devoted to.

"Lady Jenae, Goddess of Fire and Hidden Knowledge, are you there?" I asked aloud.

The candle flames flared suddenly, bathing the area around me in a warm, golden light. The air thickened, and I felt that familiar presence—like standing too close to a bonfire, yet somehow comforting rather than threatening, as well as the overwhelming pressure of the divine so close.

"Jax, my friend, my ally and my champion, you have done well. Another city has fallen to you, a true foothold on the continent, and the tower rises once more."

"Thank you, Jenae," I replied, smiling as a sudden surge of strength, of stamina and contentment spread through me, along with the hearthfire spell crackling. "It's good to actually stop for five minutes," I admitted.

"I can see that. You've done little but sprint since you claimed the Fragment of Death from Nimon."

"Yeah, it feels like it." I snorted. "Are you okay?"

"We are…busy, and tired as well," she admitted. ***"I mean not to press, but the tower…"***

"I want to bind it to your service, as I did with the Tower of Dravith."

I felt her pleasure and relief at the offer—a warm glow that spread through my chest.

"Thank you, Jax. You have no idea how much that means to us all. What we receive from the prayers of those with the caravan has helped some, please understand that. Their devotion does help us, as well as supporting us, but to bring a second tower? The city of Gaij becoming the home of the Pantheon of Flame on Carrmor will be a relief."

She hesitated, and I sensed concern beneath her satisfaction. ***"However, the tower's mana reserves and its capacity are greatly diminished. What you have restored is but a fraction of its former capacity."***

"I know," I admitted. "The manawell is dead, and the collection systems destroyed. I'm planning to bring the collectors from the legion encampment here and attach them to the tower. Then they'll continue feeding mana into the tower as it repairs itself. But is there a way to restore it more quickly?"

"There is."

The flames from the candles suddenly shifted, flaring out and blurring together, extending to form a single sheet of flame that hung in the air as I stood. It was like standing next to a vertical flamethrower, until the center of the fire suddenly collapsed away inward, revealing a black hole into nothingness, that slowly became filled with stars.

"You have earned a significant number of my marks of favor over the last few months, and even after those you've spent so far, you still have over six thousand marks available—and there'll be a lot more to come once you have the local population swear to us, as well as the mana that they can bring. You have nearly a million mana that can be spent to unlock stars as well."

"Damn," I breathed. "I knew I'd not spent it in a while, but…"

"Jax, the tier system is a simple one, with the first costing ten thousand mana and five marks to unlock, then each tier beyond that costing five times the previous, meaning that you have several stars to unlock at the very least here, and that's only if you choose to spend them all on specific directions.

"You could, with nearly six and a half thousand marks, and a million points—or near enough—unlock, for example, a pair of second-tier, and then a pair of third-tier stars, and still have enough left over to unlock the last two tier-one stars, of Exploration and Magical Research."

"Shit…" I muttered, then shut up as she went on.

"Lastly, Jax, you have a great many gods who are personally invested in your situation, and, more to the point, a group that includes representatives from some of the greatest crafting races the realm has ever seen. Noticeably, people who a certain god would very much like to be introduced to. Perhaps there would be a way to leverage that, into using some of the technologies you could unlock, to develop a transportation device?"

"Uhhh…"

"Just think about it." She sighed. ***"And think about how much EASIER AND QUICKER you could get Oracle to the Cradle of Feshcan'un, if only you HAD AN AIRSHIP HERE."***

There wasn't much of a way she could have been more blatant, and I nodded, smiling despite myself. I'd been planning on getting preparations in place for Tenandra to land here when she arrived, but that was a good point, why not build our own?

They'd be rough and slow compared to Tenandra, but that didn't mean slow compared to a wagon or horses…

"I'll have a think and see what I can come up with. But Jenae? My Goddess?"

"Yes?"

"Thank you." I damn well meant it. "Are you and the others ready to meet the people of the city tonight?"

"Oh, let me think," she mused. ***"I mean, we're desperately short of mana and followers, and there's thousands here who could help us…would we like to meet them? Hmmm…that's a hard one…"***

"All right, all right." I snorted. "I can take a hint, you know."

"No, Jax, you really can't," she replied. ***"Not unless you're beaten over the head with it. But yes, we would very much like to meet these new prospective supporters tonight. And perhaps you'd like to do something with the altars of the other gods that currently sit in the temples dotted around the city as well?"***

"I'll take care of that too," I agreed. "I'll greet the former slaves now, and then have an hour's rest, while the succubai and their people spread the word, and then we'll introduce you all here, then," I offered, getting a sense of pleasure and agreement, and a little surge of a fresh divine blessing of warmth and health again, before the sense of her presence faded away.

I took a deep breath, then smiled as Oracle stepped in, wrapping her arms around me, and I leaned down, kissing the top of her head.

"Two more jobs, then we can rest." I sighed, as the Constellation of Secrets faded from sight. "Make that three. I need to check the Constellation as well."

"And speak to the former slaves, then have a meeting with everyone and lead a service to the gods." She snorted. "Good thing you're not busy, right?"

"Exactly," I agreed, smiling tiredly. "Okay, on with the show…"

CHARACTER SHEET

Name: Jax Amon				
Title: Godslayer				
Class: Mage Imperator (Fire Focus)			**Renown**: Imperial Scion, Prince of Dravith, Master of Himnel and Narkolt, Godslayer, Mage Imperator	
Level: 52			**Progress**: 417,882/13,000,000	
Patron: Jenae, Goddess of Fire and Exploration			**Points to Distribute**: 64 **Meridian Points to Invest**: 1	
Stat	**Current points**	**Description**	**Effect**	**Progress to next level**
Agility	100	Governs dodge and movement.	+1000% maximum movement speed and reflexes. Gained Temporal Fluidity	N/A
Charisma	61 (56)	Governs likely success to charm, seduce, or threaten	+51% success chance in interactions with other beings	51/100
Constitution	125 (123)	Governs health and health regeneration	2460 health, regen 160 points per 600 seconds (each point invested now worth 20 health). Gained: Genetic Storage	N/A
Dexterity	100	Governs ability with weapons and crafting success	+100% to weapon proficiency, +100% to the chances of crafting success. Gained: Master Craftsman's Touch	N/A
Endurance	73 (670)	Governs stamina and stamina regeneration	2190 stamina, regen 53 points per 30 seconds (each point invested now worth 30 stamina)	89/100
Intelligence	206	Governs base mana and number of	2260 mana, spell capacity: 102 (100 + 2,	N/A

		spells able to be learned	+200 mana from items). Gained: Hyper Cognition & Mana Manipulation	
Luck	79	Governs overall chance of bonuses	+69% chance of a favorable outcome	92/100
Perception	110 (100)	Governs ranged damage and chance to spot traps or hidden items	+100% ranged damage, +100% chance to spot traps or hidden items.	N/A
Strength	90 (87)	Governs damage with melee weapons and carrying capacity	+90 damage with melee weapons, +90% maximum carrying capacity	88/100
Wisdom	105 (95)	Governs mana regeneration and memory	+1400% mana recovery, 16 points per minute. Gained: Mana Manipulation	N/A

CHAPTER TWENTY-THREE

We left what was going to become the cathedral of Gaij, having passed on a few requests to the staff and succubai regarding decorations and so on, then headed through the lower floor.

We were on our way to the gardens when Sehran and Daralen fell in on either side of us, and on the way, yet again, I damn well missed having Seneschal as part of the tower.

Hell, I missed all our people. I knew that back home, Restun and the others would be manically busy, and I even almost missed that mad bastard yelling at me. But that was just crazy talk.

I had a sudden horrible thought that Thomas might have actually surpassed me now, and that when Restun and the others all made their way to me—I was the damn prince, after all, and I knew he'd come to find me soon—I was going to pay for "taking it easy" the last few weeks without him beating twelve shades of shit out of me daily.

Thankfully, Seraphina had been "coincidentally" hanging around only a few rooms away, so I was shocked out of that terrible thought when I saw her, saving me sending Sehran to get her, as I'd been about to.

"Seraphina, great timing there. I need messengers sent throughout the city, please."

The mistress glided forward, her midnight-blue skin now glowing with renewed vitality since being freed from the tower's constant drain. "What message would you have spread, my prince?"

"Tonight, in one hour, I'm dedicating the new cathedral to the Pantheon of Flame. All citizens are welcome to attend, to meet the old gods and renew their faith. And while that's happening, I need to find out where the altars to Nimon and the dickheads of the dark are inside the city." I straightened and tugged down the weird-ass doublet/shirt thing that I was wearing in place of my armor and shook my head at it in disgust.

"Damn, I felt more comfortable in my fucking armor. But hey, that's life. All right, if you can sort that out, please, then I need to address the freed slaves gathered outside."

She nodded, a small smile playing at her lips. "Consider it done. The messengers will be dispatched immediately." She paused, head tilted in thought. "Perhaps we should prepare for a significant turnout. The people have been without access to these gods for centuries."

"Yeah," I agreed, running a hand through my hair. "Make it clear, please, that meeting the gods is contingent on being a citizen as well, for everyone's safety, and work with Daralen to have your people and the legionnaires organize a way to move people through in groups if needed. I don't want to turn anyone away, and frankly, the gods need them.

"That being said, though, those who support us and help us get the nice toys and presents, like a healing spell being cast on the entrance…unfortunately, if the people haven't sworn, then it could injure them when they cross that line. Too bad, so sad."

Daralen spoke up smoothly. "We'll handle it, my prince. If the cathedral cannot hold them all at once, we'll create a procession."

"Perfect. For now, let's talk to the former slaves. They deserve to hear what comes next directly from me, and hopefully we can recruit at least some of them to the legion."

Outside, the grounds of the tower had been transformed into a makeshift camp almost as soon as the gates had been opened, with thousands of newly freed people drifting in and clumping up, unsure what they were supposed to do, or where to be.

Many still wore the threadbare rags that marked their previous lives, though I noticed Varnen's people had already begun handing out some new clothing and at least blankets to everyone.

I jumped up, powering my bound with a little Soaring Majesty, and landed easily atop a raised platform that had been part of the gardens for who knew how long.

Oracle flew up next to me, though she stepped back. Both Sehran and Seraphina flew up as well, though I winced internally at the fact that of all of us, only Daralen, when I gestured to her to join us, had to climb up.

I should have thought about that better.

I smiled and waved, as a hush fell over the crowd. They watched with a mixture of awe, wariness, and hope that I'd seen countless times before on the faces of the newly freed. I knew what they were thinking: liberation was wonderful, but what came next?

For me, the thoughts I was having as I snatched my hand back from the balustrade that ringed this raised section were suddenly very different.

This was an ornamental place, elevated high enough that anyone gathered in the gardens below could see those up here nice and clearly.

Usually that was a great thing, for speeches or whatever, but out in the fallen ruins of the empire, they'd often been used as pulpits to sell slaves from.

Here? In a pleasure garden ran by the succubai?

I carefully blanked my thoughts, and snorted as Oracle, sensing exactly what I'd just thought, sent me a mental image of me standing here alone, naked.

"Well, that's just added to my nightmares. Fuck me, it's like being at school all over again," I sent back to her with a little laugh, before I got started, deciding that formal was the best way to go for this one, for now at least.

"Citizens of the empire," I called out, forcing a smile as my voice carried across the grounds with a little magical enhancement courtesy of the love of my life. "Yesterday, you were slaves. Today, you are free men and women, with all the rights and protections of imperial citizens."

I paused, looking out over the sea of faces.

"I am Prince Jax Amon, heir to the Imperial Throne, and I thank you for your trust in swearing the oath to me and to the empire. I know many of you did so without fully understanding what it meant, driven by the moment and the sudden freedom you found thrust upon you."

I gestured to the tower rising behind me, gleaming in the afternoon sun. "The empire you've joined isn't the one you've heard whispered about in myths or bedtime stories. It's not a distant memory or a faded glory. It's alive, it's growing, and it begins with each of you."

The crowd stirred, occasional murmurs passing through it like ripples on a pond, but most just stared stonily, used to a cost being associated with anything and everything in their lives.

"As citizens, you now have rights that cannot be taken from you. You cannot be enslaved again, you cannot be denied justice, you cannot be harmed without consequence. Your property is yours, your lives are yours, your choices are yours." I let that sink in for a moment. "The legion, and I, will fight to ensure that you are as safe as can be. But citizenship also brings responsibilities.

"You must follow imperial law, which is being posted throughout the city even now. These laws are simpler than you might think, the heart of which are: don't harm your fellow citizens, don't take what isn't yours, and," I allowed myself a small smile, "don't be a dick."

This earned a ripple of nervous laughter, breaking some of the tension.

"That last one is my favorite, because it's a sort of 'catchall' law. There are more laws, don't get me wrong, and they're phrased a little more…traditionally, but that one is that way for a very good reason.

"It requires a little self-reflection. You ask yourself the question, that if the situation you're in was flipped around, would what's happening be seen as you being a dick. If you're deliberately taking advantage of another, and I don't mean making a fair profit on selling something you made, for example, but price gouging and setting up to drive the prices up to make your product desperately needed by everyone, but also horrifically expensive? That'd be a dick move.

"You see how simple that is? You make something, you work out a fair price for it, and a fair profit, and then you move on. You don't fuck each other over, because as much as we might be a dysfunctional one, we're all a family. That means treating those around you as your brothers and sisters.

"You might not like them at times—gods know I had enough arguments with my brother and I've been pissed at the man, but I always love him. Anyone who wants to fuck with him? They come through me first.

"*That's* the heart of the empire. We're a family, and anyone who wants to enslave you again? They come through me and the fucking legion to try it."

I let that hang in the air for a few seconds, seeing the looks on people's faces and smiling despite myself.

"Now, each of you have to decide how you're going to contribute to the empire that protects you. Some might want to return to your previous occupations, but as free people paid fair wages. Some might want to learn new trades. All these paths are open to you."

I straightened, my voice growing stronger. "But I also offer you new opportunities. The Imperial Legion needs strong arms and brave hearts. The tower needs those who would learn magic and serve. If you have experience with magical artifacts or engineering, I need you especially, so please, come to me after this gathering."

I gestured toward the horizon. "Sonra, the city of tents and herds, has also joined the empire. Their people and their great herds will soon arrive at our gates, as they're literally, even now, marching to join us."

Murmurs of concern passed through the crowd at this announcement.

"I see your worry, and I understand it. In ordinary times, such massive herds would mean trampled fields and wasted land. Hell, some of you might have passed through Sonra before and you'll be well aware of the damn smell—it's horrific, I know! But these are not ordinary times." I smiled broadly.

"We have magic that we'll be teaching to a handful to help with that—real, practical magic that will transform this region." I walked to the edge of the platform, looking directly into the eyes of those nearest me.

"The herds of Sonra will circle this city, grazing as they go. But where traditionally it would take years for the land to recover and become fertile again, we will speed this process. We will teach volunteers a simple spell that will turn the earth and accelerate the breakdown of waste into the soil."

The murmurs changed tone, surprise and interest replacing concern.

"Imagine it—instead of masses of bloated flies and fields of literal shit, there will be fields more fertile than any in living memory, producing harvests double or triple their normal yield. Crops growing stronger and faster than ever before. This city, once dependent on imports, will become an exporter of food to all nearby regions."

I began to pace, warming to my subject.

"This means wealth flowing into Gaij, not just out. It means caravans departing for other cities loaded with our surplus, returning with gold and goods from afar. It means security for all, as these caravans will travel with guards enough to deter all but entire armies. And as they go?

"They'll be hunting down slavers! If they meet them in the wild, they'll be freeing those slaves. If they meet them in cities? Well." I shrugged. "Maybe those profits will be used to buy those slaves and bring them back here to be free."

I smiled then, and shrugged again. "You'll be wondering about me being willing to fund the slavers to free the slaves, right? Well, that's simple math for me. You see, it doesn't matter how much we spend to free those slaves, and how much the slavers gain from us 'buying' the slaves from them, because as we build, as we conquer more of the cities around us? That wealth is going to come pouring back into imperial coffers, because each and every slaver we get our hands on, where we have control, we'll be hanging.

"Letting them hold our gold and silver for now until we come to free our brothers and sisters and claim it back? Well, that's no great hardship, now is it? They're just keeping it warm for us."

I stopped and spread my arms wide. "And all these positions…the farmers, herders, guards, caravan drivers, merchants, and most importantly the legionnaires? They all need people. They need *you*."

The crowd was listening intently now, hope beginning to replace uncertainty on many faces.

"The empire doesn't force citizens into roles they don't choose. Your freedom means you decide your path. If you wish to strike out on your own, you may do so with my blessing. You'll be given food, clothing, and a little coin to help you with a new start."

I paused, letting them absorb that.

"But if you stay, if you help build this new world we're creating, you'll find opportunities that couldn't have existed before. Mages who tend the earth and who call down fire from the heavens. Craftsmen creating tools and goods, and one day, great ships that sail the skies with long-forgotten imperial knowledge. Legionnaires protecting our borders. Scholars preserving knowledge. All needed, all valued, all free."

I lowered my voice, making them lean in slightly to hear as whatever magic was in place let me still be heard across the gardens.

"I won't lie to you. The path ahead isn't easy. We have enemies. The Dark Legion still exists. The drow, though they've been banished from our territory, plot against us. False nobles from Earth seek to reclaim what they see as their birthright. But together, united, we are stronger than any of them."

I straightened, my voice rising again.

"Tonight, in the cathedral within the tower, the Pantheon of Flame, the nine original greater gods of this realm, along with two others who have joined them, will manifest to accept our worship. Those who wish to attend are welcome. Those who have not yet sworn the oath but wish to do so will have the opportunity after this, and upon swearing, will be welcome to attend as well."

I looked out over the crowd one last time.

"Yesterday, you were property. Today, you are citizens. But tomorrow? Tomorrow, you can be the foundation upon which the empire resurgent rises. A slave I freed months ago stands on my imperial council, higher than any city lord. Freed slaves serve at the highest levels of the legion, and its lowest. We have crafters, chefs, and a thousand other professions. The choice of how you serve is yours. The opportunity to be more than you ever dreamed possible is yours. The future is yours for the taking!"

I stepped back from the edge of the platform, and for a moment, silence reigned. Then, starting from somewhere in the middle of the crowd, a cheer rose. It spread outward like wildfire, building in volume until the very air seemed to vibrate with it.

Daralen stepped up beside me, a rare smile on her normally stern face. "Well said, my prince. They needed direction, and I think you've managed to give them a little hope along with it."

I nodded, watching as legionnaires began to organize the crowd, fielding questions and directing those interested in various opportunities to different areas. "Yeah, I figured they'd had their choices taken from them for too long. Now they just need to know all the options available."

"You're getting better at this," Oracle whispered, standing on her tiptoes to kiss my cheek as I leaned down.

"Well, let's be honest, I couldn't have gotten much fucking worse, could I?" I snorted, getting a smile from her.

As the gathering began to disperse, those who had not yet sworn the oath were brought forward. Oracle and I administered it together—only needing one potion, thankfully—and we watched as face after face transformed with the oath that connected them to the empire and to me.

A small number—maybe thirty out of the thousands—just outright declined, accepting the offered provisions but choosing to make their own way. I watched them go with mixed feelings.

Part of me wanted to convince them to stay, partly because as much as I was carefully not saying it, they fucking owed me, and also partly because I wanted them to be protected. But I understood it. After a lifetime of servitude, some needed to just leave, to run.

"They might return," Oracle said softly, sensing my thoughts. "When they see what we build here, when they witness the truth of what we've said."

"And if they don't?" I sighed.

"Then they exercised the freedom you gave them," she replied. "And as much as it feels like a bit of a slap in the face that they're using it to turn their backs on us, that's freedom, and it's their right."

I nodded, gently squeezing her hand before turning to greet the small number who had been led to the side of the dais, the last group I needed to talk to before the evening's ceremony.

There were fifteen of them, that was it, in a gathering of perhaps ten thousand, which said just how fucking rare their kind was here. But finding fifteen more gnomes in all of this, and especially fifteen apparently entirely sober and possibly even sane gnomes?

Frankly, it felt weird, as they were led—very nervously from their side—into the tower to sit down with me in a smaller, private area.

I saw the fear on their faces, the way that they kept glancing at the doors, and how they watched the legionnaires, and especially me.

They were genuinely expecting to be forced into whatever I wanted, I realized. I sighed, speaking as they huddled in a small group, staring.

"Look, I can see how shitty your lives have been just by seeing you here, so I'll make this as painless as I can, all right?" I asked, unsurprised when they didn't respond, beyond huddling slightly closer together. The two in the center looked like they might be crushed to death at any time.

"Are any of you from Sonra?" I asked, getting a blink from one who quickly tried to hide his reaction, while the rest just stared, not understanding. "They've sworn to me, by choice, and none of them were compelled," I said gently to the one who'd reacted.

"Cleq and Greg are heading here with the others, and they've come out of hiding. If you know who I mean, then you know how big a thing that is."

Most didn't, including Seraphina, who frowned, clearly having missed this secret despite her spies. But the gnome in question hesitated, then nodded once that he understood.

"Okay, so for you all, tonight is going to be a little more special than it will be for most," I said, moving on. "If you're aware of your ancestral god, his name is Svetu, and he'll be here tonight, I hope, but if you'll hold on, I think he might help us here."

I got to my feet, then knelt in the middle of the room, casting the communication spell and reaching for the God of Invention and Creators.

"Lord Svetu, are you busy?" I asked.

"Dammit, boy, I always am!" He snapped. ***"What is it now?"***

I couldn't help but snort, as I went on.

"Well, bugger you then, you miserable old git," I sent, sending a lot of amusement along the path of communication as well so that he'd know it wasn't an insult. But as tired as I was, I knew I couldn't shield the way I was feeling. If he wanted informality, fuck it, he could accept the good with the bad. *"I found fifteen gnomes who are terrified, but who have sworn to the empire, and I thought you might like to meet them, considering they're creators and magical specialists, but never mind. Sorry I disturbed you."*

"Wait, what?"

There was a pop as the air was displaced. Suddenly, the sense of divine presence washed over us all, as Svetu Himself was there, once again, in what I thought of as "His" form, a slightly larger gnome.

When I say slightly larger, admittedly, he was about three meters tall, but in comparison to the usual size the gods appeared, he was very clearly a gnome.

"Ah! I am Svetu!" He blinked in surprise, staring at the fifteen of his people who basically threw themselves to the floor, crying out in both fear and hope. ***"What's wrong with you?"*** He asked, clearly confused to all hell.

"They've been enslaved, beaten and tortured for most of their lives—all of it for some, I'd bet—and now they're free and fucking terrified," I explained, glaring at Him. "I was hoping that seeing their patron god would reassure them, but clearly that's a bust."

"Dammit, boy, you should know I'm not good at these things!" Svetu groaned. Then there was another pop and He was a normal-sized gnome, now waving His hands like He was calling a group of children in for a story on a mat. ***"Come on…up, all of you. Stop, just…just, just stop that!"***

"Sehran?" I asked the succubus.

She nodded, starting to sing, and a few seconds later, a pair of her sisters from outside the room drifted in, adding to the melody.

I spoke to the now thoroughly confused and terrified gnomes. "You're all safe, and we're not a danger to you, not to any of you. There are other gnomes, as well as other races, coming here to join us, and you'll be reunited with them all soon. As to Svetu, He's the god of your ancestors, and He came here to meet you all, to help you, not to threaten or harm."

Oracle stepped forward and went among them, smiling and reaching out, helping them to their feet and speaking softly, while Svetu and I retreated a little.

"What happened to them?" He asked.

I shook my head. "Honestly, if it's anything like it was on Dravith, then it's like I said. They were enslaved and forced to work constantly, beaten and tortured, their friends killed. They were made to believe that everyone, everywhere would kill them and enslave them again if they tried to escape.

"There are villages that Lucian spoke about, that were constantly fucking raided over and over again, until they managed to develop enough defenses that they're practically insane, but that as soon as they leave? For anything? They're captured and enslaved.

"I got a quest back there, you know that?" I glanced at Him. "To find and rescue enough gnomes that I can raise them to a viable breeding population again, because their society is collapsing through being fucking raided so much. *That's* how shitty their lives have become. They're both terrified of the outside world, and desperately need us."

"And you allowed this to happen?" Svetu snarled at me, turning and glaring.

"No! Fuck's sake, I've started doing everything I can to *reverse* it, and to help these people," I snapped back at Him. "But it's because of what the hell I can do. And for every quest I focus on, I have to let two or three slide because there's only so many damn hours in the day!"

"Don't growl at me, boy…" He warned me.

"Then don't snap at me for not doing enough when I'm doing more to help them than their own patron fucking god is!" I snapped back. "Fuck's sake, man, you didn't know? Why the hell do you think the other gnomes are all terrified of Giint? He's your damn champion. He's as mad as a box of frogs, but he's also a freak of nature to them! He's bigger, stronger, and utterly fearless, while the entire rest of their species live on nothing but drugs, adrenaline, and terror!

"He's the *best* of them, and holy shit that's a terrifying prospect! Have you even looked at the rest of your chosen people? Did you go to them and try to help, or have you been playing with your inventions and fucking hiding?"

"It's thanks to me that we're still alive, boy!" He thundered, His heavily haired eyebrows dipping as He stared at me furiously. ***"You think I have any time to waste?"***

"No, and neither do I!" I snapped.

"So, what you're both saying, and the fact you're having an argument in front of the still scared gnomes, is that you're both doing the best you can, right?" Oracle asked.

We both spun to glare at her for interrupting, before realizing who she was and what she'd just said.

"Well…" I started.

"I suppose…" Svetu agreed.

"So, perhaps you'd both like to speak to the gnomes and then they can go and have some quiet time in a room nearby and have some food and a little calmness?" she went on, and we both nodded.

"Excellent. Perhaps, Lord Svetu, you'd like to remind them that you look favorably on them, and that you'll be issuing them some quests very soon, personal ones, that'll revolve *around helping the empire*, and then Jax can tell them how much they'll be helping you by serving the empire as well, and *everyone* wins, then we can all get on with the evening?"

"Yeah." I nodded, as did the apparently mortified god who stood next to me.

Svetu did as she'd asked, then gave them all a quick blessing, before promising that He'd be watching over them personally from now on. And then, after shooting me a brief glare, and nodding at Oracle, He went on to say that the empire was allied to the gods, and that helping us helped Him, and that in turn helped them all.

Lastly, He promised that His chosen champion, an example of all a gnome should aspire to be, was coming, and that he was less than a month away now.

That was both terrifying and wonderful, as far as I was concerned.

Finally, after that, the gnomes were led out by the succubai, and Oracle, Sehran, and I managed ten minutes to have a little rest.

Wonderful that Giint and the others were only a few weeks away, and terrifying that yeah, Svetu *Himself* thought that mad little bastard Giint was still someone for the others of his species to aspire to be like.

I'd seen him half eat a raw fuckin' icedrake while stripping it for parts, not to mention ripping steam goblins apart, shrieking about "spare parts"—and that was only the shit that sprang instantly to mind.

All in all, it was traumatizing as fuck that anyone thought that mad little bastard was anything like *housebroken,* never mind something to look up to.

All too soon though, we were off again, moving through corridors that were suddenly jam-packed with people, as it seemed like the succubai had managed to get *everyone* interested in the event.

If I was honest, though, seeing the outfits some of the succubai wore and the very clear offers and promises being made by them as I passed them in conversation, it was obvious that what a lot of people were here for was them, not me or even access to the gods.

The cathedral of the tower was magnificent, even in its barely decorated state. Unlike the rest of the tower, which had been repaired to functional efficiency, the cathedral had been upgraded slightly in the last hour, and made into one of the few areas to receive even the slightest additional attention beyond "functional and barely that."

As Oracle and I entered through a side passage, I caught my breath at the transformation. The succubai had outdone themselves in the hour since I'd announced the service. Tapestries depicting each deity hung in their respective alcoves. Braziers of copper and gold burned with fragrant oils. A central altar had appeared from somewhere and it gleamed with fresh polish. Finally, carved wooden benches had been arranged in concentric semicircles facing it.

"It's beautiful," Oracle whispered, her hand tightening on mine.

Seraphina materialized from the shadows, looking pleased with herself. "It's just a little something we managed." She smiled. "We were able, over the centuries, to secure various artifacts and items of the old gods, and we hoped, that's all. The gods may have been banished, but they were never forgotten."

I nodded my appreciation. "It's perfect. Thank you."

She gestured toward the main doors. "The people have begun to gather. There are…more than we anticipated."

"How many?" I asked.

"Thousands." She shrugged. "Far more than can fit within these walls, even with standing room only. The legionnaires are organizing them into groups, as planned, but I fear many will be disappointed at the wait."

I considered this for a moment, then shrugged. "No, they won't. We'll make it work—we have to. Every single worshipper who the gods gain through this is a tiny bit of power. Get enough grains of sand, and you can crush anything under the weight."

I approached the central altar and placed my hands upon it, closing my eyes and reaching out with my senses. The tower responded to my touch, its lingering and limited mana flowing through the stone and into me, creating a connection.

Oracle reached out to the tower as well, laying one hand atop mine, and then again on the altar.

"Jenae, Goddess and leader of the Pantheon of Flame, I dedicate this tower to you and your followers!" I called. I felt the response as Jenae and the others moved in: the tower shivered slightly, before growing markedly warmer.

"Oh my, I suspect clothing may become optional if this continues…" Seraphina sighed, playing at waving her hand in the air. "Such a *shame*. What do you think, dear…should we discard it now…?"

That was directed at Sehran, who opened her mouth to speak before the pair burst out laughing at the look on my face.

"I hate you all," I muttered, shaking my head in disbelief at the byplay, before I raised my voice. "Open the doors!"

The first group was ushered in, about five hundred people filling the benches and standing spaces. Their faces reflected wonder as they gazed around the cathedral.

I stepped onto the raised platform behind the altar, Oracle at my side, and lifted my hands for silence.

"People of Gaij, citizens of the empire, welcome to the Cathedral of Eternal Flame," I began. My voice carried easily through the enhanced acoustics, and then echoed outside as Oracle did something to help it. "For seven hundred years, the gods of the original pantheon have been diminished, banished, or forgotten. Tonight, we change that."

I gestured to the alcoves surrounding us. "These are the spaces dedicated to the Gods of the Pantheon of Flame, nine of the original deities who guided the empire at its height. Jenae, Goddess of Fire and Hidden Knowledge. Sint, God of Light and Order. Lagoush, Lady of Water and Healing. Tamat, Mistress of Assassins and Dark Deeds…"

As I named each deity, I felt it as the gods' attention fell upon us all, the tower shivering with the weight of so many divine presences.

"Tonight, I dedicate this tower to their service, binding it to them as I bound the Great Tower of Dravith, creating a beacon of divine power on this continent."

I turned to the alcove that was set aside for Jenae, and I sank to one knee. "Jenae, Mistress and Goddess, hear my voice and come forth to receive the worship of your people once more!"

One by one, the alcoves filled with divine presence. Jenae was the first, of course. Her flames danced around Her as She materialized in Her red-enameled armor, making it clear that She was both feminine in its cut, and a warrior goddess.

Sint appeared next, His form massive and glowing with white light, His features stern but benevolent, bound in silvery steel with a white surcoat. Then came Lagoush, Her form armored in greens and blues, yet with a cape that seemed to flow like water, and the others after Her, each god taking shape in their designated space.

Gasps and cries of awe rose from the gathered crowd as the pantheon revealed themselves. Some fell to their knees in worship; others stood frozen in shock.

Jenae stepped forward first, Her voice resonating through the cathedral. ***"We accept this tower as our sanctuary on Carrmor, and acknowledge Jax Amon as our champion and the rightful heir to the Imperial Throne."***

Sint moved to join Her. ***"The flame of the empire burns bright once more. We return to guide our people and lend our strength to its rightful ruler."***

One by one, the gods stepped forward, each acknowledging the tower as their new home on this continent and confirming my position, which was kinda nice of them, making it clear that if anyone wanted access to and approval of the gods, they needed to at least respect me.

When the last of them had spoken, I turned back to face the crowd.

"The gods have returned to Carrmor! They accept this tower as their sanctuary and you as their people. If any of you wish to speak to a specific god, to offer your prayers or your following, now's the time. Step forward, and speak, but then please, move along, as there are thousands waiting behind you to do the same."

"We ask that should you wish to serve us, then you accept that you support the empire that defends and carries out our will." Jenae's voice flowed through the air and out into the corridors beyond. ***"If you come before us, unwilling to also swear to the empire, then we shall turn our faces from you, as you have turned from us."***

That was a hell of a change, and fuck me was I thankful for that. Looking up at Her, I saw the little smile and the slight inclination of Her head as She acknowledged it. I pressed my fist to my chest in thanks, realizing that yeah, I'd damn well forgotten to cast the cleansing fire spell at the entrance as I'd intended to.

I watched the gods, as they began speaking to people; thrones appeared under them as they sat and waited. The people stepped up, speaking quickly, then knelt one at a time to offer a prayer, before moving on, as the lines streamed past.

Darakin actually looked surprised by how many stopped at his alcove, including the leader of the Mercenary's Guild, and I mentally marked that one out to have a conversation with soon.

For the next goddamn *six hours*, people came forward in a steady stream, standing before me to recite the oath to the empire if they hadn't already, and them moving on to speak to the gods.

They themselves occasionally reached out to touch a particularly devout worshipper, blessing them with small gifts of power or insight. The sight of these divine benedictions only increased the fervor of those still waiting.

When the first group had finished, they were ushered out through side exits to make room for the next; on and on the line flowed. The process continued well into the night: group after group entered, witnessed the divine manifestation, and any stragglers swore the oath, before they departed with renewed purpose.

By the early hours, literally thousands had passed through the cathedral. The gods remained, growing visibly stronger with each oath sworn, each prayer offered. The binding between the tower and the pantheon deepened; mana flowed through the structure in new patterns, reinforcing the repairs we'd made and began to heal sections we hadn't yet reached.

As the last group filed out, exhaustion threatened to overwhelm me. Oracle slipped her arm around my waist, subtly providing her support.

"It is done," Jenae declared, Her voice carrying through the now-empty cathedral. ***"This tower is now a true bastion of the pantheon on Carrmor."***

"Thank you." I bowed deeply to the assembled gods. "And thank you again for the open support. It really helps."

"It's only the beginning," Jenae cautioned, her flames flickering. ***"We made the decision to back you, Jax, just as you did for us."***

"I know," I acknowledged. "But still, it means a lot."

Tamat, always the most vicious of the pantheon, stepped forward. ***"It helps everyone,"*** She said flatly. ***"The army of Kronk still gathers. Your path to the Cradle of Feshcan'un remains blocked. And now that you've declared this tower as ours, every enemy will know exactly where to find you."***

"Let them come," I replied, straightening despite my fatigue. "We'll be ready."

The gods exchanged glances, a silent communication passing between them. Finally, Sint spoke again.

"Rest now, champion and friend. You've done well this day. Tomorrow, we will discuss the road ahead."

With that, the divine manifestations began to fade, retreating into their alcoves but leaving a lingering presence in the cathedral. The tower itself seemed to hum with fresh energy as I drew in a deep breath.

"We're done, my love," Oracle whispered to me.

I smiled down at her, picking her up in my arms, and started to walk, feeling honestly like I was desperate to just stop and collapse. But I was always good for just one more walk, with her in my arms.

As we reached our room—half a goddamn hour later; I'd forgotten how far away it was or I'd have slept in a damn antechamber and fuck it all—I paused at the window, looking out over the city. Thousands of pinpricks of light showed where people were gathered, still awake, and many still celebrating the return of the gods.

The energy of the night's events had transformed it, giving the people something they hadn't had in centuries: faith in something greater than themselves. Something that wasn't a fucking mad god who had destroyed their world once already.

CHAPTER TWENTY-FOUR

The next morning started with a bang, both figuratively and wonderfully, as I woke with the very welcome sensation of Oracle's mouth around me.

I lay there for a few minutes, just enjoying the feeling of everything being right and wonderful with the world. Then I joined in and returned the favor, before breaking several of the various pieces of furniture around the room, and finishing us both off on the balcony.

Admittedly, when we'd calmed down and cooler heads were again available to consider things, we both realized that our current quarters were a *lot* closer to the ground than at home in Dravith, and no longer surrounded by vast forests. Instead, we were surrounded by a fucking city, one that had mages and plenty of people with enhanced perception skills and abilities.

A mental note was made that next time, we stay inside the room, instead of out where we might be seen. But honestly, by this point, so many people had probably seen us over the last year or so that it was past a joke.

So, we decided, *fuck it*, and just got on with the day.

Breakfast was a wonder, though I had needed to spend a little time with the cooks explaining just how desperately important a full English fry-up was, and that experimenting with it, *especially* by adding in fucking fruit to a fry-up, was an abomination.

If I wanted fruit, I'd not be having a fry-up, after all.

One thing we'd found with the succubai was that they were indeed creatures of the night. Or at least, here they were. Given the choice, they were up all night partying, and then sleeping off the hangovers through the day.

As such, I was glad to find that the serving team were at least as well organized as Seraphina was, and an invitation was sent out to the merc leader.

Half an hour later, he showed up, clearly suffering from the bright light in the garden, and reeking of booze.

I was tempted to leave him in that condition just to make the negotiations easier, but he'd sworn to me already, so I decided to cut him a little slack. I hit him with first a Complex Heal, and then a Scour, as soon as he'd taken his seat with us.

He let out a low groan, before swearing that I'd saved his life.

Oracle asked how, and we were treated to a ten-minute story that was almost entirely certainly made up on the spot, involving an anteater, three raccoons, something called a "greater hartenate"—whatever that was—and a jar of lube.

I managed to get that you could ride the hartenate though, from the amusing gestures and miming, before he finished with the mystical words: "So I told him, hold my beer…"

He shrugged and I shook my head, deciding right then and there that I needed to introduce him and Mal as soon as possible, and then run for it, as they'd either become fast friends or have killed each other by morning.

"So, how can I serve, my prince?" he asked.

"We're going to have a lot of jobs for you," Oracle said. "We asked around the city, and basically everyone said that if something needs to be done, no matter the cost, then it's the Mercenary's Guild to come to."

"We try, and I like that the reputation has gotten so far." He smiled, but I noticed the way he looked at the plates as they were being cleared away, longingly.

"What's your actual *name?*" I asked him. "I mean, we've been told that everyone calls you either just 'Captain' or another rank. Nobody actually seemed to know your name."

"Ah, well, I prefer to be known as…" He gestured vaguely.

"We already had you swear and be questioned, so I know that you've not broken any laws I care about," I pointed out.

"It's not that. It…" He sighed. "It's that image is everything, that's all."

"And your name doesn't strike fear into the hearts of your enemies?" I asked.

"It's Timber." He shrugged. "Started out as Corporal, then Sarge. Captain just seemed to stick, and everyone always introduced me as that, which I saw got a lot more respect than…" He shrugged again.

"Never thought about shortening it to Tim?"

"It's shortened already." He winced. "And let's face it, 'Tim' isn't really a name to strike fear into the hearts of your enemies."

"Seriously, what the hell was the full—"

"Timberlake Chatinos."

I winced, seeing why he'd fucking give that up. "Anyway, let's move on, *Captain*."

"With pleasure, sir." He smiled and then nodded quickly as Oracle asked him whether he wanted some breakfast.

"We're not big on ceremony," I admitted. "Seriously, have something. It's all good."

"Then thank you, sir, I'd love something to break my fast."

As the staff walked him through options, I looked at him. He was tall, and leanly built—a runner's build, I'd have called it back home—with short-cropped dark hair, a solid five o'clock shadow of stubble, and broad shoulders. He sat back in the chair comfortably, clearly taking us at our word to relax, and with the hedges behind him that ringed the little gazebo thingy we were sitting in, and the leather and silk he wore, he looked every inch the dashing gentleman warrior.

Once he'd ordered food, though, we got down to brass tacks, as the saying went.

"We need you to be an advance for us," I said. "We want you to take your forces and move out to the south. We're well aware that the slavers are going to be panicking when word spreads of what we've done here. And there's also a solid expectation that when our trade caravans move out to the other cities—and there will be some, make no mistake—those slavers and others will see a way to even the score.

"I'm going to have the caravans heavily guarded, but a lot of those guards are going to deliberately look scruffy as hell. We're talking legionnaires in what looks like rusting and shitty armor, but in reality, it's anything but. Mercenaries, people will think, and poor ones, but they'll be legionnaires, and they'll all have magic."

"And what do you want me for?" he asked.

"You know my feelings on the guilds." I smiled.

"'Those fucking parasites,' I think you called us."

"And by and large I meant it." I nodded. "But that's because there's nothing keeping groups like the Caravaneer's Guild from literally murdering caravans that start up and do routes they don't like."

"I know that's a story that gets around, but it's just a rumor." He shook his head. "We looked into it once and—"

"It's a fact, believe me," I growled, before shaking it off. "Seriously, in a few days, you'll be able to speak to the survivors of such a shitty trick. But, I know that you set up your guild and you're the only owners, along with your partners, so you moving to another city and setting up a branch there to 'escape' me? After I've made my position clear? It makes sense…"

"And what am I really going there for? Because, don't get me wrong, I'm open to it, but I like the look of what's happening here, and I'm looking forward to being involved as you take the field." He leaned back, squinting at me.

"You're going to be our muscle." I smiled. "You go there, first to the city to the south, I think, and you set up your guild—when I looked at it, you're the only merc guild, right?" I paused.

"There are others, less well organized and more of gangs, but yeah, when I saw the gap in the market, I went for it," he admitted.

"Excellent. All right, so you set up as a merc guild in that city, what's it called?" I paused again, cursing my lack of knowledge of the greater area. I knew I'd been told it before but…

"Lembiq," he supplied. "It's a wood elf city in the middle of the great forest. It's also a border city between the northern free cities, the Demos League, of the east and the kingdoms of the south. Main trade goods are ores, gemstones, and slaves coming from the north, and luxuries and finished products from the more 'civilized' areas in the middle of the continent and to the south.

"They also produce their own stuff, obviously, though its mainly as you'd expect, being a forest city, hides, alchemical ingredients and the like."

"Thanks for that." I sighed. "All right, so you go there, and you set up shop. You're there to avoid me and how unreasonable I am, yadda, yadda. You set up as your mercenary outfit and you start taking jobs. Let it be known you'll take whatever jobs you want to take—you do you, boo."

He frowned at me, and I went on.

"The idea is that you set up running and you make a fuckload of money, you recruit the people you want, and you do the jobs that you want. I want you there so that when slavers, etc., decide that they want to raid my caravans, you're the person they come to, to augment their forces, or you're the one who hears about it.

"We'll be setting up spy networks in the various cities, and the upper levels of them will know who you are…" I saw the look of concern on his face and I went on quickly. "But they'll be constrained by oath not to name you to another who's not one of us, so that's secure.

"The idea here is that you'll become part of the spy network. You'll gain from it because one thing they'll be looking for will be juicy contracts and imperial sites for you to raid. You'll be able to hit those sites, and hide the loot that travels back to us on those caravans. And don't worry, you'll be taking a nice fee from each mission and getting a percentage as well. My intention is you're going to be getting approached to raid our caravans, and you'll get to spread the word of those raids to the spies, who'll take care of it.

"If the raid is big enough, maybe you're paid to set up and take part in the raid; then you assist the legion instead and slaughter the group. Essentially, I want you there as a combination spy and safety lever, that if the shit hits the fan? You're there to be pulled on."

"It'd ruin my reputation, something that we're there building and might take months," he pointed out, frowning.

"If we need to have you take steps publicly? Yeah," I admitted. "And that's why this is a discussion, not a 'these are your orders' situation. But think about it. We're going to be taking these cities. We're going to be taking this fucking *continent*. I want you in place so that when we come to the city, if we have to take it by force? You're there to take out the guards and targets inside when we come knocking."

"So between now and then, I get to play at being a spy, and take my time to set up a second branch of the guild there?" he mused. "Answerable only to myself and you?"

"You'd answer to whoever runs my spies. On Dravith, that's a mer lunatic called Flux. If he was here, I'd have him in charge in a heartbeat with his usual team, but here, I don't know who it'll be. When I do? You will. Until then, yeah, you tell me how much, and the empire will bankroll you setting up your new branch. Ideally, it'll be only the next in a chain as well, as you'll get the branch set up, some upper leadership you and I can trust, and then you'll move on, setting up the guild in a dozen cities.

"As you go, my spies will go with you. They'll protect you, and you'll protect them. You'll get juicy contracts, and some of them will be public—after all, the empire needs jobs doing as well. And if it looks like you might be getting found out? You'll have someone who can act as a client and then escape. You'll just be the mercenaries who were hired for the job, no stress."

"I like it," he said after a few seconds of silence. "I do, but it's not gonna be cheap."

"How much?"

"To set something like this up?" He shook his head. "It took me ten platinum to set up here, and I'm still paying that debt off. Or at least I was, considering it was to House Havelton…" He smiled suddenly as a fresh thought occurred to him. "Although…"

"I think considering he was a dickbag who died in the course of being a slave owner, any debts owed to him transferred to the empire." I shrugged. "Maybe that debt would be entirely forgotten if you were to serve. And as to the seed cost for the new guild…ten platinum you said?"

"To set up here," he clarified. "Could be more or less there, but roughly—"

I plucked fifteen platinum from my pouch and stacked them in piles of five on the table between us.

"And that'd be to what, rent a building?" I asked.

"In a good area, yeah. To buy it…" He licked his lips and glanced from the coins to my face and back.

"So let's say we include ten more…" I suggested. "It'd need to be the right building to be usable by the guild and my spies, right? And knowing that any profits made by the guild…well, they'd be your profits. But the loot? Any imperial artifacts, and of course sentient creatures you rescued, should they choose to, would be returned to us."

"I could go with that," he croaked.

"And things like if you were to find out about wisps, specifically, who had been captured, you'd be willing to go into debt to purchase them," I said firmly. "They'd be brought back to us here, where they'd be freed and offered the choice of assistance to return home, wherever that may be, or freedom inside the empire. And whatever debt you incurred we'd cover, including debt interest and a bonus, in platinum."

"Yeah…" He nodded quickly. "They're rare, but you know, there's always rumors."

"You'd be helping to chase down those rumors," I said. "Inside the empire, they'd be free, and protected. No forced bonding. And if they need to be bound to survive, we'd be working to heal them."

"I'm a wisp." Oracle smiled, reaching out and laying her hand on mine, but speaking to the captain. "Or I was. I evolved, but I was originally bound to a tower, and so this is something that's very important to us both, you understand?"

"Definitely." He blinked. "So just to be clear, my debts are forgiven, and that twenty-five platinum is mine, as long as I agree to set up another branch of the guild in Lembiq, and I act as worst-case support to the empire and your spies? Beyond that, I run my guild as I see fit, and I keep the profits?"

"As long as…" I started.

"Artifacts, wisps and other creatures are returned to you, and I support you. But that's it?"

"One more thing."

"Dammit, always a catch," he muttered.

"The legion."

"What about it?"

"If you get the chance, you buy any legionnaire you can out of their slavery, and you send them home to me."

"You'll cover the costs?"

"I will."

"Fine by me." He shrugged. "What about other slaves?"

"Eventually we'll free them all, but if you set up and just keep buying slaves who vanish because they return to us every time, you'll get caught in short order," I pointed out.

"Sure, but what if they didn't all return to you?" He grinned. "What if I buy them, I free them, and they work for the guild? Armorers, weaponsmiths, skilled people who just had bad luck—what if I free them, and some of them work with me? Saves me needing to recruit, and it'll give me a group of cast-iron supporters."

“To bind them to the empire, you’d need an imperial rank,” I mused.

“Captain?” he suggested with a grin.

Oracle and I both smiled as well. “Sounds like it’s time to get the ball rolling on legion intakes.”

“Intake?”

“Well, if you’re going to have a legion rank, you need to have a legion position, and that comes with certain fun responsibilities.” I shrugged. “Maybe as part of all of this you get a few new members to the team as well. Maybe we send you a few legionnaires to serve as part of your group.”

I saw the way his face fell at that idea, and I went on hurriedly. “You’re thinking of the way the legion just charged headlong into suicide again and again?”

“Damn right I am. Look, sorry, I’m in for the rest, but that’ll—”

“Never happen again,” I finished for him. “The legion that you knew…all the legionnaires in the area, in fact—especially based out of Gaij, which as near as we can tell was the epicenter of it—were saddled with additional oaths after the fall that were, frankly, fucking stupid. A noble back when the empire first fell with too much authority and too little common sense ordered them to defend the innocent or some such bullshit. Instead of it being a general thing and an obviously reasonable order, they were ordered to do it straightaway. That meant that when any legionnaire saw something, they were forced by their goddamn magical oath to deal with it right there and then.

“If they could have saved ten thousand, and all they had to do was wait to save them by an hour? They literally couldn’t do it, because of that fucking stupid oath. So, tens of thousands, probably millions have suffered needlessly. Believe me, one of the first things I’ve done with the legion at every opportunity is revoke that oath.”

“And now they’re actually more or less sane?” He frowned. “Damn, well, yeah, that changes a lot. But what about those I rescue or buy and who you haven’t freed yet?”

“Those I’ll take care of as well.” I sighed. “Fuck, we need to do that soon, don’t we?” I looked to Oracle, and she nodded.

“Best to collect in the manastones we can, and get it done in the next few days, although, maybe deal with the Constellation now that the divine situation is up to date, and then see what we can do? If you could wait until we have a collector set up and then channel the tower’s intake to do it, it’d be a lot cheaper and reach farther,” she pointed out.

“That’s a plan.” I sighed. “I hate to wait, but yeah, that’s reasonable.”

“I have no idea what you just said,” Captain Tim said, before smiling. “But if you’ll have me, I’m in.”

“We will,” I agreed, reaching out and offering my hand. He gripped my wrist and started to pump it in an agreement as old as time, before I went on. “All you have to do is prove that you can earn and hold that rank in the legion.”

“All right…wait, what?”

Oracle smiled at the serving staff as they brought his breakfast over, and spoke politely. “Thank you. Could you ask Primus Daralen to join us when she’s free, please.”

"Of course, m'lady." The serving girl smiled and bobbed a curtsy, before dashing off.

"What did you mean by that?" he asked again, and I smiled at him, before gesturing to his breakfast.

"Go on and eat," I encouraged evilly. "It's not so interesting that I want to explain this twice. When Daralen arrives, we can cover it."

He frowned, then shrugged and tucked into his food. I settled back in the seat, holding Oracle's hand and checking the details that I had available.

The changes with the new people being sworn, and the mana donated to the gods, meant that I was now at twenty-two and a half thousand marks, more than enough to unlock any of the tiers easily. But as always, the mana cost was what limited us.

The people last night had given freely, but as many as there were and the speed that they'd had to be shuffled along meant that they'd given—on average—ten points each. There were nearly thirty thousand of them, so that meant that with the mana we'd had already at just under a million, we were now at one million, three hundred and seven thousand points to spend.

With that in mind, I decided a little shopping was in order. But I blinked, hearing Oracle speaking, and I swept the details aside. Daralen was there already, and Oracle was filling her in on the plan.

"Considering the situation, I'd suggest a legion tribune as his right hand in command instead of expecting him to learn all the details of legion life in short order."

"I can do—" Tim started, and I grinned, cutting him off and winking at Daralen where he couldn't see.

"You heard him, Primus. He thinks he'd be able to keep up with the legion. So although I think that your plan is probably right, I think that he should be given the chance to prove that he's strong enough to hold a legion slot. Perhaps you could test him, when you test the other new recruits?"

"Test him, sir?" She frowned. "Do you mean…"

"I mean a physical testing…say, to the level that you'd be looking at recommending him to join the praetoria if he passed? And obviously we'll need to be sure that he's up to scratch mentally, so perhaps you could explain legion ranks, structure, and the little details that he'd have to know, as you do it, and then test him at the end?"

She blinked, then quickly stifled a smile. "Sir, I believe there's no way that any mercenary could possibly rise to the challenge, even one such as this, with such a low bar—"

"I can do anything she can," he blustered, and I nodded thoughtfully.

"Okay, so how about this. If he passes, oh, say the physical and gets seventy-five percent of the test right, then we grant him access to a fast track of legion training and then he goes without a legion handler.

"If he fails that, though, then he'll have to accept that the legion training is of a higher caliber than his, and he also accepts a tribune or centurion as his right hand, a permanent representative of the empire, who'll be empowered to speak in my name when need be?"

“Easy.” He grinned. “I can do anything your legion boys and girls can do.”

“Excellent. In that case, Daralen, when do you want to start?” I asked.

“Now seems best, sir.”

“Now? But…” He looked at his half-eaten breakfast.

Daralen smiled at him. “If it’s easy, then it’s not an issue, you having a little food in your belly, is it? Or is it true that after you drank last night, a mercenary is just too weak to keep up?”

He climbed to his feet, glaring in response, bowed slightly to Oracle and me, and then followed Daralen as she clapped her fist to her chest in salute to us, then led him off.

“Nicely done,” I murmured, winking at Oracle, then stealing an untouched sausage from his abandoned plate, dipping it in a fried egg and then settling back. “So, while he learns to regret his mum and dad ever meeting, let’s look at the Constellation of Secrets…”

CHAPTER TWENTY-FIVE

I sat cross-legged in the corner of the tower's cathedral. I'd needed somewhere that was both not too quiet, as I'd lose myself to the task and waste forever, but also quiet enough that I wasn't going to be pestered by people every five minutes.

Or so I hoped, anyway.

With the polished marble floor cool beneath me, I shifted slightly to get comfortable, and again, decided that I was just going to start wearing my damn armor all the time because now, sitting without it? It just felt weird.

Everyone took the hint when I sat down at the back of Jenae's space and left me alone. Well, apart from Oracle, who watched silently from a cushioned seat near the wall. Light streamed from a dozen flaming braziers that had just popped up at some point overnight, and I felt the comfort of them, illuminating the space with a warm glow that reflected off the marble.

Forcing calm, I took a deep breath, closed my eyes and pulled up the Constellation of Secrets. As I focused, the air before me twisted. A flicker started it off, as if the world right there was made of parchment, and someone on the other side had lit a candle underneath it.

There was a radiance, then the world darkened at a point, and suddenly charred, followed by the glow of burning paper.

It raced out, creating a void that hung there before me, both so small that it was barely big enough to see into, and simultaneously somehow wider than a cinema screen.

I gazed into the infinite void before me, seeing Jenae's offered gifts of knowledge mapped in the stars.

The void's vastness stretched in all directions, and almost all of it was obscured by a rolling, grey fog, as if I looked down at the surface of the sea at night.

There were hints in the fog that it was moving, that the stars bounced and glimmered, reflections that drew the eye and then vanished. I had to fight down the urge to try to roll the fog back as far as possible by just choosing things quickly to see more.

At its center burned a single red star—the point of origin, marking me as the Chosen of Jenae. Around it, in a perfect circle, were six stars of varying brilliance. Four burned with steady light: Enhanced Construction, Governance, Personal Enhancement, and Crafting. All stars I'd already unlocked. They burned brightly and happily, small attendant planets circling them. The remaining two—Magical Research and Exploration—hung cold and dead, just waiting to be unlocked.

I studied the connections between the illuminated stars, tracing the patterns of knowledge I'd already unlocked, moving from one to another.

From Enhanced Construction, a single planet orbited—Mundane Construction. Its steady blue-white light represented the knowledge I'd gained: a 5% increase in construction efficiency throughout my lands, and the blueprint for the Greater Glasshouse.

From Governance, another planet circled—Population—granting improvements to governance for my people and the blueprint for the Seat of Power.

Personal Enhancement had yielded Mental Training, giving me five ranks to distribute across my skills and the blueprint for the Imperial Academy.

From Crafting, the world of Non-Magical Crafting orbited steadily, providing a 1% chance for my craftsmen to break through to a higher tier when creating items, along with the blueprint for the Crafter's Hall, which I made a mental note needed to be built here as well.

Four stars, four planets, each an aspect of imperial knowledge that had already strengthened my position. But there was so much left to unlock, and as always, I knew time wasn't going to wait for me.

"How many marks of favor do we have again?" My voice sounded distant to my own ears, half in this realm and half in the void of the Constellation.

Oracle spoke up. "Twenty-two thousand, five hundred and forty-nine marks, and one million, three hundred and twenty thousand and fifteen points of mana."

I nodded, adding it up quickly. "Two more first-tier stars at ten thousand mana and five marks each, then as many more planets as we can unlock at the same cost. That's…" I frowned, working through the numbers.

"One hundred and forty thousand mana and sixty marks total," Oracle supplied. "Well within our means. But you might not want to do them all at once. Remember, this is going to be a lot of knowledge and a lot of upgrades all at once. It could hurt."

"I can handle it. Well, probably," I said with more confidence than I felt. "With Sonra and Gaij claimed, and word spreading through both territories, we're gaining marks faster than ever. Better to have these abilities now, when we need them most, and it'll let people on Dravith know that everything's okay as well."

Oracle's concern flowed through our bond, but she didn't argue. Instead, she moved closer, her hand finding my shoulder. "I'll be right here if you need me."

I smiled, drawing strength from her love, then returned my attention to the Constellation. First things first—complete the first ring by illuminating the two remaining stars.

I focused my will on Magical Research, channeling the required mana and marks into the connection. The star flickered, then began to glow, slowly at first but with increasing intensity as the energy flowed into it. Lines of fire traced across the void, connecting the star to the central point of origin.

The star flared with brilliant white-blue light, and knowledge flooded into my mind—understanding of arcane principles, methodologies for researching new spells, ways to enhance existing magic through study and experimentation. It was exhilarating and overwhelming all at once.

Congratulations!

You have unlocked Magical Research from the Constellation of Secrets.

All magic within your territories will benefit from increased efficiency. Spell research conducted by mages who venerate you and your work will

progress 5% faster, and spells cast within the territory gain a 2% increased chance of critical success.

You have also received a bonus rare blueprint!

The Arcanum Library:

The Arcanum Library serves as a repository for magical knowledge, allowing researchers to access a vast collection of spells, theories, and accumulated wisdom more efficiently. Those who study within its walls gain a 10% boost to magical comprehension and spell learning.

Construction materials required:

- **300 Steel Ingots**
- **150 Orichalcum Ingots**
- **400 Glass Panels**
- **75 Manastones (average or higher in size)**
- **500 Units of Marble**
- **200 Books of Magic (minimum quality: uncommon)**
- **10 Golem Cores**

Note: The Arcanum Library will automatically catalog and organize all magical books and scrolls placed within its walls. When fully operational, it also provides a 5% reduction in mana cost for all spells researched within its confines.

I blinked at all the information; my mind raced as I tried to make sense of it all. The Arcanum Library would complement the Imperial Academy perfectly, forming a hub for magical learning and advancement throughout my territories, but…as much as the wording was ambiguous, it wasn't about to suddenly sprout all the reading materials needed.

It was literally a library building that would help people, not a vault of unknown spells, which was a little bit of a kick in the knackers. I'd need to fill it myself.

The next stage, though, that was the more wondrous bit.

The point of view tilted, and I seemed to fall, still aware of the marble beneath my increasingly numb-growing ass, and yet seeing and almost feeling myself dropping from the heavens to the first world as it rolled past on its stately procession.

The world that came into view, I knew, somehow, represented spell creation.

For such an incredible concept, it seemed…well, fucking mundane, actually.

I fell from the sky toward a small village, where the streets were clean and the gardens bloomed. But the houses were ordinary: they were well made and had nice touches—little flourishes and were clearly not rush jobs—but they were just…normal?

That was when I saw a woman step out, kissing her children goodbye, and smiling.

The kids waved, then ran off, well fed and dressed—but again, nothing special. It all looked that way, right until the woman, while carrying on an easy conversation with the people in the garden next door, lifted her right hand and gestured, and a tear in space appeared, through which she stepped as if it were nothing.

Following her, I saw the way she strode onward, lifting her right hand again and gesturing, speaking a word here and there in the language of magic, as armor and shields snapped into place for her.

She lifted from the ground, a solid lens of air taking her weight and setting her flashing through the sky as she spoke to others, in the distance.

Now, on both sides, I could see the green forest burning. Great clouds of smoke billowed up into the sky and flaring cinders floated on the wind, as demons—not sapient and aware like Sehran, but bestial and feral—raged and screamed, chasing people through the undergrowth.

The woman gestured, speaking rapidly. Spikes of air, distortions barely visible, flashed up from the ground behind the fleeing people; the demons ran into, and through, the trap.

They fell in neatly sliced sections. Blood and ichor spurted as the woman spoke again. This time, the bodies vanished into ash, floating free as the running people were suddenly confronted with portals that opened before them.

They shouted joyously and raced through. The brief glimpse I had of the other side looked more like a doctor's waiting room with a smiling receptionist.

Then the portal snapped shut. The woman started to chant again. This time, her hands moved, and the world around her blurred.

Demons, when they appeared, simply collapsed into ash; that ash floated down, coating the ground that absorbed it.

I blinked, seeing a much more advanced version of the Environmental Cleanse spell we'd used, as the forest was cleared, cleaned, and then the waiting trees were repaired, regrown, and blessed.

All of it was as casual as I might lob a basic lightning or firebolt, and yet I could see that the woman was changing the spells on the fly, constantly.

Literally, she cast a spell then adjusted, and recast, altering the spell second by second to make it as powerful and yet efficient as possible. In the distance, here and there, I could see others doing the same.

She was literally one of a thousand or more, and this was normal to them. They were opening portals to save people and casually eliminating entire demon armies, as if this was just what they did.

Presumably while planning what to have for dinner when they got home.

I was seeing the potential that spell creation, when it was unfettered by ignorance and instead was simply an incredibly normal thing, could achieve.

Nodding that I understood, I immediately felt myself being drawn upward again. I stared out across the miles of previously devastated forests, entranced as the mages regrew them, providing lush forests and fields in seconds.

The clouds parted for me, and I lifted into brilliant sunlight. The warm sun nearby shone down upon the world as it pirouetted away beneath my feet. A second world appeared in the distance, gently turning.

This time, I felt something different as the world drew closer by the second. I blinked; it was divided into areas that were clearly along the line of specializations.

Falling to the ground, I watched as a continent of ice carved by below me, the frozen edges harsh and yet glimmering.

The firelands rose in the distance, and I stared, then smiled. The feeling of "home" thanks to my affinities prickled at the edge of my consciousness.

The sensation of this world was spell *modification*, and I nodded as I saw the difference, how the people here simply loved and lived in temperatures that should have reduced them to sooty smears floating away.

If the last world was about creating any spell you needed on the fly and just "doing it," this one was all about modifying what you had. Instead of studying ten thousand spells, it was about only knowing a few, but being capable of tweaking them until the end result was a thing of wonder.

I saw someone casting a spell that seemed to be based on the simplest firebolt spell, but instead of it causing destruction, it…it shifted, streaking through the air to pop into a thousand colors that floated free.

Children nearby laughed and sent up their own versions, the same spell seen a thousand different ways as blues and greens, yellows and reds all the way to gleaming whites popped in the air.

A half second later, another of the children changed the spell, apparently modifying the bit that "threw" the contained firebolt through the air. They instead threw themselves into the air, waving goodbye and vanishing from sight, as others played and danced.

It was only one example, but everywhere I looked, I saw the same basic spells. But instead of them being used as they were created, they were being adjusted on the go with a level of understanding that was frankly terrifying.

These were children who were changing elements of a spell at a speed that no archmage could possibly match—*kids*.

The thought of what an adult warmage could manage?

Fuck me, that was scary.

I looked about, hoping to see one, but as before, when I understood the concept, I was lifted into the sky, the world falling away beneath my feet. I sighed, then shook my head, unable to keep the smile from my face as a kid started juggling what looked like magma while singing a silly song.

Fucking kids.

As I breached the orbit of the world and it fell away behind me, I turned to watch the next world incoming. This one should be Magical Research. As it spun into view, I nodded, seeing at last a world that met my expectations, more or less.

This was a realm of high spires, of lush, rolling hills and deep oceans, where nothing was unreachable, as mages sat and discussed their reality in comfy chairs and smoked pipes.

I saw experimentation, understanding, and codification, as these elders learned and studied, and then taught the next generation learning the how and why of magic, not just how to monkey around with it.

I saw great halls were people of all ages debated academic principles, and they defended their discoveries while others denied and ridiculed.

I saw centuries of investigation, as children picked subjects and spent their entire lives learning, all striving to add a single page to the records of the world, and I saw the absolute fucking pride as they managed it.

This world was all about developing the understanding that surpassed the other two.

Where the first world believed they knew everything, and so they lived simply, happy with what they'd accomplished and the sure knowledge they could use that to save the universe, the second was all about change.

They wanted to run and play, climb and blow shit up, because they saw the beauty in the broken and learning from it. The last? As it fell away beneath my feet, it was the theory that lay beneath it all, instead of the practical side of experimentation. They studied and learned from others, codifying it and setting it in stone for those yet to come.

All three versions of spellcraft were important, and this, I sensed, was more about me and my vision for the empire than anything else.

Did I want my people to be convinced they knew it all, and therefore stagnant, believing in perfection once they reached a set level of understanding, or did I want them to strive constantly?

I wanted the second, that was for sure. But that didn't automatically preclude the last. Between the second and third, between modification and theory, there was more of a "do we figure this shit out with practice or study" as a mentality, and there?

Well, that made it simple.

I chose spell modification first, receiving a solid five percent increase across the board to the speed that we all evolved our spells, and smiled, reading over the blueprint I received.

Congratulations! You have received the uncommon blueprint:

Spell Weaver's Sanctum

The Spell Weaver's Sanctum provides a specialized environment for analyzing and modifying existing spells. Mages working within the Sanctum can combine aspects of different spells with 12% greater success rate and reduce the mana cost of modified spells by 8%.

Construction materials required:

- **150 Orichalcum Ingots**
- **200 Units of Crystal Glass**

- **75 Manastones (average or higher in size)**
- **40 Units of Enchanted Wood**

Note: Each Spell Weaver's Sanctum is capable of supporting up to five mages working simultaneously.

Reading and rereading it, as well as staring as the details filtered through my mind, I nodded to myself. This Spell Weaver's Sanctum wasn't so much a spell-school, as somewhere to experiment.

It was somewhere that a spell could be cast and released, and then the mage could observe the effect from a dozen angles, watching and learning as it failed or succeeded. I liked it. Admittedly, it wasn't anywhere near the rare or legendary blueprints, but getting even an uncommon for free was nice.

Then, grinning because I could, I selected Magical Research, accepting the cost of ten thousand mana and five marks of favor, and gained five percent increase to the speed of learning new spells.

Congratulations! You have received the uncommon blueprint:

Arcane Symposium

The Arcane Symposium serves as a gathering place for magical theorists to share and debate ideas. Knowledge discovered, debated, and shared within its walls spreads 15% more effectively throughout the attendant territory, and collaborative research conducted there progresses up to 10% faster.

Construction materials required:

250 Units of Marble

100 Units of Enchanted Wood

50 Manastones (average or higher in size)

30 Orichalcum Ingots

Note: Regular symposiums held within this structure would gradually increase the magical aptitude of all participants over time.

I guessed that was basically where academics gathered to argue with each other, and I nodded. Definitely useful, that…we didn't want tom many lunatics wandering the streets, after all.

Lastly, with the same spend again, I unlocked Spell Creation, and gained a five percent increase to the likelihood of new spells actually being a success.

None of these sounded like big changes, they didn't, but when you looked at it and understood the meaning? It was *huge*.

The chance to evolve your spell came through hard-earned experience in using it. For the more basic spells, it was when you did "little" things like cast the same base version one hundred times in a valid situation.

Like you wouldn't gain from casting firebolt a hundred times against the wall, because that was one situation; you saw how it reacted and affected the world around it, and then you moved on.

No, you had to use it a hundred times in *combat*, if that was the nature of the spell, and that was a different animal entirely.

A hundred opponents, a hundred different situations where the armor, the speed, the environment all mattered, and then you evolved that spell.

That was fine for the weaker, more bog-standard spells. But things like my Mana Cascade? That would take years, possibly literally *decades*, to reach the most basic level of improvements, and the opportunity to shave five percent off that?

Fuck to the yes.

I accepted it all, then grinned as I received a blueprint. It was uncommon again, not that good, but it was a magical fucking building, and one that could be built to bring a bonus to my people wherever I wanted, so hell to the yes, I'd take it.

Congratulations! You have received the uncommon blueprint:

Arcane Focusing Chamber

The Arcane Focusing Chamber allows mages to experiment with new spell formulations in a controlled environment. Spells created within the chamber require 10% less mana for their first casting and are 15% less likely to result in catastrophic failure during development.

Construction materials required:

- **200 Units of Crystal Glass**
- **100 Orichalcum Ingots**
- **50 Manastones (average or higher in size)**
- **30 Units of Shadow Silver**

Note: The Arcane Focusing Chamber could be linked to the Arcanum Library for an additional 5% boost to spell creation efficiency.

Damn that was nice! The boost to magic alone was good, seriously so, but the differences that could be incorporated into the towers made it so much more that it was unbelievable.

I had to get these blueprints back to Dravith somehow, and not just because I wanted to see Cai's face when he tried to figure out where he was going to get all the orichalcum from.

I vaguely remembered that Seraphina had said that they had some here, but beyond thinking 'oh great, we might need to swipe that' I'd not thought about it again.

I forced myself to keep going, those details could be reflected on later, and I reached for the final star—Exploration. Again, I channeled mana and marks, watching as the star ignited with a golden glow that seemed to pulse with adventure and discovery.

Congratulations!

You have unlocked Exploration from the Constellation of Secrets.

Your explorers and scouts will benefit from a 5% greater chance to discover resources when surveying new areas. Undiscovered locations of significance will have a 3% higher chance of being revealed on newly discovered maps within the territory.

You have also gained access to a bonus rare blueprint:

The Navigator's Spire:

The Navigator's Spire serves as a central point for exploration and mapping. Maps created or updated within its walls gain supernatural accuracy. Explorers who begin their journeys from the Spire gain enhanced resistance to environmental hazards (+10%) and increased stamina regeneration (+15%) for the first week of travel.

Construction materials required:

- **250 Steel Ingots**
- **200 Orichalcum Ingots**
- **300 Glass Panels**
- **50 Manastones (average or higher in size)**
- **400 Units of Marble**
- **100 Units of Sunstone**
- **5 Golem Cores**

Note: The Navigator's Spire, when fully operational, can generate detailed maps of surrounding territories up to 100 miles from its location, gradually filling in blank areas over time. The rate of map generation increases with the number of explorers who report their findings back to the Spire.

Now that I knew I was going for them all, I reached out to the world as I fell toward it. The first one glowed bright, and I smiled to myself, before hesitating just before I accepted the choice. I'd check it first, and then just accept when it was a star I already knew, just in case.

The world that came into view was incredible. Glorious island chains ran left and right, and between them, riding the waves like joy-filled dolphins, came the ships.

They raced ahead of the wind, people running this way and that, calling to each other in great songs as, above them, darting through the sky, came narrow-beamed vessels that seemed to race on moonlight.

I heard them calling out to the ships below; then they dipped, diving into the seas with barely a splash, ranging deeper and deeper, then returning, meeting their seabound counterparts and sharing great tales.

The sun and stars were their guides, and the islands? They moved!

Each and every one of them moved in a constant gentle pattern that at first seemed insanely random.

As the seconds passed, though, I saw that it wasn't—it wasn't at all. Instead, it was all a predictable pattern formed by currents and by buried landmasses. I felt the pull of the ocean and rode the swell of the tides.

This world—Cartography—was all about the joy of mapping, or finding a new place by always knowing where you'd been, and therefore being able to find it again.

As I rose from the seas, watching as the ships fell away beneath me, I stared in wonder. My blood sang to return, to take up an oar or to grab a rope, and help these people map the unmappable corners of the ocean.

The next world in line, as it rose and fell and I blinked in wonder, was revealed as Resource Identification.

That sounded far less esoteric and much more mundane. But fuck me, it was incredible in its own way. And if there was only one of these to choose? I'd have had this one straightaway.

For a start, it'd have saved poor Giint a lot of icy-cold fountain-showers, because it was all about seeing what was actually there, and why it could be used with something else.

It was about seeing the reddish-brown discharge that flowed like the earth was bleeding from a nearby riverbank. A section of the earth had fallen free in a storm, and was even now rushing away, the mud and plants boiling and churning; in the clay and rock that was uncovered, a reddish-brown smear was left, discharging into the water.

To anyone else, it looked like weird dirt—that was it, a mess that would hopefully soon be washed away, and that grass would grow across.

To the experienced eye, though? It was an indicator of *iron*. The rust that bled free, being carried away downstream, wouldn't last forever, but now as the long-buried ore was brought closer to the surface, it left tantalizing hints, for those who could make sense of it and read the signs.

I saw how certain plants, as days blurred past, becoming weeks and months, grew stronger.

I saw the flowers that pushed higher than their comrades, feeding on minute traces and minerals in the ground, that would have been weaker without them.

Years passed in the blink of an eye. Short, squat dwarves ranged across the hills, travelling up the river and finding no signs of the bleeding earth that had long since faded.

Instead, they saw flowers. They tasted the sparkling clean water and spun tiny compasses, smiling broadly at something so meaningless as a set of slightly taller flowers. They found a virgin iron ore mine.

Resource Identification wasn't just about going "that's iron": it was about seeing how it affected the world, and opening your eyes to see it all as you roamed the wilderness.

I saw it and I loved it. Saw the multiple ways I could use it as well, directly for my alchemy. I knew, for example, that mugwort *preferred* this kind of an environment, but not why.

If I could figure that out? I could then start looking at maps and predict where I'd find concentrations of alchemical ingredients, and from there?

I could start planting gardens, building specialized plots that could grow everything we needed.

The understanding was enough. I lifted into the air, and I smiled to myself, determined that I was having this, and was going to make the most of it.

The last planet that spun in stately procession was Pathfinding, and this combined the two approaches of exploration, more or less.

I watched the people of the world observing everything around them, cataloging, making notes and being sure that they understood how and why, while their partners? They were split into two groups: one that was filled with wanderlust, a determination to see it all, while standing by their side was someone who observed, made notes and conferred constantly.

They judged the world, they understood it, and then when they set out to explore, they didn't need maps made by others, because they could track the wheel of the stars.

They understood why the waters grew warm and cold, and they followed the currents. When they made changes, they also remembered the old paths, and when they decided to return, they cut across them almost effortlessly.

It was a wonder to behold, and when I saw that this was the median point that came from wanderlust and examination, I was again lifted from the world below.

This time, as I reached out and selected all three worlds, bringing them each to vibrant life, I was rewarded with increased Perception and Wisdom—five points to each personally, and an increase of two points to each for each scout, resource gatherer, or similar profession in the empire.

That was a *hell* of a bonus, especially for my people. The second and third notifications popped up as well, making me blink as I realized that with just tagging all three worlds, I wasn't getting a breakdown of what and why. Instead, I just *got*.

Well, regardless, the last reward—making me think that Wisdom had been for one, and Perception for the other—was Luck. That was an increase in seven for me, and one for everyone who swore to the empire, which was a fucking hell of a boost.

I wasn't going to ask how that worked, as the cost must have been incredible. But Jenae wasn't screaming and shouting at me, so I was going to press the hell on, and I quickly read over three new blueprints.

Congratulations! You have received a bonus uncommon blueprint:

Cartographer's Workbench

The Cartographer's Workbench provides specialized equipment for creating supernaturally accurate maps and can be created in any location. Maps created using this workbench have a chance to reveal hidden features 15% more effectively and maintain their accuracy even when mapping magically obscured areas.

Construction materials required:

- **150 Units of Enchanted Wood**
- **100 Units of Crystal Glass**
- **50 Orichalcum Ingots**
- **30 Manastones (average or higher in size)**

Note: The Cartographer's Workbench produces maps that update in real-time when linked to explorer teams carrying specially crafted focusing crystals.

*

Congratulations! You have received a bonus uncommon blueprint:

Prospector's Mapping Table

The Prospector's Mapping Table serves as a base for resource-focused exploration. Expeditions drafted using this resource have a 15% increased chance to locate rare and valuable resources, and analyze resource quality with 20% greater accuracy.

Construction materials required:

- **200 Steel Ingots**
- **150 Units of Stone**
- **80 Orichalcum Ingots**
- **40 Manastones (average or higher in size)**

Note: The Prospector's Mapping Table includes specialized equipment for identifying and evaluating various types of resources, from precious metals to magical reagents.

*

Congratulations! You have received a bonus uncommon blueprint:

Wayfinder's Rest

The Wayfinder's Rest serves as quarters for travelers and explorers. Those who begin their journeys from such a location gain a bonus hint of supernatural guidance, reducing travel time by 15% and decreasing the chance of encountering hostile forces by 10% for the first 48 hours.

Construction materials required:

- **250 Units of Stone**

- **150 Orichalcum Ingots**
- **100 Units of Crystal Glass**
- **50 Manastones (average or higher in size)**

Note: The Wayfinder's Rest could be constructed inside a similar structure inside your territory, creating a network that further enhances travel efficiency.

They…they could all be built inside another building. They were all supplemental to each other, and, fuck me, if I built them in the spire? And then the spire itself atop the tower here?

Shit, they'd all support one another!

I blinked, stunned by the variety and usefulness of the blueprints, then cackled to myself, imagining Mal's face when I idly pointed out all the loot that could be gained from these. That fucker was going to lose his shit when I solved all the resource issues we'd been struggling with!

Never mind anything else, this was worth it just for that!

With all six stars of the first ring now illuminated, the Constellation shifted subtly. The stars seemed to align perfectly; their light grew brighter, pushing the fog farther back, revealing other stars that slowly bobbed and dipped, each dead and silent.

I could sense new pathways forming between them—the pathways that would lead to the second rings growing in strength. But rather than giving in to temptation, I forced myself to focus, and go back to the first ring.

I could jump ahead, I knew that I could, but I also felt—and I suspected this was a hint from Jenae—that if I did? I'd be missing a trick.

Each of the first tier had granted incredible improvements, and now? I'd be insane to just leapfrog ahead, when I could still afford to do so once this stage was done.

Better to do it right, rather than fast.

Before advancing to the next tier, I needed to fully complete the first by unlocking the remaining specializations—the planets that orbited each star.

I'd seen now that the blueprints were building on one another; they could enhance one another and those who used or rested in them.

I had plenty of points, and well, why the hell not? I wouldn't be able to do this for all the stars further on—the cost jumped by five times for each ring I extended into—but with the bonuses being as solid as they were, it just made sense to do it for the first ring, right?

I turned my attention back to start with Enhanced Construction—it was at the top of the starscape, after all—where Mundane Construction already orbited. Two more planets remained: Magical Construction and Warfare.

Channeling mana and marks into the connection, I watched as Magical Construction began to materialize. As it formed, my mind swam, a sensation of stress, of too much filled me. Suddenly, I was back looking down from above. Instead of flying to the planets, I instead received visions that flowed into my mind—buildings that channeled ambient mana for various purposes, structures that enhanced the magical abilities of those within, towers that could project defensive shields over entire settlements.

I felt it as I unlocked Magical Construction, knowing that it was part of what I desperately needed to bring about the tower's rebirth, and I sighed as the notifications streamed up, skimming them.

All magical structures built within my territory would be 5% more efficient at channeling and utilizing mana. Magical enhancements to buildings would last 8% longer, and all of that—simply through a little alignment of information, a tweak or two here and there—made me aware of just how easily Jenae had improved the tower back home to increase its mana intake by more than twenty percent.

Congratulations! You have received a bonus rare blueprint:

Mana Conduit Network

The Mana Conduit Network allows for the efficient distribution of mana throughout a settlement or fortress. When installed, it reduces the mana cost of all structure-based magic by 7% and allows mana to be channeled from a source unit to any connected building.

Construction materials required:

- **150 Orichalcum Ingots**
- **300 Units of Purified Copper**
- **75 Manastones (average or higher in size)**
- **50 Units of Crystal Glass**

Note: Each segment of the Mana Conduit Network spans up to 100 meters. Multiple segments can be connected to create a comprehensive grid throughout a settlement.

That one? Hell, I couldn't stop smiling. I wasn't going to say it, but this was blatantly Jenae helping, because the one thing I'd been starting to really worry about was how the hell I plugged in the collectors to the tower.

Did I just slap it on the roof and hope it didn't fall off? Did I add it at ground level and hope that leaning it against the tower would be enough?

Now I knew. I grew these fuckers and connected the collectors to the tower, and also, I used them to connect the genesis chambers to whatever I needed.

This time, I didn't get any other bonuses, but fuck me, this was a rare one, so I wasn't complaining at all!

Without pause, I directed my attention to the final specialization of Enhanced Construction: Warfare. The planet materialized slowly, its surface seeming to ripple with the chaos of battle even as it formed. Knowledge of defensive structures, siege weapons, and strategic fortifications flowed into my mind.

This time, I did receive a slight improvement—namely, all defensive structures within my territory would gain 5% durability. Siege weapons crafted by my people would deal 3% additional damage.

Congratulations! You have received a bonus uncommon blueprint:

Bastion Walls

Bastion Walls incorporate advanced defensive features including reinforced gate houses, improved archer positions, and highly limited mana-channeling capabilities. When fully constructed, they provide a 12% boost to the effectiveness of defending forces.

Construction materials required (per 100 meters):

- **500 Units of Stone**
- **100 Steel Ingots**
- **50 Orichalcum Ingots**
- **25 Manastones (average or higher in size)**

Note: Bastion Walls can be upgraded with additional features such as enchanted barriers or automated defensive mechanisms as higher tiers of knowledge are unlocked.

As I completed unlocking the specializations for Enhanced Construction, the strain began to build. The constant flow of knowledge and the persistent drain on my mana reserves were taking their toll. But I forced myself to press on, turning my attention to Crafting.

I'd already unlocked Non-Magical Crafting, so I focused on the remaining two specializations: Magical Crafting and Consumable Crafting. The former materialized as a planet that gleamed with inner fire, pulsing with potent enchantments.

I unlocked Magical Crafting from the Crafting specialization, and this time I did them separately so that I could see what each was.

Now, all enchantments created and layered into something physically created within my territory gained the chance to be 5% more powerful—it wasn't a guaranteed success, after all—and enchanted items gained a 3% chance to gain an additional minor benefit. Whatever that meant.

Congratulations! You have received a bonus uncommon blueprint:

Enchanter's Workshop

The Enchanter's Workshop provides specialized equipment for creating and embedding magical properties into items. Enchantments created within this workshop will last 10% longer and be 8% more powerful than those created elsewhere.

Construction materials required:

- **200 Orichalcum Ingots**
- **100 Units of Crystal Glass**
- **60 Manastones (average or higher in size)**

- **50 Units of Enchanted Wood**

Note: The Enchanter's Workshop could be upgraded to specialize in specific types of enchantments as higher tiers of knowledge are unlocked.

Next, Consumable Crafting formed, appearing as a swirling blend of liquids, herbs, and energies that continuously flowed into new combinations. I ran my hands together in glee at the thought of the improvements to my potions.

Potions, scrolls, and other magical consumables created within my territory would now benefit from a chance to increase by 5% in potency. That was cool, but also crafters would have a 3% increased chance to create consumables of higher quality than their skill would normally allow. Fuck the recipes, after all.

Congratulations! You have received a bonus uncommon blueprint:

Alchemist's Laboratory

The Alchemist's Laboratory contains specialized equipment for creating potions, elixirs, and other consumables. Items created within this facility last up to 15% longer before expiring and have a 10% chance to yield additional doses during creation.

Construction materials required:

- **150 Units of Crystal Glass**
- **100 Orichalcum Ingots**
- **40 Manastones (average or higher in size)**
- **60 Units of "Rare" or greater Herbs and Minerals**

Note: The Alchemist's Laboratory reduces the chance of volatile reactions during experimental crafting by 25%.

Moving to Governance, I focused on the two remaining specializations beyond Population; Economy and Law. Economy manifested as a planet crisscrossed with trade routes and bustling markets, somehow carrying with it the sense of the complex flow of resources and wealth through a society, which was impressive as hell all on its own.

I grinned as the notification informed me that all commercial activities within my territory would have a chance to gain 3% greater profits. Tax collection efficiency would increase by 5% without increasing how pissed the people were, which was also nice.

Congratulations! You have received a bonus uncommon blueprint:

Imperial Exchange

The Imperial Exchange serves as a central marketplace and financial institution. Trade conducted through the Exchange receive favorable terms, increasing profits by 8% for all parties. The Exchange may also provide secure banking services and standardize currency throughout your territory.

Construction materials required:

- **300 Units of Marble**
- **150 Steel Ingots**
- **100 Orichalcum Ingots**
- **50 Units of Precious Metals**

Note: The Imperial Exchange can generate a steady income stream for the treasury based on the volume of trade it processes.

Next, Law formed as perfectly balanced scales, radiating an aura of justice and order that seemed to impose structure on the void around it.

Criminal activity within my territory would decrease by 3%. Judicial proceedings would conclude 5% more fairly and efficiently, which made me shake my head in wonder even as the ache behind my eyes grew stronger and developed into a full-on migraine. How the hell that was possible I didn't know, but fuck it, some things I guessed I just had to take on faith.

Congratulations! You have received a bonus rare blueprint:

Hall of Justice

The Hall of Justice serves as the center for the judicial system. Cases tried within its walls have a 15% greater chance of reaching the correct verdict. The building's enchantments additionally make it impossible for witnesses to knowingly speak falsehoods while testifying, without considerable pain.

Construction materials required:

- **350 Units of Marble**
- **100 Orichalcum Ingots**
- **80 Manastones (average or higher in size)**
- **50 Units of Crystal Glass**

Note: The Hall of Justice houses up to 20 justicars and their staff, providing quarters and research facilities to support their work.

I paused, the strain intensifying. My connection to the Constellation wavered slightly; the stars seemed to flicker at the edges of my vision. Oracle's concern flowed stronger through our bond, but I sent back reassurance. I was tired, but not at my limit...probably.

Turning my attention to Personal Enhancement, I focused on the two remaining specializations beyond Mental Training; Physical Training and Skill Training. The former manifested as a planet that radiated vitality and strength, its surface in constant motion like rippling muscles as distant figures sprinted across its ever-changing surface.

Just focusing on them made the pain flare and I shook it off, moving ahead quickly, reducing the details down still further.

All physical training within my territory, if those doing it really tried, would now yield up to 5% better results. My people would also have a 3% increased chance to make breakthrough improvements in their physical capabilities. How, I didn't know, but Restun would probably punish me one way or the other.

Congratulations! You have received a bonus uncommon blueprint:

The Champion's Grounds

The training grounds provide specialized facilities for physical training and development. Those who train within these grounds have a chance to gain physical attributes 10% faster and have a 5% increased chance to develop uncommon or higher physical talents.

Construction materials required:

- **250 Steel Ingots**
- **150 Units of Stone**
- **100 Units of Enchanted Wood**
- **30 Manastones (average or higher in size)**

Note: The Champion's Grounds include specialized areas for different types of physical training, from strength and endurance to agility and combat techniques.

Finally, Skill Training formed, appearing as a constantly shifting display of talents and abilities being honed to perfection.

Skills developed within my territory, I saw, would improve 5% faster, and my people would have a 3% chance to discover hidden aptitudes when learning new skills.

Congratulations! You have received a bonus uncommon blueprint:

Master's Hall

The Master's Hall serves as a gathering place for those who have achieved mastery in their respective crafts and skills. Those who study under masters within this hall will gain skills 15% faster and have a 10% increased chance of developing unique techniques.

Construction materials required:

- **200 Units of Marble**
- **180 Units of Enchanted Wood**
- **50 Orichalcum Ingots**
- **25 Manastones (average or higher in size)**

Note: The Master's Hall accommodates up to 30 master-apprentice pairs at any given time, with specialized facilities for various disciplines.

The strain was becoming horrendous now. My connection to the physical world around my body grew tenuous as more of my consciousness was drawn into the Constellation.

With the final specialization unlocked, the entire Constellation pulsed with power. The completed first ring shone with harmonious light, each star and its orbiting planets working in concert. New connections began to form between adjacent stars, extending pathways for the next ring to emerge.

But the strain became overwhelming. My mind wavered, my grip on the Constellation beginning to slip. Through our bond, I could feel Oracle's growing alarm, her presence in the physical world reaching out to steady me.

With a monumental effort, I withdrew from the Constellation, pulling my awareness back into my physical body. I gasped as reality reasserted itself, the cool marble floor suddenly solid beneath me. My body felt leaden, drenched in sweat, but my mind buzzed with the vast knowledge I'd absorbed, even as my body cried out in pain from staying so still for so long.

"Jax!" Oracle was at my side, supporting me as I swayed. "You pushed too far!"

"Worth it," I managed, my voice hoarse. "The knowledge…the potential…"

"You idiot! We need you alive to use it!" she cried, though her relief was evident through our bond. "You've been in a trance for nearly seven hours, and I've been trying to get your attention for the last three!"

"Seven hours?" I blinked in surprise. It'd felt like minutes within the Constellation. "Did I…?"

"You completed the first ring," Oracle confirmed. "All six stars and their specializations are now unlocked. I could feel the knowledge flowing into you." She hesitated. "And something else was happening toward the end—new connections forming."

I nodded wearily. "The foundation for the second ring. I could see the pathways beginning to form between the stars, and I felt…something…?"

"It can wait," Oracle said firmly, helping me to my feet. "You need rest, sleep, and food before attempting anything else. And no more, Jax—we need you more than we need a damn building! One star a day at most from now on!"

I nodded, exhaustion running rampant in me. My stomach felt like it was trying to eat my fucking belly button.

My mind, though, raced with possibilities. The blueprints alone would change Gaij beyond recognition: the Arcanum Library, the Navigator's Spire, the various specialized workshops and training facilities. But the true power lay in the systemic improvements across my territories: faster construction, more efficient magic, better governance, enhanced training methods, more effective exploration.

The Constellation of Secrets was incredible, but fuck me, I felt like I'd been cored like an apple.

It was worth it, though. With the first ring complete, the path to even greater knowledge was opening before us.

CHAPTER TWENTY-SIX

Two full days passed before I felt ready to attempt the second ring of the Constellation of Secrets. Two goddamn days of recovery, of integrating the knowledge I'd gained, and of planning with my small group of advisors how best to utilize the blueprints and capabilities now at our disposal.

Mostly, though, I slept, and I recovered. That was how bad I felt after it.

Construction had already begun on several of the new facilities, with priority given to the Greater Glasshouse—food security being seriously important, sure, but this was a safety measure for more than just us, as we had the entire goddamn herds of Sonra on their way—and the Arcanum Library, which would serve as the foundation for our magical advancement.

It was also a hell of a carrot to dangle before the mages of the city, and that alone got them working their arses off.

After I'd spent all the first day unconscious, and then yesterday in bed or at best sitting in the gardens with a basically fried brain, I was getting caught up on things on the morning of the third day, when word came in that the first of the mana collectors was ready.

While I'd been out of it, the legion and the golems had been busy. First off, the single legionnaire with the two war golems who was sent after the guildmaster returned, and they did so with a bag full of literal rotting skulls.

Apparently, when they'd seen what was closing on them, they'd unleashed hell on the poor legionnaire, who'd basically stayed back, letting them wear themselves out and expend everything against the two golems that moved in.

Dozens of single use spell scrolls had been used, most of which none of us had a clue about, except that red lightning was apparently a thing, and the fuckers had been smart enough to use extreme heat and then extreme cold on the golems as well.

One of them had been entirely destroyed, and the other had been cracked badly enough to its core that it was eventually scrapped, as the cost of repair was even longer than the cost of building a new one from scratch.

It had marched up and proffered the bag as evidence it'd gotten the fuckers, though, and one of the stains that covered it from head to toe was clearly blood.

I decided that was more than enough, and the legionnaire who'd turned the wagons around and had brought them back got a bonus. The staff who had fled with the guild were very willing to return with him and be judged as well, rather than face summary judgement in the field for some strange reason. And so, in addition to a trio of Fenris automatons, taking our total on this continent to five; we'd also gained a number of artifacts and miscellaneous coins, some records and other random shit that they'd been determined to get out of our reach.

Daralen had dealt with the issues around the law by the simple expedient of putting Optio Gilpin in charge of the judiciary system, and then making sure that all the judges knew the laws as they stood under the empire. Then they were sworn to uphold those laws, and had them bring anything that was borderline or nuanced to Gilpin for oversight.

It'd resulted in the prisons being emptied almost entirely by this morning, because by the time those who had committed a capital offense were made to swear, and then questioned, they'd then been immediately executed, had their sentence commuted, or they were released into the legion's "tender" care.

That tender care was very much in evidence as the legion quick marched in through the main gate, carrying the first of the multi-ton collectors.

They'd arrived at the former legion, and now former Dark Legion encampment to find that Nimon had apparently ordered them to destroy everything and flee.

That, however, was why they also took ten war golems and six servitors and crafters. The war golems were sent after the Dark Legion with a small cadre of legionnaires to make sure the job was done—cue more smears on the paint of the golems and a handful of scratches and two more lost golems.

It made it clear just what the difference between the golems facing opportunistic wankers, and experienced and paranoid people were.

When the tower had fallen it had apparently had dozens to hundreds of the various types of golems, and over the centuries since then they'd been gradually whittled down again and again.

Thankfully, we were back to producing them now, meaning that we could afford to send golems in place of living people into the meat grinder and while they did that, the crafters and servitors repaired and then disassembled the various equipment.

Most of it was carried back by the golems, but to prove a point, those who were on the legion shit list were allowed the opportunity to help as well.

The five collectors were installed in the gardens on all sides of the tower, and the ruined remaining three were fed into the tower as raw materials to help make the next five, each of which were to be attached to the tower higher up.

Thanks to the conduits technology I'd received from Jenae—I'd made damn sure to announce that there was going to be a ceremony tonight in thanks for the gods and goddesses' help—we now had a way to connect them all to the tower. Although it'd take a few more days to get it all working, we were making progress.

Once the first connectors were up and running, that would bring in enough—we hoped—to keep the tower charged. Then the second tier would provide the extra needed to help the tower grow and power new things.

I'd also found time to deal with a handful of additional details, as lying about with a brain that felt like it'd been given freezer burn meant that I was both left with a lot of time on my hands, and very little to do, as Oracle and the others insisted I rest.

Mainly, though, I planned, gave basic orders and left it up to others to make sure they worked, and I got ready.

I'd seen other notifications when I'd received the blueprints in the Constellation, but I'd been a bit busy and had banished them, mainly. Instead, I gave orders and directions, explaining the overall plan as much as I could to Daralen and Seraphina and just getting ready to be wiped out again.

Now, laid back on the bed in our quarters, I worked my way through them, ignoring most. The kill notifications, for example, were just fucking insane. Despite all of them, I didn't gain a fucking level.

Admittedly, I needed twelve million a level, but still!

The notifications that actually meant something to me were clear, though.

You have completed a repeatable Quest: Rescue the Legion! (2)

You have freed more of the legion, hunting down and rescuing them from a life of captivity that they would never have imagined when they first signed up to protect the empire. Go forth, Prince of the Empire, and earn your legion's devoted worship.

Reward: 219/50 Legionnaires, 50,000xp

I flicked through the next few replacement quest notifications and brought up the last in line, smiling that it was a repeatable that looked to be increasing nicely.

You have received a new Quest: Rescue the Legion! (5)

Your legionnaires languish in unjust slavery, but they yearn to be free! Go, Jax Amon, Prince of the Empire, find those who offered their lives to serve: free them, heal them, and raise them to the light. In doing so, you will gain far more than it costs you.

Rescue members of the Imperial Legion!

Reward: 19/200 Legionnaires, 500,000xp

Half a million XP for rescuing people I'd have been rescuing anyway? Hell to the yes. I saw Jenae's hand in that as well, as clearly the faster I leveled, the better.

Next was a notification that I'd not seen earlier, because obviously it'd been waiting until I fulfilled the bonus requirements before it popped up. Thank you, my allied gods, for that sneaky positioning.

You have completed a Divine repeatable Quest: My God is Better than your God (5)

Jenae and the Pantheon of the Flame have witnessed your conquering of the city and Tower of Gaij and are proud of your devotion. For the capture of the city, the elimination of the enemy stronghold, and the suppression of the Pantheon of the Dark, you have completed this quest.

Bonus: Recover the Legion Encampment of old and return its foundries and constructors to operational status: 1/1

- **Kill the Leader of the Dark Legion in Gaij**: 4/1
- **Kill enemy Priests, Clerics, and Paladins**: 20/20
- **Capture the city of Gaij**: 1/1
- **Capture the Tower of Gaij**: 1/1

Bonuses have been given for exceeding the original numbers.

> **Reward:** Territorial Claim increased, 30,000+ Citizens, Access to City treasuries and capabilities, 3,000,000xp

There was even the next notification in line, which made it clear what the hell was going on:

> **You have received a Divine repeatable Quest: My God is Better than your God (6)**
>
> The dark power of Kronk grows like a tumor. No longer satisfied with raiding the caravan routes or smaller villages and settlements that surround it, the city of Kronk has turned its gaze westward, to Gaij.
>
> Kronk's army masses, its siege weapons are being prepared, and supply lines created. Beware, prince of the empire, because Kronk's finest shall be at your gate in less than two weeks!
>
> Destroy, capture, or otherwise defeat the army of Kronk, then deal with its homeland to secure a second territory on Carrmor!
>
> **Bonus:** Claim the Cradle of Feshcan'un: 0/1
>
> - **Kill the leader of the army of Kronk**: 0/1
> - **Kill enemy officers**: 0/50
> - **Capture the city of Kronk**: 0/1
> - **Throw down the altars of the Pantheon of the Dark**: 0/50
>
> *Bonuses will be given for exceeding these numbers.*
>
> **Reward:** Territorial Claim increased, 40,000+ Citizens, Access to City treasuries and capabilities, 6,000,000xp

That was a little bit of a kick in the tits—it seriously was. Mainly because it made it damn clear that, first of all, I couldn't just rock on and head for the Cradle with Oracle, and second, that I needed to be here for at least the next two weeks, and then we'd need to get to Kronk and sort that shit out as well.

But, as we'd sort of had thrown at us already, we'd decided that we also needed to make something along the lines of our own prototype airship here. And as nobody on this continent had apparently even considered anything beyond the ancient prax as being capable of flight, and they were seven hundred plus years buried and broken? Well, that just gave us a nice little way to get things moving.

If we could make it work.

That gave me both some hope and some serious stress, because if I was marching into a basically fresh war, I needed to get every damn advantage in place I could.

As such, that meant getting everyone working here, and things running smoothly, and then finally spending those points.

After a long morning of meetings—one which Oracle insisted I have a break of half an hour after each to just rest and meditate—I finally pulled up my character sheet, and read through it all. I'd done well, I had to admit that, considering the sheer fucking number of points I'd amassed, and the absolutely mental number of centuries I was about to surpass.

I had sixty-four points, as well as a meridian point, so I decided that making the most of those was the best step.

The first target was Perception. Sure, there was an argument for others first, but my Perception was levelling slowly, naturally, and the thirty-four points in that would help me to spot a lot of the problems that were going to be coming along, or so I hoped.

It'd also help a hell of a lot with my magic and alchemy, so fuck it. That left me with thirty points, of which I needed seventeen to get my Agility to the hundred mark as well.

Thirteen points left, and Dexterity needed seven of those to reach a century, leaving me with six. I dropped the last six points into Strength, because that was something I could level on my own, and had been doing consistently, but a little extra there was always going to help.

With Oracle and Sehran sitting ready, I lay back on the bed and triggered the changes. I held my breath and braced myself as the changes began to take hold.

One second, I was fine; the next, it felt like my body had been dropped into a pit of molten glass. I arched off the bed, muscles seizing in uncontrollable spasms as my nervous system went haywire.

Oracle's worried face hovered somewhere above me, but her features blurred and distorted. My vision flickered like I was a crackhead who'd found a kilo of bath salts and tried to do it all at once.

"Jax!" Her voice sounded distant, underwater. "Stay with us!"

I tried to respond, but my tongue felt too large for my mouth. My skin burned as if it were being peeled away and reattached, cell by cell. Inside my skull, something shifted—a physical feeling of something inside, where *nothing* was supposed to fucking move, definitely moving! I felt neural pathways being remapped, reconnected, and rebuilt from the ground up.

Time lost all meaning. It could have been minutes or hours that I writhed, caught in the vise grip of transformation. Somewhere in the haze of agony, I felt cool hands holding me down, heard Sehran's songs as she tried to help me endure through it.

The pain in my eyes was the worst—like tiny needles were being driven through the back of my eyeballs into my brain. Colors I'd never seen before flashed across my vision, afterimages trailing like ghostly fingerprints, despite my damn upbringing and twenty plus years of experience telling me that there were seven fucking colors in the world and that was it, goddammit.

Just when I thought I couldn't take it anymore, something snapped into place with an audible click that only I could hear. The pain didn't exactly stop—it transformed, becoming something electric and alive, racing through my body like lightning seeking ground.

I gasped, drawing in a desperate breath as awareness flooded back. The world around me seemed impossibly sharp, every detail etched with crystal clarity. I could see the individual threads in the bedsheet, count the tiny cracks in the bedframe, and feel every cell of Oracle's skin as she touched me, worried eyes scanning my face.

"Holy fuck," I managed to croak. My voice sounded strange, even to my own ears. "That was…intense."

"You were convulsing." Relief washed over Oracle's features. "Dammit, Jax, that was even worse than the last time."

"Three centuries at once will do that," Daralen commented dryly from somewhere near my feet. "Congratulations on not dying, my prince."

I tried to sit up, and my body responded with a fluidity that startled me. It was like thinking about moving and being moved simultaneously—no delay, no hesitation. My muscles felt like liquid metal, flowing rather than contracting.

"Easy," Oracle cautioned, reaching for me as did Sehran on the other side of the bed.

But I was already upright, blinking as my vision adjusted. "The notifications," I said. My tongue felt oddly precise in my mouth. "I need to see what happened."

I pulled up my status screen and was momentarily disoriented by how differently I perceived it now. What had once been flat text seemed to float in layers, the information organized in a three-dimensional space that my brain somehow intuitively understood. I focused on the waiting notifications, and they expanded before me.

Congratulations!

You have achieved your fourth Primary Century in Agility through point allocation and as such have gained a new Ability!

Temporal Fluidity: When activated, your movements exist partly outside normal time. You can perform up to three physical actions in the span it would normally take to complete one. This doesn't increase your overall speed, but allows you to chain movements together with supernatural precision and timing, essentially compressing multiple actions into a single moment.

Cost: 250 mana per second active, per bubble of compressed time.

I blinked. The meaning came along with the text, as I saw myself creating unique bubbles of space-time around myself, around a fixed target point, that enabled me to strike faster and faster in it. To the outside world, it'd look like a blur, but to me? I could hammer an opponent, provided they didn't have a similar skill.

For a second, I wondered about why I'd not faced anyone with something like this; then I saw it.

Each of my abilities was adjusted and improved upon depending on the last.

This wouldn't have worked without my Hyper Cognition; I just couldn't have thought fast enough. Likewise, without Mana Overdrive, I couldn't have carried it out.

That made sense, sort of, as to why I wasn't coming up against people with these skills, considering I was fairly sure that the average human got three or at most four points per level.

I got seven, and I got additional bonuses through being Jenae's champion. Then add in that, unlike most people starting to "build" their stats at a set point, like when they're ten or twelve years old or whatever, I'd been mixing spending points and accruing them through exercise for about a year and I'd passed level fifty.

Most people? Even most legionnaires ended up fighting only occasionally, spending a lot of time recovering from injuries, or travelling and training. Me?

I conquered fucking cities and fought gods. Of course I was growing at an insane rate. I barely had time to process this, though, before the next notification appeared.

Congratulations!

You have achieved your fifth Primary Century in Dexterity through point allocation and as such have gained a new Ability!

Master Craftsman's Touch: Your hands and mind have been gifted an innate understanding of how objects fit together and can be manipulated. When crafting, you have a chance to "see" the optimal structure of any item you're creating, allowing you to craft at up to twice the normal speed and with a 35% chance of creating an item one quality tier higher than your skill level would normally permit.

Constantly active Enhancement: When actively focusing (15 mana per second), you can temporarily manipulate small objects with telekinetic precision within arm's reach.

And finally, the third notification appeared:

Congratulations!

You have achieved your sixth Primary Century in Perception through point allocation and as such have gained a new Ability!

Essence Sight: You can now perceive the underlying magical structure of the world around you. This ability grants you a 10% chance to identify spell structures, see mana flows, detect magical concealment, and recognize the intrinsic magical properties of objects and beings. With concentration, you can temporarily perceive through solid objects by following mana traces.

Cost: 20 mana per second for basic activation Enhanced Focus; 50 mana per second to see through solid objects or examine complex magical structures.

I stared at the notifications, trying to absorb the implications as I stopped reading them aloud. Three new abilities, each building on the foundation of what I'd already achieved. The potential applications were staggering—in combat, in crafting, in understanding the magical world around me in ways I'd never imagined.

"Three centuries," I whispered, dismissing the notifications with a thought. "That's…a lot."

"How do you feel?" Oracle asked, her hand finding mine.

I took a moment to actually feel myself, and not in a fun way. The lingering pain faded slowly, replaced by an awareness of my body that bordered on unsettling. Every muscle fiber, every joint and tendon felt perfectly aligned, waiting for direction. My fingers twitched slightly, and I realized I could feel the texture of the air between them.

"Different," I finally said. "Like I've been rebuilt from the inside out." I looked around the room, and the details that jumped out at me were overwhelming—the subtle currents of air, the faint traces of magic lingering around Oracle and Sehran, the way light bent around objects in ways I'd never noticed before.

"Try something," Sehran suggested, tossing a small object toward me.

Without thinking, I activated Temporal Fluidity and felt both Mana Overdrive and Hyper Cognition coming online as well. The world didn't exactly slow down—instead, it felt like I existed in multiple moments simultaneously. In one fluid sequence, I reached out, tapped Oracle on her forehead and then the end of her nose, all in such a blur that she barely had time to blink; then and only then, I caught the small coin that Sehran had tossed to me.

"Holy shit," I breathed, staring at her shocked expression. "That was…that was three distinct moves, but they felt like one."

"It did to me too," Oracle admitted, her eyes wide. "Your hand was almost a blur, but not from speed—more like…I don't know, like you were doing everything at once."

I closed my eyes, then reopened them, deliberately activating Essence Sight. The world transformed. Colors shifted into patterns of energy that flowed and ebbed through everything. Oracle blazed like a supernova, her wisp nature manifesting as intricate spirals of mana that coursed through her human form. Sehran was different—darker, more concentrated energy that pulsed with a rhythm entirely its own.

But the most stunning revelation was the room itself. The tower walls weren't just stone—I knew that; I always had, but still—they pulsed slightly…as if they were *alive*. Continuously feeding on and redirecting the trace mana that flowed through them. I could see the network of energy running through the entire structure, branching out like a vast circulatory system.

"I can see…everything," I said, my voice hushed. "The mana flows, the way it moves through the tower, through you all. It's…it's beautiful."

I deactivated the ability, blinking as my vision returned to normal—though "normal" felt lacking now, like I was seeing less than was truly there.

"What about the other one?" Sehran asked. "The crafting ability?"

"Honestly, I think I'll need to try crafting to make it work. I've got no idea how to do anything with it unless I do that. But still, it's going to really help me with the potions."

Oracle smiled, though I could see concern lingering in her eyes. “Three new abilities is a lot, though, Jax. You should rest before trying anything more strenuous.”

I nodded, though rest was the last thing on my mind. My body hummed with energy, my senses hyperaware of everything around me. But she was right—I knew she was right…rest, give it a few hours for my body to settle. Because I was starting to feel like a rubber band that’d been stretched too damn far, and then?

“Yeah,” I agreed, settling back against the pillows. “Rest first. Then we see what else we can unlock through the Constellation of Secrets.”

As I closed my eyes, I couldn’t help but smile. Three centuries, three new abilities, and we were just getting started. The Constellation of Secrets still waited as well. And once that was done? The last of them, my meridian point, was yet to be activated.

It shouldn’t be much of a change, it really shouldn’t, but I instinctively knew doing it now would be a step too far.

I slept for perhaps four hours, far longer and deeper than I expected to. But when I woke up again, it was to the sound of low conversation next door in a small sitting room adjacent to our bedroom, and to the heavenly smell of bacon.

I managed to get up on my second attempt, my first being too quick and so fluid that I almost knocked myself out on the bedside table as I fell. A handful of seconds later, I’d gotten to my feet, and I was moving around the room okay, feeling my muscles stretch and relax.

About to head for the door, I suddenly caught a whiff of myself after laying around in bed, dressed no less, for another four hours. I hit myself with a Scour, and then stripped, hit myself again, and redressed in clean clothing.

By the time I was lacing up the front of a shirt, the door cracked open and Oracle stepped in, holding a plate of sandwiches and a cool glass of fresh apple juice.

I knew it, because *goddamn*, my Perception increase had made that incredibly clear. Every scent, every movement, suddenly spoke volumes. She came to me, setting things down and then just cuddling in; I kissed her, relaxing slightly, enjoying the fresh scent of vanilla and coconut that wafted from her. I smiled.

She always knew how to ground me.

Five minutes or so passed as we said nothing, just relaxing together, before begrudgingly, she spoke up. “Are you going to do it now?”

“I think I have to,” I admitted. “I left it all too long, knowing that I’d be wiped out by it, and now every hour that passes gets us closer to the next fight.”

“You could do this later,” she pointed out.

“When?” I asked honestly. “Seriously, Oracle, when would I do it? We’ve got the army of Kronk—fucking stupid name for a city, that—but we’ve got that army supposedly heading here, and soon. I can’t afford to be out of commission right now, not at all, but more to the point, the things that we’re getting access to through these unlocks, and through the Constellation? We need them.

“Hell, the bonuses from the academy will be lifesaving, sure, but in the short term? There’s no way we could have managed all of this without the conduits we unlocked. For all we know, there’s another one that’s just as game-changing waiting to be unlocked next. And those little five percent increases? Twenty days, and we get an extra day’s production from any mines, or crafters or whatever.

"A single day might be the difference between success and failure, and that's before we even look at the coming changes in our lives. Even if Kronk didn't exist, I'd be doing this now, because the thought of me being broken and out of action when the baby comes? Hell to the no."

"Well, that's something we need to talk about as well." Oracle winced. "Jax, sit down."

"Is everything okay?" My heart grew leaden in fear.

"It's okay, everything's okay, don't worry," she quickly reassured me. "For now, it's okay."

"For now?" I questioned quickly. "What does that mean?"

"It means that we might need to stay here in the short term, Jax, thanks to Kronk—and yes, I saw the notification and passed word to the others, so don't worry—but we can't stay for long," she said. "I'm feeling changes, both in my body and in my core. The parts of me that are still more wisp than human are full…overfull, in fact. And if I were a normal wisp? I'd be splitting, reproducing through fission, I think Thomas called it."

"Tommy knows as much about fission as I do rocket science," I said. "He's heard the word and thinks it makes him sound smart, so just tell me what you mean, please, my love."

"The tower is active," she said. "I've not been around something so active since we became pregnant. And now, feeling it drawing the mana in all around us? I need to go elsewhere, soon."

"We need to leave?" I blinked.

"Definitely before the baby comes." She nodded. "It'll have aspects of us and our physical forms, but it'll also be a mana-based form. And until it learns to stabilize itself, it's going to be weak against mana intrusion, or…" She looked at me pointedly. "Mana drain."

"And the tower is draining a small amount of mana from all around us." I nodded that I understood.

"Not a small amount," Oracle corrected. "I wasn't around when the Tower of Dravith was grown, but I bet that it was the same as this is now. The tower is draining the mana from the area to fuel its regrowth, and it's taking a lot more than can ambiently regrow.

"It's forming a vacuum, sucking inward, and while more seeps across the boundary of the draw from outside, trying to fill the void, it's a lot slower than normal."

"We need to get you away from here." I cursed that I'd wasted so long in stupid contemplation and unlocking.

"No," Oracle repeated. "Jax, we need to stabilize the city, and we need to defeat that army. Then we leave. I've got at least a few weeks left, and even if I felt that I had to start labor now, we could still take a wagon and be out of the tower's reach in a few hours. It's not that strong, after all."

"So we stay for a little…" I didn't feel good about it, though.

"Exactly." She nodded. "We stay for a little, fight the army, get that airship up and running, and then we go. I've spent some time talking with the gnomes, when you were out of it, and what we came up with…well, it's not going to be pretty.

It's going to be a lot slower than Tenandra is, but they think it'll also be a lot faster than riding a horse, or a wagon, and definitely far faster than walking.

"For a start, if things go the way the gnomes think, then we'll be able to travel continually without having to stop to make camp. And when we're aboard, you can work on your potions and I can work on my projects, our people can train…all of it.

"It makes sense, but I needed you to know, to understand that if I suddenly say 'we need to leave' you knew why, or if anything happens to me, you know to get our baby away from here as fast as possible."

"Nothing's going to happen to you," I swore grimly. "Never."

"That's sweet, my love, but we both know you can't promise that." She sighed.

"If anything happens to you, I'll tear the realm apart to get you back, and you know that."

She smiled, nodding a little amusedly and kissed my cheek, before motioning to the food and drink.

"I know, my love. But right now, if you're going to do this, best to get it out of the way. Eat, drink, and then lay back down. I'll get Sehran. She helped to keep you going last time with her songs as well."

With that, she kissed my cheek one last time, and was up and moving, hurrying from the room into the sitting room, and then bringing both Sehran and Daralen back.

A few more minutes were lost in a progress report—training, the condition of the city, some repairs that were being done to the outer walls, and the golems' progress on connecting the genesis chambers under the tower and replacing the damaged equipment.

Once all of that was done, I lay back, smiling at how excited she'd been at the thought of the new "old" legion equipment that was coming.

The armor wasn't going to be entirely replaced by the chambers, unfortunately—at least, not fully. There were several units that *could* make armor, but they produced a lower grade "scout" armor that was made for the legion of old, and only certain parts.

The cuirass, for example, was available, as were the pauldrons. The vambraces and rerebraces weren't available with the units we had. The legs? Sure. The boots? Nope. As such, there was an absolute shitload of metals and minerals being provided and run through the units. They were churning them out the far side at a rate of a single finished chest, shoulders, and legs in just under an hour—twenty-five in a day.

Now, that wasn't much when you considered we needed about fifteen thousand, and had perhaps ten days to two weeks at most.

But when you then realized that the rest of the city's armorers were working around the clock to keep up, and they were barely managing that and they were only making the other bits?

It was impressive.

Then add in that the swords, shields, maces, axes, and crossbows were being made in another machine, and a third was making bolts and arrows?

It became a little more impressive.

Finally, add in that there were five more machines that could be set up to do similar that were being made or repaired, and in a few days, we should be able to get up to somewhere around seventy a day.

Again, not perfect, but for troops that had fuck all? It was going to be a hell of a change. For now, they were wearing armor that had been looted, repaired, scraped together, and dug out of haylofts and from under beds.

I was also amused that "Captain Tim" had lasted seven hours in training—far longer than I expected—before giving in and begging Daralen for a second-in-command from the legion.

From the nudge-nudge that I saw Sehran giving Oracle and how she gestured at Daralen where the legion primus couldn't see, I got the feeling that there might be a little more than "training" going on there in the future between those two, and I stifled a grin.

All that to say that when I lay back, the world was more or less back up to date, and I was ready for the Constellation again. I drew in a deep breath, and then reminded myself that Oracle was with me, as was Sehran, their presences an anchor through our shared bond. Jenae had also sent word that She would be watching this attempt closely—"just to observe," She said—but I knew that She'd also offer a little subtle guidance if needed.

"You're certain you're ready?" Oracle asked, a touch of concern in her voice.

I nodded. "As ready as I'll ever be. The second ring is ready." I smiled at her, knowing it, even without looking. "Besides, we've still got more than enough marks and mana for at least three second-tier stars, possibly four. But I think today, unless something calls to me, I'm going to keep it to two, just in case."

Oracle nodded, though her concern remained evident. "Just be careful. I'd have insisted on no more than two, if you'd been too stupid and mulish to see that yourself. But either way, please, Jax, remember that this is going to be way more complex and higher leveled than the last tier, so stop at one if you need to, okay?"

"I understand," I lied. "And I'll stop if it becomes too much."

"Brace yourself," Sehran murmured.

I snorted. "More like 'bite the pillow, I'm goin' in dry!'"

CHAPTER TWENTY-SEVEN

I smiled, then I closed my eyes and reached out to the Constellation. It appeared more readily now, as if eager to continue our work together. The first ring gleamed with completed knowledge, each star and its orbiting planets shining in perfect harmony.

Between adjacent stars, faint pathways of light had begun to form—bridges of knowledge connecting different domains. I studied these connections carefully, feeling the potential in each.

Enhanced Construction connected to Magical Research, forming a pathway that seemed to pulse with the potential for something new, an enticing blend of building and arcane knowledge.

From Magical Research to Crafting, another pathway glimmered, hinting at the joining of theoretical understanding and practical creation.

The pattern continued around the ring: Crafting to Governance, Governance to Personal Enhancement, Personal Enhancement to Exploration, and completing the circle, Exploration back to Enhanced Construction.

Six potential new stars, each drawing from two domains of the first ring. I focused on the connection between Enhanced Construction and Magical Research, figuring that this would be the natural starting point. As I channeled mana and marks into the pathway, it began to strengthen, solidifying into a more defined bridge of knowledge.

At the midpoint between the two first-ring stars, a new point of light began to form. It started as a mere spark, then grew steadily, drawing power from both source stars until it blazed with its own unique light—neither purely Construction nor purely Magical Research, but something newborn from their union.

Congratulations!

Arcane Architecture represents the fusion of Construction principles with Magical Research, allowing for the creation of structures that are inherently magical in their very design. Buildings created using these principles will channel ambient mana more effectively and could sustain more powerful enchantments with less degradation.

All buildings within your territory that incorporate magical elements can be adjusted and attuned to be 8% more efficient and 10% more durable. Magical structures will require 5% less maintenance over time.

I had gained access to three new worlds that shimmered and solidified as I stared: Sentient Structures, Dimensional Expansion, and Mana Redirection.

More importantly, I'd also received a bonus *legendary* blueprint:

Congratulations! You have received a bonus legendary blueprint:

The Nexus Tower:

The Nexus Tower serves as a central hub for magical energies, collecting ambient mana from the surrounding area and redistributing it to connected structures. When fully operational, it can increase the magical output of all connected buildings by 15% and reduce their mana consumption by 10%.

Construction materials required:

- **500 Orichalcum Ingots**
- **300 Units of Crystal Glass**
- **200 Manastones (high quality or better)**
- **10 Lunarium ingots**
- **50 Units of Etheric Resonance Crystal**
- **10 Greater Golem Cores**

Note: A Nexus Tower can support a network of up to twenty connected magical structures within a five-mile radius. Multiple Nexus Towers may be linked to create larger networks, with diminishing returns for each additional tower.

The knowledge of Arcane Architecture flowed into my mind, a complex tapestry of principles that merged the structural integrity of buildings with the fluid dynamics of magical energies. I saw how foundations could be laid to naturally channel mana from the earth, how walls could be constructed to amplify magical resonances, how entire buildings could be designed to function as massive spell components.

The Nexus Tower blueprint alone was revolutionary—a structure that could serve as the beating heart of a magically active settlement, enhancing everything connected to it. I could already see the real world uses as well: defensive perimeters with enhanced magical barriers, farmers' fields with growth enchantments, entire districts where magical crafting and research would flourish.

Best of all? Slap one of these bad boys on the hull of an airship and just unleash fucking hell from the ship's cannons.

I wanted to, but I didn't linger on these possibilities for long. The connection had been established successfully, and it was time to pick a world to unlock, and then to move on.

I stared into the void, feeling the familiar tug as my consciousness seemed to drift forward, drawn toward the first of the three worlds—Sentient Structures. As before, I found myself falling, my perception shifting until I plummeted through clouds toward an urban landscape unlike anything I'd seen before.

The city below me wasn't just built of stone and wood; no, it was *alive*. The outermost sections were still growing in response to the residents' desires, the innermost looking like they'd spent long years adjusting and refining until every inch was a work of art.

Buildings breathed. Walls shifted subtly, adjusting their thickness and composition in response to weather conditions. Doorways widened or narrowed as people approached, recognizing residents and adjusting their dimensions perfectly. Windows tinted themselves against harsh sunlight or cleared for better views of beautiful sunsets without anyone touching them.

I dropped closer, watching in fascination as an elderly woman approached what looked to be a governmental building. The steps leading to its entrance flattened themselves, becoming a gentle ramp as she neared. The doors swung open without her needing to touch them, and lights inside brightened to compensate for her fading eyesight.

"That's…incredible," I whispered to myself, though no sound escaped me in this vision. I snorted, shaking my head at the thought of this back home on Earth.

Elsewhere, a damaged structure was healing itself. After what must have been some kind of attack, the building's outer wall was regenerating, stone flowing like liquid to seal cracks, reinforcing weakened sections with denser material drawn from deeper within its mass.

As I drifted through the city, I realized the buildings weren't simply reactive—they were intelligent. In a public square, a structure was having a conversation with its occupants, lights pulsing in patterns that somehow translated to language. The people responded not with fear or surprise but with the casual joy of speaking to an old friend.

I paused, hovering near what appeared to be a training facility. Inside, the room *itself* participated in the exercise: floors shifted to challenge balance, walls provided handholds when needed and then retracted them to increase difficulty. The building wasn't just a space for training—it was an active participant, a teacher.

Then I saw it—the connection point between building and creator. A mage stood with palms flat against a foundation stone, eyes closed in concentration. Mana flowed from his hands in distinct patterns, not crafting a spell but something more fundamental—a consciousness. He wasn't enchanting the building; he was awakening it, giving it purpose and awareness.

The vision shifted, and I found myself inside a home during what appeared to be an emergency. A child had fallen ill, and the house itself responded: walls shifted to create better airflow, the temperature adjusted for comfort, even the damn bed changed its shape to better support the fevered child. A doctor hurried in, a pulse of information flowing from the building to the doctor, identifying strains of illness. The building was a caretaker, a guardian.

"They're not just structures," I whispered in awe. "They're literally alive. I mean, they're not thinking, not fully, but…maybe they're like AI?"

I remembered all that shit: when I left Earth, AI was just starting to take off and everyone was either panicked over the potential, or, well, excited about it. But maybe this was the ultimate expression of that?

There was no threat here, just a sort of peaceful, benign interest and a desire to help.

As this understanding crystallized, I rose again, the world falling away as the next world drew me in. The empty void around me between worlds seemed, as always, to be full of magnificent peace instead of the panic-inducing vertigo it should have.

Fuck's sake, I was in the cold of space, after all. I should have at least been a little chilly. Instead, it was just serene and peaceful.

I had a sudden vivid memory of that Stanley Kubrick film, *2001: A Space Odyssey*. It was that same serene sense of scale, or smooth movement, and inexorable change.

This time it was Dimensional Expansion that unfolded below me, an entirely different interpretation of the merger between Construction and Magical Research.

From the outside, the buildings of this world appeared unassuming, even humble—small cottages, modest towers, simple halls that would barely house a family. But as I descended through the roof of one such structure, my perception shifted again and I gasped.

Inside, the space expanded impossibly. A cottage no larger than my quarters back at the tower contained a sprawling manor. A simple tower held an entire university, with great halls and libraries stacked in configurations that defied conventional geometry. What should have been a modest temple opened into a cathedral that could house tens of thousands.

I watched a builder at work, fascinated by his methodology. Rather than stacking stone upon stone, he worked with folds in space itself. With complex gestures and carefully applied mana, he stretched interior dimensions while anchoring them to more modest external boundaries. He wasn't building with wood or stone; he was building with the void itself.

In one particularly insane demonstration, I saw a team of architects gathering around what appeared to be a simple stone arch. As they channeled mana into the keystone, the archway became a portal, leading to an entirely separate structure that existed in a pocket dimension, tethered to the physical world only through this single connection point.

"The ultimate solution to urban crowding," I mused, thinking of the cramped conditions in parts of Gaij. "Or the perfect way to hide something valuable."

Even more impressively, I saw how some spaces were linked to multiple access points. A single grand library could be entered from buildings across the city, or even from different cities entirely, creating a network of knowledge accessible to all yet physically impossible to locate in conventional space.

The applications were mind-fucking.

Secure vaults that existed outside physical reality, training grounds that could simulate any environment, living spaces that could expand to accommodate growing families without requiring new construction: the only limit seemed to be the architect's imagination and mana capacity.

Again, the vision shifted as soon as I understood it, pulling me upward and then down toward the third and final world: Mana Redirection.

This world gleamed with visible currents of energy flowing like rivers through the air, coursing across the land in great streams and eddies. The buildings here weren't particularly amazing to look at, nor did they bend the rules of space. Instead, they served as dams, channels, and locks in an elaborate system of mana control.

A tower stood at a confluence of mana streams, drawing them inward and spinning them into a concentrated vortex before sending them out again in measured, controlled flows. A series of small cottages served as distribution points, each taking a portion of the stream and feeding it to different districts of the city.

In the central square, a grand structure that resembled a fountain collected ambient mana from the surroundings, purified it through a complex internal filtering system, and then released it in a spectacular display that wasn't just beautiful—it was functional, providing magical energy to everything within its reach.

I hovered above a workshop where craftsmen were installing conduits into the walls of a new building. The pipes weren't for water or sewage—they were crystalline channels designed to carry mana throughout the structure, connecting it to the city's greater network. With proper installation, the building would never lack for magical energy, no matter what enchantments or workings its occupants performed.

Most head fucking was the recycling system. Spells cast within these buildings didn't simply expend their mana and disperse it. Instead, the structures collected the residue, refined it, and returned it to the network, creating an efficiency that would make the most conservative mage weep with joy.

"It's not just about the individual building," I realized. "It's an entire ecosystem of magical energy."

In one particularly impressive display, I watched as a mage channeled defensive magic through an entire district during what appeared to be an attack. Rather than having to hold the spell himself, he simply initiated it, and the city's mana network amplified and distributed it, creating a shield that would have required dozens of mages working in concert to maintain conventionally.

A second mage sighed, getting up from his seat, and cast a single spell, linking it to a panel that looked like a tablet computer. The spell hit the screen and vanished like it'd dove into water; then outside, on the walls, a thousand similar panels reproduced the spell, hammering the invaders into glass and soot, before that in turn was sucked into the walls and recycled again.

Glancing at the mage, I saw he'd not even bothered to watch, and was instead sitting, reading a scroll again.

The more I looked, I saw how the system responded to need. During emergencies, mana flowed more heavily to defensive structures and healing centers. During festivals, it redirected to entertainment districts and public spaces. The entire city breathed magic, using it as efficiently as a body uses blood, directing it where it was needed most at any given moment.

The vision began to fade, and I felt myself being drawn back to my physical form. The knowledge settled into my mind like sediment after a flood: sticky, rich, and ready to be used over and over again.

I knew what I wanted. The worlds of Dimensional Expansion and Mana Redirection were incredible, offering solutions to problems I hadn't even fully accepted I had yet. But Sentient Structures? That was something else. The idea of buildings that could think, adapt, and serve not just as spaces but as active participants in the empire's growth…that was a power I couldn't ignore.

Especially here, with a great tower that had no wisp. Hell, it was a solution for all the great towers, as well as any other structure that had enslaved custodians. I could free them and ask them to help me train the new sentience. If they chose not to?

Hell, I could hardly blame them, but at least there was another option now.

With that thought at the top of my mind, I reached out and selected Sentient Structures as my focus. The connection formed instantly. Knowledge flooded into my mind—architectural principles that incorporated consciousness matrices, foundation stones that could serve as primitive brains, methods for imprinting purpose and personality into the very materials of construction.

I felt the strain building again, but I was determined to continue. The second ring of the Constellation was open to me now, and I intended to explore it—one connection at a time. Besides, sure, there was a little strain, but it wasn't that much, now was it?

As the notification confirmed my choice, I couldn't help but smile at the possibilities. Soon, the Tower of Gaij wouldn't just be a structure I controlled—it would be a willing, conscious ally in my plans for the empire.

Congratulations!

You have unlocked Sentient Structures from the Arcane Architecture specialization.

All buildings within your territory that incorporate consciousness matrices will have a 7% increased efficiency in their designated purpose. The complexity of tasks that can be delegated to Sentient Structures increases by one tier.

You have also received a bonus rare blueprint:

The Awakened Citadel

The Awakened Citadel serves as both fortress and guardian, with a fully developed consciousness capable of independent decision-making within parameters set by its master.

The Citadel can manage its own defenses, redirect internal resources as needed, and even communicate with its inhabitants to coordinate during emergencies.

Construction materials required:

- **400 Orichalcum Ingots**
- **200 Units of Crystal Glass**
- **150 Manastones (high quality or better)**
- **100 Units of Soul-Resonant Stone**
- **5 Lunarium Ingots**
- **5 Greater Golem Cores**
- **1 Sentience Matrix Crystal (legendary quality)**

Note: The Awakened Citadel develops its personality based on its master's character and the experiences during its first year of consciousness. Regular

interaction during this formative period is crucial to ensure proper development.

I stared at the list of required ingredients or construction materials or whatever. Most of it was obvious enough, but a "sentience matrix crystal"? What the hell was one of those?

Fuck it. I shook it off, figuring I'd ask Jenae after this, and I moved on, turning my attention to the next pathway. I'd decided that as things had gone with the first ring, I needed to unlock all six of stars on the second ring at some point, though maybe I'd not unlock every option in them.

As such, I was going to go straight ahead and unlock the one between Magical Research and Crafting. That was the most obvious one for me right now, mainly because if we could improve our creations, be that weapons and armor, potions—or hell, the buildings themselves—that would keep more people alive.

Again, I channeled fifty thousand mana and twenty-five marks, watching as the connection strengthened and a new star began to form.

I suspected that the seeming "ease" of accessing such rare and wonderous buildings and creations was offset by little details like it taking a year or ten's damn hard production to make a single one of them, but I shook that off and moved on.

Congratulations!

Artifice represents the perfect union of magical theory and practical crafting, enabling the creation of items that transcend traditional enchantment to become truly magical in their fundamental nature. These artifacts blur the line between crafted item and spell, often developing unique properties over time.

All magical items created within your territory have a chance to be 10% more potent and 15% more durable. Crafters gain a 5% chance to imbue items with semi-sentient properties that allow them to adapt to their users' needs.

I blinked as the star before me flared to life. Rolling walls of flame and spouts of expelled gasses were unleashed in a flash of nuclear rebirth. I stared in wonder as I gained access to three new worlds, each slowly thawing from the cold depths of space: Self-Evolving Items, Bound Servitors, and Artifact Resonance.

Congratulations!

You receive a bonus rare blueprint:

The Artificer's Forge

The Artificer's Forge combines the principles of traditional smithing with advanced magical theory to create a workspace where truly extraordinary items can be crafted. Items created within this forge gain a 20% chance to develop unique magical properties beyond their intended design and a chance to be 25% more likely to achieve artifact status.

Construction materials required:

- **400 Orichalcum Ingots**
- **200 Units of Dragon-Fire Imbued Brick**
- **150 Manastones (high quality or better)**
- **100 Units of Lunarium**
- **80 Units of Elemental Essence (minimum 20 of each primary element)**
- **5 Greater Golem Cores**

Note: The Artificer's Forge may only be operated by crafters who have achieved at least journeyman status in both their crafts and in greater magical theory. Be warned! The forge will also bond to its primary artificer, enhancing their capabilities but limiting its use by others.

The knowledge of Artifice was even more complex than Arcane Architecture, combining intricate crafting techniques with advanced magical theory in ways that made almost no sense to me. I saw methods for weaving spells directly into the materials of an item during its creation, techniques for binding elemental essences that would continue to grow and evolve, ways to create items that could learn from their users and adapt accordingly.

I saw swords where every section, from the coal that was used to heat the ores to the leather that formed the scabbard, was filled with specialized, researched, and studied spellforms, resources, and elemental cores.

I watched as a sword grew from a simple weapon to something that the gods would fear and that stars would shudder and hide their light from.

The Artificer's Forge could revolutionize our magical crafting capabilities, allowing us to create items that would have been legendary even in the height of the old empire. Weapons that grew with their wielders, armor that adapted to different threats, tools that anticipated their users' needs…the possibilities were staggering.

But…it was something that would bind to a single user. If I gave this to Thorn, for example, she could create armor of wondrous might…and for anyone else working at the forge? It'd be just a good forge.

As much as this was incredible, in some ways, it was also a nightmare.

How many crafters would curse her name? How often would someone doubt that anything she ever did was just the magic, not her own skill?

No. No, this had potential, but it was also a possible poisoned chalice. And that wasn't down to Jenae; that was because of the gulf between how the gods saw the world and how we, those who lived here, saw it.

I felt the familiar sensation of transition as my consciousness was drawn toward the first world: Self-Evolving Items.

The star field around me blurred, and then I plummeted through layers of clouds toward a landscape that shimmered with potential.

This world wasn't defined by its architecture or natural features, but by what its inhabitants carried. As my perception settled, focusing on a bustling marketplace, I saw items that defied conventional understanding of crafting. I suspected that if I looked hard enough, I'd find "made in Taiwan" under something here.

A warrior walked through the crowd, a sword sheathed at her hip. What caught my attention wasn't its craftsmanship—though that was exceptional—but how it changed. As I watched, tiny runes along its blade shifted position, reorganizing themselves in response to something only they could sense. The metal itself seemed to ripple occasionally, like liquid caught in a moment of transformation.

When a commotion broke out—a thief attempting to flee with stolen goods—the warrior drew her blade. It gleamed in the sunlight, but more remarkably, it adjusted. The previously straight edge developed subtle serrations, perfect for catching and holding the thief's clothing. The pommel extended slightly for better balance during the pursuit. These weren't dramatic transformations, but precise, purposeful adjustments, and as she ran, others around her shifted as well.

People's clothing flared to prevent injury as the thief shoved their way past, the item the thief had stolen grew heavier, and doors nearby slid shut and locked themselves. In the distance, as the thief rounded a corner and vanished from sight, the warrior, even clad in heavy armor, was closing step by step, as their armor changed and adjusted, disappearing after them.

It was a thousand different details all merging at once, and yet the difference? It reminded me of all those nanite movies, right before they went rogue, when everything was incredible.

I drifted closer, my attention caught by an elderly scholar hunched over ancient texts. His glasses adjusting themselves had caught my eye: the lenses thickened or thinned as he moved between different documents, aligning to his changing needs. When he reached for a quill, the frames extended tiny supportive struts down his nose, anticipating his change in posture.

"They're learning," I whispered to the void around me. "Not just responding to commands. Fuck me, they anticipate what people are going to do, what they need."

My attention shifted to a young apprentice mage struggling with a spell. The wand in her hand seemed unremarkable until I looked closer. With each attempt at the incantation, minute changes occurred in the wand's composition—channels shifting, the core material redistributing slightly. It was optimizing itself, adapting to her specific magical capabilities and the particular spell she was attempting.

When she finally succeeded, the wand stabilized its new configuration before subtly inscribing the pattern into its own substance, learning and remembering for next time.

A smith caught my eye next, working at a forge unlike any I'd seen before. Rather than shaping metal with hammer and tongs alone, he seemed to be…conversing with it. His hammer strikes were gentle, almost suggestive, and the metal responded not just to the physical force but to his intent.

As I watched, he completed a breastplate that gleamed with more than just polish. He presented it to a waiting customer, who smiled and pulled it on immediately. Not only was it cool enough that they didn't, you know, scream, burst into flames, or die from the experience, but it was already changing again.

The armor adjusted, tightening here, loosening there, until it perfectly fit. But more impressive was what happened when another warrior, clearly a rival, approached with a glare. Without any visible command, the breastplate hardened, thickened subtly at vital points—preparing for the demonstration of strength that was clearly coming.

"The items aren't just tools," I whispered. "They're symbiotes. They work with the host, or the user or whatever. Fuck me, that's incredible."

I saw gardening implements that developed specialized edges for different plants, cooking pots that adjusted their thickness based on what was being prepared, and quills that changed their cut based on the type of script being written.

Each item contained the seed of evolution, embedded during its creation, that allowed it to grow beyond its original purpose.

The last thing I saw was a family heirloom, just a little pendant passed from a mother to her daughter. As the girl took it, the metal warmed and the design shifted slightly, changing to match the style of the new owner while maintaining hints and connections to its history. The jewelry wasn't just decorative; it was a living goddamn record of its lineage, evolving as it moved from generation to generation.

As I learned this, realizing the potential, I was lifted away, drawn up and through the clouds again toward the second world. As I went, I stared back, hoping for a hint of the potential this shit offered to an alchemist.

Nothing popped out to demonstrate it though, so I turned and faced ahead, seeing the next world as it spun into place: Bound Servitors.

This world had a distinctive energy. Where Self-Evolving Items had felt collaborative, Bound Servitors radiated with purpose and devotion. I descended toward what appeared to be a grand estate, where the boundary between item and entity had been beautifully blurred.

A nobleman sat in his study, dictating a letter. Instead of writing it himself or speaking to a human scribe, he addressed what appeared to be an ornate desk set. At his words, a quill rose of its own accord, dipped precisely into an inkwell, and began to transcribe with perfect penmanship. When he paused to reconsider a phrase, the quill hovered patiently, sometimes suggesting alternatives by quickly scribbling options in the margin.

Outside, the estate's grounds were maintained not by human gardeners but by tools that worked independently. Shears trimmed hedges with artistic precision, rakes gathered fallen leaves, watering cans moved from plant to plant, each seeming to know exactly what was needed where.

"They're not just enchanted to move," I observed. "They have purpose—almost personality."

I watched a woman enter her home after a long journey. Before she could speak, a teapot began heating itself, cups arranged themselves on a tray, and a comfortable chair pulled itself out invitingly. These weren't random magical animations—they were coordinated, anticipatory, designed to serve specific needs with almost loving attention.

The boundary between servitor and sentience seemed delicate. These weren't golems or those magical servants—what did they call the fuckers…homunculi? No, these still remained objects, but objects imbued with enough purpose and awareness to act independently within their defined roles.

They were magical AIs again: useful, and not, well, shitty copies designed by corpo scumbags to rip us all off. I kept looking, seeing more everywhere I looked.

Next was a battlefield I glimpsed briefly: soldiers loaded up not just with weapons but with entire kits of bound servitors. Medical bags that could apply basic first aid without guidance, arrows that could adjust their flight paths or blunt their heads to avoid injuring allies, shields that positioned themselves better to block incoming threats even when their bearers were distracted. The advantage this gave them over their more conventionally equipped opponents was insane.

In a workshop, I saw the creation process. An artificer worked with intense concentration, not just crafting an object but infusing it with purpose through elaborately structured spells. Unlike normal enchantment, which layered magic onto a completed item, this process integrated purpose from the very beginning—essence and function developing at the same time, creating an object that understood its role at the most fundamental level.

"They're not golems, waiting to be told what to do. They're…they're almost AI, but the potential that we were all sold, not the bullshit." I compared these elegant, specialized servitors to the more generalized golems I'd encountered. "And they're not just following commands—they're watching, waiting and helping. They're seeing what we need, and doing it before we know we need it."

As the vision shifted again, pulling me toward the third and final world, Artifact Resonance, I cast a glance behind me, wondering whether it was possible, or whether this was the path to a magical Skynet.

The thought of all those things going mental and killing their creators was a terrifying one.

The final world ahead of me vibrated with harmony; every object seemed to hum with connection to something larger than itself. As I descended into a bustling city, I saw how items carried by different people seemed to acknowledge each other, subtle pulses of energy passing between them like secret greetings.

In a council chamber, advisors to some ruler gathered, each bearing what appeared to be a symbol of office. As they assembled, their artifacts—rings, medallions, scepters—began to resonate together, creating a harmonious field of energy that enhanced clarity of thought and honesty of purpose. The items weren't just symbols; they were participants in governance, ensuring the council functioned at its best and watching over them.

This, again, was a hoped-for and feared outcome of AI. But instead of ruling these people, they existed only to help.

A military company marched through the streets, their weapons and armor creating a synchronous field of protection that was stronger than any individual piece could generate alone. I watched as they encountered a threat—some kind of magical attack—and their equipment responded in perfect coordination, shields reinforcing each other, weapons drawing power from the unified field to strike with devastating effectiveness.

"It's like they're all parts of a hive mind—each aware, but the more that join together, the more they can do," I muttered, watching the interplay of energies.

In a magical academy, students wore simple amulets that seemed unremarkable until they gathered for lessons. As they worked together, their amulets linked, creating a shared pool of mana that any of them could draw from.

More experienced students' artifacts strengthened the capabilities of those worn by novices, creating a system where learning itself was enhanced by connection.

I watched a family having dinner, their table setting more than mere plates and utensils. As they shared their meal, subtle energies flowed between their heirloom dishes, glasses, and cutlery, creating an atmosphere that enhanced the flavors of the food and the warmth of their conversation. These weren't powerful magical artifacts in the traditional sense—they were every day, almost cheap items that gained significance through their connections to one another and to the family they served.

Most impressive was what I glimpsed in a temple—worshippers bearing small tokens that, individually, held little power. But as they gathered in prayer, these tokens resonated together, amplifying their mana and creating a tangible connection to their deity. The principle wasn't limited to religion—I saw similar resonance in guild halls, markets, even taverns where regular patrons' personal cups somehow made the drinks they contained more satisfying when used together.

In a master artificer's workshop, I finally understood the underlying principle. As she crafted what appeared to be a wedding ring, she incorporated elements that would specifically resonate with a matching ring she'd completed earlier. But she didn't stop there—she added layers of resonance that would connect with the couple's future home, their eventual children's cradles, the tools of their respective trades. She wasn't just creating an item; she was establishing a node in a potential network of connection that would grow throughout the couple's life together.

"It's not about the power of any one piece," I realized. "It's about the bonds, the openness and willingness of each bit when they work together."

The vision began to fade, drawing me back toward my physical form. The knowledge of Artifice settled into my mind—complex, rich, and filled with possibilities I'd never considered before.

I knew immediately which specialization I wanted to unlock first. While Self-Evolving Items and Artifact Resonance offered incredible potential, Bound Servitors represented an immediate, practical advantage we desperately needed, even as it scared me shitless with the whole Skynet scenario.

Hell, *all* those sections scared me in one way or another. I hesitated for a few seconds, before shaking it off. If I could make a set of alchemical tools that helped me? That alone could save lives.

With our resources stretched thin and challenges mounting on all sides, having objects that could independently perform critical tasks would be invaluable.

Crossbows that could be set up on the walls to fire on the enemy, gates that could lock and open when needed…I'd seen this in similar ways before: the crystal doorways of certain structures, as an example, in the prax and the towers.

They knew who I was, and they let me through, and yet they were fucking *doors*. How the hell they managed that was beyond me.

I reached out, selecting Bound Servitors as my focus. The connection formed; knowledge flooded into my mind. Filled it with hints for imbuing purpose during crafting, techniques for establishing rules that would guide independent action, ways to create items that could interpret and fulfill their owners' needs without constant direction.

Congratulations!

You have unlocked Bound Servitors from the Artifice specialization.

All items created with servitor enchantments within your territory will have a 10% increased operational duration and a 7% greater range of autonomous function.

The complexity of tasks that can be assigned to Bound Servitors increases by one tier.

You have also received a bonus rare blueprint:

The Majordomo's Kit

The Majordomo's Kit consists of a coordinated set of Bound Servitors designed to maintain and protect a significant property without human oversight.

The kit includes self-operating cleaning implements, guardian objects that can detect and respond to threats, maintenance tools that can perform basic repairs, and a central controlling item that coordinates all activities and can communicate with the property's owner.

Construction materials required:

- **300 Orichalcum Ingots**
- **200 Units of Enchanted Wood**
- **150 Manastones (high quality or better)**
- **100 Units of Soul-Receptive Material**
- **5 Lunarium Ingots**
- **10 Specialized Tool Components (minimum masterwork quality)**
- **1 Binding Matrix Crystal (rare quality or better)**

Note: The Majordomo's Kit develops its operational priorities based on patterns established during its first month of service. Special attention should be paid during this period to ensure the kit understands the property owner's preferences correctly.

As I absorbed this knowledge, my mind was already racing with applications. The Tower of Gaij could practically maintain itself with a properly implemented Majordomo's Kit. Our artificers could create medical kits that would treat injuries without requiring a healer's presence, weapons that could defend unconscious soldiers, tools that could continue with the shitty, time-consuming jobs even when their users needed rest.

It was all incredible, and yet…the pain.

I could feel it building, and the distant worry of Oracle and Sehran. I felt the eyes of Jenae on me, and I swore I could almost feel her hand outstretched, ready to stop me if I continued on much further.

I wanted to.

Fuck me, I did. But, I'd seen that these new technologies all needed things we didn't have. They all brought incredible bonuses, but they needed friggin' *lunarium*, for example, which I was fairly sure was that metal from the moon…you know, the one that they traded for *in thimble sizes.*

Ingots of it could create weapons that evolved already. Without needing all this additional bullshit.

I wanted to continue, I really did, but I had to be realistic. Nothing I was getting here was going to help us in the short term. Better to stop now, without the rest of the day or longer being written off, and instead continue this when I was on the makeshift vessel—provided I could get it working—or when the baby was born and I was back in Dravith, a portal locked down to our people that could carry me from here to there in an eyeblink.

The real gain here was the percentage increases, not the blueprints I was seeing, and I'd forgotten that in the short-term dopamine hit of powerful structures.

For whatever reason the stat points I'd gained when I'd used the constellation last weren't included this time around, which was annoying, but I got the feeling considering how absolutely tailored to me these blueprints were, that was why.

If the cost of things I really needed being given instead of toenail clipper blueprints, was that I didn't get the stat points, I could be a big boy and live with that.

I went to stop. Then, grumbling, I decided I'd have one last look and *then* stop. I could do that, right? I fucking lied to myself.

I moved on to the next connection, between Crafting and Governance. This pathway seemed subtler than the previous two, yet as I channeled power into it, wincing in building pain, the emerging star burned with a steady, profound light.

Congratulations!

You have unlocked Infrastructure from the second ring of the Constellation of Secrets.

Infrastructure represents the systematic organization of crafting and resources within a governed territory, creating networks of production and distribution that function with unprecedented efficiency. This goes beyond

simple logistics to create self-sustaining systems that anticipate needs and adapt to changing conditions.

All production chains within your territory will grow to be up to 12% more efficient. Resource allocation improves by 8%, reducing waste and ensuring supplies reach where they are most needed. Construction projects gain a 5% chance to require fewer materials than initially calculated without sacrificing quality.

I had gained access to three new worlds, each of which would unlock further options: Adaptive Supply Chains, Crisis Response Systems, and Resource Optimization. Lastly, I got a bonus *epic* blueprint:

Congratulations! You have received a bonus epic blueprint:

The Grand Manufactory:

The Grand Manufactory serves as a central hub for coordinated production, with specialized facilities to assist in all manufacturing and crafting within the territory. Materials processing, component creation, and final assembly may be shifted to take place under a single roof, with magical conveyance systems moving resources and products through each stage of production.

Construction materials required:

- **600 Steel Ingots**
- **300 Orichalcum Ingots**
- **200 Units of Enchanted Wood**
- **150 Manastones (average or higher in size)**
- **100 Units of Glass**
- **8 Greater Golem Cores**

Note: The Grand Manufactory may be specialized toward different production focuses (weapons, armor, magical items, etc.), with each specialization providing additional bonuses to its specific field.

Infrastructure brought an additional dimension to my understanding of governance—one focused not just on laws and people, but on the physical systems that supported civilization. I saw intricate networks of supply and distribution, methods for anticipating resource needs before they became critical, ways to ensure that every citizen had access to what they needed when they needed it.

The Grand Manufactory would transform our production capabilities, turning what had been scattered workshops and individual crafters into a coordinated industrial force.

Shit, it would take the system that I was most impressed with, the armor and weapons facilities I'd been so proud of Daralen and others for getting moving, and it would basically supersize it. With a factory like that, we could equip our army in a fraction of the time, produce magical items in unprecedented numbers, and ensure that no resource went to waste.

My strength was more than just flagging now, and I forced myself to speak, both to Oracle and Sehran, and also to Jenae.

"One more," I croaked. "I just need to pick a specialization and then…"

"No, my champion." It was Jenae's voice, and the Constellation of Secrets suddenly poofed into sooty smoke, fading on the breeze. ***"The Constellation is closed to you now, for a month, and then we can reevaluate it. You have pushed too hard, too far, and too fast. You must rest, consolidate your gains, and most of all, you must prepare.***

"I gave you the space to lead as you would desire, but I cannot stand by as you damage yourself with my gift. I am well aware of the addiction of knowledge, and I sense it in you now, the need to unlock more, to improve. Yes, I am cognizant of the improvements you see yourself bringing. But no more. Now, please, rest, Jax—rest and prepare, for tomorrow you will receive the news of the march of Kronk, and all that can be done, must be."

With that, even as I tried to speak, to rouse myself to take action and spread the word, a warmth flowed through me, and I fell—not physically, but mentally, consciously—as the world drifted away from me, and I retreated into a deep, dreamless sleep.

CHARACTER SHEET

Name: Jax Amon				
Title: Godslayer				
Class: Mage Imperator (Fire Focus)			**Renown**: Imperial Scion, Prince of Dravith, Master of Himnel and Narkolt, Godslayer, Mage Imperator	
Level: 51			**Progress**: 9,784,997/12,000,000	
Patron: Jenae, Goddess of Fire and Exploration			**Points to Distribute**: 0 **Meridian Points to Invest**: 1	
Stat	**Current points**	**Description**	**Effect**	**Progress to next level**
Agility	100	Governs dodge and movement	+1000% maximum movement speed and reflexes. Gained Temporal Fluidity	N/A
Charisma	61 (56)	Governs likely success to charm, seduce, or threaten	+51% success chance in interactions with other beings	29/100
Constitution	125 (123)	Governs health and health regeneration	2460 health, regen 160 points per 600 seconds, (each point invested now worth 20 health). Gained: Genetic Storage	N/A
Dexterity	100	Governs ability with weapons and crafting success	+100% to weapon proficiency, +100% to the chances of crafting success. Gained: Master Craftsman's Touch	N/A
Endurance	73 (670)	Governs stamina and stamina regeneration	2190 stamina, regen 53 points per 30 seconds (each point invested now worth 30 stamina)	4/100
Intelligence	206	Governs base mana and number of spells able to be learned	2260 mana, spell capacity: 102 (100 + 2, +200 mana from items). Gained:	N/A

			Hyper Cognition & Mana Manipulation	
Luck	79	Governs overall chance of bonuses	+69% chance of a favorable outcome	41/100
Perception	110 (100)	Governs ranged damage and chance to spot traps or hidden items	+100% ranged damage, +100% chance to spot traps or hidden items. Gained: Essence Sight	N/A
Strength	83 (80)	Governs damage with melee weapons and carrying capacity	+83 damage with melee weapons, +80% maximum carrying capacity	3/100
Wisdom	105 (95)	Governs mana regeneration and memory	+1400% mana recovery, 16 points per minute. Gained: Mana Manipulation	N/A

CHAPTER TWENTY-EIGHT

I woke slowly, stretching luxuriously as the silken sheets moved. The coolness of the patches I'd not been laying in contrasted nicely with my bed-warmed body. I yawned, enjoying the additional warmth of the sunlight that streamed in through the balcony doors that had been left wide open overnight.

It took me awhile to get my brain rebooted and going again, and feeling the strain—it was like I'd been hammering it at the gym, but in my skull instead of my muscles—and so I just lay there for a few seconds, staring at the ceiling.

I thought about all that additional knowledge, all those unlocks and all the worlds shared with me…and I thought about how fucking stupid I was.

Why the hell did I just keep going? I mean, I always pushed one step further, then just another, and then I found myself in goddamn bed again, with my brain feeling like a bowl of porridge and no clue how I'd gotten here.

I just knew I was going to get some grief for this.

I sat up, blinking, and looked around the room. I was alone, and I sighed, before "feeling" for the others with the bond.

Knowing instantly that Oracle—thanks to the bond—was only a few doors away and that she and Sehran were close enough that if something happened, we could be to each other in seconds was great.

Then I snorted, realizing that a second reason I was feeling low wasn't just that I'd put my brain in the blender and pressed "puree" again. It was because I had to admit to myself that waking, naked in my bed and alone just wasn't the same when I didn't have Bane or Tang to traumatize by flashing.

It was a stupid thing, and if I had to try to explain it to anyone else, I knew that that it'd make me sound like some kind of degenerate—not because I was happy being naked around other males, but because I wasn't involved or trying to be with any of them.

Even thinking it through like this it felt and sounded wrong, but the simple truth was, I missed my friends. I missed knowing that Bane was right there, hiding behind a chair and watching the world as I slept or worked or whatever.

Knowing that he was always just there, and that if an assassin tried to get to me, they'd be in for a world of hurt? That was a relief, frankly. Although I could feel Bane and the others drawing closer by the hour, I also knew damn well that they weren't here yet and that it'd be weeks more until they arrived.

I sighed, climbed out of bed, and hit the bathroom, did the necessities and then Scoured myself with that most useful spell. On a whim, I stepped out onto the balcony to feel the warmth of the sun on my bones, and stretched, shivering as a sudden errant and high up breeze hit me.

It was cold—surprisingly so, considering how warm the sun was—but that was the nature of the world, when you were over half a mile up.

That—of course—was when two of the resident succubai chose to streak past, and I mean "streak" in the sense of fast movement. They were clothed, or at least as clothed as they tended to be.

They got an eyeful of me, though, and I almost shouted about how cold it was up there reflexively, then decided that it'd be a lost cause.

My morning thoroughly derailed and with me feeling disgruntled, but without any real reason for it, I got dressed, and addressed the real issue that was squatting right in the back of my mind.

Being told no like a puppy chewing a shoe by Jenae and having my access to the Constellation of Secrets revoked wasn't something I was happy about, even more so because I damn well knew that she was entirely right to do it.

I knew I was approaching my limit. The more intense data dumps and the upgrades that were coming from higher tiers were having more of an effect as I went on. But the improvements?

A five percent increase in productivity was the same as an extra half a day of work achieved every ten days.

When you were needing to fight a battle, that was a hell of a difference.

Regardless, though, I made myself go all "whoosah" and channel out the annoyance and irritation, and get on with my day. I still had a lot of things to get done and…

"Jax, can we talk?"

I was so close to shouting "Fucking now what?!?" as the divine voice echoed in my ears, that I had to physically swallow it down. But I knelt and bowed my head, as was appropriate, as Sint reached out to me.

"Lord Sint," I greeted him, and I felt as much as heard the snort of amusement.

"Jax, although I appreciate the deference, I can also feel the annoyance and irritation radiating from you. Is this a bad time?"

"Honestly, no," I admitted. "I'm sorry, Sint. I'm just a little grumpy with myself this morning."

"Have you considered why this might be?"

I stifled the urge to shout "Yeah, because you're all constantly pestering me." Mainly because it really wasn't true. They gave me plenty of space, and when I shouted to them—or let my mouth get me in the shit—they came and helped straightaway.

Hell, Darakin had spent days training with me, and He'd really helped me to take the next step from where I was, to closer to actual godhood.

As such, well, I needed to grow up.

"I think it's just a lot of little things," I admitted. "It's the effect of dozens of little jobs and feeling that I'm the wrong one to be dealing with most of them all the time."

"That is, I believe, called 'life.'" He sounded amused. ***"You get true sustained peace and quiet, usually only when you are in the grave. As such, though, and with understanding the position you are in, I have a suggestion, if you'd hear it?"***

"Always." I nodded, and smiled, genuinely this time. I did like Sint, after all. "And sorry for being a dick."

"You're fine. It is the nature of your position that you are constantly the 'man of the hour.' Had you sought this role for yourself, I would offer you quotes about 'getting what you have striven for,' but considering I am well aware that you have simply taken the next logical step to protect those you love, I feel this would be an unkindness.

"Regardless, a little advice before we get to the real reason for my visit, if I may, is to ask that if you feel you are the wrong person for these tasks, why are you doing them?"

I shot an annoyed glare upward, and opened my mouth to make a comment about him picking a fucking side, when He went on.

"I do not mean 'why are you the prince.' I believe you are the right man for the role, most definitely. No, what I mean is why are you seeking to make these decisions and lead these projects yourself?"

"Because they need to be done."

"They do. As an example, I presume that Primus Daralen is your choice of right hand to lead the siege when the enemy are at your gates, and you will intend on taking a more 'involved' role?"

"Yeah," I admitted.

"Then why are you creating a bottleneck with you being involved and giving these orders directly?" He asked calmly. ***"Why not give those who have the relevant skill the job and simply ask for a report once per day? You repeatedly comment that 'Amon didn't do this shit' and you insist that you are offloading the day-to-day smaller jobs, but then you frequently do not."***

"I…" I paused, then groaned as I saw what I was doing, *again*. "I do this," I admitted. "I want to be involved and so I run from project to project, and try to be involved and then I can't give all the attention I need to any one aspect, and it suffers."

"I suspect that is an unkindness, but yes, you are attempting to run everything, despite the burdens upon you. To put it another way: are you the leader of this city? Or do you intend to be, long term?"

"Hell no." I snorted. "I'm expecting that Seraphina will run it, but—" I sighed, seeing what He was getting at. "But in that case, why doesn't she start right now?"

"I see that you do not need my advice here after all."

I could literally feel the bastard smiling at me.

"Thank you." I sighed. "Right, for me, I have a few things that I *need* to be doing and that's working on my magic, training and getting the gnomes on track. Beyond that, I don't know what else I'm needed for directly, but I do get the point."

"Delegation is a skill, Jax, and it's something that you must work at to maintain. You spent your life relying only on yourself or your brother. And now, here, with the added pressures of rank and people bringing these problems to you for a solution, it is only natural that you would seek to deal with it. You must focus and delegate, though. It is that or drive yourself mad with the strain. As things stand, with you being unavailable, others have taken up the slack, but they do so with an expectation that you will return and direct soon. As such, these tasks are not being completed, just dealt with. I recommend you spend a little time formally handing them over, and then focus on what you, and you alone, can do."

"Yeah. I get it." I grunted. "Seraphina has been running the tower for seven centuries, and the city for a lot of that as well, even if unofficially. So, why the hell am I wasting my time doing what I'm not that good at? Hell, I've seen her running this way and that behind me, and I figured she was dealing with the extra details, and I was glad. But now? I could just leave her to deal with it all and give me a daily report, couldn't I?"

"My, what a good idea," Sint rumbled, amused.

"Yeah, right." I snorted.

"There is more, Jax. We are limited in what we can share, without breaking the rules, especially with an intervention called and the additional scrutiny we all must labor under. But as you stand to hear of this news soon anyway—in less than a day—I may share it now without censure. The Dark Legion of Nimon rides to attack you as well."

"Oh, for fuck's sake, seriously?" I groaned. "Anyone else? Has the fucking Easter Bunny found a pair of Uzis and is marching too?"

"I know not the status of the 'Easter Bunny,' but the Dark Legion marches with a full five thousand in strength, an entire legion. They approach from the southeast. Their stronghold in that direction—again, should you examine a map, you would find it, so this does not break the rules—has been emptied to provide these forces. They were dispatched some time ago, with the intention of taking Gaij."

"Five fucking *thousand*?" I groaned. I mean, we had more troops, overall; we were somewhere between fifteen and twenty thousand in total. But of those, we had less than six hundred in the legion that were to the point that I could really rely on them the way I would full legionnaires, and then it was the city guard, who were frankly as much use as tits on a fish

The rest of our forces were either freed slaves, fighters, or people who wanted a change of direction, and although they were all undergoing legion training as aspirants, they were literally green in the ways of the legion.

Fuck, it wasn't like I could just stand them on the wall with spears and tell them to stab anything that climbed over it.

These were going to be facing a fully trained legion of the dark dickheads.

Against Kronk? Yeah, between my troops' backgrounds as slaves and fighters and the walls, I was confident in them holding their own, certainly. And the magic we'd begun teaching them would be a game changer, but fuck me sideways!

"Just so. However, to make things more interesting, it appears they will arrive approximately a day after the army of Kronk, and they are sworn enemies, meaning that when Kronk finds out about the legion, they are likely to divert to attack them, or…"

"Or more likely, they'll want to take the city as fast as possible so that they have a secure place to defend against them," I finished for Him. "Is Kronk's army on par with the Dark Legion?"

"Not even close," He said firmly. ***"The Dark Legion is made up as you have experienced before. The elites, their core, are more than capable of eliminating Kronk's armies with just the fodder and them. The 'true' Dark legionnaires, as discussed previously, are on par with your own legionnaires."***

"Fuck."

"However…" He almost sounded musing as He clearly tried to drop hints, ***"were the armies of Kronk to encounter the walls closed and held against them,***

and they were to lose their scouts, so as to be unaware of the Dark Legion's presence…"

"Then they'd be ground up like beef against our walls by the Dark Legion, and then we fight a weakened Dark Legion." I grunted as that option clicked into place, and I felt a hell of a lot better suddenly.

"That's still going to be hard, but it could be a lot easier than the alternative. We can up the troops' training, and then blood them against Kronk so they're not as frightened… Shit. Let the Dark Legion kill what's left of Kronk and tire themselves a bit; then we kill the Dark legionnaires, and both Kronk and their stronghold are left weak, ready for us to march in and claim them both."

"Precisely."

"Okay, thank you, Lord Sint. That's going to help a lot. So, you didn't come here to deal with me being a grump, so what can I do for you?" I asked.

"Indeed, I do enjoy our chats, but you are right. Tamat made you an offer some time ago, and this needs to be resolved."

"She did?" I muttered, then grunted. "Shit, yes, the fragment of divinity!"

"Precisely. I understand your reticence. It is a highly powerful fragment, and frankly, as things stand currently, ten percent of Illoth's power is significantly more than ten percent of Tamat's. I say this outright, and upfront, so that there are no misunderstandings.

"The fragment is literally ten percent of her power and divinity, though, and the relevant issue for you, as your semi-mortal form is incapable of corralling or making use of such powers at this stage, is that although it makes little difference to you now, you feel that giving up a more powerful fragment is a loss to you, is this correct?"

"Actually, no," I said. "Look, Sint, it's not that I'm trying to fuck anyone over—it's just that I've been running all day, every day and I keep putting things off because there's so much that always needs to be done. As to the fragment, is it going to make much of a difference to me if I give her this one and take a separate one of hers?"

"In terms of power right now? No," He said. ***"The divine powers that it could grant you are easily replaced by another fragment, and one that you would, frankly, be better suited to. The issue becomes that Tamat stands to gain significantly from this, and the pair of you have always had an…interesting relationship."***

"We piss each other off by breathing," I translated.

"Quite," He agreed. ***"So, the fragment right now will make little difference to you, but when you begin to ascend fully, and you have all ten fragments, then the relative power of a fragment will become much more important. This more powerful fragment would significantly increase your power at that point."***

"Which might be ten centuries or more from now, might never happen, or might be in a month the way things are going," I pointed out. "But Tamat could make use of that power now and it'd help you?"

"It would help us far more than you might understand. Tamat could involve herself directly in your world far more, but she could also take direct action against our enemies here and now…much more potent actions."

"So it's a no-brainer." I groaned. "And I've been putting it off."

"You have, but there are also two more factors to discuss before you make a decision." He hurried on, before I could say more. ***"Chief amongst them is that first the fragment that you choose to bind must be sundered from Tamat, and this is no small task. Should you choose to do this, it will significantly weaken her. And for the period between her sundering and the new fragment being bound, she will be both vulnerable, and, at least in part, mortal.***

"As such, it is possible, even likely, that another will attempt to attack her, and harvest more from her. This is a risk that she and you must run, because the call of a fragment that is unbound, unlinked, and free to be claimed is as ambrosia to the gods. Even for us, her fellows and her sworn family, to have such an incredible temptation is…unwise.

"Traditionally the fragments are exchanged only through direct combat, and they transfer at the point of death. For you, during the fight with Nimon, you appeared to be unaware, and again when you fought Illoth, for us, it was as if everything that we needed, desired, and required was available for a hundredth of a second.

"That was all, and yet in that time—I say this with shame, but you must understand—even I considered attacking you. I believe that I could have refused the temptation even had it been there longer, but understand this: the power and compressed divinity that you so cavalierly offered to show me and to bind in front of me upon the cupola of Himnel was a temptation beyond all others, and that was safely hidden within yourself, where we all know—the gods, I mean—that if I was to kill you and attempt to claim it, it would simply be lost.

"Still, despite all of that, all that I am, and all that you may yet be, I was tempted. I felt the yearning and ravenous need of my hunger. That is the risk that you face. Should you do this, should you and Tamat agree to trade these fragments, that power will be out in the world, in a condensed form, ready and viable for plunder. We cannot shield you when this happens, for to do so would be to expose you to our most primal urges as well.

"So think on it, Jax, before you make this deal. It could cost you everything, should Nimon or one of the others strike before you can claim it and escape.

"Lastly, and I warn you on this, despite knowing that this is not Tamat's intention, but knowing of the hunger and need, when you hold out a fragment, unbound and available, her every instinct will be to strike you down and take it, while keeping her own, despite the agreement. The risk is not small."

"Okay, so risky as fuck for a little gain to Tamat, and none to me," I said softly. "I'm sorry, Sint, but that's not really a good deal for me."

"No. As it stands, there is a significant risk to you. Should you agree, however, there are also two upsides to it. First and foremost, the fragment you bind grows more powerful when it is bound in a place of its own power. The Fragment of Death, as before, on the field of battle surrounded by thousands of the recently killed, surged and then was absorbed into yourself, granting you a significant boost in an already highly powerful fragment."

"And this one is what?" I tapped my fingers on my chest, feeling the fragment inside me, but very deliberately not summoning it out.

"It is a fragment of true darkness, not merely the absence of light, as many believe it to be. As such, a place that you could bind it, would be…difficult to reach. You would likely be forced to make do with a less appropriate locale, and the fragment would, instead of gaining power, be weakened."

"Great, so I need to trade it or somehow find somewhere that's a heart of darkness, joy!" I muttered.

"The fragment that Tamat offers in its place is up to you. She has two that would be suitable. One is a Fragment of Death, and the other is Honor."

"Uh…"

"To most mortals, there are eight primary foci: Light, Darkness, Life, Death, Fire, Earth, Water, and Air. The secondary foci are literally personifications, as are the first, of aspects of creation. The difference is that the more that these fragments are focused upon, the more their aspect is revered and a core aspect of someone's life, the more their mana is tinged with it.

"As more and more of a particular aspect gathers, it either condenses—eventually—into a focal point, or it is in turn fed upon by another form. If it is the first, then as that focus grows in power and belief, it will be imbued as a fragment of divinity.

"This is where the fragments originally come from, and why there are different aspects. It's also why there are others that seem so…" Sint seemed to struggle with the words before going on. ***"It is why there are aspects and fragments that are not bound to gods, and why a fragment taken from Nimon is not simply a Fragment of Death. There are chances for it to change to other aspects that He has gathered to Himself over the years, either from capturing them from others who had in turn gathered them, or by gathering them Himself."***

"Okay, what if it was the second thing? Fed upon by another?" I asked.

"In that case, it would be a more powerful foci that pulls that devotion and that aspect to themselves. Death, should it naturally occur, doesn't simply begin focusing down and every graveyard become a home for divine aspects of death.

"Instead, that energy, that aspect, is fed to Nimon. In this case, with His assumption over the aspects that should have been Tamat's, She is weakened and the power that naturally accumulates and joins Her, is lessened.

"Instead, it is collected by others, and in this case, the darkness fragment would increase Her pull over Her own aspect again, weakening the pull of the others and making their loss Her gain."

"And this being a Fragment of Honor, is that not something that should be with you?"

"I certainly wish for it to be." He snorted. ***"However, I am unwilling to take the risk to you or Her that sundering that free and then offering it to me would require. I would instead simply recommend that such a fragment would offer you significant gains. After all, have you ever considered why Nimon was so willing to aid Sanguis and the others in their unwise plotting?"***

"Because he's a dick?" I suggested.

"Well, perhaps that is part of the reason, I agree. However, a more factual answer, please."

"Oh, I still think that's a fact," I admitted, cheering up as I got an opportunity to call the God of Death names, knowing he might be listening. "He's a dick."

"He is." Sint sighed. ***"However, He also took that step after repeatedly warning us that He would not permit an over-god to arise, unless it was Him."***

"Uh-huh?" I agreed, not getting it.

"Jax, how many worshippers do you think the average god had at the height of the empire?"

"Absolutely no clue."

"I was amongst the most powerful, and I had over a hundred million who paid service to me."

"Cool."

"Please, Jax, that's very offensive," He snapped.

"Sint, I'm sorry…I'm not getting it. And it wasn't meant as being a dick—I just don't get the point here. You having a hundred million supporters is cool."

"I was amongst the most powerful of the gods, and I had over a hundred million followers. Yes, I gained from the aspects as well, but primarily, I gained from my followers. Consider that, and then ask yourself how many billions lived in the empire."

"Billions?" I muttered. "Damn, I didn't…oh shit."

"You didn't realize because it wasn't relevant to you," He agreed. ***"Well, this is why it is, Jax. Nimon will fly into an absolute rage when He becomes aware that you understand this secret, as it is one that He has worked to ensure no other would discover, and it is something we would not share unless it was necessary. But consider your position, and for the love of all reality, do not throw this secret in His face. I am shielding this conversation to keep it private.***

"One reason that Nimon destroyed the realm was to prevent Amon from ascending. You have sensed that he had reserves of power that were frankly incredible, and that the imperial throne has abilities linked to it, yes?"

"Yeah, definitely," I agreed. "But I thought he absorbed the fragments and therefore couldn't ascend?"

"He shouldn't have been able to. Despite bleeding that power off into artifacts and into a system that he and his mages created to enable the throne to store power, a power that you're tapping into, still, he was ascending.

"He was not made aware of the reason, nor of the potential, as we too feared the One Who Could Come. That was our mistake, though, as a being who was raised from the empire, who could be all that the empire embodied, when that belief and power could be tempered with compassion? That could be a worthy god indeed."

"You're saying that I could ascend because I would be the focal point of the empire?" I asked slowly. "That the belief and faith of the citizens would raise me up?"

"It could, though it would take time. Think of it as several centuries or so per fragment, a hundred million or so of those who support you, each respecting you, and that would indeed help your ascension, even should you never again harvest a fragment from another god. However…"

He paused, and I sensed the focus, that this was important and to make sure I listened to this. I got the feeling that however he was making sure that Nimon didn't hear any of this was costing him.

"Should you, instead of sitting back and waiting, and simply passively accepting that reverence, harvest specific fragments that were to align with your ascension? Honor, Order, Loyalty, War, and more…then each and every day, more and more power would be fed into you. For each citizen who prays to one of us, per day, their excess mana would feed you.

"For the average citizen, a hundred mana is their limit, but that is their maximum. Should they not use that mana for anything, they still generate it, daily, in the hundreds of points.

"Those points that are then lost to the ether, add to the ambient mana flow of the realm, and they in turn break down into the relevant form. Should their lives be ones of brutality, then that infests their mana, angling it to that, and converting the realm to a more brutal place. But…"

I got the hint and took it up. "But if I had aspects of honor and order, and the realm was a more honorable place, I'd be fed constantly by that mana."

"It would not be added to your normal manapool, but it would gather around you, feed you, and assist you. It would be power that could help when the time is right, much as you have unknowingly called upon it in the past."

"So really, as shitty as this is going to be, I need to do it?" I asked.

"That is a decision only you can make, but I would recommend it indeed," Sint admitted. ***"Perhaps wait until your companions arrive, however, as they are in turn chosen of the gods, and their mode of transport is indeed powerful. Also, remember that although you will indeed be likely the only one of them suited to battle a god, your first fragment comes with the ability to prevent another god from fleeing from you.***

"As such, should one of the lesser gods decide to attack, you may entrap them and face them on your terms, while your companions face any followers they choose to bring."

"Because you and the others will need to be elsewhere," I finished for him, nodding. "Okay, so basically, I've got an opportunity here that's high risk, but it could give me the kind of power that Amon had, and although it's not going to be easy, I could do it in a hell of a lot less time. Then, given that the dark dick will be pissed about it, we run a higher risk of something nasty happening, right?"

"We do, but remember, Jax, that the effect upon the realm was not simply linear. Although he gained much power in the short term because of the huge number of deaths, he also lost power, and a tremendous amount of it, as death is a natural part of existence for the mortal races, and he gains the vast majority of his power from that. With less living here, there were less deaths. So he benefited from a massive surge, but then encountered a drastic dip in the mana being fed to him.

"The rest is from worship, yes, but as most of the creatures of the realm died, the power that goes to him currently is nothing compared to the power that he had before the cataclysm, and has since lost.

"Have you never wondered how we were able to hold him off? After all, he should be able to defeat us with ease, if we are as weak as we are, compared to him at his height. Since awakening, we have each began recovering our aspects and growing our strength, so although we have little compared to the power we wielded at our height, we are still, after all, gods."

"Got it." I nodded slowly. "Okay, so yeah, do you want to tell Tamat that she's got a deal for the Fragment of Honor? And we'll do it once I've gotten Oracle safely to the Cradle and she's given birth, and our friends are with us? That way, if the shit hits the fan, at least she's got them to get her away and protect the baby."

"I think this is a wise plan."

I felt the approval as Sint's voice rumbled through me.

"While I've got you here, I have another question, if you don't mind?" I asked.

"Ask," He encouraged.

"When we're looking at expanding the city, at getting Sonra to maybe settle here, do you think that Lagoush would help with Her priests—if we taught people magic that worked for Her, I mean…nature- and growth-based spells—and then guided them to be priests for Her? Do you think She'd be willing to help by letting them circle the city in an ongoing pass, casting growth spells and basically making the grass grow a lot more?"

"I suspect She would not be averse to it, provided you taught and recruited such priests, and then they followed Her, as each spell would be in essence a prayer to Her as well. However, you would be best speaking to Her directly about this," He said.

"I will." I sighed. "And thank you again."

"Be well, Jax. And again, I agree with your plan to move forward with the governance of the city."

The sense of his presence faded, and I sighed, nodding that I agreed.

The next two hours, the first part of my damn day, was basically taken up by a little kiss and a cuddle with Oracle—nowhere near long enough or fun enough—and then a more official talk with Daralen and Seraphina.

I'd been thinking of this off and on already, and I'd had a lot of it sorted out in my head, but sitting down with them more formally and discussing it really helped.

"Okay, I've got good news and bad," I started with, trying to be as upbeat but realistic as possible. "Good news first. I'm going to stop interfering with the running of the city and hand it over to you, Seraphina, and the legion and our armies to you, Daralen."

"So, I'm to run the city?" Seraphina asked again. "As we agreed?"

"Exactly," I said. "I'm sorry that I've probably been jumping on your toes of late. I've been trying to deal with things as I saw best, but frankly, I'm also so used to running and constantly 'fixing things' that I have an issue letting go."

"You're a prince. It's expected." She smiled. "But you accept that I will rule here, that I can give orders to the council?"

"You can *create* the council," I clarified. "Disband those you think aren't suitable, and run this city with the intention that it is going to be the local heart of the empire.

"When Sonra arrives, as we discussed, I think the best possible win here would be to join them to Gaij, and then from there, for you to create a blended council, one that has both the elders of Sonra and your own people in it, as well as possibly spreading out a lot more. I know you've got a lot of land here, and it's pretty good, but there's not much of it under cultivation. Is there a reason?"

"The noble houses," she replied. "They decided that the land around the city and that which was naturally the greenest and most 'attractive' should be made into parks and their own estates."

"Then you fix that," I said. "How far out is Sonra?"

"They should arrive tonight—the leaders, at least," she said. "I sent an invitation to them to join us here in the tower for a council of war and to discuss the potential gains."

"Excellent, considering they're sworn to me already. I guess that's sorted now as well. So they should come…"

"They have agreed, and they sent word that there would be the full council attending," she said.

"Perfect. Okay, so they're coming tonight. Who else would you have in your council?" I started, then I shook my head. "Actually, you know what? Don't answer that—this is your council." I forced myself not to interfere.

"Thank you." She smiled. "I will invite the elders to form a city with me, with them to rule the outer aspects with their herds and a set position, and the surviving nobility to hold the majority of the city, and the tower as the capital of the city, a sort of manor house, if you will, that will also house the legion." She gestured to her silent—so far—partner in the meeting, Daralen.

"So, again, at Lady Seraphina's request, I ask for clarification, my prince," she said. "I am to run the defense of the city?"

"You are, and you are to take over the legion's traditional roles. A member of the legion of each city will be a member of the council. Sorry to jump in on that point after saying I was out, Seraphina, but that's important."

"I understand. And she would have been offered a post on my council anyway." The succubus smiled.

"The primus of the legion is more experienced in war than I'm ever likely to be, and as primus, you have the rank and skills to lead the defense. Let's face it—I'm a fighter and a mage. I'm shit useless at leading in big battles, and frankly, I'd love to have Romanus here with us. He's the legion general back in Dravith, and that's not to say…"

"I understand." Daralen sighed. "I wish my own general was here. But in the meantime, until one of sufficient rank is found or raised, I can lead."

"Great, glad to hear it." I smiled. "Look, I'm not just palming off my responsibilities here, but let's be honest. You two know more about your respective duties than I do. Daralen can train and lead an army better than me, not to mention defending fixed emplacements, and Seraphina, you…well, you know this city in and out. And you live for the intrigue and shit, don't you?"

"I enjoy it," she admitted.

"It makes my teeth ache and I want to stab everyone." I snorted. "That's how I feel about it all."

"Perhaps better not to attend many council meetings then?" she suggested, smiling archly. "Not unless I specifically invite you, and then I'll make sure there are people you can vent on close at hand?"

"I'll agree to that." I snorted. "Okay, that's the carrot, and here's the stick. The bad news is that we're not only dealing with Kronk. The Dark Legion has dispatched an entire legion to face us here. Five thousand troops, including the fodder, their regulars, and last of all, their elites."

"Oh shit," Seraphina whispered, her eyes widening slightly. "That's not…what I would have hoped for."

"No, but it's what we've got," I agreed. "The advantage, as I understand it though, is that Kronk and the dark dicks hate each other, so if the legion arrives and finds Kronk at our gates, they're more likely to attack them than join them, is that right?"

"I would expect so. They are confirmed enemies, both having raided each other indiscriminately for many years. Only Kronk's location on the edge of the Plain of Bones, with no water or food in the area outside of their walls, have kept them from being conquered in the past," Daralen verified.

"Excellent. So what I'm thinking is that the outriders would be perfect to cut off the supply lines for these forces, and kill their scouts." I smiled. "With both armies blind and low on supplies, they'll have to attack each other on sight, and then we clean up the survivors. Does that work?"

"The overall plan is…workable, but the details…" Daralen winced.

"That's why I'm leaving it to you," I said. "You can do this far better than I can, Daralen. But what I *can* do is help Oracle to teach our forces magic. And I can train, I can make potions, and I can act as a focal point, as the dark dickheads will charge heedlessly at me given the chance. I have some fairly powerful magics I can use on them."

"You're also the prince of the empire, and the one person we cannot afford to lose," Daralen countered. "As such, yes, you will be used when needed. You are a force multiplier all on your own. *However…*I'd ask that you stay out of the fight unless I direct, and you remain where I say. No running off to start fights with gods." She managed a smile with that one, and I grinned as well.

"I think I can agree to that. So, moving on, do you need anything from me?" I looked to the half-orc, and she shook her head.

"I'll take over the planning, though there will likely be a need for a formal, public investment of power in us both, to avoid the appearance of us simply assuming power."

"Tonight," I said. "Let's do that tonight. We can have the elders of Sonra meet us in the gardens for dinner, and we can all go over it."

"Excellent." Seraphina smiled maliciously. "I'll make sure that the remaining members of the old council who have been problematic are seated near you."

"Fuck."

CHAPTER TWENTY-NINE

The rest of the afternoon was consumed by small jobs, me basically giving approvals to people for the limited projects I was keeping control of, for now, like the airship, which I'd barely been involved in so far, and sorting things like gathering up all the altars to the other gods in the city and smashing the shit out of them.

I'll admit the experience of destroying Illoth's altars—making sure there were no hidden spiders—and then putting them in the latrines was great.

It was even more fun when I was informed by a terrified servant at the tower that a massive leg had been seen, sliced into sections and dumped in the latrines that had recently been built for our trainee legion aspirants.

People were pretty panicked and confused, until I rocked up, ready for the deed, with a tatty book under my arm—one that had been rescued from the idiots from my world—and I made a show of first hurling all the bits of the altars to Illoth into the latrines, then shouting at the sky:

"Pass the word to Illoth, will you? I'm gonna have a big smelly shit on what's left of her avatar, and the remains of her altars!" I bellowed. "In fact, tell Lolly the Turd Spider that we're all going to do it, and this is just how respected she is!"

Then I went and had an incredibly satisfying shit.

There were a lot of other little details that I had to get into place, such as the mages, sitting down with them and explaining to them that yes, Oracle was a wisp—partly—and that no, they weren't going to be using her to learn each other's spells.

Oracle had warned me to behave myself before we'd gone into the meeting, and explained that because of the way her kind were viewed, it wasn't personal, and she'd accepted that.

I was seriously unamused, but she asked me to be good, because we needed the mages, and I respected that.

There was only one absolute fucking idiot who was so excited about the "opportunity that she represents" to him and the other mages, that I ended up breaking his leg.

He'd gone on about it, and I'd been calm and fairly well-behaved when I'd explained that no, she was a person, and not a fucking training aid. He'd just waved my comment aside, as if I were just confused and needed to be told right from wrong.

Then he'd explained—as if to a child—that my own ancestor Amon had had the wisps collared and bound to assist the empire, and that this was no different. And then he went on further, suggesting that there'd been rumors of other wisps far to the east somewhere beyond Kronk, and perhaps once I'd captured Kronk, he would come there and help me to find those wisps, and make use of them. That way, he wouldn't have to share mine.

The others around him had started to move their chairs away, much in the same way that they would have if one of their number stood atop the highest peak of the tower, waving a lightning rod and shouting that all gods are bastards.

I stood, very calmly, moved around the table, my emotions encased in a very brittle composure. Then I stepped into one of the vacant spaces next to him, put my right hand on his left knee, took hold of his left ankle, and then yanked hard enough that both the knee shattering and popping free and the bone breaking were almost the same sound.

Then I grabbed him by the back of the head, slammed his face into the table and pinned him there, while I casually broke each of his fingers, holding him in place, still saying nothing in the absolutely terrified room. Finally, I squatted so that I was roughly on a level with him, staring into his one functioning and clearly panicked eye. He broke off from howling in pain when I started to speak.

"What you referred to was a travesty that Amon himself regretted to his dying day, and the woman you're talking casually about inflicting that upon is the love of my life," I said almost politely.

"She asked me to show restraint in this meeting, or else you'd already be dead, and *exceedingly* painfully. So let me explain this as carefully as I can, so that this misunderstanding never happens again."

I stood, leaving him staring up from his pool of blood, snot, and tears, as I walked back to my seat and sat.

"I stand against slavery in *all* its forms. I am absolutely *furious* that I even have to put the oaths upon you all, and yet even as *light* a leash as that is, you constantly fucking prove to me that you *need* it.

"So, to be very clear, should any of you utter fuckwits ever attempt to cage and abuse a sentient, sapient being of any race, I will make your final days of torture, dismemberment, and death into something that people will point to in a thousand years as an example of excessive force.

"The next one of you absolute fuck-nuggets who so much as looks at Oracle in such a way, will die the absolutely most painful death I can arrange. She is a wonderful, caring person and is possibly the most intelligent person I know. She—and let me be *very* clear—she is the one who keeps me from turning this entire realm into a smoking fucking ruin when I lose my temper. And, in case you forgot, I have the heads of two gods as examples of just how badly I can lose my patience.

"If these reasons weren't enough for you, then the fact that I love her with everything I am, and she will be the mother of the crown prince or princess of the empire, should make things plain.

"When this shit storm is over, I will be marrying her, and she will be the empress. She is already among the highest ranks in the empire, and you are alive now, literally right fucking *NOW*...because she asked me to show restraint."

I sucked in a long, calming breath and then smiled around the table.

"Finally, if all that and your own limited morals haven't made it obvious that bringing this back up to me is a bad idea, let me point out that should you be linked, one of you idiots to another, then the first of you who decided to strike could erase the others' consciousness in a blink of an eye.

"You would die, your mind erased—unless you believe that the other mages sitting around this table are so utterly trustworthy that you are entirely safe from them?"

Silence.

"Excellent. Does anyone have anything they want to add to this conversation?" I smiled again. "No? Okay then, let's move on. And someone get rid of that." I made a vague gesture at the slumped, heavily bleeding, and utterly shit scared, as well as crippled, mage.

"My love, I think they understand, and I doubt they'll say such offensive things again," she assured me, clearly speaking to the rest of the room, as she hit the mage with a healing spell. "After all, can you imagine if he said those things and I'd not thought to calm you down first? Or if the optio of your personal squad heard him?"

"I hear she's got a formidable temper," Daralen commented dryly from her seat. "She's the Valkyrie, isn't she? The one who forged her own path and is the champion of the Goddess Vanei?"

"That's the one," I muttered, straightening.

"Or Bane, the Champion of the Goddess Tamat," Sehran interjected. "He'd really take that kind of thing badly, mind you. You know, I can't think of a single legionnaire who wouldn't have gutted him for even saying that?" She nodded at the fat fool.

"Or Giint," Oracle added, and even I had to snort at that, as the mage, stammering apologies, managed to get himself to his feet long enough to flee the room. "He's the champion of Svetu, God of Invention, and I dread to think what he'd have come up with. He once ate an icedrake's face."

"Raw," I added. "Anyway, look, everyone, I'm sorry, but I hope I've made my lack of acceptance for this shit clear now?" I glared around the room. A lot of very scared people bowed their heads and made sounds of agreement.

"Excellent. So, I didn't call you here for that shit. I called you here to make it very clear that Lady Seraphina and Primus Daralen speak with my voice. If they tell you you're now a basic recruit because you need to understand what they go through, then I'd suggest you start running with the other recruits, because the alternative is that you come and explain your position to me. Privately. Would anyone like to arrange a private discussion?"

More fucking silence, deep enough to swim in.

"Great! We're making progress then. Do I need to be involved here further or are you all going to help support the legion to the very best of your capabilities?"

There were a handful of seconds of effusive declarations of support, and then I waved them all out.

"Was that what you were looking for from this meeting?" I asked Seraphina, who'd remained silent until now and then burst out laughing.

"Jax, my prince, those miserable old men and women have been a thorn in my side—they or their ancestors—for the last seven hundred years. To see them so thoroughly cowed was worth everything you have asked of me. I have mentioned this before, and casually, but I ask again now, having spoken to many of my sisters. Some are content here, bound to the tower, and knowing that we may now live here, literally, instead of merely surviving and being glorified mana batteries.

"The others, nearly thirty of them, wish the freedom to explore this realm, and to grow again, even despite the risk of being banished should we fall in battle. As such, I formally ask that my sisters be permitted to meet legionnaires who are interested in a binding." She looked at me carefully, as if unsure what I'd say.

"Daralen?" I looked at her, and the primus blinked, surprised.

"Yes, my prince?"

"Have you any issues with this?"

"It's not something that's common," she said after a few seconds of consideration. "But it's also not something that's against any rules. And the bonuses gained for those from such a bond are substantial."

"Enough to offset the loss of their mana," Sehran interjected. "At least, my Jian thinks so."

"Yeah, I bet he does." I smiled at her, and I nodded. "As long as Daralen has no objections and it's very clear in the contract that the legionnaire has to want this, and the terms, then I think it's a good idea."

"And if we were to invite others?" Seraphina pressed.

"Others?"

"Oh, you sneaky devil!" Sehran purred.

"It is why we were here, after all." Seraphina smiled, then shrugged. "Sorry," she said when she realized not everyone was following. "When we came here from the hells, it was both for a little fun on our side, and to earn power, which we certainly did. The issue is that we should have grown too powerful to return, and now, as we recover from the long centuries of assisting the tower, we can start to grow again.

"If my sisters choose this, they could grow to be among the strongest of our species, should they feed enough. Although we're not interested in starting a war back in the hells, there are…shall we say, attractions, to a reordering of things? If I was to end up back there now, I would have to fight for my place again.

"One day, I will want to return, and when I do, I'd rather have as many of my sisters, and our brothers the incubai, as strong as possible and ready to fight as well."

"So break this down for us all," I said. "What do you get and what do we get?"

"We, the succubai, have a chance to explore the world and grow in power. If we die and are sent back, we will be as strong as possible by the time we return," she said without preamble. "The advantage to your empire—sorry, *our* empire, as I'm now a citizen—is that you get dozens of succubai to fight alongside you, and possibly hundreds."

"How hundreds?" I asked, seeing the smile.

"Well, we can open a portal home, provided we have the mana, and we can offer our families the chance to visit." She shrugged. "What could you do with a hundred succubai casting distraction spells, Primus?" she asked Daralen, who blinked, apparently coming back to herself.

"I could destroy an army ten times the size of my own," Daralen said. "My legionnaires would have an extra layer of protection, and more than that, they'd have, well…"

"Walking, talking companionship." Seraphina smiled. "Don't shy away from that side of it. After all, we are the demons of lust and lascivious behavior."

"It's not just a job—it's a hobby and our favorite game." Sehran grinned.

"Exactly." Seraphina shrugged. "So, are we permitted to offer the binding?" she asked me, and I hesitated, then nodded.

"On one condition."

"Name it."

"Sehran reads the contracts, and makes sure there's nothing sinister in there."

"Oh, that's not a condition. That's common sense!" Seraphina approved. "Granted."

"Then fine. Spread the word then, Daralen, and if we have more legionnaires who are interested than we have succubai, then you have permission to open portals and so on. Sehran, you're in charge of monitoring that, okay?"

"Thank you." Sehran smiled. "Am I okay to include my own family and close friends in the call?"

"Fuck it, go wild." I shrugged, then remembered who I was talking to. "*Reasonably* wild," I amended, sighing, and wishing for a brief second that if only I'd been in this position before I met Oracle, I could have had a lot more fun.

Then I remembered that I'd have died. Either from all the shit that happened, or through sheer excess and exhaustion.

The other minor meetings around the tower went much the same way, except that the tale of my annoyance with the mages apparently spread and after that, people were a lot more respectful.

When the first of the wagons crested the lowest hills and started down toward the city, a group from the legion and the outriders who had travelled with us set off, riding out to Sonra and joining them, before escorting the representatives who wanted to come—on horseback—to join us for dinner in the tower.

Obviously the centaur—Sharn—chose not to ride a horse, although the thought did make me giggle internally at the mental image for a few seconds.

By the time the little group reached us, I couldn't help but smile. Marteen, Toren, Othair, and the old bugger Horace had ridden up with Cleq; the rest of the council was present just behind them. The animated little goblin took the time to wave at people and clearly enjoyed being "out of the closet." Riding a horse alongside Sharn, I spotted Greg, the second goblin, and striding along beside him, apparently refusing to ride a horse, was Bravimoth, the old orc.

When it came to the Kreonar twins, Daven and Malik, I still had no clue which was which, and Reth Suntari rode next to Ilena, the group in turn surrounded by legionnaires and outriders.

By the time they wound their way through the cobbled streets and they were on the final approach to the tower, the heavens opened, just to fuck with everyone.

That meant that the last hundred meters or so up to and through the gates, and then into the gardens, were conducted under the kind of heavy rain shower that was occasionally described as "thunderous" and more often as "fuck me, it's a waterfall."

The outside pavilion that was set up for us all had a roof, which was great, and it made damn sure that anyone who had planned to hang around to try to listen in was dissuaded of the idea on the grounds that unless they were a fish, they'd have problems.

I was ready to call it off and move us all inside, when Seraphina stepped up and welcomed everyone to the city, and took point, assuring us all that these happened occasionally, and it was entering the season for it. As such, the tower was prepared.

The serving staff set up a covered walkway that led from the nearest tower entrance to the pavilion, and as everyone shook the water off themselves, and out of hair, manes, and fuck knew what, we gathered under the awning, and watched as people raced this way and that, trying to escape the deluge.

"Damn," I muttered as a pair of legionnaire aspirants jogged across the grounds, passing from the flagstones to the already soaking grass with a clatter then a squelch, their shields held overhead as the rain drummed off them, while a full legionnaire ran alongside, roaring at them to "Keep it up, maggot."

"Ah, Prince Jax." Greg greeted me as he scurried across the carpet, wiping rainwater from his face. "I was pleased to see that our faith in you was justified!"

"Oh?" I asked.

"With taking control of Gaij so quickly!" He beamed.

"Shit, yes, of course. Sorry, Greg, it's been a busy week. It's good to see you, my friend. How was the journey?" I asked, forcing myself to do small talk.

We talked a little as the others arrived, doing the whole smiles and gripping of wrists, general talking about inconsequential crap, and then after three of our guests had tried three separate times to set up a private chat to discuss Gaij's governorship, I decided that enough was enough.

"Shall we have a quick chat now about the wider situation, and then we all know where we stand?" I asked the group, getting a smile from Seraphina as she knew that this was where she got to go from "the entertainment" to "the boss."

A few minutes later, once we all had seats and drinks, with the promise of food to come, I introduced Seraphina as the Mistress of Gaij, and then sat back, smiling as I saw a few hopes crushed.

The buggers should have come with me then, rather than staying back with the caravans.

Seraphina thanked me, confirmed that she was the mistress of both the tower and Gaij, the ruler of the city, etc., and then offered them all an olive branch in that she was setting up a council to rule here with her, and that she'd deliberately not filled the positions, until she knew where Sonra stood.

That was the sign for me to take over.

"Okay then, as you all know, I'm not a great speaker, and I'm not interested in spending forever dropping subtle hints to see who supports what.

"The situation is this. We've received word that Kronk has dispatched its army, and seems to think they can take over here. It's not a raid—it's the vast majority of their forces."

I left that hanging there for a few seconds before I went on.

"We expect them to reach us in about eight days. They have enough forces to encircle the city, though only lightly. Numbers-wise, they have around twenty thousand under their banner, and the majority are battle tested and experienced, though mainly as raiders."

I looked around, and then gestured to Daralen, who spoke up smoothly.

"We have, between our own forces, the forces of Gaij, and the legion aspirants you brought with you, some eighteen thousand fighters, but they're also, by and large, inexperienced, and are yet to even be fully armed."

There was even more of a silence at that, until Ilena spoke up, furious.

"And you allowed us to move the herds here, knowing that the forces you face are enough to completely encircle the city? That we are incredibly slow moving, and yet still you wasted days of travel where we could have been heading away from this invasion force?" She was practically incandescent with rage, getting louder and more strident by the second.

I could understand it; from her point of view, we'd put them at risk for no reason.

"Yes." Daralen smiled. "There are also reports that a Dark Legion is marching on us as well, five thousand strong. We found this out only a few hours ago."

"What?!" she practically screamed.

I took over, standing and drawing every eye. "It's not ideal," I agreed. "Neither is the situation with Kronk, but we have significant advantages, and there are ways we can turn this around, as well as slaughter the bastards. But before we can get to that, we need to make the current situation clear to everyone.

"First, we need to sort out the separation, or lack thereof, of Gaij and Sonra," I said with a smile, getting another look of shock. "Don't worry, this is a good thing, I think, and I'm asking for your agreement and your input, not ordering."

"I told you this was a bad idea!" Sharn, the centaur, hissed to Greg.

"We will listen, my prince." The little goblin sighed. "But please, do not make us regret our choice to join you so soon."

"That's a decision you'll make either way, but let's just jump right to it. So, for the majority of your existence, Sonra moved. Much as the tower under Seraphina hid its secrets, so did you, and that was why you moved. Am I right in saying that?"

"It was one of the reasons," Greg agreed, tapping his nails on the table, before smiling half-heartedly at a staring server who apologized and slid in from the side, putting a platter down near him, bowing then retreating. "The other was born of necessity. The herds must move, or starve."

"Exactly." I smiled. "What if the herds didn't have to do that? What if the city of Gaij could become a permanent home for them?"

"We would strip the area available in less than a month, and it would take at least three to recover, even in the height of summer, and that doesn't consider the droppings." Cleq shook her head. "The herds leave bountiful deposits that encourage greater growth, but it takes time, and the population of your city would starve if we permitted the herds to graze as they would."

"If the growth time was limited to three months," I agreed, smiling. "We have a spell that can turn the earth, and leave it clean, reinvigorated from the shit, and ready for planting. As the herds graze, we could do this right behind you, planting as they go."

"It would reduce the time taken for the ground to recover from the passage, but the time required to resprout and grow, not to mention the spell's range and the limitations on casting it wouldn't be addressed," Cleq said. "And unless you plan to spend the rest of your life following the herds in an endless rotation? What would be the point?"

"The point is that we have access to this magic, and we can teach mages who will follow the herds, in their dozens," I said. "The spell, cast over and over, day by day, is one that would gain them experience, as it's having a solid effect on the realm and is completed each time.

"That means that they will grow more powerful in time. They will learn, and the nature mages will adapt, discovering their own evolutions to the spells…can we agree on that? That it's possible to do this?" I sat down and accepted a drink, then looked around as the representatives of Sonra nodded or showed they acknowledged that.

"The issue is numbers." Ilena spoke up. "Are there that many mages in the city? Enough to walk behind us day after day, and cast these spells constantly? I don't think there are. And even if there were, the sheer cost in hiring such mages…"

"They're already among you and the city," I said. "You're aware that Oracle is a wisp, or she was."

"Because of who and what I am, I retain access to magic in a way that you don't have." Oracle spoke up. "I can teach a spell to three people in minutes, or up to an hour, depending on the levels of complexity. If Jax and I were to dedicate a full day to this, twenty hours of constant work, we could give you sixty mages with that spell. Those would be ordinary citizens, each with their wisdom and intelligence traits, but no magic prior to this.

"They would learn this spell, and be able to level through continually casting the spell. As they learn, the spell drops in cost, evolves, and they become better at using it. More to the point, as they pass, the land is left fallow and ready to be planted, with the life-giving droppings of the herds buried in it.

"The crops and the grasses will grow back faster and stronger, granting more bountiful harvests each year. If the herds moved around the city in a tight circle and this was cast, and then in a wider, and wider circle as you went, the estimate is that you'd complete a single circuit in a month. Then the next circuit in three months, then six, then twelve. Does this sound right?" Oracle asked.

Cleq looked to Sharn, who grumbled a little, but nodded.

"Great, so moving on from there, that's the first pass." I smiled. "We have a second pass that we could then make, because we have an advantage that we've not been making the most of.

"We have access to the gods, after all, and we could ask them to aid us in this—specifically, teaching people who were interested to be priests for Lagoush, and then having a second pass by priests who could cast spells of growth."

"Would the goddess do this?" Sharn asked carefully.

"I believe she might, if we approached her in the right way, and considering that she's already offered to help the city, provided I complete certain quests for her."

"It gains you a permanent home." Oracle went on, picking up the thread of the conversation. "You wouldn't have to leave the city, if you wanted to live here, and there are both spaces inside the city walls and space inside the tower itself."

"The Elsecaller and your other artifacts would remain under your control," I said, "but there are sections of the city that were recently damaged and other sections that were taken from the nobles. Entire estates are available, and could be either given over to you, or razed to the ground and could then provide a solid home inside the walls.

"The outriders would be folded into the legion, as light cavalry." Daralen took up the discussion when I looked to her, clearing her throat and standing. "Though they would remain under their current leadership, joining the chain of command overall, and benefitting from both access to magic—the mages of the city are currently teaching classes to the legion aspirants—and gaining full legion backing."

"What would that mean?" Reth leaned forward on the table and steepled his fingers as he looked from one side to the other. "Specifics, please."

"The Dark Legion took control of an old legion encampment, and they were using it to provide for their forces" I said with a grin. "All the devices that were created in the last days of the old empire, that provided most of the armor and weapons the Dark Legion. Well, not any more. We took it back and it's now producing the legion's new gear." I smiled. "There's a lot to be made, don't get me wrong, but it'd mean, once we're up to speed, that your outriders could be equipped in full legion scout armor, and your beasts would be armored as well, where it makes sense."

"And the magic?" he asked.

"We can only teach so many a day, but I think we could add them into the training schedule," I replied. "The advantage of a hundred light cavalry who could run from a fight, and then flank and bombard the enemy over and over from a distance with magic missiles?" I shrugged.

"We could raid the supply lines with little risk," Reth said. "Cutting the enemy off and weakening them."

"Exactly," I agreed.

"This is how Sonra has typically fought when others have tried to take us—by moving on, and the riders whittling them down over time, or sheltering near cities that have owed us favors. If we were to settle here, we would lose much of our freedoms, and many would not wish to stop," one twin grumbled.

"They don't have to. But, as you say, having access to a city of your own, that your people are safe inside of has to be a tempting thought." I shrugged. "Okay, let's roll this back a bit. We're offering you the advantages to doing this, and we're discussing how it *could* work. The first question should be: do you *want* to?"

"For many of us, yes, it would be nice. There have been many discussions for many years about Sonra settling, though the issues with the herds means it was theoretical only," Sharn admitted, surprising me that the grumpy centaur was the first to say yes.

"However, we are a nomadic people. We were born with the lust for the open plains, even if, by necessity, most of us have not seen such, for our entire lives," she finished.

"Because you've been kept hidden in the center of a giant rolling tent city." I nodded. "I get that, and why you might want to settle down and actually be able to travel outside of your enclosed area. I get that you want to, but this is a situation that gives you the best of both worlds. First, you get a secure place to live in, and second, you become known in the area and to the citizens.

"For those of you who are typically regarded as…" I paused, thinking of the subtle way to say it.

"Monsters," Greg said simply. "Most believe we are monsters, as our distant cousins, although appearing similar, frankly are monsters, and would kill us as happily as you."

"Exactly." I shrugged. "Most people will think you are, and so they'll react accordingly. In the empire's lands, you'll be seen out and about, engaging in normal life, and people will get used to you, as well as learning that you are other citizens. You'll be protected from them, and they from you, meaning you can explore and live a bit, which you won't be able to do anywhere else. That's the advantage there. But, as you say, you're viewed as monsters, so it won't happen overnight. The other side is that for those who want to travel, to explore, we're going to be producing caravans of our own soon, and reaching out to the other cities.

"Those who are interested could run those caravans, as either honest traders, or as spies, as we'll be sending out both kinds." I smiled, seeing the surprise on a few faces. "We'll also be looking to set up diplomatic alliances with other cities, and we'll also be looking to reclaim the deserts, but we're talking these things in the short term."

"And in the long?" Reth asked pointedly.

"They join us, or they're our enemies," I said. "I'd be willing to accept neutrality if I thought for a second it'd last. Allies, I'd love. But the simple truth is that we're in a war of the gods here, and the enemy need to be pushed off this continent. If they want to accept imperial laws and swear to be allies, swear the oath of citizenry and become part of the empire as a subsidiary kingdom that bends the knee? Fine with that."

"Few would choose such a thing," Greg pointed out.

"And I know that, which is why we'll be conquering them all eventually." I shrugged. "I didn't start out planning to rule the realm, but I know that there are others out there attempting to do it, to conquer enough that they can claim the imperial throne and try to take it from me. As such, there are only two sides for now: with us, or against."

"I told you we shouldn't have done this," Sharn said caustically to Greg, before clambering to her feet and trotting off, clearly furious.

"There are concerns, my prince," Reth said. "We have been free for seven hundred years, and yes, we have sworn to you, but…"

"But I'm asking a lot." I nodded. "I know, and I'm sorry. Look, think about what I've told you. We knew about Kronk, though not if they were coming for sure until yesterday, and for the Dark Legion only a few hours ago. We understand if you choose to flee, to take the herds and leave, heading in a different direction. I won't stop you." I saw the looks of hope on a few of their faces.

"But if you do this, there's nothing to stop Kronk from bypassing us and heading for you. Hell, there's nothing to say that we're definitely their target." I shrugged.

"I *think* we are, because they're headed this way. But they might just as easily be after you. And when they begin chasing you down…now, we'd come to your aid immediately as you're imperial citizens. But if they bypass us and head straight for you, we're all going to lose a lot of people: you because advance scouts or whatever might reach you first, and us because we'll have to face them out in the field instead of from behind these walls."

"And if we agree to settle down, and we move into the city?" Greg asked shrewdly. "You have a use for us and a safe place for the herds?"

"Yes and no." I smiled. "A use? Most definitely. I've got access to a lot of information and to advanced golems, and we're working on producing native airships. Those of your people who are gifted in artifact creation and engineering would be a massive help there. If we can make the prototype in the next week or so, we'll have a platform that we can use to fly over the enemy. We can literally slaughter them in their thousands by launching spells at them from above."

"And the other side?" he asked grimly.

"We can fit everyone and the animals inside for only a short time," I admitted. "The people? We have the space. The herds? Not so much. I'd suggest that a section of the herds be protected, the best of the best, and the rest are split into two groups: one to be slaughtered for meat, and the other to provide the mounts for the cavalry."

"You ask us to gut the great herds, and for what? To protect your people?" Ilena covered her face in her hands. "You take our heritage and our way of life, and you force us to serve. Why didn't we listen to Sharn?"

"You didn't listen because you all saw a way to gain," I snapped. "You saw a better life for yourselves and you made the decision, and now, thanks to the actions of fucking Kronk and the dark dickheads, you're seeing the fucking risk!"

"But—"

"Have any of you considered the rewards?" Seraphina asked suddenly, drawing their attention.

"What rewards?" Greg groaned. "Please, show me the rewards!"

"Literally, we have discussed the dissolution of your way of life, but let's consider the advantages, shall we?" she asked smoothly, sitting forward.

I took the hint, leaning back to watch.

"First, as our prince has said, you would gain a position on my council, and a permanent home. For some, this might be meaningless, but for most, you can see the path to true wealth here. On the council, you will serve the empire, certainly, but you will also have an opportunity to advance the cause not only of your own interests, but of your species.

"Have none of you dreamed of the day that gnomes and goblins could have shops that are their own? That orcs could walk the streets and be respected?" she asked curiously. "I'm opening the door to many of my sisters binding themselves to the legion, and those of you who know how lethal we can be will understand that such a pairing means that the legion will exponentially grow in strength.

"After all, imagine the airships that you build"—she gestured to Cleq and Greg—"scouring over the enemy; imagine them preparing to defend, or to counterattack…then a hundred of my kind distract them, all at once.

"A hundred of us, reaching out to twist their minds, and then you attack, killing your enemies in their thousands with little risk." She shrugged. "That is just the first line of the assault, but let's continue this. As Prince Jax has said, he wants hundreds, and eventually thousands, of legionnaires all able to cast spells.

"When a thousand legionnaires fire a volley of Magic Missiles—a spell that produces between three and seven explosive, though weak, darts for each casting—and then they do this again and again?

"Tell me, how long would Kronk's army withstand five or ten thousand missiles all being fired into them, over and over again? Would their armor hold? Or would it be reduced to battered scrap? Would their mages, who often turn the tide of battles on their own, be able to defend them? Or would they be killed instantly? Would they even choose to fight after seeing what they faced, or would the remains of their army break as soon as the legion took the field?"

Silence reigned for a few seconds, before she went on.

"What would you do, my Lord Reth of the outriders, when you lead three or five hundred of your riders to strip and loot supply wagons by the dozen? When you lead your forces to harry and slaughter their enemies on the field with impunity?

"How many hundreds of slaves would you free daily? Leading them back to freedom and a real life, while taking a portion of the slavers' wealth as your own loot? Make no mistake, the empire is a massive beast, and one that must be fed and served. But it's not necessarily something that you can't benefit from supporting. Ask yourself what you want.

"You have an opportunity here to gain the kind of rewards that you have never imagined, and yet you focus on the changes and the risks, instead of the rewards. Ask yourself, what do you want, and then how can the empire assist you to get it?

"For those who want to continue to roam, Sonra can be that still. Not all of you have to settle down, or any, if that's not what you want. But if it is? We could create a city that has the advantages of both Sonra and Gaij, as well as the benefits of the empire!

"For myself, I wanted the tower restored, and my sisters free. For those who didn't know—and how could you—we were bound here by our old contracts, and forced to assist the tower. To do that, we constantly channeled our mana into it, trying to keep one step ahead of entropy. Now? For less than a week, Prince Jax has been in the city.

"The tower is growing, dozens of floors larger already. And it is again drawing its own mana. The locals who have harvested, used and abused my kind—in ways we weren't happy about"—she added with a throaty laugh—"well, those are now paying the ultimate price. That was our price, and he met it easily. He conquered the city in a handful of days with the smallest contingent of all. So, ask yourselves, what can he do with the support you could give him?

"What do you want out of this? You're asking 'Will the herds be safe enough?' with his plan, when you should be asking, 'What are the herds for?'" She shrugged.

"Are they only to exist for breeding and eating? Is there a specific aim to their breeding you are working toward, or are they there simply to grow and protect you, to give you a screen to hide behind and a way to afford to live?

"The legion needs mounts, and you'll be paid handsomely for them, I'm sure. The city needs food, and I will pay a fair price with pleasure. Beyond that, what are the remaining herds actually for? What, if not to breed the best that can be bred?"

"Sonra already breeds the best," Ilena snapped.

"And yet, what if you had access to the very best that can be recovered?" Seraphina purred. "If for every city and province that is conquered, their best were singled out and brought to you? The greatest of each herd could be provided to Sonra to breed the next generation. Instead of Sonra being known as the home of the great herds, what if Sonra and Gaij merged, to create the greatest of all cavalry?"

"The legion needs riders," Daralen said abruptly. "The best of the best, and they'd be equipped, trained, and respected for it. For any warrior, to know that you would be making a difference, and to improve, to learn, and better yourself, should be an easy choice."

"It should but…" Reth sighed, shrugging, "not all wish to improve. Many simply wish to exist."

"And for those, we're starting caravans." I rejoined the conversation. "We'll be reaching out to the other cities, setting up trade and more. Hell, change my mind on conquering them, give me an alternative, and I'll listen, *happily*. Show me that not all are scumbags trying to take advantage, and we can find another path."

"You would consider that?" Greg asked me, and I snorted.

"Are you kidding?" I shook my head. "Fuck's sake, I'm about to be a father, and even before that, all I wanted was to keep my people safe. If there's a way to do that where the war could end and we could all actually stop and relax? I'd take it in a heartbeat. The problem is that the offers we've had so far have all been by scumbags I wouldn't trust with a boiled egg, never mind the lives of those I love. Seriously, I don't want to spend my children's lives at war constantly."

"Plural?" Oracle asked, smiling suddenly. "As in, multiple children?"

"Hell yes. Who'd want to be an only child?" I asked. "Fuck that. I love my brother, as much as I want to punch him some days. I want a lot of kids, and I'll damn well enjoy the practicing as well."

"And just like that, we're moving off the topic." Seraphina smiled. "Please, consider what we've said tonight, but understand that we are at war. War is a terrible thing, but when we win this—not if, when…remember that we are led by a prince who has killed gods in single combat, so *when* we win—consider the next step. There will be an undefended Kronk, a city known for its wealth and raiding, that needs to be taught a lesson. And then the strongholds of the Dark Legion on this continent are open to us as well. Remember that if you choose to continue travelling, or even if you settle and integrate into Gaij now, you don't have to stay in the long term. You could stay now, and then decide to roam again when more of the territories have been conquered."

"Remember, as imperial citizens, you have the right of protection from the legion," Daralen said. "And that right could extend to sending legion units with you as you travel." As she said that, she glanced meaningfully at Reth, who nodded that he'd taken the hint.

"Very well. Perhaps we should call it a day at this point and actually relax and have dinner together?" I suggested, looking around. "Instead of arguing on and going in circles, perhaps we should all take the night to think on our positions, and what we need and want out of the situation, and then you can take that up with Seraphina, Daralen, or me, depending on the need, with Seraphina for the city and surrounding territory, Daralen for the legion and armies, and me for the empire."

"And who would we speak to about the airship?" Greg smiled mischievously. "That, *I* am interested in."

CHAPTER THIRTY

The sun was tinting the sky from midnight blue to a dusky pink as I made my way toward the massive workshop Seraphina had provided to the gnomes.

For what felt like forever, I'd been dealing with shitty little details, chasing idiots who just needed something explained one more time, and now? After all of yesterday fucking around with getting things into place, I was finally doing what I needed to.

Oracle was working with the legionnaires, teaching still more of them magic, and Sehran was spending the entire day working on contracts, with both the local succubai and the buggers still in hell, making sure that no matter what, we gained out of the situation.

But me? Today I was finally going to see what those crazy bastard gnomes had done with the airship designs Oracle had given them.

I pushed open the massive double doors to the workshop, a cavernous space that had once been used to store siege weapons, if the faded murals on the wall were any indication. The smell hit me first, making me cough and wince—a pungent mixture of machine oil, heated metal, various unidentifiable chemicals, and the unforgettable aroma of unwashed gnome.

"Hello?" I croaked. My voice echoed off the stone walls. "Anybody conscious in here?"

A head popped up from behind a workbench. The gnome's wild white hair stuck out in all directions and what looked suspiciously like a pair of goggles made from crystal decanters were strapped to his face.

"Visitor!" he shrieked in a voice far too high-pitched for the early hour. "The prince! The prince is here!"

Another head appeared, this one belonging to Greg. The goblin's yellow eyes blinked rapidly as if he'd just woken up.

"Jax," he said, his voice scratchy with exhaustion. "You're early. We weren't expecting you until after the morning meal."

"Greg?" I snorted. "Fuck's sake, is that you? I thought you were coming here later?" I admitted, stepping farther into the workshop. "Figured I'd check on the progress before my morning ass-kicking from Daralen."

"You were meeting me here," he agreed. "I simply chose not to wait for you. Cleq and I came here directly from dinner last night."

I looked around, trying to make sense of the chaos. The workshop floor was covered in scattered parts, half-completed mechanisms, and what appeared to be at least a dozen different drafting tables covered in schematics. Several gnomes were passed out on cots shoved against the far wall, while others worked in what seemed like a fever dream, muttering to themselves, swearing and occasionally breaking into manic giggles.

One of the mad little bastards was smoking.

I don't mean he had a pipe or a joint or whatever—there was literal smoke drifting off him constantly; he stood stock-still, staring at the wall and grinning.

"What in the actual fuck is going on here?" I watched as one gnome tightened a bolt with one hand while drinking from a beaker of fluorescent-green liquid with the other.

"Progress!" came a voice from an attached room.

I turned to see Cleq stepping through the doorway, her usual clean and tidy appearance replaced by oil-stained overalls. Her fingers, black with oil or grime to the middle of her hands, flexed like claws as she grinned at me. "Glorious, chaotic progress."

She gestured toward the center of the workshop, where something large was covered by a massive tarp. "Would you like to see what we've accomplished so far?"

"That's why I'm here." I sighed, following her toward the covered object. "Though I thought you fuckers were coming here with me, and you were just curious, not planning to take over."

Greg scurried ahead, grabbing one edge of the tarp. "Prepare to be amazed," he said, with far more enthusiasm than seemed warranted given his obvious exhaustion. "Or confused. Possibly both."

He and Cleq pulled the tarp away with a flourish, revealing…well, I wasn't entirely sure what I was looking at.

It was big, certainly. The frame was roughly the size and shape of a large farming wagon, but that's where any resemblance to normal transport ended. The bottom was lined with what appeared to be dozens of crystal tubes filled with swirling energy. Multiple canvas bags—inflation chambers, I presumed—were attached to the upper frame, but instead of the elegant balloon shape I'd expected, they looked more like lumpy potatoes strung together. A series of what looked like propellers were mounted at various points around the frame, their design unlike anything I'd seen before.

Most bizarre was the control area—not a helm as I'd expected, but a circle of chairs facing outward, each with its own set of levers, pedals, and gauges.

"What. The. Fuck," I said slowly. "Is that?"

"Isn't it magnificent?" cried one of the gnomes, bouncing up to stand beside me. "We've completely reimagined the concept of aerial locomotion!"

"You've completely reimagined something, that's for sure," I muttered, circling the contraption. "Will it fly?"

Cleq shrugged. "Theoretically."

"Theoretically," I repeated. "So you haven't tested it."

"Well, not as such," Greg admitted. "We've tested components. The lift chambers work wonderfully in isolation. The propulsion system has also been bench-tested."

"But not together?"

"We're building the first airship the realm has seen in seven hundred years," Cleq said defensively. "There's bound to be some…improvisation required."

"No—no, you're fucking not," I growled. "Dammit, I described what the airships we have back home look like! I told you how they work, and goddammit, Oracle and I even drew them plans!"

"Did you?" Cleq blinked in confusion. "What happened to them?"

"I don't fucking know, do I?" I growled. "What had they managed to get working before you arrived?"

"Not much," he admitted, bewildered. "They were in a heap, drugged up to their eyeballs and were arguing whether the moon was a giant cart, and if so, how they could steal it."

"Oh, for fuck's sake," I whispered, rubbing at my face and trying to maintain my calm. "Why did I think this was going to be any different?!"

I took a deep breath, trying to remind myself that I'd asked them to do the almost impossible on an insane timeline. "Walk me through it," I said finally. "Explain how this fucking version is supposed to work."

This set off a flurry of activity as gnomes and goblins crowded around, each trying to explain their particular contribution. After fifteen minutes of increasingly technical and contradictory explanations, I held up my hands.

"One at a time," I shouted. "Fuck's sake. Cleq? You start. Simple version."

She nodded, pointing to the crystal tubes along the bottom. "These are manastone accelerators. They draw ambient mana from the air and compress it into a usable form. The compression creates both lift and propulsion energy."

"We've enhanced them with the principles you shared from your tower's collectors," Greg added. "They're far more efficient than anything we've created before."

Cleq continued, pointing to the lumpy canvas chambers. "These are buoyancy chambers. They're filled with a gas lighter than air, created by a chemical reaction we trigger at launch. They provide most of the lift."

"And those?" I pointed to what looked like metal wings folded against the sides.

"Stabilizers and additional lift surfaces," one gnome piped up. "For maneuverability at higher speeds."

I walked around to examine the control area. "And this setup? Why so many stations?"

"Ah, that's the beauty of it." Greg's voice rose with excitement. "Unlike a traditional ship where one person steers, our design requires coordinated effort. One operator controls elevation, another handles forward propulsion, another manages the stabilizers, and so on."

"So it takes six people to drive this thing?" I asked incredulously.

"Seven, actually," Cleq corrected. "The seventh coordinates the others. We've developed a communication system using these speaking tubes." She pointed to a series of brass pipes connecting the chairs.

I pinched the bridge of my nose, a headache forming. "So you need seven specially trained people just to keep it in the air?"

"Well, yes," Cleq admitted. "But think of the advantages! No single point of failure. If one operator is incapacitated, the others can temporarily compensate."

"Unless it's the coordinator," I pointed out.

"Details." Greg waved dismissively. "We can train backups."

I walked around the contraption again, trying to envision it in flight. It was ungainly, overcomplicated, and frankly, looked like it had been designed by a committee of drunk madmen—which, given the state of some gnomes, wasn't far from the truth.

But underneath the chaos, I could see genuine innovation. The manastone accelerators were either incredible or utterly moronic—I didn't know which. The propulsion system, although bizarrely configured, had sections I recognized from some of the imperial designs Tenandra had talked about before.

"Have you thought about the power requirements?" I asked. "Even with these manastone accelerator thingies, you'll need a hell of an initial charge to get this thing in the air, right?"

"Ah!" A gnome with a particularly impressive mustache jumped forward. "That's where you come in, Your Highness! We've calculated that with your mana capacity, you'll provide the initial charge needed for liftoff and for ongoing flying. The accelerators will eventually take over to provide the forward momentum but you'll be used to keep it in the air."

I blinked, feeling a spike of horrified anger. "You designed this assuming I'd be your battery starter? And then you think that I'll spend the day, doing what? Just holding it up?"

"Well, you or another handful of powerful mages." The same gnome smiled. "But yes, that was the most efficient solution, and it'd be worth it!"

I shook my head, torn between admiration for their creativity and frustration at the practical complications. "How long until it's ready for a test flight?"

Greg and Cleq exchanged glances. "Three days?" Greg suggested.

"Two if we forgo sleep entirely," Cleq added.

"Oh, that's a good idea!" one gnome shouted. "No more sleep!"

"Bags!" another yelled, before yanking a handful of powder out of a bag that I saw all the gnomes had on their hips. A cheer went up as the others started doing the same.

"Wait!" I shouted. "Don't you fuckin'…"

I was too late.

All the gnomes in sight had buried their face into a handful of what looked to be commercial-grade Colombian marching powder. A deep inhale, a round of coughs that sent floating powder arcing through the air, and one by one, the gnomes started to fall over, utterly fucking unconscious.

"And how many people do you have working on this?" I asked Greg, looking around at the scattered gnomes. "Tell me you've got more?"

"Fourteen gnomes and now two goblins," Greg replied, shrugging. "Plus occasional help from some of your tower or city craftsmen who wander in when they're free."

"Ohmyfuckinggod," I whimpered. "ARE YOU SHITTING ME?"

"What's wrong?" Cleq frowned.

"Prince Jax, we're trying to create something never seen before—" Greg chastised me.

"NO!" I roared. "Fuck's sake—no, you're not." I dropped my voice and held onto the ragged edge of my self-control, barely managing not to pick him up and shake him. "Greg, I need paper, or parchment or whatever, and I'm going to draw you what I want you to build, okay?

"I want you to build it with these gnomes, any craftsmen you need, and any golems that you need. And Cleq, didn't you mention there were more gnomes with Sonra? Get them in here. All of them."

"But many of them aren't engineers," she protested.

"Doesn't matter. You need bodies—people to fetch tools, hold things in place, run errands. Anyone who can follow simple instructions." I turned to Greg. "And what's in those beakers you're drinking from?"

"Gnomish stimulant," he replied cheerfully, before blinking myopically. "Keeps them working through the night!"

"And scrambling your brains," I whimpered. "All right, it's okay, we can do this…"

The gnomes were already starting to kick and twitch. I realized that if we were to get this done, I'd just found the place I was going to be spending most of the next few days.

"So…" I snatched a piece of charcoal from the pocket of a gnome who was beginning to giggle hysterically, and I started to draw. "We need a shape that's simple, something that we all know how it works, and that's designed to hold everything we need. That's why it's a ship…"

"A wagon!" corrected Greg gleefully.

"Because a ship is designed to hold…wait, what?" I broke off.

"You say a ship is designed to do all of that? I agree. However, do you see many ships here, my prince?" Greg grinned at me. "The local artisans and our own people are experienced at building wagons. They have no experience with ships."

"I…see." I sighed. "Okay, so a wagon, a big fucking wagon, with a pointed bow…*front*." I cursed and put my fingers together, making them into a wedge. "It needs a bow like this, to break through the wind or it'll be constantly fighting against it, all right?"

"Of course!" He smiled. "I see what you mean now. Never fear!"

"Ah, like this?" Cleq interlaced her fingers and showed me.

I shook my head, forming the wedge again, then moved on.

I spent the next hour going through the design with them, identifying areas that could be simplified. By the time I needed to leave for my training session that Daralen had suggested, we'd outlined a modified plan that seemed at least marginally more practical.

"I'll be back this afternoon," I promised as I headed for the door. "Try to make some actual progress by then, not just more…innovations."

Greg nodded solemnly, but his eyes were already drifting back to a schematic one gnome was enthusiastically waving. I gritted my teeth, having a feeling my instructions had already been forgotten.

Training with Daralen and the legion was, in many ways, more straightforward than dealing with the gnomes—though yeah, more painful. She'd set up a training area in one of the tower's courtyards for me, a space large enough for several dozen legionnaires to drill all at once, and in this case, for them to spar with me.

When I arrived, she was already there, shouting orders at a group of "lucky" recruits who were attempting to maintain a shield wall against her veterans. The poor bastards were getting demolished, but they were learning fast—each time they reformed, their line held a bit longer.

Daralen spotted me and gestured for one of her subordinates to take over. "My prince." She approached with a formal salute that was somewhat undermined by the gleam in her eye. "Ready for today's lesson?"

"Depends," I said curiously, squinting at the group. "Is there a reason there's so many here?"

Her lip quirked up. "I thought we might try something different today—full contact, no mana or abilities—and see how you fare against multiple opponents."

I raised an eyebrow. "And the recruits?" I didn't really want to hurt anyone, but I also was unwilling to waste my training time with people I'd have to be careful not to hurt constantly.

"They were the winners of a little 'friendly' competition. As such, they get a break from training to see what real sparring is like when you climb the ranks." She smiled and nodded toward the far side of the courtyard, where three figures waited. "You'll be facing veterans today. Edin, Tullus, and Verana."

I knew Edin—she'd been with us since Marrow, a solid fighter with a mean right hook, I vaguely remembered. The other two were strangers to me, but the way they carried themselves spoke of years of combat experience.

"All at once?" I asked, failing to keep the surprise from my voice.

"Unless you're scared." Daralen smirked.

"Fuck you." I grinned. "Let's do this."

I walked to the center of the training area, where a circle had been marked out in chalk. My three opponents took positions around me, each drawing training weapons—blunted, but still heavy enough to break bones if they connected with enough force—while I accepted a wooden version of my naginata from Daralen.

"That should make the spar less lethal, but don't break it. Rules are simple," Daralen announced. "Stay in the circle. First to surrender or be rendered incapable of continuing loses. Magic is not permitted."

I nodded, hefting the naginata and spinning it, getting a feel for its balance and reach. It was a little lighter than mine, but felt uncomfortably solid as well, like it'd shatter instead of taking a blow. I shrugged. What would be, would be.

"Begin!" Daralen shouted.

The veterans moved immediately, coordinating their attack with the precision of those who had trained together for years. Edin came at me head-on while the other two circled to flank me. I blocked Edin's initial strike, then was forced to duck as Tullus—a burly man with a shock of white hair—swung for my head.

We were all wearing the standard "training uniform" of the legion—nothing fancy, and certainly nothing unique or marked up. The legion for the last few decades hadn't had the luxury of making things like that.

Instead, it was a pair of rough shorts, a sleeveless top, and soft-soled shoes—a bit like lace-up boots—all in a kind of "off-white" that spoke of a lack of chemical processing.

It was important, though, because the weapons we all used were dipped in fresh ashes or charcoal, so that even a glancing blow left a mark.

It was a pain in the arse at times, because you ended up touching things without realizing and then finding out just how much you scratched your chin or adjusted your package by the marks you left each time. But it was good for this.

The veterans advanced slowly, tightening their circle and constantly moving, trying to get at least one of their number into a position that I'd not see them coming, while the other two feinted to get my attention. I felt a flicker of grudging respect—they were good.

For the next few minutes, it was all I could do to keep them at bay. Every time I focused on one, the others would press their advantage. I managed to land a solid hit on Verana's shoulder, but took a blow to my ribs in exchange. My enhanced Constitution meant I could take more punishment than most, but that didn't mean it didn't hurt like hell.

"Is this really the best you've got, my prince?" Edin taunted, circling me with her practice sword held low. "I expected more from the man who killed a god."

"Just warming up," I grunted, parrying a thrust from Tullus.

I decided to change tactics. I was waiting for them to come to me, staying put and letting them dictate the fight, which I'd never do normally, so the hell with it. I charged straight at Edin, shifting my grip on the naginata to right-handed only and holding it halfway down the length, then spun and leapt at Verana again. This time, I lanced out with the naginata, almost throwing it, letting the haft slide through my fingers until I was down to the last foot, then clamping down hard.

The sudden lengthening of my weapon by over three feet was enough to throw off Verana's timing, allowing me to slam the tip of my practice naginata into her sternum. She staggered back with a charcoal mark across the front of her clothes, making it clear she was "dead."

One down.

I spun to face the other two. The world seemed to slow as I pushed hard, moving as fast as I could, executing a complex series of strikes that left Edin overextended and vulnerable. A quick sweep of her legs sent her to the ground, even as I twisted and lashed out with a snap kick, catching the last blade as it came at me, and kicking it aside.

Tullus proved more challenging. Despite his size, he moved with surprising speed, and had clearly been waiting for this. He kept his guard tight, moving as quickly as he could, throwing punches as much as he used his weapon and trying to drive me back to where I knew Edin was setting up to ambush me.

The thing was…I wasn't even pushing that hard. I caught myself waiting, ready for the "real" attack to come. I wasn't fully committing, expecting that it'd be clear when it came, that there was more that the legionnaires were planning. But it wasn't until I realized why I knew that Edin was waiting, that it all came to a head in my mind.

I knew Edin was waiting, because I remembered where she'd fallen, and then I'd used the sound of her breathing, the crunch of the gravel, and even the reflections off nearby metal and glass to keep an eye on her, while devoting most of my attention to looking for a hidden attack behind Tullus's more open ones.

For a few more minutes, we sparred, before the details clicked. I cursed mentally. After a series of feints that made it clear that he wasn't holding anything back, I simply overwhelmed him with a barrage of strikes, each one carefully calibrated to force his defense in a specific direction until I created an opening.

The final blow was a punch that I pulled, but that caught him across the jaw—not hard enough to break anything but definitely enough to ring his bell. He staggered, then collapsed to the dirt of the circle, even as I spun, wrenched the practice blade out of Edin's hand as she lunged at me, and then swept her legs from under her. She flipped to the ground with a crash that left her senseless, and Daralen held up a hand to stop me.

"Match to Prince Jax," Daralen announced, stepping into the circle. "Your technique is lacking, but your speed and strength are more than enough to make up for it. Did you trigger an ability?"

"No," I said. "I'm sorry, Daralen. I didn't." I helped Tullus to his feet. "I think we might have a problem with the training, though."

"The point of training," she said dryly, "is to ensure you survive when those advantages aren't available."

I was about to retort when I felt a familiar presence—a pressure in the air, a sense of anticipation that made the hairs on my arms stand up. The legionnaires felt it too; their postures straightened as they instinctively looked around for the source.

"Your mortals have the right idea," came a booming voice from the center of the training ground. ***"Technique matters."***

The air rippled, and suddenly Darakin stood before us, the God of Battle resplendent in gleaming armor that seemed like a second skin to him. His face—as always—was both handsome and otherworldly, subtly "wrong" in its perfection; the feeling of pressure that came from him made it damn clear that the being that just stepped out of thin air was nothing mortal.

"Lord Darakin." I bowed my head slightly. "Come to critique my form again?"

His laugh was like thunder, making several of the younger recruits flinch. ***"Come to give you a proper challenge, my friend. These mortals…"*** He gestured dismissively at the veterans, who had dropped to their knees. ***"I mean no offense to them, for they are impressive for their kind, and are adequate for basics…but you need more. As you were before your fight with Illoth, they sufficed. Since absorbing more of the divine, even when only holding your fragment and not fully absorbing it, they are no longer suitable."***

Daralen, to her credit, recovered her composure quickly. "My lord, we are honored by your presence. Would you…care to observe our training methods, as we try to adjust and assist the prince?"

Darakin's smile was all teeth. ***"Observe? No, Primus. I intend to participate."***

He turned to me, and the gleam in his eye was unmistakable. ***"Unless, of course, Prince Jax is too busy?"***

"Never too weary to get my ass handed to me by a god," I replied, resigned to what was coming. "Though maybe we could use a larger space? I'd prefer not to destroy this courtyard when you inevitably send me flying through a wall."

Darakin laughed again. ***"Prudent, though I shall limit myself to you, as always. The great field beyond the eastern gate should suffice."*** He looked at the kneeling legionnaires. ***"Bring your warriors. It is good that they should see your prowess."***

With that, He vanished. The air snapped closed behind Him like a door slamming.

Daralen stared at the space where He'd been, then at me. "Does this…the gods just popping in for a chat with you…does this happen often?"

"Honestly? More than you'd think." I sighed. "Come on, we'd better not keep Him waiting. He'll get cranky."

An hour later, I was flat on my back, staring up at the cloudy sky and trying to remember how breathing worked. Around me, a circle of a hundred of the legion watched in stunned silence as Darakin paced, critiquing my performance. Beyond them were at least a thousand of the aspirants who looked, frankly, fucking terrified that they might be expected to spar with either of us one day.

I knew this, because there'd been a perfect moment to observe the crowd when I spun, almost lazily, through the air, my weapon casually disarmed from me and my feet kicked out.

"And your guard drops when you prepare for an overhead strike," He was saying. ***"A minor tell, but one an experienced opponent will exploit. As I just demonstrated."***

I managed to raise a hand in acknowledgment, still not quite able to form words. My entire body felt like one massive bruise, despite the fact that Darakin had lowered Himself to my level, creating an avatar with my exact points in identical areas, so that He could "help" me.

The god sighed, then reached down and hauled me to my feet with casual strength. *"You're improving,"* He said, his voice pitched so only I could hear. *"But not quickly enough. War is coming, Jax. Not just with Kronk and the Dark Legion, but others. The realm gathers itself, and you must be ready."*

I nodded, finding my voice at last. "I'm trying…but there's only so many hours in the day. I've got a city to prepare, an airship to somehow make functional, and a pregnant partner who's pushing at least as hard and who I'm worried about."

Darakin's expression softened slightly. *"The child grows well. Oracle is strong. Focus on what needs your attention most urgently, and trust your people with the rest. And as to the airship? Perhaps speak to Svetu. He loves a challenge, after all."* Then His gaze hardened again. *"But do not neglect your training. I will return tomorrow."*

Before I could protest, He stepped back and addressed the assembled legionnaires. ***"You fight well, mortals. Your discipline is commendable. Remember that in battle, it is not merely strength but coordination that brings victory. Move as one, strike as many."***

He turned back to me, dropping His voice again *"Until tomorrow, champion."*

With that, He was gone, leaving only a lingering sense of sudden emptiness in the air.

Daralen approached, her expression carefully neutral. "Well," she said. "That was…instructive."

"That's one word for it," I groaned, feeling my ribs where Darakin had landed a particularly vicious blow. The bugger had pulled the blow, using the flat of his swordstaff instead of the blade, but it'd still broken at least four ribs. Thankfully, healing magic was a thing. "Sorry about the interruption to your training schedule."

"Are you joking?" She snorted and gestured to the legionnaires, who still stared at the spot where Darakin had stood. "My troops just witnessed the God of Battle Himself demonstrating combat techniques that they can use, and the difference between a trained and untrained combatant. That's worth a month of regular drills in terms of motivation."

I hadn't thought of it that way. Looking at the legionnaires, I could see what she meant—there was awe in their expressions, yes, but also a new determination. They'd seen what they were striving toward, however hard it might be.

Mind you, they'd also seen their prince get his fucking head handed to him as well, and I damn well suspected that Darakin had upped the level by a lot.

When we'd trained together last time, it'd not been as fucking one-sided…had it?

"Glad to be of service," I said dryly. "Now, if you'll excuse me, I need to go drown myself in healing magic and rum before I check on our flying monstrosity again."

Daralen nodded. "I'll continue with the recruits. Will you be joining us again later today?"

"Fuck to the no." I sighed. "Between the airship and meetings with Seraphina about the city's defenses, I'm booked solid. Tomorrow, though."

"Tomorrow," she agreed. "When your divine instructor returns."

The way she said it made it clear she'd be ensuring every available legionnaire was present to witness my next beating. *Perfect.*

By the time I returned to the workshop that afternoon, it had transformed. Where before there had been perhaps a dozen or so workers, now the place was swarming with activity. Gnomes were everywhere—standing on ladders, crawling under machinery, arguing vehemently over schematics. I spotted Greg in the center of it all, directing traffic with the authority of a field marshal.

"What happened here?" I asked as I approached.

He turned, his yellow eyes bright with excitement. "We took your advice! Cleq went to Sonra and brought back every gnome we had—fifty-three in total. Plus another dozen goblins with mechanical aptitude."

I looked around, noting the more organized workflow. "And the stimulants?"

"Limited to emergency use only," he assured me. "We've implemented shifts as you suggested, though some refused to leave in the middle of delicate work."

I nodded, making my way toward the airship. The tarp was now gone, and I could see substantial progress had been made just in the hours I'd been absent. The frame looked to be entirely different, resembling a wider, longer wagon.

Cleq appeared at my side, wiping grease from her hands with a rag. "We've simplified the control system," she said without preamble. "Down to four operators instead of seven."

"That's still three too many," I pointed out.

"It's the best we can do with the time constraints," she countered. "Any fewer and the controls become too complex for a single operator to manage effectively."

"Bullshit." I snorted. "I managed to fly a ship on my own, and that's normal back there, a single control console."

"Ah, but this was with a wisp to—" she countered.

I cut her off. "No. Tenandra is unique. The rest of the ships have a single pilot and that's it. Well, except for the dreadnought, but that's about the same size as the tower laid on its side."

"So big…" she murmured, her eyes shining as inspiration struck.

"Whoa—no…no, you fucking don't, all right! This is the project—THIS. You can make a giant ship later! This one, this needs to fly first and it needs to be using mana crystals! I'm not draining the mages to fly it!"

"But the cost…!" she groaned.

"The whole point of this is that it can carry all our people when we need to go, it can be fast, and it's a platform for the mages to bombard the enemy below from. If it's slow as shit and the mages are exhausted by flying it, then there's no point!"

"But this is the prototype!" she implored. "We need to figure out how it works before we can build a better one!"

I couldn't argue with that—not without delaying the project even further. "Fine, but don't forget that I need the damn thing to fly and get us to the other side of Kronk! Now, what about stability? That design isn't exactly aerodynamic."

"We've reshaped the buoyancy chambers." She pointed upward, where gnomes were busy reconfiguring the canvas chambers. "More streamlined now. And we've adjusted the weight distribution to improve handling."

I walked around the contraption, noting the improvements.

It was…well, it looked like someone had heard of the zeppelin, and then decided that it wasn't ballsy enough, and needed a wagon attached underneath, with a wide walkway that ran around that, and…a set of lawn chairs nailed into place on the front, because apparently having a great view was one of the most important considerations. "Fuck my life," I muttered, rubbing at my face, then cursing as I realized that I'd managed to get the soot on my hands again, and I could taste it on my lips. I dragged down a long-suffering breath, then hit myself with a Scour, and then turned back to her. "What about the power requirements?"

"Still substantial for initial liftoff," Greg admitted, joining us. "But we've modified the manastone accelerators to require less input. A single strong mage could now manage it without risking burnout…perhaps a thousand mana into the accelerators."

"And the capacity?"

Cleq consulted a sheet of calculations. "Currently designed for four passengers plus minimal cargo. We could increase that, but it would reduce speed and maneuverability."

I shook my head. "Four is fine for a prototype. The goal is proof of concept, and the next one will be the real transport. If this works, we can build larger versions later."

A commotion at the far end of the workshop caught my attention. A group of gnomes were arguing ferally over what either had to be the propulsion system, or an on-board washing machine and tumble-dryer combo. They were gesturing wildly and occasionally shoving each other, building up to what looked to be a full-blown fight.

Yup, before I could say anything, the smaller of the two—both appeared to be women—landed a punch that smeared the taller's nose across her face in a blur of claret.

"Problem?" I asked idly as they both screamed and started to beat each other.

"Creative differences." Greg sighed. "The traditionalists want to stick with a simpler propulsion. The innovators are pushing for their new 'thrust vector' concept."

"And in plain Common that means…?"

"Spinny blades versus directed mana jets," Cleq translated. "Both have advantages. The rotary system is more reliable but less maneuverable. The thrust vectors provide better control but are untested at scale, and they occasionally explode."

I watched the argument escalate, then made a decision. "If you can stop the 'occasionally explode' side, then use both."

They stared at me. "Both?" Greg repeated.

"Fuck it, why not? Don't get me wrong—you need to sort out the whole 'exploding' issue first, but rotary propulsion for forward movement, thrust vectors for fine control and emergency maneuvering. Best of both worlds."

The gnomes and Cleq exchanged glances. "That…could actually work," Cleq admitted. "It would add weight, but with the improved buoyancy chambers…"

"It solves the control redundancy issue as well," Greg added, warming to the idea. "If one system fails, the other could compensate enough for emergency landing."

I watched as they hurried off to share the compromise, feeling oddly proud of my diplomatic solution. Maybe I was getting better at this leadership thing after all.

For the next few hours, I moved between different work groups, offering suggestions where I could and mostly trying to stay out of the way of the true experts. The gnomes, for all their eccentricities, were brilliant engineers. Once given a clear direction and freed from the need to reinvent the entire concept of flight, they made terrifying progress.

By early evening, the airship—still unnamed, as the gnomes couldn't agree on what to call it or whether, like Oren had once told me, it should have a name before the maiden voyage—was taking proper shape.

The control systems were being installed, the propulsion mechanisms tested individually. Greg estimated they'd be ready for an initial ground test by the following evening, with a test flight two days after that.

Then, if all went well, they would start on the "real" version at that point, and it'd be a few more days when they put that together. It was going to be smaller than I wanted, much less maneuverable and more expensive as well. But if they could pull it off, it'd be enough to get us into the air and ready to unleash hell.

Just in time for the arrival of Kronk's forces.

As I prepared to leave, intending to grab some food before collapsing into bed, a messenger arrived. "Prince Jax." She saluted. "Lady Seraphina requests your presence in the Grand Hall. House Granth has arrived and seeks audience."

I suppressed a groan. House Granth had been expected at some point. Hell, they should have been here before this, all things considered. I'd totally lost track of the time I'd told them to make it to me by, but their timing couldn't have been worse. I was exhausted, sore from Darakin's "training," and had been looking forward to at least a few hours of rest.

"Tell her I'll be there shortly." I rubbed my temple, where a headache was forming. "And have someone bring some fucking alcohol to the hall. I just know I'm gonna need a damn drink to deal with this."

The messenger nodded and hurried off. I turned to Greg and Cleq. "Keep pushing forward. I'll check in again tomorrow morning."

"We'll have something even more impressive to show you by then," Cleq promised.

"I know. Look, both of you…thank you." I shook my head. "I know if you'd not decided to play with this project, I'd be even further up shit creek without a paddle, so thank you for taking it over. It means a lot."

"It is our pleasure, my prince." Greg smiled toothily. "And we gain from this as well. After all, when the basic versions have been figured out, then comes those that are used for real. For many of us, the herds were…a cost of our safety, as were the walls that kept us hidden.

"The lack of the smell is one that I am pleased to experience. And knowing that one day these creations may let us sail the skies, free from any danger? It is wonderful," he finished.

"Yeah, about that…" I smiled. "Believe me, there's plenty of danger up there as well, and when something fails, the result is messy. Like 'crater in the ground and everyone is dead' levels of messy," I pointed out.

He just smiled.

I sighed and then left the workshop, knowing that I was going to need to deal with more blatant political bullshit next, considering the message hadn't been "Wilhelm is here to swear fealty and behave himself"—it was "House Granth is here."

Fucking complications.

CHAPTER THIRTY-ONE

I got back to my quarters and took the few minutes needed to hit myself with Scour, and then pulled on fresh clothes and ran a hand through my hair, knowing full well I still looked like I'd been dragged through a hedge and then beaten senseless by the God of Battle—which wasn't far from the truth.

With Darakin's "training" session, I'd have been crippled at the very least, and taking this meeting from my bed if not for healing magic, though, so fuck it. I made my way to the Grand Hall to meet House Granth.

The hall had been transformed since we repaired the tower, and every time I entered it, it was different. Seraphina had clearly spared no expense, having the ancient chamber restored to something like it must have looked back in the day when she'd first come here. Though it made me smile to see that with the current version, she'd prepared a small throne-like chair atop a half dozen raised steps at the far end for me, instead of the lounger thing she'd had before.

Clearly, by the way that she stood close to it, but not sitting, it was intended for me, I assumed anyway. But it was also clear that once I'd gone—I'd not be taking up residence here long term, after all—she'd be using it instead.

It was a simple way to get herself a throne, and one that was entirely legitimate as well, and understandable. Sneaky fucker.

The marble floors gleamed, freshly polished, while newly sewn or repaired tapestries depicting the old empire's triumphs hung from the walls. Imperial banners—my banners, technically, though I'd never really considered them that way before—hung alongside the new symbols of Gaij that Seraphina had commissioned: a golden tower, surrounded by black, with a ring of red around it and the buildings of a stylized city picked out against the red.

House Granth stood, waiting in a tight formation near the center of the hall.

The man I took to be Gaspar stood, grim-faced and formal. His hair was touched with distinguished silver at the temples, though his face was hard-edged. Behind him stood a small group, including a younger man who bore only a vague resemblance to him—probably Wilhelm's father—a damn pretty woman with long blonde hair I took to be his mother, and Wilhelm himself, looking very uncomfortable a step behind Gaspar, positioned between and slightly ahead of them.

Behind them, in a sort of horseshoe pattern, stood the members of what I guessed were the "main branch" family, older men and women, carrying themselves with hard postures and ramrod straight backs, glaring at pretty much everyone.

They also looked incredibly pissed that Gaspar had presumably invited Wilhelm into the spot right next to him, as I got the feeling that the way they were standing was very deliberate.

Seraphina stood nearby on a raised dais, her posture impeccable and her expression carefully neutral. Four succubai attendants flanked her, their wings furled tightly against their backs and hands clasped behind them in a formal stance.

"House Granth," she announced as I entered, "Prince Jax Amon, Heir to the Imperial Throne, master of Dravith and Lord of Gaij."

Gaspar stepped forward and executed a quick bow as I walked past him that I could tell was technically correct but somehow managed to convey that he considered it an unnecessary formality. Considering that I barely knew a good bow from a bad one, that was saying something.

"Prince Jax." His voice carried that aristocratic inflection that immediately set my teeth on edge. "It is a pleasure to see you again."

"Bollocks. And I'm not going to lie and say that it's great to see you," I responded with a raised eyebrow. "Last time I saw you, I'd just been forced to fight for my life while you placed bets for amusement. So let's do this, Gaspar. What do you want?"

"House Granth comes to claim its ancestral holdings and position within the imperial hierarchy."

"Your ancestral holdings," I repeated, not bothering to hide my skepticism. "And where exactly would those be?"

"House Granth controlled extensive territories on this continent, as well as others in the empire, and we simply seek to recover them," Gaspar replied smoothly.

Wilhelm stepped forward slightly. "Mine prince, if I might speak?" When I nodded, he continued, "Ve understand zhat much has changed since zhe cataclysm. Ve merely seek recognition of our historical claims, but modified to account for zhe current realities."

His tone was respectful without be begging, a hell of a contrast to his grandfather or whatever Gaspar was, and his barely concealed arrogance. I studied him for a moment, remembering our brief encounter in the arena, and the times we'd met since. He'd fought well, with honor and skill, and when I'd defeated him, he'd not been a dick about it. Instead, he'd genuinely wished me luck, going so far as to offer me a necklace his mother had given him for luck.

I forced my irritation down, and nodded.

"Okay, so what exactly does House Granth bring to the empire besides outdated land claims?" I focused my attention back on Gaspar.

"We bring our considerable resources, knowledge, and military capabilities," Gaspar replied. "House Granth maintained and preserved imperial techniques and spell knowledge that will have been lost to this realm for centuries. Our house includes skilled mages, craftsmen, and warriors trained in Earth's modern combat techniques combined with traditional imperial methods.

"And most importantly," he added with a hint of smugness, "we bring legitimacy. House Granth stands among the oldest and most prestigious noble families, our lineage unbroken since the founding of the empire."

I leaned forward slightly. "Legitimacy," I repeated coldly. "You believe I need your approval to rule? That the support of the gods, of Amon himself naming me his heir and the right of conquest doesn't matter, but you supporting me does, is that right?"

"Not approval, exactly." Gaspar's tone suggested that was precisely what he meant. "But the support of the true nobility would certainly strengthen your position. The common people respect tradition, after all."

I couldn't help the laugh that burst from me. "The common people? Fuck's sake, Gaspar, the realm respects strength, and they want protection. And I'll tell you what they do respect, though—leaders who stand against their enemies rather than flee to another realm *to escape a cataclysm they fucking caused!*"

His jaw tightened at the barb. "The nobility did what was necessary to preserve imperial bloodlines and knowledge during a catastrophic event."

"One you fucking created!"

"Not all of us were involved!" Gaspar snarled. "We were forced to flee or die. What would you have done? We survived and protected our line!"

"And now you've returned to claim your rewards." I snorted. "How convenient."

Wilhelm stepped forward again. "Prince Jax, if I may zpeak plainly—ve seek partnership, not confrontation. House Granth has much to offer zhe reborn empire, particularly in zhe face of zhe approaching zhreat from Kronk."

"Kronk?" I asked, eyeing him.

"Vere you unaware?" He blinked, then he bowed. "Mine apologies, Lord Jax. Ve believed you knew, but zhere is an army marching on you already. Our informants say zhat Kronk has dispatched eight zhousand troops…"

"It's closer to twelve," I corrected absently, having gotten that update from Daralen already. "And there's also five thousand of the Dark Legion marching as well, though they'll arrive after Kronk."

"Ah, mine apologies, mine prince, perhaps zhis is mine error zhen. Regardless, ve could assist you, vith modern tactics, modern veapons…"

I watched him for a second before nodding slightly and looking back to the head of the house. "Wilhelm speaks more sense than you do, Gaspar," I remarked. "What specifically does House Granth offer against these immediate threats?"

Gaspar seemed about to deliver a sharp retort, but Wilhelm continued before the head of his house could speak and ruin their momentum. "Ve have detailed knowledge of defensive wards zhat ve vould be villing to share and zhat may be useful to counter large-scale assaults. Our mages know many spells, and zheir aid with defensive spellcasting could help significantly, as could our limited, zhough extremely powerful Earth veapons."

With Kronk's army approaching, the wards might be useful, as would their knowledge of modern manufacturing. But honestly? Not hugely. I wasn't willing to let these pricks near my airship project, and I didn't doubt that the wards would need a lot more time to be set up and powered than we had, and…I glanced at Oracle, who had remained silent since we arrived.

"What do you think, my love?" I asked her.

"I like Wilhelm. Gaspar? Not so much," she admitted. *"Can we get one without the other, or without the rest of the family?"*

"Probably not."

"Well, in that case, can we use them where the fighting is thickest and 'accidentally' forget to reinforce them?"

"I wish." I sent her a mental chuckle. *"What do you think, though, seriously?"*

"Maybe see what they can do, give them a chance, and make it clear that they behave or they're out?"

"Good plan."

"Impressive claims," I said aloud. "And what do you expect in return?"

"Recognition of our ancestral claims—adjusted for current realities, of course," Gaspar repeated, with a glance at Wilhelm. "Restoration of House Granth's place in the imperial hierarchy, with appropriate authority over our traditional territories. And a position on your council befitting our status."

I studied him for a moment, sensing the trap. "And if I decline these terms?"

Gaspar's smile didn't reach his eyes. "Then we would be forced to seek alliances elsewhere. Other noble houses have established territories on this continent. A unified nobility would be a formidable force. I believe one has already made such an offer to you, and was refused. I'm sure they would appreciate all we could bring."

The threat was barely veiled. I leaned forward, my voice hardening as I decided that now was the best time to make things evident regarding our respective positions.

"Let me be perfectly clear, Gaspar. I don't *need* the old nobility's blessing to rule. Hell, it'd probably make my life harder. The empire rises again because the people are helping me to do it, and because the gods themselves have blessed it, not because a handful of aristocrats who abandoned their responsibilities seven centuries ago have decided that we can't live without them any longer."

Gaspar's face tightened with poorly concealed anger, but Wilhelm placed a hand on his arm.

"Perhaps," Wilhelm suggested, "ve could discuss more specific terms? Our leader speaks of zhe house's traditional position, but ve recognize zhat circumstances have changed dramatically since zhe cataclysm."

I thought about it for a few seconds. Having them on board could be useful; hell, just a brace of RPGs at the right time could turn the tide of the fight, after all. And having someone who was involved in all the plots and shit that the noble houses seemed to breathe constantly would be good, as it'd mean I didn't need to worry about that shit.

The other side was I didn't *like* Gaspar, I didn't trust him, and my fists were itching to smash his teeth so far down his throat he'd be shitting them out.

"Be calm, my love. Remember, we need all the help we can get, and we can always leave them here and go back to Dravith when the time comes. He'll have to abide by the rules you set," Oracle sent me, and I grumbled, mentally, at her.

"Here's my offer," I said finally. "Swear allegiance to me and the empire. Provide your defensive knowledge immediately to help prepare for Kronk's arrival. In exchange, I'll consider your land claims—subject to verification and current occupation—and request House Granth is considered for a position on *Seraphina's* council—understand that I won't be remaining here to rule, so it's not my council, after all—though not with the authority you've requested."

"Unacceptable," Gaspar snapped. "House Granth does not bow like common supplicants. We are imperial nobility."

"You are refugees from a dead era," I corrected. "The empire where you had control and rights is long gone. Under the new one, there's gonna be nobles, sure, but they earn their place, and they rise as high as they deserve—no higher, Gaspar.

"The empire I'm building is going to work for everyone we can manage. We're going to protect the weak, raise up strong children, and send the creatures of the night running. If you earn that spot? You can be part of it all and rise literally as high as you want. Or you can cling to your bullshit rights and be left in the dust. Don't fucking test me."

Wilhelm stepped forward again, his expression troubled as Gaspar glared at me. "Prince Jax, might I suggest a compromise? Perhaps ve could establish a probationary period during vhich House Granth demonstrates its value to zhe empire, after vhich our position could be formalized based on our contributions?"

"A reasonable suggestion," I agreed, liking the idea. "But any arrangement would still require House Granth to swear the imperial oath, binding all members to loyalty to the empire and its laws."

Gaspar's face darkened further. "I will not bind House Granth to unspecified terms before our position is secured."

I shrugged. "Then you know where the door is. Try not to let it hit you in the arse on your way out."

"Lord Gaspar," Wilhelm said quietly but firmly, "you invited me to take part in zhis meeting, because you believed I might learn something, or see something zhat you missed. Mine advice is zhis: perhaps ve should consider zhe prince's position. Zhe threats facing Gaij are immediate. Our knowledge could save lives, and it vould prove our value."

The tension between them and certainly between the others and Wilhelm was thick enough to cut with a knife. Gaspar clearly hadn't expected to be contradicted publicly, and sure as shit not by a member of the lesser branches of his own house.

"Wilhelm has a point," I agreed. "And let's be clear on this, Gaspar, because frankly it's been a busy day and I'm only halfway through it. You bring information and knowledge that would be useful, but without me, you're about as welcome in these lands as the plague. You need to get somewhere to live, and with your weapons, you can do that. Hell, you can probably take most smaller towns over easily…maybe, with a lot of planning and luck, even a city.

"That's as far as you could go, though, and you know it. You've got a dozen hangers-on who have done nothing but glare at me since I arrived, and you're bringing a sense of entitlement that's the last thing I need.

"Could you help me? Yeah, you probably could. And I know your modern weapons certainly could—though I doubt you have much. And again, let's be honest here—an RPG is great, as are assault rifles, but once you're out of ammo, they're fancy metal ornaments. Magic and armies here are what will carry the day, and although you've got a little to add, it's nothing compared to what you're asking.

"If I accepted your demands, you'd gain access to imperial sites, you'd have authority over them, and you could easily supplant any of the local nobles who are members of your old house, which through genetic drift and intermarriage, is gonna be most of them on this continent. You're wanting me to give you the keys to the fucking kingdom, for a song, a promise, and basically bugger all else.

"As such, the answer is no. You want to go join the other dickheads and fight me later? Go for it. I'll regret killing Wilhelm and his family as I get the feeling he's a good guy I could work with. For what it's worth, you're nowhere near as much of a bellend as my father, which gives me some hope.

"I'd do it, though, if that's what I have to do, so I'll say it again. Don't fucking test me. Go away, have a think what you can realistically offer me and what you want in return, and we can talk again. Or not." I sat back in the throne, my hands resting comfortably on the arms below. I waited, preparing to activate a half dozen different abilities and spells.

Gaspar looked as if he wanted to argue further, but Oracle chose that moment to step forward.

"Lord Gaspar," she said, her voice calm and reasonable, "perhaps you would like time to consider Prince Jax's offer, and while you do so, we could provide food and drinks, as well as somewhere to rest?"

After a moment's hesitation, Gaspar nodded stiffly. "We will consider your…proposal, Prince Jax. Though I must warn you that other houses will not be so accommodating."

"And I'm fine with that, because if I'm honest? I'm looking forward to slaughtering most of them, just like I did Malakai," I replied with a thin smile. "Seraphina will have one of her people show you to appropriate accommodations within the tower, and we can talk later."

As House Granth was escorted from the hall, I noticed Wilhelm glancing back with an expression I couldn't quite read—something between apology and hope—and I sighed when the doors closed, looking to Seraphina and Oracle.

"Well, that wasn't fun," I muttered.

"Definitely not." Oracle sighed, massaging her back. "I'm exhausted. And that timing? He's either lucky or stupid, and I don't know which."

Seraphina stepped in close, her expression thoughtful. "As nobles of the old empire, they could be useful, if you could bind them to serve honorably," she pointed out. "They could be used to activate old ruins and imperial sites, spread the rule of the empire, and even claim locations in your name."

"And their arrogance could be lethal," I countered. "Especially if they're willing to help our enemies."

"On the upside, though, we'd have a diplomat we could send to negotiate who we're not going to be upset about if they got beheaded." Oracle smiled, before going on more seriously. "Wilhelm appears to genuinely understand that they've got no rights with us."

I nodded, standing and taking Oracle in my arms, giving her a brief kiss, before looking to Seraphina. "Keep a close eye on them, please. I want to know if they try talking to anyone else."

"Already arranged," she assured me with a slight smile. "The rooms prepared for them have certain…advantages. The walls have ears, as they say."

"Good." I stretched, wincing as my muscles protested. "Now, if you'll excuse me, I need to go back and see how our flying monstrosity is progressing. With any luck, the gnomes will have built something that won't kill us all the moment it leaves the ground."

"Weren't you just there?" Oracle frowned.

"Honestly, I'm terrified of leaving them for *any* amount of time to get into trouble. If I'm there, I can still meditate and try to figure shit out, or get food, and then I'm ready to spar as well. If I'm here?" I glanced to the side, seeing a good dozen people already hanging around, looking hopeful.

"Unless you're here to see Seraphina, go to Othair," Oracle ordered them firmly. "He is dealing with the prince's schedule and will arrange slots where appropriate."

That got them moving, though most looked pissed, and she turned to me as soon as they were out of earshot.

"As soon as he arrived, I had him set up and told him that he needs to decide who gets access to you. If they waste your time, then he's failed, and you'll consider this as a trial, and then find someone better to do that job in the future."

"That's evil." Seraphina smiled. "For someone like him, simply being in the heart of such power is the most powerful drug of all, so to imply that anyone who wastes your time is his fault? He'll be the most terrible gatekeeper imaginable."

"Sounds damn good to me." I grunted. "He's not stopping people who actually need to see me though, right?"

"No, but he's filtering out the timewasters who primarily just want to be seen talking to you." Oracle sighed. "I've been getting the legionnaires to chase them off as well. And you don't want to know how many dinner invitations we get."

"Have they been pestering you?" I asked her. A building feeling of annoyance for timewasters made me stick my jaw out, ready to fight someone, when she laughed and shook her head.

"No, I'm working with the legion all day, so I have them stop anyone interrupting me at all, and then gather up all the invites. They dump them on Othair's desk when I remember to send them over."

"Well, that's something then," I grumbled.

"A point, though," Seraphina interjected calmly. "Attending some of these dinners—or hosting your own—would be wise. These are the people who matter in the city. And before you say that everyone does, you know what I mean is that they can either help you, and me, to achieve your aims, or they can make it far harder. Genuinely, it would help."

And that was how I ended up being forced into agreeing that we'd have a damn formal dinner in three days' time.

Fortunately, in the meantime, I managed to run for it back to the "comforts" of the drug-addled gnomish—and goblin-ish—workshop.

It was in a state of controlled chaos when I arrived. Gnomes scurried across scaffolding and platforms surrounding what was now clearly recognizable as an airship frame, albeit one with certain…unconventional design elements.

The wagon-like base I'd last seen had been streamlined. Its front now sported a pointed prow that would indeed help cut through air resistance. Above it, the inflation chambers had been completely redesigned, arranged in a slightly more aerodynamic configuration that actually looked to be moving in more of a zeppelin style rather than the lumpy potato sacks of the last version.

Greg spotted me immediately and hurried over, his yellow eyes bright with excitement despite the obvious exhaustion on his face. "Prince Jax! You're just in time for the preliminary activation test!"

"Already?" I asked, surprised. "I thought you said it would take at least another day."

He grinned, revealing his pointed teeth. “We’ve been working in shifts around the clock. Cleq brought in every gnome and goblin with any mechanical aptitude from the Sonra caravan. Progress has been…explosive.”

“Fuck’s sake, that’s what worries me,” I muttered, following him toward the center of the workshop where Cleq was directing a team of gnomes making final adjustments to what I guessed had to be the control system.

“Ah, Prince Jax.” She greeted me without looking up from her work. “We’ve simplified the control interface considerably since yesterday. Now it only requires three operators instead of seven.”

“That’s still two too many,” I pointed out.

“Well, it’s the best we could do with the time we had,” she snapped. “One pilot controls direction, one manages altitude, and one coordinates the mana flow. Any fewer and it’ll probably explode.”

“You know what? Three sounds good,” I agreed with a snort of amusement.

I walked around the craft, inspecting the modifications. The propulsion system had been completely reconfigured, with what appeared to be both propellers, looking like something from the Great War, and directed mana jets positioned at strategic points around the frame.

“You went with both systems,” I approved.

“Your suggestion was quite brilliant.” Cleq finally looked up from her work. “The rotary system provides steady forward thrust while the mana jets offer fine control and emergency maneuverability. If one system fails, the other serves as backup, and we should be able to turn faster than a horse!”

I nodded, moderately impressed despite my concerns. “Power requirements?”

“Still substantial for initial liftoff,” Greg admitted, “but we’ve modified the manastone accelerators to require less input. A single strong mage could almost certainly now manage it without risking burnout.”

“Or much burnout,” Cleq hedged.

“Well, obviously, there’s a margin for error.” Greg beamed.

“And the explosions,” Cleq pointed out.

“There were only three!” Greg sighed. “And almost everyone survived!”

“Except the ones who blew up.”

“Well, *of course* except the ones who blew up!” He rolled his eyes. “Anyway, moving on…”

“And the payload capacity?” I asked slowly, not sure whether I should get between the pair when they were arguing in case I got bitten.

Cleq consulted a sheet of calculations. “Five passengers plus minimal cargo. We could increase that, but it would reduce speed and maneuverability.”

“Again?” I asked. “Look, we agreed, the goal is proof of concept, not troop transport. If this works, we can build larger versions later, but we’re gonna need them, all right?”

A commotion near the rear of the craft caught my attention. Two female gnomes were engaged in what appeared to be a rapidly escalating technical disagreement, complete with emphatic gestures and increasingly creative insults.

“Why is that familiar?” I asked, then blinked. “Weren’t they doing that earlier as well?”

"Standard gnomish creative differences." Greg sighed. "The fueling system for the mana jets is the issue this time, I think. One prefers direct manastone or conduit transfer. The other insists on a buffered approach."

Before I could respond, the smaller of the two gnomes landed a punch that sent her colleague sprawling. Rather than intervening, the surrounding gnomes simply adjusted their positions to give the combatants more room.

"Is this…normal?" I watched as the fight escalated.

"For gnomish engineering? Absolutely," Greg replied with surprising cheerfulness. "Technical disputes are traditionally resolved through demonstration of superior force. It's quite efficient, really—the winner's design is implemented without further debate."

I shook my head, deciding not to interfere with their "process." "When do you expect to be ready for an actual test flight?"

"Tomorrow, if all goes well with today's systems check," Cleq said. "We'll test the engines and lifting mechanisms today, then the integrated systems tomorrow. And if those prove satisfactory, we'll attempt a short, controlled flight the following day."

"Just in time for Kronk's advance scouts to reach our outer perimeter," I noted.

"We'll be ready," Greg assured me. "Though I should mention one limitation—the craft as designed is primarily a reconnaissance platform and limited troop transport. It won't accommodate large numbers and we have no weaponry planned."

"It's better than nothing," I said. "Don't worry about the weapons. The plan is to have legionnaires who can cast spells aboard, and they can fly overhead, picking off juicy targets."

"That's a thought…what about looking down?" Greg asked suddenly. "You know, actually being able to see the ground below. Should we use slings for the legionnaires?"

"Of course not!" Cleq swore. "That would be incredibly inefficient. They'd be constantly having to kick their legs back and forth to get any momentum going with a swing!"

"Well, what if we swung them? Have two people above each one, swinging them back and forth."

That got them both thinking, as Cleq scratched her chin, musing. "The view would be incredible."

"They might fall off."

"Well, we just have some spare people aboard, just in case." Cleq groaned. "Honestly, do I have to think of *everything*?"

It took a couple of seconds to realize that while I was thinking of a sling that legionnaires could be attached to, to look down from the underneath, the pair were actually talking about a swing, like in a child's playground.

The worst part of all of this was that Greg and Cleq were elders of their race and representatives of Sonra. I was used to the mad shit that gnomes came up with; I was actually hoping the fucking goblins would be better, which probably said more about me than them.

The lift test was a success, in that the bag on the top inflated to about twice the size of the frame and it lifted about six inches off the floor before letting out a fart-like noise and collapsing to many cheers, and one of the prototype engines exploded when it was tested. Again, to the sound of much cheering.

Eventually I gave up and went back to the tower, got some food and a drink, and chased Oracle around the bedroom a bit, just because why the hell wouldn't I?

The next morning came about far too fast, and after a brief breakfast, I kissed my love goodbye, answered a few questions and gave far too many orders, and then set off for the workshop again.

Nearly four hours of arguing had passed when a tower messenger arrived, saluting crisply. "Prince Jax, your presence is requested for training with Lord Darakin. He awaits you at the eastern field."

I suppressed a groan, my muscles already protesting at the thought of another session with the God of Battle. "Inform him I'm on my way," I told the messenger before turning back to Greg and Cleq. "Continue with the tests. Don't blow anything up, kill anyone, or do anything stupid. I'll be back later."

"We'll have something impressive to show you," Cleq promised.

"Just make sure it flies and doesn't fucking explode!" I reminded her. "Everything else is secondary, you mad bastards." That last part was muttered, but I knew she got it by the big grin she gave me.

Darakin was waiting for me on the training field, His divine presence drawing the eye of everyone around. A crowd of hundreds had gathered already, and not just legionnaires this time, but citizens of Gaij as well, drawn by rumors of yesterday's display.

"Prince Jax," He boomed as I approached, His voice carrying across the field without effort. ***"You return for more lessons."***

"Apparently I'm a slow learner," I replied with a rueful smile, rolling my shoulders to loosen them for the inevitable beating to come.

Darakin laughed, the sound like distant thunder. ***"Not slow. Merely learning. There's a difference."*** He drew his weapon—a massive sword that seemed to shift form slightly as it moved through the air. ***"Today we focus on countering superior reach and strength. Many of your coming opponents will possess both."***

I nodded, drawing my own weapon, my naginata. After all, it wasn't like I was going to try to kill him for real. He was a god, so unless I really tried, the worst I could do him was a minor injury. Plus, that crack about "superior reach and strength" was ridiculous. I had a naginata, he had a sword, and…the massive sword, as I eyed it, lengthened even further, reaching at least ten feet to my naginata's seven. I sighed. "I'm ready."

What followed was an hour of the most intense training I'd ever experienced. Darakin drove me relentlessly across the field with a series of attacks that tested every limit of my speed and endurance. Each time I thought I'd found a pattern to exploit, He would change tactics, forcing me to adapt instantly.

"Better!" He called as I successfully deflected a particularly vicious overhead strike. ***"You're anticipating rather than merely reacting. Did you feel the strike before it arrived? Be honest."***

"I think so." I scratched the back of my neck, considering it. I'd managed to get into that sense of oneness, the void, where there was nothing—no thought, no emotion…just emptiness—and when I'd been there, I'd held him off for what had felt like seconds, but I knew was longer.

"It was…" I paused, thinking of the word for it, when He grinned.

"I thought you had! Excellent! Again!"

I didn't waste breath responding, focusing instead on maintaining my footing as He pressed forward again. My muscles burned, sweat pouring down my face, but I refused to yield ground easily.

As the session progressed, I became aware of a disturbance at the edge of the field. Glancing over during a brief respite, I saw Gaspar and Wilhelm watching intently, having apparently decided to observe the training.

Darakin noticed my distraction and followed my gaze. ***"Your noble petitioners seem interested in our work,"*** He observed. ***"Perhaps they wish to learn as well."***

Before I could respond, He renewed His attack with even greater ferocity, forcing me onto the defensive once more. I managed to parry three consecutive strikes before mistiming a counterattack, leaving myself exposed. Darakin's practice sword connected with my ribs, sending me staggering back several paces.

"Focus!" He barked. ***"Your opponent will not politely wait while you attend to distractions."***

I nodded, centering myself and reengaging. The next exchanges went better, as I managed to land a glancing blow on Darakin's shoulder—an achievement that drew murmurs from the watching crowd.

The god acknowledged the hit with a slight nod. ***"Improvement. But still too hesitant in your follow-through."***

We continued for another half hour before Darakin called a halt. I was dripping with sweat, my limbs trembling with exhaustion, but feeling the familiar satisfaction of having pushed my limits.

"You learn quickly," Darakin said, His voice pitched for my ears alone. *"But time grows short. The darkness gathering in the east is greater than you yet realize."*

"The Dark Legion?" I asked, catching my breath.

"They are but a shadow of what comes," He replied cryptically. *"Rest for the remainder of today. Tomorrow, we will work on integrating your abilities with your physical combat skills."*

As Darakin stepped back, I became aware that Gaspar had approached the edge of the training circle, Wilhelm trailing behind him with a concerned expression.

"Impressive display," Gaspar called out, his voice carrying a note of condescension. "Though perhaps somewhat theatrical for practical purposes?"

Darakin turned slowly to face him, and the air temperature dropped several degrees. ***"You question my methods, mortal?"***

Either oblivious to the danger or too arrogant to heed it, Gaspar continued. "Merely observing that actual combat seldom resembles such choreographed exhibitions. House Granth's warriors train in more pragmatic techniques."

Wilhelm's face had gone pale. "Lord…" he murmured urgently, tugging at Gaspar's sleeve.

Darakin stepped toward Gaspar, his form seeming to grow larger with each stride. The crowd around them shrank back instinctively, legionnaires and citizens alike recognizing the god's mounting anger.

"You believe you know combat better than I, mortal?" Darakin's voice was terrifyingly hushed. ***"You, who have hidden from actual battle for centuries? Who fled and dishonored his own house, when you failed to apprehend the murderers in your own midst?"***

Gaspar finally seemed to recognize his mistake, but pride wouldn't let him back down completely. "I meant no disrespect. House Granth has its own combat traditions, that's all," he bluffed, realizing that his attempt to show me up in front of my supporters had backfired…massively.

"Show me," Darakin commanded, His voice brooking no refusal. ***"Demonstrate these superior techniques."***

The blood drained from Gaspar's face. "I…that is, I'm not properly attired for—"

"Now," Darakin interrupted, gesturing to one of the nearby legionnaires. "***Provide this one with a training weapon."***

The legionnaire hurried forward, offering a practice sword to Gaspar, who took it with visible reluctance.

Wilhelm stepped forward as if to intervene, but Oracle appeared at his side, gently restraining him, and making me smile that she'd come to watch me.

"This is unwise," she murmured to Wilhelm. "But necessary."

Gaspar stepped hesitantly into the training circle, holding the practice sword awkwardly. Despite his bluster, it was immediately apparent that his combat experience was limited at best.

Darakin didn't even bother drawing his weapon. ***"Attack,"*** He commanded.

After a moment's hesitation, Gaspar lunged forward with a clumsy thrust. Darakin sidestepped effortlessly, His hand closing around Gaspar's wrist with crushing force. In one fluid motion, He disarmed the noble and swept his legs from under him, sending him crashing to the ground.

"Pathetic. Again!" Darakin ordered as Gaspar scrambled to his feet, retrieving his weapon with trembling hands.

What followed wasn't training by any stretch of the term but abject fuckin' humiliation. Darakin systematically dismantled Gaspar's every attempt at offense, demonstrating just how vast the gulf was between mortal combat skills and divine mastery. He didn't inflict serious injuries, just painful and obvious ones, which He then ordered be healed, before He went again, and again…and again. Each takedown was calculated to maximize Gaspar's embarrassment before the watching crowd.

Finally, after Gaspar had been dumped unceremoniously onto his backside for at least the tenth time, Darakin stepped back. ***"House Granth's combat traditions are not impressive,"*** He declared, His voice carrying to every corner of the field. ***"Perhaps your knowledge is better spent on matters other than warfare."***

Gaspar struggled to his feet, his fine clothes now covered in dust and grass stains, his face mottled with shame and anger. "You…you had no right—"

"I have every right." Darakin cut him off. ***"You questioned my authority in my own domain. Consider yourself fortunate that I chose to educate you rather than eliminate you for your impertinence. Were you not striving to show your worth to my ally, I would have eliminated you and every one of those who have shown such a lack of honor!***

"Only three have I seen in your house so far who deserve such largesse as being recognized by the prince, let alone a member of the divine, and yet still you have shown little sense and less honor in your attempts at manipulating them.

"Be warned, Gaspar of House Granth. Your kind were permitted access to events and respect by dint of your relationship with Amon, your forebear. Since your failure to avenge him, and your dishonorable existence, you have lost that respect entirely. Take this warning to heart: should you feel the presence of the divine, and not be protected by Prince Jax, fall to your knees and beg for a swift end."

The god turned his back on Gaspar, a dismissal so complete it drew a collective intake of breath from the onlookers.

"Prince Jax, we will continue tomorrow. Your noble petitioner should leave my presence before I reconsider my mercy."

Gaspar stood frozen for a moment, then threw down his practice sword and stormed away, shoving past Wilhelm and the gathered spectators.

Wilhelm hesitated, then moved forward and bowed deeply to Darakin. "Zhank you, Lord Darakin, for your mercy und zhe gift of your instruction," he said clearly, before hurrying after Gaspar.

"He could learn much, that one," Darakin muttered in an aside to me.

"Wilhelm?" I asked, and he nodded. "Yeah, I like him too, despite everything."

"He shows potential, though so does the meanest ore. It is the treatment it receives and the form it is guided to that matters as much as the base material."

"Yeah, you're not wrong there, mate." I snorted, then winced, realizing how I'd spoken to him, and that we were essentially standing almost shoulder to shoulder, slagging off someone who had annoyed us, and discussing if his kid was a waste of skin as well.

"Regardless of the end of our allotted time today, the spar was both enjoyable, and I believe, helpful to you?"

"Definitely," I agreed, thinking about the difference between sparring with him and the legionnaires. "When I was training with the others…" I tried to think of a tactful way to say it, not wanting to complain about the legionnaires who'd been genuinely giving it their all.

"They are mortal," He said. ***"As you leave that state behind, you will find that each step along the road increases your power by a significant degree. You will find that although your own stat sheet is still showing results, it is…less accurate than once it was as well."***

"Crap, you mean I'll need to reset it again?" I asked, remembering the difference on the ship when I'd done that before.

"No," He said simply. ***"Such things are not meant for the gods, and they are always less accurate. Simply respect it as a recommendation now, instead of a law. Be well."***

With that, he turned and strode from the field, vanishing between one step and the next. With the primary draw—a literal god kicking the crap out of their prince—gone, the crowd started to disperse, and Oracle approached me.

"That could have gone worse," she observed with a smile, standing on tiptoes to get a kiss. "You're all sweaty."

"You don't normally complain." I smirked at her, then wrapped my arms around her and held her tight as she pretended to try to fight me off.

"Usually that's because we've both been getting sweaty!" she huffed, finally breaking free and glaring up at me. "It's less fun when it's just you."

"But you liked seeing me spar," I pointed out.

"You're half naked and fighting a god. I don't think anyone's man is going to be beating you on those grounds." She tossed her hair and acted like one of those hoity-toity princess types for a few seconds. "I'll accept you're not as pathetic as the others who want me, and you'll do for now."

"For now?" I laughed, and she grinned.

"Sorry, I've been teaching a succubai life-sensing spell to the legion scouts, and their minds…" She shook her head, blowing out a breath then grinning. "It's a mess in there!"

"I bet." I frowned. "Wait, couldn't they have hurt…"

"It was Sehran," she assured me, and I relaxed, knowing that Sehran would never hurt Oracle. "Anyway, I think a little humility for Gaspar was important to learn."

"I agree, but think how much easier our lives would have been if he'd killed him." I picked up my shirt and looked at it, seeing the rips and the damage, then sighed. "Pants it is then." I shrugged, dumping my sweaty and bloody rags to the side with the other rubbish to be cleared away at the end of the day.

"True," she conceded. "Though I suspect Gaspar's pride might not survive it yet. If he decides to mouth off about Lord Darakin…" She shrugged, then smiled at the possible repercussions.

We both turned to look at the crowds, seeing whether we could spot the pair, then nodding as Oracle pointed at Wilhelm's retreating figure. "Wilhelm seems different from Gaspar. More thoughtful."

"I noticed that too," I agreed. "He tried to warn Gaspar before the situation escalated. And he's shown more sense in the past too, but it could be fake."

"Honestly, I don't think so, and we still need to learn more about the families." She sighed. "We know that Falco were more or less honorable and fled because there was no choice—or at least we think so. They weren't involved with the attack on the emperor, I mean. What if Granth were the same?"

I nodded, then glanced toward the tower. "I need to clean up before checking back in on the airship test. Do you want to join me?"

"I wish." She sighed. "No, it's back to teaching for me. Although, if we could get a deal struck with Granth, we could make use of their mages in the legion training, which would be nice…"

CHAPTER THIRTY-TWO

The next morning dawned clear and cool, which was a damn nice change from the summer heat. I'd just finished a light breakfast when a tower attendant arrived with news that Gaspar had requested an audience.

A private one.

"Did he say what it was about?" I asked, surprised that he'd recovered his composure so quickly after yesterday's humiliation.

"No, my prince," the attendant replied. "Only that it was a matter of great importance that he wished to discuss with you alone."

I exchanged glances with Oracle. "What do you think? Trap?"

"Possibly," she mused. "Though, honestly, if he watched you fight yesterday, I don't get what he thinks he's going to accomplish."

"I'll grant it," I decided after a moment's consideration. "But I want guards outside the door. Oracle, I'd like you nearby as well, just in case."

The attendant bowed and departed to deliver my response.

I turned to Oracle with a weary smile. "Want to bet he's going to threaten to take his toys and go home?"

"Too easy—there's no way our life is that simple." She snorted. "Though there's a small chance that Wilhelm has finally managed to talk some sense into him and he's actually willing to negotiate in good faith."

"Miracles do happen," I agreed, though with little conviction. "Though I fuckin' doubt it. Sehran?"

"Yes?"

"Go see Greg. He'll be at the workshop, no doubt. Ask him if he has another of those truth stones. I don't know where the hell I put mine…"

An hour later, I found myself waiting in a small meeting chamber for Gaspar's arrival. The room had been chosen deliberately, with multiple exits and clear sight lines. There were also two rooms nearby with Oracle, Sehran, and a shitload of legionnaires hanging about inside "just in case."

Gaspar arrived perfectly on time, which surprised the shit out of me, as I was expecting a power play to make me wait for him.

"Prince Jax," he greeted me with a bow that was a little less…*weird* than the last one. It was quick, perfunctory, and as though he wanted to get it over with as soon as possible. The way his fingers twitched and clenched said the same, and…I realized that it was my Perception. Since I'd boosted it to a hundred, I was noticing far more than I normally did.

"Thank you for agreeing to see me." His voice was clear, but again, abrupt, as though he'd rather be anywhere else other than here.

"Lord Gaspar," I acknowledged, gesturing to the chair across from me as I sat down in my own. "You wanted to speak privately?"

"Yes, thank you." Again, his tone was quick, precise and clipped. He sat, looked around the room as if making sure we were alone, then checked again, eyes narrowing.

I smiled. "Nobody is waiting in stealth," I assured him, rubbing the stone in my pocket idly. "Would you like me to cast a spell to prove it?"

I almost cursed as soon as the words were out of my mouth. I'd been thinking Flames of Wrath, but as he wasn't sworn to me, he'd burn as well. Thankfully, he took me at my word and shook his head.

His movements were careful and deliberate; for several minutes, he just stared at his hands, which were clasped tightly on the table before him. When he finally spoke, his voice was uncharacteristically subdued.

"I've been a fool," he said bluntly.

Of all the things I had expected him to say, that hadn't even made the list. I maintained a neutral expression, fighting not to say things like "Ya fuckin' think?" and instead waiting for him to continue.

"Yesterday's…demonstration by Lord Darakin was enlightening in ways I hadn't anticipated," Gaspar went on. "It forced me to reconsider certain assumptions I've held for far too long, as were the obvious, well, repercussions."

"Such as?" I prompted, when he fell silent again.

"Such as the notion that the old nobility could simply reclaim our former positions through right of birth," he admitted. "The world has changed more profoundly than I was willing to consider. The gods walk among us again—they did on occasion in the deep past, but it was considered a rarity, and only their upper priests or Grandfather met with them truly. For the rest of us, it was only at the highest of feast days, when they chose champions, or if they decided to take direct action."

He looked up, meeting my gaze directly. "I've spent the night reconsidering House Granth's position and what we truly have to offer in this new era, and what it can offer us."

"And what conclusions have you reached?" I asked, still suspicious of this apparent transformation.

"That our future lies not in clinging to past glories, but in adapting to present realities," he replied. "To that end, I have a proposal that I believe would serve both our interests."

I leaned back, studying him carefully. "I'm listening."

"I propose to step aside as head of House Granth in favor of Wilhelm," Gaspar stated. "He would swear allegiance to you and the empire, placing all House Granth's resources at your disposal. In exchange, you would recognize our ancestral claims—modified to account for current realities, of course—and accept Wilhelm as a loyal vassal, with a position on *your* council, not the local one, but the imperial senate, provisional for five years, at which time if he's not earned a full place on it, you can dismiss him."

"And your role?" I asked.

"Advisor to Wilhelm, nothing more." Gaspar sighed, before sitting forward. "I've come to recognize that my…temperament is perhaps not well-suited to the diplomatic challenges of this new age."

I couldn't help the skeptical expression that crossed my face. "That's quite a change of heart, Gaspar. Why should I believe it's genuine?"

His lips thinned. "Because I'm not a complete fool, boy. Yesterday made it abundantly clear that the balance of power has shifted. The gods have chosen their champions, and you are among them. Fighting against that tide would be suicidal. Not to mention the obvious threat that was made."

"Which one?" I asked.

"Which one?" He scoffed. "There were so many that you forget? The one that the God of Battle made to eliminate my house! He literally threatened to kill everyone in my house, bar three, and considering the way it was phrased, it was clear who! My grandson Wilhelm is...he's a good man. A better man than I deserved, considering how we've treated him. Both him and his parents, my son Kurt, and his wife Penelope.

"They were never interested in the family 'business' as you might call it, just… Do you want to hear this or not?" He glanced up from his fingers.

"Sure," I agreed, then held a hand up before he could start. "Look, this is sounding like a hard conversation."

"The hardest a man can make." He grunted.

"Want a drink with it?" I picked up a small bell from the table and rang it.

"By all that is holy, yes," he growled.

A few seconds later, when a member of the serving staff had entered and been sent with orders to bring strong local spirits, I gestured for him to continue.

"Fine, uh, thank you," he forced out, before taking a deep breath. "I guess I should start at the beginning then."

"It's a very good place to start," I replied softly.

"Heh, well, I was the forty-third in line, born to Cerin, Amon's fifteenth son, and the elven maiden Caramantha, a little over two thousand years ago. Local time being what it is, I honestly couldn't tell you much more specifically than that, but the point is that I never expected to be in line for greatness.

"Unlike many, by the time I was born, the empire was already old. The process of pacifying the outlying lands was well in hand. My father died from a wyvern attack that led to most of their species being culled from the steppe, and I inherited my title younger than most. That was probably why, when I was old enough to understand the choice, I decided to devote myself to a gentleman's pursuits."

"You were a scholar?" I asked him, blinking.

"Bite your tongue, boy," he snapped, then grinned as if embarrassed. "I was a lothario and a wastrel, spending more on pleasure gardens and whores in a month than most cities earned. I spent decades, centuries even, involved in the most fun and debauched of surroundings. And although I was offered many bindings over the years with many succubai, I refused all but unconditional fun, deciding that I had no real rank, and no real responsibilities, so to hell with it.

"In Amon's earliest days as emperor, he wanted his children to follow in his footsteps. They were to serve in the legions, fight and hunt monsters, expand the borders and protect the innocent and weak." He shook his head.

"By the time I was born, all that had changed. My elder half-siblings were already as sunk in debauchery as it was possible to get, and Grandfather had given up on most of us. We were given an honorary title, some lands, and were essentially left to our own devices, summoned to the capital once every five years to give a report to the chamberlain, who would decide whether we'd earned the right to face Grandfather.

"I did it twice, and never again. The man was a bloody hellion, and scared the crap out of all of us," he muttered, rubbing the back of his neck, then breaking off as the door opened and the same serving man reentered with a decanter and two glasses. He picked up the story again once the man had left, and this time, he held his glass in his hands, clearly trying to decide whether to speak or drink. "When I first faced him, I expected to be praised, and instead he asked me what I'd done.

"I told him of the increase in profits from my city and the surrounding areas. I told him of trade routes and of the growth of the empire. He asked me again what I'd done, and I didn't understand. He told me to go, and that next time I came before him, to consider my actions and not to waste his time."

He drank his drink down in one, knocking the amber liquid back like it was water, then making a face that was all surprised acceptance. "Not bad," he admitted.

"Not bad at all," I agreed, tasting mine and nodding.

"So, the next time I saw him, I'd pushed my people. I'd demanded more profits. I'd sent out bigger caravans. And when they'd been raided, I'd sent out the legion to deal with it. I told him of the new products we had, of the maps and discoveries our traders had made, of the explorers' progress, and he asked me again what I'd done, and what I learned.

"When I repeated the same, trying to get him to understand, he threw me out, and I was furious." He knocked another glass back. "I left the capital, and I never returned, not until Sanguis summoned us all. When he did, I was invited to a party, and I was told that there was a new order rising. That we'd been overlooked for too long, that we'd been ignored, dismissed and despised by an uncaring parent.

"And he was right. We'd all been ignored. In my case, that casual dismissal had driven me back to the edges of the empire, and I spent the next thousand years stewing in my anger and the contempt that I'd been shown until Sanguis summoned us all.

"By the time Sanguis told us all these things, we were ready to listen. The emperor was old, after all, and *obviously* senile. He'd ask the same question of all of us, and we were forbidden to discuss our answers. But it was obvious who his favorites were, and it was rarely any of the main branch."

He shook his head. "That should have told me something. That there were clear favorites was the way of life, but who they were, and what? That was clear, if you had eyes to look. Jamis, Legion Primus Praetoria. Elbetta, a golem architect. Ren, the general of the Northern Legion. And, of course, always his favorite, Samanth, a merchant's daughter discovered to have been born out of wedlock, and raised to the imperial family when her bloodline was discovered. She refused all the benefits of court, or so it seemed, and built a merchant empire.

"Those he loved, and he lavished gifts on them. When I was told that they'd be taken care of as well? By Sanguis, I mean? I was overjoyed. I was also stupid and petty, in that I never gave a thought to how, or what would happen beyond that—simply that Sanguis, the first born, the leader of us all and the prince of the realm, said it would happen, and that was enough.

"What he was going to do was never clear, or at least not to most of us. I think we all thought there was going to be a meeting of the senate, some kind of action to prove to Grandfather that he was wrong, and too old, and then he'd be put aside. Certainly, that was what we believed would happen with the favorites.

"When it all happened, the coup? It was over in a rush…legionnaires fighting legionnaires, monsters in the palace grounds, magic the likes of which I'd never imagined, the gods themselves falling and being banished. And then? The moon." He spat to the side, then apparently thought better of it and apologized.

"Go on," I told him, pouring us both another glass.

"Sanguis told us all that we'd been betrayed, and to bring anything we had that was powerful and to follow him. He would save us all, and he did." He shrugged. "He marched us through the portal to your realm, to his fallback position, a location he'd prepared to hide in if it'd all gone wrong. Once we were there, with everything we knew failing and falling apart, it was obvious to a few of us that we'd made a terrible mistake.

"Falco tried to kill Sanguis on the spot, but he's always had more bravery than sense. Sides were taken, and in the first hour after we arrived and the portal was closed, more noble blood was spilled than in the last thousand years before it.

"By the end of it, we'd all fled in separate directions. None of us trusted the others, and we'd all grabbed anything we could—artifacts, weapons, whatever. A few had their guard, or a few treasured servants, but that was it. We were suddenly in a different world, one without mana and with no clue what we were to do.

"Roll forward a few centuries and we were all in touch again, setting up our own private fiefdoms and doing everything we could to keep them safe from our brothers and sisters, aunts and uncles. A limited truce was reached. Although we all still tried to kill each other with assassins and poisons, or mercenary bands, by and large, we were content with the way the world was going."

"You were happy to stay there?" I asked him disbelievingly.

"Long term? No. The lack of mana made every day a miserable existence in some ways, though the new world brought us much in the way of compensation still—men and women to warm our beds, precious treasures, and technology." He shrugged. "I participated in the process to get us all home, but it was out of fear that if I didn't, I'd be left there, alone, while my brethren grew fat and happy raiding my cellars."

"Cellars that were destroyed?" I asked, and he waved that aside.

"To me, and to the others, they were still there. Of course we knew there'd be damage. We knew there'd even be rebellion and the possibility of people trying to break the empire apart was raised. But it was the empire! It existed for thousands of years, and held hundreds of millions, billions even at its height. Even with the capital destroyed, with Amon gone, it would endure."

He shook his head. "We believed it—I did. Nothing that anyone said would dissuade me, and in truth, nobody tried very hard. Why would they, after all? For most of my closer children, it meant that when we returned—not if, *when*—then they would be the nobility of a vast and powerful empire. If they managed to convince me that this was ridiculous, then I'd either fly into a rage or depression, spending anywhere from months to decades in it.

"When Kurt and Penelope had their boy, I was in one such slump, and I ignored them long enough that they simply raised the boy without our familial input, more or less. He was raised on the stories of our home, but that as he and his parents weren't in the direct line, of my first born and all the primo genesis that involved, they simply accepted that it wasn't for them, and became hardworking members of the family.

"We mocked them mercilessly for it, behind closed doors, and occasionally openly, but, well, what happened, happened. When I watched our name be drawn, and I had to choose one of the family to sacrifice? I chose Wilhelm, knowing that he was likely to die, because at least then it wasn't one of those I genuinely cared about, and…" He hung his head in shame.

"When you spared him, the relief was incredible. But, more than that, the reaction of Kurt and Penelope? They tried to leave the family—to just leave, to get away. I let them…a little. I moved them to new roles. I twisted things so that they were close enough that I could reach them, and yet, I gave them the space they wanted."

"And then you killed a thousand people to open a portal?" I asked him grimly, and he blinked at me in surprise.

"Well, no?" He frowned.

"What?"

"How do you think we got here?"

"By portals using blood magic," I growled.

"Well, partly right, yes, but also, no." He smiled for the first time, looking genuinely amused. "Yes, there were some human sacrifices, and I made sure my people knew it, and that word would reach the other families as well. But in most cases, it was animals. And the humans…we emptied the prisons. Those closest to our chateaus had always had our people inside them ready, if such a situation was to occur, but believe me on this if nothing else. No 'innocents' died to bring us through. Animal sacrifices were the majority. Self-aware beings grant the most mana to the realm, but ten times the number of lesser creatures could grant it as well.

"We killed thousands of animals and hundreds of criminals to return, expecting a realm that would be overjoyed that we'd returned. And what we found?" He sat back. "They treated us like you do. Like scum, like it was all our fault, when we were as much victims as any other." He stared at me, seeing something else, though, as he spoke, his voice growing softer.

"For nearly two thousand years, I asked myself what my grandfather wanted me to say, and I had no clue. Last night, in a fit of rage, I asked the same question to Wilhelm, like I have all my other children over the years, and do you know what he told me?"

"He told you what he'd done," I said just as softly. "Not what the people in his lands had done, not the accomplishments of others, but what he'd done with his own two hands."

"He did," Gaspar admitted, glaring at me. "Of course you'd see it straightaway, damn you. He told me exactly that, and I almost flew into a rage. I gave him all these opportunities, offended and pushed back my firstborn and all my other heirs to give us a chance, to offer you Wilhelm and show we could be valuable to you, and he gave me *that* as an answer."

"What did you do?"

"I told him to get out, and I sat there, drinking in the dark of my room. The words went round and round all night long. He told me, just like he had as a child, and when I'd dismissed him, thinking he was just too simple to understand, instead I saw the truth. He'd told me that he'd learned to ride a horse, or his bike, that he was studying the sword, that he did all these things, and instead of hearing his stupidity, I heard his intelligence."

"And now you're willing to give him your house? Just like that?" I asked skeptically.

"No." He shook his head. "I'm accepting that this is his house, not giving him anything. Yesterday, in an attempt to bluff that my house was strong, I didn't consider that I offended a literal god. I was too caught up in the things I 'knew'…like that Grandfather would never permit Darakin to actually harm one of his children."

"And then you realized that he's dead." I nodded, seeing it. "You've been lying to yourself ever since it happened, haven't you?"

"I think we all have," he admitted sourly. "All of my children certainly did, except for that boy and his parents, who worked to stand on their own two feet. And while they did, me and mine have suckled on the teat of the empire like a parasite, giving nothing back. This is our chance. If he does well, he'll lift our house, and we with it. If he fails…well, that's why we want concessions."

There was truth in his words—I could sense it thanks to the stone—but also calculation. Gaspar hadn't undergone a complete personality transformation overnight, but he was being honest. Or at least I thought he was, considering the bloody stone in my pocket was staying happily warm. There'd been a few bits where it'd shivered as he came close to lies, but I'd guessed it was more by omission or lack of understanding than outright malice, and so I'd said nothing.

"All right, so what're the concessions you're looking for and what of the succession?" I asked. "Your previous demands were…" I snorted.

"We would accept whatever position you deem appropriate in the succession…it's more that we are acknowledged as being within the good graces of the empire again, and our rights to our old lands returned," Gaspar replied carefully.

"As far as I know, there was nothing in them that would help the empire now, over any other territory. They were, though, my home, and the only place I ever loved, so I want it back. We would administer it as an imperial fiefdom, complete with taxes and under your rule, all laws to be observed. Wilhelm would be the ultimate lord, though I would rule in his stead as my own condition, and when he's there, or we're here and so on, I serve as his advisor. And, naturally, we would expect recognition commensurate with our contributions."

I considered his proposal in silence for several minutes. Having Wilhelm as the formal head of House Granth would be far more manageable than dealing with Gaspar's ego and ambitions. The younger man had shown more flexibility and pragmatism than his grandfather, and seemed genuinely interested in constructive collaboration.

It just seemed too fucking easy, that's all.

"If I agree to this arrangement," I said finally, "there would be conditions."

"Of course." Gaspar nodded.

"First, the oath Wilhelm swears would bind all members of House Granth, including you, and you'd all swear the oath of citizenship. You know this isn't just a formality—it's a magical binding that would prevent direct action against me or the empire. I don't know exactly how that prick Sanguis did it, but I think it took Nimon's help, or he'd have died taking action against Amon."

Gaspar's jaw tightened slightly, but he nodded. "Understood."

"Second, although I would recognize your ancestral claims, subject to verification and current realities, Wilhelm's and therefore your place in the succession would be determined by me, not by historical precedent, and it'd be at the back, for now at least. Though, I'm willing to change that when you prove yourself."

"Acceptable," he agreed—though, by the clenched teeth, I could see it cost him.

"Third, House Granth's resources—including any technologies, spell knowledge, or other assets you brought from Earth—would be shared with the empire as needed, particularly for our immediate defense against Kronk and the Dark Legion. And your troops and mages, as needed, are mine to command."

"We would, of course, contribute to the common defense," Gaspar replied. "Though once there's no need for us here, if those troops have been expended or their weapons lost, you'd provide a legion escort for missions we go on. I think that's fair. Such as sending us to try to negotiate or eliminate the other houses, and provide an appropriate escort when we go to reclaim our lands."

I leaned back, considering. The offer was better than I'd expected, and yeah, hell, send him to negotiate, and if he died? Absolutely no loss at all. I mean, I'd not want to lose honest legionnaires, but him? That was a win as far as I was concerned. That crack about reclaiming his lands was obviously what he was after. A "legion escort" to do it was blatantly meant as a full fucking legion or more to go and conquer his old lands, but…I mean, I'd have to claim them anyway, right?

That was probably what he was ultimately after anyway, I realized.

If I took his troops and used them all, their weapons and so on, then I'd need to replace them. A hundred or so modern mercs or a few thousand legionnaires, all with magical training, just weren't in the same league.

I still didn't trust Gaspar's sudden change of heart, not at all. Wilhelm, though…yeah, maybe him I could take a gamble on. And at the end of the day, let's face it. If I needed to, I could kill them all. And Darakin was already pissed at them, so I didn't see them lasting long if they did try something.

"Very well," I said finally. "I accept your proposal, with one additional condition: the transition happens immediately. Wilhelm becomes head of House Granth today, not at some undefined future point."

Gaspar hesitated, then nodded. "Agreed."

"Then we have an accord. Seraphina will arrange a formal ceremony tonight to officiate the transition and Wilhelm's oath-taking, as well as that of all your people. In the meantime, I expect a full accounting of whatever defensive knowledge House Granth possesses that might help us against the approaching armies."

"It will be done," Gaspar promised, rising and bowing again.

As he turned to leave, I added, "And Gaspar? This is the only chance House Granth gets. Don't waste it."

He paused, then nodded once before departing. As soon as the door closed behind him, Oracle entered from the adjoining chamber, softly closing the door behind her.

"Do you believe him?" she asked.

"Not entirely," I admitted. "But I believe he's pragmatic enough to recognize when his current strategy has failed. And I do believe Wilhelm genuinely wants to be part of building something new rather than clinging to the past. He's got something planned, though."

"I get the hope, but that his excuse for the last two thousand years of achieving nothing being that he was basically stupid and trying to fake it so that the other houses wouldn't attack him?" Oracle shook her head. "He's not that stupid."

"Maybe, maybe not," I disagreed. "I think he's wanted to believe something so long and he's never had to grow up that maybe yesterday was the final straw that was needed, that's all."

"I hope so," Oracle whispered. "I like Wilhelm."

"Me too. All right, let's check on the gnomes' progress before the ceremony tonight. I want to see if our flying contraption is any closer to being airworthy."

The workshop was humming with activity when we arrived. The airship now hung suspended from the ceiling by heavy chains, its inflation chambers fully expanded and its engines running at a low idle. Gnomes scurried over every surface, making final adjustments and conducting what appeared to be pre-flight checks.

Greg spotted us immediately and hurried over, his face alight with excitement. "Prince Jax! Lady Oracle! You're just in time!"

"Time for what?" I asked warily, noting the almost manic gleam in his eyes.

"The maiden flight!" he exclaimed, gesturing proudly toward the craft. "All systems are functional, and the initial tests exceeded our expectations!"

I stared at him in disbelief. "You're joking. Yesterday you said it would be days before it was ready for an actual flight."

"We worked through the night," Cleq explained, appearing at Greg's side. Her clothes were stained with oil and her eyes were bloodshot from lack of sleep, but her expression was triumphant. "The systems test went perfectly, and once we started, we couldn't stop until it was complete."

"Define 'perfectly,'" Oracle requested.

"Well, there was one small explosion," Cleq admitted. "But we identified the cause and resolved it immediately."

"And the prototype is fully operational now?" I asked, still skeptical.

"Absolutely!" Greg assured me. "Phizzik is preparing for the test flight as we speak."

I looked toward the craft and saw a particularly wild-looking gnome settling into the pilot's chair, strapping himself in with an elaborate harness while muttering excitedly…and stroking the metal.

"Is he…talking to the airship?" I asked.

"Phizzik has a special relationship with his creations," Cleq explained diplomatically. "He's also our most experienced test pilot."

"Our *only* test pilot," Greg corrected under his breath. "The others are dead."

"The flight plan is quite conservative," Cleq continued. "Just a short circuit of the tower's perimeter at low altitude to demonstrate basic functionality. We'll conduct more extensive testing tomorrow once we've evaluated today's performance."

"Wait, one pilot? I thought you needed three?" I asked, suddenly spotting that there was only one of the buggers behind a console now…you know, exactly like I'd fucking told them to do it.

"Well yes, until we ran out of pilots and had to make it work for just one," Cleq said, as if that were obvious.

I watched as the remaining gnomes got ready, making final adjustments before scurrying clear of the craft. A section of the workshop's roof had been retracted, creating an opening large enough for the airship to pass through.

I didn't ask how the hell they'd found the time to make the roof retractable, but considering the size of the airship now, I was betting it'd ended up too big to get through the doors and the mad gnomes had found a way to do that too.

"All clear!" called one of the gnomes supervising the launch. "Initiating sequence in three…two…one…"

The engines roared to life, the sound surprisingly muted given their apparent power.

I heard a groan from the side. Glancing over, I saw three mages—young ones, given the scraggly beards and obvious lack of wealth—all collapsing to the floor, exhausted.

The craft began to rise steadily as the chains were released, its movement controlled and precise. So far, at least, it seemed to be functioning as intended.

Phizzik's voice echoed through the workshop as he screamed down: "Systems nominal! Lift ratio at 112% of projected! Mana flow stable! Initiating forward motion with flappy things!"

The airship moved smoothly out of the workshop and into the open air above. The propellers chopped at the air and drove it forward while the mana jets burped in frantic patterns to keep it level. From below, it looked surprisingly elegant despite its unconventional design, though I half expected it to explode or split in half at any time.

"It's actually working," I murmured, genuinely impressed.

"Did you doubt us?" Greg asked with mock offense.

"Given that yesterday it looked like the bastard offspring of a potato farm that had fucked a wagon? Yeah, you could say I had some concerns," I replied dryly, before going back to staring at the contraption as it limped into the sky. "Fuckin' hell, they actually did it…"

CHAPTER THIRTY-THREE

The afternoon sun beat down on me, turning the sweat pouring off my body into a clammy slick that made me almost lose my damn grip as I ducked under Darakin's swing.

The God of Battle's massive blade whistled through the air where my head had been, and I felt the breeze of it passing my ear.

"Too slow!" Darakin thundered, His form perfect as He pivoted with impossible grace and reversed direction, bringing His weapon around in a vicious arc that would have taken my fucking head clean off if He'd been really trying.

I caught the blow on my naginata, my arms trembling with the effort. The weapon's shaft creaked ominously under the pressure, and I heard the collective gasp from the crowd of legionnaires and Gaij citizens who'd gathered again to watch me get my ass kicked by a literal god.

"Better," Darakin acknowledged, pressing harder. ***"But still not good enough."***

I twisted suddenly, breaking the lock and rolling under his guard, coming up behind him. I struck at his exposed back, only to find my blade meeting empty air as Darakin simply stepped aside like the fucker had always known what I was going to do.

A boot crashed into my ribs, sending me sprawling across the dirt. Pain lanced through my side—nothing broken, but I knew from experience it would bruise spectacularly if I let it. Instead, I rolled to my feet, spitting dust and feeling the grit between my teeth as I reassessed the massive, armored form standing before me.

Darakin stood ten paces away, His practice blade held loosely at His side, a slight smile playing at the corners of His mouth. ***"You're learning to anticipate, but you still rely too much on what you see rather than what is."***

"What the fuck does that even mean?" I muttered, circling warily, trying to keep my breathing under control. My naginata felt heavier with each exchange, though I knew that was just fatigue setting in.

Darakin's smile widened. ***"It means you're training your eyes when you should be training your instincts. You manage to hold the void for longer and longer each time, but for war, to truly be the weapon that you know you can be, you must embrace it."***

In a blur of motion, He closed the distance between us. His blade came down in an overhead strike that I knew would have chopped me in two had it been real.

This time, I didn't try to block—that was a fool's game against His strength. Instead, I stepped *into* the strike, throwing His timing off just enough that the blade passed harmlessly to my right. I brought my naginata up in a sharp thrust that caught Him in the shoulder.

For a moment, surprise flickered across Darakin's face, quickly replaced by satisfaction. ***"That's more like it!"***

The next exchange was brutal. I abandoned conscious thought, letting my body flow from one movement to the next, matching Darakin's supernatural speed with my own enhanced reflexes. Letting the void fill me: emotion, fear, concern, anger…all of it seeping away.

For several long minutes, we danced across the field, blades clashing in a rhythm that seemed almost like staccato gunfire.

Every muscle in my body screamed as I pushed beyond my limits. Sweat stung my eyes; the taste of blood was in my mouth from where I'd bitten my tongue earlier. The world narrowed to nothing but the next strike, the next parry, the next heartbeat.

Then Darakin changed the tempo, and I found myself overextended, my guard open. The god's practice blade stopped a hairsbreadth from my throat, cold metal kissing my skin.

"Death," Darakin announced, then stepped back. ***"But you lasted seventeen minutes in close combat, Jax. This is not a small amount of progress."***

I lowered my weapon, chest heaving and lungs burning. "Seventeen…minutes? Fuck…me, it felt…like…a heartbeat," I wheezed as everything crashed back in. "How the hell…do I feel…like this?"

"You are used to your stamina being one of your greatest strengths, but in truth, no matter the opponent, combat, especially higher combat, is exhausting. Seventeen minutes, Jax, in close combat against the God of Battle. I say this not to be offensive, or to rob you of the achievement, but there were places I could have stopped the fight."

"I…bet…"

Darakin nodded, His expression turning serious. ***"To do so, however? I would have to have used more than just skill. Adding in an ability, a gift of the divine. When you face mortals in the field, their skills will be lesser. And this is not pride talking, but fact—I am the God of Battle, Jax. If you were to be able to best me, then what would I be?***

"More to the point, what would you have become? Time flows differently in battle. Seventeen seconds can be an eternity when blades are drawn, never mind sixty times that. Remember this when Kronk's forces arrive."

The mention of the approaching army sobered me immediately. "Two days," I said quietly, wiping sweat from my brow. "Maybe less if they decide to pick up the pace…"

"They won't," Darakin assured me. ***"Your outriders have done good work. But yes, the time approaches. You should—"***

He frowned in annoyance as a messenger approached, a young legionnaire who couldn't quite hide his awe at the God of Battle's presence. I recognized him as one of the newer recruits by the fact his armor was still shiny as hell and clearly hadn't been broken in.

"Prince Jax…my…my Lord Darakin…" The legionnaire saluted nervously. "Primus Daralen requests your presence at your earliest convenience. The gnomes have completed another stage of the airship's construction and wish to demonstrate it."

I nodded, my ribs protesting as I straightened up. "Thank you. Tell her I'll—"

"You'll rest," Darakin interrupted firmly. ***"And heal those injuries before you go anywhere."***

I grinned, and then was about to make a comment like "Yes, Mum," but the look on his face silenced me. You don't argue with the God of Battle when He gives you that look. Not if you want to keep all your limbs attached.

"Your warriors need you at your best," He continued, voice softening slightly. ***"Not limping around with cracked ribs and a shoulder that's half dislocated."***

I blinked in surprise, rotating my shoulder experimentally and wincing at the sharp pain that shot down my arm. I hadn't even noticed when that had happened.

"Fine," I conceded. "I'll take a minute to catch my breath and heal. But I need to see what those crazy gnomes have cooked up. We're running out of time before Kronk's army reaches us."

Darakin's massive hand clasped my uninjured shoulder. ***"You've learned much since we began, Jax. More than you realize. But remember—the greatest battle you'll face is not against Kronk or the Dark Legion, but against your own impatience."***

He paused for a moment, His eyes distant, then sighed and went on.

"Jax, there are times that we sense the future—not full prescience, you understand…more a hint, a sense—and for the empire, I sense an approaching darkness, a terrible one. We all do. We have no details. We cannot tell more, because it touches upon zzzzzzzz, and as such, we cannot explain more. I'm sorry."

"What?" I frowned. "Whatever you said, it was all…I couldn't hear it." I shook my head. "It was like a buzzing, a noise that was just wrong."

"Because you are not ready for those secrets yet, and our requested intervention is in place, of course." He sighed, closing His eyes and drawing a deep breath before going on. ***"I cannot explain further, nor share more with you, beyond to say that our own futures are tied to it, and as such, as for all the gods, our sight is blurred. None may know the moment of their death, nor their true future."***

With that cryptic piece of advice, He stepped back, His form already beginning to fade. ***"Until tomorrow."***

And then He was gone, leaving me standing in the middle of the training field, sweaty, bruised, and wondering how the fuck a god could just drop wisdom like that and then literally disappear before I could ask what the hell he meant.

The legionnaire messenger cleared his throat. "Shall I tell Primus Daralen you'll be delayed, my prince?"

"Yeah." I sighed, rolling my aching shoulder. "Tell her I'll catch my breath and then I'll set off. Oh, and Legionnaire?"

"Yes, my prince?" He smiled as he straightened.

"Never interrupt the God of Battle when he's sparring with me. It's not a time to distract either of us."

"Ah…of course," he agreed, nodding jerkily, then wincing as he saw—as did I—the handful of optios and full legionnaires waiting to give him presumably the same advice, but clearly with a lot less patience.

"Good man. Now go get Oracle for me. Tell her I got banged up and could use some healing."

"At once, my prince." He nodded, saluting again, fist to chest, before sprinting off, desperately trying to outrun those waiting for him.

I limped toward the edge of the field where a water barrel stood. Plunging my head into it, I let the cool water wash away the sweat and dust. When I surfaced, gasping, I found Sehran there, her wings folded neatly against her back, an amused expression on her face.

"Enjoying yourself?" She held out a cloth.

I took it and dried my face, wincing as I hit a tender spot. "Abso-fuckin'-lutely. Nothing like getting the shit kicked out of you by a god to start your day off right," I lied.

"Your day started nearly twelve hours ago," she pointed out. "And you've been in three separate meetings since dawn."

"Details," I muttered, taking a long drink from the water ladle. "Where's Oracle? I need to get patched up before I go see what new death trap the gnomes have designed."

"She's in the tower with Seraphina and Cleq. They're discussing something about the herds and grazing patterns." Sehran's expression turned serious. "The Sonra elders are getting nervous. They agreed to move some of the herds inside, and slaughtered a portion of the beasts they raised for that, but they're keeping the rest. They're moving north slower than they'd like, though. They want to make sure that Kronk doesn't find out about the herds being so lightly defended up there."

"Smart." I nodded. "That's Seraphina and Sonra's problem, though. They agreed to split the herds?" I asked, having literally not been in the meetings since handing control over to Seraphina.

"They did. Half of the best of the herds were moved into the estates on the east side that the mistress sorted out for Sonra, and the rest are around the tower. The grass is vanishing faster than it grows, but there's enough dried food for them for a month. That should be a lot more time than they need."

"Damn well better be." I grunted. "Fuck, I need to have another meeting with the gods. I keep putting that off."

"You're either constantly running or fighting," she pointed out. "Unless you can magic more hours into the day, there's not much more you can physically do."

"I know, but still." I shrugged. "Fine, so the best of the herds are secure, and the rest?"

"A bit less than a third were lined up and culled. It was a hard day for Sonra, and I think that's why Greg and Cleq are hiding with the gnomes, to be honest. They were your main supporters with the Council of Sonra and they're not popular, but the group all agreed that it needed to be done."

"Shit," I muttered.

"The meat was salted and prepared. Thankfully, part of the tower's working areas include cool rooms for meat, as none of the usual butchers and their storage areas could have worked for so much. There's an ice mage who's just keeping the ice in there topped up as well. But it looks like there's a lot of steak for everyone for the next few months."

"Always an upside." I grinned, then shook my head, muttered "Fuck it" under my breath, and hit myself with a heal, feeling the shoulder grate before it popped back into place.

"Gods, that's better," I whispered.

"Why'd you ask for Oracle?" She cocked her head to the side. "You can heal, I can heal—hell, half the legionnaires here can heal now."

"I wanted to get that kid outta here before they murdered him." I grinned at her, nodding toward the still clearly annoyed legionnaires. "Besides, I like having Oracle close by."

"She's busy," Sehran pointed out.

"She is," I agreed. "She's also pushing herself too hard, and the half an hour it takes for her to travel to me and then a little downtime, before she gets back to work, is a break, even if it's not a very relaxing one." I grinned. "Plus, I might get to look down her top and that always cheers me up."

"Me too." Sehran sighed. "I still think you should let me watch you both."

"No, because then it's a small step to helping and joining in." I grunted. "You want to play, go play with the other succubai."

"You think I haven't been?" She smirked.

"You have?" I blinked.

"Of course!" She laughed. "Seriously, Jax, I am a succubus. Jian knows this. As much as I play, he's the one I love, him and Tenandra. But when it comes to fun? He'd love to watch me with the others, and I've already arranged a dozen of us for a night as a treat for him and Tenandra."

"Fuck me, his heart's gonna give out," I muttered at the mental image.

"I think it'll be another organ that fails first!" She laughed throatily. "Anyway, as much fun as this conversation is, are you ready to hear about the contracts?"

"For the succubai?" I asked.

"Well, it's not for the ale." She grinned. "I've reviewed them, and rewritten them so we get a blanket contract for all those who want to join, and…" She hesitated. "Do you want to see the full contract or just hear the highlights?"

"Just give me the highlights," I told her. "You promised to do the best you could and you've been using these things for centuries longer than I've been alive. The legionnaires will have to read and agree to them, and I want you to explain them to any volunteers, but just give me the broad strokes."

"Okay, all succubai or incubai who join, do so on the understanding that they serve the empire first, then their individual master, and that you are the heart and head of the empire. They accept that each contract is valid until dissolved by the legionnaire and demon together, and that you have veto to banish and break the contract at any time if you feel that they've taken advantage somehow. They agree to limit their activities to private areas with their bound one, unless otherwise approved, and they understand that you and Oracle are exclusive and aren't to be pestered."

"You added that one in for all of them, but not you, eh?"

"I need something out of the deal." She laughed. "Seriously, though, the last bit I liked especially. For each bonding, as they'll have a chance at possibly tens of thousands of mortals to feed on—with the war coming—and your willingness that they can learn magic here, they agree to provide five times their body weight in orichalcum." She smiled mischievously. "What metal was it you desperately needed to make all the imperial buildings like the academy again?"

"You fucking wonder." I stared at her, seeing the proud smile that tugged at the corners of her lips. "You absolute fucking wonder! How many want to join?"

"I have a hundred legionnaires as the trial group, and six hundred or so succubai and incubai who want in." She grinned. "I had to cap it at that as the portals were getting out of control and we'd need specific mass-produced scrolls to provide the portals. You don't want a massive unregulated portal to the demon realms, after all."

"No, we don't, but that means…" I paused. "How much does a succubus weigh?"

"That's a rude question for any lady, even us." Sehran gasped, pretending to be shocked.

"How much?"

"For the hundred we have as volunteers, we'll get at least five hundred ingots," she assured me. "The outriders want in as well. As do, well, at least a third of all your forces. The rest will as well, given the chance, I think, but it'd be a bit of an issue when you turn up to the other cities and try to play the imperial lord card, when half your armies are demonic."

"We'll keep it as the hundred for the control group, but…" I hesitated. "Fuck it. Ask Reth of Sonra if he's happy with fifty of his riders getting access to your kin as well, and if so, we have two groups to test. Limit it to that."

"I'll pass that along." Sehran nodded. She hesitated, then added, "There's also a message from Wilhelm. House Granth is prepared for tonight's ceremony."

I grimaced. "Fuck, sparring drove that from my mind. Gaspar is still officially stepping down?"

"So it seems," she confirmed. "Though some of the family aren't happy about it. Three of them have already left the city in protest."

"Let me guess—the ones who thought they should inherit instead?"

Sehran's smile was all teeth. "Precisely. Shall I have them…followed?"

I considered it for a moment, then shook my head. "Not yet. If they're smart, they'll just go sulk somewhere. If they're stupid enough to cause trouble, we'll deal with them then."

She nodded, her wings flexing slightly—a sign I'd learned meant she was disappointed. The succubus might be bound to Jian, but that didn't mean she didn't enjoy a good hunt now and then.

"All right." I sighed, rolling my shoulder again. "I need to go see the gnomes, and I'd better not keep Primus Daralen waiting too long."

"Definitely!" Sehran smiled, then paused. "Do you want to walk, or fly?"

I smiled. "I'll walk. It's a bit shit to leave my escort here and it'll let me clear my head a bit. You go."

With a final nod, Sehran spread her wings and took to the air. Her form rapidly receding as she flew ahead to the tower. I watched her go, seeing a creature as happy in the air as on the ground, and shook my head. Even with my Soaring Majesty ability, I could never match her natural grace in the air.

Sighing, I gathered my gear and started the long walk back to the workshop, hitting myself with a Scour. Legionnaires folded in around me, keeping people back and maintaining a watch over their prince. *Seventeen minutes.* It didn't sound like much, but in a normal fight, that was a lifetime. Against Darakin? Fucking hell.

Sure, I believed him when he said that he could have done more to stop me, that he could have picked it up or used an ability, but damn, he was the God of Battle!

If I'd been able to defeat him, he was right. What the hell would I become?

Two days until Kronk's army arrived. And somewhere beyond them, the Dark Legion marched as well. I needed to be ready. I'd make damn sure I was, but the more I thought about it, the thought of thousands of enemies that I could literally unleash hell upon?

I was starting to look forward to it, and that was scary in a whole different way.

What the hell *was* I becoming?

By the time I reached the tower, deciding that I needed more than a bloody Scour first, and definitely a change of clothing, Oracle was waiting for me in our quarters, a stern expression on her face that softened slightly when she saw the bloody state of me and my clothes.

"Seventeen minutes," I announced before she could speak.

Her eyebrow arched delicately. "What?"

"Seventeen minutes I lasted against Darakin today," I clarified, wincing as I shed my sweat-soaked, straining top. The blood had congealed and stuck to me like, well, congealed blood.

"Congratulations," she said dryly. "You're now lasting minutes against a literal God of Battle. Maybe in a few years, you'll manage to not get cut to pieces?"

"Your confidence is overwhelming," I replied, but there was no heat in it. She was right, after all. "How're you feeling today?"

Her hand moved unconsciously to her belly, still flat beneath her flowing dress. "I'm fine. The baby's fine. Stop changing the subject and tell me why you didn't heal yourself."

"I did."

"Then why the hell did you ask me to meet you here?" she growled, glaring at me, even as she hit me with a heal of her own.

"Because I love you, and I feel like I never see you," I admitted. "And it made you take a break as well."

"I'm fine." She sighed. "Really, Jax, I am. I'm just a little tired, that's all."

"And so am I, so a ten-minute break before we go see what madness the gnomes have cooked up won't kill anyone. I hope."

That ten minutes—where we just sat and talked, had a drink on our balcony and relaxed—passed far too fast, and all too soon we were climbing to our feet again. "Well, the gnomes have something to show us, and then we've got the House Granth ceremony before we can relax again."

Oracle's expression tightened slightly. "Are we sure about this, Jax? Giving Wilhelm control of House Granth?"

I shrugged, reaching for a fresh shirt. "Not entirely, but it's better than leaving Gaspar in charge. Wilhelm's shown more sense so far, and he actually seems to want to be part of what we're trying to do here."

"And if he's just playing the long game?"

"Then we'll deal with it," I replied. "But honestly, I think he's as genuine as we're going to get. And he acted honorably when we first met. Also, right now, we need all the allies we can get."

She nodded, though I could tell she wasn't entirely convinced. "I know. I just don't like it. It seems…too convenient and too quick for Gaspar."

"Trust me, I know." I snorted, remembering my own father. "I don't think he's given up on his scheming, not at all, but I think he's trying to play it from the other side, that's all."

"How?" Oracle asked, helping me finish dressing.

"If he's as dumb as he seems, but thinks he's smart, then him giving up a little power now to get control of his ancestral lands is wise, because he can run there and leave us to either be wiped out, or when we win, he gets to be a loyal supporter there.

"If he takes those he actually cares about out of the city and to wherever, but has Wilhelm name him his heir, then when Wilhelm dies, he's back in control, but with his lands and authority intact."

"You think that's what he's planning? To let his own children die for his ambition?" she asked, clearly horrified.

"Honestly, not sure," I admitted. "If it was Sanguis? He'd do it in a heartbeat, if he could bring himself to give up his power in the first place. But this seems logical. And we'll soon know, if he tries to fuck off and leave us with just Wilhelm and a small number of their guards."

"We'll know when he starts pushing for those roles, and a legion of his own," Oracle mused. "If he's what he's painting himself as, wanting to retire then he'll want a nice house and a lot of gold to basically relax and do nothing. If he wants more, and he's trying to set us up, then he'll soon ask for forces to 'prove himself'."

"Yeah, you know what though, I think we should give it to him if he does." My smile grew. "We just make sure that we put a second-in-command under him who we trust implicitly, and they have orders to take over if need be. After all, if he's willing to go about eliminating our problems for us, let's let him."

"Use him to put all the effort in?" Oracle asked, and I nodded.

"What's that saying, no man works harder for another than he does for himself? Let's allow him to think he's working for himself, and let him work his arse off. If he's doing this, now that we've guessed the pattern, we should be able to make the most of it."

"And if Wilhelm is kept safe…" Oracle grinned. "Then he's earning wealth for the house, and through that for the empire anyway. All we need to do is make sure that Wilhelm is as honest as he seems, give Gaspar careful orders, and make sure that we keep an eye on them all."

"Gods, I feel better now that's sorted," I muttered. "I was worrying about that."

"Me too," Oracle admitted, standing on tiptoes to kiss me, then nodding to the door. "How about I tell the legionnaires we're flying, and then they can start running?"

"Well, I walked all the way here," I agreed, smiling back. "I'd love to fly with you."

As soon as Oracle had passed the word, we strode out onto the balcony. The constant breeze up here whipped the narrow collar of my shirt as I squinted at the gleaming city beyond.

The sun was beating down, the coolness of the morning gone under the relentless hammer of the sun. Most of the actual building materials used here were either marble or that grey granite, and then they were covered in some kind of plaster, thick white stuff that reflected the light.

The roofs were generally tiled, oranges and reds leading this way and that, though here and there I saw thatch as well, and occasionally gleaming with bronze or iron.

Why the hell they'd do that, I had no clue, as a metal roof had to make the houses below sweatier than Satan's taint, but fuck it.

As Oracle stepped up by my side, beaming, I jumped into the air with her, just enjoying a few minutes with the woman who would one day be my wife.

The sun, the heat, the actually surprisingly beautiful city that was laid out below us…for a long few minutes, as we flew, all was perfect.

Below us, the city of Gaij was a hive of activity. Legionnaires and their aspirants drilled in formation on every large, available open space that wasn't covered by Sonra's wagons or herds.

Civilians hauled supplies to the walls or worked to reinforce buildings, carry feed, set up materials, and who knew what else. The energy was tense but purposeful—everyone knew what was coming, and they were determined to be ready.

As we landed in front of the workshop the gnomes had been building the airship in, I could already hear the familiar sounds of argument and construction. It was oddly reassuring, though, as that was because as long as the gnomes were arguing, they weren't all dead from some catastrophic explosion, which made visiting a slightly more stressful thing as well.

Daralen stood outside the massive doors, her expression a mixture of resignation and amusement. She snapped to attention when she saw us touch down.

"My prince," she greeted me formally, her fist against her chest. "Lady Oracle."

"Fuck's sake, you can relax, you know, Daralen." I smiled. "What have the mad bastards done now?"

A corner of her mouth twitched before she managed to stop it. "It might be better if you see for yourself, my prince. They're…enthusiastic about their progress."

That could mean anything from "they've created a revolutionary new propulsion system" to "they've accidentally made a flying bomb that could level the city." With gnomes, you never knew.

"All right." I sighed. "Let's see it."

The massive doors swung open at Daralen's signal, and we stepped inside the cavernous workshop.

The scene that greeted us was controlled chaos. Gnomes scurried everywhere, shouting instructions, carrying tools and materials, climbing over what appeared to be…

I stopped dead, staring upward.

"Is that…is that what I think it is?" Oracle breathed beside me.

"Holy fucking shit," I whispered. "They actually did it."

The airship hung suspended from the ceiling, massive and gleaming. But it wasn't the ramshackle collection of parts I'd seen last time. This was sleek, its hull polished to a mirror shine. The inflation chambers above had been completely redesigned, no longer resembling half-deflated potato sacks stitched together but forming a single streamlined cigar shape. The propulsion systems were integrated seamlessly into the hull. And the control deck?

"Prince Jax! Lady Oracle!" Greg's voice pulled me from my stupor. The little goblin hurried toward us, his face split in a wide grin. "What do you think?"

"I think…" I struggled to find the words. "I think it's nothing like what you showed me last time. Fuck's sake, that was only yesterday!"

"We fixed it!" he announced proudly. "After you left, Cleq realized that we'd been overthinking the entire design. We went back to your original descriptions and simplified everything."

"How many operators?" I asked skeptically, remembering their insistence on multiple stations.

"Just one!" he declared. "Well, one pilot and one engineer to monitor the engines. But that's it!"

I blinked in surprise. "Only two? You were insisting on seven when we started!"

"Seven was impractical, we told you that, but you insisted! I think you'll find this works a lot better," he corrected, as my glare slid off him like water off a duck's back. "But one is optimal! Cleq noticed that the description of airships you gave us had a single pilot as well, so we redesigned everything around that concept."

"And it still works?" Oracle's voice betrayed her skepticism.

"Oh yes!" Greg bounced excitedly. "We've done hover tests already. The lift chamber inflation works perfectly, and the mana accelerators are providing steady power. We're ready for a full test flight!"

I exchanged a glance with Oracle, who looked as surprised as I felt. "That's…impressive," I admitted. "I thought you said it would take days more."

"Days? Ha!" Greg waved a dismissive hand. "Once we figured out the right approach, it all came together. None of that overly complicated nonsense. Simple, elegant solutions!"

I blinked, then spotted a trio of golems on the far side and grinned. "How many golems do you have now?"

"Forty-three." He grinned.

"Fucking hell." I swore. Forty-three golems could build a damn *city* in a few weeks. They didn't stop, they didn't rest, and looking at them, these were all at least level three versions, and capable of basic independent work.

Months ago I'd seen two of them before taking an airship's hull apart to replace the cladding and it'd been the work of only a few days for them to do what would have taken weeks for "normal" engineers.

Given what I'd seen of gnomish engineering before, simple and elegant weren't words I'd have associated with their work, so something still didn't add up.

"Did something change after I left?" I asked suspiciously.

"Well..." Greg glanced around, then lowered his voice. "Svetu *might* have visited, and gave out some quests."

That explained it. The God of Invention and Creators must have gotten tired of watching his chosen people fumble around and decided to intervene.

"I see." I nodded. "And did Svetu have any suggestions for improvements?"

"Just a few small ones," Greg admitted. "He said our original design was 'an abomination against the principles of flight' and that we should 'stop being overcomplicated idiots and build something that won't instantly explode.' Then he suggested a few modifications."

I bit back a laugh. That sounded exactly like the cranky old bugger.

"Well, I'm glad he was helpful," I said diplomatically. "When can we test it?"

"Right now!" Greg declared. "We're opening the ceiling port and we've already cleared the space. Phizzik is just finishing the pre-flight preparations."

I looked up at the massive opening in the workshop's roof, then back at the airship. It still seemed impossibly advanced compared to what I'd seen before, but if Svetu had been involved, perhaps it really would work.

"All right." I nodded. "Let's see it fly."

Greg beamed and turned to shout instructions to the other gnomes. They scrambled to their positions, checking final connections and clearing tools from the workspace.

"Are you sure about this?" Oracle murmured beside me. "The last time they tested something, some of them blew up, didn't they?"

"I think that was the time before, but Svetu's involved now," I replied quietly. "That changes things. Besides, we need this to work. We're running out of time."

She squeezed my hand in understanding. We both knew what was at stake. Without the airship, reaching the Cradle of Feshcan'un would be nearly impossible, especially with armies moving across the land.

A wild-haired gnome—Phizzik, I presumed—was carried, semi-conscious and drooling into the pilot's seat and strapped in, while another took what I guessed was the engineer's position behind him. The rest of the gnomes cleared the area, moving back to what they presumably considered a safe distance.

The seconds stretched out into minutes, before Phizzik jerked awake with a scream; twitching, he stared around wildly, then nodded, as if everything was as it was supposed to be.

"Initiating launch sequence!" Phizzik called out, his voice carrying through the workshop. "Inflation chambers at full capacity! Mana accelerators online! Mages...go! Releasing moorings in three...two...one..."

I saw a pair of mages standing at the back of the room suddenly collapse, looking like someone had hit them with bricks. With a series of mechanical clanks, the chains holding the airship in place disengaged. For a heart-stopping moment, the craft dipped slightly—then steadied, hovering perfectly in place.

"It's working," Oracle whispered, squeezing my hand tighter.

"Engaging upward spinny things at fifteen percent," Phizzik yelled. The propellers began to spin, slowly at first, then faster. The airship moved upward with surprising grace, ascending steadily toward the opening in the roof.

The craft cleared the opening without incident, emerging into the open sky above. Through the gap, I could see it circle once, twice, its movements smooth and controlled.

A cheer went up from the assembled gnomes.

Greg turned to me, his eyes shining. "What did I tell you? Perfect!"

I had to admit, I was impressed. "How fast can it go?"

"We estimate about five miles per hour at full speed," Greg replied proudly. "And it can maintain that pace for up to twelve hours before needing to recharge the manastones."

"Range?" The tactical implications were already spinning through my mind.

"About seven hundred miles round trip, depending on wind conditions and payload, holding up to fifteen," he answered. "If you can supply enough manastones or storage, then there'll be more than enough to reach the Plains of Bones and return, or go farther, though I think a rebuild might be needed after the first full flight, when we see what works and what doesn't."

That was better than I'd dared hope. If these figures were accurate, the airship could potentially get us to the Cradle of Feshcan'un and back—assuming we could navigate the dangers in between.

Above us, the airship continued its graceful circuit of the workshop, then began to descend toward the opening. As it reentered the workshop, I could see Phizzik's face split in a manic grin, his hands moving confidently over the controls.

The landing was as smooth as the takeoff, the craft settling gently onto its landing struts as the moorings were reattached.

"Well?" Greg demanded, practically vibrating with excitement. "What do you think?"

I looked at the airship, then at Oracle, then back at Greg. "I think it's fucking amazing," I admitted. "How soon can you build more?"

His face fell slightly. "Ah, that's the thing. We don't have enough materials for more than one more, and that would take at least a week to construct."

"What about the prototype?" I asked, thinking that we could rebuild that and…

"This is it. We rebuilt it each time."

"Okay, well, if you can even manage one more, that might be enough," I mused, already calculating. "We'd need two—one for Oracle and me to reach the Cradle, and one to keep here for defending the city, if possible. But if you can't, then you can't. Have you got spare parts for it? If something happens?"

"We've already started gathering materials for the second one," Greg assured me. "Now that we have the design perfected, construction should be faster. But the problem is materials like orichalcum, lunarium, and platinum. They're all needed for the engines…"

Phizzik had disembarked from the airship and was bustling toward us, his wild hair even more disheveled than before. "Perfect flight characteristics!" he announced without preamble. "The control response is excellent, the lift-to-weight ratio is optimal, and the mana flow is steady. It's ready for operational use!"

I nodded, impressed despite myself, and smiled at the gnome who had a totally different speech pattern from any I'd seen before. Usually they were all drugged up to the eyeballs, and even here, most had been. Clearly whatever got him off, the opportunity to fly shit had him operating on the sharp edge. "Good work, all of you. Seriously, this is incredible."

The gnome beamed with pride. "We aim to please! Now, when would you like to schedule the first official flight? We should test it with a full payload to ensure—"

"Tomorrow," I interrupted. "We need to be sure it's fully operational before Kronk's forces arrive."

"Tomorrow?" Phizzik echoed. "There are still calibrations to be done, fine-tuning of the—"

"Tomorrow," I repeated firmly. "Do whatever calibrations you need to do today. By sunrise, I want it ready for a full test flight with passengers and cargo."

He hesitated, then nodded, beaming. "Yes! Yes, we can do this, and then, the world! We get to explore it all!"

"Good." I smiled, clapping him on the shoulder. "I knew you could do it."

As the gnomes returned to their work, already arguing about last-minute improvements, I turned to Daralen, who had been silently observing the entire time.

"What do you think?"

"I think it's terrifying and possibly about to change everything I know about war," she admitted.

"It is, but it's not something to worry about in other ways. The legion used to use these, you know?"

"These?"

"Well, no, they were cities. Huge, flying war-cities called the prax," I said. "This is nothing compared to them. But the legion weren't less because there were flying weapons. If anything, they were more needed."

"I hope so, though I'd like it if the realm would stay still for five minutes before the next realm-shattering invention was unleashed, please." She smiled, clearly tired, but still up for the task, and I nodded.

"I'll see what I can do once we've destroyed the armies and conquered Kronk." I winked. "Of course, there'll be a baby here then as well, and that's going to be a change for everyone, I hear."

"Well, no starting wars just to escape changing their soiled linens." She smiled softly.

"Dammit! I had high hopes for that one working." I sighed. "All right, if you're gonna be a party pooper, anything to report?"

She straightened. "The city defenses are at eighty percent readiness, my prince. The walls have been reinforced, and we've positioned the limited ballistae at strategic points. The mages are continuing to train the legionnaires in basic combat spells, with good results."

"What about the outriders?" I hadn't heard from Reth and his scouts in a few days beyond the brief details Sehran had shared.

“Six teams are deployed, harassing Kronk’s supply lines and eliminating scouts,” she reported. “They’ve been remarkably effective. Reth reports that the main army is still approximately two days away, moving at a standard marching pace and seems uninclined to hurry.”

“And the Dark Legion?”

Her expression tightened slightly. “Based on tracking, they’re likely to arrive about a day after Kronk’s forces. But we think they already know about Kronk.”

“You think they’ll attack them?”

“Knowing what I do of the Dark Legion and Kronk, I think they’ll attack each other on sight.”

Perfect timing, if everything went according to plan. “Excellent. And House Granth?”

“Preparations for tonight’s ceremony are complete,” she confirmed. “However, there have been…complications.”

I raised an eyebrow. “What kind of complications?”

“Three of Gaspar’s children have left the city. I didn’t know if you knew. They’ve taken a small contingent of guards with them—about fifteen, all armed with Earth weapons.”

I frowned. “I thought they were still in the city. Dammit. Any indication where they’re headed?”

“None yet,” she admitted. “But I’ve dispatched a team to track them. I’ll report as soon as we know more.”

I nodded, considering. Armed nobles with a grudge could be a problem. But, more likely, if Gaspar was indeed playing games, it’d be an attempt to get them out of the way with some weapons and deniability. “Keep me updated, but focus on the preparations for Kronk’s arrival. We can deal with disgruntled nobles later.”

“Understood, my prince.” She hesitated, then added, “There’s one other matter. Wilhelm has requested a meeting with you before the ceremony.”

“Did he say what about?”

“No, but he seemed…troubled.”

Interesting. “All right, I’ll see him in an hour. Where is he now?”

“In the guest quarters with his family,” she replied. “His father and mother are with him.”

I nodded. “Good. Have them all sent to the small council chamber in half an hour…and make sure there’s food. Damn, I’m starving after that session with Darakin.”

Daralen smiled slightly. “Already arranged, my prince.”

“You’re a lifesaver, Daralen.” I sighed. “Keep an eye on the gnomes, would you? Make sure they don’t get too creative with any last-minute improvements.”

“Of course,” she agreed, though her expression suggested she’d rather face Kronk’s entire army singlehandedly than babysit a workshop full of manic gnomes.

As we left the workshop, Oracle fell into step beside me. “You really think that thing will fly all the way to the Cradle?” she asked quietly.

“It has to,” I said. “And if I have to get out and fucking push it, I will. We’re running low on time, and I don’t care what it takes. We’ll do it.”

CHARACTER SHEET

<table>
<tr><td colspan="5">Name: Jax Amon</td></tr>
<tr><td colspan="5">Title: Godslayer</td></tr>
<tr><td colspan="3">Class: Mage Imperator (Fire Focus)</td><td colspan="2">Renown: Imperial Scion, Prince of Dravith, Master of Himnel and Narkolt, Godslayer, Mage Imperator</td></tr>
<tr><td colspan="3">Level: 52</td><td colspan="2">Progress: 417,882/13,000,000</td></tr>
<tr><td colspan="3">Patron: Jenae, Goddess of Fire and Exploration</td><td colspan="2">Points to Distribute: 0
Meridian Points to Invest: 1</td></tr>
<tr><th>Stat</th><th>Current points</th><th>Description</th><th>Effect</th><th>Progress to next level</th></tr>
<tr><td>Agility</td><td>100</td><td>Governs dodge and movement</td><td>+1000% maximum movement speed and reflexes. Gained Temporal Fluidity</td><td>N/A</td></tr>
<tr><td>Charisma</td><td>61 (56)</td><td>Governs likely success to charm, seduce, or threaten</td><td>+51% success chance in interactions with other beings</td><td>51/100</td></tr>
<tr><td>Constitution</td><td>125 (123)</td><td>Governs health and health regeneration</td><td>2460 health, regen 160 points per 600 seconds (each point invested now worth 20 health). Gained: Genetic Storage</td><td>N/A</td></tr>
<tr><td>Dexterity</td><td>100</td><td>Governs ability with weapons and crafting success</td><td>+100% to weapon proficiency, +100% to the chances of crafting success. Gained: Master Craftsman's Touch</td><td>N/A</td></tr>
<tr><td>Endurance</td><td>73 (670)</td><td>Governs stamina and stamina regeneration</td><td>2190 stamina, regen 53 points per 30 seconds (each point invested now worth 30 stamina)</td><td>89/100</td></tr>
<tr><td>Intelligence</td><td>206</td><td>Governs base mana and number of</td><td>2260 mana, spell capacity: 102 (100 + 2,</td><td>N/A</td></tr>
</table>

		spells able to be learned	+200 mana from items). Gained: Hyper Cognition & Mana Manipulation	
Luck	79	Governs overall chance of bonuses	+69% chance of a favorable outcome	92/100
Perception	110 (100)	Governs ranged damage and chance to spot traps or hidden items	+100% ranged damage, +100% chance to spot traps or hidden items. Gained: Essence Sight	N/A
Strength	90 (87)	Governs damage with melee weapons and carrying capacity	+90 damage with melee weapons, +90% maximum carrying capacity	88/100
Wisdom	105 (95)	Governs mana regeneration and memory	+1400% mana recovery, 16 points per minute. Gained: Mana Manipulation	N/A

CHAPTER THIRTY-FOUR

The small council chamber was surprisingly cozy compared to some of the grand, drafty spaces that were usually used for formal meetings. Someone—probably Othair, knowing how organized that bugger was—had arranged for a fire to be lit in the hearth, and the dancing flames cast a warm glow over the polished wooden table and the simple but good quality decorations.

Wilhelm was already there when I arrived, along with his parents. I immediately recognized his father, Kurt—the same sharp features as Wilhelm, but with silver threading through his dark hair and deeper lines around his eyes. His mother, Penelope, was tall and fair-haired, her bearing regal despite her obvious nervousness as she bobbed a curtsey.

"Prince Jax," Wilhelm greeted me, rising quickly to his feet. "Zhank you for finding zhe time to be meeting vith us before zhe ceremony."

"It's okay. It made a lot of sense to. Kurt and Penelope, I presume?" I asked.

"Oh mein Gott! Ja, mine mother, zhe Lady Penelope, and mine father, Kurt of House Granth." He visibly colored, clearly mortified he'd not introduced his parents.

I laughed, offering them both a hand to shake.

"It's fine, seriously," I assured him, taking a seat across from them, and they sat as soon as I had.

A servant appeared with a tray of food—bread, cold meats, cheese, and fruit—and placed it on the table before silently withdrawing. I helped myself to a hunk of bread and some cheese, my stomach growling audibly. "You'll have to forgive me—for the dinner—I'm bloody starving. So, what's on your mind?"

Wilhelm exchanged a glance with his parents, then cleared his throat. "Ve are…concerned about tonight's ceremony."

"Having second thoughts?" I kept my tone neutral, despite the jolt of alarm that ran through me. If the most reasonable member of House Granth was getting cold feet, either he'd seen the same thing we had, or he wanted out.

"Nein, nein," he hastened to assure me, looking genuinely distressed at the suggestion. "I am honored by your trust, and committed to serving zhe empire. But…" He glanced at his father, seemingly searching for words.

Kurt leaned forward, his expression grave. "Vhat my son is trying to say, Prince Jax, is zhat ve are concerned about potential…complications." His Germanic accent was clear as well, but the pronunciations were more blatant.

"You mean the three who left?" I asked bluntly, tearing off a piece of bread.

Wilhelm nodded. "Ja. Marcus, mine uncle, and Eleina and Thorin, mine cousins. Zhey vere next in line as Gaspar's son und next two children, but zhey have always resented our branch of zhe family. Zhey believe mine father betrayed zhe house by pursuing commerce rather zhan politics."

"They'll need to be watched," I agreed, "but they're not my immediate concern. What else is bothering you?"

Wilhelm fidgeted slightly. "Zhere are...divisions within zhe house. Not everyone is pleased vith Gaspar's decision to elevate me. Some believe it shows veakness. Others...vell..."

"They think there's a game being played," I said. "And what do you believe?" I watched his face carefully.

He met my gaze directly. "I believe it shows visdom. Gaspar realizes zhe old ways no longer serve us. But I worry zhat others might see tonight as an opportunity to...express zheir displeasure."

"Are you expecting trouble at the ceremony?" I asked, my mind already calculating the additional security measures we might need.

"Not open violence." Penelope spoke up for the first time, her voice soft but clear, some kind of Nordic accent this time. "But perhaps...demonstrations of loyalty to the old order. Coded messages. Alliances forming."

"Political theater," I summarized. "Is there anyone specific I should be watching?"

"Demetrius," Wilhelm replied immediately. "He is Gaspar's cousin and arrived on Earth vith him. He has been his advisor for many years. He does not approve of me, or of our alliance vith you."

I nodded, making a mental note. "Anyone else?"

"Soren and Althea," Kurt added. "Gaspar's younger children. Zhey remain in zhe city, but zhey are...unpredictable."

"We'll keep an eye on them," I promised. "Is that all that's troubling you, or is there something else?"

Wilhelm hesitated, then seemed to come to a decision. "Zhere is one more zhing. I...I am not certain I am ready for zhis responsibility."

Ah, there it was. Not politics, but personal doubt. Fuck knew I could relate to that more than he realized.

"No one ever is," I said honestly. "But from what I've seen, you have more sense and more honor than most of your house combined. That counts for a lot."

"But I have no experience in leadership," he protested. "I vas never groomed for zhis role. I studied business and zhe sword. I dreamt of a life of glorious battle on zhe front lines, possibly von day rising to command a legion. Not politics."

"Which might actually be an advantage," I pointed out. "You haven't been corrupted by centuries of noble scheming. And frankly? Running a house isn't going to be that different from running a business. You manage resources, make strategic decisions, and take care of your people."

He still looked uncertain, so I pressed on. "Look, I didn't ask for any of this either. One day, I was just a guy looking for his missing brother; the next, I was apparently the heir to an empire. But you adapt. You learn. And most importantly, you surround yourself with people you can trust."

"Like your Primus Daralen?" Wilhelm asked.

I nodded. "Like Daralen. Like Oracle. Like people who will tell you when you're being an idiot, not just yes-men who'll agree with everything you say."

For the first time, a small smile appeared on Wilhelm's face. "Mine father has never hesitated to tell me vhen I am being stupid."

Kurt chuckled. "Zhat's a father's right, as vell as his job, mine son."

The tension in the room eased slightly. I took another bite of cheese, chewing thoughtfully.

"So here's what's going to happen," I said finally. "Tonight, Gaspar will officially name you his heir and step down as head of House Granth. You'll take the oath of citizenship, as will everyone else in your house. There might be some grumbling, maybe some pointed comments, but as long as everyone behaves themselves, it'll be fine."

"And if they don't behave?" Penelope asked quietly.

I met her gaze steadily. "Then they'll deal with me. And I'm much less patient than I used to be. And frankly, Lord Darakin is already pissed with your house—specifically *not* you three, just so you know. But the rest? He'd probably be overjoyed if they were to act up, as then he knows I'll invite them to spar with us for some fun and he'll slaughter them all for shits and giggles."

"It is that bad?" she asked, and I hesitated.

"Well, he doesn't *like* them," I clarified. "Especially not Gaspar. The rest? They're on his shit list, that's for sure. As I say, you're not. I'd recommend keeping it that way."

"Any advice as to how, mine prince?" Kurt asked with a faint smile.

"Act with honor." I shrugged. "Honestly, I like the guy—god, I mean—he likes a good fight and has no patience for politics. Probably why we get on so well."

"I shall do mine best." He nodded, seeming satisfied with this answer.

"After the ceremony," I continued, "we'll have a formal dinner, and then a more private council meeting to discuss the defense of Gaij against Kronk's forces. I want you there." I nodded to Wilhelm. "And your parents, too, if you want, but I expect Gaspar will push for inclusion as well. That's up to you."

"I zhought as much," he agreed.

"Well, we've got a fairly good idea of the game he's playing, and we're going to give him enough rope to hang himself, put it that way, so deal with things in your house as you see fit. If you decide you need a little more weight behind you, come see me, Seraphina, Oracle, or Daralen, depending on what you need. Me for, well, the empire, obviously, Oracle because she's better with magic and frankly subtlety. Daralen if you need the legion or military advice, and of course, Seraphina for the local politics and city angle."

"Mine zhanks," Wilhelm agreed quickly. "Ve vill do vhatever ve can to help."

"Good." I popped the last piece of cheese into my mouth and stood. "Now, if there's nothing else, I need to get ready for tonight. So do you."

Wilhelm rose quickly and bowed, his parents following suit. "Zhank you for your time, Prince Jax. Und for your confidence."

I nodded, studying him for a moment. Despite his uncertainty, there was a core of strength to him that I respected. He might not have been raised to lead, but sometimes the best leaders were the ones who didn't seek power in the first place.

"Just remember," I said as they turned to leave. "You're not alone in this. And neither am I. That's how we survive, mate. You impressed me already. That's on you, nobody else."

Once they'd buggered off—and I gave them a minute to clear the corridor ahead of me so there wasn't that awkward "I've already said goodbye now we need to walk out together" scenario—I headed back to our rooms to get ready.

The Great Hall of the tower had been transformed for the ceremony. Tapestries depicting the history of the empire hung from the walls, their vibrant colors catching the light from hundreds of candles and magical light sources. The imperial banner—my banner, technically—dominated one wall, while the new symbol of Gaij hung opposite. Between them, the crest of House Granth had been mounted, freshly polished and gleaming.

Seraphina had arranged the seating with the precision of a battlefield commander, placing potential troublemakers where they could be easily watched and separating rival factions with neutral parties or stationing members of her people or the legion in the spaces between. The succubai stood at strategic points around the hall, their wings folded behind them and actually dressed demurely—for them—but their eyes alert.

I took my position on the raised dais at the front of the room, Oracle on the left beside me, looking stunning in a gown of midnight blue that set off her pale skin and made her eyes seem to glow, while I wore black and red. I'd been clear on the style, and it'd ended up looking more like a military uniform than a damn courtier, thankfully.

Daralen stood at Oracle's left, her armor polished to a mirror shine, while Seraphina took her place on my right, the Mistress of Gaij in her official capacity.

The hall gradually filled as the nobles and officials of Gaij arrived, along with the representatives from Sonra—there were some looks at that, considering the suits that had to have been planned well in advance to make Greg and the others look so smart.

Lastly there were the newly raised members of the merchant class, and anyone else who hadn't yet learned to be too wary of me and formal occasions yet. Last came the members of House Granth, filing in with the precise formality that only old nobility seemed to manage.

Gaspar led them, his bearing regal despite the obvious strain on his face. Behind him came Wilhelm, flanked by his parents. The rest of the family followed in strict order of precedence, their expressions ranging from solemn to openly pissed.

I noted a particular glare from one old bastard I mentally pegged as Demetrius, Gaspar's elderly cousin. Next to him, Soren and Althea—Gaspar's youngest children, according to Seraphina—wore carefully neutral expressions that didn't quite hide the calculation in their eyes. The rest of the family spread out to their assigned seats, a sea of finely dressed nobles with centuries of scheming in their blood. I forced a smile, while mentally sending Oracle images of us fireballing the lot of them into cinders.

She responded to it with one of her on her knees for me while I sat on the throne, and my smile became a lot more genuine, as I realized it was an offer—provided I waited until everyone was gone—not just teasing.

Once everyone was seated, I stepped forward, raising my hands for silence. The murmuring in the hall died away, all eyes turning to me.

"Citizens of the empire," I began, my voice carrying easily through the hall. "We gather tonight to witness a historic occasion—the formal recognition of House Granth as a noble house of the empire, and the elevation of a new head for that ancient house."

I nodded toward Gaspar, who rose and approached the dais. He looked older up close, and tired.

"Lord Gaspar," I addressed him. "You come before us to pledge your house's allegiance to the empire. What do you offer in service?"

Gaspar bowed, the gesture precise and measured. "House Granth offers its knowledge, its resources, and its strength to the empire. We bring the wisdom of centuries and the technology of Earth to aid in the restoration of imperial glory."

It was a formula Seraphina had suggested—acknowledgment that they served the empire, not the other way around. Gaspar recited it without stumbling, though I could see it cost him something to do it.

"And who shall lead House Granth in this service?" I asked, though we all knew the answer.

Gaspar turned to face the assembled nobles. "I, Gaspar Granth, having led this house for nineteen centuries, do hereby relinquish my position as head of House Granth." A murmur rippled through the crowd, quickly silenced as he continued. "In my place, I name my grandson Wilhelm Granth, son of Kurt, as the new head of our house, to lead us into this new era of cooperation with the empire."

The murmur grew louder. I saw Demetrius's face darken with anger, while Soren and Althea tensed. But no one spoke up in challenge—at least not yet.

Gaspar beckoned, and Wilhelm rose from his seat, approaching the dais with measured steps. The contrast between the two men was striking: Gaspar, the ancient aristocrat with privilege and power baked into every line on his face. Wilhelm, younger, less polished, but with a directness and honesty that was a hell of a lot better in my eyes.

"Wilhelm Granth," Gaspar intoned formally, "do you accept the responsibility of leading House Granth in service to the empire?"

Wilhelm drew himself up, his voice clear and steady despite the trace of accent. "Ja, mine lord I do."

"Then kneel," Gaspar commanded.

Wilhelm sank to one knee before him. Gaspar removed a heavy signet ring from his finger—the symbol of his authority as head of the house.

"With this ring, I pass to you the authority and responsibility of House Granth, and I take my place as no longer your lord, but your advisor instead." His voice carried to every corner of the hall. "May you lead with wisdom and honor."

He placed the ring in Wilhelm's open palm. Wilhelm closed his fingers around it, then rose to his feet. The two men faced each other for a long moment, a wordless communication passing between them. Then Gaspar bowed—genuinely, not the perfunctory gesture he'd offered me—and stepped back.

Wilhelm turned to face me, squaring his shoulders. "Prince Jax, as zhe new head of House Granth, I pledge our allegiance to zhe empire und to you as its prince und heir of Eternal Amon."

"Before your pledge can be accepted," I said formally, "you will swear the oath of citizenship, binding your fate to that of the empire. Are you prepared to do so?"

"I am," Wilhelm replied firmly.

"And does every member of House Granth present also agree to be bound by this oath?" I raised my voice to address the entire delegation.

There was a moment of tense silence. Then, one by one, the members of House Granth rose to their feet.

"We consent," they chorused, though some voices were noticeably less enthusiastic than others.

"I ask you all, any who haven't taken the oath so far, to take it now, or to leave the room," I said loudly. Then I looked to Oracle and she nodded, as I raised a mana potion to my lips.

Wilhelm was first, kneeling before me. I placed my hand on his head, feeling the slight tremor that ran through him as he started to speak. Behind him, the others did as well, as Oracle pushed the oath out to them all.

"I swear upon pain of death, to faithfully execute all that the Emperor decrees, and that Prince Jax Amon speaks for the empire until his ascension. I swear upon my soul that I shall stand for the Empire when it calls. I shall be strong when the weak need me, generous when the poor are at hand, and merciless when my fellow citizens are threatened. I shall worship the Gods of my fathers, respect my elders, and raise up my children to stand tall.

"I am an Imperial Citizen. I claim the right to call upon the Legion in my hour of need, to hold those who wrong me to justice, and to be avenged if I cannot be saved."

"I swear to obey Prince Jax and those he places over me; I will serve to the best of my ability, speak no lie to him when commanded otherwise, and treat all other citizens as family.

"I will work for the greater good, being a shield to those who need it, a sword to those who deserve it, and a warden to the night."

"I will stand with my family, helping one another to reach the light, until the hour of my death or my lord releases me from my Oath.

"Lastly, I will not be a dick!"

I felt the magic of the oath take hold, binding them all to their word, before speaking to Wilhelm again. "Rise, Lord Wilhelm Granth, citizen of the empire and master of House Granth, ally of the throne. I formally return control of any lands inside the bounds of the empire to you, and I name you Earl Granth, adding you personally, though not any heirs you may name at this time, to the line of succession."

That last bit was a fun addition, and I saw the sudden naked fury on Gaspar's and Demetrius's faces before they smoothed it away.

Gotcha, motherfuckers.

"House Granth is now formally recognized as noble subjects of the empire, with all the rights and responsibilities that entails. Lord Wilhelm, as head of your house, you, personally, are granted a seat on my council and an advisory position in matters of imperial governance."

Wilhelm bowed deeply. "Zhank you, mine prince. House Granth vill serve faithfully."

"Then the empire thanks you, and this audience is concluded," I said.

He stepped back and bowed, then backed away, before turning to rejoin his family. With the formal part of the ceremony complete, the tension in the room eased slightly. Servants appeared with trays of drinks, and the quiet murmur of conversation resumed as people began to mingle.

I stepped down from the dais, Oracle at my side, and moved among the guests. Seraphina stood next to me, and Daralen next to Oracle, both in case of issues and for the political look of the thing.

Personally, I'd rather have Sehran, but as Seraphina had pointed out, too many succubai sent the wrong message. Still, it was important to be seen, to take the measure of the various factions, and—most critically—to keep an eye on the potentially troublesome members of House Granth.

Demetrius kept his distance, his face set in a rigid mask as he conferred quietly with a small group of the older nobles. Soren and Althea, on the other hand, seemed to be making a deliberate effort to be sociable, though I noticed they stuck mostly to members of their own house rather than mixing with the locals.

Wilhelm moved through the crowd with surprising grace, greeting people warmly and making introductions. His parents stayed close, offering quiet support when needed.

After making the obligatory rounds, I found myself face-to-face with Gaspar. He looked tired but satisfied, like a man who had just set down a heavy burden.

"It went well," he observed, accepting a glass of wine from a passing servant.

"So far," I agreed. "Though I notice Demetrius doesn't look particularly happy about the change in leadership."

Gaspar sighed. "Demetrius has never been happy about anything in his entire life. He'll adjust, or he'll find himself increasingly isolated. The oath won't let him act against the empire directly, and Wilhelm has more support than he realizes."

I nodded, scanning the room again. "And your other children? Soren and Althea?"

"They're ambitious," Gaspar admitted, "but they're not fools. They know this is the best path forward for the house. They'll support Wilhelm, even if only for their own advancement."

"I hope you're right," I said. "We have enough enemies without adding internal strife to the mix."

"Speaking of enemies." Gaspar lowered his voice. "What's the latest on Kronk's forces?"

"They'll arrive the day after tomorrow, according to our scouts, unless they pick up the pace," I replied. "And the Dark Legion a day behind them."

He nodded thoughtfully. "Will you stay and fight, or take the airship to the Cradle?"

I raised an eyebrow, surprised he knew about our plans. "News travels fast."

"I make it my business to know things." He shrugged. "And it doesn't take a genius to work out why you need an airship so urgently."

"We fight," I said firmly. "The airship is to be used as a mobile bombardment platform if we need it, though now that I know it's the only one we're going to be able to build for a while, I'd be unhappy to use it for anything other than an emergency, until we use it as a faster method of travel to get us to the Cradle after the fight is won."

Gaspar nodded again, seeming satisfied with my answer. "Whatever you decide, Wilhelm will support you. He's a good man, better than I ever was. Perhaps better than our house deserved."

There was something close to regret in his voice, and for a moment, I saw not the scheming noble but simply an old man facing the end of his relevance. It was almost enough to make me feel sympathy for him.

Almost.

Then I remembered the look on his face when I'd not named any heirs of Wilhelm to the line of succession, and I squashed that ruthlessly. Either he was a complicated man and didn't himself know what he wanted, or he had plans and was playing a game.

Either way, I'd need to watch the fucker.

"Just make sure he has the support he needs," I said. "And keep an eye on the rest of your house. I don't want any surprises."

"You won't get any from us," Gaspar assured me. "We've sworn the oath. We're bound to the empire now."

"So was fucking Sanguis," I growled. "I mean it, Gaspar. Don't fucking try me."

"I wouldn't dream of it, my prince." He pretended shock, then bowed and moved off.

"That one is a threat," Seraphina said through a beaming smile as she moved in closer, appearing to all the world to be smoothing some lint from my collar. "He never lies, but every statement…"

"It's careful." I nodded. "Either he's a natural politician—and fuck me, that's an insult and a half—or he's just such a sneaky conniving bugger that…wait, that's a politician again, isn't it…"

Seraphina grinned, and we all moved on.

The highlight of the evening for me—while I was dressed and around others, anyway—was Sharn.

The centaur wore a fitted suit and frankly, looked fucking incredible.

I'd never seen a horse wearing trousers before, and just getting into the thing must have been a nightmare, but the look at the end…

"Lady Sharn." I greeted her. "You look…"

"Incredible!" Oracle gushed.

"Really?" Sharn asked, clearly not sure about us, but for the first time since I'd met her, she looked nervous and actually vulnerable. "You're not just saying that?"

I pulled out the truth stone thingy, made sure she could see that I was actively channeling into it, and spoke. "You look incredible, I promise."

The look of relief on her face, and the genuine thanks, not to mention the tears in the corners of her eyes, made me think that maybe, just maybe, there was a chance for us to get along after all.

Until now she'd been a bit of a hardass, but the more I thought about the risks they'd taken and the changes I'd forced on them, the less I could blame her.

Now she was in a place that she'd certainly never been before and doing things that must be about as alien as discussing poetry would be for me.

The rest of the evening passed without incident. The formal dinner that followed the ceremony was a subdued affair, with polite conversation and careful lies and smiles.

By the time the last course was cleared away, I was more than ready for the real business of the night.

"Lords and ladies, honored guests," I announced, rising from my seat, "I thank you for your company tonight. However, there are things that need my attention. Lord Wilhelm, if you would join me, along with Primus Daralen, Lady Seraphina, Lady Oracle, Lady Sehran, and Lord Reth and Lord Greg of Sonra, for a council meeting."

There were a few murmurs of surprise at the inclusion of Sonra's representatives—and their titles—but no one objected openly. The named individuals rose from their seats, following me as I left the dining hall and made my way to the council chamber, where the actual work was waiting.

CHAPTER THIRTY-FIVE

The council chamber was larger than the small meeting room where I'd spoken with Wilhelm earlier, with a massive table of polished wood dominating the center of the space. Maps of Gaij and the surrounding territories covered one wall, while another held detailed plans of the city's defenses.

Had the fight been intended to take place inside the tower, we could have used the new creation table, and seen everything down to granular detail assembled on it.

Or we could in a few more days, as it was nearly finished, the damn thing having proven much more complicated than we'd expected.

But, given that the enemy would need to have made it over the far walls, through the city and then over the tower walls, I decided that using old school, regular maps was just fine.

Once everyone was seated, with Othair, my chamberlain, and several other officials taking positions around the periphery of the room, I got straight to the point, slightly surprised that Gaspar hadn't come along and had instead allowed Wilhelm to bring Kurt.

"We have limited time, so I'll be brief," I began. "Two days from now, Kronk's army will reach our walls from the east. Roughly a day after that, the Dark Legion will arrive from the southeast. Our immediate priority is to prepare the city for siege while maintaining the airship test flight schedule, and funneling more resources into preparing it."

I turned to Wilhelm. "Now that the formalities are out of the way, you need to know the full situation. The most important detail for the empire, and us personally, is that Oracle is pregnant."

Wilhelm's eyes widened slightly, but he nodded for me to continue.

"Under normal circumstances, this would simply be a reason for celebration," I explained. "But given Oracle's unique nature and the general shit storm that will quickly surround our child, there are complications. The safest place for the birth is the Cradle of Feshcan'un, an ancient site of power, and we know this because the gods have personally intervened to recommend we go to it."

"Vhich lies near Kronk?" Wilhelm surmised, his expression growing grave.

"Exactly," I confirmed. "Beyond Kronk, across the Plains of Bones, through a stretch of desert, and in territory believed to be uninhabitable. That's why the airship is crucial—it's our best hope of safely reaching the Cradle, and frankly, it'll be a hell of a lot faster. We could have made it—just—in the timescale we had, but Kronk and now the dark dickheads have screwed that up."

"Might ve ask as to zhe timescale? Und vhat can House Granth contribute to zhis effort?" Kurt asked, his practical business mind already at work.

"Your Earth weapons give us a significant tactical advantage," I replied. "But ammunition is limited, I'm assuming?"

Wilhelm nodded. "Ve have approximately two zhousand rounds for each assault rifle, six hundred for zhe handguns, und zhirty RPG shells total. Vonce zhese are depleted, zhey cannot be replaced."

"Then we need to use them strategically." I turned to Daralen. "Primus, give us the current defensive assessment."

Daralen rose, moving to the map of Gaij on the wall. "The city's defenses are at eighty-five percent readiness. The walls have been reinforced, and the legion is positioned at key points throughout the city. We've also prepared fallback positions in case sections of the outer wall are breached, and we've closed the numerous smugglers' routes in and out of the city. Anyone who tries to use them is in for a shock."

She pointed to several marked locations. "Our intelligence suggests Kronk's forces will approach from the east, following the main road. They have approximately twelve thousand troops, primarily infantry with some highly limited, poorly provisioned cavalry and a dozen siege engines, ranging from catapults that will need to be assembled to a few gnomish creations."

"Vhat do ve know of zheir capabilities?" Wilhelm asked.

"Limited magical support. Kronk is primarily a city that was settled by deep dwarves, driven up from the depths by something; then, given the limited morality of their kind, others migrated inward and essentially formed the raiders' capital," Daralen replied. "Their mages are few and poorly trained. Their real strength lies in sheer viciousness, and their limited siege equipment. They know how to take a city, even if they lack finesse, though generally, they limit themselves to towns, and less well defended targets. Why they've chosen to attack us is anyone's guess."

"And the Dark Legion?" Reth inquired, speaking for the first time, sprawled in a chair and looking weirdly wrong in formal clothing, instead of his usual leathers and armor.

"Smaller but more dangerous," Daralen said. "Five thousand troops, but better trained and with significant magical support. Their elites alone could turn the tide of battle if given the opportunity."

"What about our own forces?" I asked, though I knew the answer.

"Eighteen thousand total that I'm willing to field. A few thousand more we could field if it was an emergency, but who are untrained and would fall easily," Daralen reported grimly. "Ten thousand legion and aspiring legionnaires, five thousand city militia, and three thousand from Sonra, primarily cavalry and archers."

I nodded, doing the mental math. Against either Kronk or the Dark Legion alone, we'd have solid odds. Against both simultaneously, things would be dicier, but that was seriously unlikely. Even if it happened, though, it should still be fairly straightforward. We both outnumbered them *and* had the advantage of the walls.

"Here's my suggestion." I leaned forward. "We use House Granth's ranged weapons as a reserve force, should we lose a section of the wall. Their firepower can decimate enemy formations attempting to breach the defenses. The RPGs should be saved for any siege engines that get within range, and only as they're being used, as that should be the most demoralizing for the enemy."

Wilhelm nodded in agreement. "Ve can position our best marksmen at key points along zhe walls. Zhe assault rifles have significant range und accuracy advantage over bows."

"Good," I approved. "Reth, what's the latest from your outriders?" I asked, even as Daralen growled next to me.

The Sonra representative leaned forward, grinning savagely as I blinked at Daralen in confusion. "Six squads in the field, my prince, and they've been devastatingly effective. The legionnaires have adapted to horseback far better than we anticipated."

"That's because they're tough motherfuckers." I grinned, earning a slight nod from Daralen.

"Indeed," Reth continued, his enthusiasm clear. "The addition of magical support has transformed our capabilities. Each squad has eliminated multiple enemy patrols and supply convoys, using healing magic to recover quickly and magic missiles to strike from beyond normal bow range."

"Any casualties?" I asked.

"Minimal," he replied. "Three wounded, none killed. The Explosive Compression spells have been particularly effective against grouped enemies."

"Yeah, they will be." I grinned even wider, then saw the look of confusion on the faces of Wilhelm and his parents. "It's a variant on a gravity missile, or a mortar. Fire it, and on impact, it explodes outward, burning anything nearby, then collapses inward again and crushes everything within reach until it runs out of mana.

"Continue the harassment operations until Kronk's primary force arrives in sight of the walls, then withdraw to the city. I want all our forces inside the walls before the siege begins, Reth."

"As you command," Reth acknowledged, though he looked less than happy.

"There a problem?" I asked.

"We're cavalry," he pointed out. "If there's a siege, they're going to block the exits and if we're inside, we're useless."

"I have to agree, my prince. Do you wish to hear my plans?" Daralen asked, and suddenly the growl and the looks of annoyance from her were made very clear.

I swallowed hard, took a deep breath and then nodded. "Shit. Actually, yeah, I do. Daralen, my apologies. I gave you command of the city and then I totally just started taking over it again. Please." I gestured to the table, moving back.

"Thank you, my prince," she murmured, though the smile she gave me suggested she understood. "So, as discussed, the two forces are closing on the city currently. Reth's outriders—supplemented by legionnaires—have eliminated the scouts for Kronk and the majority of those for the Dark Legion, as well as successfully cutting Kronk's supply lines.

"There was an attempt to sever the Dark Legion lines as well, but they were far heavier defended, and it was judged better to maintain the advantage of secrecy. Kronk appears to be unaware of their old enemies marching on them from the south-east, but the Dark Legion are most definitely aware, and have picked up the pace.

"It's possible for the dark dicks, as you call them, to arrive before Kronk, but given the distances and speed, I judge this unlikely. Instead, Kronk will arrive late tomorrow night, should they choose to continue marching now that they're close, or midday the following day, should they decide to make camp and then travel later.

"Most likely, they'll arrive at some point the day after tomorrow, and then the Dark Legion that evening. The most likely scenario is that Kronk and the Dark

Legion will attack each other on sight, and Kronk's army will be pushed up against our walls and slaughtered. At which point the Dark Legion will spend a day licking their wounds, and then will attempt to use Kronk's siege weapons and attack us."

I nodded. "Thank you, Daralen. What's your plan for the defense?"

"Similar to your own, my prince, in that we close the gates and remain inside, with the more powerful explosive weapons held in reserve until ready. However, I would have them held back, out of sight, until the two armies are decisively engaged, and then I'd ask that we use them on the Dark Legion only."

"Okay, why?" I asked.

"The Dark Legion are the most likely victors in any battle between them and Kronk, even if Kronk have brought their elite troops—they have a single company of Minotaur berserkers, and two mercenary groups, one of deep dwarf sappers and one a group of fleshcarven."

She paused. "Are you aware of the fleshcarven?"

"Nope," I admitted, getting shakes of the head from most of the others, while Reth hissed in recognition.

"They are revenant souls, summoned through the veil, and into bodies stitched together and reanimated by a particularly disgusting form of blood magic. They exist only to kill. When the body they are contained by is destroyed, they attempt to take a fresh host.

"The legion has faced their kind before. Magic weapons are the best, but the simplest way of dealing with them, frankly, is to make them the Dark Legion's problem."

"Let them both fight it out." I nodded.

"These are the elites of Kronk, and it's unlikely that all three companies will be here, but we need to be ready if they are. The sappers are the easiest to counter, given that with the Dark Legion approaching they're unlikely to have time to set up and achieve anything. But if they do, we simply bombard them with the Explosive Compression or similar spells," she said.

"The Minotaurs are their best at close combat, and the legion are likely to counter them immediately with their own elites, while the fleshcarven will be targeted by area of effect spells, and fire. The revenants cannot survive outside of a body in this realm for more than a handful of seconds…"

"They suffer from the same limitations as we do," Seraphina explained. "They require mana to survive. But where we can essentially hold our breath and last a few minutes if our bond is severed, they require it to interact with any form at all.

"As soon as their host is damaged, they begin to leak mana. Once they run out, they must acquire a new host immediately or be returned through the veil. If they can do neither, then their soul fails and they are lost forever."

"So if they attack us, they become sniper targets." I looked to Wilhelm. "Preferably when they're as far out as possible, and then they can either feed on their allies, or die. Simple."

"Exactly," Daralen confirmed. "We'll keep our forces behind the walls, providing minimal resistance to Kronk's initial approach. Once the Dark Legion arrives and the two forces engage, we'll wait. Then, as the legion gains the upper hand, focus limited attacks on them, essentially trying to keep the two sides as evenly matched as possible, and let them kill each other. When there is a single victor, we unleash hell upon them."

"Sounds fun," Seraphina whispered.

"While the majority of our forces do this, the cavalry is sent north. They wait for the signal, and essentially stay out of the fight as much as possible, unless there is a direct opportunity to counter charge that cannot be denied. They are to remain in reserve, ready for the fight to come, until we call for them, at which point they swoop down and eliminate the enemy as they attempt to regroup."

"Communication could be a nightmare," I pointed out.

"We have succubai." Seraphina smiled. "My sisters would be happy to fly out and relay orders when needed."

"That's a point." I nodded to Sehran. "Do you want to fill everyone in on the situation with your friends?"

"I'd love to." She smiled. "As you'll have noticed, Lord Wilhelm, Kurt, the mistress of the city and I are succubai. I've been told there are a lot of legends about our kind in your realm. Are you aware of who and what we are?"

"Demons of lust." Kurt stood a little straighter, clearly not approving.

"That's very accurate." Sehran agreed with a wide smile. "But it's a little limiting. Yes, we are demons, in that we come from the hells and that's another realm alongside this one. We need mana to survive here, but unlike most of the denizens of our realm, we prefer not to take it by force.

"We spend a limited amount of time here, in this realm, and once we grow too powerful, we are blocked from returning. Frankly, our realm is either very exciting and violent, or exceedingly boring, and there's little in between.

"That means that when we're summoned here, we tend to view it as a bit of a vacation. We get to have a lot of fun, we get fed vital life-bearing fluids and mana, and we're often given little gifts that we take home with us. If we enjoy our time here, and our summoners have enjoyed theirs, they tend to invite us back. Where we come from, the kind of sexual rules and limitations you have here simply don't exist, and well…"

"We're lust demons," Seraphina finished for her with a throaty chuckle. "It's both a description and a job title, and we tend to revel in it. What my little sister is trying to say is that for our kind, visiting this realm is a cause for celebration, and one that is viewed with considerable jealousy by the others who aren't picked.

"Add to that, should we die here, our souls are anchored there, and we are reformed, meaning that no matter how bad the experience, we literally shrug it off and get on with our lives. For us, though, that we're both virtually unkillable here—permanently, I mean—and we are literal lust demons means that when Prince Jax asked if we might have any of our other sisters—or brothers—who would like to come for a visit, over six hundred leapt at the chance."

"Legionnaires, like any soldiers in any army across all of reality, are both constantly looking for an advantage, as well as some sexual relief. I'd had a lot ask if we knew any others like Sehran who might be interested in a warlock pact, and we laughed it off. But when we stopped and thought about it, it was obvious that was a mistake," I said.

"We can distract, buff our bound masters, and some have gifts that are related to fire, as a general rule," Seraphina explained. "Fireballs, breathing fire, flying, that kind of thing…"

"And with a hundred and fifty succubai and incubai ready to jump up and wave at just the worst moment, I'm betting the enemy won't know what hits them." I smiled. "There were six hundred who volunteered, but we limited it to a hundred of the legion and fifty of Reth's outriders, for now."

"Add in that there are also now four hundred legionnaires with at least Magic Missile spells under their belt, I think that the standard five darts, cast four hundred times, in a single volley will cause significant damage." Oracle smiled.

"It sounds…like you expect a slaughter," Wilhelm admitted. "Of zhe enemy."

"We're hoping for it," I admitted. "I still don't get why they're doing this, as neither force is really a threat, more a holding action."

"Could zhat be zhe plan?" Kurt asked. "Simply zhat both sides are planning to hold you here until zhe birth or similar?"

"And vhat of your journey to zhe Cradle?" Wilhelm added. "Vhen vill you depart?"

I exchanged a look with Oracle before answering. "The airship will be ready for a full test flight tomorrow. Truthfully, I have no intention of leaving the city until this is resolved one way or the other, but…"

"But time is not on our side," Oracle finished for me, her hand moving unconsciously to her belly. "The birth would be months away if I was human, but I'm not, not fully, and we just don't know how long it'll be. Lagoush recommended we don't waste any time, though; and we have to think that's for a good reason. We had planned to take the caravans and a large force, but the journey will be dangerous no matter what method we use. Even with the airship, it's likely to take a week or more."

"I understand." Wilhelm nodded. "Perhaps mine father could assist vith zhe airship's final preparations? He has experience vith complex mechanical systems from his business ventures on Earth."

Kurt straightened in his chair. "I would be honored to help, mine prince. I am no engineer, but I have overseen many technical projects and know how to test for reliability."

"Fuck yes, please. Have you got any experience with gnomes?" I asked. "They're brilliant, but sometimes they get caught up in perfect solutions rather than practical ones. We need that ship to be reliable, not perfect."

"I vill see to it personally," Kurt promised. "I have not met gnomes before, but if zhey are as legend states, it shall be a vonderful experience."

"Legend?" I wondered whether he meant accurate family ones or the traditional European ones.

"Zhere are many legends of zhe helpful tinker people," he explained, and I barely stopped myself from laughing.

"Ah…uh, yes. They're certainly that. Greg here has been overseeing the work as well and…" I turned, realizing that Greg had come in with us but had been silent the entire time.

I moved to look at him, finding him in the chair he'd taken on arrival, head bowed and fast asleep. "Damn," I muttered. "Uh, Reth?"

"He's exhausted." Reth sighed, shaking his head. "He's been sleeping less than two hours a night for days to help keep the airship project on track, so, if we can, maybe let him sleep?" he suggested.

"Othair, can we get him to a bedroom, and tucked in please?" I glanced over at the chamberlain. "He's worked miracles and he damn well deserves that sleep."

"I shall see to it, my prince," the fussy little man promised, rising to his feet and summoning a legionnaire to do the heavy lifting.

"Thank you," I said sincerely. "Now, Daralen, let's go over the details of the defensive positions…"

For the next two hours, Daralen led the discussion and worked through every aspect of the coming battle—troop placements, supply management, evacuation plans for civilians should there be breaches, and coordination of magical defenses. By the time we finished, it was well after midnight, and everyone looked exhausted but focused.

"Without more information, there is little else we can do here now," she concluded, rolling up the last of the maps. "I would recommend everyone get some rest. Tomorrow will be busy for all of us."

As the council dispersed, Wilhelm lingered behind with his father. "Prince Jax," he said quietly, "I want to zhank you again for your trust. House Granth vill not let you down."

I studied him for a moment, then nodded. "I believe that. Just remember what I said earlier—being in charge isn't about having all the answers. It's about finding the right people who do, and listening to them. Take me—I'm not the brightest, I give shitty speeches, and honestly, I forget things all the time…"

"We still need to speak to the gods," Oracle reminded me.

"Dammit. See what I mean?" I sighed. "The thing is, though, I'm trying to learn to delegate to those people I trust who can do these things. I keep an eye on them, but need to let them do the things I can't. I need to watch and learn, and then every so often, I get to go buck-ass wild and kill a fuckload of enemies." I grinned as they both blinked, having not expected that.

"Believe me, it keeps the rest honest," I admitted in a low, confiding voice, with a slow wink and a smirk. "plus, well, Sint gave me some pointers on delegation that I'm trying to follow, and I can do the same for you."

"It vould be mine honor," he promised, then bowed again, and followed his father from the room.

When everyone else had gone, leaving only Oracle, Daralen, Sehran, and myself, I sank back into my chair with a long sigh.

"Well," I said, "that went better than expected."

"For now," Daralen cautioned. "The real test comes when Kronk arrives."

"Always the optimist." I grinned tiredly.

"Always the realist," she corrected, though a hint of a smile played at her lips. "Will you be joining the airship test tomorrow?"

I nodded. "I need to see it in action with a full payload before making any decisions. Speaking of which, we need to sort a crew of succubai out for the test, so that if it does come apart and crash, they can fly free without dying."

"Then I suggest you get some rest," she advised, rising from her seat. "Dawn comes early, and there's much to be done."

With a formal salute, she departed.

Sehran smiled and stood as well, giving us both a hug, before leaving to give us a little time alone together in the council chamber.

"She's right, you know," Oracle said softly, coming to stand behind my chair, her hands resting lightly on my shoulders. "You need rest."

"So do you, but I know." I sighed, leaning back into her touch. "But my mind won't stop racing. Less than two days until Kronk arrives. Three until the Dark Legion. And once we've slaughtered them all, we get to try to find a mythical missing fucking hedge or whatever it is."

Oracle's fingers worked at the tension in my shoulders, her touch gentle but firm. "One step at a time, Jax. That's how we've survived so far."

I reached up, covering one of her hands with my own. "We'll make it," I said, trying to convince myself as much as her. "Somehow, we'll find a way through."

"I know we will," she replied, leaning down to place a kiss on the top of my head. "Now, come to bed. Tomorrow will take care of itself."

As we left the council chamber, arm in arm, I tried to focus on the progress we'd made. House Granth was officially sworn to me. The city defenses were nearly complete. The airship was functional. And though the armies of our enemies approached, they would face each other before they faced us.

Two days. That's all we had left before the storm broke upon us. Two days to prepare, to plan, and to pray.

Two days to get ready for war.

CHAPTER THIRTY-SIX

The time between waking up the next morning, and the horns ringing out across the fields, as the army of Kronk came down out of the hills, was an utter blur.

I'd managed one more sparring session with Darakin, and the test flights with the still-unnamed airship were going well. But the vast majority of that time was spent running back and forth, trying to be useful, while also trying not to get in the goddamn way.

The gods had made a contribution to everyone's day—in the best possible way—after Jenae gave up on me ever finding time and calling out to her. Instead, she summoned me and "all the faithful" to an open-air service in the gardens of the tower.

She and the other gods blessed artifacts that Svetu—totally unknown to me—had ordered be made, and they were handed out to our people.

There were *forty-fucking-thousand* of them, and thanks to the inrush of people from outlying towns, villages, and so on, there still weren't enough for everyone to have one. They were simple, a literal symbol of the god that you wished to serve. Over a full day and a night, people were funneled through and allowed to pick one, and then they went to their chosen god and prayed to them, linking it.

That made it so that every prayer that people made to them while wearing the damn thing got the mana where it needed to go. Which was great and all, but when I found that the little turd had passed it off as my order to a bloody entire blacksmiths to do it as the utmost priority, and as such, over three hundred people were now missing their helmets?

Not fucking amused at all.

The upside was, though, that they were then able to offer "little" quests, to just about the entire city.

From "secure the home" to "kill the invaders," "preserve rations" to "craft armor" and a thousand other quests, people were working like they never had before, and I'd even gained out of it as well.

Congratulations!

You have been given a Quest by the Goddess Jenae: Protect Gaij!

The Goddess Jenae has granted you a quest! The city of Kronk has ever been a thorn in the side of the true and honest people of Gaij, and everyone else as well! Now, marching to your capital to sack and burn it, are ten thousand plus reasons to conquer their city in turn, or...burn it to the ground with cleansing fire!

Defeat the invading army: 0/1

Remove the threat posed by Kronk: 0/1

Reward: Secure borders, Safer trade routes, 5,000,000xp, loot, and a more experienced and stronger workforce! (Possible additional rewards based on performance.)

Then came the second offering as well, making damn sure that I knew that Jenae was fudging the books a little by splitting them into two separate quests.

Congratulations!

You have been given a Quest by the Goddess Jenae: Protect Gaij! (2)

The Goddess Jenae has granted you a quest! The Dark Legion, Nimon's chosen servants, have decided now's a great time to demonstrate their disapproval with your heretic ways!

A full legion has been dispatched to burn your city to the ground and salt your fields. Not one soul is to be left alive within your borders, and that's exactly how the Dark Legion prefer it!

Defeat the invading army: 0/1

Destroy the Dark Legion Stronghold of Versilas: 0/1

Reward: Secure borders, Safer trade routes, 5,000,000xp, loot, and a more experienced and stronger workforce! (Possible additional rewards based on performance.)

All things considered, yeah, I'd take a basically "free" additional ten million XP, considering there was no way I could leave the fuckers to run rampant here.

The last quest, though…that was the doozy.

Congratulations!

You have been given a Quest by the Goddess Jenae: Bring balance to the Realm!

The Goddess Jenae has granted you a quest! The wisps, long believed to be the most innocent of all creatures in the UnderVerse, are on the edge of extinction, driven into hiding, captured, tortured, and driven insane by the demands placed upon them. There are now less than a thousand wisps known to exist.

Their breeding methods are partly to blame, due to the abnormally high number of fully grown wisps who die in the process.

Discover, recruit, and protect a viable breeding population to assist Oracle in the birth of your child, and welcome a new species to the realm!

Discover, recover, and protect wisps: 0/50

Secure their home: 0/1

Reward: A chance at an easier birth for Oracle, Balance being restored, Unknown, Unknown. 5,000,000xp

That was clearly the one that was the absolute priority, but considering the obvious phrasing and the fact that we'd been as good as told that there were wisps in the Cradle already, that decided it. I'd accepted all three quests, and I'd gotten back to work.

Now, as I stood at the top of the tower, the wind whipping my hair as I stared out across the city, the walls, then fields—mainly ruined already, I admit—I watched as the army of Kronk raced down from the foothills, and ran hell-for-leather across the plains.

"Are they really going to run all the way?" I asked after a minute, watching as they kept coming. "Fucking seriously?"

They didn't march as an army; they didn't file in rows or ride as one. They spread like a swarm of locusts, running here and there in groups and just…

"That's Kronk," Daralen said in a disgusted voice. "They have no concept of order. There's no common unified command, no strategy, nothing beyond pointing the mass at the enemy and then setting them loose."

"That can't work well for them," I said. "It just can't."

"It does." Seraphina sighed. "If you take into account that Kronk's masters view the citizenry as scum. They don't care about the losses. They'd be fine with the entirety of the 'regular' troops dying to take Gaij. Losses of five-to-one would be more than acceptable for them. Even ten- or twenty-to-one would be fine if there was a big enough prize to claim."

"But they've got no chance," I growled. "They have to know this."

"No, they don't," Daralen said calmly. "I'm sorry, my prince, but remember that the entirety of the city either swore to you or were forced out. Some of them will have fled toward Kronk, attracted to that ethos. But there weren't many who refused, and those who did mainly went south or toward the villages and towns farther out, hoping that you'd forget about them and they could live there still."

"So?" I asked.

"So they don't know. Those who were forced out will have taken word that you took Gaij, but with a small force of, at most, three hundred. There were attacks by the drow and the Dark Legion, and they'll assume other civil unrest as well, because without the oaths, and without the general goodwill that you've managed to build among the population, that's the normal way of things here.

"That means that, because Sonra didn't arrive until after that, they are most likely unaware of our true strength. If they have even heard that Sonra is here at all, that'll simply make them more desperate to attack, as they'll think that any forces that are here, are part of Sonra, and that if they can kill them all, they get to loot Sonra first as well."

"So…they're literally expecting that we've only got a few hundred to defend the city?" I wondered, a smile tugging at the corners of my mouth.

"Plus the city guard, which is two thousand or so, on average. Expect maybe fifty percent losses with the taking of the city by you, in their numbers, and yes. They're likely expecting the city to hold at most two thousand defenders, probably less."

"If that's their expectation, how will we know?" I asked.

"The elites." She pointed to the top of the hills as a new group came into sight. "We'll know what they're expecting by how many elites they field. If they brought all three of their units, but let the chaff run at the walls to die just to distract us, then they're expecting not to need them. If they brought only one or two of the elites, then it's truly going to be an absolute slaughter."

"And the Dark Legion?" I asked hopefully. "Do you think…"

"They're aware of Kronk's forces." She shook her head. "That's after the outriders have been careful to eliminate their scouts at every opportunity. That suggests either they have spies in place in Kronk, or scouts who are both better at their job than the outriders *and* damn lucky. More likely, it's magic or divine intervention."

"Great. But regardless, five thousand against us, and that's after they eliminate Kronk and tire themselves out. Damn, I like those odds."

"We can hope," she said. "The Dark Legion and Kronk have hated each other for centuries, making it highly likely that the Dark Legion was dispatched when they heard Kronk was planning this, simply to try to catch their army in the field, unable to run away. But there's always room for a surprise."

"No plan survives contact with the enemy," I agreed. "Okay, are we ready?"

"As ready as we can be," Seraphina said, and Daralen nodded.

"Then spread the word. Close the gates, and let's get boiling the oil," I ordered, rubbing my hands in evil glee.

"By your command." Daralen crashed her fist to her chest, then marched off.

I watched the army for a few minutes longer, seeing the way that they streamed like locusts, and I shook my head at the total lack of control.

"Twelve thousand people, and only three units at best, that are under control, with the rest just free to do what they want," I muttered. "It's madness."

"It is." Seraphina sighed. "It's incredibly wasteful, but as we said, Kronk doesn't care. As far as they're concerned, there's a valuable core and then there's people there to soak up the arrows and the oil. The more of them who die, the less they have to share that wealth with. And remember, the city is mainly under the control of the deep dwarves."

"Yeah, about them—who and what's the story there?"

"They were driven up by the drow about three centuries ago, and they established the city there, then started raiding, is the simple answer." She shrugged, sitting on the edge of a crenellated section of the roof.

"Where surface dwarves form tight-knit groups around family or beliefs…or ale…the deep dwarves are obsessed with wealth. To them, anything that another can take by force is rightfully the property of the stronger side."

"Charming," Oracle muttered.

"As a race, they are…less concerned with family than most. Where those races, such as the high elves, that normally secret themselves away from the others do it for racial purity reasons, the deep dwarves do it because they are physically incompatible with most other races.

"There have been attempts to summon us for mating in the past—the deep past, you understand—but there are…difficulties with the dwarves, more related to size than, like the drow, capability."

"They're that small?" I grinned.

"No, actually. They're incredibly large. And when you combine that with bones that are naturally reinforced with minerals from the depths, a form of heat resistance from the depths, and their ability to manage the pressures down there as well? The result is that rape isn't a thing for them, or at least not in the way that results in half-breeds."

"Seriously?" I blinked.

"They tend to kill their victims during the act. As they're also significantly stronger than most surface dwellers, they view all the races that are not their own with utter contempt. Anyone who wants to live in their city can—they don't care who moves in—but if a deep dwarf wants something, they'll take it. It'll either be a fight to the death or submission…and the submitting party will be beaten regardless.

"The deep dwarves are naturally long-lived and slow to breed, with a need for greater pressures to carry a child to term than the surface world can provide. As such, there are pressure zones in the city where only the strong can go—or they'll die—and that's where the dwarves tend to congregate.

"Beyond there, they don't care who's living in the city, as long as there's food, ale, and people to fight. It means that the city has become an absolute breeding ground for scum, villainy, and raiding. With an outlook like that, you can understand why the dwarves don't care if the rest of the army die."

"Because the spoils and loot only belong to whoever's strong enough to hold it anyway," I agreed. "Why don't they just kill everyone else in the city and keep it all then?"

"Because they need people to work the farms, to do most of the raiding, and to bring them goods. They know they're hated and reviled, and they hate being outside the pressure zones, so they need the people out there. They just don't like them. From a dwarf's point of view, I'd imagine it's a case of blinking and there's another hundred, then blink again and there's a thousand more humans."

"Mad shit," I muttered. "Is there anything we can do?"

"Not really." She shook her head. "It's lunchtime, so I'd suggest a light meal, and then possibly a trip to the wall or the barracks to try to cheer people up. But beyond that, there's nothing to do until they reach our walls, in about…" She looked toward the incoming swarm. "Two hours?" she guessed. "A few will reach the wall sooner, but they'll be alone, and they're more likely to mill around and do nothing."

"Is that a ladder?" I pointed to one group that seemed to have stopped to fight among themselves.

"Looks like it. I'd imagine a small group carried it all the way here, and now that bigger one wants it." The fight was short and brutal, and the bigger group soon started running toward the walls again, leaving a dozen bodies still on the field behind them, to be trampled by others.

"Wow," I muttered. "We really don't have to do much here, do we?"

"Not really." Seraphina smiled.

"How about we have that lunch and you invite Wilhelm and his father to join us, let them feel useful, and then maybe take Wilhelm to the wall and let him get a little experience with you by his side?" Oracle suggested. "That way he gets it, and those on the walls get to see that you're there with them?"

"That's a good idea," I said.

"We all know you'll only mope around otherwise." She smiled, before leading us off the roof. "Lunch first though!"

Lunch was a surprisingly normal affair, considering the enormity of what was happening beyond the walls. But I'd long ago learned that everyone had their own way of coping with the wait before battle. Personally, I'd have skipped it entirely, but Oracle insisted I eat something, and Wilhelm and his father seemed genuinely appreciative of the invitation.

They asked a few questions about what we were facing, and I let Daralen answer most of them. Her crisp, unemotional assessment was far more useful than my tendency to describe every enemy as "dickheads" or various highly accurate alternatives.

She excused herself after a light starter and headed to the wall, while the rest of us ate a little more, though none of us really tasted anything, despite doing our best to look as relaxed as humanly possible.

Still, I could see Wilhelm's tension growing as we ate. His eyes frequently darted to the windows as if he could see the advancing army through the walls.

"Have you ever been in a siege before?" I asked him, as servants began to clear away the last of the plates.

"Nein," he admitted. "I have fought in small skirmishes since ve arrived from Earth, but nothing like zhis."

"It'll be educational. I've been on both sides, attacking and defending now." I smiled, standing up. "It's up to you, but I'm going to go to the walls and do a little fighting—which I know sounds ridiculous—but honestly, at this point, and considering all we know about the enemy, this is probably the best time for you to get some real experience. If you're up for it?"

Oracle caught my eye as I rose, and she smiled, the tension in her shoulders visible, but she spoke up regardless. "Have fun, and don't lose your temper. We need them to commit to the fight so they're not watching for the Dark Legion, remember? If you scare them off, you'll only have to chase them down later."

"You're no fun." I grinned. "Well, you coming or staying?" I asked Wilhelm, and he smiled, clearly excited, as he stood with me.

"It vould be an honor, mine prince," he said.

"Seriously, though…try not to get killed," Oracle said softly to me. "I'd hate to have to raise our child alone."

"As if you'd let me die." I leaned down to kiss her. "You'd storm the afterlife and drag me back by my ear."

"Damn right I would," she murmured against my lips.

Twenty minutes later, Wilhelm and I were climbing the steps to the eastern wall, where Kronk's forces would make first contact. I could hear the growing roar of the approaching army even through the thick stone: a chaotic blend of shouts, war cries, and the thunder of thousands of feet pounding the earth, all with a collection of bugles, horns, and toots from fuck knew what that made it sound more like a scramble at a festival for the bar, rather than a serious assault.

Daralen was already there, surveying the field with a critical eye. She acknowledged us with a brief nod as we joined her at the battlements.

"How's it looking, Primus?" I asked cheerfully, taking in the scene before us.

The view from the wall was both impressive and slightly comical. Kronk's forces spread across the field like a disorganized anthill someone had kicked over.

Small groups charged ahead, larger ones lumbered along at various speeds, and everywhere there were isolated skirmishes as different factions fought over weapons, position, or seemingly nothing at all.

There were humans, orcs, elves, dwarves—just about every race was somewhere in the mix—and even a handful of monstrous ogres. Streaming around them were goblins that looked to be guiding their bigger cousins, despite them occasionally being stood on.

"It's pathetic," Daralen replied bluntly. "They've divided themselves into at least thirty separate assault groups. None appear to be coordinating with the others, and the majority are so poorly equipped they might as well be naked."

"But zhere are so many of zhem," Wilhelm breathed, his eyes wide as he took in the sheer scale of the attacking force.

"Numbers mean nothing without discipline, and less than a hundredth of the army can use the limited ladders they have at a time." Daralen pointed to where several groups had collided with each other, dissolving into a confused melee. "Watch."

As we observed, the fastest of Kronk's forces approached the walls, carrying crude ladders and grappling hooks. They moved in groups of twenty to fifty, shouting war cries that were more enthusiastic than intimidating.

"Are we going to blood the new recruits?" I looked to Daralen.

"We are." She nodded. "It will give them experience under the best of the controlled conditions we can provide, as well as take the edge off the fear for those who are in their first fight." She raised a hand, signaling to the officers stationed along the wall, and barked an order that was quickly repeated down the line. "Legion aspirants to the front! Veterans to support positions! Prepare for wall defense!"

The change was immediate and impressive. Veteran legionnaires who had been manning the battlements stepped back, allowing the newer recruits to take their places. But they didn't leave—instead, they positioned themselves directly behind the recruits, close enough to step in if needed.

"Zhis is zheir first fight?" Wilhelm muttered to me. "I've fought a dozen times now, und I'm still feeling zhe fear. Vhat manner of man vould not?"

"Honestly, after a while, you'll learn to be more afraid that they'll fuck up and do something you're not prepared for," I admitted, squinting at the forces and looking for anything out of the ordinary. "I've been here for, oh, six or eight months now? Longer? Honestly, I'm not sure, but I've been in a fight at least once a day on average, often dozens of times, and by now…" I shrugged. "As I say, it all blurs. In fact, since I took the city until now is one of the longest times I've had without a fight since I got here."

"Mein Gott," he muttered under his breath.

"Put it this way, my levels now are what, sixteen million experience for the one I'm working on now?" I grinned at him. "I plan on having that in the next two weeks at most."

"Zhat is…terrifying." He shook his head. "But I vould not complain at earning zhat much experience!"

"I bet. Anyway, this is how the legion trains," I explained to Wilhelm as we watched. "Veterans are there, stepping up and ready to guide the recruits through their first battle. They can move in if things go up shit creek, but mainly they're there for moral support, and to instill the fear of the gods—or, more importantly, their optios—in the recruits. By the end of today, these legion aspirants will have actual combat experience, but in as safe a way as possible."

Wilhelm nodded, studying the formation with interest. "And you are confident zhey vill hold?"

"Against this rabble?" I snorted. "Absolutely. Just watch."

The first of Kronk's forces reached the base of the wall, hoisting their ladders with more enthusiasm than skill. Many of the ladders were too short, others broke under the weight of the first climbers, and a few actually fell backward, crushing the men beneath them.

Those who managed to get their ladders in place began to climb, shouting encouragement to one another. Above them, the legion recruits waited, spears and swords ready.

"Hold," Daralen commanded, her voice carrying easily over the din. "Let them tire themselves on the climb. Plenty of time to push the ladders aside when we've taught a few the error of their ways as well."

The recruits obeyed, though I could feel the stress that filled them. Behind them, the veterans remained calm, occasionally murmuring advice or adjustments of stance, and more often than not, either taking the piss, or telling terrible jokes to relieve the stress and pass the time.

The first of Kronk's climbers neared the top of the wall, his face red with exertion, breathing heavily from effort. As his head cleared the battlements, I strode forward on impulse, drew back, and punted him full force.

"Not today, thank you!" I bellowed after him as he fell, taking a handful of others with him, before I turned and strode away like I didn't have a care in the world.

"Vhy…" Wilhelm asked quietly, and I leaned in closer as I spoke.

"Nobody was expecting it…broke the ice a little with how obviously easy it was," I whispered as the next visitor showed himself. This time, a recruit thrust forward with his spear, catching the man in the throat. He fell backward with a gurgled cry, vanishing from sight.

All along the wall, similar scenes played out as more climbers reached the top, only to be met with disciplined resistance. Most died before even setting foot on the wall, speared or cut down as they crested the battlements.

"Form up!" Daralen called, as a few lucky attackers managed to scramble onto the wall. Considering she was deliberately holding people back from the edge to give them the chance, it was obvious that none of the experienced legionnaires thought anything of the enemy at this point. "Shields forward!" she roared.

In small groups, the aspirants stepped up, often casting nervous glances at their "buddies" as the experienced legionnaires waited close by.

The recruits locked their shields together, creating a wall of steel. And behind them, the veterans watched carefully, only stepping in when a recruit was obviously overwhelmed.

I watched a young legionnaire—barely more than a boy—face his first opponent, a burly man with a crude axe. The recruit's shield technique was textbook perfect, but the wild swings of his opponent were throwing him off-balance.

"Footwork!" shouted the veteran behind him. "Remember your stance!"

The recruit adjusted, planting his feet more firmly, and when the axeman's next swing went wide, he thrust his sword into the man's unprotected side. The look of surprise on the recruit's face as his opponent fell was almost comical.

"First kill," I murmured to Wilhelm. "He'll never forget that moment."

"It seems…too easy," Wilhelm observed, frowning. "Zhese attackers, zhey are not even properly armored."

"That's Kronk for you, apparently," I replied, scanning the battlefield. "The bulk of their army is just cannon fodder. They waste lives like we'd waste water by the pool."

I noticed a few scattered groups of deep dwarves among the masses that stomped toward the walls, their shorter, stockier forms distinctive even from a distance. Unlike the chaotic rabble around them, they moved with purpose, barking orders that were largely ignored by the human forces.

"Those are some of the deep dwarves Daralen mentioned." I pointed them out to Wilhelm. "Not their elites, though—probably just overseers sent to make sure the attack happens."

"Zhey do not seem concerned about zhe losses," Wilhelm noted.

"They're not." Daralen joined our conversation. "To the masters of Kronk, these lives mean nothing. They're expendable tools, nothing more. Their aim is to tire us out, and hopefully take a few of us with them. The actual warriors will come later."

While we watched, I found myself enjoying the simplicity of the current fight. The recruits were finding their rhythm now, growing more confident as they dispatched climber after climber. The veterans had to intervene less and less, content to offer advice rather than direct assistance.

"Zhis is going well," Wilhelm remarked, watching as a recruit expertly deflected a spear thrust and countered with a killing blow.

"It's going exactly as expected," I replied. "These aren't soldiers—they're just desperate idiots thrown at our walls to tire us out and use up our resources before the actual attack comes."

"And vhen vill zhe actual attack be?" he asked.

"Tomorrow," Daralen answered before I could. "Today, they send the fodder to test our defenses and wear us down. Tomorrow, they'll bring their elites and siege engines, once panic has had a chance to spread in our ranks."

"Panic?" I snorted.

"They expect that we have less than a tenth of our actual numbers, and healers are rare. In a traditional siege, there would be many injured from today, bleeding out, crying and begging for help; those who have little experience would be driven from the walls by the sight, further weakening us."

A section of the wall to our left erupted in shouts as a larger group of attackers managed to gain the battlements. I saw a recruit go down, blood spraying from a wound to his neck, as a particularly burly attacker carved a space for his companions.

"Time to step in," I said with a grin, banging the base of my naginata on the solid stone of the wall.

"My prince," Daralen cautioned, her tone brooking no argument. "You are not to engage unless absolutely necessary. I have veterans moving to reinforce that section already."

I started to protest, but she cut me off with a look that would have withered most men. "You are the heir to the imperial throne. You cannot take the field against the common rabble."

I sighed, knowing she was right but hating it nonetheless. "But…"

"Wait until their elites take the field, then destroy *them* instead." She grinned suddenly, a feral look that cheered me right up. "Trust in me. When the aspirants feel that they've got a handle on the battle, and the real test comes, so will the elites. When they see how far they've come, then I want to show them how far they have left to go, and how high they can truly climb."

"Oh, I like that." I grinned.

"You vould let zhe prince take zhe field against zheir elites?" Wilhelm sounded surprised.

"First, I am a realist," Daralen said. "Never give an order you know won't be obeyed, and I have not the rank to stop him. Secondly, I know you've watched him sparring against Lord Darakin. Do you honestly believe their elites are a threat to him?"

"Vell, no, I suppose…"

"Exactly. You, however, need experience, my Lord Granth. Will you take the field?"

"I…" He hesitated, then grinned almost nervously. "I vould be honored, Primus."

The veterans had indeed moved to fill the gap, their experienced sword skills making quick work of the attackers who had gained the wall. Within moments, the breach was contained, and the bodies of the slain were being unceremoniously tossed back over the battlements.

Three recruits had died, bleeding out before they could be healed, but all the others were back on their feet. As I watched, a nearby optio was collared by Daralen, and Wilhelm was placed under their care.

I winked and nodded to Wilhelm, who grinned back, and I returned it. For him, this was even safer a fight than it was for the aspirants. Unlike them, he wore full plate and was trained in its use; most of these idiots had much more basic gear, including their weapons.

"He'll do well," Daralen said to me quietly. "Better to blood him now, and have him associate the legionnaires as his companions than stand atop the roof and watch."

"Definitely," I agreed.

Over the next hour, the pattern remained largely the same. Waves of poorly armed attackers would reach the walls, attempt to scale them, and die by the dozens. The recruits grew increasingly confident, requiring less and less guidance from the veterans behind them.

After another hour, I moved along the wall with Wilhelm, watching the fighting techniques of both our forces and the enemy. Wilhelm stayed close, asking occasional questions and clearly antsy to jump back in, but being restrained from the fight simply by a lack of opportunity.

"They're running out of steam," I noted, as we returned to the command post. The attacks had become less frequent and more halfhearted. "Either that, or they're regrouping for something bigger."

"Probably both," Daralen said. "The main body of their army has seen that the wall won't fall today, and they need a better way in than ropes and ladders, or at least a lot more of them. These were just the eager ones."

"Or zhe sacrificial ones," Wilhelm suggested. "Perhaps zhey vere sent forward to test our defenses?"

"If there was that much control on the other side, I'd agree, but I have to go with Daralen's advice here. They're too uncoordinated," I disagreed. "If that was the plan, it was a clusterfuck. They've learned nothing except that we can kill them easily."

Daralen pointed to movement at the rear of Kronk's forces. "They're bringing up their siege engines. Basic creations, but goblin and captured gnome work unless I miss my guess. They'll be powerful, but expensive in terms of mana to use, and they'll do damage if they get close enough."

I studied the approaching machines. They looked like short-armed giant crossbows, a catapult without a counterweight and three battering rams, mostly, with a few smaller things mixed in. Nothing that posed a serious threat to the reinforced walls. But yeah, I could see that they'd be enough to cause problems if we let them get up to the actual walls, or fire.

"Archers!" Daralen called; along the wall, bowmen stepped forward, nocking arrows. "Target the teams pushing the siege engines. I don't want the engines themselves damaged! On my command…loose!"

A hail of arrows arced over the battlefield, raining down on the men struggling to push the heavy siege equipment forward. Dozens fell, and the advance of the machines ground to a halt.

"Again!" Daralen ordered, and another volley followed the first.

The concentrated arrow fire took a heavy toll on the exposed siege crews. Without proper shields or cover, they were easy targets, and the siege engines themselves began to falter as more and more of their handlers fell.

"Wilhelm," I said, "have you had any training with a bow?"

He shook his head. "Zome, but I am not particularly skilled. Mine talents lie more vith zhe sword und spear."

"Same here," I admitted. "I can just about hit a barn at ten paces, but anything beyond that is wishful thinking."

Wilhelm laughed, seemingly relaxed despite the battle raging below. "Perhaps ve should stick to vhat ve know, zhen."

"Sounds like a plan," I agreed. "Though I'm starting to think Daralen isn't going to let me do much of anything today."

"She is right to be cautious," Wilhelm observed. "You are too important to risk unnecessarily, and even zhen, it comes to making a point. Zhere is too much zhat can go wrong in a battle like zhis."

I was about to reply when a commotion farther down the wall caught my attention. A group of particularly determined attackers had managed to secure a much better ladder against the wall and were climbing rapidly, led by a deep dwarf whose armor gleamed dully in the afternoon sun.

Ropes were attached to the surrounding blocks and supports attached the ladder, making it much harder to push aside, as well as…

"Are those rungs moving?" I blinked as I saw the speed the little bastard was flying up the ladder.

"It looks like a gnomish invention," Daralen offered.

"Looks like we might get some action after all." I nodded toward the disturbance. "Let's see how they handle that."

The deep dwarf was first up the ladder, his stocky frame surprisingly agile as he vaulted over the battlement. Armed with a heavy war hammer, he immediately engaged the nearest recruit, who barely managed to raise his shield in time to block the first crushing blow.

Even from our position, I could see the recruit's shield buckle under the impact. The deep dwarf was stronger than he looked, and far more skilled than the rabble that had come before him.

"That recruit needs help," I muttered, starting to move in that direction.

"He has it," Daralen said calmly, pointing to where a veteran was already moving to assist. "Watch."

The veteran legionnaire stepped in smoothly. His sword flashed as he darted in quickly, deflecting the hammer to the side, and then slammed his shield into the deep dwarf, managing to shove him back only a foot or so. The aspirant, recovering his balance, thrust his spear at the dwarf's exposed side, scoring a glancing hit that drew blood.

The dwarf roared in anger, swinging his hammer in a wide arc that forced both legionnaires back. Behind him, more attackers were cresting the wall, creating a small but dangerous beachhead.

"Centurion!" Daralen called. A new officer stepped up, crashing his fist to his chest and standing ramrod straight. "Take your squad and reinforce that section. I want those attackers thrown back immediately."

"Yes, Primus!" the centurion barked, then led a dozen full legionnaires into the breach.

The fight was fast and brutal. The centurion sprinting in from the side triggered an ability—Shield-bash, I thought it was—and covered the last few feet in a blur, slamming his shield into the deep dwarf and sending him reeling back.

He might be heavier, or denser or whatever than a regular dwarf, but he wasn't made of fucking steel, and he'd have needed to be to shrug off that blow.

The others fell upon the attackers with disciplined efficiency, their coordinated attacks easily slaughtering the disorganized invaders. Even the deep dwarf, for all his strength and skill, couldn't stand against the group of trained legionnaires working in concert.

I watched as he parried one thrust only to be caught by another, the blade slipping between the plates of his armor. He staggered, blood flowing freely, then was driven back against the battlements by a Shield-bash. A final thrust sent him reeling back to the edge, blood streaming from gaps in his armor. The centurion lopped off his right hand, left hand, and then his head in short order, before planting a foot and shoving the corpse backward to topple off the wall. A sudden scream rang out as the heavy little bastard took someone else off the ladder as well, cut short as they crashed to the ground below.

"Clean and efficient," Daralen noted with pride. "Just as it should be."

The rest of the attackers had all joined their leader, either killed outright or driven back over the wall. The breach was sealed, and the legionnaires resumed their positions, though now with more veterans mixed among the recruits at that section.

"How are our casualties?" I asked as Daralen rejoined us.

"Minimal," she reported with satisfaction. "Climbing slowly—there's nothing we can do about that—but eleven dead, thirty-two wounded, most not seriously, and all are getting healed and given a break before being shoved back into the fight. The recruits have performed admirably."

"And the enemy?"

"Difficult to count precisely, but the field is littered with their dead. Around twelve hundred at least, and that's just what we can see from here."

I nodded, surveying the battlefield. The ground before the walls was literally fucking covered in bodies, most piled under or around the ladders where they had fallen. Blood darkened the earth in spreading patches, and the moans of the wounded rose in a grim chorus.

"Look zhere," Wilhelm said suddenly, pointing to the distant horizon. "Vhat is zhat?"

I squinted, following his gesture. At first, I saw nothing but the hazy outline of hills against the sky. Then, gradually, I made out movement—a dark line slowly taking shape along the southeastern ridge.

"Daralen?" I asked, though I already suspected the answer.

She pulled out a small spyglass and studied the distant formation for several seconds. "The Dark Legion," she confirmed grimly. "Right on schedule."

Unlike the chaotic mass of Kronk's forces, this new army moved with deadly precision, rank upon rank of soldiers in perfect formation. Even at this distance, they were unmistakable—the golden highlights of their officers, the regimented blocks of infantry, and the banners bearing Nimon's symbol.

"They've made good time," Daralen observed. "At their current pace, they'll reach the battlefield by nightfall."

Below us, Kronk's forces were still focused on their increasingly halfhearted assault on our walls. They hadn't yet noticed the new threat approaching from behind them.

"I have to ask. Zhould ve varn zhem?" Wilhelm asked, his expression troubled. "Give zhem a better fighting chance?"

"And deny ourselves the advantage?" Daralen replied. "I think not. Every member of their army lost to them is a warrior we no longer have to fight."

I nodded. "Fuck to the no," I agreed with feeling. "Both armies came here for blood—better that they get it from each other. The longer they fight each other, the weaker they'll both be when we have to face whoever's left standing."

"It seems…cruel," Wilhelm said softly.

"It's war," I told him. "And if we want to survive it, we need every advantage we can get."

As if on cue, a horn sounded from Kronk's rear lines—someone had finally spotted the approaching Dark Legion. The reaction was immediate and predictable. What had been a disorganized assault became pure chaos as panic spread through the ranks.

Some groups immediately abandoned their assault on our walls, turning to flee back toward the hills. Others, perhaps not understanding the new threat, continued their attacks with increased desperation. A few, braver or more disciplined than the rest, began trying to form defensive lines facing both our walls and the approaching legion.

"Now it gets interesting," Daralen said, watching the confusion unfold below.

"They're caught between hammer and anvil," I agreed. "Our walls and the Dark Legion."

"Zhey'll be slaughtered," Wilhelm said softly.

"Yeah, I hope so," I said with feeling, watching as the Dark Legion began to accelerate its march, clearly eager to catch Kronk's forces in the open.

"They're too close to the walls. They'll never be able to reform their lines to defend themselves…" Daralen said musingly. "In fact, the command tent is right there, at the rear, right in the path of the Dark Legion."

"Well, that's gonna really ruin Kronk's day, isn't it!" I said cheerfully, before nudging Wilhelm with my shoulder. "You'll like fighting these ones—they're a lot more fun to fight," I assured him.

"I zhought zhey vere zhe elite troops of zhe God of Death." He sounded unsure.

"That's why they're the most fun." I nodded. "They sent, oh, about five hundred after me in a forest a few months back."

"How did you escape?"

I frowned at him.

"He killed a third of them alone, and would have killed the rest, had not Nimon, in a blatant breach of the rules, taken a direct hand," came a voice from behind us.

I turned, grinning as Darakin stepped out of nothingness to stand by my side.

"Yeah, man, that was a good fight." I smiled wistfully. "I bet you wish you could have joined in."

"I did. We were forced to watch and not interfere, though your request at the beginning, I confess, had much to do with mine own changing of allegiance."

"What was it?" I frowned, trying to remember.

"You asked Sint to tell people that you died a hero, even if, and I quote, you 'weren't one really.'"

"Well, yeah." I shrugged, a bit embarrassed at that bit being shared aloud.

"Did you hear that, Legionnaires?" Darakin called out, his voice rolling like thunder to suddenly ripple across the walls. ***"Your prince believed that he was unworthy of the moniker of 'hero,' despite him having saved thousands that day alone from slavery. Despite him ordering all those who should have been protecting him to run, so that he could hold off the enemy, alone, willing to give up his own life, to buy those he had rescued a chance at freedom."***

"I had help…" I said, looking around. "Fuck's sake, man, don't make it sound like that…"

"Alone, standing on the field of battle, he killed over TWO HUNDRED of the Dark Legion, including seventeen of the Dark Chosen, the most elite of those foul troops. He was level twenty-seven!"

That got some wide eyes as legionnaires elbowed one another and stared.

"Most of you here today are higher leveled than that. You have years, even decades, more experience with your weapons. And before any of you suspect that his victory was because of his divine nature, at that point he had not yet claimed a fragment of Nimon's fell power!

"Many of you, who stand here today, have more experience than he did then, more years of training, and standing to either side of you are your battle brothers. You have strong walls and good steel, while he had only the forest, the darkness, and the storm. I ask you, Legionnaires! How many of you will write new legends today?

"How many of you will turn to your children, nay, your grandchildren, in years to come, and say 'I was there'? How many of you will have their names recorded in song and deed, as living legends who helped the empire to rise again, as a phoenix from its ashes?"

There was a roar in response, and he nodded.

"Remember that, brave souls—remember that you are the true legion, the strong line between the innocent and the evil. Stand tall, believe in yourself and those who your prince has put over you, and you shall earn your name in glory this day!"

As his voice echoed off the walls, I glared at him, before shaking my head. "Fuck's sake, Darakin, what was that all about?"

"I bring news, and there is little time to impart it." His voice dropped to me alone.

"What's wrong?" I frowned.

"The god Baphomet." He shook his head. *"He was ever a craven and foul cur, but today has he gone a step too far. He has appeared before the leaders of Kronk's army, and has ordered them to step aside, permitting their most hated enemy, the Dark Legion, to pass through their lines, to assault you directly. The Dark Legion are aware, and have been ordered by Nimon to pass through those lines peacefully."*

"What?" I grunted, feeling like I'd been punched in the gut. "Why?"

"The dwarves of the deep might have little care for gods that are not their own, but their Minotaur allies serve Baphomet. When the dwarves refused his order, the Minotaurs slaughtered their allies in his name. They now stand tall in the command tent, and their orders are even now being sent."

"And Nimon is laughing his arse off, I bet." I swore. "Fucking hell, that rat bastard!"

"My prince?" Daralen frowned, and I waved to her to wait.

"His direct and craven intervention means they shall be punished and that we in turn can aid you further, sharing this information now, and robbing them of some of the advantage they gained. Beyond that, there is little that we can do, other than warn you that Baphomet intends to send his force before you to encircle

the rest of the city, leaving the Dark Legion both access to the siege weapons, and to prevent you from escaping."

"Motherfucker," I growled. "What do you think?" I asked Darakin directly, looking him in the eye. "Can I take him?"

"It...would be unwise." He reached out and laid a hand on my shoulder. *"You have improved much, but the others you have faced have been fools and cowards, inexperienced in war, while Baphomet glories in it. Soon, my friend, you could...but not yet."*

"Then I guess we need a change of plans." I sighed. "Thank you, Darakin. One last thing. Are they setting up for the night or…"

"They march for your walls now. They have been ordered to ensure that not one stone stands atop the other by morning, and they intend to see it done."

CHAPTER THIRTY-SEVEN

The god nodded to me, then stepped back, shimmering as he faded from sight, and I nodded respectfully back to him, before turning to Daralen and speaking quickly.

"Nimon and Baphomet broke the rules. I can't explain it, not fully, but they aren't supposed to take a direct hand. They have, though, and that freed our allies up to share information that we couldn't find out or get any other way.

"Kronk is going to stand aside, and they're leaving their siege equipment. They're going to loop around the city and make sure we stay bottled up for now, while the Dark Legion take their gear and use that and their own to storm our walls."

The Dark God Nimon has personally intervened to declare any follower of the Pantheon of the Flame, any citizen of the Empire, or any citizen of Gaij who does not rise up and seek the death of the Apostate Jax, as an Enemy of the Church.

All sanctified soldiers of the Church will receive +3 to Strength, Agility, and Endurance when facing the forces of the Apostate and his hated Gods. Killing any member of those forces will make this buff permanent. Furthermore, this buff will increase by +1 for every additional kill those soldiers make.

Kill on, Holy Warriors!

"Motherfucker!" I snarled, stepping forward. "All right, that's how you want to play it, is it?"

"Jax…" Daralen started.

"Fuck this shit. Daralen!" I bellowed, making sure everyone around could hear me. "Deal with the assault, and stay the hell back. I'm gonna introduce myself!"

"Jax, no!" she shouted, but it was too late.

I strode forward, stepping up onto the crenellations and throwing my hands out to the sides.

"OI, FUCKFACE!" I yelled into the dying light of the sunset. "I KNOW YOU'RE THERE, NIMON! COME ON, DON'T BE SHY!"

"I give you one chance, apostate, for the sake of those souls cowering behind you," came the reply. ***"Kneel, beg for my forgiveness, and perhaps I shall make your passing clean. Those curs behind you may leave, once they have sworn to never again raise a hand to my chosen.***

"Refuse this most generous of offers, and they shall be maimed, their hands and staff cut off, their eyes put out, and their tongues torn loose. Then they shall be set loose to wander the realm, begging for the mercy of their betters."

The proclamation rang through the air, and I didn't bother to look back at the legionnaires behind me. Though, if I were honest, through the rising anger, there was a little voice that reminded me about that dickhead of a tribune, Alister, and the way he'd stabbed me in the back on Nimon's orders.

"Ah, we're back to that bullshit threat, are we?" I shouted at the sky, noting the way that my words rolled as someone—Jenae or one of the gods, I was willing to bet—lent a helping hand. "Well, it's not the first time you've tried it, but let's count the successes, shall we? You tried that here, on this continent, and we came and fucking healed all those we could find. That's a zero there, my son!

"As to you and me? I mean, fucking *really*? How many times have you tried this shit now? What's it gonna take for your people to learn that you're just a little bitch? Do I have to add in the next duel that you're gonna wear a dress and pigtails after you lose? Do I need to put you over my knee and spank you? Or is that what you're hoping for, eh?"

Thunder rolled hard enough, my eardrums vibrated.

"Fuck me, that one hit home, didn't it? Or was that the sound of you getting your rocks off? Seriously, at what point do you fucking grow up, learn to shut your cock holster and fuck right off! You've sent five thousand of your little princesses all in their prettiest dresses to come visit me, and now I'm gonna have to beat them like redheaded stepchildren, all because you can't accept you lost.

"You lost when you murdered Amon, because he came back through me. You lost when you banished your brothers and sisters, because they came back and despite a seven-hundred-year fucking nap, they're still kicking your arse six ways from Sunday!

"You lost when you tried to have me killed, and you lost when you tried to do it yourself. You sent Illoth to do the job you couldn't manage, and what's left of her avatar is buried in my fucking latrines!

"At this point, the only thing you've managed to do well is show what a useless, piss-poor excuse for a god you are. The only way you could make it even worse is for you to step up and take a direct hand again.

"So what's it gonna be, bitch! You gonna throw some more lightning around, maybe fart out a little thunder and run away, or you ready for a fucking rematch? Come on, Nimon! Get your arse down here and face me again. Let me add another trophy to my wall, or get your arse outta here and have Illoth get back to trying to burp Asmodeus's cock out of you!"

It wasn't my most inspired speech, I had to admit, but the thunder and lightning that echoed across the sky was more than enough to draw every eye, as I pointed to the siege weapons in the distance, that were even now being abandoned by the forces of Kronk.

I wasn't about to let the Dark Legion take possession of them, though—no fucking way. They were magical weapons, and as such, they needed power. They needed mana, and I'd just drawn a massive target on my back.

I needed to keep the enemy watching me, not watching the city. I needed our people to view it as I'd just challenged the gods, and that was why both sides were allying against us.

What killed more warriors than the clap was fear.

If they saw both forces that they believed were going to fight each other suddenly joining together and being led by their personal gods, everything Daralen and the others had accomplished today in stiffening their backbones could be undone as fear burned its way through our ranks.

Now, instead of that, they saw me challenging the gods—I'd been very careful not to name or involve Baphomet in the challenge, because if there was one person I genuinely believed had the measure of my skills, it was Darakin, and he clearly didn't think I'd win that one. Hopefully what they'd see was both armies attacking us after I called out their gods and walked away from it. That'd stop the fear, or at least dull it enough that the others around them could counter it.

All they needed was one more push…

I crouched, then triggered Soaring Majesty. I flashed through the air, naginata in my right hand and left hand glowing as I muttered under my breath, summoning Pyroclastic Blast into that hand and then hurling it into the staring deep dwarves.

They'd clearly not wanted to leave their siege equipment, but the sight of me flying toward it, hurling fireballs that exploded and coated everything nearby in essentially lava, had the desired effect.

A handful ran for it, even as others bellowed for their allies to stand fast, and to fight.

The loudest of the group was the next lucky winner as my spell crashed down literally atop him, causing him to vanish beneath the glowing rock. What was left of him burst into flames.

On all sides, those who had been gathering, ready to stand and fight, were hurled from their feet, screeching in agony as their armor or flesh was superheated by flowing liquid rock.

I was more than four hundred meters away from them, flying directly across their forces, when the first of the enemy mages tried to counter me.

A trio of lances shimmered into being, each around a meter and a half long, and shining like they were made of gold. They flickered, unevenly, pulsing as the mage tried to build the spell.

I grinned, realizing the actual issue he, she, or it was facing.

All spells had a maximum distance. Beyond that, they tended to fail. That could mean that they unraveled and fell apart, or they exploded, often very nastily.

I didn't seem to have that problem in the way that most mages did, mainly because I was linked to Oracle, who, as a creature of magic, was incredibly gifted at using it.

Also, I had Amon's memories of centuries of magic studies, and I was a demi-god, so, you know, go me.

Most other mages didn't have any of those advantages, though, let alone all of them, and as such, because they were using spells that they'd been taught instead of spells they'd created themselves, they had no chance of effecting anything beyond a set range.

That range was dependent on the mage involved, but for most, it was around a hundred to two hundred meters, unless they were very good.

That meant with around three hundred meters between me and the greasy-haired cockwomble, he was frantically trying to stay hidden behind his friends, while getting closer.

This was complicated by the fact that his "friends" had seen me hit a target at least six hundred meters away twice with massive globs of liquid fire that exploded and did serious damage to everything around the target, and they apparently decided that they didn't really like the guy that much after all.

All of this to say, that by the time I'd approached to within about two hundred and twenty meters of him, he was still straining to hold his own spell together, while I'd had the time to cast another of mine.

This one was a fun one that I hadn't used in a while, mainly because it tended to leave such an effect on the area and result in any surviving enemies having nightmares and a life-long need for therapy.

It was a spell that if the *Canadians* had a chance to use it, they'd have embraced it wholeheartedly, and Earth would have had yet more sections of the Geneva Convention added wholesale.

I sighted my spell on the center of the little group, and directly on the forehead of one of the few members of the group who were still trying to protect their charge in the incredibly stupid-looking multicolored robes.

The spell blurred as it shot across the intervening space in the blink of an eye before smashing into his helm, and smashing the guy—or girl or whatever; I wasn't going to judge them on their sexuality, just their fucking stupid life choices. Then it went active, rippling out, locking gravity into place and beginning to unwind.

The soldier was crushed to the ground, *literally.*

Originally, they were about six feet, and had been wearing shiny silvery armor. Half a second later, it looked as if they'd been a balloon covered in tinfoil, that had a bowling ball dropped on it.

Claret splattered the area, as ten lines flashed out after the shell of the spell detonated, flinging them loose. Each of the lines held a single seed at the end, and that seed was the fun part.

The closeness of the idiots around the mages—I'd noticed that several more were nearby, as they all bolted out of hiding in every direction—meant that some of the seeds ended up embedded in other warriors or figures. One embedded itself in the back of a mage's head where she'd been sprinting away from the display.

The lines each rolled out secondary connecting lines that moved in turn, reaching for one another and creating a ritual circle that covered about ten meters. Then, the next phase went active, and a burst of black light flashed outward, then tore inward as the gravity seeds powered up.

The luckier of the group, inside the AOE, were the handful who were killed when the dipshit who had drawn my attention lost control of his spell and it detonated, burning several to death and sending him to the ground, stunned.

Of the others, a few were crushed flat a half second later; killed instantly by the gravitational anomalies, which was probably a blessing. The most unlucky though, were those who were caught in a nexus of forces, as the seeds went fully active.

Each of the seeds had a flickering pulse of positive or negative charge, set to around thirty Earth gravities. They rapidly pulsed from one to the other, yanking anything nearby at thirty gravities, and then switching to shove outward and away.

That created waves of gravity pulling this way and that, hurling people, and then rapidly *bits* of those people in different directions. Some were caught between several nexuses, their bodies being torn and flipped, crushed and burst, hurtling from side to side.

Finally, after what must have seemed like an eternity for them, though was only seconds for the rest of the realm, the final phase went active, and two hundred gravities of force was expended across all the seeds.

Everything in its radius was cratered into the ground. Those standing nearby but outside of the AOE were thrown from their feet as the earth split into a chasm at least ten meters wide from the force of an earthquake never before experienced.

That clinched it: most of those who had stayed and were ready to fight now decided they'd rather be elsewhere.

Kronk's soldiers were in an uproar. Half had refused to stand down; the shocking sight of their hated enemy marching to their rear was seen as a challenge, and fully five thousand rushed at them as the Minotaurs roared orders and struck out at any who refused them.

The fleshcarven made their presence known, as well, as dozens of them fell on their closest "allies" in Kronk's armies and started to feast, after their masters' attention wandered.

The dwarven sappers, if they were even there, were nowhere to be seen—or at least *I* hadn't spotted them. But as I threw out still more spells, the utter absence of any direct action by Nimon clear for all to see, the Dark Legion broke into a run. Rank after rank raced forward, as I poured on the speed, determined to get to the siege equipment first.

The air whistled past me as I shot through the sky, angling myself like an arrow at the abandoned siege weapons. On the far side, the battlefield churned with chaos—Kronk's disorganized forces clashing with the disciplined ranks of the Dark Legion, while the Minotaurs bellowed orders and cut down any who refused to obey Baphomet's commands.

Explosions suddenly detonated in the front lines of the fight between the Dark Legion and Kronk's forces. I stared, then swore.

Their mages were bombarding the front lines, missile after missile that blew great holes in their own fucking side as much as the enemy's just to open it up, and I could already see blurs streaking through the gaps.

Dark Chosen, the elites of Nimon's forces. Some, like Thomas had been, were built around massive strength—berserkers who could take on dozens at a time. But the ones I could barely track, I just friggin' *knew* were going to be stabby-stabby bastard rogues.

I glanced back toward the walls of Gaij, where Daralen and the others would be watching this insanity unfold. I hoped they understood what I was doing—drawing attention away from the city, forcing both armies to focus on me and showing my people that they weren't all that.

If not, Oracle, Daralen, Seraphina…the list of people getting involved in kicking my arse when I got back was going to be ridiculous.

The siege engines were less than two hundred meters ahead now. I could see figures scrambling around them—not deep dwarves anymore, they were running for it, but a mix of heavily armored soldiers who had to be Kronk's own and the first of the Dark Legion's advance troops, close enough that they were going to get there before me at this rate. They had to have been dispatched specifically to secure the weapons.

"Not fucking today," I muttered, adjusting my trajectory to land directly beside the largest of the catapults.

I hit the ground rolling, coming up with my naginata swinging in a wide arc. Two of the nearest soldiers staggered backward. They hadn't expected me to actually land among them—probably thought I'd keep my distance and throw more spells from afar.

"Prince of Gaij," one of them called out, as he ran at me, his voice distorted by the ornate helmet that covered his face, complete with two fucking stupid little wings coming out of either side. "The gods have ordered your death. Surrender, and your suffering will be—"

I didn't let him finish. Launching forward, I raced across the short distance, then slid to the side as he swung a greatsword overhead, clearly thinking to split me in two.

For me, it was as if he were mired in treacle. I let the blade hit the ground, then kicked my left foot off the side of it, as it sank into the earth, driving it deeper. I spun, lopping his head off, my naginata's blade sliding neatly between the plates of his armor at the throat.

Blood sprayed as I completed the cut; his head launched into the air carried atop a short but highly colorful fountain of claret.

I spun and changed my grip on the weapon, flipping it around and gripping it by the head. Swinging hard, I smashed the metal-clad base into the dropping head with all my might.

"He shoots!" I roared, as the blow landed. The helmet deformed around the impact; it rocketed to the side, slamming into a rogue who appeared at the last second, having been mid-leap when he saw the helmet coming.

It crashed into the side of his head. The cloth hood did nothing to slow the metal. The rogue was flipped end over end, his own head crumpling with a sickening sound.

"HE SCORES!" I yelled, before ducking as a light of crossbow bolts streaked by on their way, now off to terminally inconvenience someone else.

There was a brief scream from behind me, and I couldn't help but grin, figuring that another stabby-stabby bastard rogue had gotten what was coming to them.

"Anyone else want to chat?" I flashed a grin that I knew was all teeth and no humor. "No?"

In response, the freshly arrived Dark legionnaire elites attacked as one—seven elite warriors moving with practiced coordination. These weren't the rabble who had been climbing the walls; these were the real deal, Nimon's chosen killers.

Until now, I'd been working to the limits of my natural power but without using my abilities, instead just pushing as hard as Darakin had been showing me I could.

Now I triggered Mana Overdrive and felt the familiar rush as my senses sharpened and time seemed to slow around me. Colors became more vivid, sounds crisper, and every movement of my enemies appeared telegraphed seconds in advance as my body surged with strength and power.

The first swing came from my right—a heavy mace aimed at my ribs. I twisted, letting it pass within inches of my side, then shoved the wielder from that side, just where he was off-balance, and into the path of his friend, who brought a hooked halberd around and into his former ally's armpit. Then I brought my naginata around in a sweeping arc that forced the next attacker back.

Another came from behind, sword thrust aiming for the area where the armor was less able to cover, just below my kidneys, due to the limits of mobility.

"Hyper Cognition," I whispered. The world slowed further as my mind accelerated to inhuman speeds.

Now I could see not just their movements, but the patterns—the way they worked together, the small signals they used to coordinate their attacks. I could predict where each blow would land seconds before it was launched, and beyond them, the displacements in the air and the way that light shimmered as the rogues closed.

The sword missed me by a hairsbreadth as I sidestepped, then pirouetted to face my attackers. The five warriors had formed a loose circle around me, cutting off any escape routes. I didn't need them.

"You know what your biggest problem is?" I asked conversationally, as if we were discussing the weather rather than trying to kill one another. "You're not used to fighting someone who isn't afraid of you."

They didn't respond, instead launching another coordinated assault. Two came at me from the front while a third tried to flank me. I parried the first thrust, ducked under the second, and fed mana into my weapon, igniting it to a fiery glow. I spun my naginata in a tight circle that caught the third attacker across the chest, stumbling him backward with a deep gash through his armor that was cauterized even as it left the body.

"That's two!" I counted aloud.

My focus shifted to the catapult beside me. Now that I was closer, I could see what I was looking for—a compartment built into the base of the mechanism, where small, glowing stones were secured. Manastones. The source of power for these siege weapons, and potentially far more valuable than the machines themselves.

"No, no, no," came a sharp voice from behind the catapult. A robed figure stepped into view, another mage, this one wearing the insignia of Nimon's chosen. "The Dark God foresaw your intention, heretic. These weapons are ours now."

He raised his hands, and the air around the catapult shimmered with protective magic. At the same time, the warriors pressed their attack with renewed vigor.

"Everyone's a fucking critic," I muttered, deflecting a sword thrust and countering with a slash that took the warrior's arm off at the elbow. "That's three!"

More soldiers poured in from all directions now—the Dark Legion's vanguard had reached us, and reinforcements were arriving by the second. I needed to move fast.

I feinted left, then spun right; my naginata cut a deadly arc through the air. Two more of the elite warriors went down, one clutching at a throat wound that sprayed blood in a crimson fan, the other crumpling as the blade found the gap between helm and breastplate.

"Five," I said, my voice eerily calm, even to my own ears.

The mage was chanting now; his spell grew in complexity as he wove layers of protection around the siege equipment. I couldn't let him finish.

My fingers curled around the haft of my weapon as I summoned a spell I'd used so many times that it was instinctive by now. I could probably cast it while balls-deep with my fingers busy and a bacon sandwich in my mouth.

Frostfire Circle of Cleansing crashed into the ground under me, rolling out to six meters on a side, and nicely underneath his own shield, before flaring to life and setting fire to both him and the others around me.

"That's cheating," the mage stupidly gasped, clutching at his robes where the mana had burned through them. "How…"

"Oh, *seriously*? That's what the fucker whose god is breaking all the rules says," I shot back, ducking under another sword swing and driving my elbow into the attacker's face with enough force to shatter his helmet's faceplate. Blood and teeth sprayed as he collapsed. "Six."

The last of the elite guards backed away, reassessing his options. Around us, more Dark Legion soldiers formed a perimeter, their movements controlled and disciplined even in the midst of chaos.

"Nimon Himself has ordered your capture," a new warrior called, his voice steady despite the carnage I'd unleashed on his companions. "You cannot escape."

"Watch me." I launched myself at the catapult, naginata first, mana pouring into the weapon, and I activated its shield killer capability.

The shield spell the mage had been casting burst like a soap bubble. I landed beside the manastones and grabbed the glowing treasure. Six of them, each pulsing with stored power.

The last elite guard charged me from behind, his sword raised for a killing blow. Without looking, I thrust my naginata backward, feeling the blade sink deep into flesh. I twisted, wrenching it free as the warrior collapsed.

"And that's seven," I finished, conversationally, to the burning and screaming mage, as I pocketed the manastones. Then I stepped to the left slightly and leaned back; a thrown blade arced through the air to clang against the metal of the siege equipment, before tumbling to the ground.

More soldiers were closing in fast—too many to fight head-on, even with my abilities. I needed to create some distance.

I leapt to the next siege engine—a massive ballista—and repeated the process, tearing open the compartment and retrieving another four manastones. As I worked, I used my free hand to cast another spell, a second gravity seed, one that I'd hold to detonate after I was clear.

"You want these so badly?" I called out to the approaching soldiers. "Come and fucking get them!"

I triggered Soaring Majesty again, propelling myself skyward just as the first wave of soldiers reached the siege equipment. From above, I watched as they swarmed over the machines, trying to get high enough to reach me.

Thirty meters up, I unleashed the spell again.

The effect was immediate and devastating. The seeds detonated in sequence, creating a rippling field of gravitational distortion that tore through the siege equipment and anything unfortunate enough to be near it. Metal twisted and warped, wood splintered, and bodies were crushed or torn apart as competing gravitational forces pulled them in multiple directions at once.

The explosion radiated outward, sending a shock wave across the battlefield that knocked even more enemy soldiers off their feet. The siege weapons—all of them—were reduced to twisted scrap in seconds, as I fired off one more of the spells to be sure.

I angled myself toward the walls of Gaij, leaving chaos in my wake and grinning evilly inside my helm. Behind me, the Dark Legion was regrouping, but their prize was gone, destroyed rather than captured. And in my pouches, I had the manastones. Sure, ten weren't many, and there might have been more hidden nearby, but it was ten more for the airship, and that meant I was ten closer to having my love safe.

Worth it.

The flight back to the walls took only a few minutes, considering I was no longer frantically burning mana like a rocket had been shoved up my arse.

I spotted Daralen standing at the command post, her expression a mixture of exasperation, grudging admiration, and barely hidden and controlled fury.

Wilhelm was beside her, his eyes wide with awe as he watched my approach.

I landed on the battlements with a theatrical flourish, removing my helmet and raising my naginata high as legionnaires began to cheer.

Behind me, the battlefield was in chaos—Kronk's forces and the Dark Legion now fully engaged with each other, the group that should have circled the city clearly deciding to join their friends and fight the dark dicks instead, and the siege weapons nothing but smoking ruins in their midst.

"I was going to kill them all myself," I announced, my voice carrying easily over the wall. "But then I decided that wouldn't be fair to all of you."

A ripple of laughter ran through the assembled soldiers, tension bleeding away as they realized what I'd accomplished.

"The Dark Legion thinks they're special because they serve a god," I continued, turning to face them fully. "But they're not. Fuck's sake, we have eleven of them!

"Those dark dickheads bleed just like anyone else. I've faced them before, as Lord Darakin told you, alone in a forest with nothing but my weapon and my wits, and I sent hundreds of them back to Nimon in pieces."

I gestured to the battlefield behind me, where the remains of the siege weapons still smoldered.

"You are the legion! The finest warriors this realm has ever seen. You stand on these walls not because you had to, nor because you're greedy, thieving bastards coming to loot and pillage. No, you stand here because you chose to defend your homes, your families, and your future. When those bastards reach our walls—and they will, when they've finished slaughtering those who were nearly their allies—they won't be facing just me. They'll be facing all of *you*."

I looked across the faces before me—young recruits, hardened veterans, all watching me with growing determination.

"I mean, fuck me, how unlucky can they get? Not only are they going to face *me* in battle, and I just fucked their shit up with barely any effort, but they get to face *you* as well, *and* your friends, *and* the optios who trained you!

"They get to face the mad shit the gnomes have been cooking up, they get to face our magic and our fresh steel, and lastly, that's all after they've climbed a fucking ladder and had their teeth kicked in!

"I've got half a mind to send half of you home, just to give them a chance. But no, they listened to that yellow streak of piss Nimon, and they came here. Now it's time for them to make that climb, to drag their sorry arses up here, and face us…

"And may their fucking cowardly, pathetic god show them mercy when they do, BECAUSE WE WON'T!"

A cheer erupted along the wall, weapons raised in salute. I caught Daralen's eye and gave her a small nod. The message was clear: I'd bought us time and destroyed their siege capability, but the actual fight was still ahead of us.

As the cheering continued, I pulled one of the manastones from my pouch, holding it up so it caught the light.

"Well, will you look at that?" I called out, grinning like the madman I probably was. "I guess those bastards lost some loot and I found it. Fucking terrible shame, that. I wonder what you'll all loot from your kills?"

That thought started an even louder cheer.

CHAPTER THIRTY-EIGHT

The fight beyond Gaij's walls had turned from a fucking mess of madly charging idiots, into a mass of idiots who were now pressed tight against the well-formed ranks of the Dark Legion. And even from here, it was clear they were running headlong into a meat grinder.

What had begun as two distinct armies—Kronk's disorganized lunatics and the Dark Legion's disciplined force—had become a churning maelstrom of violence as the forces that should have been allies tore into each other.

The Minotaurs, bearing Baphomet's blessing, had betrayed their deep dwarf companions at his order, only to find themselves caught between the walls of Gaij and the Dark Legion's advance anyway, when half their force mutinied and refused the command to stand down.

They were left with the option of hoping sense prevailed, or finding themselves left alone at the end with a blood-crazed Dark Legion army, when it'd cut its way through their only allies.

I leaned with my arms folded atop the battlements. Oracle, having arrived a few minutes ago, joined me, watching the carnage unfold.

The manastones I'd recovered from the destroyed siege engines had already been sent to the gnomes, ready to be used by the airship if they needed it.

"That was incredibly stupid, you know," Oracle said quietly, her eyes never leaving the battlefield. "Even by your standards."

"It worked, didn't it?" I replied with a grin that probably looked as exhausted as I felt. The adrenaline rush of the fight had faded, leaving behind the bone-deep weariness that always followed a fight interrupted, and using my abilities like that.

I'd healed both the damage that Soaring Majesty and the debuff that came with Mana Overdrive had done, but still, I was tired, and honestly a bit low.

What had looked like being a much easier fight had needed a helping hand, but now as our enemies slaughtered each other, we were left to watch, as literally thousands upon thousands died horrifically.

"It worked this time," she conceded, finally turning to face me. Her expression softened slightly, though I could still see the worry in her eyes. "You can't keep throwing yourself at every problem, Jax. Some fights aren't yours to win alone."

Before I could respond, Daralen returned, her face set in the carefully neutral expression she wore when she was particularly pissed off but forced to deal with an idiot officer.

It looked remarkably like the face that Lydia made right before she chewed me out, now that I thought about it.

"That was an impressive display, Prince Jax," she said, her tone clipped. "Though perhaps a little warning next time would be appreciated, as would the chance to talk you out of it!"

"There wasn't time." I nodded toward the battlefield. "I'm sorry, Daralen, but they were about to secure those siege engines. If they'd gotten them intact, controlled by an army that actually had a fucking clue, our walls would have been in serious trouble. And you felt the fear rising in our people. I had to do something."

"A speech would have been something!" she started. "Spells cast at this range are unlikely to work, but even that would have been *something*. What do you think the effect on morale of seeing their prince fall in a fight that he had no reason being in would have been?"

"I—" I started.

"Prince Jax, you gave me command of the defense. Is that still your intention? That I lead?" the half-orc growled.

"It is," I agreed, wincing. I knew I wasn't going to like this.

"Then until such time as I give you a different command, you are to stand down and be a bloody symbol to the defense, not a gods-be-damned target out on a field!"

Wilhelm nodded in agreement, still wide-eyed from watching my aerial acrobatics. "Zhat vas…incredible," he admitted. "But zhey are right, mine prince. It vas a foolish risk."

"Fine. Daralen, you win. I'll stay here until you agree I need to step up. But you and I both know I can only agree to that if things go well! There's a hundred scenarios where you need me doing exactly what I just did. When the shit hits the fan, you'll order me in there—you give your word, or I'll take command and they'll all have to make do with my shittier tactics! Agreed?"

"Jax…" she growled.

"Do you agree, Primus? That when you need me in there, when you need your biggest, most incredibly stupid and lethal weapon in the fight, you'll use me? Or are we both wasting our time?" I snapped back.

"I agree!" she snarled. "But until then, you'll respect my authority and plans and you'll wait for orders!"

"Fine!"

"Fine!" she snapped back.

"Now that everyone's happy," Oracle smiled sweetly, "perhaps we could stop arguing in front of the children?"

I looked around, seeing how many of the legionnaires on all sides were staring at us, wide-eyed, and I forced a chuckle, before waving it off.

"Back to your posts!" Daralen roared. "Or do I see legionnaires with too much time on their hands?!"

That got everyone moving, and she turned, glaring at a group of ten directly behind her.

"This *is* our post, Primus!" a centurion at the front shouted, crashing his fist to his chest in desperate salute and not daring to look at her.

She glowered at him, then at the others, before turning her back on them and staring out across the battlefield.

"Dammit, Jax, you have *no* idea how much you scared the hell out of us all," she eventually admitted to me.

"We do." Oracle gestured to Sehran, who I hadn't seen before, but I now noticed was hiding off to one side. "He does it all the time. The optio of his squad spends half her life cursing him and the rest leveling like…what was it Thomas said? Oh yes, 'numbers go brrrr.'"

"I can believe it." Daralen sighed.

"I don't do it deliberately, you know," I half apologized. "I just see what needs to be done, and I, well…I do it."

"The hardest part, Jax"—she said, and I grinned at her dropping the "prince" bit again—"is that I can never tell if you're a born tactician, that you see the weakness in the split second that it appears and you move to deal with it on instinct, understanding and assessing the risks in that fraction of a heartbeat—"

"I think—" I started to say, and she went on.

"Or you're a complete moron sent here by the gods to punish a poor legionnaire for poor life choices," she finished.

"Such as?" Oracle asked.

"Joining the legion, for one," Daralen grumped.

"I'm not all that," I admitted. "But I do see things, and I react, that's all."

"Do you understand the effect? The risks?" she pressed.

I hesitated, then nodded. "I think I do." I moved on as she opened her mouth to speak. "I mean it, Daralen. Amon shared, well…so much with me, with *us*. Oracle and I are bonded, and she has access to a lot of the memories he poured into me.

"What he gave us is mainly magic, not 'wow, that's magic' but I mean he gave us magical knowledge, information, theories and thousands of years of fireside chats with mages and lunatics alike. We've got half-formed theories and totally debunked stupid ideas, all rattling around inside me—ten thousand years of knowledge forced into a brain that's not even thirty yet. It means that I know things, things I shouldn't. I've been able to manipulate spells in ways I probably shouldn't have been able to since the very beginning, when he was just a mad voice in the back of my head that occasionally screamed or wept.

"In the end, though, as he named me his heir, he was sane, or enough that he understood, and he tried to give us everything we needed. Most of what he shared was magic, as I say, but he also fought hundreds of thousands of times. From battles that left entire continents devastated, to barroom brawls, they're all there, just faded and half-mixed in with others.

"The effect is like that." I gestured out over the walls, as they battled back and forth across the ground I'd recently painted with the innermost thoughts and feelings of their friends. "Sometimes I think things through and I make conscious decisions, but most of the time?" I shook my head. "I just see the gap, see the lever that with a little push can change the course of the fight, even if only in a small way. And before I think about it, my hand's on it and I'm fucking heaving. Does that make sense?"

"Unfortunately." She sighed. "Are you sure you don't want to lead this fight? If you have all those memories…"

"They're a chaotic jumble." I shook my head. "Amon trained for three hours a day with any and every master of a weapon he could find. If I had those memories right, I'd be able to kill the entire enemy army with a butter knife, never mind a proper weapon, but I don't. It's the same with magic. He was a master of mana, and could have reached out and snuffed out the entire enemy army's leadership with a single spell from here with ease.

"The things I've seen him do? They're incredible. Some of them were with my body, but me? I'm learning, and every little baby step I make, I get to understand a bit more about the way it all fits together.

"It means I'm probably learning faster than I should. I know my magic is definitely more powerful than a 'normal' mage, but beyond that? I need to be taught. I need you to explain how and why it works or it doesn't, because if you don't, I'm gonna make some serious fuckups," I finished.

"Like zhe way you almost got caught by zhe Dark Legion zhere?" Wilhelm asked me.

I shrugged, scanning the chaotic melee below. "Not really. Those Dark Legion elites? They're good, but they're predictable. They fight like fools. They've hardly ever faced anyone who didn't piss themselves in terror as soon as they see them, and they rely on their abilities too much. They fight in ways that are clearly patterns. The stealthy stabby-stabby bastards always think that if they're invisible, then you can't see them…"

"Vell, zhat is literally vhat it means," he pointed out.

"But if you look for displacement, the splash of mud, the way that the grass bends, or the wind blows around something?" I shook my head. "When it all comes together…the smell on the wind, the sound of their breathing, the tremor through the ground…once you recognize those patterns, they're easy to counter."

"But still—" Daralen began.

"Look," I interrupted, pointing toward a section of the battlefield where the fighting had abruptly ceased. "Something's happening."

In the midst of the carnage, a space was clearing. The Dark Legion's forces were pulling back in perfect formation, blowing horns and creating a perimeter around what appeared to be a command group. The Minotaurs of Kronk, recognizing an opportunity, were calling their forces to halt as well, though that was probably because so many of their forces had discovered that running headlong at an enemy who's trained and experienced when you're in cloth and waving your freshly found sword in the air and screaming isn't a strategy for a long and profitable life.

"They're regrouping," Daralen observed, holding a spyglass to her eye. "No, wait…they're parleying."

"Parleying?" Wilhelm repeated, incredulous. "After all zhat?"

"The Minotaurs serve Baphomet," Oracle reminded him. "It's probably taken all this time to get enough control over their forces that people would actually listen."

"Slaughters will have that effect," Daralen agreed absently, still scanning the distant gathering.

I narrowed my eyes, focusing on the group. My enhanced Perception allowed me to make out details that would have been invisible to others at this distance, and damn I loved having hit the century in it.

The Dark Legion's commander—a tall figure in ornate armor with distinctive golden scrollwork—faced a massive Minotaur whose horns reflected the fading light with gold and gemstones.

"Kronk's losing badly," I observed. "They've lost almost half their force, and they have to know the Dark Legion will slaughter them all if they keep fighting. Think they're negotiating surrender terms?"

"Or trying again for that alliance," Oracle suggested grimly. "Against us."

I nodded slowly, my mind racing through the possibilities. "They're keeping their distance from our walls, beyond arrow range. They think they're safe to just stand there and talk, don't they…" A slow, wicked grin spread across my face as an idea took shape. "I think it's time we reached out and touched them again."

Oracle caught my smile and started smiling as well as she felt the briefest shape of my plan. "Jax, what are you thinking?" she asked for the benefit of the others.

"They're all gathered together," I replied, my voice low with anticipation. "Every leader, every powerful mage, every elite warrior…all in one place."

"Please don't tell me you're going to fly back out there and challenge them," Daralen said firmly.

"No, he's thinking of using that gravity spell again." Oracle grinned evilly.

"It's a perfect opportunity," I explained, my fingers flexing as I thought it through. "One spell could decapitate both armies at once."

"At that range?" Daralen asked, skeptical. "Can your magic reach that far?"

"With enough power behind it? Yeah," I replied confidently. "Don't get me wrong, it'll be expensive and fuck me, I won't get more than a handful of them off. But we've got plenty of mana potions, and the risk is well worth the reward. After all, they've got to be convinced they're safe from us at that range."

Oracle studied the distant gathering, her expression thoughtful. After a moment, she nodded slowly. "It's definitely worth trying. And we'd be here with you, Daralen, so no risk from him going out there. I'll help him, but as we agreed, only if you give the order, Primus."

"Do it," she said after a brief pause.

I raised an eyebrow. "You're not going to try to talk me out of it?"

"When has that ever worked?" she replied with a faint smile. "Besides, if you manage this, the result will be utter chaos in their ranks."

"I'll help you as well," Oracle said. "Hold on, and let me…"

I felt her reaching into me, her consciousness gently tweaking the spell as I started to get it locked into place in my mind, adjusting this bit, tightening that…

Without further discussion, we were off, shaping the mana into the complex pattern required for the gravity seed spell. The process was different than normal, when I just slapped it together and hurled it loose. The distance from here to there was nearly nine hundred meters, well outside the range of the average mage. Hell, a hundred meters was a limit most never surpassed.

At this range, any flaw in the spell's structure could cause it to unravel before reaching its target.

Oracle worked through me, continuing to add and twist, strengthening and stabilizing the growing spell matrix.

"Ready?" I asked when the spell had reached its peak potential, the mana within it compressed almost to its breaking point. The spell seemed to shiver, eager to be released.

"Now," Oracle confirmed, her voice tense with concentration and laced with glee.

With a gesture that sent relief pouring through my extended arm, like a growing cramp that was prevented just before it could take hold, I launched the spell.

It streaked across the battlefield like a comet, a barely visible distortion in the air that left a trail of shimmering heat in its wake.

For a breathless moment, I thought it would reach its target unimpeded. Then, just as it neared the gathered leaders, a bare seventy or eighty meters from them, a shimmering barrier was revealed.

The spell impacted with a flash of blinding light, the shield interrupting it and causing it to detonate prematurely.

The gravity seed exploded out, close enough to unleash havoc, but nowhere near as close as I wanted. The protective shield failed under the strain, and the mages who had erected it were caught in the spell's area of effect.

I watched in grim satisfaction as they were crushed by the gravitational forces. Their bodies compressed horribly before being torn apart by competing gravitational waves, and all those nearby fled in panic.

The leaders, though, the *true* targets, had been well outside the spell's reach. They spun, all watching as chaos spread; a handful of warriors on both sides blamed the other side and started to attack again. They reacted to that immediately, shouting orders to their troops as they tried to work out the source of the attack.

"Fuck," I muttered, already gathering mana for a second attempt. "Missed the main targets."

"Stop," Oracle ordered, grabbing my arm. Her face was flushed with rage and concentration. "They know what we're capable of now. They'll be getting others and more shields—"

"And that's why we don't give them the time!" I argued. "They're blaming each other. We can—"

"No!" she insisted. "Trust me, Jax. Give me a second to prepare a surprise. They'll be expecting the same attack from the same source. If they figure it was us, they'll think that was it, at most. If you fire again now, it might stand a chance of getting through, but if they have one shield, they might have more. Let me get ready."

I hesitated, then nodded, trusting her. Oracle closed her eyes, her hands moving in intricate patterns as she began laying the groundwork for not one spell, but two.

"When I tell you," she said without opening her eyes, "cast your spell again, aimed at the same target. Make it exactly as before."

"They'll be expecting that." I repeated her earlier words. "They'll have shields ready."

"Exactly," she replied with a smile that was all teeth and no warmth. "Just be ready."

The enemy forces had indeed regrouped, their mages forming a protective circle around the leaders. I could see the way that they were taking up station, no doubt creating more shields, maybe even overlapping in layers of protection.

I tried to replicate exactly what she'd done, but even as I did it, I knew it was weaker and less polished. It should hold together though, or so I hoped.

I completed the spell, then held it, flexing my jaw as I stared at the group as they got their forces back under control and pointed in our direction.

The longer we waited, the shittier our chance, I was sure, as I spotted others hurrying in from across the camps.

"Oracle…" I pushed, through gritted teeth.

"Now," Oracle commanded suddenly, her eyes snapping open.

Without hesitation, I launched the second gravity seed spell, channeling as much power into it as I had before and more. It streaked toward the enemy position. And, as expected, a powerful barrier intercepted it, though this time, it was closer to the target.

The shield was positioned less than fifty meters from them when it flared into existence. Still, a dozen or more Dark Legion soldiers and a handful more mages were caught in the blast, their bodies contorted grotesquely before being pulverized.

But even as my spell was intercepted, Oracle unleashed her own. Instead of a different spell, or a new form of attack, she fired off not one, but two of the exact same spell, just spaced two seconds apart.

The first crashed into a second barrier, again shattering it and taking out the mages who had cast it. But the last?

It streaked on, passing through the now cleared air like vengeance given furious form!

Just as it looked like this attack would succeed, reality itself seemed to tear open. A massive form materialized between the spell and its target—a towering Minotaur, easily fifty feet tall, with bronze skin that gleamed like metal and horns that curved upward like scimitars.

Baphomet.

The god caught Oracle's spell in one massive hand, crushing it like a gnat. The resulting explosion of magical energy washed harmlessly around His divine form as He turned His baleful gaze toward the walls of Gaij.

"**COWARDS!**" His voice boomed across the battlefield. The sound was physically painful to mortal ears, as was the pressure that He exuded. "**YOU HIDE BEHIND YOUR WALLS AND STRIKE FROM AFAR! YOU ARE WEAK! FACE ME IF YOU DARE, CHAMPION OF PATHETIC, WEAKLING GODS!**"

He punctuated His challenge by crashing His fists against His chest, the sound like thunder rolling across the plain. Every soldier within a hundred meters on both sides had fallen to their knees, bowed down before the manifestation of divine power; even His own Minotaurs cowed and averted their eyes.

"Don't even think about it," Oracle hissed, seeing the look on my face.

"He's challenging me directly," I argued, already considering doing exactly what I'd promised Daralen I'd not do. But hey, this was the get-out clause, right? Something only I could do? "If I refuse—"

"You'll live if you refuse," Daralen interrupted bluntly. "My prince, you're powerful, but that is a god who glories in the fight, not one that you have tricked into facing you unprepared. A challenge that Lord Darakin himself warned you aren't ready to face, yet."

"She's right," Wilhelm added, his face pale with fear. "Zhere must be another vay."

I gritted my teeth, caught between my pride and my common sense. Refusing a direct challenge would damage morale, make me appear weak in front of my troops. But accepting…

Before I could decide, the air around us changed, growing warmer, almost comforting despite the tension. A feminine voice, familiar and ancient, spoke directly into my mind.

"Stand down, my champion. This is not your battle to fight."

Jenae, Goddess of Fire and Hidden Knowledge, had joined the party.

The sky above Gaij erupted in flame—not a destructive inferno but a display of divine power that formed a protective canopy over the city. And beyond that, around and above, below and before the dome, the feeling, that incredible pressure of divine presences, washed out. It was the Pantheon of the Flame, here to take part in the confrontation below.

Jenae's voice rang out, audible to all on the battlefield, but clearly aimed at the gods, both on our side, and our enemies' side.

"Baphomet has crossed the bounds set by divine law, and in full view of the intervention. He has physically manifested to interfere in a war between His followers and our own. By the ancient compact, this grants us, as well as the right of direct intervention in turn, a zzzzzz—" Whatever she just said was clouded and blocked out; the sounds seemed to be lost in a shimmering ringing sound before she was back, carrying on as if uninterrupted.

"And as our first involvement, we shield this city. In punishment for your transgressions, though, for our second, we summon a divine champion to take the field in response! You demanded to face a champion, Baphomet, but for breaking the compact, you have forfeited your right to set terms!"

A pillar of flames roared into the sky, a hundred meters from Baphomet and closer to us. A figure stepped through—Darakin, God of Battle.

He stood, now matching Baphomet in size, not in His more human and frailer "equal to me" version but in His full divine form manifested. He wore full plate armor that gleamed like molten bronze, His features stern and implacable as He strode across the battlefield, His footsteps shaking the earth.

The Dark Legion and Kronk's forces scattered before Him, desperate to avoid being trampled underfoot as the god marched directly toward Baphomet.

"Fool," Darakin's voice thundered. ***"Your arrogance has doomed you. Did you think we would not respond in kind?"***

Baphomet roared in defiance, but there was a new note in His voice—uncertainty, perhaps, as well as challenge and anger.

"You have broken the compact," Darakin continued, now standing before the bull-headed god. ***"And in your own stupidity, you have given me an opportunity I have long craved!"***

With a gesture, Darakin created a glowing tether of pure energy that shot from His chest and embedded itself in Baphomet's. The Minotaur god bellowed in outrage, trying to dodge, to step aside and deflect it, but found Himself bound, unable to move farther away.

"I invoke the right of divine combat," Darakin declared, His voice echoing with power and joy. ***"You will face me here and now, and as the cost of your***

arrogance, for interfering in a war between the mortals directly, should you fall, then shall I claim a tenth part of your essence, a fragment of your divinity, as my prize. Should I fall, to balance the scales of the realm, then may you claim the same from me."

Baphomet struggled against the tether, His muscles straining. ***"YOU CANNOT FORCE THIS! I REJECT—"***

"You cannot reject what you have already accepted by your actions," interrupted an unfamiliar voice, cold and implacable. A new entrant, and one that sounded different from all that had come before. Almost neutral and bored by the events. ***"You show your ignorance, little bull. Now you must pay the price, or earn your prize. Long ages it has been since the compact was broken so blatantly, and as such, you are given this choice. Accept the challenge, or forfeit double to your challenger."***

"I demand redress!" came Nimon's voice, suddenly booming. ***"Should my champion win, I demand that Darakin must cease all training of the apostate whelp!"***

"The terms are acceptable and agreed," the new voice agreed, ***"in exchange for the forfeit being doubled. Let the combat commence."***

A dome of shimmering energy suddenly encased the two gods, separating them from the mortal world. For a few seconds, they were completely obscured from view. When the barrier cleared, both deities stood ready for battle.

Darakin had manifested a short spear and round shield. Baphomet wielded a massive double-bladed axe, its edge gleaming with malevolent energy.

"Holy shit," I whispered, my eyes wide as I watched the two gods circle each other. "This is actually happening. Fuck me, I need beer and popcorn!"

"Divine combat," Oracle whispered beside me. "Literally, Darakin against Baphomet…this is insane!"

The entire battlefield had fallen silent, mortals on both sides frozen in awe at the spectacle unfolding before them. The gods themselves had gone to war!

CHAPTER THIRTY-NINE

Baphomet struck first, His axe whistling through the air in a blow that would have cleaved a fuckin' mountain. Darakin stepped to the side and shrugged it off with his shield. The impact of the massive axe crashing into the ground sent a shock wave across the battlefield that knocked dozens of nearby soldiers off their feet.

Darakin stabbed out, His spear passing a hairsbreadth off Baphomet's left ear as the Minotaur twisted; then He was pulling His axe free, the haft being driven into Darakin's shield with a clang that felt like it shook the realm.

As Darakin stepped back, resetting, Baphomet followed, grabbing at the spear and catching it behind the head, trying to use His massive muscles and weight to His advantage.

Where Darakin was solid muscle, but in excellent proportion, not too thick in the shoulders or the waist, Baphomet was literally a bull.

Solid muscle, with power that, if a blown landed, it could end it all.

He bellowed, yanking the spear forward and off to the side, using His axe haft to hold Darakin's shield against His body. He drove His head down and forward, attempting to gore His opponent with His massive jet-black horns.

Darakin went with the motion, releasing His spear but twisting and letting Baphomet push Him seemingly off-balance. Then Baphomet screamed, throwing the spear aside, and stumbled back, grabbing at a dagger driven deep into the meat of His left thigh.

Darakin strode to the side, sliding the toes of His right boot under the spear where it lay—three Dark legionnaires crushed by its length—and kicked it up into the air, catching it and returning it to a ready position as He called out: ***"First blood to me, Baphomet! And so shall be the last!"***

The Minotaur god roared in absolute fury, hurling the dagger aside—and killing one of His own supporters in a move that had luck's name all over it—then He lumbered forward, His axe gripped in both hands.

The fight was incredible. Each movement was faster than mortal eyes could track, each blow powerful enough to level buildings. The ground beneath them cracked and heaved, unable to withstand the forces being unleashed.

Baphomet fought with raw fury, every attack meant to overwhelm with sheer power. His axe carved furrows in the earth when it missed, and each roar from His bull-like throat sent soldiers on both sides cowering in terror.

But Darakin? He fought with the precision of a *master*. His spear darted in and out, finding gaps in Baphomet's guard, drawing divine blood that glowed like liquid gold. His shield deflected the most powerful blows. And where He couldn't block, He simply wasn't there, stepping aside, His movements a dance of deadly grace.

A particularly powerful swing from Baphomet's axe missed entirely, the momentum carrying the bull god off-balance. Darakin seized the opening, His spear thrusting forward to pierce Baphomet's shoulder. The wound wasn't deep, but it was serious. The damage was enough that it'd make His arm weaker and slower, preventing the big bastard from making certain moves.

Baphomet bellowed in pain and utter rage, retaliating with a wild swing that Darakin only barely managed to throw Himself back to partly avoid.

Still, the tip of the axe carved a shallow furrow across his armored chest, staggering the God of Battle. For a moment, it looked as though Baphomet might make the most of His advantage, but Darakin recovered quickly, deflecting the follow-up strike with His shield. His spear licked out again, cutting a shallow wound across the same thigh He'd opened up earlier.

"Look at the soldiers," Oracle whispered, pointing to the edges of the divine combat.

The shock waves from each collision between the gods wreaked havoc on the mortals caught too close. Dark Legion soldiers and Kronk warriors alike were being hurled through the air or crushed beneath the debris thrown up by the gods' movements. Those with any sense were retreating as fast as they could, but many had been too in awe, or simply too unlucky to move in time.

The battle continued, each exchange more violent than the last. Baphomet landed a powerful blow that cracked Darakin's shield, only to take a spear thrust to the other thigh in return. Both gods were bleeding now, their blood sizzling where it touched the mortal realm.

"Darakin's winning," I observed, watching the fight with professional appreciation. "He's wearing Baphomet down."

"Are you sure? It could be a feint," Wilhelm pointed out, his voice hushed with awe.

"Baphomet's movements are slowing," I disagreed. "He's putting everything into each attack, hoping for a knockout blow. Darakin is pacing himself, making each strike count. And look at the wounds. He's—"

"He's being led around by the nose, and Lord Darakin is bleeding him dry," Daralen assured us all. "And I think Baphomet knows it."

As if confirming her assessment, Darakin pulled out a lightning-fast combination, a Shield-bash that knocked Baphomet's axe aside, followed by two rapid spear thrusts that opened deep wounds in both of the bull god's massive arms.

Baphomet roared in pain, His axe slipping from weakened fingers. Before He could recover, Darakin's spear flashed upward, opening the Minotaur god's throat in a spray of golden blood that hung in the air like…well, a god's fucking slit throat.

Baphomet staggered, clutching at the ragged wound, His eyes wide with disbelief. He fell to his knees, the earth shaking with the impact.

Darakin stood over His fallen opponent, His expression grim but satisfied. He reversed His grip, and drove the spear through the god's chest and impaled Him, staking Him to the earth, still kneeling.

Then He strode to the side, collected His dagger, and almost casually, gripping one of Baphomet's horns for leverage, He sawed Baphomet's head from His shoulders.

Raising the gruesome trophy high, Darakin's voice boomed across the battlefield: ***"SO FALLS THOSE WHO BREAK THE DIVINE COMPACT! I***

CLAIM MY PRIZE—A TENTH OF BAPHOMET'S ESSENCE, A FRAGMENT OF HIS DIVINITY!"

A golden light erupted from the fallen god's body, coalescing into a pulsing orb that floated toward Darakin. The God of Battle reached out, gripping it, and the light was absorbed into His form. For a moment, His divine presence grew even more intense. Power radiated from Him in palpable waves. He threw back His head and roared His triumph to the early evening glimmering stars overhead.

Then, still holding Baphomet's severed head, Darakin turned to face the walls of Gaij—to face me directly.

"BROTHER!" He called, his voice thunderous with joy. ***"I ASK TO HAVE THIS FASHIONED INTO A GOBLET, BY THE SAME CRAFTSMAN WHO WORKS ON YOUR OWN AND TAMAT'S! THEN SHALL WE DRINK FROM THE SKULLS OF OUR ENEMIES TOGETHER!***

"FIGHT ON, FOR I SHALL BE WATCHING AS YOU AND YOUR VALIANT FORCES SLAUGHTER THIS PATHETIC ARMY!"

With those words, Darakin vanished in a blinding flash of light. Baphomet's headless body remained for a moment longer before it too dissolved into motes of golden light that scattered on the wind.

The divine presence that had permeated the battlefield gradually receded, though the damage remained: a circular area nearly half a mile wide had been transformed into a cratered wasteland by the literal combat of the gods.

In the aftermath, both enemy armies stood in disarray. The Dark Legion's perfect formations had shattered, soldiers milling in confusion without orders. Kronk's forces were, if anything, in worse shape, many having fled entirely during the divine confrontation, and still more clearly running now.

"Well," I said into the stunned silence that had fallen over our section of the wall, "fuck me, that was something you don't see every day."

Daralen gave me a look that suggested she wasn't quite ready for jokes yet. "The Dark Legion will regroup, my prince. As much as I'd love to lead a charge into their ranks now and capitalize on this, the cavalry are too far out of position, and the losses, should they manage to close ranks, would be excessive. They're trained for devastating losses, and they'll be desperate to show their master that they still deserve His grace."

"Even after all of zhat?" Wilhelm asked. "You zhink zhey'd hold?"

"They've lost at least a third of their force," Daralen noted, her professional assessment cutting through the awe of the moment. "Between our attacks, their own mistakes, and the collateral damage from the divine combat, they're weakened, but not yet out of the fight. Better that we allow them to bleed themselves against the wall next."

"At least Kronk's army is at, what, less than half strength?" I added. "But you're right—they'll be back. That or they'll run. They'll probably have to spend half the night reforming, but they'll hit us tomorrow. They have to."

Then I turned to Wilhelm, who still stared at the battlefield in shock. I clapped him on the shoulder, grinning. "Well, congratulations, mate. I think that's definitely one to cross off the bucket list. 'Divine combat' has to be on there, right?"

"I…I never imagined…" he stammered.

"None of us did," I admitted. "But this changes things. Darakin's victory bought us time and weakened the enemy, but it also means they're more likely to be cautious now. The first few hours tomorrow will need to be steel against steel…get them thinking the weirdest shit is now over."

I looked out over the battlefield once more, where the shattered remains of two armies were slowly retreating, dragging their wounded with them.

"Get some rest," Daralen ordered before I could. "You're right. Tomorrow, we bleed them, get them to fully commit; then, with a little luck, we unleash hellfire and damnation upon them. Hit them with a cavalry strike or three. And perhaps I'll even let you out to play as well."

"Oh, you silver-tongued devil." I grinned at her. "Yes, boss, will do!"

"Oh, shut it, you." She smiled, the expression clearly winning the fight despite herself. "Go on—get to bed, and SLEEP! Given all that happened today, I'm placing no bets on tomorrow's likely shenanigans."

CHAPTER FORTY

Dawn broke over Gaij in hues of crimson and gold, as if the sky itself remembered the divine blood spilled last night.

For me, I was up already, and not enjoying the morning the way I liked—bouncing Oracle off the walls. No. Instead, I stood on the eastern wall, watching the slowly lightening fields and the spread-out and messy camps of the enemy.

I'd managed only a few hours of restless sleep, then I'd dragged my hairy arse out of bed before first light to survey the battlefield. Oracle and Sehran joined me first for a little breakfast, and then atop the walls.

The cratered wasteland left by Darakin and Baphomet's fight stretched out below, a scar on the land that showed the difference between their fights and those of mortals, and made me damn thankful that when I'd fought them, it'd been with limitations placed on the gods' power.

Beyond it, in the distance, I watched as the two armies—because they were clearly still separate, no matter what the gods had intended—formed up for the assault.

"There's a lot less of them today." Daralen stepped up and joined me on the battlements; I glanced at her, before nodding and going back to watching them. She looked fresh despite the early hour, her armor polished and her expression focused. "No more of yesterday's chaos, it seems."

I studied the approaching formations through narrowed eyes. "The Dark Legion are still here, and they're in command," I agreed. "Look at their formations—perfect lines, proper spacing. Kronk's rabble have either gone, or they're just hanging around and watching. Hell, most of them look to be barely awake yet, and they're not liking the early start."

That was true. Where the four and a bit thousand strong Dark Legion had been split into companies, similar to the Imperial Legion—whose tactics and style they'd modelled themselves on—the army of Kronk sat around tents and cookfires, only just starting to dress.

There were—and I'd counted them—forty-two centuries standing in place. Each was a separate unit of one hundred troops—or less thanks to yesterday—and they wore near identical black armor, the main adornments insignia rankings in bronze, copper, silver, and gold.

"Why the differences in the armor?" I asked Daralen, glancing over.

"You can tell you hit your century in Perception," she grumbled, lifting her spyglass and peering through it. "Ah, do you mean from the second from the lead company, then two left and back to the fifth row?"

"Yeah." I counted the ranks and nodded. "Those ones."

I could see that they looked different, but not how…just that they were.

"They're ours," she growled.

"What?"

"The encampment claimed here, the one that the Dark Legion took? The constructors couldn't be changed by them. They didn't have the authority to alter imperial constructors, so they just kept them churning out legion armor and weapons, then they painted them black and stuck spikes on them."

"You're shitting me?" I asked.

"No."

"Well, that's great news then!" I said louder, having just spotted that of the others on the wall around us, a lot were doing their best to listen in while trying to look like they were doing anything but.

"My prince, I fail to see how that's good news," Daralen replied, clearly confused but trying to be polite and not tell me I was a fucking idiot in front of the troops.

"They're laid out in five companies of a hundred across and nearly ten companies deep," I pointed out. "With three rows in our armor, and them being five across, that gives us roughly fifteen units, which is one thousand five hundred or so Dark legionnaires, right?"

"Your calculations appear correct," she said stiffly. "All wearing stolen armor that was gifted to us from the empire."

"Exactly!" I grinned, holding my helmet in my left hand and then using it to gesture to the enemy. "That's fifteen hundred sets of legion armor we just have to fix up and clean, free! Let's be honest here…sure, some will need to be fumigated, and they all need the rats scraped out of them, but even factoring in the cost of repairing them, that's gotta be at least a thousand free suits for our people just there. Literally marching up and ready for the taking.

"Now, I don't know about you fuckers, but I love my legion plate. And seeing that there's a load of spare parts right there?" I shrugged. "My legion armorer back home—Thornapple—would be overjoyed! Especially when you consider that there's what, four and a half thousand of the enemy there, and then less than three thousand of Kronk's army left in total?

"Hell, we've got them outnumbered, and that doesn't even include that they've got to climb the walls and try to face the REAL legion. I've got half a mind to go back to bed and leave the aspirants to deal with this alone. They're already better than half the dark dickhead's troops!"

"Do you hear that?" Daralen bellowed, and the legionnaires and legion aspirants around us stiffened instinctually to the voice of their mistress. "Prince Jax is considering taking the day off, as there's that little a challenge to be presented by those out there! Well, I say that each of you better damn well distinguish yourselves before my eyes, or it's shit duty for the lot of you! What do you think, Prince… ten dark legionnaires each?"

"I think the aspirants should get a nice, easy target. Let's say they only have to kill five each, then they get to step back and relax, while the experienced legionnaires show them how it's done!" I shouted. "What do you think, aspirants? Can you kill five of the enemy today? Considering half of you have magic as well?"

"Ten!" an optio nearby barked suddenly, gesturing to his small squad of nine others. "My boys and girls will get ten each!"

"Twelve!" another shouted.

"That's more like it!" I boomed. "Let's make it interesting, though. If a thousand of you all kill even five, just a pathetic *five* each, that's almost the entire army out there done already! What do we do for forfeits then?"

"I think anyone who kills their five gets their ales paid for by anyone who got less!" someone shouted out from behind me.

I turned slowly, looking back over my shoulder, as silence fell. Whoever had shouted it clearly panicked that they'd crossed the line.

I pointed my naginata, held in my right hand, in their direction, and grinned.

"I LIKE IT!" I shouted. "But you know what? Let's go one better! Everyone who kills five gets their ales paid for, for the next two days, by the *empire*. And anyone who gets ten? Those who got less have to buy them theirs for the next week!"

That got a cheer. And as word spread, the cheer just kept going again, and again, and again.

The sound of the cheering forces atop the wall as the Dark Legion started to march forward drowned out their horns, and I grinned at Daralen.

"Well, what do you think?" I asked her in a lower voice.

"I think if the aspirants kill two each, I'll be overjoyed," she admitted grimly. "They'll be facing mainly experienced, highly trained, and vicious opponents in heavy armor, rather than the unskilled and practically naked rabble of yesterday."

"So how do we increase the odds for them?" Oracle asked softly.

"Considering they spent the night building those." She pointed to several large, covered structures being pushed toward our walls by teams of soldiers. "They're siege towers, aren't they?"

"And battering rams," Daralen added, gesturing to the covered rams that were now becoming visible. "Four that I can see, likely headed for different gates to try to divide our defense."

"They're being smarter today," I admitted musingly. "But they're still outnumbered, so why the hell do this?"

"They clearly think they can breach the walls," Sehran nodded, "but they can't. I mean, not unless they're going to pull another divine trick like yesterday?"

"No." Daralen grinned suddenly. "My prince, the simplest rule in life is often the most misunderstood and forgotten, and is incredibly important in warfare. 'Never attribute to malice what can be explained by stupidity.'"

"I don't get it," I admitted.

"We agreed yesterday that they probably didn't have accurate numbers on our side, then we forgot about that on the grounds that they were receiving divine intervention, correct?" she asked, a gleam in her eye.

"Yeah," I agreed, nodding.

"Well, the question becomes, that if after yesterday, none of the enemy gods are willing to be involved in the fight anymore—which I'd certainly assume, given the loss they faced, and how pissed off the God of Death seemed to be over it all—then do we know if any of the gods thought to share our new, more accurate numbers?"

We all puzzled our way through that for a few seconds, before I started to grin.

"They haven't told them. They still think we've only got a thousand or two at most, and if they send their armies to the other gates, then we'd have to be stripping the wall to respond to them. They don't need the gates to fall to let them in; they're thinking that if we strip the walls to defend the gates, then their siege towers can roll right up and through.

"They'll be expecting a fight but that there's only a few thousand at most to fight—and that they're all practically new recruits or guards. Fuck me sideways with a buttered loaf, they probably think that the 'real' fight was yesterday with Kronk! They're expecting to roll right over us, and that's why they're making sure we can see how many of them there are. They're forming up in nice lines to intimidate us!"

"They have to have magical ways to see in, though?" Oracle suggested, her voice borderline excited and fearful, clearly optimistic but not daring to give in to that hope fully. "I mean, the scroll of Eagle Sight you used before, something like that would enable…"

"The gods said yesterday that they were shielding the city from Nimon and all his kind." I laughed. "I bet they spent all the time coming here focusing on Kronk with any scrying spells they had. That's why Reth and the others couldn't catch many scouts. Fuck me, this is perfect!"

"How do ve make zhe most of zhis?" Wilhelm had stepped up when we were talking, having joined us—along with Gaspar, unfortunately—at my wave.

"We give them *exactly* what they expect to see," Daralen said. "Jax, I need to issue orders quickly, and with no time for discussion…"

"Do it," I ordered. "You're in command, Daralen. Just send me and mine where you need us."

I turned away from the wall, facing the assembled legion officers who had gathered for the morning briefing.

"Primus Daralen has command of the defense," I reminded them, though none needed it. "Follow her orders without hesitation. The enemy has lost much of their strength, but they're desperate now, and that makes them dangerous."

"What of you, my prince?" asked one of the centurions, a grizzled veteran who had survived more sieges than most.

"I'll be where I'm needed most," I answered. "But make no mistake—this is the legion's fight. Your fight. Yesterday, the gods themselves fought for us. Today, you get to show them that their faith in you was justified."

A murmur of approval ran through the assembled officers. I nodded to Daralen, yielding the floor to her.

"Four centuries to the eastern gate," she ordered crisply. "Three to the north, three to the south. The rest will form reserve forces ready to reinforce any section of the wall that comes under heavy attack. BUT…I want half of the forces on the walls to make a show of running from them, as if ordered to those gates, then to take up station behind and below, ready to respond as needed. Archers will focus fire on the siege tower crews first, then the battering ram teams. Magic is to be held until I give the order."

She continued detailing assignments, positioning our forces to meet the coming assault. As she spoke, I studied the faces of the officers. There was tension, certainly, but also determination and a quiet confidence that hadn't been there before. Witnessing Darakin's triumph yesterday and now the feral grin on their primus's face had bolstered their spirits immeasurably.

When Daralen finished, the officers dispersed to their positions, leaving me with Oracle, Wilhelm, and Seraphina, who had joined us during the briefing.

"The succubai are ready as well," Seraphina added. "Positioned throughout the defenses, with instructions to focus on distraction spells when the enemy reaches the walls."

"No," said Daralen quickly, countermanding those orders. "How many have made a pact now? How many do we have?"

"One hundred and fifty legionnaires and outriders, and forty-three succubai who are bound to the tower," Seraphina said proudly, looking at Sehran, who beamed. "You did well, little sister."

"Nearly two hundred succubai…" Daralen breathed. "How many are in the city?"

"All. The outriders who left with Reth yesterday are all the unbound."

"Okay, we've got two hundred riders in the city, what, fifty of which have bound succubai…"

"And incubai," Seraphina pointed out.

"And incubai…whatever." Daralen shook her head, dismissing the difference. "At this point, I care more about their skill set than what's in their pants. They're demons of lust, and even the most female-focused of my legionnaires could be tempted by an incubus, for a few seconds, is that correct?"

"It is, but it would require a lot of effort on the incubai's part," Seraphina admitted.

"But they could distract them, for at least a handful of seconds?"

"Definitely."

"Excellent." The legion primus smiled widely. "Prince Jax, I need you to be visible on the wall, and feel free to use all the spells you want. Make it look like you're trying to hold the army back alone. Although I want you to remain as safe as possible, I accept that you're going to make a spectacle. Do it and make sure the enemy are as focused on you as possible. Now, Seraphina, what I need is…"

I turned back to the battlements, watching as the enemy forces drew steadily closer. They moved with purpose now, the siege engines protected by large groups of Dark legionnaires who bore huge shields and marched in tight formation.

"Here they come," I said to Oracle, smiling, and confident in Daralen in a way I wasn't in my own plans on this scale. "Okay, my love, looks like it's down to the two of us to give them a warm welcome."

The next fifteen minutes passed in tense preparation as the enemy marched slowly and methodically across the battlefield. Unlike yesterday's chaotic rush, this was a disciplined military operation. The Dark Legion's commanders had clearly taken control, ignoring the forces of Kronk beyond ordering them into the lead, with the Dark Legion marching behind them, clearly expecting to use their "allies" as disposable arrow magnets.

The bulk of their infantry formed protective screens around those who were pulling the siege engines, with groups of archers positioned to provide covering fire. Blocks of marching infantry split off and streamed to the left and right along the wall, or got ready to take their turns, be that with ropes and ladders or running up and through the siege towers.

Behind them all, I could see their mages in small groups—fewer than before, thanks to our attacks yesterday, but still dangerous: four groups of them, with two heading left and right, and two more staying with the command team and marching along behind the siege towers, respectively.

When they reached the effective range of our wall defenses, Daralen stepped up and bellowed the order: “Archers! Fire at will!”

A volley of arrows arced from our walls, followed by another, and then another as the limited archers we had—more than half were out of sight still, waiting to give a nasty surprise—sent hundreds of arrows raining down on the approaching forces.

Most slammed harmlessly into raised shields, but a few found gaps in the formation, felling soldiers who were quickly replaced by others.

The enemy responded with their own volleys, forcing our defenders to duck behind crenellations as arrows whistled overhead, or to raise shields and wait the rain out.

They had roughly five hundred archers. They worked as one, trying to sweep the walls clear, focusing on a side, peppering that area and forcing our own archers there to huddle down, while those to either side on the roof returned fire.

The exchange continued as the siege engines drew steadily closer to our walls. Dozens died on our side before the healers could get to them, but the enemy lost far more.

“They’re hitting multiple points simultaneously,” Daralen observed, her voice calm despite the tension as we constantly feared we were missing a trick somewhere. “Trying to divide our defense, to weaken us for the towers.”

She was right. The two siege towers were approaching different sections of the wall before us, while the battering rams headed for the northern, eastern, and southern gates. The attack was well-coordinated, designed to stretch our forces thin—if we had fewer forces than we did. As it was, two-thirds of our forces were ready for the fight…just out of sight in nearby streets or buildings.

The first serious casualties came when Daralen looked at me and gestured to the siege tower. “I’d like to reduce the towers to one for this. Can you take the other one out?”

I snorted and stretched, before starting my own spell, as Oracle, who’d spent the last few minutes casting and preparing, unleashed hers.

The first spell she’d done was a simple one, but damn it was effective: a shield, just to protect us and the command group against the inevitable retaliation.

The second and third spells were two of the same gravity seed spells that she fired—not at the closest siege tower, but the wheels along one side of the farthest.

The spells streaked through the air, slamming into the ground a few meters shy of the tower, then exploding outward. Where they’d hit, they took out a small number of the marching infantry. But as the ten gravity seeds went active, pulling and pushing and gradually manipulating space-time all around the base of the tower, the wheels that were already under tremendous strain bearing the weight of the tower, first twisted, then cracked, two or more opposing forces levering them in different directions.

The siege towers were massive constructions, but relatively simple in themselves: a box, with ten wheels on a side—each of the wheels reinforced over and over with metal—and an axle that ran from one side to the other.

The front of the box, when looking at it head-on, was about fifteen meters across, with a rope attached for the bearers to pull on, to drag the tower forward.

Three of these ropes ensured the tower was pulled at speed, and then infantry ran alongside, their own shields raised to protect the slaves who pulled the towers from arrows and so on.

The tower itself was, as noted, a box, square with an open rear and filled with stairs that ran upward and then switched back, a platform at the top letting the warriors who used it run to the next set of stairs, and then up to the next level again.

They were simple: three sides—the front, left, and right—were solid wood, with banded metal across it, and then the structure was doused with water by a water mage as it rolled forward, clearly as a counter to the traditional way of dealing with these things on Earth, which was to set fire to them.

Then they just repeated the design for the next box atop and the one beyond, until they reached the height they needed. Then they just dropped the front when they reached the wall and used that panel as a bridge to run across and overwhelm the defenders.

The problem they had was that they had to keep a number of defenders inside as it moved, to balance it, and they and the overall tower all came to a hell of a weight.

Then when the slaves tried to pull the tower forward, and one entire side of it was suddenly being crushed into place, the structure being put under ungodly pressure, the result was best described as "crrrrack" and "ohshitohshitohshit" for anyone too close to the tower at the time.

Certainly for the unlucky bastards inside.

The rest of the structure tried to keep going forward, while one wall and the wheels of one side stopped dead, and began creaking and shattering in place.

That meant that the entire tower twisted slightly, then gave way in spectacular fashion, before collapsing, certainly killing the poor fools inside it, and well, a lot of those who had been marching alongside as well.

As almost an entire century vanished beneath falling wood, the mages took the bait that we knew they would.

They'd moved to within a hundred and fifty meters of the wall now—their own magical shields were up and taking occasional arrows—but most of the time, they were simply being protected by a bunch of Dark legionnaires with tower shields angled overhead. They were close enough for a few of their number, clearly those with the most experience and power, to start firing at me and Oracle.

The lightning bolt that hit our shield was good, I had to admit. It was powerful enough that it darkened our shield and hid the rest of the battle from our sight, as I'd made the most of doing to enemies before.

I didn't know whether they were planning for that, or they were simply trying to take the shield down, but that was when I finished my spell.

I didn't need to be able to see, not when I'd had so long to prepare and lock the spell into place. I grinned, hidden behind the wall of darkness that the first shield provided. I popped the mana potion, downed it, and slipped my helm on, taking a deep breath and gripping my naginata. Then I triggered Mana Overdrive and Hyper Cognition, and released the spell, one of my new favorites from my Mage Imperator class.

The swirl of crimson energy that burst out from my feet, enveloping me and hurtling me across the field of battle, to appear right in the middle of the clustered mages, was both incredibly cool, and incredibly confusing. The cool was for me and mine, I mean.

Confusing?

Well, the mages certainly looked confused when I bounded out of a sudden swirl of crimson smoke and started to carve the shit out of them all.

The first figure I faced was beaming at the walls, pointing at the "damage" his lightning spell had managed. And then I was there, my naginata lopping his hand off, then continuing around to take the head off the figure next to him.

I'd appeared in the middle of their group, with five mages on my right and four on my left, a century of Dark legionnaires around the outermost of the "ring" here, and then thousands beyond that on all sides.

Possibly not the wisest of places for an imperial prince to appear, but as I grabbed the mage I'd just de-limbed by what was left of his upper arm, and dragged him into the way of a second mage who had nearly finished casting, he proved his worth as a meat shield.

The spell, some variant on a fireball, was disrupted by the screaming body of his companion staggering into it. The mage casting it, unfortunately, lost both his focus and control.

That meant that the fireball detonated, washing out across the group and those who'd been staring in shock at my arrival, and treated everyone to a little excess heat.

I, fortunately enough, was on the other side of my fresh meat shield, and happened to be the chosen champion of the Goddess of Fire, which meant that for me, it leaped all the way to "whoo-boy, that's warm" instead of "number 57, extra crispy."

As the remaining mages on all sides either lost control of their own spells they'd been building—and with explosive results—or I chopped into them, Oracle's next spell took hold.

The biggest advantage of having such an incredibly gifted spellcaster as Oracle bonded to me—besides the obvious ones—was that she had access to all my spells. That meant that as I punched, kicked, and stabbed with joyous abandon, my sped-up awareness and my ability to move faster than a regular human could even perceive now enabling me to dodge blow after blow and carve myself a little breathing room, Oracle had cast the same spell again.

Tactical displacement flared around me, and I vanished from sight as the entire group of mages and their escorts were still dying, burning and enveloped by failing spells.

Then I reappeared, this time a meter behind the second group of mages, the ones who were held back to protect and support the leaders of the armies.

There was a brief pause where I wanted to vomit, my mana bottoming out, or close to it; the world spun, my inner ear screaming that this shit just wasn't right.

Then I finished pulling the potion—a greater mana potion capable of restoring five thousand mana at a time—free of my bag, shoved my helm up and downed it, then winked at the single mage who had spotted me, slid the helm back into place, and threw my now-empty potion vial at her.

She flinched and raised a hand to stop it, batting it aside. Then she realized what had happened and started to scream a warning.

The mages here were almost seven hundred meters from the front, half a mile or so, and they were frankly bored to shit and resigned to just watching the fight unfold, mentally spending their gold already.

As such, not one of them had the foresight to even have a shield spell in place, and the eleven of them who were spread out, half sitting in folding camp chairs—dicing, arguing, and two reading fucking books—were utterly unprepared for me to appear.

I cast a single spell, and beyond that it was all physical, as I laid about me with the naginata. My first victim lost her head—literally—dicing. The blade passed through her neck from behind and barely slowed, before I lunged forward and drove it into the guy sitting to her right, taking him in the chest as he started to stand.

I swung it around, shifting my stance and bringing the blade around over my head, leaving my right hand loosely gripping and my left tight. Then I brought it down, drawn back on my left side, driving the metal-clad base into the rib cage of a figure on that side with bone-shattering force directly over his heart, before extending forward as far as I could and taking another in the gut.

I dragged the blade free to the right, sending that mage to the ground, screaming as his intestines, carved literally in half, tumbled free to the dirt below him. I spun, bringing the blade around and taking another head.

Then I pulled it back, released with my left hand and pointed at the command tent where the enemy leadership were just starting to see the issue. I unleashed Flames of Wrath upon them.

Admittedly, yeah, it was more a pain and surprise spell, as anyone in command of the Dark Legion at this level were going to be double hard bastards. But I didn't have the time to cast the gravity spell, and I needed to keep my mana for Oracle.

The next ten seconds were lethal for the mages. The last of them died as he tried to run. My blade erupted through his chest from behind, as I heard Oracle speaking through our bond.

"And three... two... one..."

I paused, looking at what was left of the command tent as the leadership, all burned to one degree or another, and both furious and obviously panicked, screamed orders. Then I vanished.

Time allotted to the entire attack was less than a minute. As I stepped back from the crimson flare of power, to stand next to Oracle, Sehran, and Daralen, the legion raised another cheer.

"So, was that what you had in mind to distract them?" I asked the primus, pulling my helm off and grinning at her before kissing Oracle soundly.

"My gods." Daralen sighed. "What I'd give to be able to use that ability tactically."

"That's what it's for," I admitted when Oracle had stepped back, grinning, and I pulled a potion from my bag, grimacing before I downed it. "Gods, I'm gonna get PTSD over mint at this rate. Anyway, the issue is that it costs around a thousand mana to send me there and the same back. If I could do it with a century I would, but the cost?" I shook my head.

"How was it used in the past? Or is it one of your own creations?" she asked.

"No, it's one of the standard spells created for the imperial Mage Imperator class," I explained. "The way that all spells work is that the more experience you gain with them, the less it costs and the more you can do with it. From Amon's memories, I'll eventually be able to literally pick out entire legions and reposition them on the battlefield at will.

"The issue is that it's void magic, and anyone else who's experienced in such a spell can interfere with it, if they're quick enough and skilled enough. For me to move an entire legion would probably take hours, if not days of casting to get ready, and then the cost would be incredible."

"Doable using the tower's mana collectors, though," Oracle pointed out. "If the tower was at full capacity, it'd be a simple thing: have two Mage Imperators ready, one who transports the legion to the target area, then the second who claws them back five minutes later."

"You could literally eliminate the enemy leadership in seconds." Daralen sighed. "They'd be unable to defend against such an attack, and they'd have to spread out their forces to prevent its effectiveness, weakening their armies."

"If we could pull it off," I agreed. "As it is, though, we did manage one thing."

"More than one, I think?" Seraphina suggested dryly. "I believe the morale boost of seeing you slaughter half the enemies' mages was significant."

I looked around, seeing the grins and the slightly stunned looks on the faces of the legionnaires nearby.

"Back to your posts!" Daralen bellowed, seeing it as well. "What, are you guardsmen or LEGIONNAIRES? The enemy are coming, Legionnaires—do something about it!"

"What did you mean?" I asked Seraphina when Daralen turned back.

"Well, you just removed the limited magical protection that the majority of the army had, didn't you?" she asked, and I nodded.

"Yup, and that means that unless the commanders have an artifact to shield them, then it's time to start making the most of that." I scratched at my chin. "What do you think, Daralen, Oracle? Do we cast the gravity spells into the middle of their forces and break those pretty lines up, or do we use them on the commanders and take them out first?"

"The commanders," Daralen said firmly. "Without whoever took over after yesterday, the army is a headless mass. They'll be unable to respond to the changes as we begin the second phase. Admittedly, I'd not considered the use of that spell, or I'd have changed a few things around, but as it is, it's a pleasant surprise."

"What would you have done?" I asked her curiously.

"Is the spell dependent of size, or mass?" she replied.

"Uh…"

"Is it more expensive if you sent multiple bodies, or is it larger and smaller bodies that effect the cost?" she clarified.

"Uh, a bit of both?" I admitted. "I could probably send two or three of us at a time, as the portal opening is a major part of the cost; then the target moving would be less. But on the other side, I'd be totally out of mana and be fucked until I could down more mana potions and…"

"But you could send a single large object there, if there wasn't a need to bring it back?" she pressed.

I blinked. "Yeah?"

"Then you could send either a war golem into the middle of the enemies' leaders, totally unexpectedly, or you could send a gnomish bomb?" she pointed out.

"Fuck me, I could," I muttered. "I never even thought about that."

"Fortunate you have me then." She smiled. "You'll note that all four gates have ten war golems standing behind them, ready for any unexpected breach, and that there are five more standing there."

I looked where she pointed, then grinned as I spotted the five hidden war golems.

"That's gonna be a nasty surprise for anyone who manages to break a gate down," I pointed out, and she snorted.

"Please, Jax…the gates are at absolutely no risk. Those golems are ready for a breach, but if any breaches occur, I'll eat my helmet. No, I merely wanted to point out the difference in planning versus unplanned and last-minute attacks.

"Lord Wilhelm, are you taking part in the defense?" she asked him.

Wilhelm stiffened, clapping his fist to his chest as he'd seen the legionnaires do. "Yes, Primus Daralen," he barked, getting an annoyed look from Gaspar, who stood behind him and to the side.

"Excellent. You may move three centuries to the right. You'll find Optio Macius. He recently lost his second, and I believe both he and you would benefit from that. Keep your section clear of the enemy, Legionnaire!"

"Yes, Primus!" He grinned, clearly overjoyed, and clapped his fist to his chest again, before striding off, Gaspar in tow trying to reason with him.

"Now that we're free of those two," she said to me. "Their weapons…we have control of them. Are they as truly devastating as you've suggested?"

"You saw them in action in the fight for Gaij when we were ambushed here," I pointed out. "In tight quarters and when you're unarmored or not expecting them, they're lethal. With good armor, and especially if it's enhanced as mine is, then it's a lot less so."

"Excellent. In that case, we'll be keeping them for the second-to-last wave. When I give you the signal, I want those remaining mages taken out, please, my prince—though I'd appreciate it if it was done with you remaining there." She pointed at the ground by my feet, and I snorted.

"I can fire the same gravity seed spell at both groups, but I can't guarantee I can get them, not from here," I pointed out.

"When I give you the word, do your best," she said firmly. "Sehran, Seraphina, are your people ready?"

"They are," Seraphina declared, and Sehran nodded.

"Then as soon as the battle is joined, be ready," she said. "I see no reason to increase the risk to my aspirants at this stage, so we'll simply eliminate the enemy in one go."

I turned to Oracle and smiled, watching as the front lines of the enemy began to climb the walls to the right and left, most having no clue that they were dead meat.

"Gods, I love having good subordinates," I quipped.

"As do I, when I can get them," Daralen agreed calmly. "However, it seems the enemy's leadership still draws breath?"

"Fuck," I muttered, and Oracle and I started to cast.

CHAPTER FORTY-ONE

The first two spells we sent off hammered into a shield that was clearly artifact based, considering the speed it'd been erected and the way that it still stood, despite the two hits.

The third spell was Oracle's, and it punched into the shield, taking it to the edge of overload and darkening it. The fourth was mine, hitting just as the shield began to recover. The fifth and sixth were Oracle's, punching through the again weakened shield, and then hitting a fool in very shiny armor full in the face before it exploded.

We watched in silence as the spell unraveled and flung its gravity seeds out. Then it began to power and flip, sending the burned and clearly stressed remaining Dark Legion leadership flying in all directions.

It was a paladin, I guessed, who was the last to fall; certainly, his armor was the fanciest. And the distant scream that we could dimly make out even from here, as his armor crumpled like tinfoil under a boot, definitely made an impression.

As his sword, flung out in the last seconds, flipped end over end, landed tip first, buried in the grassy hilltop and quivered to a halt, I turned back to Daralen, only to find that she was deep in conversation with someone else, passing more orders and apparently had just expected that as she'd given the order, that was it, done.

"I think we got them," I said to Oracle, turning back and squinting through the dust cloud that had risen from the impact. "At least, anyone important enough to give orders…"

As we watched, the command tent tilted suddenly as something inside apparently gave way. The tent collapsed sideways, revealing a struggling lump inside, that eventually fought their way clear of the tent, only to stand, stunned, atop the devastated hilltop.

They lasted perhaps five seconds, before turning and running as fast as they could pump their arms and legs, down the far side of the hill and out of sight.

"Yeah, I think that's a success." Oracle smiled. "Any other targets for us, Daralen?"

Daralen shook her head with grim satisfaction. "No, you did well, but this next phase belongs to the legionnaires. They earned this, after all. Time for us to move along."

Around us, the battle continued unabated. To our right and left, in a wide front along the wall, the remains of Kronk's army had made it and were attempting to scale it using ladders and grappling hooks.

Their assault was desperate and disorganized—these weren't the disciplined soldiers of the Dark Legion but rather a rabble of idiot individual warriors and mercenaries. They'd lost most of their army and all their leadership—bar a handful of the Minotaurs and fleshcarven—the previous day. Apparently, any of the survivors who had half a brain had deserted overnight, and it showed in their haphazard approach.

Squinting, I noticed that the fleshcarven who I'd been expecting to be the major threat today were entirely missing, and the Minotaurs…

"Looks like they had a falling-out over creative differences," I muttered, nodding toward the Minotaurs, where a much smaller group, and clearly badly mauled, bellowed and shouted at their companions, trying to drive them to climb faster.

"Daralen…" Oracle started, drawing her name out.

"No, you can't have all the fun to yourself." The legion primus smiled despite herself.

"But I'm pregnant," Oracle tried.

"That just proves you already had fun, and you make poor life choices," Sehran replied in a stage whisper that carried. "Swallow next time!"

"And you can't get pregnant if you let him put it in your—" Seraphina added in the same tone.

"And that's enough of that!" I said loudly. "Fuck's sake, considering we know Oracle shouldn't have been able to get pregnant regardless, maybe it was from the times we did those things that it happened!"

"That's a good point." Sehran nodded thoughtfully. "I think you'll need to experiment to make sure you know how it happened, actually."

"Oh, I know how it happened," Oracle admitted. "But I think the experimentation is a wonderful idea!"

I stared at them, my mouth open slightly as I replayed the conversation and realized that I did not, under any circumstances, want to talk her out of said experimentation.

No, I would take one for the team, and be unspeakably brave about it.

"On a change of subject before Jax picks Oracle up and runs off to get started, I think they actually think they've been lucky to survive this long," Sehran observed dryly, watching as the first of Kronk's warriors reached the top of the wall nearby, only to be met by waiting legionnaires. "They have no idea what's going to come, have they?"

The scene playing out along the battlements was almost comical. As each of Kronk's warriors hauled themselves up over the wall, they were met not by the handful of terrified guards they expected but by fully armored legionnaires who dispatched them with mechanical efficiency. Legion aspirants stood in the front line, side by side with veterans, stepping up to gain combat experience whenever an opportunity presented itself.

Even the city's regular defenders were joining in, guards who'd not joined the legion, preferring the much less stringent rules and standards of their old roles. After the previous day's fighting and seeing the gains their companions who had joined had made, though, they were discovering a taste for it.

They fought with more enthusiasm than skill, but against the unarmored and exhausted warriors of Kronk's army—running across the battlefield and then climbing thirty meters up a rope, while your entire body surged with fear and adrenaline was tiring work, after all—it was more than enough.

To our left, the single surviving siege tower had reached the wall. After our display of destructive magic against the first tower, the Dark Legion had diverted every available soldier to protect this remaining one. It had crawled forward slowly but steadily, and now its drawbridge crashed down onto our battlements with a thunderous boom.

Dark legionnaires poured out. Their black armor gleamed in the morning light as they charged forward, screaming war cries filled with bloodlust—and straight into the waiting war golems.

Five massive constructs stood in formation, each holding a bow that no human could have drawn. As the first wave of Dark Legion soldiers burst from the tower, the golems loosed a volley of mana bolts. The magical projectiles tore through armor as if it were parchment, leaving smoking holes in breastplates and helms. The entire first wave fell before they had taken three steps onto our wall.

Dark Legion berserkers, their elites, staggered forward, some missing limbs, stunned and staring as they tried to take in the utter slaughter that had just taken nine in ten of their companions and almost the entire remaining "elite" forces of the army.

Then the golems fired again. The almost electrical buzz of the bows charging built up, then cut out as they fired. A zip and boom noise echoed as the remaining survivors were blown off the wall or back into the siege tower in tiny bits.

The second wave hesitated, but only for a moment. With commanders shouting at their backs, they charged forward over the bodies of their fallen comrades—and met the waiting legionnaires who had moved up behind the golems.

"Well, that worked better than I'd expected," Daralen commented dryly, watching as the golems stepped back to allow the legionnaires to engage. "Looks like the Dark Legion's armor is less effective against mana projectiles."

All along the wall, similar scenes were playing out. The Dark Legion and Kronk's remaining forces fought with determination, but only a small number made it onto the walls, and where they did, they were being slaughtered.

Add to that, they remained blissfully ignorant that they were facing only a fraction of our true strength. Most of the legionnaires, both veterans and aspirants, remained out of sight still, with fresh ones moving up only as people were injured and passed through to receive healing.

Daralen raised her hand, and a yellow signal flag rose and then waved from behind her. She called out, one of her abilities as a legion primus enabling her to pitch her voice to carry almost effortlessly. "Archers! All archers to the walls!"

I shook my head, knowing that if we had Romanus there, with his War Leader ability, he'd have been able to do it without the use of the flags at all, but clearly Daralen had gone down a different path.

The order was relayed along the battlements, and suddenly thousands of archers who had been concealed earlier emerged from doorways and stairwells. They took up positions along the wall, nocking arrows and awaiting the next command.

"Target the rear ranks!" Daralen ordered. "Force them to bunch up!"

Volleys of arrows arced over the heads of the enemies directly engaging our forces and fell among those waiting to climb the ladders or enter the siege tower. Predictably, they began to press forward, seeking shelter from the deadly rain at the base of our walls—exactly as Daralen had intended. Lifting their shields overhead to try to protect themselves.

"They're compressing nicely," she observed with professional detachment. "Seraphina, how do your eyes see it?"

The succubus shaded her eyes, studying the enemy formations. "They're packed in tightly now, especially near the tower and the gates. I'd say there are at least thirty or forty men per ten square meters in those areas."

Daralen nodded and turned to Seraphina. "Excellent work. If you could signal the cavalry now, please?"

Seraphina nodded to one of the other succubai, who launched herself into the air. What looked like a long banner, or several stolen bedsheets stitched together, trailed from her ankles.

She climbed higher and higher, then started to fly round and round, making sure that the bright-red length of cloth was visible before screaming a single word that I wasn't able to make out, but made a bright-white light flare like the sun for a few seconds.

Then she flew back down, panting but grinning as she landed nearby. A legionnaire I recognized helped her to free her legs.

Vislen, I remembered; then I snorted in amusement when he caught my eye and winked. He'd helped Sehran to get the remnants of the altar from Lagoush's temple on the way to Sonra, and he'd apparently really enjoyed having that dirty bugger of a succubus in his brain.

Now he'd clearly found one who wanted to bond with him. Looking her over, briefly, I could understand the wide smile on his face.

Long legs and a fashion model's high cheekbones, but with a porn star's figure, and the obvious sex drive that a demon of lust had, meant that yeah, I could also see why he winced as he straightened, pressing one hand to the small of his back, even through the armor.

I was willing to bet he was living his best life right now.

"And now," Daralen called, "those trained with Explosive Compression, target their midst!" A red flag rose and was repeated along the wall, rippling out as the order was repeated, and a fresh set of legionnaires stepped forward, starting to cast.

I grinned as Sehran joined them, winking at us as she took advantage of the opportunity.

Along the wall, legionnaires who had been trained in the spell stepped forward. Unlike the more complex gravity seed that Oracle and I had used, Explosive Compression was a simpler spell that could be taught in only an hour, provided Oracle was willing to, or had the time, to link with them.

It created a focused burst of pressure that detonated outward, then sucked inward, compressing everything around into a small area. And as we'd expected, it was devastating when targeted at groups of tightly packed enemies.

Nearly a hundred legionnaires unleashed the spell simultaneously, targeting the densest clusters of enemy troops, and the effects were horrific.

Bodies were crushed against one another, armor buckled, and people screamed as they were compressed by the magical onslaught. When the pressure released an instant later, those at the edges were dropped, wheezing, panicked, only to be hit by the second one hundred who unleashed next. Those who had believed they'd survived, and were frantically, desperately thanking their god for that small mercy, were now targeted and thrown violently outward, colliding with their comrades or dashed against the stone walls, before being sucked back inward.

"Archers! Continuous volleys!" Daralen ordered as the shield walls that had been protecting the enemy were completely abandoned.

As the enemy struggled to regroup, arrows and crossbow bolts rained down upon them. With their formations broken and many of their shields lost, destroyed, or abandoned in the chaos, they made easy targets. Hundreds fell in the first minute alone, pierced by multiple shafts.

"Third wave of compression!" Daralen called. Another barrage of spells hammered into the increasingly disorganized enemy ranks. "Boiling oil!"

That was the breaking point. What was left of the cohesion of the Dark Legion finally shattered, their discipline overwhelmed by the relentless magical assault and the mounting casualties. Some groups tried desperately to fight their way up through the siege tower, seeking to engage us directly rather than remain exposed to our archers and mages.

Others began to waver and fall back, at first in small groups and then in larger numbers, as their friends were suddenly lost under sheets of boiling oil, poured over the side to wash across them.

"This is fucking beautiful." I grinned at Daralen. "You were absolutely right about them never realizing our true numbers."

Daralen's smile was thin but satisfied. "War is as much about perception as reality, my prince. Although, I'll admit, that they had no clue about the numbers of those trained with basic spells helped hugely. Regardless, it's time for the final act. Seraphina?"

The succubus nodded and made a sweeping gesture with her arm and let loose a piercing wail that hovered over the battlefield like the last gasp of a tortured soul.

All along the wall, nearly two hundred succubai and incubai moved forward from where they'd been waiting.

They took up positions along the battlements, and as one, they began to sing.

The sound that filled the air was unearthly—beautiful and terrible at once. It washed over the battlefield like a physical force, and I could immediately see its effect on the enemy.

Hell, I could feel it on our own troops, and they'd been ordered back so that they stood behind the line, hands over their ears and turned away.

When it came to the enemy, many simply stopped fighting, their weapons lowering as they stared up at the wall in confusion and desire. Others shook their heads violently, trying to clear their minds, but their movements became uncoordinated, clumsy.

"Gods," Wilhelm whispered beside me, his own expression somewhat dazed. "Is zhat vhat it's like for zhem to use zheir powers against us?"

"No." I smiled, looking up at Sehran as she lifted into the air. She and a handful of others who were stronger than the average, sang a counterpoint that was designed to lessen the effect on our side of the wall. "Look there." I pointed, and he looked up, then blushed and looked aside.

"Mein Gott, mine prince, you should not look at your companion so," he chastised.

I burst out laughing. "First, I meant notice that she's singing a counterpoint for us all. Literally, she's reducing the effect on us, as are a dozen others."

"Oh, mein Gott, I must apologize. I zhought…" He'd gone from a faint blush to fully crimson now.

"And as she's a succubus both in name and nature, honestly, she probably wore that very short skirt deliberately in the hope that people would look up. When dealing with a succubus, remember that *not* looking is the act more likely to cause offense."

Seraphina nodded, looking pleased. "Normally we would target individuals, but with so many working in concert, they can affect an entire army—briefly, at least—and Jax is right. Looking is actively encouraged, and should the sight leave you with a desire to do more than look, you would be welcome to come to my quarters after the battle."

She smiled suggestively, and I had to stifle a grin as I turned away, seeing the mixture of horror and honest temptation on Wilhelm's face.

The battle hadn't stopped, though, and Daralen didn't waste the opportunity the distraction had given. "Magic missiles! Now!" she barked. A gold banner was hoisted, again going up in relays along the length of the wall.

Those legionnaires trained in the spell stepped forward. Unlike the complex and costly spells that Oracle and I wielded, Magic Missile was an incredibly basic combat spell that was both cheap and useful.

Individually, each dart did little damage, or at least it did to an armored figure. They could kill, and easily, but they were like scalpels.

Attack an unarmored figure with a scalpel, and you were going to do a lot of damage. Try it with someone in full plate armor, and unless you were very lucky in placement, they were going to shrug it off and kick your ass.

That was the difference on a base level, but then add in that the scalpel exploded when it hit…again, small but significant damage. And combine that with the placement rule—stab it into a neck or the joint of the armor—and you killed or disabled instantly.

Try the same thing on the middle of a breastplate, and you were the one who was going to end up dead when they shrugged it off.

The legion had been drilling with the spells constantly, though, and at that order, nearly four hundred legionnaires launched almost two thousand golden darts of pure magical energy.

It formed a brilliant display that momentarily outshone the sun itself. They streaked toward the enemy in perfect arcs, each crashing into a target that was stunned, disoriented, or reeling and injured already.

Where they struck, they exploded with concentrated force. Dark legionnaires, who would have been staggered by a single blow, vanished under the impacts of dozens.

They were thrown backward by the impacts, their armor dented or punctured. Entire centuries were obliterated in that single volley. The battlefield below became a charnel house of broken bodies and shattered equipment.

"Torches!" Daralen bellowed.

A handful of legionnaires tossed flaming torches into the oil that covered many of the enemy, setting light to them and further breaking their morale as their friends died, shrieking.

Any semblance of order among the enemy forces collapsed. The Dark Legion, once the pride of Nimon, broke and ran. Kronk's remaining warriors, never disciplined to begin with, were almost all already dead, and those who weren't were in full retreat, fleeing toward the distant hills.

"Again, missiles!" Daralen barked, and a second volley of magic missiles lanced out from our walls, catching the fleeing troops in the back. More fell, and the retreat became a rout.

All along the wall, the enemy sprinted like their arses were on fire. Companies that had been dispatched left and right, heading to the other gates, were treated to the same punishment, the same orders having been relayed along the wall over and over.

That was when I heard it—the thunder of hooves approaching from behind the enemy lines. Our cavalry, some two thousand strong, had circled wide around the battlefield and now charged into the retreating forces from their unprotected flank.

The slaughter was merciless and complete. Caught between our walls and the advancing cavalry, with no leadership to rally them and their morale shattered, the enemy forces were cut down where they ran. A few tried to surrender, throwing down their weapons and raising their hands, but in the chaos of battle, many were cut down before our officers could establish control. In all honesty, it wasn't like we tried very hard.

Within twenty minutes, it was over. The field before Gaij, which had been thronged with enemy soldiers at dawn, was now littered with their bodies. A few small groups had managed to escape the encirclement, fleeing into the distant hills, but they posed no threat—and would likely not survive the journey back to whatever lands they had come from.

Silence fell over the battlefield, broken only by the moans of the wounded and the orders of officers directing the collection of prisoners and the recovery of our own casualties.

I leaned on the battlement, suddenly exhausted as the battle-fury drained from me. "Well," I said to no one in particular, "that was…efficient."

"Indeed," Daralen replied, removing her helmet. Her face was streaked with sweat, but her expression was one of profound satisfaction. "Total victory, with minimal losses on our side."

"I didn't even get to use the gnomish airship as a flying platform to rain down hell upon the idiots," I complained, though there was no genuine disappointment in my voice. "I had this whole plan involving fire spells from above, you know?"

"There will be other battles, my prince," Daralen said diplomatically.

"I suppose." I straightened up and stretched, feeling joints pop, before raising my voice and shouting so that people could hear. "Well, I think it's time for a fucking drink, don't you? And the empire is buying!"

A cheer went up from the legionnaires within earshot, and I grinned at them. "That's right! Free ale for everyone who killed at least five of the enemy today!"

"You'll bankrupt the imperial treasury," Oracle murmured, slipping her arm through mine.

"Worth it," I replied, kissing her cheek. "Besides, did you see how they fought? Even if they didn't hit their quota, I think we can forgive it."

"There's one last job to do," Daralen said formally to me. "My prince, will you accept the surrender of the enemy? They are badly wounded, and lie beyond the walls, in pain."

"In pain, you say," I grunted, knowing exactly what my upbringing said I should do, and what I knew was *right*. "Well, I do think it's wrong to leave them in pain," I said. "Sehran, would you and Seraphina and your brothers and sisters like to go and minister to the fallen? You know, permanently put them out of any pain they're in?"

"Oh, I think I speak for all of our people…" Seraphina said with a wide smile. "When I say that not one of them will ever be in pain again."

"Excellent. Glad we're on the same page. Go have fun."

They came to our door, with a plan to murder and kill my people. The end they would get from the succubai was probably more gentle than they fucking deserved.

We began making our way down from the wall, surrounded by dozens of legionnaires and joined by Wilhelm, and a somewhat subdued Gaspar.

"Ja, I counted seventeen," Wilhelm was saying to Oracle. "Zhat's confirmed kills. Do you zhink zhat's enough to impress Primus Daralen?"

"I think you impressed everyone today," my love assured him, patting his arm encouragingly.

As we reached the street level, legionnaires and city folk alike parted before us, many cheering or saluting as we passed. Word of our victory was already spreading through the city, and although we'd lost some, the vast majority—thanks to the joint action of better equipment, training, walls, and healing spells—would all fight again.

"You know," I said to Oracle as we walked toward the central square, "I think this calls for more than just ale. We should have a proper feast, celebrate properly."

"After everybody has had a chance to clean up," she agreed, wrinkling her nose. "You smell like a combination of blood, sweat, and ozone."

"The authentic aroma of victory," I declared grandly, making her laugh.

Behind us, Daralen was already organizing parties to clear the battlefield, tend to the wounded, and secure any surviving prisoners. The practical work of the aftermath would continue for days, I knew, but for us?

No, tonight we celebrated, and tomorrow, we put together a crew and set off. The Cradle of Feshcan'un was calling, and we were running out of time. Still, Gaij was safe. The armies that had threatened it were shattered beyond recovery. And most importantly, we had demonstrated beyond any doubt that the empire was more than capable of defending what was theirs.

As we reached the steps that led up into the tower, I turned and looked out over the throngs of people gathering. I grinned as I raised my voice to address the growing crowd.

"People of Gaij! Today you witnessed the power of the empire and its legion! Today you fought alongside the finest soldiers in any realm, and together we have achieved a total fucking victory that will be remembered by our enemies—well, the handful who live, anyway!"

The cheers that greeted my words were deafening.

"Tonight, we celebrate! Tomorrow, we begin rebuilding! And forever after, let it be known that Gaij stands under the protection of the empire!"

More cheers, and I grinned at Oracle. "Anything I'm missing?"

"Short and sweet," she agreed, reaching up to kiss my cheek. "Though I think you missed mentioning something important."

"What's that?"

"That the empire is buying the drinks." She winked as she settled back on her heels.

I laughed and turned back to the crowd. "And tonight, the empire pays for every round! Drink well, for you've earned it!"

The resulting roar of approval could probably have been heard all the way back on Dravith. As I stood there, arm around Oracle and surrounded by friends and allies, a sense of relief washed over me.

This was what it meant to be a prince of the empire—not just the power or the privileges, but the responsibility to protect and the joy of victory shared with those who had fought beside you.

"Come on." I tugged Oracle toward the tower and our quarters. "I think we've earned that drink. But first, I need a bath, and you!"

CHAPTER FORTY-TWO

The night was pretty raucous, as only a city that has been under siege and survived it in a short time can be.

Traditionally, from the little I understood about Earth's past, and from asking around here, when there was a siege of a city, it typically ended in one of three ways…when it was a success for the defenders, anyway.

First, they survived after long months under siege; that was the second most common one, and in that situation, the populace were generally closer to "famine victim" in mentality and physicality than they were to riotous celebrant. As such, minimal celebration, maximum "let's just get on with things," and a general feeling of hatred for the enemy going around.

Option two, the city stands, but it's taken a few weeks of hard fighting, to a few months. There's been enough supplies that nobody starved, but still there's been a lot of people who died—like half the population or so, on the walls—and there's also rampant plagues thanks to the unburied dead. And in an additional extra "fuck you" to people because we were in the UnderVerse, there were even odds that the excess death mana would spawn randomly rising undead or a lich might wander by and start raising all the corpses.

In that situation, there were frequently second sieges started, as incredibly shitty as that sounded.

Option three was what we'd pulled off, where the leadership were either so skilled, so lucky, or had a hidden superweapon, that the siege ended quickly, before the hunger and losses had a chance to really bite the population. Instead, you got what we had: an entire city that was expecting months of deprivation and hardship got a message saying "oh don't worry, those mo-fos are all dead" and people exploded in celebration.

That meant that when Oracle and I were laid on the bed in our quarters a few hours later, listening to the sounds drifting in through the open balcony doors, panting and sticky, trying to catch our breath, it was clear that nobody was going to be any use in the morning.

A little later, we moved out onto the balcony—still naked—and sat, enjoying a drink and watching the city half a mile below.

There were dancers in the streets; there were literally what looked like street parties going on—and I mean *parties*. This was a city that had expected to lose a load of its population, and were instead told "Oh yeah, don't worry about it…the baddest motherfuckers in the area, the Dark Legion, *and* the army of Kronk, known far and wide as mad motherfuckers, have all been slaughtered to a man, with almost no cost on our side."

Then add in that yeah, the city was under the nominal control of a tower full of succubai, and you got, well, what looked like a hell of a party.

I guessed that divorce rates and pregnancies were going to be going through the roof after tonight, and that was just what I could see from here.

The gardens of the tower had been stripped pretty much to the ground. Their impressive and manicured lawns, trees and foliage that had concealed many a tryst were now completely bare, thanks to the herds that had been temporarily moved into the city. And now, with the fight literally over, someone had apparently already had the bright idea to move most of the herds out of the way, use that Environmental Cleanse spell and turn the grounds into, well, a lust-filled demon party.

From here, I could pick out a dozen legionnaires I knew, and I deliberately stopped gazing around, out of the inability to look Daralen in the eye in the same way after I might have seen her involved somewhere below.

I hadn't seen her, but all things considered? It was just because I'd blinked and then turned away.

Hell with it—wherever she was, she deserved some fun as well, and so did whoever she was with.

Oracle and I relaxed for a few minutes, but then found that we just couldn't take it anymore and moved back inside, firmly closing the doors and going to bed. Because, as all the world knows, the last thing you're interested in, after a great sex session, was the sound of other people still going at it.

Especially when they were legionnaires and succubai, two *incredibly* naturally horny groups, who were also capable of dedicating incredible effort to annoy and outdo their friends.

Tomorrow was going to be a day chock-full of people limping and sitting down *very* carefully, I already knew.

By the time we woke again, the sun peeked through the blinds and the noises outside had mostly died away. That wasn't to say stopped; within the first three seconds of opening the balcony doors, I heard a voice raised in orgasm, *again*. But at least it was only one, and not fifty or more.

We had a leisurely morning, getting over the events of the last few days, and then we went down to breakfast, finding a great many people in the main hall, all in various stages of celebration from still drinking, to recovering, to unconscious in the corners.

I was pleased to see that the old favorite pastime of soldiers everywhere, namely drawing a cock on their unconscious friends' faces, was a thing here as well. I took the time to find a quill and ink, and write "caution: men working at rear" on one of the guys' foreheads to much laughter.

It was the little things that made life good.

I also realized that a second reason I felt a lot better about things was that I could feel the approach of Bane and the others as well.

I could feel that it was my usual lunatics, what seemed to be about forty others—which I was figuring was the ship's crew—and my entire usual squad, which was just an incredible relief.

Thomas wasn't among them, which I was both sad and proud about. Sad, because he was my brother and I loved the big, ugly bastard.

Proud? I knew him; he'd have wanted to lead the mission to get to me, and instead he'd stayed behind, probably because he knew he had responsibilities that nobody else could manage.

That or Belladonna had found some new lingerie and he'd decided I was a big boy and could find my own way home while he lived it up and drank all my beers.

Even odds, really.

There was a lot of good cheer, generally, and that situation was only heightened when I sat down with Seraphina and Sehran—the pair had taken to spending a lot of their time together, and I was wondering whether Jian was in for an even more tiring reunion than he was expecting—when Seraphina moved to kneel before me, head down and started to speak.

"My prince, Lord Jax, Imperial Scion and Master of the Tower, Lord of Gaij and Sonra, and Leader of the Empire, thank you."

"For what?" I asked, a bit nonplussed by the titles. It was kinda a thing here that because there were so many, I didn't really pay attention to how they were phrased, though I imagined there'd be a few lords who would be kicking off if they were said in the wrong order.

"For seven hundred years, we were trapped here," she said. "We fed on the tower, and in turn fed that mana back into it, enabling both ourselves and the tower to survive, though it was an unsatisfying existence for both, barely enough for us to live and keep the tower from collapse," she said formally.

"When you made your offer, that you would bring an end to the infighting, heal the tower, and grant us power over the city, we hoped, but we barely dared believe. If we'd had another viable choice, we'd have taken it, but as long as we'd struggled and suffered alone, it also meant that we recognized a lifeline when we saw it.

"We discussed it in private, and we decided that should you break faith with us, and kill us all, at least that was the worst that could happen. That we would no longer be here, but returned to the hells, and although we would miss this life, we could also begin to grow again.

"Yesterday, you showed us the might of the empire, you showed humility, and you showed that we are more than just toys for your kind, a momentary distraction. You showed that our hungers and needs were valid, and that the enemy, having attacked us, having intended to take everything from your people, weren't deserving of mercy.

"Others would have made excuses and enslaved them. They would have been called something else, but they would have been slaves, and we would have been told to continue to live as we had.

"In giving them to us, you gave us power. Sehran assured me that you knew that when we feed, we gain stats from our victims, that weaker targets are worth less, of course, but even they can help us to grow. You gave just less than two hundred succubai and incubai, almost a thousand souls, almost all of which were Dark legionnaires, men and women who had spent decades letting their darkest desires run free."

She smiled up at me, and I took her hand to pull her to her feet, opening my mouth to tell her it was okay, and that she'd helped me, that they'd fucking well deserved what they got, and a dozen other things.

Instead, Oracle spoke for us both.

"You're our ally, and our friend, Seraphina," she said. "Your people's needs are just as valid as any others, and we'll do our best to help you when we can."

"Thank you." Seraphina smiled, sitting back down and shrugging a little self-consciously. "It's been a long time since I knelt to anyone—with my clothes on, anyway." She winked. "But I wanted to thank you, and well, it felt right."

"Thank you." I said, "If you'd not taken that chance on me, then this might have all turned out very differently." I shrugged. "That's the fun of partners, I guess. We all stood to gain from it, and..."

I faltered, frowning as a feeling of wrongness, of concern, rippled through me. Then a voice whispered in my ear, making me sit upright.

"Jax, we must speak," came the clear voice of Lagoush.

"Goddess, what's wrong?" I asked.

"I suggest somewhere more private. And quickly," she replied firmly.

I nodded and stood; Oracle rose as well. I gestured to Seraphina to stay, but nodded to Sehran when she glanced at me. I headed for the door, the other two in tow. That feeling of unease continued to build.

"Jax, Lagoush must make a request of you." Jenae's voice echoed in my ears, and I felt that it was private, and that only she and I were speaking as she went on. *"The decision is yours to make, and I understand if you refuse it. As the future emperor, you will need to weigh the decision carefully, but...listen with an open mind, I ask."*

"Of course," I assured her. "Can you give me a hint?"

"No, this is for Lagoush to ask. But Jax?"

"Yeah?"

"Consider it carefully. There is no right or wrong answer here, though Oracle may feel differently."

Then she was gone. The sense of her presence vanished like smoke on the wind, as we passed through the main doors and out into the corridor.

I glanced left and right. The corridor, like most of those in the tower on the lower floors, was wide enough for ten to march abreast and for three men to stand on each's shoulders, with space to spare.

It gave the lower floors a feeling of space and solidity. Where it could have easily felt like the weight of the structure above was going to crash down at any second, it instead gave the feeling of massive strength.

I took a right, then opened the first door we came to. A pair of legionnaires sat at a small private table, arguing good-naturedly over drinks.

They shot to their feet as their prince entered, which, as one was in the middle of settling his armor into place, made sections fall off and clatter to the floor with a noise fit to wake the dead in the small room.

The legionnaire whose armor it was looked mortified, but they both clapped fists to chest in salute, stiffening and moving slightly closer together, to try to shield the table behind them, covered in coins and dice, from view.

"I need the room," I said tersely. "Sorry, but I need you to grab your gear and leave, now."

They saluted and grabbed everything as fast as they could. The strain in my voice made it clear that I didn't give two shits about their dicing or whatever else they'd been doing.

Within a minute, they were gone, and the door closed. Sehran had the presence of mind to tell them to stand on the far side, making sure nobody interrupted us, and that they were to forget anything they might hear.

Seeing this was important, not a noble or an officer throwing their weight around for something stupid, they nodded, taking up station and hurriedly finishing dressing. As the door closed, I heard one of them call someone else to get the rest of their squad as well.

Then the air before us shimmered and parted like a waterfall, as Lagoush stepped forward. Unlike before, when we'd done the whole formal greetings and She'd shown herself to throngs of the faithful, appearing a dozen meters tall and in iridescent scale mail and plate armor, instead She appeared of a height with Oracle, and She sat on the table without preamble, facing the three of us.

She was barely five foot, and wore what looked like leathers with armored sections mixed in, a bag on Her left hip and sword over Her right shoulder. A long, wide-bladed knife, almost long enough to be a shortsword, was on Her right hip; over Her left shoulder was an empty quiver, though what She normally had in it I had no clue.

She had sea-green and grey eyes that seemed to change as I looked into them, and pale, almost translucent skin. Her hair was almost white, and was bound with rings that looked to be polished mother-of-pearl.

All in all, had She not given off the unmistakable presence of a divine being, She'd have turned heads, but not because everyone assumed She was a goddess.

Instead, it'd just have been that She looked like a badass.

"Goddess," I said formally, and I sank to one knee.

"Please, Champion of the Flame, there is no need," She assured me, a smile, clearly forced, on Her lips. ***"I'm sorry, I'd hoped to leave you to rest and recover more, but time is short."***

"What do you need?" I asked Her.

"Do you remember the quest I gave you?"

A shiver ran through me as my already blinking notifications got a prod from a divine being.

I opened it, as She obviously wanted, and nodded.

Repeatable Quest discovered: Recover Lagoush's Artifacts

There are a number of artifacts that were gifted by Lagoush to help the Tower of Gaij and the surrounding territory.

The goddess wants them either returned to her, reconsecrated to her worship or destroyed. Should they be destroyed, the power that has been invested in them will be mostly lost, but that which will reach her will enable a single boon to be granted to the Empire as thanks.

Recover, reconsecrate, or destroy the Divine Artifacts of Lagoush

Reward: 1x Greater Boon, 250,000xp

"Jax, there is little time, and I apologize again, but something is attacking a small group who recently declared for me. They found another artifact, which is how I became aware that the Cradle still existed.

"I am limited, heavily so, by something that holds the Cradle, as are the others. We can sense much of the realm, but areas where another has extended

their control to deliberately shield the area from us are almost impossible to pierce, at least without an incredible expenditure of mana.

"The Cradle of Feshcan'un is one such place. We believed at first that it was simply too far from our reach, that as you claimed territory and dedicated it to us, then we'd be able to reach out and extend our sense there. In some areas that is true. But as I say, it appears now that someone or something is preventing our gaze from falling upon the Cradle." She hesitated, then went on.

"There are three such areas on the continent that would have served to assist you in your upcoming birth, Oracle. One is the Cradle, and I still believe it is the best choice. A second is the valley of Parsen'tar, where the headwaters of the river Synclin meets the forest. The last is…"

She glanced at me, as if waiting for me to explode, then went on.

"The last is the headwaters of the river Gaij, ninety miles to the northwest."

"Okay, I don't have that on my map…" I said slowly, pulling up my mental map that I'd gained when I first arrived here and checking it, regretting that the fucker only showed me places I'd been, and then glaring at it, as Lagoush clearly did something and caused all three points to flare with a bright star.

The Cradle was a couple of hundred miles to the east, and as I watched, a greyscale area around it began to bleed through, filling the map.

I watched as the boundaries that had been simply blank, a sort of "terra incognita" as the old maps would have shown it, for several hundred miles in all directions suddenly faded out, being replaced by vague drawings of hills and forests, rivers and lakes, with mountains being faint outlines.

"We cannot show you what we, too, do not know," Lagoush said softly. ***"To our eyes, that which is important is not the same as that which you see. We can see important details, things upon which the realm turns, with crystal clarity. But those even a meter beyond it? All is a fog.***

"The world I have revealed to you is as it once was, and lives on in my memories only," She admitted. ***"We—I—did not offer this before, because it could be totally different now, and what I tried to guide you to could instead be a cave a mile underground, or a mountaintop now. I have no way of seeing. Do you understand?"***

"I do." I nodded. "Though if you'd told me about that fucking place to the northwest before now, we could have checked it out on the way past," I groused. "Fuck's sake, we passed it by what, thirty miles? Less?"

"I did not direct you to it, because I felt what I believed to be a resonance, but when I called to them, they did not answer. None of the others did either, but by far the strongest was the Cradle, and…" She hesitated, and I went on for her.

"And if we'd found whatever we needed to the northwest, we'd never have come to Gaij," I growled. "Or at least not yet, and you want the fucking artifacts, is that it? You know, you do a piss-poor job of talking your allies into shit when you—"

"They're wisps, aren't they?" Oracle said softly, cutting me off.

"What?" I blinked.

"I believe so." Lagoush nodded, but She held up a hand as well. ***"I do not know. I must be clear, Oracle, Jax—the resonance feels like your kind, Oracle, but they have not answered when I called to them, not until now."***

"What changed?" I asked.

"They answered?" Oracle spoke over me. "They're definitely—"

"I don't know," Lagoush said firmly. ***"Yes, there are wisps there, in the Cradle, and yes, they have answered. They are under attack, with more of their number dying by the hour. They are hunted, and some of those who have been captured are being harmed, that's all I know.***

"They call for me—they beg me to aid them. To extend my grace from here, to a location I have no control over, is horrifically expensive. The mana required, the mana lost in such an attempt…"

"But you have to help them!" Oracle demanded. "You have to! They're—"

"I'm trying to!" Lagoush shouted. ***"Dammit, that's why I'm here! Stop interrupting me and let me explain!"***

The walls seemed to shake with the power of Her voice, and we all backed up, wincing, then sighed as we were hit with a quick heal, even as Lagoush dropped Her face into Her hands, taking a deep breath.

"Please, listen to me," Lagoush said, her voice filled with brittle calm. ***"I ask that you break the artifacts held in the Vault of Stone and grant their power to me. In doing this, I will gain enough power to temporarily aid those who call out to me, who I believe are wisps, but until I reach them fully, I cannot be sure.***

"For now, all that I know is that two of their number have gained access to a fragment of an old altar of mine. Their resonance matches that of the others, and so I believe that all there, or at least some, are wisps and they are dying, begging for me to help them."

"Jax, we have to…" Oracle turned to me, desperate, and I got what Jenae had been warning me about before. This was something that was going to have a cost, either way.

"What are the artifacts?" I asked Lagoush, and She nodded grimly that She understood what She was asking.

"There are three, none so powerful that I could offer to take only one. The first two are fertility enhancers. Use these in temples that worship me, and they will spread their blessing in a small radius, around a hundred meters on a side from the temple. I'm aware that doesn't sound like much, but it will have a significant effect. Those who are attempting to breed, be they of any species, will find that they have an easier time of it, and the offspring that are the result of any union blessed within the radius will be less likely to suffer miscarriage, weakness, or infection. Any child who is conceived within its radius will gain a permanent bonus of plus one to their Luck and Constitution stats."

"Fuck me…" I whispered. "Tell me that's per level?"

"No." She shook her head. ***"But ask yourself, Jax, how many points in Constitution do you think a baby is normally born with?"***

"Fuck," I muttered, realizing that at best, it had to be one or at most two. For any children conceived in a hundred-meter radius of the artifact to be born with at least two points, possibly three?

For a start, the way that babies were always needing to be protected from anything, like a cold, would be null and void. Shit, them just having the plus one to Luck meant that as a kid they'd be preternaturally lucky, and therefore much less likely to catch a bug in the first place.

Then they'd grow up stronger, and they'd, well, they'd be blessed indeed from such a start.

"There's two of those?" I asked, and She nodded. Just thinking of the potential of that made my head hurt, considering that they could be put in sections of the tower that had hundreds of rooms in that radius, considering it was in all directions, and we could literally take advantage of that.

Hell, just the thought of the babies who were going to be coming from last night's celebrations and who could have been blessed by being near these fucking things now was enough to make my fists itch.

"The Vault of Stone is on the second floor beneath the tower," Lagoush went on quickly. ***"Any conceived within reach of the lower floors since the tower was dedicated to us all will gain that blessing."***

"That's something," I growled. "Dammit, though, why not tell us about this before?"

"I gave you the quest," She said. ***"Do you think we spend all day lounging on clouds and watching you?"***

"Well, no, but fuck me, it feels like it at times!" I growled. "Okay, sorry, but damn, that's a hell of a blessing to give up. What's the other one? It's weaker, I hope?"

"No." She shook her head. ***"It is a gift that was created for my healers to carry into battle, wars specifically, and so long as it is given mana, it will prevent infections from developing..."***

"For how far?" I growled.

"Five hundred meters."

"Fuck me!" I cried. "Fuck me sideways with a 747 and extra cheese-whip! What the hell were you thinking to not tell me this before?!"

"That's why the tower is how it is?" Sehran asked shrewdly.

"What?" I snapped, looking at her.

"Seraphina told me that wounds suffered around the tower and outside in the gardens don't fester. She said it was one of the reasons everyone wanted to be in the tower, considering that after the cataclysm, when healers were rarer than platinum, simply being inside the walls here killed infections. She thought it was the tower, but it was this, wasn't it?"

"It is," Lagoush admitted. ***"There are other artifacts in there, though none so powerful. It was a holding area for the tower to give out as needed. I'd imagine that it was simply forgotten about as one of the many doors that the succubai could never open. The mana conduits in the ground were all that kept it functional at all for so many centuries, so the tower fed the artifacts the mana they needed before the succubai could siphon it off. This one, unlike the others, needed only mana, not my blessing as well."***

"Jax..." Oracle said softly, looking at me in supplication. "This is important. You know I'd never ask normally, but this is our baby..."

"It's your people." I nodded. "Wisps who might be the difference between our baby surviving being born and not."

"Exactly!" She nodded desperately.

"But to give these artifacts up, means hundreds, possibly thousands of children who might be born here will be born weaker, and unluckier than they could be," I finished.

"Hundreds of children a year, in a city the size of Gaij, hundreds of children, who are more likely to die in childbirth, or to infection, or to falling down the stairs—all left to suffer, because we chose our own child over theirs," I said in a monotone, as the possibilities spread out before me.

"Exactly," Lagoush admitted. ***"In time, those artifacts could make a difference to the empire, and not a small one. People who grow up blessed with additional health and luck, quickly find their lives attracting other gifts. Think of the beautiful people in your own world, the way that they have an easier life in every way…"***

"They get things a lot easier." I nodded. "It's not all easy, because they get treated differently because they're beautiful. It gets assumed that they only have the job because they're hot, or they blew the interviewer, but fuck it, when the alternative is that they don't even get the interview? When they get their drinks bought at the bar, meals bought, they get invites to places and modelling contracts…" I shook my head.

"It's not as easy as saying they're hot so they get a better life, it's always good and bad, but on the balance of it, yeah, I'd rather be lucky and handsome, than unlucky and fugly. And once you've got those two things from you being a baby, you're going to grow up a lot better off than those around you. When you do that, well…"

I stared into the distance, then blinked as Lagoush stepped forward, suddenly the same height as me as She gripped my shoulders, staring into my eyes.

"Jax, focus! I'm sorry, I know this is hard. I know the cost to you and the empire. But if you don't do this now, and I mean now, then there is no point! I feel them dying, Jax! My children, they call out to me. They pray, and I CANNOT HELP THEM!"

As She spoke, She grew again. Her eyes darkened to the color of the storm-tossed seas, and the light in the room faded measurably as the goddess, in Her panic, spread Her essence around.

The walls beaded with moisture; the scent of a wild ocean—the depths stirred up, full of sea salt and brine—filled the room. I saw in her eyes the genuine fear, the horror of those who had called to her and who she couldn't answer.

At the end of the day, though, the decision was mine, and we both knew it. I felt Oracle's horror and hope, and I saw the tens of thousands of children who could be born without those gifts, and the shorter, uglier lives they would suffer because of it.

I saw the risk to my unborn child, a child who existed, right now, and who would be helped by this, even as untold others would be harmed.

They wavered in the balance, for a long second.

And then I remembered another time. Mere months ago, when I'd needed Lagoush's help. When my brother was dying, being cored apart by Nimon's dark gifts turning against him, and Lagoush, despite not needing, or *wanting*, a champion had blessed him and taken him as hers.

He wasn't the kind of a guy who would have been picked by Lagoush, not at all. She was all about the sea, about the water and healing; she was called the Lady of Calm Waters for a reason.

Jenae and me? Sure, not just the situation, but we were both hotheads as well, at times. Sint? Probably; we got on well, and fuck knows me and Darakin were getting to be friends. But my brother and Lagoush?

He was more about spoiling the water by dipping his balls in it than cleaning it and making it healthier.

She'd done it, though, because She could help there and then, even if it cost her a perfect champion in the future.

That, and knowing that the children who were yet to be born could be helped in other ways, made it easier.

"Lead the way," I said to Lagoush.

She almost wept in relief, before spinning and rushing to the door.

It opened with her gesture and the corridor beyond was lined with legionnaires. Dozens of them stood there, and as they saw the goddess, they stared, open-mouthed; then they moved as She rushed out, leading us all.

We ran behind her, dashing down the corridor, taking the stairs two and three at a time: Oracle flying, Sehran sprinting, and my boots ringing as they hit the marble.

People scattered as we raced past, seeing the focus and feeling the divine presence. Less than a minute later, having triggered Mana Overdrive, I blurred past them all, picking Oracle up and carrying her in my arms as I ran faster and faster. Eventually I skidded to a halt, as the door materialized before us.

We were two levels down, beneath the ground floor. The door here had been sealed so long it looked more like it was part of the wall, rather than an actual door.

Dust had seeped into the cracks; spiders had danced and left webs, their remains and the husks of their meals there for so long that it'd been long lost to the darker areas of the tower and forgotten. But as I approached, willing the door to open, a cascade of dust, debris, and fossilized fragments rained free.

The doors opened slowly, grating across the floor and filling the air with the sound of resisting stone. Beyond, in the darkness of the vault, a dozen magelights flared bright, each shining like the sun.

Lagoush moved, flashing through the gap, reforming on the far side and racing past stacked treasures without care.

I saw stacks of platinum ingots, chests of coins, bags of rubies, and ropes of aquamarine. On all sides was wealth, but in the back, stacked in a secondary chamber, I saw, pushing through the doors, a smaller section of shelving.

Two golems stood to attention on either side, their charging cradle still drinking in the mana that was needed to power them, and between them?

Five artifacts.

Two were collections of bowls, some deep, others shallow, and clearly meant to be stacked in a way that allowed the water to flow from one to another; then presumably it'd make its way back up by some arcane plumbing method.

That or magic.

Of the two, magic was less confusing than fluid dynamics and plumbing, to be fair.

The third item was a single rod, about half a meter long, with three snakes wound around it, their eyes closed and tongues extended, checking the air.

That, Lagoush snatched up first, then She turned to me, offering it. ***"Please, Eternal, shatter this! Use your ability!"***

"Which one?" I asked, confused to all hell.

"Any!" She begged. ***"If I use my power to destroy it, it will cost me that much at least. I need all that I can gain!"***

"Use mine," Jenae whispered into my ear. *"Use fire, and I will guide you."*

I reached out, summoning fire to my hand, having genuinely no clue what the hell I was going to do with it, beyond summoning it. I felt the weaves shift, a glove that encircled my hand, my palm at least, and that radiated outward, formed.

I felt fingers of air, of earth and water, all shifting, being used to redirect, to guide, as the central fingers of fire grew fatter and longer.

The temperature in the room spiked, then continued to rise, faster and faster. Sweat broke out across my body. Oracle and Sehran backed up, even Lagoush shielding her eyes as my mana dropped faster and faster.

The artifact, though, as I took it in that hand, plucking it from hers as She backed up, hissing in pain, melted almost instantly. And as it did, a surge of power that threatened to knock me from my feet was unleashed.

Lagoush sucked it in, drinking it down like She was breathing in every last speck of air in the world, and I felt the relief in Her as She healed Her hand.

I've got a fire goddess helping me to create fire, and then me reaching out and taking something from a water goddess *with that damn hand?* Yeah, go me—no way to tell *that* was going to hurt her, was there? *Fucking idiot*, I mentally cursed myself, before turning to the remaining two artifacts that she'd indicated. I reached out, melting their forms and freeing the power in them as well.

Ten seconds later, it was done, and I released the weave, realizing that I'd not gotten a new spell notification, sure, but Oracle and I had definitely learned something there.

"I will reach out to them. I will protect them, as best I can, but…" She paused, looking at me beseechingly.

"But don't fucking hang around and get our arses to the Cradle?" I asked Her, and She nodded, clearly relieved.

"I'm sorry, Jax. It was not my intention to force you into this choice. For what it's worth, although I am unable to tell much of the situation, the resonance suggests there are the most wisps there of any of the three sites, and it is genuinely the site that I believe offers you the best chance at a successful birth.

"There are wisps there, as well as many other magical creatures, and the site is filled with an overabundance of life. I sense a need, a rush that you must reach that place quickly. One that I can rationalize only as that when the time for the birth comes—which I believe to be rapidly approaching, should you not seek to delay it—such a place would be for the best."

"I get it," I assured Her. "I do. I just don't like it. Next time, fucking *tell* me. We'd still have gone to Gaij. I still needed to get that bitch Illoth out of the territory after all, but you not telling us means that we didn't stop to see if those wisps would join us as well!"

"They are likely hidden deep within the earth, trying to avoid such as you and your companions, but I understand. I will discuss the options with you next time, my ally. And Jax?"

"Yeah?" I asked.

"Thank you," She whispered, before vanishing as She stepped backward.

"Jax…" Oracle started, clearly struggling with her words.

I shook my head. "It's okay," I assured her. "It was the right thing to do. We can't let people die today, for a chance to make others' lives, who might never be born, slightly better in the future. I just hate being railroaded into it, that's all."

I paused, then shook my head. "Okay, look around here quick, then we need to get to Seraphina and Daralen. That airship better be damn well ready, because it looks like it's time for a trip."

The next ten minutes was spent cataloging the contents of the room, and that was as long as I was willing to waste. That there were so many artifacts and valuable things was great, but honestly, the vast majority was potential wealth, rather than actual usable crap.

By which I meant that there were stacks of ingots, mainly platinum, there were a shitload of coins, and yeah, an utter buttload of gems. There were some necklaces, some rings and chains, and a load of what I'd have termed on Earth "costume jewelry" because it was blingy as hell, and that was it.

Admittedly, here, it wasn't costume. These were genuinely the real deal: a moonstone the size of a hen's egg, for example; diamonds that filled a small chest; more rubies than I could shake my dick at—and I could really shake my dick. But the one thing they weren't, was magical.

Except for the two remaining artifacts, there was little in the room that was magical, and what was, was crap.

Magelights, for example. Great, they lit the dark places up. Whoo. They weren't manastones, though, and that was what we needed to power the airship.

Gems? Perfect condition, all graded and polished and ready to be set into things, presumably for enchanting, given that one artifact was designed to contain the pressure of enchanting something to enable you to fit more into a smaller space.

The second artifact was a weird one as well, considering it was a single-use sort of a nuclear option, and one that I was willing to bet damn good money was here literally in case the succubai got out of line.

It'd disrupt any and all mana in the area for a short period of time, stunning anyone trying to use a spell, and disrupting all mana that was actively in use outside of a structure.

I was sure that this had been deliberately designed as a counter in case the succubai tried something, as it'd stun them, wipe out any spells that were active—and that'd free anyone who was being bewitched by them at the time—and yet it was designed specifically not to damage mana that was protected inside something solid—you know, like the way that the mana behind the walls of the tower would have been.

It was a sort of last reserve, I was betting, a way to break them free of the tower if they were found to be lying somehow and playing silly buggers.

I slipped it into the bag along with a few thousand in gold and platinum, but the rest was frankly fuck all use.

I had nearly ten thousand gold on me now, and considering I tended to conquer cities and then take what I needed? Yeah, shopping wasn't really a biggie for me at the minute.

I used the city treasury as my own, and I tended to eliminate a few noble houses wherever I went on general principles, and that served to prop up the treasury as well.

Lastly, well, I kept getting into fights—through no action on my part, obviously—but when you did that, and against armies, well, there tended to be a lot more loot left over.

That loot went into the treasury and got handed out in bonuses and so on, but the upshot was that there really wasn't much of a need for wealth beyond "better if I have some in case of emergencies I can't just stab in the face."

That was why, half an hour after that, I was sitting in the throne room, with my advisors around me, and I was checking my armor over.

I'd been channeling as much mana into it as I could on a regular basis over the last few weeks—ten here, a hundred there—and although that didn't sound like much, it really added up.

The armor was almost back to pristine again. The scuffed, battered, and broken sections reformed and gleamed with promise, even as I checked the articulation on an elbow joint.

"No," I said to Wilhelm's entreaty. "I'm sorry, mate, genuinely I am because if it wasn't obvious already, I do like you and I'm learning to trust you as well. But seriously, there's space for twenty people on the airship, and that's the maximum.

"This was always intended as a prototype that would be expanded upon, but there's only so much that can be done in a short period of time. As it is, when I add in a basic crew, which it damn well needs, that takes up five slots.

"Then comes me, Oracle, and Sehran, and we're down to twelve, less if we want to go faster, which we desperately need to do. So I'm capping it at seven more.

"With that, even if you had a hell of a lot more experience than you do, I'd be saying no to you, because you're the head of your house, and I need you to stay here and support Seraphina."

He opened his mouth, and I shook my head.

"End of discussion, mate."

He sighed, before bowing his head and tapping his fist to his heart in salute.

"I can pass my duties to another here…" Daralen suggested, stepping forward.

I shook my head. "No, Daralen, there's little that's as important right now as the next generation of the legion. I want you here to make sure that's done right, to protect the city, and to make goddamn sure that no matter what happens, we've got a home here," I ordered.

"Yeah, I know that you're the primus. Yeah, I know that there are literally no legionnaires here who have your level of skill, and that's why I'm leaving you behind. This is now your home, the home of the legion on Carrmor, and we cannot lose it again. Understand that. You have everything you need here to rebuild the legion stronger than it's been since the fall.

"Mages, artifacts, armor and food, cavalry, support and everything that the legion, and a fledgling empire resurgent, could need is literally here. I need you to keep it safe. In six months, you'll have a force based here that can wipe the floor with any other city. That can take on five times its number in open battle, and that's before you start looking at weapons like the airships.

"Hold the city, Daralen; train those we have and recruit more. Make it so that in six months they've got the basics down, and I promise you, you'll not recognize the legion you grew up in. We'll bring them back, all those who were taken from us and enslaved, and we'll make their captors fucking pay. Trust in me, protect the city, support Seraphina, and help to get the empire back on its feet.

"My people from Dravith are nearly here. Another week, more or less, and they'll arrive. Keep your eyes open and you might see them passing. Once we have them with us, and real transport, aboard the ship, that's when we start to speed up the retaking of this continent. We find somewhere that has a portal, we capture it, and then open it between here and Dravith, start moving legionnaires and equipment through, secure both sides.

"As I say, six months, and you won't recognize the legion, but it'll be in the best possible way, I promise," I finished, before forcing a smile.

"Yes, my prince." She nodded, tapping her fist to her chest in salute. "But you need protection, for Lady Oracle, if nothing else."

I nodded as I saw what she was doing there, both stroking my ego by saying "Hey, *you* don't need it, I know" and pointing out that the love of my life damn well did.

"I'm not stupid," I said. "I know we need others. Given the choice, I'd take a goddamn full legion of five thousand. But we need to be fast and there's limited room. My squad are a week out, and they're going to be going a hell of a lot faster than this rust bucket is going to go. Chances are they'll overtake us before we arrive. But if we don't, as much as I want to help these wisps, I have to be sensible about this. If the shit hits the fan, we won't be landing to help them.

"Instead, we'll follow at a safe distance if they're raiders, and then when my people arrive, we'll make a plan. Maybe that plan will be to come back and get you, I don't know, but with that in mind, I want you to take a day here to get things in order, and then I want you to start preparing.

"Kronk will be the first target. I want a solid five thousand legionnaires and a thousand cavalry ready to smash it into the ground. Once that's done, we're going to start working our arses off, and I mean that. This isn't the end here, as I leave Gaij—it's the beginning.

"I expect to be back in a week, possibly two at the most, but either way, not long. Once we know that we're safe—that the baby is, I mean—then we'll be back and we'll be digging in."

I looked around, seeing the looks on their faces, these people who had come so far with us, in such a short period of time.

I saw Marteen, Hoarce, Toren and Daralen, Sehran as always, and Oracle, and Seraphina and her people. I saw Othair, who just saved me no end of shit, Wilhelm, and his scheming shitehawk of a grandfather.

There were Greg and Cleq, the goblins, who—freed from their need to be the sensible, well-behaved, and upstanding citizens of Sonra, examples of all their race wasn't—had apparently reverted. They no longer felt like they were judged for their appearance instead of their skills, and as such had regressed to almost feral, in their time with the gnomes.

Well, you know, feral like all engineers, deciding that nothing had enough features until it was totally fucking broken.

These people, and literally thousands of others, had come this far with me. I really didn't want to leave them all behind, but that was life.

"I'd recommend that you take five legionnaires then, and two of the succubai." Daralen stepped forward, drawing my eye. "I'd say seven legionnaires, given the chance, but we all know how powerful a distraction at the right time can be. As such, Vislen and his partner Kato, Orden and his partner Hador—for both your heavy support and a succubai and incubai, respectively."

I nodded, and she went on.

"Then, given that you refuse to let me accompany you, I'd suggest the remaining three be a centurion—Lembas—who took to the mage training like a legionnaire to ale, frankly, so I'd recommend you spend some time on expanding his repertoire. And Bern and Toci, both stealth skilled as line legionnaires and experienced as scouts, or as you'll no doubt insist on calling them, 'stabby-stabby bastards.' Though, in this case, Toci is dual-classed as a ranger, and Bern as an assassin, intending to sell her life as dearly as possible executing the enemies of the legion."

"Sounds good," I agreed. "How long until they can be ready?"

"They're legionnaires, Prince Jax." She fixed me with a glare. "They're already ready, and they're waiting at the ship."

"Glad to know I get a say in things then." I snorted. "Fine, anything else I need to do before we set off?"

"Just promise that you'll be careful." Seraphina stepped up and enfolded Oracle in a hug, and that started the ball rolling as everyone started professing care, concerns, and wishes to be there at the birth.

Considering that, first of all, we still didn't know how the hell this whole thing was going to work, or when, it was a bit weird, not to mention that traditionally, the whole demons and baby thing was generally a no-no…you know, unless one was intended as a snack for the other.

It was four hours later that we set off. We were held up slightly because one gnome—having been informed that he wasn't chosen as crew—had tried to replace the engines with something less powerful so that he could instead put them on his own side project.

The real delay was getting the crew who had been picked to stop beating him long enough to find out where the hell he'd stashed the parts, and then reattaching them.

Othair and Marteen had gone nuclear with their respective skills, and although there might have been a manastone in the city still by the time we left, if there was, it was *very* well hidden.

"Just in case" bags of holding had been provided to Oracle, which included the very best of the produce from several bakers and chefs, and a half dozen of the weirdest and most incredibly vibrant fruits that could be found.

I'd been given a shitload of local coffee, and already made bacon sandwiches. Literally. A stack of a hundred, and that just made me all warm inside.

Mainly because by the time we finally lifted into the air, I was already down to ninety-six.

CHAPTER FORTY-THREE

The airship had changed so many times now that I was constantly half expecting that when I opened our door, it'd be a different room beyond. But thankfully, as the sun rose on the third day, it wasn't.

Its layout was a little weird, mainly because as Oracle and I were ostensibly the most important people on the ship, we were given our own quarters, which was fine by me.

Unfortunately, the size and layout issues meant that our quarters could just about fit in the bed, and a seat, and that was it. When the seat was unlatched and lowered down, the bed had to be lifted and locked away to make room for it, and when the bed was down from its latched position on the wall, well, you couldn't open the door.

The window was a single porthole that I could maybe get my arm through up to my elbow, if I lubed it up, and had no glass. That meant that because of the height we were at, it tended to get colder than a witch's tit in there.

It was private, though, and that was appreciated.

The next room was the "common room," which meant it was the area that everyone got to be, almost all the time. As that included the crew and my people, that tended to be around twelve people in just enough space for twelve people to lay down, provided they didn't mind each other's elbows getting friendly.

There were three doors from that room, not counting the one into our room, and they led out to the right and left, respectively, if I stood with my back against our door, and forward.

Left and right led out onto a narrow walkway that ringed the enclosed quarters and had been originally intended as a place for people to fire off spells from, and straight ahead led into the cockpit.

That was it.

The entirety of the ship, for five straight days, while we travelled at a speed that was only a little faster—or so it seemed to me, in the words of the great Blackadder—than an asthmatic ant with some heavy shopping.

Admittedly, yeah, all right, that was a slight exaggeration…medium shopping carried by a horse, but come on. I'd been on planes and I could fly; being here while we trundled along?

The pilots changed shifts every six hours, with Phizzik being both the lead pilot and the overall boss, with a pair of engineers and two other pilots who seemed to be there for window dressing.

That, or at least as near as I could tell, Phizzik never slept, because day or night, when I looked into the cockpit, there was the mad little bastard, working away.

That meant that between the roughly five miles an hour and that we didn't need to stop for the night, we were making good time.

Horses and so on needed to stop for the night, and yeah, all right, issues like rivers and forests and so on weren't really a problem up here.

I tended to start my day with a coffee and a shit over the side, which was in itself a hell of a trick, and I could fly.

Then I spent some time with Oracle helping to teach the others spells, and then arguing with them about said spells. Then we passed a little time on target practice, which involved all of us lying down on the boards outside and firing off random spells aimed at monsters we spotted on the ground, unusual and possible threatening beasts, or more frequently, trees and the local equivalent of a pigeon.

No matter where I went in all of reality, those fuckers were there.

I'd also tried to read my notifications, and then I'd scrapped them all in a huff.

Congratulations!

You have killed the following:

- 17x Church of Nimon Slave Aspirants of various levels for a total of 23,112xp
- 22x Church of Nimon Soldier Aspirants of various levels for a total of 204,095xp
- 28x Church of Nimon Sanctified and Blessed Soldiers of various levels for a total of 247,957xp
- 22x Church of Nimon Dark Chosen of various levels for a total of 542,991xp
- 31x Guards of Kronk of various levels for a total of 127,114xp
- 82x Mages of various levels for a total of 926,116xp
- 63…

It'd just gone on and on. Once I'd checked that, yeah, I gained a single level out of it all…honestly, I didn't really give two shits beyond that.

Congratulations!

You have reached level 52.

You have 7 unspent Attribute points and 1 Meridian point available.

Progress to level 53 stands at 417,882/13,000,000

I'd been at nine million and change out of the twelve million I'd needed for my next level, and as one of the commanders of the forces who defeated a combined army of a little over seventeen thousand, yeah…

I'd fucking well *earned* those points. Sure, there were only seven, and I needed more than that to achieve another century anywhere. But I was at eighty-three on my Strength, and adding seven to that brought me to ninety, which made me feel a little better about how close it was getting.

Beyond that came the meridian point, which, as always, I'd wanted to spend on something cool. But given that I had the time to deal with everything now, I decided to slot that in as well.

PRIMARY

Brain: 1/10 Spell Cost Reduction: -5% (Primary Bonus: 1 spell slot per point.)
Head: Primary Node: Additional points invested will reduce mana cost by 5%.
(Note: Air Elemental Core results in increased mana regeneration by 50%, self-control decrease of 5%.)

SECONDARY

Eyes: 1/10 Vision Improvement (Secondary Bonus: +10% chance to notice important visual details.)
Eyes: Important details will glow to your vision. This will level with the relevant skill.

Ears: 0/10 Hearing Improvement
Ears: Important sounds will become clearer with concentration. High levels will aid in translation.

Mouth: 1/10 Vocal Improvement
Mouth: Your voice will become 10% more likely to have a desired effect on a target—soothing, seducing, persuading as required.

Nose: 0/10 Tracking and Detection Improvement
Nose: Scents will be stronger, aiding in tracking.

Heart: 1/10 Health Increase
Heart: You will gain an additional ten points of health for each point invested in your Constitution.

Lungs: 2/10 Stamina Increase
Lungs: You will gain an additional ten points of stamina for each point invested in your Endurance.

Stomach: 0/10 Sustenance Improvement
Stomach: You will gain the abilities to resist poisons by 5% and to gain sustenance from more sources.

Legs: 1/10 Speed Increase
Legs: You will gain a boost of 10% to your speed, as well as better stability over various terrain.
(Note: SporeMother Core results in a gain of 10% to your speed in darkness. Speed in daylight will be decreased by 20%.)

Arms: 1/10 Strength Increase
Arms: You will receive a boost of 25% to your carrying capacity and your damage output with melee weapons.

Hands: 1/10 Dexterity Increase

Hands: You will develop crafting abilities at a 10% increased rate, along with a greater chance to succeed in crafting complicated items.

Again, not a hard choice, given that I had only my nose, ears, or stomach left to unlock. Gaining protection from five percent of poisons with stomach was nice, sure, but ears might actually help me to hear when some sneaky stabby-stabby bastard was sneaking up. And nose…well, anyone who's spent much time around soldiers, or legionnaires, in any enclosed space knew damn well that being able to smell things better would actually be a curse.

I was going to leave that one for last, if I had any say in it.

All of this to say, that the day was going fairly well. I'd gotten up to date on a lot of things, and, yeah, it was seriously irritating that I had no room to do anything, but I was getting better at meditation.

I wanted to spend it doing alchemy…well, no, that was a lie.

I wanted to spend my time doing *Oracle*, and eating lots of good food, drinking great rum and then possibly having some more sex, before settling down with the squad—my squad, though these guys were nice enough—and having some more drinks and basically relaxing.

What I was doing instead, at first anyway, was meditating, and then as time went on, it was listening to music.

That had been a hell of a surprise, because when I started sorting through my bags of holding, I'd found a bunch of random shit that was useless.

So, over the side it'd gone—littering wasn't really a thing here, and the random discovery of a two-handed greatsword in the middle of a field with no tracks leading to it might actually be the start of an exciting quest in someone else's life yet.

No, the real discovery was something I'd totally forgotten about until now, and that was going to change Ronin's…all our lives for the better.

My *phone*.

I'd forgotten that the damn thing was in there. With the solar cell attached to it, all it needed was a little time in the sun, and boom.

That was it—the lives of everyone aboard were made infinitely better as I set it in an empty bowl so the sound was amplified.

The hours flew past as I sat and navel-gazed, trying to find that moment of epiphany, and the others, well, survived, essentially.

Vislen and Orden, who had bonded to a succubai and an incubai, respectively, seemed to enjoy spending a lot of time out of sight of the rest of us. Sehran and the other two demons often went flying when they weren't "otherwise busy."

Oracle and I occasionally did the same as well, but most of the time was spent listening to music, and sitting on the boards outside—when it wasn't raining—and watching the world passing by beneath us.

Hours passed by at a snail's pace, and at Oracle's pushing, we spent a lot of the time asleep as well.

It was torturous instead of restful, though, as every so often, we'd receive word from Jenae or one of the others, to let us know that more of the wisps had vanished.

She wasn't sure whether they were dead, or taken somewhere beyond their senses, as the full area was shielded to hide it. But the one thing we did know was that the gods were growing increasingly desperate, and that something was hunting them all down.

Vanei had lent her power over the air to ensure we had swifter passage, and Svetu had made some very clear upgrades to the engines, and then spent some time with the gnomes, explaining exactly what they had to do and no more.

Then he rejoined us for about four hours and rebuilt that engine from scratch, after retrieving it from the field it'd crashed into after ripping itself free.

Fortunately, the damage was minor, as it'd burned through the manastone it'd been powered by in short order.

Tamat and I talked—several times, in fact—and we agreed as soon as the site was claimed and everything was settled, then we'd exchange fragments.

Jenae forbade me looking over the Constellation of Secrets, explaining that I'd basically strained my brain—*again*—and I needed time for the mass of information to settle, but that in a month or so, I should be good to go again, and so I just…watched.

We flew over the plains, then forests, across low hills covered in scrub brush and then over valleys that sank down out of the ever-present wind and that were sheltered places of incredible life.

For nearly a full day, we followed a river, seeing thousands of animals, beasts, and monsters. And once, for one of the most nerve-racking five minutes of my life, we flew alongside what was apparently a lesser dragon.

The terms "greater" and "lesser" were misleading when it came to dragons, because this fucker was around the same size as a medium lift troop transport plane back home. It swooped in, clearly thinking to make a meal of this new and unusual prey, then spotted us and flew off, apparently disgusted that its "snack" was "infested" with humanoids.

Jenae had something to do with that, I was fairly sure, but as she didn't say, I didn't ask, and that meant in my mind, I owed no more favors.

This entire mission was a fifty-fifty thing for me, because on the one hand, yeah, we were going here to make it easier for Oracle to give birth, and we needed that.

On the other? The gods were desperate for us to get there and make contact with these wisps. I was pretty sure a big part of that was that if I claimed the area, and converted it back to their control—it'd long been a source of power for Lagoush in the past—then it'd result in a massive boost in their relative power.

So again, I didn't ask, and they didn't offer, so no further debts grew in my mind.

It was mid-morning on the fourth day when Kronk came into view, distantly and only for half an hour. But when it did, it was going to be a target for the empire at some point.

We'd passed the trails that the army had used coming to Gaij on the way, and we'd even passed over some survivors of the fight going back the other way—when people had asked whether we were still at war with them, considering they were deserters, I'd agreed that we were and they'd all gotten some experience bombarding their enemies with spells, which was fun.

Kronk itself, though—that was a shithole. As soon as I saw it, I agreed it had to go.

The area for the last fifty miles or so had been pretty shitty. It wasn't "back to the desert" levels of nasty, but it clearly felt like it. The ground was cracked and dusty; the grass was scrub and patchy. And the trees?

They were rare and far between, as well as gnarled, twisted things.

The little we did see growing were the fields that were clearly used to feed Kronk, and even they were hard-pressed to grow anything at all.

All in all, it was as if the land around us had been sucked dry of all life. The more I looked at Kronk, the more I was convinced that if it wasn't being done by that shithole of a city, then it certainly wasn't being helped by it.

Himnel was a shithole, let's be clear on that, and it, like Kronk, spewed masses of smoke from thousands of chimneys all the time. The streets were grey and cobble-lined, and the oppressive air of hundreds of years of brutality and slavery was ingrained into the very stone.

It was a *forge-city*, though. It'd been created, always, with the plan that the entire city was there to produce, to make things for the empire to conquer the continent of Dravith.

Kronk? Even the name was shit. But staring at its distant high walls, the cloud of sulfurous smoke that spewed upward, the literal crap that poisoned the river that flowed by it, and the lines of rust, where the metal walls wept red and orange regret into the dirt, all of it just combined to make me want to smash it from existence.

A single caravan toiled south from the city, and that was on the far side, but even from here, I could see that it included slave wagons. I had an irrational need to call down fire on the entire smoking, stinking shithole as soon as possible.

I sat morosely on the boards that ringed our little world, and stared down as the ground became increasingly dreary and lifeless.

I'd heard people say that the desert was dull, that they couldn't stand it. I kinda got that, though I wasn't bothered by it. Different folks liked different places, and that was life.

Personally, it was the mountains that called to me; something about the bones of the world being on display, I liked. The desert? It wasn't where I'd choose to spend a great deal of time, but I also saw beauty in it, in the way that the sky was so huge and the striations of color everywhere you looked.

I liked the gentle susurration of the sand as it spoke across the thousand dunes, and where there was life, it was hard.

It was used to every step being life or death, and making the most of a single drop of moisture. I looked at that, and I could respect it.

The more waterlogged areas that we'd passed across? The rivers and the huge abundance of life in the woods and forests, the plains and the hills?

I liked that as well, partly because I liked the grass, and partly because I knew there was food, shelter, and things to play with down there.

But this?

This endless plain of cracked earth that was even bleeding out the color of the land and leaving bare dirt behind? This was more hellish than hell ever could be for me.

I saw bones clearly, even from a hundred or so meters in the air, as we passed the half-buried and alternately fresh piles left behind by the deaths of tens of thousands and more.

I saw dips where just-out-of-sight things had set up and waited for prey, and I saw the places those creatures in turn had died.

There were pits that had been dug and abandoned, clearly long dry, where at a guess people had tried to find water. Here and there, as the hours passed by and the miles flashed away beneath us, I saw the remains of caravans.

There were the remains of pack beasts, ranging from horses to creatures I had no names for, and always, there were the rotting dead.

For whatever reason, the dead didn't seem to rise here as much, and where they did?

They wandered aimlessly.

Like the zombies of old movies, where they limped and staggered, moaning and gnawing at the air, except that even that effort seemed beyond these. We took to putting them out of their misery as we flew past.

Finally, on the sixth day, as the sun dipped toward the horizon, we saw the first hints of the Cradle, and the boards were filled with desperate people, wanting to see anything different, and for a little while, hope rose in us all.

How fucking wrong we were.

CHAPTER FORTY-FOUR — THE FINAL CHAPTER

By the time we reached the edge of the Cradle, it was obvious that something beyond nature was keeping this place intact, as with a sharp line, the blasted, devastated land that we'd crossed for hundreds of miles was suddenly vibrant with life.

Leaves and vines that passed over the invisible line withered and died, but inside? Inside, they *thrived*, shifting in unseen breezes.

"That gives me the fuckin' willies," I whispered, holding onto a guide rope and leaning out, staring down as we crossed over and continued in toward a distant lake, and peering down over the railing of the airship.

Below us, a riot of green exploded out. Trees that should have been impossible, given the condition of the ground a mile away, soared skyward, their branches heavy with fruit. Vines twisted and coiled around every surface. Even from this height, I could see animals moving through the dense canopy—far too many for everything I thought I knew about territory and animals.

Fuck me, I wished instantly I could open a portal back home and have David Attenborough step through. Though the shock would probably kill him.

I didn't care what anyone said; that man was a national treasure. Exposing him to risk would be like burning the *Mona Lisa* to light a cigar.

"It's like looking at another world," Oracle murmured beside me, one hand resting protectively on her belly, and I reached out, taking her in my arms and nodding, scanning the perimeter.

The transition made my every sense scream that it was wrong, it was almost surgical in its precision. One side: death. The other: frantic, desperate life.

"Circle around," I ordered the pilot, who unsurprisingly was again Phizzik. "I want to see the entire boundary before we find somewhere to land."

Vislen approached, standing as close to attention as could be managed on a pair of planks that creaked constantly in the wind. "My prince, there's something wrong about this place," he said formally, a sharp change from using my name and telling me shitty stories for the last several days as the small group had grown closer.

"You think?" I grunted. "The air feels…charged." The fine hairs on my arms stood on end beneath my armor. "Like the entire valley is about to be struck by lightning."

"Not just that," Vislen continued, his gaze fixed downward. "Look at how the animals are moving. It's not natural."

He was right. Even from our height, I could see herds flowing across clearings like water, predators chasing prey with a manic intensity. Everything was moving too fast, living too desperately.

"It's the life," Oracle said suddenly, her voice hollow. "This place is stealing and concentrating the life—it has to be!"

"What do you mean?" I asked.

She gestured at the wasteland we'd just crossed. "That shouldn't exist. Not naturally. This place—the Cradle—it's pulling everything into itself. Mana, life force…everything…for hundreds of miles. It's the only thing that makes sense. But it didn't used to be like this, surely? Lagoush said it was a paradise, a place of safety and abundance. But this? This is horrible."

A chill ran down my spine. "And the gods sent us here? To make it easier for the baby? Fuck's sake, maybe we don't want to land…"

Oracle's eyes met mine, uncertainty flickering across her face. "They said the wisps were here. That they needed our help. And that they could help us with the baby. Jax, even if we have to just rescue them and then leave again, fly straight back to Gaij…"

"Can't!" Phizzik shouted over the rushing of the wind as we were buffeted by something.

"What?" I shouted back, then sighed as he spoke normally, the sudden surge of wind dying away.

"Can't just go back," Phizzik explained. The mad little bastard grinned like he was living his best life, his hat crushed down atop his head and goggles covering his eyes. "Bag failing, not enough gasses. We lands, mebbie a day to make repairs, then we go again."

"What?!" I snarled. "When the hell were you gonna tell us this?"

"Now." He shrugged, unconcerned. "Why tell you before? You got more gas?"

"No!"

"Then what difference it make?"

"It makes a hell of a fucking difference, you mad little bastard!" I roared. "I need to know this shit! What if we have to fight down there!"

"Then fight." That was all he said, shrugging again.

"Jax…" Oracle dragged out my name warningly as I clenched and unclenched my fists, thinking longingly of throttling the little bastard, before forcing down a deep breath and finding some calm.

"Phizzik…" I started, and a second gnome, one of the engineers, spoke up instead.

"Engines drain the stones," he said. "Too much power needed, too many leaks, too little control. Phizzik change direction every few seconds, fires the engines again and again, drains mana, but means less weight on bag, keeps bag as full as possible on way here, tanks emptying and need refilling. All takes mana. We land, use stones, refill bag, all good."

I glared at him as I worked through this in my head and then cursed, looking up at the bag overhead.

I vaguely remembered overhearing a conversation about the zeppelin-like bag, how it leaked too much, having to have the gasses replaced all the time, but I thought they'd fixed that.

Or more to the point, I'd *assumed* they had. Fuck.

"Fine. Find a landing spot near the lake, then get to work refilling the bag!"

Sehran moved closer, her wings twitching nervously as she nodded forward. "Jax, something's down there. The lake at the center, can you see it?"

I looked where she pointed. In the heart of the valley lay a massive lake, its waters shimmering with an unnatural blue-green luminescence. Even from this distance, I could make out movement beneath the surface—multiple shapes patrolling methodically.

"Are those…people?" Orden squinted.

"Jax, they look like mer!" Oracle said in a rush, perking up. "Maybe they can help!"

"Maybe," I agreed grimly. "Or maybe they're why the wisps are dying. Fuck's sake, we don't know anything about this place!"

I paused, then closed my eyes and reached out to Lagoush, planning to ask her about the mer, hoping that she'd made contact with them. She was the Lady of Water, after all. I frowned, trying again, as the spell fizzled out and failed.

"Oracle…" I said slowly. "I can't reach Lagoush, or Jenae. None of them!" I tried the spell again and again, feeling it just unravel each time. The hairs on the back of my neck rose in response to the failure.

"I feel it too." She swallowed hard. "There's something here, something that's trying to block all magic."

"Phizzik, is the ship…" I started to ask.

He stared at me in panic at out of the little cabin, as he pulled levers and yanked on the yoke. "Not good!" he screamed. "Very not good!"

"Fuck! Can we get out of here?" I yelled at him.

He shook his head quickly, reverting to more gnomish in chat than usual with his stress. "No fly. Best Phizzik can do is maybe no crash and all die?"

"Do that," I ordered. "Land as well as you can. If those who can fly get off, will that help?"

"You weigh more than ship?" he snapped; I looked at him, and he went on. "Ship weigh much, much, and no want to fly now. If you can lift ship, great. If not, we crash."

"Fuck!" I snarled. "All right, everyone who can fly, start ferrying everyone who can't off!"

"What are you going to do?" Oracle asked me, feeling that I was going to do something.

"Try to slow us down," I growled, knowing that I could do it, a bit at least, as my own flight was more lifting myself with magic, rather than…*magic*.

Fuck, it needed magic, and here…

I tried to lift myself using Soaring Majesty. It worked, sort of, but it cost me far more than it should. I snarled as I accepted that no, I wasn't going to be helping to save the day, Superman style.

"There," Lembas called out, pointing toward the northern edge of the lake. "I can see structures."

I followed his gesture. Half-buried in the vegetation, stone pillars rose like skeletal fingers from the jungle floor. Even from here, I could see they were ancient—weathered by time yet still standing, defiant against the encroaching vegetation.

"That has to be the temple," I called out, before banging on the side of the cockpit and jabbing a finger in the direction of the structure. "We make for the temple! There, you little bastard!"

Phizzik nodded, his eyes magnified through his goggles, as he yanked on some levers and pumped others.

As we dropped lower, the air grew thick with pollen and spores, a miasma of life that clogged the lungs and made my eyes water. The smell was overwhelming—decay and growth locked in an accelerated cycle, the scent of overripe fruit and fresh blood mixing in the humid air.

"Everyone, check your weapons," I ordered as we approached the landing site. "I don't know what we're walking into, but be ready for anything."

Oracle stood beside me, her hand finding mine. "Jax, I can feel them—the wisps! They're in pain…they're afraid."

I squeezed her hand. "We'll find them," I assured her. Then, stepping up to the edge, I grabbed Lembas and jumped, using my mana only to speed my descent as much as possible when I absolutely had to, as we fell. As we approached the ground, I used it again, to slow to a manageable speed, before dropping the slender legionnaire off, and then hurtling back up.

Both succubai and the single incubai were all doing the same, carrying those they could, and then returning for others. I had to snort in amusement despite everything at the way that the gnomes clung to the leather straps that made up most of the clothing of the demons.

We managed three trips, as Phizzik—screaming, kicking, and beating on the controls—kept the airship mostly level, coming in for as graceful a landing as was possible.

Which was to say…not very.

In the end, with the engines dead, the balloon thingy deflating, and all the mana being sucked free, Phizzik still managed to not *entirely* crash in a small clearing, disturbing a flock of birds that erupted from the canopy in a cloud of iridescent feathers, before the bag ruptured and a sound like a gigantic fart ripped through the area as it deflated completely.

It sure as shit wouldn't be taking off again anytime soon, and it was only that the gas used to inflate the balloon section either wasn't flammable or that it was all expended that saved us from an untimely and very fiery death.

That wasn't the weirdest bit, though. From the moment I hit the ground, I felt a vibration running through the soil itself, as if the land were shivering in panic.

Oracle landed next to me, but as soon as she did, she looked like she wanted to throw up.

"Are you okay?" I asked her, and she nodded, clearly fighting to control the urge, before forcing a smile.

"I'll be fine. I just don't like this, Jax. It feels wrong."

"You're right about that," I muttered, before raising my voice. "Is everyone okay?" I called out, looking around, and then shaking my head at the state of the gnomes. They were racing to the ship now, almost before the damn thing had settled fully in the remains of several trees—the lunatic looked to have hit them deliberately—and they were screaming the pilot's name, and that they told him this would happen.

The bit that got me was when I realized that they apparently were overjoyed by this.

When I spotted that Phizzik was screaming similar things at them, and demanding they rebuild to his plan, not their own stupid ones, it made it clear this was the normal response to a crash with the crazy little bastards.

"Fine! You crazy little fuckers stay here and try to figure out a way of fixing that mess," I snapped at the gnomes, fighting down the urge to wade into the middle of the chaos and start kicking them all, before turning to the others. "Vislen, Orden, you're our vanguard. Kato, Hador, protect our flanks. Lembas, I want you watching for magical threats, but save your mana if you can. I don't like the way this place feels. Bern, Toci, scout ahead but stay within sight. Sehran, stick with Oracle."

They moved into formation without question, professionals all. I drew my naginata, feeling its comfortable weight as we stepped into the jungle. I settled my helm atop my head, feeling strangely more "me" these days when I was in full armor and expecting a fight.

The overgrown undergrowth closed around us immediately, freakishly dense. Vines reached toward us as if sentient, and more than once I had to slash through growth that seemed to appear between one step and the next. The sounds of the jungle pressed in—chattering, screaming, growling, hissing—a cacophony of madness on all sides that made me feel like a massive Austrian actor was going to burst out of it at any second and scream "Get to the chopper."

We hadn't gone fifty paces before we met our first natives, who were clearly on their way toward us to investigate the crash.

They melted from the underbrush like humanoid ghosts: lumpy, pallid figures with overlarge eyes and six-fingered hands that ran like gorillas, knuckling across the ground and staring at us almost sideways on. Their skin was stretched too tight across swollen joints, and growths distorted what I'd swear was their almost dwarfish features.

Overlarge ears and nose, thick lips—not a one had hair of any kind—added to the impression.

"Don't move," I ordered my people, lifting my empty left hand and holding it palm out to show I wasn't a threat. "We mean no harm," I told them, despite being literally heavily armed and armored.

The creatures chittered amongst themselves, a rapid-fire language that sounded like breaking glass. One stepped forward, tilting its head at an impossible angle, almost ninety degrees sideways.

"You. Metal-skin. Why come?" Its voice was surprisingly musical, though the words were awkwardly formed.

"We're looking for the temple of Lagoush," I replied. "And for the wisps who live there."

The creature hissed, its companions shrinking back into the foliage. Several shrieked in anger or fear at the mention of it. "Temple. No! Bad place. Much pain."

"What do you mean?" Oracle stepped forward.

The creature's eyes immediately fixed on her belly, and I felt a sudden tension ripple through them.

"New life," the creature whispered, creeping forward slowly and reaching toward Oracle's abdomen.

I stepped between them, naginata raised in warning. "No," I said flatly. "You don't touch her."

The creature hissed, then backed away. "Temple that way." It pointed farther into the jungle, then shook its head, and seemed to deflate a little, going on in a quieter voice. "Find wisps. Find pain. All same."

With that cryptic message, the creature hooted at its companions, then vanished back into the undergrowth, leaving us alone in the stifling heat.

"What the fuck was that?" Kato muttered, wiping sweat from her brow.

"I don't know," I admitted. "But they confirmed the wisps are at the temple, and they didn't attack us. That's a good sign for now. Let's keep moving."

I spoke to Oracle and Sehran through the bond, nervous that the gnomes were about to be jumped. *"Do you think we're okay leaving the gnomes unprotected?"*

"I think so," Oracle said softly. *"I didn't sense any aggression from them. It was more nervous and a sense that they wanted to protect something. When you told them about the wisps, it knew, and it seemed sad. I think they've gone home."*

"They have," Sehran agreed, before shaking her wings in a shrug. *"Or at least they're going somewhere. I can sense so much life around us right now it's blocking out details, but I can sense them moving away, not circling around."*

*"Jax, the gnomes **might** face a threat, but we know we **will** face one. I think we have to push on with everyone. Once it's dealt with, we can come back and protect them,"* Oracle pointed out.

I cursed as I realized that she was right.

I nodded and we pressed on, following the direction the bald dwarf thing had indicated. The jungle grew denser, if that was possible, the trees twisting into unnatural shapes as we approached the temple grounds.

On all sides, fruits hung from branches, swollen and bursting with over-ripeness that was almost painful to look at. In dozens of places, the bulging fruit seeped and dripped something to the forest floor that reeked of rot, making me think that the life that was being twisted and forced into everything was accelerating it all to the point that it matched pears and bananas.

Back home, there were only two states for a pear to be—underripe and mush—and the changeover period between the two lasted about twelve seconds, and only occurred when nobody was around.

If there was a banana nearby? Just buy it and put it straight in the bin; don't waste your time expecting to eat it. That was my experience. And here?

This was that times five *thousand.* Fruit was literally so overripe that it was starting to rot on the vine.

"Don't eat anything," I warned, seeing Hador reach for one. "Nothing here is natural, and I don't think that's gonna be healthy."

Oracle stumbled suddenly, one hand clutching her stomach. Her face contorted in pain as she gasped.

"What is it?" I asked, panicking and staring around as I moved in closer, trying to tell whether someone or something was doing something to her.

"The baby," she gasped. "It's…oh by the gods, I think its reacting to this place. The mana! I can feel it squirming, moving. It has to be that the mana is affecting it."

"Shit, do we fly?" I asked her, looking up at the sky that was barely visible through the trees. "Just go, try to get clear?"

"No…" She shook her head, biting her lip, and gripped my hand tightly for a few seconds, before blowing out a long breath and straightening.

Sehran was there as well and steadied her. "I've got her, Jax," she assured me.

I nodded, but didn't move away.

"Jax, it's okay. I'll be okay." Oracle forced a smile. "Let's just find them, yeah? We need them, and then maybe we go. Or maybe this is what Lagoush meant. Maybe this is how it helps us."

I nodded slowly. "Okay, but if this gets worse, we're out of here. I can always come back on my own and check it out later. Just tell me if you feel it getting worse, okay? I mean, we're almost there. Look."

Stone pillars were vaguely visible here and there through the trees, and I guessed that, given the massive and obviously artificially straight sides to the blocks, they had to be part of the temple we were looking for.

As we got closer, it was obvious that yeah, what we were seeing was the outermost edge of the temple, and that it'd fallen long ago.

Vines were wrapped around massive blocks that were themselves half sunken into the verdant earth, overgrown by moss and grass, insects buzzing and climbing across them.

Most of the structure had been consumed by the jungle. Vines and roots cracked through ancient stone, pulling it apart even as they held other sections together.

As we approached, I reached out to Jenae, hoping, but no. There was still nothing, only silence where her presence should have been, and a sense of mana unraveling as I tried to reach out to her.

"Oracle," I sent through the bond, not wanting to worry the others. *"Can you feel the gods?"*

She closed her eyes, concentrating, then shook her head. *"No. Something's still blocking them."*

Something powerful enough that it could hide from the gods and block them once we were inside its reach… A chill ran down my spine. *"That's not good."*

We reached the temple steps, which descended into what looked to be a collapsed courtyard, or maybe a cellar or something.

Water from the lake had seeped inside, creating a shallow pool that reflected the overarching trees and the clouded sky above. It covered the entire place, but was only a few inches deep, or so it seemed. The air was getting thicker with mist, making it difficult to see more than a few meters at most.

"Spread out," I ordered tersely. "Let's make sure we're not taken from behind."

"Unless we're lucky…"

I didn't even bother to check which of the succubai that had been—it was just par for the course now—but what I'd thought was Sehran's signature style was clearly a lust demon thing. It made me feel almost proud of the way that Tommy and I had been quipping that shit all our lives.

As my people moved into position, I helped Oracle down what was left of the slippery steps. The moment her foot touched the water, ripples spread outward, and the mist before us parted as they approached.

They must have been waiting for us, a dozen or more ethereal forms, each glowing with inner light. They shifted constantly, amorphous bodies that seemed unable to decide on the right shape or color.

Wisps.

They were *definitely* wisps, sure, but they weren't like Oracle.

Their forms wavered, unstable; patches of darkness spread through their luminescent shapes like bruises. Some were barely bright enough to see, clinging to existence by sheer will.

"You came," one of them whimpered, floating forward. Its voice sounded like wind through dead leaves. "We called, and you came."

"Lagoush sent us," I agreed, observing them carefully as they spread out into a half circle, watching us. Something was wrong here, but I couldn't put my finger on it. When Oracle tried to move forward, her left hand rising toward her people, her distant cousins, I pulled her back. "She said you needed help."

"Yes," the first wisp replied, its form flickering. "We are dying. This place…it feeds on us."

"No! No magic!" another wisp hissed suddenly, flaring into a form of spikes and jagged edges threateningly and surging forward, apparently noticing Lembas laboriously preparing a spell. "No magic here! They will find us!"

Lembas froze, looking to me for direction. "It was only an identify spell. I was just going to try to heal them…?"

I nodded that I understood, then went on, as he lowered his hands.

"It's all right. We won't use magic, for now. What, though? What will find you?" I stepped forward, then backed up when their lights became tinged with red and more black.

They drew back quickly.

"I'm sorry, I don't want to startle you, but we came to help you, and for you to help us," I said, as reassuring as I could.

"I'm one of you," Oracle said softly, reaching out again. "I evolved. I was healed and I've grown. We—"

"Quiet!" another hissed. "You have to be quiet, be small…"

"You can't help us. So many lost, eaten…"

"Tell us," Oracle beseeched. "Tell us and let us help you, then you can help us as well!"

The wisps conferred among themselves, their light dimming until they were barely visible in the mist. Finally, the first one returned to us.

"The hunger in the water," it said cryptically. "It takes us. Changes us. We have lost many."

Oracle stepped forward, one hand extended. "I'm like you. I can help—"

"NO!" The wisps recoiled violently. "No magic! It, *they* will sense you!" The leader calmed itself, floating closer to Oracle; its voice changed as it apparently sensed something. "Like us, but not? You carry new life! *Special* life. You…you need us, yes?"

Oracle's hand instinctively moved to her belly.

"You can sense our child?" I glanced from them to Oracle's belly and back.

"We feel it," the wisp replied. "A bridge between worlds. Like us, but more. Much more."

Oracle gasped suddenly, doubling over in pain. "Jax…" she choked out.

I held her, scared and totally unsure of what the hell I should do here, whether they were hurting her or…

The wisps surged forward as one. "We can help," their leader said decisively. "We *will* help, but not here. *Inside*. Where it's safer."

I hesitated, torn between suspicion and Oracle's obvious distress. Her face was twisted in agony, her form shivering as the baby within her reacted to the mana-saturated environment.

"Fine," I decided. "But my people come too."

"Only her," the wisp countered. "And you. And her." It indicated Sehran. "You are linked, we feel it. The others must guard the temple. There are…things…in the jungle. They come from the water and all around. They would take her if they could. If we can't defend us, they'll come…they will take her, take us all."

"The hell they will," I growled. "They've never faced imperial legionnaires."

"Then they must protect us! Protect the entrance, here!" the wisp insisted.

I hesitated, then nodded.

I didn't like it, but Oracle's condition and her uniqueness meant that we genuinely just didn't know what was happening. She could be getting ready to give birth, or deteriorating rapidly. "Vislen," I called. "Secure this courtyard. No one gets past you, understand?"

He saluted, immediately organizing the others into defensive positions.

Sehran stepped up and took Oracle, lifting her in her arms and starting forward. "You need to be ready. I've got her."

I hated it, but she was right.

"This way," the wisp urged, leading us deeper into the temple.

We followed it through crumbling corridors, and down long-lost halls. Across sections where the floor was covered in stagnant water and the walls in mold, and then into rooms that looked like the former inhabitants had barely stepped out for a coffee.

We passed chambers where roots had burst through walls and ceilings to create natural arches, and where the original stonework looked determined to last out the ages.

The entire structure seemed alive, somehow. The feeling, even transmitted through the standing water that came up to my knees now, pulsed with the same frantic energy that permeated the jungle outside.

Like a panicked heartbeat that was only getting faster.

Finally, after a few minutes of careful travel, and having gone far enough I was close to refusing to go any farther, not without calling the others in to join us, we reached what appeared to be the temple's inner sanctum.

It was a rough circle. It'd probably been a perfect one, once, but the walls alternated between carved and ornate, and lost beneath flowing rivulets of water and collapsed sections, or ancient vines that had pushed their way through who knew how long ago.

The floor was a foot deep at the shallowest with rippling water, and the roof and walls added to it constantly. Drops fell; the massive stones overhead bowed unsubtly inward. Frankly, the whole place made me want to run.

At the center stood a low stone bier, still intact despite the chaos around it, even with a section of the wall directly behind it having fallen and created a pile of rubble bare meters from it.

Dozens more wisps waited here, most of these even more damaged than the ones who had greeted us. Some were barely more than fading and flaring sparks, clinging to existence out of pure stubbornness.

"Bring her," the leader instructed, sounding excited, flaring bright next to the altar.

I hesitated, my instincts screaming that something wasn't right here. "What exactly are you going to do?" I demanded.

"Stabilize her," the wisp replied. Its voice warbled in and out like a bad radio reception. "The baby draws too much mana here. It will tear her apart if we do not help. It feeds on her mana. When the mana is too twisted, it feeds too hard, and will kill her."

Instantly, I felt a surge of fear, of distrust, worrying what these fuckers were going to try to do. We'd spent so long keeping everyone away from her, and now I was supposed to just trust that because they looked like wisps, we should let them close, that we should…

Oracle clutched my arm. "Jax. It…it's okay. We need to trust them. I know what you're feeling, I do, but I can feel it. They're my kind. It'll be okay…please—" She gasped and clutched my hand as another wave of pain hit her.

I bit down hard on the fear, on the panic, and forced myself to nod. To trust that if *anyone* was going to know what to do here, it was Oracle. I had to trust her.

Reluctantly, Sehran and I helped her to the altar. As she lay down, I looked at the rubble, seeing that it was new, or it looked recently piled up anyway, compared to the rest of the chamber.

"Is that safe?" I asked. "The roof isn't going to come down, is it?"

The wisps gathered around Oracle, their light pulsing in unison. I kept my hand on my naginata, eyes scanning the chamber for threats.

"The baby comes too soon," one wisp murmured, as none of them even bothered to answer me. "The Cradle awakens it."

Sehran moved closer to me, her voice low. "Something about this doesn't feel right…"

I nodded slightly, hesitating, not wanting to complain about the wisps in the bond and have Oracle hear and worry more, but aware if I said it out loud they'd hear it too.

The temple shook violently. Dust and small stones showered down from the ceiling.

"What was that?" I demanded of the wisps.

The lead wisp turned to me, or I guessed it was the same one, its light flickering. "They come! The taken ones."

"We begin!" another of the wisps croaked, its light looking diseased and twisted in comparison to most of the others. "The baby! Our future, we save!"

"Yes!" I nodded. "You have to save them both!"

"Protect," it hissed. "Too many come, if we stop. Both die. ALL die. Us, her, the baby…you must protect!"

A distant scream echoed from the courtyard, followed by the clash of weapons and shouts of alarm, then the boom of spells, and more shouts.

I looked down the passage, hating that I was leaving our people to fight while I stood here, but there was nowhere else I could be.

"Jax, go." Oracle sagged back and let out a groan of relief. "It's okay, I can feel it…what they're doing, the wisps, it's helping."

"I can't…" I said, torn, and glancing from her to the passage and back. "Oracle, I can't leave you…"

"You have to, my love. I'll be okay… Don't worry, you have to do this… Do it for our baby!" she ordered, taking my hand in hers and squeezing as hard as she could as she panted with the pain. "I won't be alone…don't worry."

"Jax, I'll keep her safe," Sehran promised me.

I looked to her and then back at Oracle, my throat dry and heart hammering as a horrible feeling that I might lose her rose in me. That I might be away fighting off some stupid beasts and she could have a heart attack and die or whatever while giving birth.

"Fuck's sake!" I snarled. "Fine! Sehran, you keep her safe. I'll just…" I looked to the passage and back.

"I'll be fine, I promise." Oracle forced a smile. "Please, Jax, just go…save our people and then hurry back."

I gritted my teeth, then leaned in and kissed Oracle, hard.

"Stay with her!" I ordered Sehran, already running toward the exit. "I'm trusting you!"

Then, silently through the bond, I sent another message, even knowing that Oracle would hear it.

"I don't trust them. If you have to kill them all, then do it. Just keep her safe!"

"I will," Sehran sent me, and I nodded to myself, sprinting as fast as I could.

I raced through the corridors, naginata drawn, following the sounds of battle, leaping over rotting crates and long fallen debris. It seemed to take forever, but eventually I burst into the courtyard, and chaos greeted me.

My people stood in a defensive circle, fighting against a horde of creatures that poured from the jungle. Some I recognized as something like the pale beings we'd encountered earlier, but others…

Others were wisps, or had been. Their light was corrupted, black tendrils writhing through their luminescent forms. They moved with terrible purpose, landing on my people, screeching and forming into frantic, half-seen shapes, trying to tear at their flesh.

The pale things were clearly in terrible agony as well, their eyes rolling, their veins distended. They screamed in pain and fear, all the while attacking wildly.

I saw a flash and heard a boom as a goddamn wisp, one who had barely been bright enough to pick out, flying toward my people, suddenly detonated, spending its life to attack us.

"Prince Jax! Thank the gods!" Vislen shouted, blocking a blow from what appeared to be a mutated mer—its four arms wielding coral blades, its tendrils a mix of flailing madly and limp noodles. "They came out of nowhere!"

I leapt into the fight, naginata slicing through corrupted flesh as I fed it fire mana and started hacking. The mass of different creatures fought as one. My stomach tightened and my balls tried to reach my heart internally at that horribly familiar sign, as I desperately tried to remember why.

"Lembas!" I barked. "Frostfire Circle of Cleansing, now!"

He nodded, fingers sketching complex patterns as he began the spell we'd only recently taught him. The creatures sensed something and surged toward him with renewed fury.

I intercepted them, my naginata a blur of motion as I triggered Hyper Cognition and Mana Overdrive at once. I carved a path through their ranks, sub-vocalizing and casting my own as well, planning to overlap the circles. That was when I saw the black ichor that sprayed from a wound, splashing down, then running together, coagulating, reforming…or, in my case, when it touched the flaming blade of my naginata, bursting into incandescent fire.

That color. That consistency. I knew it. I knew them and why this was so horribly wrong.

"It's Xenefier!" I screamed in warning. "Don't let their blood touch you! Fuck, we need fire! Burn it! BURN IT ALL!"

They ran at us, all of them in a desperate, frantic wave. Lembas was the first to fall, a coral-tipped spear punching through his left knee, making him scream and lose control of his spell.

He collapsed, shaking, unused to the horrific backlash of a failed spell and already in tremendous pain from his knee. Before I could do anything, a misshapen, hairless ape-thing landed atop his chest, slamming a section of ornate carven rock down atop his helmet and crushing it almost flat.

I felt him die, even as I slammed my own circle into place, and my people fought on. The corrupted wisps darted overhead, screeching, then diving, driving themselves into us and detonating, or unleashing half-formed spells that clearly did more damage to them than they did to us. Their bodies—infected by Xenefier—clearly couldn't use their mana properly.

For every creature we cut down, two more emerged from the jungle. They were herding us, I realized—trying to force us away from the temple entrance, desperate to get down it, toward…

Suddenly, a scream echoed from deep within the temple—Sehran's voice, filled with pain and anger. I felt the agony that overwhelmed her, and…and I felt Oracle's fear and pain.

Oracle.

My love.

The sense of her flared and then filled with pain, before starting to move.

My blood turned to ice. I spun toward the temple, only to find my path blocked by a wall of corrupted flesh as the trees above disgorged dozens more of the ape-things.

They crashed down, splashing into the shallow water; more than half broke bones on impact, opening terrible wounds. But the black gloop forced them to rear up and fight us anyway.

The others were being grabbed, pinned as these things deliberately opened wounds in their own flesh and poured their sentient goo over them. Screams rose and then died as it soaked into their eyes and ears, sinking into their bodies and hijacking them.

"FIGHT!" I roared, abandoning all pretense of defense as I charged forward, naginata sweeping in wide arcs. Creatures fell before me. Their bodies dissolved into puddles of black ichor, even as the fires rose from my spell. The ichor flared into screaming, burning death. "FIGHT, LEGIONNAIRES!"

I lashed out on instinct, hammering them again and again, striking out with fire, with naked force.

I threw mana out, unformed, sending cracks spiraling out in the rocks as pure concussive force hurled everything from me.

I reached the temple steps, taking them three at a time, when a mental blast hit me like a physical blow. I staggered, vision blurring. A familiar presence invaded my mind, making me miss a step and crash into the wall, tumbling and falling.

The child will be mine.

The voice was ancient, patient, filled with terrible hunger. Xenefier…or that was what we'd named it. The original Malthus entity, the thing in the city that we'd burned—but not managed to kill.

I pushed the presence from my mind through sheer will, forcing myself back to my feet and continuing my headlong rush into the temple. The corridors seemed to stretch endlessly, twisting and turning and feeling like they were ten times longer than before.

"Oracle!" I shouted both aloud and through the bond, my voice echoing off stone walls. "Sehran!"

Another scream answered me, closer now. I burst through a doorway to find Sehran pinned against a wall, black tendrils wrapped around her limbs and throat. Her wings were a torn mess, with ichor forcing its way into dozens of wounds across her body from the thing that held her.

"J-Jax," she choked out, eyes wide with terror. "Go! Get her back!"

"Where?" I screamed. The teleport spell took too long to cast, but in my fury, the half-remembered abilities of Amon fused with the Mana Overdrive and I pushed off. The ground beneath my feet cracked as I put far more power into it than I should have been able to.

I hit the thing with a shoulder. The body detonated under the impact, bones and muscles reduced to mush as it flew back. My naginata—still ablaze—slashed through the tendrils that held my friend.

I caught her as she sagged free of the wall, the frostfire circle blazing to life beneath us both as I *demanded* it exist. She collapsed into my arms, barely alive, bleeding from dozens, if not hundreds of wounds. Some of Xenefier was still within her, bulges that roamed beneath her skin.

"Wall," she managed to force out. "Not…a collapse…a *door*."

I looked to the far wall of the chamber, seeing the section beyond that bier I'd noticed earlier. Now there was a hole, where the piled stone had been before, revealed in the middle of it with a dark passage beyond.

I lowered Sehran gently to the floor, dragging a healing potion from my bag and pouring it over her wounds, even as the semi-sentient flames from the circle burnt their way inside her. Then I rammed the rest of it into her mouth and half choked her with it.

Then I was off, forcing myself to my feet and sprinting down the revealed passage. A Pyroclastic Blast hurled from my hand with bare constraints and guiding on it, crashing into the corrupted thing that I'd driven from Sehran.

I hated leaving her, abandoning her to just heal or die. I wasn't even sure I'd done enough to save her life. But at the same time, I couldn't stop, not now!

I charged through the opening, only to be met by a wave of corrupted creatures that poured from the darkness. They swarmed me, dozens of them, filled to the brim with the corruption—that thing's blood—and as I hewed my way through them, it surged and leapt from their limbs in sticky tendrils, locking onto me, seeping into my armor.

I fought with manic intensity, channeling mana into my naginata until it glowed white-hot, carving through their twisted bodies. But there were too many, and every second that passed was another second Oracle was beyond my reach.

"ORACLE!" I roared, my voice breaking with desperation. My mana surged again, slamming outward from me on instinct. The walls and floor nearby cracked under the terrible impact.

The temple shook again, more violently this time. Cracks spread across the ceiling; chunks of stone crashed down around me. The survivors were burning now, I saw, with some of them deliberately throwing themselves *into* the flames!

I saw the flames burning deeper into them, searing out Xenefier root and branch, as the hosts howled and thrashed, paying a terrible price to gain their freedom.

I saw broken bodies and death on all sides: wisps collapsing, fading into literal gasses and liquids; others crushed beneath the falling debris.

I seized the opportunity, slamming yet another circle down, feeling the strain on my mana as it dropped lower. But it worked. As everything around me screeched and beat at themselves, burning, I broke free and ran again.

If they survived, if they were free of Xenefier, all well and good. But if not? If they just died? That was the price they paid today.

The passage descended steeply, curving back toward the lake. The walls here were different, more solid, and seemingly recently excavated, and the floor, although slick with running water that surged down it, was freshly broken through, with hard edges on the steps and broken rock, instead of long worn away.

The passage opened after another two twists, revealing a vast cavern beneath the temple. At its center stood a perfect circle of black in the knee-deep water that filled it. The blackness seemed solid; the water might be connected to the lake above, but this…this wasn't. It was something insanely corrupt and wrong. Tendrils of black mass writhed up and danced, each holding a wisp captive who shrieked and wailed, being crushed in the thing's embrace.

And in the middle of it, Oracle floated, unconscious, above another altar, surrounded by corrupted wisps and mer. Their hands moved and black gunk flowed from their fingertips, trying to burrow into her, and failing, burning up on contact, as she somehow, even unconscious, fought.

"GET AWAY FROM HER!" I bellowed, charging forward.

One of the mer turned to face me—larger than the others, its body distorted by growths that pulsed with black life.

"Stop," it commanded, its voice gurgling as if speaking through water. "One more step, and she dies." As it spoke, a thigh-thick band of the gunk wrapped around her throat and constricted, making Oracle shake and thrash, even as smoke rose from the tentacle.

I skidded to a halt, rage and fear warring within me. "What are you doing to her?"

"Preparing," the mer gurgled, the air shivering with its voice. "The child requires…adjustment."

"Let her go," I growled threateningly. Mana built around me in waves of heat; I started to pull it in. Nothing conscious was happening, instead it was all on instinct. "*Now*."

The mer tilted its head, fixing on me. "You do not understand what you have created, prince of fire. This child is the bridge! The doorway. Through it, all worlds will be one."

"Xenefier," I snarled. "*I fucking see you!*"

"Xenefier is but a name you have given to the fragment you have seen of the true being," the mer corrected. "We have existed since before your gods were born. We have waited, patient and eternal, for the perfect vessel. We almost abandoned the search…" It gestured to Oracle's belly. "But now, we have found it."

Behind me, sounds of combat grew closer. Spells exploded. Someone had survived at least.

"What do you want with our child?" I demanded, my mind racing, playing for time. "Don't fucking do this!"

"Want?" the mer hissed. "We do not want. We simply *are*. Your child will become our avatar. Through it, we will feel and use mana, and then, we will be one. The one who is all. All things, all realms. All will be one."

While it spoke, I inched forward, calculating angles, estimating the distance to Oracle. I could cover it in two leaps maybe using Mana Overdrive. But the corrupted beings surrounding her…

"I'm fucking warning you!" I snarled. "Don't do this!"

The mer gestured, and I half turned, glancing back and then at it again after seeing what it'd wanted to show me. Two of its other bodies, dragging Sehran into view from behind me, made it clear that at least some of the fighting I'd heard was them taking her prisoner again. She hung limply between them, blood streaming from a deep gash across her forehead. One of the mer held a jagged blade to her eye.

"We only need the child!" the leader replied coldly. "The mother is…convenient, and will strengthen our vessel. There is much growth still to be had, but. It. Is. Not. *Necessary*. And this one…" It gestured toward Sehran with a finger. "Is *entirely* expendable."

Footsteps pounded down the passage behind me, and I allowed myself a moment of hope. *My people were coming. If I could just…*

The mer leader lifted one hand, twisting it in the air; reality seemed to bend around it, the black pool rippling violently. A doorway opened above the water—not a portal as I understood them, but a tear in the fabric of existence itself as the wisps all shrieked something, the fucking thing somehow forcing them to help as Oracle was surrounded by a greenish-black bubble of force.

"No!" I lunged forward, only to be met by massive wall of corrupted flesh as new enemies lumbered out of the figures that had surrounded her, roaring their fury and racing at me.

The first Minotaur that hit me was huge, heavily muscled. The light-brown fur or hair was thick and short, and the horns—swinging at my face—were at least half a meter long and a glossy black from tip to base.

I'd barely noticed it in the crowd, the dozens of bodies that had been by Oracle.

I slid back a few inches, the force of the massive creature's unexpected attack doing that as it grabbed onto my shoulders and shoved, the flesh all along the arms splitting and opening as the black gunk poured free.

Then I ignored the hands that grabbed me, the arms that were as thick around as my thighs and the force that he was putting into the push. I yanked my naginata in from the right, dragging it back and then ramming it through his chest in one go. My absolute fury combined with my mana sent the weapon blazing with the brightness of the sun as I ran him through.

Then I grabbed him by one horn, and yanked hard enough—one-handed—to snap the bastard's neck and yank him aside. At the same time, I ripped my naginata free. The black mass inside him caught fire, even as the tar-like substance that covered his arms poured onto me. The rest peeled back, his flesh suppurating and forming a thick and stinking barrier of fats, malformed flesh, and who knew what else, to stop the spread of the flames.

I threw the fresh-made corpse aside, and ignored the mass that poured across the armor and bulled forward. Other bodies—some hairless and pallid, aquatic, or even covered in dirt and reeking, long dead and rotting, having dug their way up from unknown places—all piled in, and I tore them apart in a frenzied rage.

Blood and viscera flew; limbs and torsos were hacked apart. And still, more and more of the black substance landed on me. Circle after circle flared to life as I struggled forward. Dozens of creatures became hundreds, and they drained the spell as fast as I could refresh it. My mana vanished into the seemingly endless void of creatures.

The touch of the black mass seared through my armor, eating into the flesh beneath, but I barely felt it. I couldn't use the most powerful of my spells. I couldn't for fear of harming Oracle, of bringing the roof down atop our heads and killing both her and our child. But this?

All I could see was Oracle, unconscious, being lifted by the light and carried toward the doorway and away from me.

"NOOOOOOO!" I screamed. Mana lashed out, unfocused, released in my rage, my need.

Creatures on all sides were thrown back. Their forms collapsed into ash, or were hurled with enough force that they left broken sections of stone where they impacted.

Every second, though, brought more of them.

Xenefier had learned, a tiny part of me realized. It'd learned how to counter me. Instead of piling everything in on me at once, they came in waves: too little to be able to kill a large enough percentage of them to matter, and too large to simply bull through.

I was limited in my spells to clear them back, and there were too many who didn't care about horrific injuries or death to be able to fight through quick enough.

I fought with berserk fury, cutting down everything in my path. But for each creature I felled, three more took its place. They weren't trying to kill me, I realized distantly—just delay me.

The mer leader reached the doorway. The bubble that had held Oracle popped; it had to clumsily grab onto her, to cradle her in its arms. It turned to face me one last time, before awkwardly dropping Oracle to the floor of the dark room beyond, its arms and chest where she'd touched clearly burned.

"When the time comes, she will be returned to you," it offered, its voice echoing unnaturally. "But the child belongs to us now. Attempt to follow, and the brood mare becomes unnecessary. Remember, fleshling, you can always breed again, but this one? This is ours!"

With that, it stepped through the doorway, and Oracle vanished from sight. The other mer followed, dragging Sehran back toward the altar.

"NO!" I screamed, channeling every ounce of power I possessed into a desperate surge. Mana Overdrive pushed my body beyond even the limits I'd reached before, too far—too far for my body as it was. Muscles tore, bones broke as I exploded forward.

I crashed through them in their dozens. The flames of the circles cleared the black blood from me, even as more and more poured from above and coated me.

"Remember…we only need the child!" came the voice again from all those around me.

The gloop exploded into sheets of flame as my rage went incandescent.

I reached the edge of the black pool just as the other mer stepped through the doorway. My fingers were inches from the edge, when it slammed shut with a crack like breaking stone.

I stumbled through the empty air, my fingers reaching, desperately grabbing at nothing, as I felt the terrible feeling of Oracle, gone. Gone so far from me that I could barely sense her at all.

Oracle was gone. My child was gone.

Behind and all around, the corrupted creatures throughout the cavern collapsed as one. The black ichor spilled from their bodies as the thing that had controlled them withdrew, and it poured into the ground, burrowing away, returning to the depths.

And as for me, I sank to my knees and I stopped as everything hit me all at once.

The world seemed to grind to a halt.

A tiny voice whispered in my ear that this was wrong.

This couldn't be.

No, this wasn't fucking right!

No. No. No. No.

If I just stayed here, stayed quiet, this couldn't have happened. I had to be wrong.

Something was going to change. The bubble would burst and all of this couldn't have happened. I couldn't have lost them.

No.

I never knew how long I stayed there, but it was long enough that many of the wisps and other creatures who had surrounded me…who had *fought* me, had awoken and *fled.*

At some point, Vislen and the others found me, bursting into the chamber, weapons ready, only to find me kneeling at the edge of the formerly black pool, staring at the empty space where the portal had been.

"My prince," Vislen began, his voice hesitant. "What happened?"

I couldn't answer him. Couldn't find words for the void that had opened inside me.

Sehran. I'd forgotten about her, but someone apparently healed her. I felt it as she stirred weakly, before shoving them aside. She forced herself to her feet, staggering and stumbling across the chamber to collapse by my side, bowing her head in shame.

"Jax…my…master." She forced the words out, tears streaming down her face and mingling with the blood that still dribbled from rents in her flesh. "I'm…sorry. I failed…you…couldn't stop…them."

I couldn't bring myself to reassure her. To say anything, beyond awkwardly, blindly patting her shoulder.

After a time, I rose slowly, every movement a supreme effort of will. My armor was a bloody mess, that black ichor having shredded my flesh and left holes in me that were yet to seal, and yet… I felt nothing.

Just empty inside, frozen and cold.

"They have her," I whispered, my voice a hollow echo in the cavern. "They have Oracle, and they have my child."

The chamber fell silent, the implications sinking in. Then Vislen stepped forward, fist over heart in salute.

"We'll get her back, my prince," he vowed. "Whatever it takes."

I stared at the black pool, remembering the mer's words. *We only need the child.* The threat was obvious: pursue them, and Oracle would die.

But there was no choice. No reality where I didn't tear apart heaven and earth to find her.

I felt it building, bubbling up from below; the pressure grew at a horrific rate until I couldn't take it any longer and the ice inside me shattered into a billion razor-sharp pieces.

I threw back my head and screamed, a sound of pure anguish and utter rage that shook the very foundations of the temple. Far above, the sky darkened as storm clouds gathered, responding to my rage and the uncontrolled power that streamed from me.

The temple shuddered, the water danced, and the walls shook. I felt the shaking of the fucking veil as power poured off me and into the ether, and it went on and on.

Finally, exhausted, I collapsed to my knees, braced on all fours as I panted, staring at my armored arms, as steam rose from gleaming, perfect plate.

In that moment, I made a silent vow. I *would* find Oracle. I would *save* our child. *And then I would obliterate every trace of Xenefier from existence.* Even if it meant burning the realm to ashes.

"Now, little one, we are even," came a fresh voice, and with it, the huff and snort of breath, the mocking derision, and casual cruelty that I recognized from the one interaction we'd had before.

Baphomet.

I felt it as he retreated, abandoning the Cradle, and the sudden feeling as the other gods finally found a way in, as whatever he'd been doing to keep them out was withdrawn.

I felt their fear, their horror at what had happened. I seethed as the rage, the anger and fear that had filled me changed me.

My soul was seared, the brittle metal that had made it up, being burned.

Impurities failed and dissolved.

Fear.

Uncertainty.

Pity.

Doubt.

All of them were lost, boiling away as the iron of my soul was forged into unbending steel.

That fucker didn't know what it'd done. In removing Oracle from my life, it'd removed the only part of me that had lines left that couldn't be crossed.

As of now, the prince that I'd been trying to become, the good man who fought to improve and save the realm? He was shut away, put into a little box in my mind and carefully set aside for when the realm was sane enough that he could be brought back out again.

For when the fuckers learned their place and not to provoke me, to prod the bear.

No, Jax was gone now. This realm had proved they didn't deserve the mercy and patience that he'd offered. They couldn't be trusted with the iron glove. With the fucking carrot.

No. Now it was time for the mailed fist.

In place of the man once known as Jax, only Amon's Heir was left.

It was time to teach them all some motherfucking respect.

THE END OF BOOK NINE OF THE UNDERVERSE

CHARACTER SHEET

Name: Jax Amon				
Title: Godslayer				
Class: Mage Imperator (Fire Focus)			**Renown**: Imperial Scion, Prince of Dravith, Master of Himnel and Narkolt, Godslayer, Mage Imperator	
Level: 52			**Progress**: 417,882/13,000,000	
Patron: Jenae, Goddess of Fire and Exploration			**Points to Distribute**: 0 **Meridian Points to Invest**: 0	
Stat	**Current points**	**Description**	**Effect**	**Progress to next level**
Agility	100	Governs dodge and movement	+1000% maximum movement speed and reflexes. Gained Temporal Fluidity	N/A
Charisma	61 (56)	Governs likely success to charm, seduce, or threaten	+51% success chance in interactions with other beings	51/100
Constitution	125 (123)	Governs health and health regeneration	2460 health, regen 160 points per 600 seconds (each point invested now worth 20 health). Gained: Genetic Storage	N/A
Dexterity	100	Governs ability with weapons and crafting success	+100% to weapon proficiency, +100% to the chances of crafting success. Gained: Master Craftsman's Touch	N/A
Endurance	73 (670)	Governs stamina and stamina regeneration	2190 stamina, regen 53 points per 30 seconds (each point invested now worth 30 stamina)	89/100
Intelligence	206	Governs base mana and number of	2260 mana, spell capacity: 102 (100 + 2,	N/A

		spells able to be learned	+200 mana from items) Gained: Hyper Cognition & Mana Manipulation	
Luck	79	Governs overall chance of bonuses	+69% chance of a favorable outcome	92/100
Perception	110 (100)	Governs ranged damage and chance to spot traps or hidden items	+100% ranged damage, +100% chance to spot traps or hidden items. Gained: Essence Sight	N/A
Strength	90 (87)	Governs damage with melee weapons and carrying capacity	+90 damage with melee weapons, +90% maximum carrying capacity	88/100
Wisdom	105 (95)	Governs mana regeneration and memory	+1400% mana recovery, 16 points per minute. Gained: Mana Manipulation	N/A

THANK YOU! (AGAIN)

Well, I hope you enjoyed that? Yes, I know, you're probably plotting murder right now, considering the situation I've left you in, and I'm not sorry! Bwhahaha!

Seriously though, At the time of writing this message in July '25, I already have book 10 written as well, and book 11 is starting work next week, so by the time you read this, you'll know that the rest of the series is nearly done, and over the next 6 months or so, and certainly by mid '26, the story will be done!

As such, I'd ask for two things, if I may. First and foremost, the story from this book on is going to be a twisty one, with the kidnapping and more, so I'd ask that you please don't ruin the surprise for anyone, and that when you read the end of book 12, you DEFINITELY don't share that.

Please do leave reviews, ratings and speak about the book publicly, sharing it on FB and everywhere else is massively important and I'd appreciate that more than you know, but please don't ruin the endings for anyone else.

And yes, for those who know, this shows that the end has always been known, to me, and I do have a plan. Shhhh!

Heh.

Thanks everyone!

-Jez
03/07/25

PATREON

Hi everyone! Okay, when this launches in June all of my Patreon supporters will have already read it, and some will have already finished book 9, and will be on the next book I've been working on as well, which is UnderVerse 10!

The highest tiers also have access to a secret project, and will be busily reading literally as I finish the chapters. So, if you want to read them perhaps 4-6 months ahead of release? Come join us on the dark side!

HOWEVER: I do want to point out one thing everyone, the app stores on apple and android platforms have enforced that a 30% mandatory percentage goes to them for any purchasing done through the **app**. So the app store Patreon subscription has increased by that amount automatically, PLEASE sign up through the website instead, it's still Patreon's website, and the increase doesn't apply there.

There's several of those wonderful supporters out there that I have to thank personally as well; Gary Mischa and Niall, thank you all!

Gary, Mischa and Niall, thank you all!

https://www.patreon.com/Jezcajiao

UNDERVERSE 10 : WRATH ASCENDANT

By Jez Cajiao

When the war started, Jax was filled with hope, a belief that everything was possible... now he has only his rage and hatred to carry him forward.

Himnel. Narkolt. Gaij. The cities that have stood against him have learned the cost, but now, as Jax is forced to stand alone, to stare into the abyss and see what his own mistakes have brought about, Kronk dares to raise its head and threaten him.

They're about to find out why he's called the Godslayer.

The gods have a plan—gather ten divine fragments, ascend to godhood, and face an evil that has survived for millennia. But divine fragments don't come gift-wrapped. They're held by demigods, tyrants, and things that make the Dark Legion look like amateurs.

Every fragment Jax binds tears him apart and rebuilds him stronger. Every victory costs him a piece of his humanity. And every day that passes, the clock ticks down.

The Continent of Carrmor is far larger and its civilization older than Dravith, but that just means there's more ruins to explore, more secrets to uncover, and more powerful enemies to crush beneath his boots.

Kronk is only the beginning. Lembiq awaits. The Dark Legion regroups. And an ancient entity watches from the shadows, counting down the days.

It's time to take the gloves off.

Coming Soon

A FOREST OF VANITY AND VALOUR

By Adam Beswick

An aggressive debt collector banished from the kingdom. Now his life depends on his ability to help the less fortunate...

Vireo Reinhold relishes collecting his monarch's proper dues. Working hard to prolong and fund the king's never-ending war, the self-centered official revels in the perks of luxury that come with his unorthodox role. But his world upends when he unearths an ancient spellbook that promises to unlock a shadowy, forgotten magic.

Embroiled in a secret affair with a fellow noble's wife, Vireo is mortified when he's forced to commit an unthinkable act. Driven into exile, no longer able to coerce the vulnerable, and with the powerful tome in his enemy's hands, the fallen agent's only shot at survival hangs on his skills at saving others.

Can Vireo redeem himself as the people's champion before they all fall to a sinister fate?

A Forest of Vanity and Valour is the dark first book in the Tales of Levanthria fantasy-retelling series. If you like fast-paced action, evil-to-good transformations, and classic stories with a twist, then you'll love A.P Beswick's ominous tale.

Buy Now!

BATTLEFORGED: FIRST CLEAR: A LITRPG APOCALYPSE ADVENTURE - BOOK 4

By MH Johnson

How to negotiate in the post-apocalypse:

1. Always try make a strong first impression. — *And few things say strength like an army of undead revenants EAGER to begin slaughtering at your command!*

2. Be clear and concise when making your diplomatic offers. Let everyone know all the wonderful benefits they'll enjoy by doing things your way! — *If they play their cards right, they might even get to keep their heads!*

3. Speak softly, and carry a BIG CANNON! — *Because the best negotiations are when your competitors are looking down the barrel of your gun!*

4. *If all else fails, you can always pull out your **DINOSAUR COLLECTION** to impress all your new friends!*

Eric has a little problem.

Someone he cares about has been kidnapped by sadistic goblins working with corrupt bureaucrats who are eager to make him pay for interfering with their plans of military conquest and economic dominion.

Good thing Eric has a BIG ARMY!

An army that's absolutely PERFECT for crushing ANNOYING little problems that threaten any girl silly enough to fall for a guy like him.

Sadly, his mother has made it clear that negotiation is the best path forward when dealing with corrupt administrators. Especially when SMART negotiations just might give his sister the breathing room she needs to fortify her own growing kingdom.

Eric is forced to agree. If nothing else, this is a great opportunity for him to level-up his Negotiation skills. And he can think of no better negotiating tactic than **GROWING HIS UNDEAD LEGION TO MASSIVE PROPORTIONS!** Preferably by including everyone's childhood favorite: **DINOSAURS!** - *Lots and lots of hungry dinosaurs!*

Eager for a fast-paced adventure with a survivor determined to get the best of everyone trying to kill him? Then read on!

Order Here

FACEBOOK AND SOCIAL MEDIA

If you want to reach out, chat or shoot the shit, you can always find me on either my author page here:

www.facebook.com/JezCajiaoAuthor

OR

We've recently set up a new Facebook group to spread the word about cool LitRPG books. It's dedicated to two very simple rules;

1: Let's spread the word about new and old brilliant LitRPG books.

2: Don't be a Dick!

They sound like really simple rules, but you'd be amazed…

Come join us!

https://www.facebook.com/groups/LITRPGLegion

I'm also on Discord here: **https://discord.gg/u5JYHscCEH**

Or I'm reaching out on other forms of social media atm, I'm just spread a little thin that's all!

You're most likely to find me on Discord, but please, don't be offended when I don't approve friend requests on my personal Facebook pages. I did originally, and several people abused that, sending messages to my family and being generally unpleasant, hence, the author page:

www.facebook.com/JezCajiaoAuthor

I hope you understand.

LEGION

Okay everybody, if you've not yet seen or heard! My wife Chrissy, and our friend Geneva and I have launched the Legion Publishers!

We're taking on new authors, as well as experienced ones, focusing primarily on the LitRPG side of things, but we're open to anything really, with one very clear rule that guides our company:

Don't be a dick.

That's it. Our contracts aren't hidden behind layers of legalese, you can find them here:

https://www.legionpublishers.com/legioncontract

If you want to reach out and ask any questions, get an idea of the support we offer, and possibly become part of the family? We'd love to hear from you, just tap the link and fill in the form:

https://www.legionpublishers.com/contact-and-submissions

Hope you're having a good one!

-Jez, Chrissy and Geneva

If you want to read any of our amazing authors work then go get them!

Theft of Decks By Lars Machmuller **Buy on Amazon**
Quest Academy By Brian J. Nordon **Buy on Amazon**
Wandering Warrior By Michael Head **Buy on Amazon**
Knights of Eternity By Rachel Ní Chuirc **Buy on Amazon**
Scarlet Citadel By Jack Fields **Buy on Amazon**
Welcome to the Dark Ages by Malory Buy on Amazon

LITRPG!

To learn more about LitRPG, talk to other authors including myself, and to just have an awesome time, please join the LitRPG Group

www.facebook.com/groups/LitRPGGroup

FACEBOOK

There's also a few really active Facebook groups I'd recommend you join, as you'll get to hear about great new books, new releases and interact with all your (new) favorite authors! (I may also be there, skulking at the back and enjoying the memes…)

https://www.facebook.com/groups/LitRPGlegion/

https://www.facebook.com/groups/GamelitSociety

https://www.facebook.com/groups/LitRPG.books

https://www.facebook.com/groups/LitRPGforum/

www.ingramcontent.com/pod-product-compliance
Lightning Source LLC
Chambersburg PA
CBHW060753210726
48292CB00013B/72

* 9 7 8 1 9 1 5 6 1 7 3 4 7 *